THE COMPLETE DAVID REECE SG9 BLACK OPS SERIES

DAVID COSTA

This is a work of fiction. Names, characters, places, and incidents either are the product of the author's imagination or are used fictitiously. Any resemblance to actual persons, living or dead, events, or locales is entirely coincidental.

Copyright © 2019, 2021, 2023 by David Costa

All rights reserved.
No part of this book may be reproduced or used in any manner without written permission of the copyright owner except for the use of quotations in a book review.

This edition published by Wire Books in 2024.

TESTED BY FIRE

I dedicate this book to my wife Helena and my granddaughter Erin who, through their love and encouragement, helped me to finish this story.

Monsters are real, and ghosts are real too.

They live inside us, and sometimes, they win.'

~ Steven King

CHAPTER ONE

YOU NEVER HEAR THE SHOT THAT KILLS YOU

Costello lay flat in the back of the white Transit van, the tripod holding the Barrett Browning .50 calibre rifle steady. He held the stock against his right cheek and shoulder, the barrel pointing between the slightly open rear doors. As he looked through the scope, the outline of the figure standing beside a car half a mile away crystallised into clarity in the crosshairs. Costello began to put pressure on the trigger, his aim square on the chest of his target.

Private Stephen Channing 1st Battalion Royal Welsh Fusiliers had been working at the Vehicle Check Point – VCP – since eight that morning and his four-hour stint was almost up. The VCP was part of a ring of manned check points that encircled the small village of Bessbrook in South Armagh. The job of the patrol was to check the vehicles entering the village, which was home to the Bessbrook Mill Army Base, and one of the busiest landing pads in the world with hundreds of military helicopter landings and take-offs carrying troops, police, supplies, and equipment around the outlying bases of South Armagh. The danger of land-mine attacks in the infamous Bandit Country of the South Armagh Provisional IRA had made it almost impossible to travel by vehicle transport. The check points around the village provided a protective shield, preventing vehicles potentially carrying explosives getting close enough to hit the base.

Stephen Channing was happy. The day was bright, and his thoughts were on relaxing in the sun on the grass near the landing pads after lunch.

Costello took the full pressure of the trigger, squeezing through. He felt the cushioned kick in his shoulder as the figure in his sights stood up straight to inspect the licence he'd been handed by the driver of the red car beside him.

The soldier felt as if someone had hit him square in the chest with a sledgehammer, throwing him backwards and knocking him completely off his feet. The pain reverberated through his entire body as the bullet punched through his flak jacket and exited out his back after destroying most of his internal organs. He blacked out before the real pain registered; he was dead when his body hit the ground. What remained of the bullet exploded against a wall behind him, sending shards of masonry in all directions.

The van moved off in the opposite direction, leaving another dead British soldier lying on the ground.

The driver of the red car could only tell the police that the soldier was already flying backwards when he heard the loud bang of the shot. Maybe it was true. You never hear the shot that kills you.

Chapter Two

Monday, 23 September 2019

She checked if she was being watched. Before she became one of their agents, years of being on the run from the British Security Services had left their scars. His voice kept coming back to her. Trust no one; always expect danger and you'll be all right.

The man she knew as Joseph had been her RUC Special Branch handler. She'd been his agent inside the top echelons of the Provisional IRA in Northern Ireland. The war was supposed to be over, yet now she felt the danger and again; she was turning to the one man she trusted.

She remembered all he'd taught her on the streets of Belfast – London was no different to any big city – she could hear his voice clearly in her head.

Use the shop windows, use the reflection in the glass to see who's behind you. Memorise the clothes people are wearing. If you're in a building, use the lift. Professionals won't follow you in because it's hard to avoid eye contact inside. Drop your keys or tie your laces, take a chance to look around you.

She used his teachings as she walked through Victoria close to the main national bus station. Opposite the main entrance to the station was the Red Lion pub. She entered, knowing it would be busy and loud, many accents lost in the crowd. She'd been here many years ago with Joseph and he'd shown her how she could walk in the front door on one street and leave by the back door on another, allowing her to confuse anyone who might be following her.

Its main attraction today, however, was the public phone at the back of the bar.

She knew the Belfast number by heart and when the voice answered, she spoke clearly, 'This is Mike, BC15, I need to speak with Joseph at the set location in London. Tell him, *Democracy*. I'll be at the meeting place at 1 p.m. each day for the next three days.'

She then hung up and walked out of the pub's back door.

CHAPTER THREE

HQ SG9 LONDON CITY AIRPORT

The brass plaque on the door said *Business Sales International*. The three-story flat-roofed building located inside the perimeter fencing of London City Airport was, in fact, the secret headquarters of Secret Intelligence Group Nine. SG9, a section of SIS, the British Secret Intelligence Service, and known as 'the Department'.

The Department had been created not long after the worst terrorist atrocity in the modern world, the 9/11 attacks on the Twin Towers in New York. And when London suffered its own attacks on 7 July 2005, where fifty-two people were killed by four so-called home-grown suicide bombers who exploded their backpacks on the London public transport system during the morning rush hour, since then there had been more attacks in Manchester and London.

The British prime minister, in agreement with his Cobra Committee, decided that Britain needed a secret organisation working outside the restrictive parameters of the existing intelligence agencies. Democratic governments around the globe were finding their hands tied by the need for transparency in their methods and the rise in media coverage meant they were scrutinised beyond anything they'd known before.

Prime Minister Peter Brookfield put the unit into the hands of the Head of MI6, Sir Ian Fraser – known to many only as C. He was given the power to recruit the team as he saw fit with the order to report back to the PM only when needed.

The fact that MI5 and MI6, along with other elite intelligence organisations throughout the world, had failed to identify the 9/11 attack meant that western intelligence agencies had to adapt to a new type of war; not only how to gather intelligence, but how to thwart the attacks and, in the case of SG9, retaliate. The CIA and the FBI were to be criticised after 9/11 for the way they kept secrets which, if they had been shared, would have shown an attack was being planned and maybe stopped. The US Government then formed Homeland Security to oversee all the American Intelligence Agencies, filter the information, and ensure those people at the top couldn't work to protect their own little kingdoms in the future. The something else that was needed had been agreed between the Western powers: to share intelligence where they could, identify clear targets, and strike back.

The Department was set up in the two years after the July seventh bombings under the utmost secrecy and on a strictly need-to-know basis.

Back then, Sir Ian and his deputy for Subversive Activity, Jim Broad, personally scoured the files of relevant British covert agencies selecting the operators who would become the core of the Department.

The vetting had been carried out by Broad, a career spy who had gone straight to MI6 from Oxford University where he'd originally met Sir Ian. Fraser had taken a different direction and had worked his way up the army becoming a trusted friend of the PM and eventually heading up MI6 after a service record that saw him as General Officer Commanding British Military Intelligence.

Broad studied the Personal Record File of one of his SG9 operatives. The file was written in a crisp civil service format, telling him a lot but, in the end, very little.

Name, date of birth, and where he'd been born, Belfast. The file described retired Detective Inspector David Reece and his time covering the intelligence training and operational background. RUC Special Branch twenty-three years during the Troubles, but what, realistically, was an all-out terrorist war. He'd served through the ceasefires, the peace talks, and the Northern Ireland Peace Agreement gathering – analysing all aspects of intelligence and, when necessary, handling the enemies of peace, even if that resulted in death.

He'd been a successful recruiter of agents and through the agents he had under his control had saved many lives and, on many occasions, prevented terrorists succeeding in their terror campaign. His skills were second to none. Firearms, bomb making and disposal, recruiting and training new agents, surveillance, counter-terrorism techniques, interviewing...

Reece was considered one of the best due to his ability to adapt and learn on the spot.

The file also showed that the impact of the dangers he'd come to face daily had taken their toll. Two failed marriages, two estranged sons from the first. Diagnosed with severe stress during a period of heavy drinking, resulting in a period of enforced leave, but somehow, with counselling and follow-up treatment, he'd come through it a changed man, the file said he was hardened to life around him, a loner who kept himself to himself.

The police service had changed since he'd joined and after taking early retirement in 2015, he'd stumbled from one type of personal security job to another, from bodyguard to the rich, to private investigations. This was when in 2017 the file of David Reece, retired Detective Inspector Special Branch RUC George Cross and Police Service of Northern Ireland PSNI had landed on the desk of Jim Broad and after some detailed enquiries, he'd brought the file to the attention of Sir Ian Fraser. Sir Ian respected the skill of his second in command and trusted his judgement, so when he'd read the file, he agreed that Reece should become an agent in the Department.

Now Broad was about to call him in for the most important mission of his career.

CHAPTER FOUR

'The ravens are in danger,' Broad said to Fraser before hanging up the secure line between their offices. The code for extreme danger to the British State, borne from the legend that if the ravens that nested in the Tower of London were to disappear, it would be the end of Britain, was not one to be taken lightly, so Sir Ian had immediately left his office overlooking the Thames and was now sitting in Jim Broad's office.

Broad had told Sir Ian to read David Reece's file on his way over so when he'd arrived, he wasn't surprised to see Assistant Chief Constable Tom Wilson PSNI, a six-foot Ulsterman, fit for his sixty years and with a head of silver hair was already there. He acknowledged Fraser's arrival with a welcoming smile. Wilson headed up what used to be the Royal Ulster Constabulary Special Branch, now called the Crime Special Department of the PSNI.

They knew each other well, having worked together in Northern Ireland when Fraser was a Five Operator targeting the same terrorists as Wilson, and both men had a deep respect for the other.

'Well, Tom, I know from our history such a request for an urgent meeting can only be for one of two reasons: something is going to blow up in my face, or the person involved needs my help.'

Fraser sat back in the chair at the top of the conference table and took a long sip of the whisky Broad had handed around.

Broad looked at Wilson. 'When you phoned this morning, you said it involved David Reece, so we pulled his file. What's it all about?'

CHAPTER FIVE

LIVERPOOL JOHN LENNON AIRPORT

Every journey begins with a single step, and this journey started in the departure lounge of Liverpool's John Lennon Airport. As usual, the Belfast bound flight was delayed, so he had time to carry out his favourite pastime – people watching. Since 9/11, terrorism was a world-wide sport, and he'd found his talents sought after.

Every nationality seemed to be milling about the departure area. Some he watched for a while, others he would pass over quickly as he worked out in his mind where they'd come from or where they were going. Most of the young people were booking on flights to hotter climates; their clothes light and cool, reflecting that their destination point wasn't within the United Kingdom. Unfortunately, he wasn't bound for a warmer climate.

While watching, he began to feel he was also being watched. Every human has this hidden sense from the time we were running with the dinosaurs as a defence mechanism in times of danger. After years of specialist training and living with danger, this gift had been honed to perfection. In the modern world of mobile phones, too many people were losing this special skill. Instead engrossed in the small screens they missed so much in front of them, and unfortunately sometimes because of this the very killers in their midst.

Slowly, he looked around. As he did so, his mind began to break down each section of the room into individual sequences. Within a few seconds he could see the security CCTV camera that typically panned the concourse had stopped and was focussing on his direction. He was sure he was the target of its interest. As he had nothing on him of a sensitive or incriminating nature, he stared back, daring the people observing to show their hand, to show why they were interested. It didn't take long. Two men in suits, both about thirty, walked towards him. Within seconds they were standing each side of him, the one to his right spoke.

'Mr Reece, sorry to bother you. There's an urgent telephone call for you in our office, if you would like to follow us?'

No identification had been offered; he didn't need to see any. Recognising the methods they were using from his own training: don't bring attention to yourself unless you need to. His trained eyes landed on the slight filling out of their suits at waistband level; they were armed, so likely Special Branch officers.

The office they took him to was small but big enough for its needs. One of the men handed him the phone and when he said hello, he immediately recognised the voice on the other end.

'Hello, David, I'm glad I caught you. I need you to get down to London asap.' Hearing the voice of Jim Broad made him wary. He reminded Reece of Captain Mainwaring from the TV sitcom *Dad's Army*; part bank manager, part soldier, looking after his kingdom and the people who worked for him. He demanded and received respect. Anyone who had taken the time to research Broad's background would know he'd been there and got the T-shirt.

'What's the matter with my mobile phone?'

'Security, dear boy.'

'I'm on my way. I'll have to get across to Manchester Airport as there'll be a better chance of getting a flight there.'

'Don't worry about that, there's a Puma helicopter on its way to you, should be there in fifteen minutes. It will bring you to the office at London City Airport and I'll meet you here. See you in a couple of hours.'

With that, the line went dead, and he stared at the noiseless handset.

What the hell is going on? he thought.

As he settled into a seat behind the pilot and they headed over the English countryside following the contours of the M6 motorway hundreds of feet below, the memory of the last time he'd been in a Puma came flooding back.

He'd been travelling with an army search team over the snow-covered hills of South Armagh in the middle of the night five years before. Although he wore the uniform of a Sergeant in the Royal Ulster Constabulary, he usually worked in civilian clothes as an undercover officer. Later, when walking through the streets of Crossmaglen – a

Provisional IRA stronghold – the uniform would give him the anonymity he needed to do his job. As they flew over Camlough Mountain, it seemed like they were flying upside down as the white, snow-covered land below looked like clouds in the moonlight except for the odd golden light flowing from the windows of the farmhouses dotting the landscape.

The operation involved them landing at the Crossmaglen Army police base then patrolling on foot to a nearby housing estate to raid the home of PIRA commander, Sean Costello, arrest him, and search the house for munitions and documents pointing to his terrorist activities.

The Puma landed on the base square and without shutting down the engines, dropped the raiding party and then accelerated towards the thirty-foot-high security fencing before pulling up into a steep climb away from the base.

The PIRA leader wasn't at home and his family couldn't, or more likely wouldn't, give any information as to his whereabouts. Reece brought back some documents found hidden behind a box in the garage, which provided little intelligence.

The whole time Reece had been in Crossmaglen he was escorted by an eight-man army patrol providing protective cover against any attack. On the way back to the base, an elderly lady passing him whispered under her breath, 'Good morning, Sergeant, take care.'

She kept walking with her head down. Reece hadn't replied; he knew she risked death if seen talking to him. But it had felt good to realise that there were decent people here in a town known for its bitterness and hatred of the security forces.

Although the search hadn't garnered the information they needed, Reece knew Sean Costello had a reputation for death – he'd been linked to at least twenty murders and Reece had interviewed him before.

Sat across the table from him with a fellow Branch Officer in the Gough Barracks holding centre. The other officer had asked Costello what he would do if they met in Costello's local pub: would he buy him a pint?

Costello said nothing but reached for a box of matches on the table and taking one out he broke it in half while looking the officer in the eye. The SB man smiled and took out a match from the same box, struck it, and placing the flame in the box, ignited the rest while never once taking his eyes off Costello and said, 'Well, this is what I'll do to you if you ever come across my path.'

It was war, and everyone knew the endgame if caught in the wrong place at the wrong time.

Big boy's rules.

That was the name of the game.

Unfortunately for Reece, they couldn't make anything stick and Costello had walked free. The biggest regret of his career was that he'd never managed to get Costello off the streets and behind bars.

Unlike the Puma journey on that winter day, this time Reece found himself looking out at green fields and small towns and villages.

They landed in a secure corner at the airport where a car waited to take Reece to the SG9 office. As he walked to the car, Reece noticed a shaft of sunlight part the clouds and light up the tarmac in front of him.

The Gods shining down, he thought, *but bringing good news or bad?* That was the question.

CHAPTER SIX

It was only the second time Reece had been in this office. The first was when he'd been invited to join the Department. On that occasion, he'd sat in front of the desk as Broad walked him through his personal file.

Sir Ian Fraser had sat quietly watching Reece and only spoke to explain why SG9 had been created, his own connection to it as head of MI6, and how Reece could help by bringing his valuable experience in combating terrorism.

Reece didn't need much convincing. He'd been in a rut, with rare skills not needed in Civi Street. His previous life, he thought, had been but a preparation for just such a job. His boys had grown up and left home, and there was no one special in his life.

Nothing to hold him back.

His answer was: *where do I sign?*

That was two years ago.

Wilson stood as Reece came around the table.

'Well, Tom, this is a surprise, but a nice one. How are you?'

'Good, Dave. It's been a while.'

'A few years. It's good to see yo—'

'All this is very nice, gentlemen,' Sir Ian interrupted. 'But we have work to do. Mr Reece, please take a seat. I'll let the ACC explain the urgency and why we had to get you here as soon as possible.'

Reece nodded his recognition of Sir Ian and in turn, Jim Broad, before sitting down next to Broad facing Tom Wilson.

'It's all your fault, Reece.' He smiled. 'If you hadn't been such a good agent handler, we wouldn't be sitting here now.'

Reece returned the smile with a raised eyebrow, showing his confusion.

'OK, Tom, what have I done now?'

'Do you remember an agent, code name Mike?'

'Yes, a damn good agent.'

Reece thought back to the first time he'd seen Mary McAuley.

Just another ordinary day on the surveillance of PIRA targets in and around Newry town twelve miles from the border with the Irish Republic and a few steps from the Bandit Country of South Armagh.

She was coming out of the house of one of his targets. Her long black hair blowing in the slight breeze. She walked with her head up. As she moved, she reminded Reece of a cat stalking its prey: quiet and with a concentration in every step.

Reece had decided to follow her, telling the rest of the team on the secure radio network to stick with the original target.

Reece smiled as he remembered his real reason for wanting to follow the woman. She was a lot better looking than the original target.

Looking at the men around the table, Reece sensed the urgency of the meeting.

'What's happened to her? Is she OK?'

Wilson opened the file in front of him and began.

'Over the past few months, our agents and technical devices in Northern Ireland have been producing information that a dissident Republican terrorist group, believed to be the Real IRA, is planning something big.'

Technical devices meant bugs…listening devices. They were easy to install in most locations and were deemed the most reliable method of intelligence collection as the information gathered came straight from the horse's mouth.

'The information shows they're in the preliminary stages of planning but to date, we've not been able to ascertain what, but we are confident it's something big.'

Wilson turned another page of the file.

'As I said, it's something big, and the one name that keeps popping up is an old friend of yours, David. Sean Costello?'

Reece's stomach flipped. He looked Wilson in the eye and just smiled.

'All our information points to Costello being back and up to his old tricks.'

Costello had been one of the top ten terrorists in the world during the Troubles. He had a reputation for ruthlessness and was linked to countless murders around South Armagh and South Down. Most of his suspected victims had died in bomb blasts and mortar attacks, but his speciality was to kill his victims from long range shootings using a Barrett Browning .50 sniper rifle.

But with Reece, it was more personal...the never-ending dull pain in his right shoulder a constant reminder of the last time he'd seen Costello. The day had been hot, but as the sun started to go down over Carlingford Lough, the air grew cooler. Carlingford Lough is an inlet of the Irish Sea which parts the Warrenpoint and Rostrevor towns in Northern Ireland from the town of Carlingford in the Irish Republic. The slimmest of intelligence from a technical source had indicated that a retired judge was the target for assassination.

The judge lived in a colonial-style house on a small country hill just outside Rostrevor, overlooking the Lough below. Reece was assigned the job of visiting the judge to tell him of the threat and to discuss upping his security. SB Officer JD had stayed in the car as Reece approached the house. Just before he raised his hand to knock, a small red Ford van drove at speed into the driveway. In the split second that followed the screech of tyres, Reece could see that both the driver and the passenger were wearing black balaclavas. He ran for the cover of his car, shouting at JD to get down. At the same moment, the front passenger jumped out of the van, an AK47 assault rifle in his hands, which he aimed at Reece then opened fire.

The rapid-fire struck the police car just as Reece made it to cover with the engine between himself and the gunman. Reece knew the engine block would give him protection and was the safest place for him to be. He took his Smith and Wesson 59 in his hand and blindly fired over the bonnet in the direction the gunman had last stood. The noise of both weapons exploded all around him. Another burst from the AK and a storm of bullets struck the car and Reece felt a thump and searing hot pain in his right shoulder. Falling backwards, he heard the bang, bang, bang from JD's H&K MP5 automatic rifle before the blackness and silence took him.

Ten hours later, Reece woke in the Musgrave Park Military Hospital in Belfast. JD stood smiling by the side of his bed.

'Thought we'd lost you for a minute there, buddy.'

Reece tried a weak smile. The pain in his shoulder now a dull throb. His mouth was dry, and he could just about croak the words, 'What happened?'

'When you yelled to get down, I only had a split second to dive out of the car to my right before the AK opened up. Then you blasted back, giving me time to get to cover and fire towards the van. The driver pulled it round and AK man jumped in, and they were gone, but not before I'd hit the back of the van and blew out the windows. They found the van a couple of miles down the road with blood in the footwell of the driver's side. The surgeon was here about an hour ago. He said you're lucky to be alive. The injury was caused by shrapnel, not an actual bullet. If it had been, in such close range, you'd have lost your arm at least. You were in surgery for eight hours. A lot of bullets hit that car, and a lot of shrapnel got you. I've buzzed for someone to come and check on you.' Just then, a young-looking doctor came into the room.

'Good, Mr Reece. I'm glad to see you're awake.' Lifting the clipboard at the end of the bed, he made a few notes on the form.

'I've made a note for some more painkillers, only to be taken when you really need them. You were lucky the round had already shattered before entering your shoulder. It missed all the vital organs, but we couldn't get all the pieces out. What's left are some small fragments and apart from some pain now and then, with a strict physio regime, you should recover full mobility and use of the arm.'

Reece took the doctor's advice and after three months away from work, made as full a recovery as he could.

Occasionally, as the fragments moved, his shoulder would give out a sharp stab of pain just to remind him of that day.

Having later discovered that the gunman was none other than Sean Costello, Reece had laughed at the thought of the surprise Costello must have felt when he found himself on the receiving end of gunfire from two trained Special Branch officers instead of an unarmed old man. His escape wasn't plain sailing as his driver and cousin, Vincent Hughes, took a bullet to the foot.

Sources within PIRA reported that both men hid in the home of a Republican sympathiser for two days, during which a doctor, who supported the cause, fixed up the wound on Hughes' foot. He would be walking with a limp for the rest of his days.

The sympathiser then smuggled the two men across the border into the Republic and the safety of Dundalk town, known by the security forces as 'El Passo' because of the number of on the run terrorists who lived and operated out of there, carrying on their murderous campaigns into the north and further beyond.

The house search in Crossmaglen, several months later, was with the intention of arresting Costello or at the very least, learning information of his movements.

As Reece listened to Wilson, it didn't surprise him that Costello was back in action or that he'd remained involved in the more extreme levels of Republican terrorism. Most sensible people had realised that enough people had died, and some sort of peaceful settlement had to be agreed. Thirty years was long enough. But people like Costello were just psychopathic killers; they didn't want to stop until every living British soul was dead. It wasn't about the Cause for him anymore, he just loved killing.

'This is where you come in, David,' Wilson said. 'Although we're being told that there is a job coming up, we don't have any details. Now, your old agent Mike comes into the picture. Have you had any contact with her recently?'

'No, not since leaving the force. Why?'

'She contacted the agent's control number this morning. She gave her code name and number and left a message asking to meet with Joseph. I was coming to London for meetings anyway, so I thought I could bring everyone up to date myself.'

Wilson played a recording of the call to the room. The men watched Reece for his reaction.

'Mike. She was my best agent at the top of the PIRA. She comes from a long line of Republicans. When I first became aware of her, she lived just outside Newry, but she originally came from the Beechmount area on the Falls Road in West Belfast.'

'How did you recruit her?' asked Sir Ian.

Reece was happy to tell these men the story, but even in a room where secrets were shared daily, there were some things about Mike he wouldn't be sharing with anyone.

NEWRY, NORTHERN IRELAND, 1992

The first day he'd followed her, she'd taken the bus to Belfast and met with Kevin O'Hagan, the PIRA Head of Intelligence, in the Europa Hotel. Realising she had access to those higher up due to her on-the-ground connections, Reece knew she could be vital to providing intelligence for their operations. After a few weeks surveying her, he knew the key to bringing her on board lay with her husband, Brendan. A drunk and a bully who thought he was higher up the chain of command in the PROVO than he was.

Coming out of a pub one night, Reece watched from his car while Brendan decided to beat her in the street. Not wanting to blow his cover, he had to suffer in silence while the poor excuse of a man pushed her around and taunted her. Reece drew the line through when Brendan took his fists to her. By the time he'd left his car and reached them, Mary was on the floor following two blows to her gut and one to her face, Brendan was about to continue his assault while she was on the ground until Reece grabbed him from behind and swung him around.

About to focus his attack on Reece, Brendan stumbled, but Reece knocked him unconscious before he managed to even form a fist.

Reece offered Mary his hand and helped her to her feet. Assessing her facial injuries, he expected to see fear in her eyes. But she was strong and all he could see was fire. He knew that when she told him to leave, she would be OK.

The next time Reece saw her she was walking in the rain about a mile away from her home. He pulled over and offered her a lift. She recognised him and although it was a short journey, he got the impression from their conversation that she was happy to see him. She was a lonely but smart woman. She tried to apologise for her husband's behaviour, but he knew from how she described his actions that the love, if there had ever been real love, had died, and she could potentially be looking for a way out.

After he'd dropped her off, Reece opened a file on the couple and discovered that although Brendan was a low-level PIRA recruit who had been implicated in moving weapons for Sean Costello and a couple of robberies, he was only alive because of Mary.

She was the one the PIRA wanted. She was unassuming. Looked to all around her like the down-trodden battered wife. But best of all, she was clean.

She'd never been arrested. Never been linked to any crime. Never even had a conversation with a police officer as far as Reece could see.

Using his sources, Reece discovered that she had a Republican background and had only agreed to passing messages on to save Brendan's head being blown off. She was loyal to her family. Regardless of what they did to her.

Reece kept an eye out for her, but it was three weeks before he saw her again. This time she was carrying her shopping and sporting a huge bruise on her face.

He asked if she was all right and she burst into tears. She was in pain. Reece then took a chance and drove to a small lay-by a few miles out of town. He asked her what had happened. She said she couldn't talk about it, especially to a stranger. Reece gave her his cover story – his name was Joseph, and he was the regional manager of a hotel chain, and he travelled around checking in on their various sites.

No longer strangers, she poured her heart out to him. There was something about him that she trusted, something in his eyes.

He offered to have a word with Brendan for her, but she refused. Said this was just a glitch and she could handle him. Besides, she couldn't leave him. She was a good Catholic girl, after all.

She asked him to take her home and when they pulled over just outside the estate where she lived, he handed her his fake business card and told her to call him anytime. He would be there for her.

About two weeks later she called him and said it would be nice to have that coffee and chat but away from the prying eyes of where she lived.

With cover and backup from a surveillance team, he met her in a café in Banbridge, a town about fifteen miles north of Newry. Expecting her to be battered and bruised and again, he was shocked at the venom in her voice when he joined up with her.

'Joseph, they want to kill you. I know you aren't who you told me you are, you're at the top of their hit list. Their units are hunting for information on you, and they will kill you.'

She'd explained that her exposure to the PIRA had turned her romantic ideas about it all to nothing. She was crushed and utterly disgusted with the likes of Sean Costello. Only a few days earlier he'd been bragging about shooting dead a retired security services officer in the street in front of his wife. And another in his home.

Both hits had been aided by information she'd personally passed to Costello. But only one of them was ordered from above, so Sean was on risky ground.

When she then found out Brendan was the getaway driver, she was physically sick. She'd prayed that the police would lift her so she could unburden herself, but they didn't.

Her last task had been to take pictures of officers O'Hagan wanted rid of to the local PIRA meeting.

She'd nearly thrown up again when she saw his face in one of the images and realised, he was Special Branch.

Reece had no choice but the tell her the truth and ask her to join him as one of his undercover agents. She was so sickened by recent events that she immediately agreed, waving off his attempts to tell her what risks were involved.

She was already at risk, and she knew that passing what information she could to Reece was far better for her soul than not doing it.

She took many risks, saving many lives over the years and as a result of the information she provided, they had recovered weapons and explosives and arrested many dangerous people.

She'd played a vital role in the Peace Process, and she was one of the best agent's he'd ever know.

SG9, PRESENT DAY

'Is *democracy* a code-word? Why did she use it?' asked Fraser.

'We give it to our agents only to be used in the case of information indicating an imminent attack on the British mainland or against a head of state which means anyone from the prime minister or a visiting Head of State to the queen and senior members of the Royal Family, hence the "the ravens are in danger" call,' Wilson replied.

'Why is she asking for you, Reece? You left Special Branch a few years ago. Does she not have another handler now?' Jim asked.

'At the time, she was placing herself in such danger that when she said she would only ever work with me, everyone agreed. It would be like shooting the goose that laid the golden egg if we didn't and she refused to help us – the importance of the information she was feeding us far outweighed the office politics. It was authorised that only after my death would she use a different handler. She knows I've been out for years so whatever she has to say now, after years of silence, it's important.'

'You'll have to meet up with her tomorrow,' said Sir Ian.

'Yes, it's a popular little restaurant near Grosvenor Square. I'll find out what it's all about. I'll report back here at six tomorrow evening?'

'Agreed,' said Sir Ian, before Wilson explained that he was needed back in Northern Ireland but asked to be kept in the loop. It would also be easier for him to learn anything new about Costello that came in if he was in Belfast.

Jim looked at Reece.

'David, I'll have a team for tomorrow—'

'I trust everyone here,' he interrupted, 'but I think until we know more, we keep this between ourselves. I'll wear a wire so you can listen in and record everything, though. Then if you need to act immediately, you can.'

'OK,' said Sir Ian. 'Let's go with David's plan and Jim can keep us all updated. I don't fancy having this bugger Costello bumping off the queen or one of the Royal Family on my watch. He needs to be stopped, and that's on you and your team, Jim. Do not let me down.'

CHAPTER SEVEN

TUESDAY, 24 SEPTEMBER 2019

Sean Costello watched the crew on the Irish Ferry from the passenger deck as they prepared to bring the ship into the dock at the Holyhead Ferry Port at the tip of Anglesey in Wales. The two-and-a-half-hour morning crossing from Dublin had been bouncy thanks to the strong winds. He'd travelled this route many times and he couldn't remember ever having a smooth crossing. It was as if the gales had made it so rough for a reason: to keep the Irish and British mainland apart.

Unfortunately, the rough sea swell had never been rough enough, and he'd spent his adult life fighting to force the British out of his country by other means and see the United Ireland he craved become a reality.

He'd opposed the so-called Peace Process Gerry Adams and Martin McGuinness had signed up for and regarded them both as traitors. They'd betrayed the Cause and Costello knew he couldn't live in Ireland while the British continued to have influence and rule over the north of his country.

He heard the announcement over the speaker system that all vehicle owners should return to the car deck ready for departure. He made his way to his small white Ford van. He'd driven from South Armagh that morning and the registration plates would show it belonged to a deceased farmer near Crossmaglen. He had died from natural causes and the family were willing to let Costello have the van for £200. In a hidden compartment in the back of the van, there was a Sako TRG-21 sniper rifle, which he'd zeroed-in between the hills near Camlough and Forkhill.

With the rifle was a 9mm Browning pistol and ammo for both weapons, along with 20lbs of Semtex explosive. All with the compliments of Colonel Omar Gaddafi and his terrorist-supporting Libyan regime.

The one good thing since the Peace Process and 9/11 was that the British Security apparatus had turned most of its resources away from Ireland and were now focused on Islamic terrorism. Costello was aware of the random security checks at airports and docks where, if you were unlucky, you could still get pulled in for questioning and a vehicle search, but he was willing to take his chances.

As he drove off the ramp and followed the line of traffic towards the port exit, he could see the police checking cars and occasionally directing one to a large drive-through building on the left. Costello knew that even if he was pulled in, the search would be a cursory one. He held his breath as he neared the checkpoint and concentrated on the traffic in front to avoid any collision. Two minutes later, he was safely through where he turned left at the port exit and headed towards the A55. He knew this journey east well and soon he would be in the safe house. He chuckled to himself. There was nothing safe about what would be going on in that house.

In fact, his plans were anything but safe for the people of Manchester.

CHAPTER EIGHT

He heard them smash down the glass front door to the flat. A few steps into the corridor was a door to his bedroom on the left. It was dark, but he knew where his gun lay on top of the bedside cabinet. He could see the dark outline of the two men filling the doorframe, both pointing handguns towards where he lay. He reached for his own gun, found it, and pointed it at the looming figures. He could get them both if he moved quick enough. He pulled the trigger. Nothing happened. Had he forgotten to slash the slide and put a round into the chamber? Had he pushed off the safety catch?

He fumbled with both the slide and safety catch and the magazine fell out, spilling bullets on the floor and the bed. He looked up at the face of the closest figure, which now resembled a laughing skull. The dark gun aimed at him flashed once, then twice, the noise deafening in the small room. Then came the all-consuming darkness...the sense of falling...down...never landing.

He woke in a cold sweat, his heart racing, a sickness in the pit of his stomach. That's how it always was. The nightmares always the same. The feeling of helplessness, even though protection was at hand. The dream still came, but the nights between were increasing. Reece turned on the bedside lamp. His Smith and Wesson 59 was still there on the bedside cabinet. He still checked it, as usual, every time he woke from the dream. There was a round in the chamber. The 9mm rounds filled the magazine, which was tight and secure.

The hotel room looked like many others he'd stayed in. He always carried a small leather bag with a few changes of clothes. His bag small enough to use as cabin luggage at airports, reducing the time he'd spend booking into or leaving airports. As always, when he booked into a hotel, he made sure to pick up a bottle of his favourite Bushmills Irish Whiskey, a bit of home no matter where he went. He loved to tell people that Bushmills in Northern Ireland at 1680 was the oldest licensed distillery in the world. The emphasis is on the word licensed. There were older distilleries, but none licensed at the time and paying tax on their product.

He looked at his Casio G Shock watch. It was four thirty. The night was still dark, but the dawn wouldn't be far off. He crossed the room and poured himself a small glass of Bush. The Pavilion Hotel in Sussex Gardens was one of his favourites when staying in London excellent value for money with close-by transport links through the capital. It was elaborately decorated, and he enjoyed the fact they provided a good breakfast in his room at no extra charge. The hotel was also close to the junction with the Edgeware Road and the area was a great favourite with him.

Despite the short walk from the hotel down the Edgeware Road to Hyde Park Corner and Oxford Street and the shopping centre of London, the immediate area provided a community feeling all of its own with a unique atmosphere. Small fruit and veg shops, old-fashioned barbers, family bakeries, and restaurants. Everything a community should have and everything in walking distance of the front door of the hotel.

After a good start to the day with a continental breakfast and leaving the hotel early, he could take his time using his anti-surveillance to make sure he had no one following him. A few stops at coffee shops along the way would also pass the time. He downed what there was of the glass of Bushmills, climbed back into the king-size bed, closed his eyes, and slept fitfully for a few more hours.

When Reece left the hotel, the morning air was fresh with a slight autumn breeze, the sun shining brightly and reflecting off the glass windows of the buildings as he passed by.

Turning right at the junction with the Edgeware Road he walked at a steady pace in the direction of Hyde Park and Oxford Street a mile away. Reece had tried to avoid the London underground since the July seventh bombings.

The nearest Tube station was where one of the suicide bombers, Mohammad Sidique Khan, had set off his bomb as the train pulled out of the station, killing six people and injuring many more.

He only used the Tube when it rained or if he needed to get across the city quickly. He never used a car in London. Traffic congestion and road works made it a nightmare to travel the roads of the city in that mode of transport. It was quicker and more enjoyable to walk getting rid of the kind of stress he would have if driving. Taxi drivers knew the short-cuts and where the roadworks were, so a taxi was OK on those occasions when no other way was possible. For now, he would walk using the tradecraft surveillance skills he was taught on these very streets by MI5 many years ago.

As he walked, he thought about how the training had developed and how it had saved his life on more than one occasion. Because of the continuing terrorist campaign in Northern Ireland during the early eighties, Special Branch officers were sent on training courses in England with the SAS and MI5. Reece had attended a Surveillance and Agent Handling course in London with MI5. The instructors taught all the tradecraft of running agents in a dangerous and hostile environment and the skills of how to watch and avoid being watched through surveillance and anti-surveillance. He'd learnt how to follow someone on foot and in vehicles. The instructors always kept the trainees away from the underground for two main reasons, the difficulty of following someone in the crowded Tube stations, but, more importantly, there was no underground in Northern Ireland so that would have been a waste of valuable course time.

Walking, you could see much more going on around you. Then there were the smells, the noise, and the air that cleared his mind, helping him make better use of the senses God had gifted him.

Today is a good day to walk, Reece thought.

Before leaving the hotel, he'd strapped the holster to his belt, inserting the Smith and Wesson with a fully loaded 9 mm clip. SG9 operators were given permission from the highest level of the prime minister's office to carry firearms on operational duties.

The one thing Reece would tell anyone who asked him about his undercover work was that the only person you could really trust was yourself. When he'd returned from the course in London, he'd gone to Newry on one of his rare days off. He'd taken his second wife because she'd badgered him to go to the town's market. The market itself was inside a square walled area with an entrance at each end from the street. While his wife inspected the stalls for a bargain, he put into practice the skills he'd been taught in London. Within a few minutes, he noticed two young men standing at the exit opposite the one he'd used to enter. He saw how they were talking while discreetly trying to look at him without drawing attention to themselves. One spoke to the other, nodded, then, taking one final look towards Reece, turned and left the market. It was that final look that confirmed his suspicions. Reece knew he was about to be set up as a target. The man leaving was the final confirmation that he was on his way to get a gun or a hit team to do the job. The other man stayed to keep an eye on Reece and point him out to the gunmen when they arrived.

Reece didn't hang about to find out for sure. His instinct, backed by the training, told him to get out of there. He quickly found his wife and whispered in her ear that they had to go now. He could see she wasn't happy about having to cut her shopping short, but she knew something was wrong by the way he took her arm and led her back to the car. Soon they were leaving the town far behind.

He'd trusted his instincts, and, on this occasion, he found out later, he was right to do so. Later, agents within PIRA brought in reports that the PIRA unit in Newry came close to killing an off-duty police officer they'd spotted in the town's market. They didn't know his name, but because he'd been spotted entering and leaving the town's police station, his face was known to them.

On his walk through the city, he was moving faster than the traffic. On at least three occasions, he'd passed the same car stuck at traffic lights on red. He came to the end of Edgeware Road and turned left towards Oxford Street with Hyde Park Corner on his right.

This part of the city was always busy with people moving at different speeds for different reasons. Tourists, workers, shoppers, always the shoppers. This was Oxford Street, this was what it was famous for, people and plenty of them.

When you walked, it had to be with your head up, dodging the many people coming your way. Not counting the stupid ones with their heads down, looking at screens oblivious to all going on around them, not caring, making others dodge around them to avoid a collision. Reece remembered a senior intelligence spokesman once saying the biggest danger from terrorism was the fact too many people walked about with their heads down, looking at screens rather than noticing what was going on in the world around them. This had the effect that the first they knew they were in the middle of a terrorist attack was when the bullets started to hit their body, or the bomb had already exploded. When it was too late to stop the attack.

Reece wanted to get off these pavements as soon as possible. Moving in crowds gave you cover but at the same time gave cover to those who may be following. He crossed the road, taking one of the quieter side streets heading in the direction of Grosvenor Square. He picked up a newspaper and found a café with a seat inside at the window.

Reece hated warm milk. It always reminded him of his childhood, when his mother would pour hot milk on his morning cereal. He liked good coffee and when ordering in cafés he always made sure to ask for a little cold milk on the side. The waitress brought the coffee. He poured the milk in himself, keeping it strong and the way he liked it. He opened the paper and between the stories and the sips of coffee he watched the people pass in the street. He'd not spotted anything that gave him any concern, but he wouldn't drop his guard. He would keep watching, observing. He was working now, and he would continue to take a circuitous route stopping in at least two more cafés before finally arriving at the final point where he would be able to observe from a distance the people moving in and around the restaurant where he would be meeting Mary 'Mike' McAuley.

CHAPTER NINE

Costello arrived at a service station on the M56 near Chester and made a call to a local number. When the man answered, he said, 'It's Paddy. I've arrived safely and am on my way.'

'Your home is ready. The keys are under the flowerpot by the front door. The fridge is stocked. Make yourself at home and I'll be there about five tonight,' the man replied.

The line went dead. Costello read the text he'd just received, giving the address and postcode of the house which he fed into the satnav, then drove onto the M56 and headed to Manchester. The street in Irlam was quiet when he pulled into the driveway of the house. He retrieved the keys from under the flowerpot and opened the door to a large garage, and drove the van inside. The house and the street were exactly what he'd asked for. There were four large houses, none overlooking another, and the house where Costello was staying was the first on the street. This meant the neighbours wouldn't notice any unusual coming and going. A street where people kept to themselves.

Costello closed the outside door of the garage, staying inside with the van. He entered the house by the internal door through the utility room, then into the kitchen. He checked out the rest of the house, which was fully furnished and of a typical three upstairs bedrooms with a bathroom, with an open-plan living-dining room downstairs.

A small garden to the rear surrounded by a six-foot panel fence completed the picture. Costello estimated that from pulling the van into the drive into the garage and closing the garage door had been no more than a minute. Prying eyes, if there had been any, would have seen little to talk about. Costello brought two items from the van into the house: his holdall and a Browning pistol which he stuck down the waistband of his trousers, pulling the fleece down to conceal it from view. He switched on the kettle, turned the TV on to *Sky News*, and settled down to wait for the others.

Chapter Ten

Reece had walked the full circle around Grosvenor Square, passing the old American Embassy twice. He'd walked through the park area of the square and sat on a bench near the statue of President Franklyn Roosevelt where, once again, he read his newspaper. He'd sampled two more coffees in nearby cafés. All his tradecraft in surveillance confirmed he was alone. At 12.30, he inserted his radio earpiece and spoke.

'Control, this is Alpha One coming online, over.'

The voice in his ear confirmed his message.

'Roger, Alpha One, you're coming in loud and clear.'

Reece replied, 'Roger, Control, moving to view primary location. Will keep you updated.'

'Roger, Alpha One.'

Reece made his way to the top of Grosvenor Street just off the square. Corrigan's was one of his favourite restaurants in London, one he'd used many times. He'd first used it the year he'd recruited Mary McAuley.

She'd travelled to London on a shopping and theatre weekend bus trip from Belfast. It gave Reece his opportunity to carry out a long debriefing of information. It also gave him the opportunity to work on her agent tradecraft; the kind she'd need to stay alive. Realistically, to make sure they would both stay alive. He'd taken her to Corrigan's on her second night when she was supposed to go to the theatre.

Mary had turned up with her flowing black hair combed to fall loosely on her shoulders and down her back. She wore a fifties style floral dress. Her brown eyes and dark olive skin gave off a Latin complexion. Reece had forgotten how beautiful she was. He'd tried to be the ultimate professional, but he knew from that night his feelings for Agent Mike would never be the same again. He briefed her on how to contact him using her code name and agent number, BC15, and helped her memorise the special agent's phone number. Never to write down anything connecting them both.

Mary took everything on-board quickly, understanding everything Reece explained to her. She was a good listener. Reece had known from the start that she was a smart woman. The more they met and talked, the more he knew the path she'd chosen had been decided after much thought and heart-searching.

The dinner in Corrigans had gone on for some time with two bottles of Chablis, a favourite of his, and one Mary seemed to enjoy as well. She'd given him a sense of what the Republican movements were thinking at that time. What they were discussing and planning with regard to the terrorist campaign and their political movement led by Gerry Adams and Martin McGuinness. The peace talks had been going on in the background with the British Government.

Eventually, the talk of violence and destruction drained from the conversation, and she began to open up and speak about her personal life. Her marriage was disintegrating. The drunken abuse from Brendan meant she'd reached the point where she could take it no longer. She wanted to leave but had no money, nowhere to live, and no one she could talk to with any trust. She was opening up to Reece in her own way, a cry for help, without coming straight out and saying so. She was a proud woman. Reece reassured her as best he could. He told her he would always be there for her, and he would help her, one step at a time, to leave Brendan and find a new life just for her.

Throughout the night, Reece had to keep reminding himself to be professional. Getting personally involved would be dangerous. But he couldn't help himself. There was something about this woman that broke down his barriers. Her beauty, her vulnerability, her intelligence. All combined to overwhelm his senses. He found himself holding her hand across the table, looking into her dark eyes, and smiling when she smiled. Reece had been through bad relationships, marriage, and divorce, so he could understand her pain, although his pain had been psychological. He could see the tears welling in her eyes.

He felt that night that he'd said what she'd hoped to hear. When he walked her to the taxi rank, she was quiet. As they parted, she squeezed his hand and, leaning close to him, she kissed him on his cheek. As she turned towards her taxi, she looked back over her shoulder and said, with a smile, that she'd enjoyed the evening and she'd call him soon.

Reece had told her in the restaurant that if she ever needed to talk to him on a matter that would take time to discuss and if she could make it,

Corrigans would be the place to meet. Otherwise, the laneways, lay-bys, and secure safe houses in Northern Ireland would have to do.

Now, as one o'clock approached, he watched her get out of a taxi further down the street and casually check around. Deciding she was clear, she walked up the street towards him and into Corrigans fifty yards away.

CHAPTER ELEVEN

Reece spoke into his mike again. 'Control, target arrived safely and moving to rendezvous, will be in touch.'

'Roger, Alpha One. Understood. Standing by.' The voice sounded loud in his ear, but he knew that only he would have heard it.

Reece walked the fifty yards to Corrigans, entering at one o'clock on the dot.

The restaurant was busy, but he was able to spot Mary seated near the window, facing the door.

Before the maître d' could ask him if he needed a table, Reece said, 'I'm OK, thanks. My friend's already here.'

Mary smiled as he sat down. 'I've always wanted to come back here ever since my theatre weekend when you wined and dined me.' Reece loved her smile. It seemed to light up the whole world. Her eyes sparkled. Her smile meant she cared when she asked, 'How are you, Joseph?'

'I'm well.' Before he could say anything more, the waiter hovered at the table.

'Good afternoon, my name is John, and I'll be your waiter today.' After presenting them with menus, they both ordered the soup of the day and the wild Atlantic salmon in a dill, garlic, and parsley sauce.

'How about some wine, Mary? The one we had the last time?'

'That would be wonderful.'

'We'll have a bottle of Chablis, and can you bring some ice water as well, please?'

'A very good choice, sir.' The waiter nodded and walked back towards the bar at the rear of the restaurant.

'Now,' said Reece. 'Where were we? I've always liked this place. Maybe it's the Irish name that reminds me of home, or maybe it's that the bar reminds me of Robinsons bar opposite the Europa in Belfast. Or, maybe, it's just that it brings back good memories all around.'

'I know what you mean. Maybe that's why I like it too. I sat here yesterday eating alone, but somehow it still felt like you were here.'

'I didn't get your message until late yesterday. But I'm here now. We can talk while we eat.'

Reece noticed that Mary had put in the effort. She'd dressed well for lunch. She wore a navy-blue trouser suit, a white-linen blouse, a dark blue scarf hanging loosely around her neck, and a simple set of pearl earrings with a matching necklace. Light red lipstick with a dusting of brown eyeshadow enhanced her eyes and olive skin. He was sure a few of the customers and staff had noticed her when she'd come into the restaurant. The waiter brought the wine, letting Mary sample a taste before pouring for both and leaving the bottle with the bucket of ice on the table.

Reece tasted the wine. Memories of the last time he'd been here with her. He'd thought that now he'd left Special Branch all those days were behind him, yet here she was again as if there had been no ceasefire, no Peace Process, and the dangers had returned. Despite the wine, his mouth felt dry, and he was sure that the throbbing pain in his shoulder was stronger than yesterday.

'So, Mary, your message was pretty specific. *Democracy is in danger*. What's up?'

She smiled. 'What, no small talk? Didn't you miss me? How have you been, Mary?'

'Of course I missed you. I always hoped you were well, and we'd meet again, but not under these circumstances. When you hadn't been in touch, I thought you'd left all this behind you. I heard a rumour you'd divorced Brendan.'

'Yes. When he went inside for that armed robbery, I was able to push it through. I sold up and moved back to Belfast. I live there now on the Lisburn Road.'

Reece knew it was because of the information provided by Mike that he'd been able to set up the operation in Newry that caught Brendan McAuley coming out of the town Post Office with a balaclava on his head and a gun and a bag of money in his hand. Reece had promised Mike that they wouldn't shoot Brendan unless he gave them no option; he didn't. When he walked out of the Post Office it seemed to him, his luck had run out when a police patrol had been passing at the same time. The operation had been set up to allow the young getaway driver to escape. This would reinforce the feeling that the appearance of a passing police patrol was just bad luck. As Brendan had carried out the robbery on his own accord, more fool him. There was no inquiry by the PIRA internal investigation team; commonly known as the Nutting Squad. Brendan was given a beating when he was on remand for doing the job without permission and losing a perfectly good pistol.

John, the waiter came again, and took their food order then, leaving with a slight bow, returned to the kitchen.

'I'm sorry I was unable to keep in touch. I've missed our chats, but I've left the force a while now,' Reece said.

'But you still work in the game?'

'Yes, but for a bigger company with a bigger remit.'

'That's good because you're going to need that bigger company with the bigger remit,' she said with a smile that didn't show her teeth.

'Is it anything to do with Sean Costello?'

'Yes, and this time he's mixing business with the Islamic crowd.'

Reece didn't expect that. Republicans and Islamic Jihad usually kept away from each other, both ideologies went about their own terrorism from different points of view.

'In what way?' asked Reece.

'Well, to bring you up to date I must go back some time in my story. What I'm going to tell you, some of which you may already know, starts in Iran and Lebanon some years ago. When Sean Costello joined the Provisional IRA, it was quickly noticed how good a shot he was and how ruthless he could be. At that time, the movement was very closely associated with other terrorist groups such as Black September, Basque Separatists, and the German Baader-Meinhof gang.

'The top players in these organisations were sent to Arab training camps throughout the Middle East, sponsored by the likes of Gaddafi and Iran. It was at these camps the best the terror groups had to offer went to finishing school, polishing their skills and making them deadly killers. This is where Costello learnt to be an even more efficient killer with all kinds of weapons and explosives. Being that kind of boiling pot for the many terrorist groups of that time, it was inevitable that friendships would be forged across the boundaries of the different ideologies. Friendships that bring me here today. I have to tell you now, one of those forged friendships will be visiting this country soon with a deadly intent.'

Reece hesitated before he took another sip of the cold Chablis.

'I presume Costello is one side of this deadly friendship. Most of what you've already said, especially where Costello is concerned. I know only too well his particular skills.' As Reece spoke, he instinctively felt his right shoulder with his left hand, squeezing the muscle gently.

'Correct, and this is where the other half comes in. Have you ever heard the name Sharon Lyndsey?'

Reece had not only heard of her; he'd been given her file by Jim Broad when he first joined the Department. The White Widow.

Reece had been surprised to see that she'd been born in the town of Banbridge in Northern Ireland in 1983. Reece had been living in the same town at that time while working in the Newry Special Branch office.

The file had told him that Lyndsey's father had been a British soldier and during her early years, she'd moved to England with the family where she'd grown up and converted to Islam. She'd married one of the London July Seven suicide bombers, Germaine Lindsay, and earned the White Widow moniker. She'd claimed not to have known anything about the bomb attacks, or her husband's involvement with extreme Islamic Jihad, and the police had accepted this.

The file went on to say that she'd taken her young family to South Africa and then to Kenya where she became an important cog in the ranks of Al Shabab and al-Qaeda. She was involved in organising the Islamic attacks in the region. She also appeared to be deeply involved in the financing of the terrorist campaigns.

Mary sipped her wine while watching Reece for his reaction.

'Yes, I've heard of her, and from what I've heard she's a nasty piece of work. What's all this about?'

'As I said, it's a bit of a long story. Somewhere along the line, she and Costello crossed paths, most likely in one of the training camps they both attended, God knows, but they met. Now they're working together to attack this country, a *spectacular* as you might call it.'

'How do you know?' asked Reece.

'A week ago, I met up with Kevin O'Hagan in Belfast. To say he was angry is an understatement. He told me that working with the Brits and Unionists was always going to be difficult without idiots like the Real IRA and Sean Costello sticking their oar in. He said there was talk that Costello was planning a big job on the British mainland and he would be working with the Islamic Jihad under the control of Sharon Lyndsey. All he knew was that it was going to happen soon and would involve them killing someone of high importance.'

'And how does O'Hagan know?'

'He's been speaking to some guy who used to be PIRA but has now moved over to the Real IRA. This guy doesn't mind attacking Brits, but not if it means getting into bed with Islamic nut cases. His words, not mine. The guy went with Costello to old PIRA weapons hide near the border in South Armagh. There they removed a sniper rifle ammo and some Semtex. Then he went with Costello to the hills near Forkhill and he did lookout while Costello zeroed-in the rifle with a few rounds. All Costello would say was that he would be away the first week of October and that he was working with some old friends from the Middle East. The guy also claimed Costello said something about the White Widow and a high-grade Brit target, but nothing clearer than that. He didn't even think it was sanctioned by the Real IRA headquarters, but rather Costello operating as a rogue warrior.'

'Do you think you'll be able to find out any more information?'

'Maybe, if I meet with O'Hagan again. But I don't think he knows much more.'

'Well, see what you can do, but don't take any unnecessary risks.'

'I'll try, but no promises.'

Reece poured them both some more wine. 'It's the twenty-fourth of September, so we don't have much time before whatever Costello is up to happens. I'll give you a secure-access mobile phone number, so you can get me at any time. Where are you staying?'

'I got a good deal at the IBIS beside Wembley Stadium. I'm going to be here two more nights, then back to Belfast.'

'Wembley, that's a bit far out?'

'Best I could do at short notice. Anyway, there's a straight run into the city centre from the station just opposite the hotel.'

'If you ever need to get over in the future, I can pick up the expenses and get you a hotel nearer the city centre. Talking about expenses.' Reece took an envelope out of his jacket pocket and handed it to her.

'There's five thousand in there.'

She started to protest as she always did when Reece gave her money. She wanted to think that what she was doing was saving innocent lives and not being a traitor to the cause, her country, or her people. Reece held up his hands and explained as he always did.

'Look, it's for expenses. Plane tickets and hotels don't come cheap. When you're on my time, I pay, not you.'

The fact that he always made it seem that the money came from him personally and not a shadowy organisation seemed to satisfy her sense of morals. She smiled and put the envelope in her handbag.

'If you need more for emergencies, let me know.'

Reece thought back to a male agent he used to run in Newry PIRA who had the complete opposite view when it came to be being paid for his information. He would always tell Reece the same sentence in Gaelic, which he would then translate.

'Talk's cheap but drink costs money.'

Agents became agents for many reasons. Some were caught doing bad things and the offer to become an agent, source, informer, whatever you wanted to call it, outweighed many years in jail; their own get out of jail free card.

Reece preferred agent or source. When he'd attended the Agents Handling Course with MI5 in London, he remembered the instructors teaching the reasons someone became an agent. They did it for two main reasons, the first being money. The money to pay the agent could increase depending on the quality and the frequency of the information they provided. If the agent's motivation was money at the start, they would work hard to bring in the kind of information that brought the biggest financial reward.

The problem with the agent motivated by money was they could end up taking too many risks and expose themselves to questions from within their own organisation. Being too nosey and asking too many questions could lead to being set up by their own people who would then give them disinformation. They would then sit back to see what the reaction of the security forces would be thus exposing the agent's double-cross. The agent would then, after torture end up in a ditch with a bullet in the head.

The second problem with the agent motivated by money was that they would start to invent the information just to get more money. A good handler would soon spot this as the agent never seemed to realise there were many other sources reporting in at the same time and when all the information was pulled together like a giant jigsaw, the false information provided by the greedy agent would stand out like a sore thumb.

If an agent was good or bad, if they could produce good or bad intelligence depended, to a large extent, on how good the handler was. The term *to babysit* was used because that's what a good agent handler became: a good babysitter. When an agent is first recruited, how long the agent produces good intelligence and how long they stayed alive depends on the understanding built up between the handler and the agent.

The handler looked after the agent as a babysitter would a child. Teaching them to walk before they can run, what to say, dangers to look for, even down to how to spend money. Many agents were lost because they couldn't handle the fact that all of a sudden, they had a large flow of unaccounted cash to spend.

A good handler taught the agent well at every aspect of the game as they arose. The handler also needed to study the agent. Know their personal background and habits through and through. What makes them tick? Do they have a drink or drug problem? Are they a gambler? Do they have problems at home? And most important: do they really listen? Can they do this without bringing suspicion on themselves by their actions or what they say? But above all, can they be trusted?

Thinking back on the agent's course, Reece would laugh to himself when he remembered the room of trainees being asked by the instructor, if they looked at all the instructors on the course were there any they would target for recruitment? The whole room, including Reece, agreed on one of the MI5 Instructor's being ideal material as he drank too much when in company and wanted to be everyone's friend. A few weeks after the course Reece was not too surprised when he saw media reports that the same MI5 officer had been arrested and charged with trying to pass secrets to the Russians.

Reece had always lived by the only trust that really mattered, to trust no one but himself. Mary McAuley came a close second. She also fell into the only remaining type of agent. The one who had been true to their cause but then the cause she aspired to had changed, had died as far as the agent was concerned. In Mary's case, fighting the British, fighting a war against soldiers and police who represented the oppression she'd grown up with, was a war she could put her name to. But when that war resulted in the deaths of more and more innocent men, women, and children, she'd changed. The men and women who had carried out her war had changed from patriotic Irishmen to a bunch of cruel terrorists, like Sean Costello, who killed for the fun of it. The cause was a banner they hid behind.

They didn't bring the Brits to the Peace Table Talks because they were winning, it was more the opposite, the Provisional IRA had been beaten by the Brits mainly by their intelligence organisations. The British had worked on recruiting good agents like Mike and using high-tech surveillance methods to bring the terrorist group to its knees. The Republican leadership had, in general, seen this coming. Each year the security forces had taken out more of their top people who were ending up either dead or serving long terms of imprisonment. The dregs that remained were not of the same calibre and therefore even easier for the security forces to pick off. When the talks came about, lowlifes like Sean Costello formed their own killing groups, making Costello a big fish in a small pond. This was the agent bracket Mary McAuley fell into. The agent who, despite still wanting a United Ireland in her heart and was willing to fight the forces of oppression, wasn't willing to kill innocent fellow Irishmen and women to achieve it.

Reece had run many agents in his time and took great pride that his tradecraft training had paid off when it came to teaching his agents how to stay alive. A number of these agents had been lifted for interrogation by the Provisional IRA Nutting Squad. Reece knew of the techniques used by this brutal group to extract confessions of collusion with the security forces from its members. There were no Human Rights or Geneva Convention rules when it came to getting the answers they wanted, so the training from Reece had saved many of his agents from the inevitable hole in the back of the head. They had tortured one lad so badly and taped his so-called confession that he'd been an informer despite the fact he'd never worked for the security forces. The lad had confessed to stop the beatings he was getting and had ended up with two Armalite rounds in the back of his head, before he was dumped in a field in South Armagh. His interrogators sent his taped confession to his parents which only added to the horror and misery they were going through at the death of their son. To add to their trials, they couldn't recognise their own son when his body was brought to the hospital because of the damage done by the Armalite rounds and the brutal beatings he'd received.

Reece understood the world his agents lived in and thought he'd left all that in the past. When he'd left Special Branch, he'd introduced his agents to their new handlers. Everyone except Mary. She'd remained steadfast in her resolve that she'd only work with him and would only stop when one of them was dead.

A long way off, thought Reece. The starter and main course had come and gone, washed down with the cool tasting Chablis, iced water, and a strong coffee. The restaurant had filled and now began to empty again.

'I like this place,' she said as she watched people leaving. 'It always has good memories for me.' Looking at Reece she said, 'You don't know how close I came to asking you up to my room when you walked me back the last time we dined here.'

Reece had thought about that night many times; he knew she was looking for a reaction.

'I've often thought about that night too. After two bottles of wine and being in the company of a beautiful woman, the man in me would have accepted your invitation. But being the professional and knowing you had travelled over with a party of people from Belfast, the risk of being seen together would have been too great. Now, we have to be professional again, but when this is all over, I would like to see you when we could get to know that other side of our lives outside all this, the personal you. Because I really do like you, more than like.'

This answer seemed to please her. Her eyes sparkled, and her face broke into a smile. She reached across and took his hand in hers.

'I look forward to that day, but for now, we have work to do.'

With that, she stood and bending down kissed Reece on the cheek.

As she left, Reece could see that same slow, purposeful cat-like sway that he'd noticed the first day he'd seen her all those years ago in Newry.

He also noticed the other men and women in the restaurant watch her as she left, but he knew none of them would have the feelings he was now feeling in the pit of his stomach.

Chapter Twelve

Costello was half asleep when he heard a car pull into the drive parking up at the side of the house and the lights switching off. Underneath the chair cushion on his lap, Costello held the Browning. Slipping the safety catch off with his right thumb he pointed the pistol at the living room door. He could hear the footsteps, the key in the front door, the closing the door, and footsteps towards the living room where he sat in quiet darkness even though it was only five fifteen the light outside had started to disappear. Mohammad entered the room and switched on the light, smiling when he saw Costello.

'Ah, Sean, my friend, why do you sit in the dark?' He turned to close the blinds. Costello noted that Mohammad had changed little since the last time they'd met in Beirut. Arabic in looks with a small, well-trimmed beard. Costello knew he was about forty now, but he'd retained his boyhood looks and smile. Now he wore the suit of a well-heeled businessman. Costello flicked the catch back on the safe, put the pistol back in his waistband, and stood to give Mohammad a hug.

'Good to see you too, my friend. How are you?'

'I'm fine, Sean, just fine, and really glad to see you. You have everything you need?'

'Yes, everything, thanks. This place is ideal. What's our plan of action?'

'Tonight, we rest, my friend. We have a delicious meal, maybe a glass of wine. As far as the wine goes, don't tell my fellow Muslims. What they don't know will never hurt them. I am devout, but when I'm a soldier, not so much. Tomorrow, we go into Manchester for a walkabout, so you get the real lay of the land, so to speak. In the meantime, I have a map of the target area for you to look at after dinner.'

Mohammad went to change out of his work suit into jeans and a roll-neck sweater. Costello thought about how the simple change of clothes seemed to change the man himself. He was more relaxed, and the conversation turned to everyday life, the weather, sport, women. He cooked a steak dinner and poured the red wine. Costello got the impression Mohammad had been nervous about today, but now that day was here, he was unwinding. It was a feeling Costello had experienced many times before. You knew what you were going to do was dangerous, but life is dangerous. Better not to think too much about what lay ahead.

Costello spread the map on the table after Mohammed had cleared the dishes.

It was a basic tourist map, but just what Costello had asked for, the kind of map that highlights all the main points of interest for tourists. Mohammed sat back at the table, and pointing to the map he said, 'This is where we need to look at tomorrow.'

'When does she arrive? When do we meet?' Costello asked.

'She'll arrive at Manchester Airport late this evening and will contact us tomorrow for a meet up. But tonight, we need to get some sleep. We'll be busy over the next few days.'

Costello folded the map, topped up his glass.

'There will be plenty of time to sleep, Mohammad. I'll stay here and go over things a few more times in my head. Like you, I want this job to go well and when I pull that trigger, I want to see the surprise in the eyes of his bodyguards and his eyes as they go dark. The scope on the rifle is strong enough to do that.'

'Inshallah, my friend, but I am tired so I will see you in the morning.'

'Inshallah, what the fuck is that?' asked Costello.

'God willing, my friend, God willing.'

CHAPTER THIRTEEN

'Control, this is Alpha One. Meeting over, all went well returning to main office, will need to speak to the Chief on return.'

'Roger, Alpha One.'

Reece was surprised to hear Broad's voice answer. It was rare for the Chief himself to answer from the operation room.

Reece hailed a taxi and asked to be taken to the business access drop off at London City Airport.

Reece sat in the back, his thoughts on his lunch with Mike. Now he was thinking of her as the agent and not the woman. For now, he was happy that he had all the information he could get out of her, and he'd locked her words in his memory ready for the cross examination he knew was coming.

Still, he remembered the words. He could see her face, her smile, hear her laugh, remember the colour of her hair, her eyes, the shape of her lips and her body as she moved. He made a promise to himself that no matter what happened he would see her again.

On arrival at SG9, Reece was directed by Broad's secretary to the Ops centre conference briefing room. When he got there, he could see Broad sitting at the large desk used for the spreading of maps and files at the briefings for operations. Sitting beside him was a man Reece only knew from media photographs, Sir Martin Bryant. Bryant stood as Broad made the introductions.

'David, let me introduce the Chairman of the Joint Intelligence Committee, Sir Martin Bryant.' The men shook hands. Reece noted the strong grip.

'Nice to meet you, Mr Reece.'

'You too, sir, and it's David.'

'Sir Martin,' Jim said. 'As you probably know, is the PM's eyes and ears in all matters pertaining to the intelligence community and one of the very few people cleared in knowing who and what SG9 is all about. He is here at the request of the prime minister, to hear your briefing from the horse's mouth so to speak and to save time when answering the questions needing clarification. Questions he knows the PM would ask if he were here himself, so you can speak without any worry about security. Now let's get down to business. How did your meeting go? What have you got to tell us?'

Reece knew something of Bryant's background. He was a career civil servant, tall, lean, and fit for his fifty-two years. He was a close friend of the prime minister, not just his ear in the intelligence community. He had a reputation for being a straight talker who didn't suffer fools easily. His dark brown hair starting to go grey at the side complimented his square strong jaw line.

Today he wore his regular three-piece blue pinstriped suit with a pocket watch and chain finished off with a blue striped tie with matching pocket hanky.

Reece thought of him as the consummate city banker. He knew that even though he couldn't see his shoes from where he sat, they would be a pair of black shiny Oxford brogues. Reece also knew that despite the appearance of the city banker, Sir Martin Bryant was a man of steel which many men who crossed his path had found out to their cost. Reece noticed his clear blue eyes were watching him with interest. Watching and listening for what was to come.

'What I've heard has me worried on a number of fronts. Mainly that extreme Irish Republican elements are now working on this operation with extreme Islamic terrorists.'

Reece then told them the details and the fact that whatever the terrorists were cooking up was so big that two opposing ideologies were willing to work together in a common cause to ensure the kind of spectacular success they craved.

It was Sir Martin who spoke first when Reece stopped talking. As Reece spoke, he'd been making notes marking them as bullet points on the yellow writing pad in front of him.

'Point one: It's a spectacular involving two well-known terrorist groups. Point two: It has to be something so big the result would be catastrophic for this country, maybe even the West as a whole. Point three: The first week of October seems to be important to them.'

'Gentlemen, can I remind you the first week of October covers the Conservative Party Conference taking place in Manchester? A conference attended by the British Prime Minister,' said Bryant.

Looks of understanding fell over the men in the room.

'I'm deeply concerned at the involvement of Sharon Lyndsey, the White Widow. She didn't only earn that name because of the martyrdom of her husband; it's also attributed to the large number of widows she's created through her terrorist actions across the world.'

'Mr Reece, I'll waste no time in briefing the prime minister. I'll also put the resources of the police and Intelligence Services at your disposal. As SG9 is a Black Ops organisation, people will be told you're working directly for me and the PM's office and for this work, you and Jim here will always have direct and secure access to me. I'll brief Sir Ian Fraser accordingly.'

Reece was surprised at this. His previous experience of career civil servants was that in cases where decisions of life and death had to be made, they quickly passed responsibility on to someone down the ladder. If things went wrong, they had their scapegoat for the blame. If things went well, they took the plaudits as they would let it be known they'd chosen the person to lead the plan. In Sir Martin, Reece could already see someone he could work with. Someone who was used to taking responsibility and leading from the front, someone, who wouldn't ask from his people something he wasn't prepared to do himself.

'Mr Reece, do you think you'll be able to get any more information from your agent?'

'Yes, she'll get back to me as soon as she has anything, and I can contact her anytime.'

'Good, do you know this Costello personally? Do you know what he looks like and how he operates?'

'The closest I ever got to him was in a shoot-out when I was hit by shrapnel in the shoulder. He was masked then, but I know how he moves under pressure. He won't give up easily, he has nothing to lose and will shoot anyone who gets in his way. He's a vicious bastard who lives to inflict pain and death on others. He uses the United Ireland cause as his excuse to kill. He doesn't have many friends. We now know even his old IRA chums are only too happy to inform on him. To them he's a dinosaur, lost in the past, and they believe he needs to be taken down.'

'We will take him down, Mr Reece, I can assure you of that. The where and when is to be decided. But we'll take him down. I want you to keep in touch with your agent and keep me updated. I also want you to take the SG9 team to Manchester to find Costello and the White Widow and if you find them, kill them both. I don't want these people arrested on our soil to become prison heroes at the expense of the British public, or, to have their so-called human rights dragged through the courts all the way to Strasburg so that unelected judges can make us the laughingstock of the world.

'Did you know that a Mossad analyst once calculated, one terrorist cost as much as a hundred expensively trained men to capture him or her? This is a cost this country can't afford. The decision was made some time ago that SG9 would be our main arm of defence against the people who want to hurt us. We have tried diplomacy, we've tried talking, and financial blackmail and, too many times, we've given in to their demands, yet they still plot to kill us. Have you ever heard of the word Kidon?'

Reece looked at Broad who nodded his head to answer.

'Yes, it's the Israeli unit of Mossad specifically set up to kill its enemies.'

'Correct, Mr Reece. Ehud Barak, a past prime minister of Israel, and also a past member of Kidon, once quoted the reason for the existence of such a unit in words I believe could be attributed to our SG9, he said, the intention was to strike terror, to break the will of those who remained alive until there were none of them left.

'Simply put, these people don't want to negotiate with us they just want to kill us, they want to destroy us in whatever way they can. So, we must find them and kill them first. Do you have any problem with that?'

Reece took time to reply. Did this make him a killer, a murderer, an assassin?

'No, I've seen enough of what they do up close. I have no problem with that.'

Reece knew that Sir Martin not only had the ear of the PM but when he spoke and gave directions, it was the prime minister who spoke.

'Good, now let's get ahead of this. I'll inform the PM that your team has full control of this operation. Whatever you need, it's yours.'

Standing, Bryant looked both men in the eyes. 'Good luck and good hunting.'

After Bryant left, it was Jim Broad who spoke first.

'Right, well, there you have it, David, a direct order from the top. This is why SG9 was formed. What do you need?'

'A four-man team, sorry, one of which should be a woman. With me as lead, that's three more. Everyone should be good with firearms and surveillance. One should also be a locksmith in case we need quiet access. Where can we run secure comms from?'

'Here, and I'll move a camp bed into my office until this is over. We will need a simple code name for the operation, have you anything in mind?'

'As it seems this is developing into an assassination attempt on the prime minister, let's call it Long Shot, it's the same for Costello and us, a real long shot if we're to be successful.'

'All right, I'll let the Gold Commander on the ground for the conference know you're coming. Five, Six, and GCHQ will all be told to keep their eyes and ears to the ground, especially with the Islamic Jihad input. I'll funnel all incoming information through here and keep you updated. Anything else?'

Reece knew there would be a lot of pressure on SG9 and especially him, so he was going to make damn sure he had everything he needed.

'An SAS CQ assault team on standby in Manchester. I'll brief them personally on what might be needed.'

'You've got it.'

'Can you also have our Special Branch and boarder people go through all passenger and vehicle arrivals into the country from Ireland in the past week? Pass on Costello's latest description and photos, bearing in mind he won't be giving us any full-frontal face displays. You could do the same for Lyndsey through Manchester and Liverpool airports. It's a shot in the dark, but maybe something will turn up. We can assume that Costello won't be on his own, so CCTV around the area of the conference might look for a six-foot white and fit looking male who may be accompanied by an Asian friend. It's rarer than you might think.'

Broad pulled up the calendar on his laptop.

'OK, let's see, the conference starts on Sunday twenty-ninth of September, with the main appearance by the PM on Wednesday the second of October, so we don't have much time. The PM will be attending the conference no matter what. You must remember the legacy set by Margaret Thatcher the morning after the Brighton bomb. She went on stage at the conference to say the terrorists would never win. Today's prime minister will say and do the same. I also remember the words of the Provisional IRA after the bombing, we only need to be lucky once.'

Reece stood and reached out his hand. Broad took it and shook it firmly. No more words were necessary, the deal had been made and both men knew what was at stake.

Chapter Fourteen

When Sharon Lyndsey's flight landed at Manchester Airport from Zurich, she'd already travelled from Iran to Tukey to Switzerland under the name Karen Webb. She'd discarded her Islamic dress instead dressing in the dark trouser suit of a Swiss banker with Gucci luggage and handbag to match. She'd dyed her hair blonde and covered her blue eyes with brown contact lenses.

Her documents matched her appearance with a genuine passport provided by an official in the Swiss Civil Service after he'd been blackmailed through a honey trap extra-marital affair with a lady working for the Islamic Jihad.

Once through the airport she took a taxi to the Hilton Hotel in Deansgate and booked in for three days under her assumed name.

Chapter Fifteen

Wednesday, 25 September 2019

It was typical Manchester weather, showers with a little sunshine peering through the clouds now and then. Mohammad had driven them both to Irlam Railway station where they took a train to Deansgate Station Manchester. Costello was now in operational mode as he liked to call it. He carried the Browning 9mm in the right-hand pocket of his green Barbour jacket. His hand felt comfortable wrapped around the pistol grip. He constantly observed the other people on the train and again as they walked across the overhead walkway leaving the station and down the steps turning right into Deansgate itself. Costello had been here years before when he'd driven a lorry with nearly one ton of HME from South Armagh, to park it up near the Arndale Centre before activating the timer which triggered one of the largest explosions in Britain since the Second World War.

He was aware he was on the British Security Service's most wanted list but a visit to Tehran and a few cosmetic snips here and there had been enough to change his facial profile, enough to allow him to move about more freely. Only someone who really knew him could spot the man below the new mask.

It was while he was in Tehran that he'd met by accident his old friend Sharon Lyndsey while sipping a cup of strong Arabic coffee outside a café in The Square of the Revolution.

She was wearing the traditional Muslim headscarf and when he called out to her, she stopped and taking a long look said, 'My God, Sean is that you?'

They had hugged and talked non-stop through three cups of coffee. The last time they'd met was in a training camp in the Becca Valley in Lebanon. She was teaching in tradecraft on how to use forged documents to get through security checks and how to set up false covers and bank accounts. Costello had been improving his skills as one of the world's deadliest snipers.

After two more meetings, the plan that brought Costello back to Manchester had been hatched. Lyndsey had hitched her star to a number of Islamic Jihad groups from Hezbollah to Al Shabab but always staying close to the al-Qaeda terrorist campaign. Like Costello, she'd always moved when one group seemed to be going soft on the West. Lyndsey had told Costello she had contacts in England who wanted to attack the British establishment where it would hurt most, its own streets. In particular, there was a small team of three men who she'd helped with false documents and money. These men were now ready to carry out attacks in England but what they needed was a good target and the proper resources to hit it, determination they had in abundance according to Lyndsey. It was then that Costello had floated the idea of a joint operation where he could supply the equipment and they could hit two targets at once. They agreed that Lyndsey would be the finance provider and the point of liaison between the two groups on the ground and Costello would be the leader of the overall operation.

Costello worried that she'd be too well-known and might be spotted in England. She'd laughed and told him she'd been there many times helping to radicalise young men to the cause of the Islamic Jihad, then helping them to train and fight in the countries where they were needed.

The three-man team she spoke of were of the highest calibre and commitment. One of them, Waheed, was a cousin of Azhari Husin, who had been al-Qaeda's chief bomb maker. He'd been killed when a house he was in at Batu, Indonesia was assaulted by their Special Forces acting on intelligence received from the Israeli Secret Service, Mossad. He'd been wounded twice but died a martyr to the cause when one of his associates detonated a suicide vest killing them both. Waheed had followed in his cousin's footsteps and was now one of Islamic Jihad's top bomb makers.

The seed of an idea had started to formulate in Costello's mind. He didn't know if he could work with a fanatic who was willing to kill himself to get the job done. To Costello, this was a waste of good talent. Talent like him, who, if with the right organisation and planning, not only gets the job done but gets away to do the same on another day and time. He was prepared to die for his cause, but he would rather live for it.

'Can you get them all to Manchester before October first?' he'd asked her.

'No problem. Two of them are there already; one of them works in an office in the city. The third man is in London, but I can have him there by the first.'

'Good, if we can do what I think we can, we'll bring about the greatest defeat of the British and the West since 9/11 and the day your husband died a martyr in London.'

'If you can do this, I'll help you all I can.'

Now, as Costello left Deansgate Station with Mohammad and walked over the walkway down into Deansgate, then past the front entrance of the Hilton Hotel, he knew what he was looking for and the questions in his head that needed answers.

The hotel staff were standing out in the street on what appeared to be the emergency hotel drill. Many of them in flimsy uniforms offering little protection against the strong, cold wind.

When Costello had told Lyndsey his idea, she'd been sceptical at first but when he went into the details, she'd agreed that with a little planning and the right team, it could be done. Lyndsey had contacted her al-Qaeda masters to brief them. At first, they too were sceptical, especially from the point of view of a Western Terrorist working closely with the Islamic group, but in the end admitted that if the operation was a success, it would be a great victory for both groups. If not a success, they would lose little and could blame Costello for the failure. Lyndsey had told Costello this and what they were thinking. He was still happy to proceed and now, with Mohammad he turned off Deansgate and continued with his recon of Manchester where in just over a week, he hoped to carry out the attack that would put the all-Ireland question back on the world political stage and the cause of Irish freedom at the forefront once again.

Chapter Sixteen

Mohammad left Costello outside the Hilton and crossed the road to the office where he worked. Costello crossed the Great Northern Square into Windmill Street where he walked to the rear entrance of the Midland Hotel. The hotel was one of Manchester's iconic landmarks. Stopping at the rear door he turned to face the square in front of him. Directly facing was the entrance to the Manchester Central Convention Centre Complex. He walked at a normal pace towards the Convention Complex main doors counting the number of places and seconds it took from the hotel doorway to the steps at the front of the Convention Centre. He noted the line of small trees that dissected his path as he crossed the otherwise open space. He turned and retraced his steps back to the hotel door, turning once more to face the open square.

This time under the peak of his baseball cap, his eyes took in a slow right to left arc. He noted the many CCTV cameras and the tall buildings.

Turning once more, he walked along the outside of the hotel towards Peter Street emerging with the hotel's main front entrance to his right. He crossed Peter Street into Mount Street towards Manchester Town Hall and Albert Square.

Halfway along Mount Street, he found the café Mohammad had told him about. The Browners Café was quiet, apart from three workmen having a full English breakfast each. Costello took a seat by the window. Outside, the rain had started to fall more heavily. The few people on the street moved to cover from the sudden shower. Costello could see why Mohammad liked the café. Apart from being quiet, the menu was simple and cheap. The people who worked in the café were all Asian and from the familiar way they spoke to each other probably family.

Costello ordered a pot of tea and a full English breakfast with extra toast. Looking outside he could see the rain had started to die down, people started to come out onto the street again but still, few of them. He took out his pocket notebook and made cryptic notes. In between bites of breakfast and hot black tea, his plan started to develop. His mobile phone vibrated in his pocket. The text read:

I'm here, Hilton Hotel, coffee at two.

The White Widow had arrived.

CHAPTER SEVENTEEN

The morning after his meeting with Sir Martin Bryant, Reece had thrown his things in his bag, checked out of his hotel, and returned to the Department HQ at London City Airport. When he entered the main briefing room, Jim Broad had already started to brief the three other people present. Reece knew everyone and had worked with them at one time or another. All were in their early to late thirties and each had a long background in the intelligence game.

April Grey, slim with blond hair and blue eyes, smiled as Reece waved a hand of acknowledgement around the table. Grey was ex-military police and someone who knew her way around a surveillance grid. The fair-haired, blue-eyed man sitting next to her was six-foot ex-14 Int and Detachment operator Joe Cousins. Reece had worked with him in Northern Ireland during the Troubles in South Armagh and Belfast, on some of the most dangerous and tricky operations ever carried out against the terrorist elements at that time.

Reece was glad to see him as he knew Cousins was one of the best locksmiths around. If they needed to gain quiet entry to any premises, Joe was the man to do it.

The final agent at the table was the kind of person nobody looked at twice. Steve Harrison could walk into a room, and no one would know he was there. He'd come to SG9 via the famous MI5 surveillance team known as the Watchers. Steve had also worked in Northern Ireland backing up the police and military surveillance units when MI5 were assisting Special Branch, usually when installing bugging devices deep into the terrorist heartlands. Although Reece had never worked with Harrison, he'd done his surveillance training under Harrison's watchful eye when he attended the MI5 courses in London. That training had saved Reece's life on more than one occasion.

Broad spoke first. 'David, I know you all know each other, so we can dispense with the introductions. I've given everyone the background as far as we know it. There is a credible threat. We have information that there may be an assassination attempt on the prime minister when he attends the Conservative Party Conference in Manchester. Now, David, I'll let you fill in the details as it's your agent who has provided the intelligence.'

'At the moment, we think the prime minister is the primary target. His personal security detail and local protection services will still be in place to protect him. Our job isn't to babysit the PM but to identify, find, and eliminate this enemy. We can't remove the prime minister from the target zone as it's the conference in Manchester, where he'll go no matter what. The intelligence we have to go on, although sketchy, gives us enough to take this threat seriously.'

'Do you think we'll be able to get any more information?' asked Harrison.

'My source is heading back to Northern Ireland with that in mind. Our immediate task is to get to Manchester, embed ourselves in the standard security setup, then familiarise ourselves with the possible target area. The operation will be overseen by Mr Broad and run from the control room here. We've been authorised to carry and use firearms. The people we're looking for will be armed and dangerous so, Big Boys' Rules, we take them out before they take us out. So, let's hit the armoury, get what we need…from weapons to surveillance equipment and report back here in one hour.'

'The code name for this operation is Longshot,' Broad said. 'Which I think is very appropriate. There's a Puma chopper ready to transport you to a secure location just outside the city. There'll be an SAS team allocated to you so if you need heavy weapons backup, they'll take care of it. Your job is to find these people and if needs be, take them out yourselves. Good luck and good hunting.'

Chapter Eighteen

When Costello left the café, he turned left and walked in the opposite direction with the Midland Hotel behind him. Now he walked into the main square in front of the Town Hall. The rain kept people off the street even though it had now stopped. Costello would have liked to sit at one of the outside tables in front of the cafés and restaurants facing the Town Hall and observe the whole area for a while, but the chairs were still too wet, so he walked on.

At the rear of the town hall, he passed a small group waving coloured flags protesting about something, but he didn't get close enough to find out what in case they were being observed by the local police. He walked alongside the tram lines that dissected St Peter's Square, passing the Manchester Library on his right. He turned at the end of the building and crossing the road, he entered the Midland Hotel through the front revolving doors.

Inside, the large open lobby was busy with customers. The main seated public area had been closed for what appeared to be a conference group having tea and coffee. Costello decided to keep walking through the reception area and down the corridor which led to the rear door out of the building. He stepped outside, stopped, and looked around from left to right. This was the exact route his target would take. He could look straight across at the Manchester Conference Centre steps and main entrance door. He estimated it would take fifteen seconds to get off his shots, no more than two accurately, as the target would be moving, and a line of small trees would protect the target from view for a few seconds during the walk.

Costello kept his head down as once more his eyes, below the line of the peak of his baseball cap, scanned the ground from left to right and back again. He took in the outline of the many tall buildings surrounding the background to the square patch of land with its concrete path and walkways where the target would cross in those few seconds. Two buildings caught his attention. At the rear of the Conference Centre, he could see the large outline of the Hilton Hotel towering in the distance; too far away to make it a viable prospect for Costello's needs. To hit his target from one of its high-up windows would be a supreme effort and too far for the accuracy he needed being almost a mile away. At that distance and height, the shot would be too shallow and with possible windage, too much could go wrong. As he looked to his right, a building of what appeared to be apartments with balconies looked more promising.

Costello set off at a casual pace in the direction of this building. As he walked towards it, the possibilities firmed up in his mind. Walking alongside the building down Windmill Street he crossed to the front of the building on Great Northern Square. Looking back the way he'd come, he could just make out the rear door of the Midland about three hundred yards away.

A few more steps took him to the front of the building with a sign that said Great Northern Tower Apartments. Access was via a button keypad and all the apartments' numbers were on a metal plate with a button next to them, allowing a visitor to press and speak for access. Costello discreetly took a photo of all this and then the building from a distance across the square. He looked at his watch. He still had an hour to use up before his meeting with Sharon in the Hilton, plenty of time for a little more thinking over a cup of coffee in one of the cafés on Deansgate.

Finding one, and as he usually did, took a seat near the back so he could watch the door and people passing by outside. Ordering a black coffee, he took out his notebook and made a few notes with a crudely drawn sketch showing where he'd walked. He then looked at the tourist map provided by Mohammad.

Now he could feel a sense of relaxation come over him; the satisfied calm that always came when he'd completed a profitable recognisance of the ground where he would operate. The next time he'd cover this ground would be with the whole team – each with a different task to complete. Each one of them would have to be sure of the part they would play and where they would be operating.

Chapter Nineteen

When Costello entered the lobby of the Hilton Hotel, he could see the White Widow seated on a settee in the café to his right. The café at the front of the building had large glass windows from the floor to the ceiling looking out onto Deansgate. The windows were slightly tinted to make it difficult to see into the building from the outside but easy to see out from the inside.

Lyndsey was almost alone in the lounge area with only a man and woman sitting in the furthest corner from where she now sat. On seeing Costello, she stood to greet him, kissing him on both cheeks. Costello sat in one of the large armchairs facing her.

'It's good to see you again, Sean, would you like some coffee?'

'Could I have a pot of tea? I've been drinking too much coffee lately.'

She called over the waiter who had been cleaning glasses behind the bar and gave him the order for a pot of tea for two. Costello noticed how the years away in foreign countries had dulled her Irish accent even more than he remembered.

She noticed Costello searching the area with his eyes.

'Don't worry, the people in the corner are American tourists. Their conversation is loud like all American tourists. I can hear them from here, they've been arguing about where to go today and tomorrow. The only security cameras I can see are one directly above them and one over the bar. The cameras are there to spot drug use or for people using their own booze from handbags. We can relax for our little chat.'

'I must say, the change in your hair colour and the contact lenses completely changes your appearance, Sharon.'

'It's a lot easier to change my appearance that way than with plastic surgery.'

'I'm inclined to agree.' He smiled.

The tea came and after pouring, she asked, 'Well, how are things going, is the safe house OK?'

'Yes, it's perfect. I just finished my first look about and everything is looking good to go.'

'So, you think it can be done?'

'The details will need to be worked out. When will the rest of the team be here for a get together?'

'I've instructed everyone to be at the safe house for eight tonight. Is that OK for you?'

'Yes, that's great. Is the finance in place?'

'Yes, all bases are covered, with extra available if you need it. The house has been paid for in advance using false ID. Of course, when we leave it, we leave it clean so no trace back to us. I presume you've brought all the equipment we need?'

'Yes, no problem, we have all we need.'

'Is there anything you need from me in the meantime?'

Costello took out his tourist map, placing it on the coffee table between them. He pointed to the map. 'This building here, it's called The Great Northern Tower Apartments, is ideal for what we need. Take a walk there yourself, bring Mohammad and work out how we get access to the building and one of the apartments to the rear above the eighth floor. Even if it means renting or buying one. At worse, we may have to take one of the apartments by force. I'll let you work that out, whatever's best. We might even organise a viewing on the day.'

'Sure, no problem. I'll text him now. Hopefully, we'll have some news for tonight's meeting.'

Costello finished the last of his tea. 'Until tonight then. I'll do one more walk about before getting the train back to Irlam.'

As he left, Lyndsey noticed he didn't look back and the two Americans were once more falling out loudly over their tourist plans. If only they knew the plans she'd just been discussing, they might be a little quieter.

Chapter Twenty

The prime minister's Downing Street study wasn't large as studies go. The desk, made of dark stained oak, sat at an angle facing the door with two large winged-back leather chairs in front. The room had the dark furnishings of a gentleman's club. The prime minister, the Right Honourable Peter Brookfield, sat behind the desk reading a report consisting of two pages of A4 marked *Most Secret* or *Red X* as these types of documents were known thanks to the large *Red X* that covered the front of the buff folder the reports came in.

Sir Martin Bryant sat in one of the large leather chairs quietly watching as Brookfield started reading the second page of A4. Bryant had always liked this room. Its size and lack of windows gave it an air of intimacy, privacy, and most important, secrecy. Bryant always associated his one-to-one meetings with the prime minister as confidential at least secret at most. The room different from the sterile rooms of his own office building and its intimacy had greatly helped him build a close bond of trust with the PM which he believed was reciprocated.

Putting the second page on his desk, Brookfield's greyish blue eyes looked back at Bryant.

'How serious are we taking this, Martin?'

The PM always addressed him in personal not formal terms as two friends to each other. Despite this, Bryant, when on business as this meeting was, always addressed the office.

'Very seriously, Prime Minister. I'm assured by the Department head that the agent providing the information is reliable.'

'But this is Islamic Jihad and Republican terrorists working together to kill me.'

'That's the assumption, sir. The high-up target, hints at Manchester being the location for the attack, the same week of the Conservative Party Conference; everything points in that direction. We believe the spectacular result, if achieved, is the bond that's bringing these groups together.'

'Will we be able to firm that up?'

'Hopefully, but as time is short, I've given the go ahead for SG9 to take the lead on this, especially as the agent in question is reporting to the SG9 officer. The operation, code name Long Shot, will run things from the Department's Operation Room at the airport. The officer in question, David Reece, will be leaving with a special team for Manchester today.'

'Has he got everything he needs?'

'I've given Broad the full co-operation of the Anti-Terror Squad in Manchester and a dedicated SAS CBT trained team at his disposal. Reece will pull the whole thing together on the ground when he gets there and report directly to Jim Broad, who will then keep myself and C in the loop.'

'Do you need anything from me?'

'No, not at this stage, Prime Minister. I've given the go ahead for SG9 to use the extreme force it was created for. The best you can do is to go about your normal government business. I'll update your security detail that there is an increased threat, unknown what exactly but to stay on their toes.'

'Well, there's no way we can cancel the Party Conference or even increase the security presence without raising questions from the press.'

'I agree, sir, this is the very reason I've given the Department the lead role on this. It's their intelligence source, their agent, their handler, and the main target, Costello, is known to Reece. Now everything is in hand and moving forward to Manchester.'

'That's good. Keep me updated, I'll be available at all times.'

Sir Martin stood to leave.

'I'm not happy about the Islamic involvement, Prime Minister. It's always unreliable but on this occasion the fact we have an agent reporting on the Republican Costello might just give us the opening we need.'

Brookfield shook Sir Martin's hand.

'Let's hope so, Martin, good luck.'

After Bryant had left the office, Brookfield read over the two pages once more and wondered how he could appear normal to those close to him knowing what the words on the two pages were telling him.

Chapter Twenty-one

Mary McAuley had decided to pay a visit to her old haunting grounds of Newry. She didn't know why but she felt in her blood that some of the answers she was looking for, and that Joseph needed, were to be found there. She'd always trusted her instincts and once again, she was to find that trust was to prove so true.

She'd deliberately taken her time walking around the shopping area in the town centre. She knew that if she was spotted, word would be quickly passed that she was in town. She bought a blouse in Dunnes Stores to ensure she had one of their distinctive green bags. After two hours of walking around and talking to people she knew, old neighbours and friends, she headed to the local Republican Club. When she entered, she noticed it had had a paint job and new chairs and tables. Since the ban stopping smoking in public places had come in, the club smelt of the fresh paint with just a hint of beer. She walked up to the bar knowing the eyes of the few men and women in the room were watching her.

'Well, hello, Mary,' said Paddy Maguire from behind the bar. He hadn't changed much except his hair was a little thinner than she remembered, and his beer belly a little larger.

'Jesus, Paddy, are you still here?'

'Club Steward, now if you please. I think the Committee thought that since I've been here since the year dot, I needed a new title to reflect the new paint job. How are you? How have you been? You look great.'

'Not bad. You know me and Brendan got divorced and he's inside?'

'Yeah, he was always a bloody fool. Dint know what a good thing he had. We all knew he knocked you about a lot, sorry about that.'

Sorry it was happening or sorry no one did anything about it, she thought.

But someone did, and it was because of him she was here.

'Well, what will it be, are you staying for a drink, do you know we even have coffee now?'

'Well, that sounds great. I'll have a white coffee please no sugar.'

Maguire pointed to a table in the corner.

'You sit yourself down and I'll bring it over.'

'Why don't you pour yourself one and we can have a catch-up?'

'Sounds like a great idea. Sean can cover the bar.'

Mary sat at the table choosing the chair with her back to the wall and facing the door, another little tip from Joseph. Now she could see anyone coming into the club, friend or foe, and from where she sat, she could also see the half-dozen people sitting in the room plus the two young men playing at the snooker table. She noticed Maguire whisper in the ear of Sean and point in Mary's direction before he arrived at the table placing a tray with two mugs, a milk jug, and a pot of coffee on the table, then he sat down opposite her, but she could see the entrance door over his shoulder.

'Should I be mum? How do you like it?' Maguire asked, but his eyes showed he had another meaning to his question than how she liked her coffee.

She thought she'd play him at his game.

'Strong, with a little milk no sugar, a bit like my men.' She smiled.

This had the desired effect and Maguire's hand trembled slightly as he poured the liquid into the mugs. Mary had always enjoyed the effect her beauty had on men, especially weak men like Maguire. When they were thinking about her, their mouths ran off in all directions trying to impress her. Mary had learnt to ask the right questions and lead them in the direction she wanted, without them realising they were being led. This was when she listened, the trick always being to make them think they were in control of the conversation.

'So, Mary, what brings you back to Newry?'

She'd been expecting the question. She knew the answer could open the whole conversation in the direction she wanted it to go or raise suspicion as to her motives if she got it wrong. She looked over the top of her coffee cup into Maguire's eyes and smiled when she replied which she knew would have the desired effect of knocking him off guard.

'Oh, you know me. Newry has some of the best shops.' She held up the Dunnes bag for effect as she continued, 'I get bored living in the big city sometimes, and I love the drive down here. I take the long way down to Newcastle then through the Mournes to catch up how beautiful it is.

Then when I get here, I catch-up on my shopping and meet with some old friends as well.'

Now she turned the tables.

'Well, the old town the people and the shops still seem the same. What about you, how have you been?'

She'd deliberately dressed for the occasion in a black button-down blouse with bright flowered pattern skirt, short heeled, red shoes, and just the right amount of make-up; not too much not too little.

It had the desired effect, Maguire started to talk and as he spoke, his answers became more unguarded especially when Mary smiled and on occasion laughed at his attempts to be funny.

'Oh, I'm OK,' he replied. 'I'm still here. The club has a good committee who look after me and listen to my problems and pay me well enough. I'm happy enough.'

'Did you ever marry?'

'Why, are you proposing, Mary?'

'No.' She laughed. 'I've had enough of that lark. Just wondering, I haven't been in here in a while.'

'No. There was one or two who came close but I'm fine and available if you're ever interested,' he said with a wink.

'No, thank you. I've had my fill of men for some time. Brendan saw to that.'

'Ah, sure that's a waste. Is he still inside? Why was he not released with the rest under the Agreement?'

He knew the answer to that question, but she'd play along, anyway. Under the Good Friday Agreement terrorist prisoners were released on licence after two years served no matter what their crime.

'Brendan was an idiot as you know. He did the robbery off his own bat without sanction from the IRA, so his crime was classed as criminal instead of terrorism. He couldn't claim membership of the organisation after disobeying orders.'

'Yes, he always was the idiot, especially with a drink in him.'

Now, Mary thought. Now is the time.

'I know he was an idiot. I was young and immature when I met him and trying to please my mother when I married him. She's old-school Catholic and wanted to see me married in the chapel where she prayed, so the pressure was coming from two fronts Brendan and my mother, and I suppose, in a way, the Catholic religion. The hope of every Catholic mother in those days. Brendan was all right in the beginning as far as husbands go. But then he started to change, and it was only later that I found out why.'

'His involvement with the boys.'

'Yes, if Brendan had one other failing, it was that he was easily led. He got involved with the wrong people who used him, who saw that he was weak and pliable.'

'You mean people like Sean Costello?'

There it was. She knew Maguire was more than just a barman. A good barman doesn't just serve beer…he sees and listens, and he learns to keep what he sees and hears for a day when he might use it for his benefit. This was just what he was doing now, she thought, in the hope of getting closer to Mary.

'Yes, people like Costello. I thought we were supposed to be at peace, that the war was over, but it seems not.'

'Ah, Costello's just a big bully. I've seen his sort many times over. Why, during the whole Peace Process he was in here threatening and blowing his big gob off. "There'll be no peace while I'm around", says he. "No peace until the Brits leave Ireland for good. Anyone who signs up to this peace deal and that includes Adams and McGuinness are traitors and they deserve to be shot".'

Mary didn't interrupt. This was exactly what she wanted Maguire to do, keep shouting his mouth off in the hope she was pleased. She let him continue his flow of words.

'Sure, Costello and a couple of his mates were in here a few times after the Agreement putting a bit of muscle about, letting it be known they'd left the PROVOS and joined this new group, this new gang…the Real IRA. Well, it wasn't long before the word went out from South Armagh telling Costello and his mates to stay away from their places of business, including here. We're just a Republican Club mind. We don't take sides. My customers just want a quiet pint and a bit of peace to drink it.'

'So, where's Costello now?'

'The last I heard, him and a few of his mates were hanging about Dundalk. I did hear that Costello still wants to carry on the war but that he is so afraid of the Brits and the PROVOS that he paid some money to have some plastic surgery done on his face, so no one will recognise him. Did you ever hear such nonsense, the big brute is so ugly it would have cost a fortune, maybe he robbed a few banks?'

Mary laughed again which seemed to please Maguire and helped lift the conversation away from the serious subject it had become.

'Well, I'm just glad people like him are out of my life. I'm like you, Paddy, a bit of peace to do my shopping and a quiet chat with friends over a cup of coffee.'

Maguire took the hint.

'Another cup, Mary?'

'Why not? I have a bit more time to spare, why not?'

It took Mary another hour of general chit chat, smiles, and laughter and finally a promise to return soon before she could escape the Republican Club and what, she had no doubt, the lecherous attempt by Maguire to keep her there.

Driving back to Belfast, the thought of Costello changing his appearance kept coming back to her. It was time to get this bastard out of her life once and for all. She would need help to do it. She needed Joseph. She would call him when she reached Belfast.

CHAPTER TWENTY-TWO

The Manchester rain had reached Irlam when Costello got back. The house was empty and quiet, and he'd gone to his room and lay on the bed, falling asleep almost immediately. When he woke it was dark outside, the noise that brought him out of his slumber was a car engine stopping and car doors closing. He reached for the Browning on the bedside cabinet. He lay in the darkness as he heard the key in the front door and voices, one was Mohammad and the other Lyndsey and one he didn't recognise. Tucking the gun into his belt beneath his T-shirt at his back, he went downstairs to find Lyndsey and two men sitting in the living room.

'Mohammad's in the kitchen putting the kettle on,' said Lyndsey.

He studied the two men sitting on the large couch. They both looked back, one smiling the other frowning.

'Sean, let me introduce you.'

Before she could say more, Mohammad came through from the kitchen with a tray of mugs and a pot of coffee.

'Good, Sean, you're here. Everyone, come and sit at the table, it will be easier.'

Doing as he asked, and with the coffees poured, Lyndsey spoke again.

'As I was saying, Sean, let me introduce you to my friends.' Pointing to the man with the smile she said, 'This is Imtaz, he's from Birmingham and currently studying to be a doctor, Imtaz this is Sean.'

Both nodded acknowledgement to each other. Pointing to the man with the frown she said,

'And this is Waheed. He lives in London and a true follower as we all are. I told you about his uncle, Azhari Husin, a true martyr, Allah be praised.'

Waheed smiled for the first time showing a gap between otherwise pristine white teeth, yet Costello noticed the frown above his eyes seemed to remain.

The colour of their skin was similar to Mohammad, the type specific to Asian men thought Costello, not as dark as an African not as pale as a European's.

They looked like twin brothers apart from the frown, both between twenty-five and thirty years old. Short beards in the style of young Muslim men, both wore jeans with trainers and a casual denim shirt. Similar in every way except Waheed was the more serious or maybe it was just because Imtaz seemed to smile more. It might have been the frown, but, Costello thought, this guy had more history in this game.

'Pleased to meet you,' they said almost in unison.

Costello noticed Imtaz had a slight Birmingham accent.

'Well, where are we now?' Costello asked Lyndsey. 'Can you bring everyone up to date?'

'Sure, only you and Mohammad know our true purpose in meeting here tonight.'

The two new arrivals said nothing just listened, paying attention to every word without any hint of expectation or surprise.

Lyndsey spoke, looking at each in turn.

'Before we start, Mohammad is going to use this device to sweep the room and your phones for bugs.'

She produced a small black electronic device like a mobile phone with two large dials on the front and handed it to Mohammad. She then took her own mobile phone, switched it off, and placed it in the empty fruit basket in the middle of the table.

'Please turn off your phones and put them in the basket.'

Everyone did as she asked, then Costello spoke.

'I thought this was a safe house?'

'It is, Sean, but like you, I've been able to stay one step ahead of the enemy by trusting no one. Sometimes not even myself. This way we can all talk freely and in confidence from the start. When we've checked the room, I'll chair the meeting, so we don't get bogged down with too much conversation.'

All nodded their agreement as Mohammad first swept the device over the phones then slowly moved round the room, paying attention to any electrical equipment, before sitting back at the table.

'All clear, we can proceed,' he said.

'Good. Now, as I was saying, I don't want to get bogged down in too much discussion of who we are and where we're from, this is not important. Let it be enough to say we're all soldiers in the great war against the infidel the Great Satan, the West.'

'If we're to fight the Great Satan as you say, why is this infidel here, I know you and I trust you. You are the great White Widow. We all know what you've sacrificed for the cause, but we don't know this Irishman?'

It had been Waheed who had spoken. Lyndsey had been expecting the question, it was one that had been asked by her masters in Tehran when she first proposed the whole idea.

'Yes, you might consider Sean the infidel and so he might be, but he is a dangerous one and one who has great skills. Skills he has used to kill our enemies and he has offered them to help us in our cause and in this operation in particular. I've known Sean for many years, and he is a great soldier in the fight against our common enemy: The Great Satan. If I'm willing to trust him and vouch for him, are you willing to follow my instructions to help us succeed in what will be a blow to the West that'll rock them to their foundations?'

Waheed looked Costello in the eyes and smiled, showing the gap in his white teeth.

'I'm happy to accept your word, and I'll work with this man to destroy our common enemy for now.'

'Is it the agreement of us all that we work together to see this done?' she asked.

Around the table each in turn replied, 'Yes.'

When he said yes, Costello looked at Waheed.

I'm going to have to watch my back with you, my little Islamic arse kisser, he thought. When this is over, if you're still alive, I'm going to put a bullet through that pretty little gap in your teeth and maybe one in that frown, right between your eyes.

Waheed could see Costello looking at him and he noticed the strange smile he had on his face.

Lyndsey spoke again. 'This team are going to strike a blow against the infidel that'll go down in history as the greatest ever.'

Costello knew the rhetoric and the inclusion of the word infidel was for the benefit of the two newcomers and not directly aimed at him, even though he knew they would class him as such.

'We're going to kill the chief infidel…the British Prime Minister.'

Imtaz and Waheed looked at each other their eyes widened, their smiles broad…the frown still there. They looked for Lyndsey to continue.

'We're going to do it here in Manchester, at the Conservative Party Conference in five days' time.'

'What, no mortars this time?' asked Waheed. Even he knew the fame of the improvised mortar attacks that had killed so many in Northern Ireland and almost killed the British prime minister and his cabinet when the IRA had mortared Downing Street itself from a Transit van parked in Whitehall.

Lyndsey continued, 'Not this time, Waheed. This is not an impossible operation, otherwise I wouldn't have come halfway round the world putting myself at great risk of capture or death. Some months ago, when I met Sean in Tehran, what began as the seed of an idea soon flourished after I'd spoken to Mohammad. He's lived in England for some time and has passed information back to his cousins in the Islamic Jihad and Hezbollah. When I spoke to the commanders in Tehran about a joint operation with Sean, they told me to speak to Mohammad and it fit perfectly with the idea. I'll let Mohammad tell you what he told me, and you'll see why we can do this if we all work together. We each have a particular talent and we are all needed for this to run smoothly. Mohammad, can you tell us where you come into it all?'

'Sharon is correct. I'm originally from Iran and a member of Hezbollah. I've lived in England for eight years, five of them here in Manchester where I went to university before getting a job with a large property agent in Deansgate. From my first days in England, I've sent home letters and emails to my people in Iran. If I wanted to send something of a sensitive nature, I would travel to the Iranian Embassy in London where the Cultural Attaché would forward it through secure channels. Sometimes, as on this occasion, the people in Iran would contact me if they had follow-up questions or instructions. Again, this was done through the Attaché, and we'd meet in Manchester. This is exactly what happened when Sharon showed an interest in this operation. When I was at university, I joined the Conservative Party as a student. I attended meetings and showed interest but nothing more than making myself known to the local Constituency Chairman. I did this because I wanted to attend the Party Conference for which I had to be cleared through a strict vetting procedure – including police checks, and a reference from my local chairman confirming who I am.'

'You sound like a spy, brother,' said Imtaz.

'You could say that. What I've been doing would probably fall into that category. I attended the last conference. As usual, I watched, listened, and reported back. I paid attention to the security surrounding the conference itself from the outer perimeter of ordinary policing to the inner perimeter of heavily armed police and specialist officers. The whole area is surrounded by high fences and barriers. To gain access, you must wear a conference identification card which has a barcode that's scanned once on access through the outer barrier gate and a second time when you pass through a large tent fitted with full body and baggage scanners. This is manned by police and conference security staff, and all this before you pass into the main conference building.

'The Midland Hotel, where the top government officials, including the PM, and party people stay during the conference, backs on to the square leading to the Conference Centre. That's where I saw the prime minister leave the hotel on the day of his main speech and walk with his bodyguards across the square – information I passed to Tehran two years ago.'

Mohammad stopped speaking, this was as much as he wanted to say at this time, now it was time to hear from others.

Lyndsey turned to Costello.

'Sean, can you tell everyone where you think we are now?'

Costello took his time looking each in the eye in turn before he spoke.

'First, let me say when Sharon and I first began to explore the possibility of such an operation, the one thing we both agreed on was that this would be an operation for serious, professional people, not a bunch of amateurs. That's why you're here. Each one of you has a proven track record of working for your cause, whatever that may be. If we're to be successful, we must work together. As Sharon has already said, even if we have opposite ideas of who the enemy is.' Costello looked at Waheed.

'The information brought by Mohammad has helped bring us here to formulate a plan of attack. We each have a part to play which will become clearer to you over the next few days. We need to be armed. If you're in danger of capture, you'll have to shoot your own way out. We cannot let the enemy know our plan. I've already carried out the observation of the hotel and conference areas, and I'll do so once more before the security barriers are put in place. I recommend that you all do the same to familiarise yourselves with the area as well.'

Costello opened his tourist map on the table and pointing to it, continued, 'This is a simple tourist map you can buy from any newsagents in the city. The beauty of it is you can pass yourself off as a tourist looking for places of interest. Mohammad, you already know the area well, so you won't need one. Waheed and Imtaz, I want you both to work together and get to know the area well, especially this location just outside the security zone. The final plan is starting to take shape in my head. If the attack is to happen successfully, it will be on Wednesday, 2 October.'

Costello let what he'd said sink in, and then Lyndsey spoke again.

'We must remember we'll all be working on the ground of the enemy. This enemy has one of the biggest and most successful intelligence and security organisations in the world. Our own security must be airtight. Mohammad will sweep the room for bugs every time we meet here. Mohammad, you, Waheed, and Imtaz will stay here until the operation day. When it's over, if we're still alive and safe, we all make our own ways back to our safe locations whether here in England, Iran, or Ireland wherever. Sean, I've booked you a room in the Hilton in the name of Mr Paul Jordan.'

She took an envelope out of her bag and handed it to him.

'There is money and a credit card in Jordan's name. I wanted you to be closer to the target area so that you can observe the day-to-day changes to the conference zone. I managed to get you a room looking in the direction of the Conference Centre. I know it's some distance between the Hilton and the Midland Hotel, but you should be able to view the whole area from the safety of your room. This arrangement will be good for our security with less travelling back and forth between here and Manchester needed. Waheed and Imtaz, you work together for now and carry out your own observations. Sean, no offence to anybody here but a white man walking about with Asian men in Manchester is not usual and could draw unnecessary attention…the kind we don't want. Sean, is your equipment secure?'

'Yes, in a secret compartment in the van in the garage.'

'Good, let's leave it there until nearer the time. Mohammad can drop of us at the Hilton now and collect some Glock pistols from our Iranian brothers for each of you. We will all be armed for the duration of the operation.'

'I'm OK,' said Costello. 'I have my Browning.' He moved his shirt to let them all see where he'd secreted the weapon when they'd arrived.

'So, Mohammad, it's just you, Waheed, and Imtaz for the Glocks. Like Sean, I have my own weapon.'

She then placed a piece of paper on the table with a set of numbers on it and their names beside them.

'These are your numbers, make sure you save each other's on your phones. Don't worry about security. If you do need to talk to each other on the phone, I'm sure you're wise enough to not be specific.'

When everyone had saved the numbers, Mohammad took the paper to the sink in the kitchen and burnt it.

'Imtaz and Waheed, your only purpose here is to work on this operation. Mohammad will see to whatever you need. Any questions?' she asked.

No one answered.

'OK, we all know our tasks, let's get to work and we can meet back here in two nights' time. Mohammad, can you drop us back in the city? Sean, can you get your bag?'

Both nodded agreements. While Costello went upstairs, Lyndsey took Mohammad to one side and whispered, 'I don't know what it is, but I have a strange feeling about Waheed. I want you to keep a close eye on him.'

Chapter Twenty-three

The hop to Manchester in the Puma was uneventful. The noise from the engines made it difficult to hold any sort of conversation. The talk was general with everyone catching up with what each one had been doing and even some chat between April Grey and Joe Cousins on buying property in the Oxford area. Reece was pleased with the team. He knew they were professional enough to know when they could relax and when they needed to be back in the zone.

When they landed at Barton Aerodrome on the outskirts of the city, Reece noticed another Black Puma parked on the grass near to where they touched down. The Aerodrome was just outside Manchester, its two grass runways about five miles from the centre of the city. Reece could see from the banners on the perimeter fencing that it was also the location for private light aircraft and helicopters, and flight training schools.

Now Barton would be their home for the duration of Operation Longshot. They, along with the SAS team allocated to them, would be taking over one of the two large hangars.

When the rotors had stopped, a man approached the team and asked, 'David Reece?'

'I'm Reece.'

'Excellent, I'm Geoff Middleton the Troop Commander. Welcome to Barton. Let me show you where you'll be staying.'

He was around six-foot tall with a shock of blonde hair; he was clean shaven with dark brown eyes. He looked fit with a slight tan, and he moved quietly without effort.

'This way everyone.'

As they walked towards one of the large dark green hangars, Reece noticed a lot of people about.

'I know what you're thinking,' said Middleton. 'How secure is this place? My thoughts exactly when we arrived this morning, but apparently, they're used to large numbers of troops and police coming and going in the run up to the conference, so no questions are asked. The hangar is surrounded by a fence with a secure key padded entrance door. The code is easy to remember: Battle of Hastings – ten sixty-six. My own little joke when I changed the code this morning, I thought what better, after all it was a long shot with the arrow that hit Harold in the eye.'

Smiling, he opened the door and waved everyone through.

Reece was beginning to take to this man. He'd seen this same self-depreciating type of humour before in people who, despite doing a very dangerous job, could still laugh at themselves and the situation they were in. The inside of the hangar was exactly as Reece expected: a large, cavernous building with no windows, doors front and rear, split into three large sections by heavy dark sliding doors from floor to ceiling, making three large, roomed areas.

'This is your living area.' Geoff pointed to the first sectioned off area. 'The middle section is the general comms area with links for us, the police, and a separate link for your team in London. All the comms links can be combined when needed. The third section at the rear is where me and the boys are bedding down. We had a basic briefing at the head-shed in Hereford this morning so once you've settled in could you come along and bring us up to speed?'

'No problem, see you in fifteen minutes.'

The section allocated to the SG9 team had all the home from home comforts you would associate with a camping trip: basic to say the least, camp beds, blow-up mattresses, a square table with six hard chairs.

No relaxing here, thought Reece.

He threw his bag on the first bed. April took the last knowing the toilet and washroom facilities were going to be the only private place to change. She'd been on many operations before and was used to such places. Reece went to the middle section of the three partitions to find Middleton and the rest of his eight-man team. Two communications officers manned the radio desk and phones. Talking to one of the operators was a senior police officer, the badge on his shirt's epaulets showing he was the Assistant Chief Constable. When he saw Reece, he came over and shook his hand.

'Mr Reece, hello, I'm Graham Lockwood, Gold Commander for the conference. Whitehall tells me I'm to give you whatever you need but as that's all they've told me. The floor is yours.'

Reece took in Lockwood; he thought he was shorter than most police officers he knew and put him at around forty but with a shock of grey hair that made him look older.

'Pleased to meet you, sir. I presume Whitehall also told you we don't have much time?'

'Yes, they did say the period covered the conference dates next week.'

Turning to the room, Reece knew the more information he could give everyone the better result the outcome would be. The seated SAS CQB team reminded him of his Special Branch days and briefings such as this. The men in front of him looked fit and alert. They would know that every piece of information would make their job that much easier and the targets that much easier to identify.

Reece brought them up to date with the intelligence he'd received from Mary. 'We don't know the numbers, exactly who they are, or even how they intend to carry out the attack, but we do know the lead terrorist is an Irishman called Sean Costello originally from South Armagh. We have old photos of him which I'll have distributed to you. We have border agencies checking for arrivals and CCTV from Ireland. We will also be checking the CCTV around the area of the conference. The photo and the information aren't for distribution to the press at this time. Geoff, I'll send the rest of my team to meet with you guys later so that you're all familiar with each other. We will be out on the ground getting to know the area around the conference and I recommend you do the same but keep it low key. If these people are already in the area, they'll be switched on and on the lookout for anything out of place and could potentially know some of our surveillance techniques.'

'We can make the conference zone airtight,' said Lockwood.

'I know, but that would do two things: Alert the press and spook the terrorists. That's why the PM has rejected any such overkill in security measures. His own security detail will be aware of a threat increase but nothing more specific than that. Our job is to find these people and stop them before they even get close to him. I'll keep you all updated on any new intelligence we receive, of course. Our communications will be filtered through London and here. Don't underestimate these people. They are determined and more than experienced in what they do, our job is to stop them.'

'Mr Reece,' said Lockwood. 'Please give your team members one of these.'

He handed Reece black armbands with the word Police in large white letters written on them.

'They won't protect you from bullets but in a confusing situation they might just save your life.'

'Thank you. May I suggest we meet back here tomorrow at 1800 for any updates? If there're any questions, I'll try to answer them?'

No one spoke. Reece knew from experience that the CQB team would spend their time checking equipment, comms, and maps, getting to know the targets and the target area. Questions would come later if they needed to know more.

'Just one more thing, Mr Reece,' said Lockwood. 'All this interagency stuff in such a small area worries me. My central command room is in the city and yours is here. I don't want us all shooting at each other by mistake.'

'As I've already said, Commander, I am in total control of this operation. Everyone will be told what they need to know and if I want people to stay out of our way they stay out of our way. I will, however, let you send one or two officers from your communications team to work here, and they can keep you up to date with anything I see fit. The operation code name is Longshot. If that word goes out over your network, everyone should be aware that Special Forces are on the ground and they're to hold fast and wait for my instructions.'

'I'm happy with that. Here, you better have these as well.'

Lockwood handed Reece two key fobs.

'There are two black, unmarked, Range Rovers fully fuelled and ready to go outside for you and your team.'

'Many thanks, sir, now we can get out and about right away.'

'I must warn you, Mr Reece, my men will be especially alert anyway, so please ensure that your people don't bring themselves to their attention unnecessarily. Your organisation is unknown to us. London told me not to ask questions, throwing the Official Secrets Act at me, so I'm not asking any questions. I'm just going to assume that you're part of the Security or Secret Service. I'm not happy. I don't like secret soldiers in the middle of my operation, and I told them so. But there it is, I've been told I have to accept it. I only ask that you keep me informed and, in the loop, as much as possible.'

'You don't have to worry about anything that's my job, just do what I tell you and we'll all get along nicely.'

Lockwood looked shocked at being spoken to this way but decided not to make an issue of it turned and left.

Reece knew Lockwood wanted to know who Reece and his people belonged to. Lockwood didn't need to know, nor would he ever know who SG9 and the Department really were. The MI5 cards were for such an occasion; giving Reece and his team the freedom of movement they needed. Anyway, the names on the cards were false though the cards genuine, a gift from MI5 to Jim Broad for use in just such an operation.

'Geoff, are your team familiar with the general area of the operation and how to get there quickly?'

'Yes. From the maps and aerial photographs, but the city roads can be busy at times, so we'll be out in vehicles at different times checking routes and traffic. We have the Puma on standby, so we can rope down if needs be and the Commander has allocated us a room in the conference building itself where I'll move some of the team when the PM is in the city.'

'Good, I'll have one of my team to come in and establish comms links. Now, we'll get out on the ground ourselves then I'll get back to you later.'

Reece went back to the SG9 team who were now settled into their section of the hangar. They were sitting round the small table where he joined them. After bringing them up to date on his discussion with Lockwood and the SAS team he told them what was next.

'Right, let's get out and see the lay of the land. April, you're with me for now. Joe and Steve, you take the other Range Rover. First stop for me is a decent coffee shop, I need a fix. Joe, can you link all our comms before you go, including through London?'

'Not a problem,' said Joe.

The mobile phone in Reece's pocket came to life. Looking at the screen he saw Mike.

'I have to take this,' he said as he walked outside the hangar putting the phone to his ear. As he pressed the answer button, his heart raced a little.

'Hello!'

'Oh, Joseph, I'm glad I got you.'

'I told you, I'm always free for you.'

'I'm in Belfast and I'm hoping to catch-up with Kevin O'Hagan. I have a few questions I need to ask him. In the meantime, I needed to bring you up to speed with something I've just found out.'

Reece listened as Mary continued to speak, telling him of her trip to Newry and her conversation with Maguire. Reece, like Mary, was concerned about Costello having a face change.

'That's very interesting. Do you think O'Hagan will know more?'

'Possibly, it's worth a try, you never know.'

'OK, but be careful, don't put yourself in any danger.'

'I didn't know you cared.'

'You know I care, Mary, maybe more than you think.'

There was a long silence on the other end of the phone before she spoke again.

'I care about you too, Joseph, maybe more than you think.'

His heart took that wee jump again and his mouth was dry all of a sudden.

'Well, just be careful. Call me back when you catch-up with O'Hagan.'

'I will do, bye.'

Reece stood for a couple of minutes after the click ending the call. His mind was racing through all the times he'd been with Mary McAuley. He knew he was trying to be professional, trying hard to keep her at arm's length, but even without seeing her or hearing her voice he knew she'd found her way into his soul, and he didn't want her to leave.

Chapter Twenty-four

Mary McAuley was having similar thoughts. She'd wanted to hear his voice and see his smile, but for now that would have to wait, she had to find Kevin O'Hagan.

It turned out to be easier than she thought. When she called his number, he answered at once and informed her he was in the Belfast City centre shopping. They arranged to meet at the Castle Shopping Arcade in the Starbucks Coffee shop in one hour. This gave her time to get home and change into something a little more casual. Unlike with Paddy Maguire, this would be more business than seduction, so the clothes would reflect that. A dark blue trouser suit with a white blouse and now that the Belfast sky had turned grey, a casual, lightweight, waterproof jacket.

She found O'Hagan already sitting at a table, ordered a latte, and sat facing him.

'What's happening Mary?'

'I've just been down to Newry for a bit of shopping and a catch-up with old friends. What one of them told me confirms what you were thinking. Sean Costello is definitely up to something big.'

'What did you hear?'

Mary told him of her conversation with Maguire and the concern she had over what she'd heard.

'Costello's up to something, I just know it.'

'I agree. It's what we suspected. Our people in South Armagh say he cleared a hide and got in some sniper practice. The talk is that he's up to something big but not on Irish soil as he's completely disappeared.'

'Maybe he knows better, Kevin, and he's lying low.'

'Whatever it is, if I know Costello, he won't stop until somebody stops him. He won't listen to reasoned argument. Either way, he's determined to be a hero, dead or alive.'

'My worry is that he destroys any good work the Peace Process has brought about.'

'One thing I can assure you about, is that the people at the top won't let that happen. Nothing will get in the way of that. Mr Costello is already a dead man. If the Brits or someone else don't get him, we will. Look what happened to Eamon Collins.'

Mary remembered Collins only too well. He was another bastard who deserved what he got. Collins was a British Customs Officer living in Newry during the Troubles. At the same time, he was also operating as a Provisional IRA Intelligence Officer for the area. During his time, he'd set up many off-duty security forces for gun and bomb attacks, assassination but realistically plain murder. They were easy targets shot in front of their friends and families.

This had been one of the reasons she'd decided to help Joseph.

Collins used his cover as a Customs Officer to allow him easy access back and forth across the many border roads. Then, like many others, he came to the notice of Special Branch and was arrested. He broke under interrogation, spilling the beans on not only his own involvement and actions but naming many of his PIRA friends, leading to widespread arrests. Eventually Collins had withdrawn the statements that had made him a super-grass saying they were made under duress. The judge hearing the trial believed him and set him free. Following his release and the collapse of the case against him, all those he'd named also walked free. Collins was ordered by the IRA to leave the country and to go into exile on pain of death for his betrayal and was warned never to return. But Collins was arrogant and believed his past work for the cause would be enough to allow him to return from America where he'd been living. He returned to the family home in Newry after writing a tell-all book and taking part in a TV documentary about his days in the IRA. But he was wrong to think he was safe or would be forgiven. The IRA, especially the PROVOs, he'd worked with in South Armagh didn't want to forgive or forget. One day, while Collins was out jogging near his home, he met with some of his old comrades who gave him a beating before plunging a large knife into his brain. Thus, all traitors of the cause meet their end. Mary knew the risks she took, but she took the risks to save lives unlike Eamon Collins who lived to take lives even innocent ones.

'I remember Collins all right. He deserved everything he got. I just thought you needed to know what I've heard as soon as possible.'

'I know, and thanks for that. If you hear anything else about Costello, give me a call. Now, I must dash. The wife's expecting me to meet her at

Primark to help her spend more money. Don't worry too much about Mr Costello, his days are numbered.'

'Sure, Kevin, see you soon.' She smiled.

When O'Hagan had left, she took her time to finish her latte, making up her mind what to do next. She realised that she'd taken the mobile phone out of her bag and had been holding it for some time. Her subconscious mind had already been telling her what her next step would be. Pressing the buttons, she sent a text to Joseph.

Need to meet, can come to you

A message came back almost immediately.

Can you get to Manchester? Can pick you up?

On my way, will phone you when boarding

Next stop Manchester and Joseph, she thought.

CHAPTER TWENTY-FIVE

The Hilton Hotel in Manchester is just like Hilton hotels the world over, clean, efficient, spacious, comfortable rooms, good staff, and pricier than they should be. The one on Deansgate filled the skyline of the city from miles around. Some would say it was ugly and not sympathetic to other architecture in the area like the Town Hall and Library in St Peters Square, but they were far enough away from the hotel not to matter. One of its main features was Cloud 23, the Cocktail Bar on the twenty-third floor with views of the city from the windows on the forty-seventh floor. With an indoor pool and fitness suite, Costello knew this would be the ideal place to relax while preparing for the task ahead.

After booking in, he found that his corner room on the forty second floor gave him the view he'd hoped for. From the window he could see through his binoculars the rear of the Midland Hotel and the top of the Conference Centre. What he could see only confirmed what he'd originally thought on his ground recce. The wind, the distance, and angle would all combine to make a shot from the Hilton almost impossible and therefore too risky if he was to be successful.

Chapter Twenty-six

Manchester was still in one of those autumn moods with bursts of warm sunshine in between the showers of rain. The temperature this time of year still wasn't cold enough for a heavy coat so jeans and a light sweater under her green Barbour jacket covered all the points needed. Deansgate always seemed to have a gale force wind blowing down it but once you entered any of the side streets or squares, this died down and it could be pleasant again. She met Mohammad in a café that looked across the square at The Great Northern Tower Apartments.

The great thing about cities everywhere, she thought, was that no one pays attention to anyone else anymore. They are all lost in their own little worlds. They either had their heads down stuck in a screen or in deep conversation with someone else to the total exclusion to everything going on around them. Lyndsey was sure that this must make it very difficult for someone involved in surveillance. To blend in they would have to make themselves invisible to the people they were following. She supposed it could work the other way if she showed she was looking for surveillance following her and not blending in with the crowd making them aware she was being aware. It was a strange and dangerous game that the fox and hounds played out. One she'd played out on two continents coming close to capture occasionally and having to shoot one of the hounds when she was cornered in Mombasa. That was why her shoulder bag felt a little heavier. The .38 pistol added the extra weight but made her feel more secure. For now, she was sure there were no hounds.

'As you can see from here,' said Mohammad over his coffee, 'the security for the apartments starts at the main entrance door with push button access. I've checked the square and there doesn't seem to be any CCTV coverage of the door. I passed by the door earlier and there appears to be a camera inside covering the entrance. I think that's so the people inside can see who has buzzed their apartment allowing them to buzz anyone in.'

'While we've been sitting here, I've seen a few people coming and going,' said Lyndsey. 'How do we get in there when the time comes?'

'I've been thinking about that. I would suggest I knock on a few doors advertising my agency and hopefully I'll get inside one for a look around. I would pay special attention to the apartments where we'd like the operation to go down from.'

'It sounds easy enough but what about your exposure, your face, your business card?'

'Don't worry, my days here are numbered anyway and this operation will be the one to expose all our comrades whether they like it or not. We will shake their foundations so deeply they would find me, so it's home to Tehran and my family.'

'Worst-case scenario, we go in the night before and take over the apartment and wait. All we'd need is two people: Sean and one other.'

'It would have to be me. With my agency credentials, I would be able to give Sean the cover he needs to get in.'

'No, we need you in the Midland and the conference area, inside the security cordon. You can update Sean when the prime minister and his detail are moving towards the target area. There's no photo on your business card so Imtaz can pretend to be you and go in with Sean the night before.'

'What about you and Waheed, what will you be doing?'

'Don't worry I've been thinking about that, let's just say I have a contingency plan which I'll explain when we next meet up. Right now, I'll finish my coffee, have another walk around, and meet Sean for a cocktail. You keep looking for ways to get us in that building. The easier the better, but no matter what we'll be in there and ready.'

Not for the first time was Mohammad impressed by this woman. Her determination, her coolness, her total commitment to the cause and the task at hand. He had no doubt she was ruthless; ruthless enough to kill anyone who got in the way.

Chapter Twenty-seven

Costello sipped his Tom Collins, the gin refreshing. To his surprise, Lyndsey had settled for a fresh orange juice with plenty of ice. From where they sat next to the window, they had a panoramic view of the city at night. The drink added to the whole feeling of calm. Lyndsey had even smiled once or twice, something he couldn't remember seeing from her for a long time. Maybe she was starting to feel more relaxed.

'I'm glad I got here early enough to get the full lie of the land before they sealed it off.'

Lyndsey brought him up to date and what Mohammad would be doing to get them access to the apartments.

'Imtaz is OK, I don't think Waheed likes me,' said Costello.

'Waheed will do as he is told. He has a strong, built-in hatred of the West since his uncle died. He hates everything with the West, but he'll do his job, as we all will. Now that the security is being increased around the conference, we all need to be more surveillance aware. I have no doubt there'll be the extra vigilance and CCTV coverage.'

'I've already made a note of the CCTV. I know where they're placed and the area they cover, even the cameras in here.'

'I know. Where we'll slip up is if we draw attention to ourselves, so we need to blend in and avoid being seen, that's what the camera operators will be looking for: something different. Ordinary Joe Public will be unaware of our presence until it's too late. They're too lost in their own little insignificant worlds to realise what's going on around them. I've seen it before in Mumbai and Africa.'

Costello smiled understanding, but his eyes showed nothing.

'That's why I'm a country boy at heart. I hate cities and the people in them.'

Looking out the window at the light below, Lyndsey understood what Costello was saying.

'That's why I live in the east. The cities are busy, but the people have time for each other, time to stop and talk, to look around, and to enjoy life. Anyway, one more drink and I'm off to bed what about you?'

'Another Tom Collins.'

Chapter Twenty-eight

Thursday, 26 September 2019

Reece and the SG9 team spent the next morning getting to know the entire Deansgate area.

Reece had been thinking back to his first days of surveillance training with MI5 in London. As a young Special Branch officer, it had been part of the three-week course. On the first day, they'd each been given a copy of the ABC map guidebook to London and told to familiarise themselves with a specific part of the city. Reece had been allocated the Victoria section as this would be where he would be training day to day. Now he was doing the same in Deansgate, Manchester. Where were the bus stops, the taxi ranks, the car parks? Where was the security strong especially at the entrances and exits?

The team had worked first in the Land Rovers, finding their way around the one-way systems, then on foot, all the time getting used to each other's voice in the earpiece each of them wore. Happy with the progress, Reece told the team to return to Barton where they could study the maps, aerial photography, and the only photos they had of Costello and Lyndsey. Reece phoned Jim Broad to bring him up to date. Broad had been in the communications room in London and had been listing in as they'd carried out their reconnaissance of the Manchester streets. Reece told him about the phone call from Mary.

'She's arriving in Manchester shortly. I'll pick her up and drop her off at a hotel, probably in the Piccadilly area as all the hotels around the conference are fully booked.'

'I hope what she's got will be worthwhile, David.'

'I'm sure whatever she has will be more than we have right now. The more information we can get the better.'

'OK, keep me updated. I have a meeting with Sir Martin Bryant at nine this evening and it will be good to have something to update him with. Call me if you need me or have something new.'

'Will do.'

Reece told the team he was heading to the airport to pick up his agent and he would brief everyone at midnight.

'Meanwhile, you should get some rest; it's going to be a busy couple of days.'

He hated Manchester Airport. Its three terminals were always busy no matter what the time. He'd just parked up in the arrivals area for Terminal One when the text on his phone told him that Mary had arrived, and she'd be out in a few minutes. He'd talked about drop off and pickups at ports and train stations with Mary in the past. He would always be outside observing her coming and going making sure she was alone, that no one was following, or she hadn't bumped into someone she knew on the journey.

The rain had stopped for now and as he stood by the Range Rover, he could see the front door of arrivals and saw Mary coming out pulling a small cabin bag. No one was following her. Since he'd spoken to her on the phone, he'd felt the anticipation of seeing her again, of being close to her, rising in him. Now, when he watched as she crossed to the carpark, his stomach turned, and his mouth was dry.

It had been ever harder for him to concentrate on the job in hand when he could see her face and remember her voice in his thoughts. They hugged as friends would – close but not too close.

'You look tired, Joseph.'

'Tell me about.' He laughed.

On the drive into the city, she brought him up to date. The conversations she had with Maguire and O'Hagan was why she was here, why she had to see him, important enough to see him in person. He reassured her she'd been right to come. The change in Costello's appearance and the fact he'd disappeared only helped to confirm he was already here. Not knowing what he looked like now worried him. It was already like trying to find a needle in a haystack, but this would make it almost impossible. He'd booked Mary into the Premier Inn in Piccadilly. It was a typical franchise hotel cheap but cheerful. Reece carried her bag to the room.

'Have you eaten recently?' he asked.

'No, I'm famished.'

'Me too. Let's find somewhere to eat.'

They found a small café near the main Piccadilly Railway Station. The food was basic, and the café didn't serve alcohol, so it was coffee for two to wash down the meal. Reece moved the conversation away from Costello. He could tell from her face the strain she was under.

'When this is all over, I'll show you the sights of Manchester.'

'When this is all over I would rather you showed me the sights of somewhere warmer.' She smiled.

There it was, that smile. His heart gave another little flutter. Once again, when he was with her, he had to force himself to be professional. Feelings get in the way, he thought.

She looked beautiful as always, dressed for business, not pleasure, this time, she still looked beautiful.

'Right, we have a busy day tomorrow. Are you up for it?'

'I'm up for it, as you say but what more can I do? I've told you all I know?'

'I've interviewed Costello in the past. We have the most recent picture of him before his face lift. You've met him, you know him personally. Between us, we just might get lucky and see him before he can do any damage. You know the mannerisms that make him who he is. He can change how he looks but he can't change who he is. He can't change his height, how he walks, what he sounds like, how he speaks, his voice, his accent. It's going to be dangerous, Mary, especially if we get close enough to confirm who he is, but I'll be with you every step of the way. Are you OK with that?'

'If he sees me first, I'm dead, at the very best I'm blown.'

'That's worst-case scenario but I intend to get to him first. A dead Costello doesn't talk. But I need your help. I need you with me on this.'

'It's nice to be needed.'

There was that wicked smile again but this time there was moisture in her eyes.

He reached over the table taking her hands in his as much to reassure her as to feel the warmth of her skin, to be close to her. She squeezed lightly back.

'OK, I'll do it but only for you, Joseph.'

It was his turn to smile.

'I'll walk you back. You get a good night's sleep, and I'll pick you up in the morning.'

'What, no night-cap?'

'Well, maybe just the one, I'm driving.'

When he left her at the hotel, he hugged her, holding her closer and for longer than normal. She responded by pulling her arms around his shoulders. It was then he knew he couldn't wait or hold back any longer. When his lips met hers, he could feel a surge of electricity flowing between them both. When they separated both were breathing heavily.

'I'm sorry, that wasn't very professional of me, but I've wanted to do that for a very long time.'

'Don't be sorry, Joseph, I've wanted you to kiss me, to hold me. What do we do now?'

His professional head kicked in, overruling his heart once more.

'I promised you when this was over, I wanted to see more of you. I want that more than ever, but for now, I need to keep my head for the job in hand. Can you understand, can you wait?'

'I don't have much of a choice. I'll wait, but not forever. See you tomorrow then,' she said as the lift doors closed and took her to her room.

Not for the first time did he admire the strength in this woman. When she'd gone, he realised he was still breathing heavily, his pulse racing.

I'll see you tomorrow and for longer to come, he thought.

Reece liked driving through cities at night. Less traffic, more time to think. Peoples' laughter as they moved between the restaurants, pubs, clubs, theatres, and parties. A city at night has a breathing, living sound all of its own.

His thoughts were still of Mary, her face, her brown eyes, and dark hair, her smile. His thoughts were interrupted by the in-car phone system.

'Hello?'

'Hello, David, can you talk?' It was Jim Broad.

'Yes, I'm using the hands-free. Just dropped Mike off. I'm on my own.'

'We have some news which might be helpful. The ports' people have been checking back over their CCTV and records as we requested, and they may have something. A couple of days ago a small white van with one male on-board landed at Holyhead port from Dublin. The van went through without a close stop check but a few things have been highlighted. The registration shows it came from Crossmaglen, but a quick check with the local police shows the real van originally came from a farm belonging to a recently dead farmer. There're some grainy images of the driver. The height and build fit Costello's description but the driver's wearing a baseball cap, so we can't be sure. The interesting bit is that CCTV was able to follow the van's movements from Wales through to the M56 then the M6 and then leaving the motorway at Warrington.'

'That is interesting. If he was heading straight to Manchester, he would have stayed on the fifty-six.'

'I've sent you the CCTV and informed the police to be on the lookout for the van. It might just be the break we're looking for. Anything new from Mike?'

'No, but I'm going to keep her here. She knows Costello better than any of us and that might just give us the last piece of information we need to complete the jigsaw of what's happening.'

'OK, if I get anything more, I'll be in touch, you do likewise.'

'Will do.'

This was going to be another long night looking at CCTV recordings before getting to bed. Reece knew all the activity of the day would make it difficult for his brain to switch off and for the sleep to come.

CHAPTER TWENTY-NINE

Mohammad had wasted no time; he'd carried out more research into the apartment block and noticed on the Right Move website that there were two for sale and a few for rent. Apartment C13-1 and apartment C6-3 both in the region of £300,000 or £1,000 per month for rental properties. The history of sales of the building showed that they had two or three coming up for sale on a yearly basis, so this was a lucky break. He spent more time digging further and identified two of the rental apartments, fully furnished for immediate occupancy. He phoned Lyndsey and arranged for her and Costello to meet with him at the apartments later that morning. Then he phoned the agent for the properties and arranged viewings for eleven at the two for sale and two of the rentals which seemed to fit Costello's requirements.

Costello was in the lounge drinking his coffee when Lyndsey sat down beside him.

She told him about her call with Mohammad.

'We can go together as the Webbs, and you can have a good look around and see what you think.'

'Sounds like a plan.'

'We'll have a better idea where we stand, and we can bring everyone up to date tonight.'

They met Mohammad outside the apartments at eleven on the dot.

'I just have to buzz the one that's for sale and the agent will let us in.'

'Introduce us as Mr and Mrs Webb, I'll do the rest of the talking,' said Lyndsey. 'Then I'll keep the agent occupied while you two look around.'

'Fine by me,' said Mohammad.

He buzzed a number on the metal keypad for apartment C-13 which was on the first floor.

'I'll buzz you in and you can take the lift to the first floor where I'll meet you,' said a man's voice.

The door opened with a loud click. When they came out of the lift they were met by a young man. Costello thought he was just out of school.

'Hello, I'm Jake, welcome.' He shook everyone's hand.

'Good morning, Jake,' said Mohammad. 'I made the appointment with your office for Mr and Mrs Webb, my clients.'

'Nice to meet you. Let me show you the first apartment which is up for sale.' He spoke as he led the way to the door.

'As I told your office, my clients would like to see both the properties for sale and to rent with a future option to buy,' Mohammad said.

Mohammad knew the commission for Jake would be larger if he sold a property rather than rent one, but the fact they would rent one with a future option to buy would perk him up. The prospect of a rental becoming a sale as opposed to a straight rental improved his commission prospects even more.

'There are eight apartments on each floor four facing front onto the square and four facing the rear of the building. All the apartments are of similar design with two bedrooms except for the top floor which has four penthouse apartments.'

Jake opened the door of number 13 and led the way, still talking as he walked.

'This apartment as you can see looks out to the rear. All apartments have a balcony. This one because it's for sale is, as you can see completely empty of furniture although all the main electric goods, cooker, fridge, washing machine are installed all included in the price.'

'Really, we're more interested in a fully furnished let for now,' said Lyndsey.

'No problem, we have two on the twelfth floor. I'll take you there now.'

Lyndsey looked at Sean, she didn't need to speak. She could see for herself the first-floor balcony gave no view of the target area.

'Great, Jake, let's have a look at them.'

It took another half hour and the inspection of the second rental on the twelfth floor, apartment C-12 for to Costello to nod to Lyndsey that this was the one. Jake had walked her round the fully furnished apartments she'd questioned him for long periods in one bedroom giving Costello the time he needed to check the view from the rear windows and balcony. He took a few discreet photos on his mobile of the main living area and from the glass doors onto the balcony using the zoom on the camera phone he could clearly see the rear door of the Midland.

The monthly rent was £1000 with a deposit of £3000 Jake told Lyndsey.

'I'm happy with that and I think this apartment is perfect. We might need a second viewing if that's all right, but it would be soon if we do.'

'Yes, that's no problem but a property like this is highly sought after so first come first served, as they say.'

'No problem. Mohammad will be in touch with you later today. How quickly can we get the keys?'

Jakes eyes lit up at her answer.

'There's just a little paperwork and once the deposit has been paid, you can have the keys right away.'

'I think it's just what we're looking for. We'll be in touch this afternoon.'

After leaving Jake and the apartment they sat once more in the café looking back towards the building. Looking at the photos on his camera it was Costello who spoke first.

'It's good. I can get a clear shot from there, at least two good ones if needed. Can you cover the paperwork? They might ask for references and credit checks.'

'The credit check I can cover. References might take a little longer and it will take them longer to check than we need but they can be provided. Cash jumps many fences, my friend. At the very least we can ask for another viewing on Wednesday morning do the job and get away. We will meet tonight to go over things and tie up details. In the meantime, I'll go with Mohammad to Jake's office and complete the forms to get things moving. A cash up front offer should get us the keys.'

'While you're doing that, I'll take one more walk from this side to the front door of the building then back to the hotel. The NCP down the street will be ideal to park the van up when we're in the apartment.'

'Until later then. Mohammad can pick us up outside the hotel about seven. I'll see you in the lounge about six thirty.'

Chapter Thirty

Friday, 27 September 2019

Reece hadn't slept well. The pain in his shoulder and the dreams woke him during the night. When he'd returned to the bunker it was late, but the team were still up. They'd been watching the CCTV sent from London tracing the van along the motorways from Holyhead to Warrington. Jim Broad had also contacted the GARDA in Ireland asking for any identification of the driver. The same request had been made of the Irish Ferries shipping line that transported the van across the Irish Sea. Reece had watched the short clips showing a man, tall and lean with the black New York baseball cap, and asked the SAS team to watch too so they had every piece of information he did. He'd also told them about the supposed cosmetic surgery.

The only photos the GARDA and Tom Wilson had of Costello had also arrived. They were of the old Costello; the one Reece knew so well from across the table in the interview room. But if he'd changed his face, as Mary had reported, they wouldn't be much use.

'Concentrate on the eyes people. It's the hardest thing to change,' he told the team. 'The CCTV also gives an idea of how he moves. He walks with a slight stoop, head down looking at the ground and keeping his face hidden from the camera.'

When Reece went to bed the team were still in the communications section going through everything they had.

Now awake, he'd taken two paracetamols for the shoulder pain and given an hour, they'd do the trick for a while. After breakfast he assembled the team.

'Today I want you to check the railway stations, bus stops, and tram routes through the city but especially near the Conference Centre. With a focus on the route in from Warrington. Walk the area again and again and get to know every nook and cranny. I'll pick Mike up and do the same, then let's all meet up for a bite of lunch. There's a Weatherspoon's beside the Town Hall; we can meet there. It will be noisy, but nobody really pays attention to anyone else, so we should be OK to talk. When you're out, don't forget never let your guard down. They're out there too. I know you won't, but I have to say it, anyway.'

'You look tired, David,' said April, saying what they were all thinking.

Reece laughed. 'I always look this way when I'm busy need a long shower and a strong coffee and that's next on my list. Let's get out there, people, and find these bastards. We don't have much time to work with so let's make it count.'

After an almost cold shower and then a large, strong coffee, Reece could feel his body recharging. Standing outside the hangar in the clear morning air, he could see the hustle and bustle of activity around the small airport. He could smell the aviation fuel and see a few of the SAS troopers jogging around the perimeter of the runways keeping up their fitness levels. Mechanics, aircrew, people all mixed together with their own worlds keeping them occupied. Parked up at the end of the runways were three small, single-engine aircraft in the corner of the field close to the farthest hangar. Next to them, a dark Puma helicopter, the one the SAS would use if needs be.

Reece went back inside for one last check with the comms team and found the troop commander with his men around the table going over the CCTV, photos, and maps. Going over the information they have he knew that's what makes them the best at what they do. The training, the shoot-outs, the flash bangs all leading to the dead opponents and successful compilation of the operations they're involved in, plan then plan again. The training, the preparation the skill all combined to ensure the best possible result.

'Have you got everything you need?' asked Reece.

'Yes thanks, as they say PPP…Piss Poor Planning is what fucks up the operation so get the plan right and we will get the job right.'

'Let all your people know that we'll be out on the ground. We need to keep our comms open and linked.'

'Will do. See you later.'

The coffee and the shower had done the trick and the paracetamol had finally kicked in, Reece felt better; refreshed, and ready for the rest of the day. Time to pick up Mary; the thought making him feel even better.

The traffic was light on the drive into Manchester which helped him make good time. He parked up and found Mary waiting in the hotel foyer.

Her dark hair hung loosely around her shoulders. Her clothing showed she was ready for a working day with denim jeans with dark blue trainers a tight-fitting jumper with a light blue short jacket.

'Good morning. Did you sleep well?' he asked.

'Yes, thank you, what about you?'

'Not bad,' he lied. There was no sense in worrying her or telling her he'd spent most of the night between bad dreams and dreams and thoughts about her, with a little shoulder pain put in for good measure.

'Are you ready for a long day?'

'Lead on, McDuff,' she replied.

'I thought we could start with a drive round the centre. Have you had breakfast?'

'Yes, I'm OK thanks.'

'Right, let's go; we can stop for a coffee later. On the way I can bring you up to date on what where we are now. Then I want you to meet the rest of the team later when they grab a bite of lunch, if that's all right by you?'

'No problem. Do they know who I am?'

'They know you're my agent and your code name. The only questions they're likely to ask will be about this operation, nothing else.'

'OK, let's go.'

CHAPTER THIRTY-ONE

The rest of the SG9 team had been out driving around the target area for about an hour. Now they picked up their target they were following on foot. Their unsuspecting quarry a young white male didn't know he was being followed; his every move noted. It was an easy way for surveillance operators to keep sharp and check their communications. Pick a target then follow them for at least one hour without raising the suspicion of the person being followed.

They followed the young man from Deansgate train station into St Peters Square. He'd spent time in some shops moving around the area with a surety that confirmed he knew this part of Manchester. The team took turns, always one in front of the target, one behind, and one keeping level on the opposite side of the street. The comms was working perfectly, and the team eventually joined up with the target when he sat unaware off them in the reference area of the Manchester Central Library.

April Grey sat down two desks to the right of the young man. Joe Cousins browsed the reference books on shelves in front of him while Steve Harrison sat near the exit doors reading today's newspaper copies. April moved close enough to see that the young man was browsing the Internet page for Ernest Hemingway and his life.

A scholar, maybe a budding writer, she thought.

'OK, guys, nearly time to get to Weatherspoon's,' said Harrison over the airwaves. 'Let's go. I think we can call this a successful morning.'

'Roger,' came the responses.

Reece drove through central Manchester and around the area of Deansgate at least four times, all the time watching the traffic, the people, the streets, and the buildings as they passed by. Up close, Mary noticed the change in him from the casual Joseph, who always, to her at least, appeared relaxed and calm, to the Joseph she now saw, concentrated, focused, quiet, intense.

'Are you OK, Joseph?'

'Yes, why do you ask?'

'You seem so distant, as if you're somewhere else.'

'Don't worry about me. I was just thinking if we don't stop these people, I could be responsible for the death of the prime minister.'

'Don't be silly. You're doing everything you can to stop them. That's all you can do; no more, no less.'

He smiled. 'Have you been to Manchester before?'

'I came once on a shopping trip to the Trafford Centre when it first opened, a long time ago. We stayed one night, then back to Belfast, not much time for sightseeing. What about you? Do you know Manchester well?'

'Not really, since I arrived, I've driven and walked around this section especially and studied maps and aerial photographs, but I'm getting a feel for the place. I would prefer Belfast or London, even though there seems to be fewer people than London and not as many foreigners, so hopefully Costello will stand out. His favourite landscape would be the countryside, empty roads, hills small towns, and villages like the place he comes from…more room to move about.'

There he goes again, she thought. Back to the work, the Joseph who can't relax, back on the job. Maybe one day she'll see him with his guard down, see the real Joseph underneath, the real man, or maybe he could never change.

'Right, let's find a parking space, then meet with the rest of the team. I'll introduce you as Mike. They already know you're my agent so don't worry about people knowing who you are, who you are doesn't matter to them. Your security is safe. They're here to do a job and you're part of the team that'll help them get that job done.'

'Nice to be wanted.'

'Don't worry, I'll look after you. You'll be with me most of the time, it's just good that they get to know you and you them. Knowing each other in the flesh so to speak makes things easier when we are out there doing the job. Anyway, I'm starving. I need a bite to eat, how about you?'

'I'm famished.'

Reece parked just of the Town Hall Square in one of the side streets and put a few coins in the parking meter displaying the ticket on the inside of the windscreen. They found the rest of the SG9 team in the Weatherspoon's restaurant already waiting at a table near the back with two spare chairs for Reece and his agent. This was the Joseph she wanted to know, was getting to know, to see him working with his team, the secret Reece. The one she thought cared, the one she wanted, more than he knew. As they entered the restaurant, she'd noticed the way he looked around without moving his head.

Would there ever be a time when the professional side would relax, just switch off, she thought as he placed his hand in the small of her back and guided her to the table where the rest of his friends were sitting. Reece introduced her as Mike and going around the table, introduced the rest of the team, first names only; no need to complicate things.

'Well, how has your day gone?' Reece asked no one in particular.

'We've had a good morning getting to know the place better,' said Joe. 'We took a dummy target from the station to the library. Good run, good comms. We're ready for any surveillance foot or mobile in this area.'

'Great, before we go on, have you all ordered, we're starving.'

'Yes, our drinks food on the way, you need to order at the bar. Our table number is 44,' said Cousins.

'What would you like?' Reece asked Mary.

'Whatever you're having.'

Reece went to order at the bar. Mary noticed the people around the table looking at her. She smiled and looked back.

'Welcome, Mike, it's nice to meet you at last,' said April.

'It's nice to meet you all too,' said Mary.

'Well, I can tell you from everyone here we very much appreciate what you're doing for us and Joseph,' Grey replied.

Reece returned and sat beside Mary, placing a glass of wine in front of her and a large diet Coke with ice for himself on his beer mat.

'Now we're all acquainted, I want to bring everyone up to date. We're still catching up on the CCTV and ANPR from the port in Holyhead to the Manchester area. The PSNI are also checking out the van, but all the family will say is that it belonged to their dead father, and they sold it to an unknown male for a few hundred quid. The police are trying to put pressure on them because it's against the law not to inform the DVLA who you sell a vehicle to, but the family don't seem too worried about not doing things by the book. The prime minister will deliver his main speech on Wednesday afternoon and he's staying in the Midland for the duration.'

The food arrived for the other three SG9 operators. Reece waited until the waiter had left before he spoke again.

'I'll work with Mike and you three should work together and I want us all to be in contact at all times. For the rest of the day, we should keep going over the ground, getting to know every inch of the ground.'

Reece continued to speak as they ate, 'We can only speculate to the who and when, but we have no ideas on the how. Answer that and we can end this and go home to our own beds.'

He knew he was speaking to professionals, no sense in teaching them how to suck eggs when they already knew the game and what was needed.

'Mike has joined us at great risk, but I've asked her to come to Manchester for two reasons. One, so we could all meet as a team and get to know each other. Two, she knows Costello personally. Even though he may have changed his appearance, she knows how he moves how he walks, how he stands, how he dresses. The habits of a lifetime that are hard to change. It might mean Mike having to get close enough to put herself in danger. That's where we come in. If she does point out Costello, we need to be ready, we need to be there. Not only to protect Mike and the prime minister but to make sure Costello and his friends don't get away. Mike knows the dangers and she is willing to take the risk. Is everyone happy with this?'

'That's what we're here for,' said Harrison. 'I hope the boss, the PM, and everyone else realises the risk we're all running. If we could get a little more information that would help.'

'Don't worry, Steve, that's what we're working on. Everyone knows the risks. There are no guarantees, but the PM has decided he won't hide from terrorism. It's our job to do our best, that's all we can do. Mike and I'll go for a walk after lunch and walk off some of these fish and chips. I want you all to go back to the hangar for eight tonight for any update.'

'Great. We will do a couple more runs around and we can all catch-up later,' said Harrison.

Reece stood. 'Well, Mike, do you fancy a walk?'

'Yes, that sound great.'

Leaving Weatherspoon's, Reece walked in the direction across the front of the Town Hall Square. For a change it wasn't raining, and the wind was slight, with the sun breaking through white clouds.

People were moving through the city, but it's not as busy as London, he thought.

'We can walk the whole block, so you'll have a better feel for the place in case you're on your own at any time. What did you think of the team?'

'Scary and quiet, but I think strong too.'

'Scary?' He laughed. 'I think they would love to hear that. If I met them cold like that for the first time, I would probably have to agree with you. The one thing to remember is they're the best at what they do. They cover each other's back, and now they'll cover yours.'

They continued to walk down Deansgate and as they passed the front of the Hilton, Costello watched them from the café lounge through the tinted windows. The man was familiar to him, he was sure he'd seen him somewhere before. The woman he defiantly knew.

'So, Mary McAuley, what brings you here and who's this man you're with? I know him, but from where?'

He left the hotel and crossed the street to follow them; keeping at least one hundred yards behind. He watched them cross the road at the bottom of Deansgate and go into the railway station. He decided not to follow them further. Having travelled through the station himself he knew it was small with nowhere to hide, it was too open an area where he risked being seen. They might be getting a train or tram, they might even come back out, so he couldn't hang around, he needed to get back to the hotel to call Lyndsey and put in an important call to Ireland.

Reece felt that sixth sense he'd felt many times before. He knew they were being watched and he'd studied the glass panel on the station wall and using its reflection he could see a man turn and go back the way they'd just come. He couldn't see him clearly, and he could be jumping to conclusions, but Reece felt certain. The man had been following them, watching them, and he was wearing a dark baseball cap. By the time they were through the entrance and Reece could risk a look over his shoulder, the man was gone.

'What is it?' Mary asked.

'I'm not sure. Stay here.' Reece ran back down the station steps and across the road in the direction he'd seen the unknown man but there was no sign of him. He returned to where Mary was waiting and watching.

'Nothing, and something, I don't know for sure but let's get back to the car.'

Reece took Mary a different route to the one they'd used, passing the Bridgewater Hall, and following the tram lines back to the Library Square. As they walked, he spoke to the team.

'Alpha One to Alpha Team, I'm leaving Deansgate Station heading back to the car near the Library Square. An unknown male with a dark baseball cap was behind us for a while on Deansgate but did a U-turn, and might still be in that area, can you check, over?'

'Roger, I'll take a look,' replied Grey.

'Just being careful. It might be nothing but felt a little strange.'

They walked the rest of the way back to the car in silence. Reece drove out of the city centre to the Lowry Centre in Salford. He used the time driving to check for followers. He was sure there were none. At the Lowry, they found a quiet corner in a café. Mary could see his eyes checking the faces of the shoppers outside.

'Are you OK?' she asked.

'Yes, I'm just being careful.'

'Who do you think that was?'

'I don't know. I'm not even one hundred per cent sure he was following us, but I'm not taking any chances. It's slim, very slim but I'm going to get the team to continue to concentrate in the Deansgate area. We can find ourselves on the CCTV too. It will show if anyone was following us. Hopefully then we will have a clearer picture. And, if it was Costello, then he had to have picked us up somewhere near there as we walked through. And he still just might be in the area. But don't worry, I checked on the way here, no one is following us, we can relax…for now.'

CHAPTER THIRTY-TWO

Costello went straight back to the Hilton having phoned Lyndsey on the way and asking her to come meet him.

'You sure it was Mary McAuley?'

'Definitely.'

'And this man. You know him too?'

'I've seen him before. I'm not sure where but I'm sure I know him. It will come to me.'

'Could he be one of us?'

'Maybe. But I don't think so. The feeling I got when I saw him was danger, something from my past.'

'Do you think they saw you?'

'No, that's why I didn't follow them into the station or get too close. I came straight back here. But I checked, no one followed me.'

'We need to find out what McAuley is doing here. Can your people at home find out? Who knows, she might be here with a boyfriend for a dirty weekend or just shopping, but it's the kind of coincidence I don't like.'

Costello didn't like it either. The unknown man still bugged him.

'Yes, it will take a few hours, but I should be able to find out.'

'In the meantime, stay in your room until I call you or you get a reply from Ireland.'

'I need to switch off for a while, anyway. I find when I do that and relax my memory chip it reboots the computer in my head it will check in and bring up who this guy is.'

He left her and returned to his room. Using his mobile phone, he dialled the number of a trusted contact in South Armagh. The familiar voice on the other end asked the caller to leave a message.

'Hi, mate, it's me call me back as soon as you can.'

Costello lay on the bed and closed his eyes.

Chapter Thirty-Three

Reece dropped Mary back at her hotel.

'I'll catch-up with you later. Do you fancy going out for a meal tonight?'

'That would be lovely. Do I need to dress up or are we slumming it?'

'Somewhere in between would be nice. Pick you up around eight.'

'See you then.' She kissed him on the cheek as they parted.

Once again, he felt the butterflies in his stomach take flight.

'Alpha One to Alpha Team, where are you now?'

It was Cousins who answered.

'We're still around Deansgate, over.'

'Roger that. Can we all meet in the café in the Town Hall in twenty, over?'

'Roger,' the team replied one by one.

Reece found another parking space near the Town Hall. Keeping the change for these parking meters was costing him a small fortune. He made a point to include the cost in his expenses sheet. Unlike James Bond, real secret agents had to account for every penny they spent, that meant receipts and forms in triplicate.

The inside of the Manchester Town Hall brought an old-world atmosphere with the building housing and excellent café and the council offices together. Reece had visited the café in the past and always enjoyed its relaxing atmosphere; the open space inside made it cool and welcoming.

The team were already there at a corner table. He briefed them again on the man he'd seen.

'What I didn't say in front of Mike was that I'm sure it was Costello. Mike didn't see him, and I can't put my finger on it but it's my gut telling me it was him. The comms people have got back to me with the CCTV coverage which they uploaded to my mobile. Mike has seen it but the quality's not great so she couldn't be sure.'

Reece showed the grainy coverage of Deansgate, and they could see Reece and Mary walking towards the station and a tall man wearing a baseball cap who appeared to be keeping pace with them from the footpath on the opposite side of the street. Although they could estimate the man's height there was no clear shot of his face even when he turned and walked back towards the camera before disappearing out of shot.

'Many times, during surveillance, you get that gut feeling as you call it, that sixth sense. It paid not to ignore it and nine times out of ten I was right to listen to it. So, what now?' said Harrison.

'Well, I think we can assume that it was Costello and he spotted me and Mike. We hadn't been walking long so he must have been somewhere in this area.'

Reece placed his map on the table.

'This is the route we walked after we left you in Weatherspoon's. I don't think he was following us too long or I would have spotted him earlier. So, if he wasn't dropped off by a car, we need to start paying attention to the main Deansgate area. The cafés, restaurants, bars, and hotels. If he has been travelling in and out of the city, if not by car, then public transport the trains and buses then we need to get Lockwood's people to step up their CCTV coverage in the area. They might even have him following me today although they should already be doing that, anyway. I'll give him my timeline for walking down Deansgate earlier see what they come up with. We might get lucky and see where he went after bugging out from following me.'

'The Hilton Hotel is smack bang in the middle of where you were walking, we should certainly check it out,' said Cousins.

Reece had been studying the map,

'Good idea, we need to take a look, but we should always work in the belief they're here. We need to be careful at all times, keep your eyes open, and everyone keep in touch.'

'David, if you're right, and I think you are, why did he stop following you when you went into the station?' asked April Grey.

'You've got to remember that essentially, Costello is a coward. All his kills are with the built-in caveat that he can catch his target by surprise, and he can get away afterwards. For him to follow me into the station would be to follow me into an area he was unsure off with a confrontation scenario he didn't know. He would have assumed I was armed, maybe Mike too. He would also have been worried that we might be meeting other armed colleagues in the station. Too many unnecessary risks. He will now be more aware of our presence, so he'll be taking more precautions, even more alert, we must be the same.'

'Do you think he knows who you are?' asked April.

'He just might remember me from our days of bumping into each other between shoot-outs and question sessions. He would know Mike, she worked with the top tier of the Provisional movement and lived in Newry during the Troubles, so he would know her for sure. I'll be meeting up with her later. Let's do a little more digging in the Deansgate area and see what we come up with.'

'As he has spotted you, he must be spooked. I think you should operate in the area using the Range Rover, the tinted windows will give you the advantage should you need it. I can check the Hilton,' April said.

'Good idea let's do that, but everyone keep in touch. Anything at all let me know. I'll bring London up to date and get the boss to speak to Lockwood and I'll have a look at the CCTV myself. Let's not forget people if you do spot this guy, we have to put him down no second chances no calling on him to surrender because he won't.'

Chapter Thirty-Four

When the phone blinked into life, Costello's first thought was that it was Ireland calling back, but instead it was a text from Lyndsey.

I will pay the bill. Booking out now. M picking us up in twenty.

Costello packed, making sure to wipe down as many surfaces as possible, so no fingerprints were left. Then he went down to meet her in the lobby, Mohammad was waiting in the car outside.

The drive to Irlam took another thirty minutes but in total silence as they all looked for the suspected security presence, but there was none. Inside the Irlam house, and after Mohammad had done another sweep, they sat around the table. Imtaz and Waheed were still in Manchester.

'Why did you follow them, Sean, why did you expose yourself?' asked Lyndsey.

'I'm sure they didn't see me. I recognised Mary McAuley and I'm sure the man she was with worked for the security forces in Northern Ireland, I can't remember in what capacity, but it will come to me. I'm still waiting on my contact in Ireland getting back to me then hopefully, I'll know more.'

'Well, we always knew there were risks, but by your actions you could have put us all at risk. I just hope you're right and they didn't see you, but we can't take chances. The fact that they were in Deansgate could be expected. McAuley can be taken care of later. If we're successful, you can have the pleasure of that, Sean. Still, it's good that you did spot them before they spotted us. If they're that close, then it could only be a matter of time before they check the hotel and even with our cover, we're at risk. I'll book us into a hotel further out from the city for the next few days. Mohammad, where are we with the apartment?'

'I have good news. I called with the estate agents like you said. The forms were fairly straight forward and after I showed young Jake the three-grand cash for the deposit, I can pick the keys up on Tuesday afternoon.'

'Were my passport and credit ID, OK?'

'Yes, everything went smoothly. I have all your documents in the car.'

'That's great. We know the area. We now have the apartment to work from we keep to our schedule. A final meeting here tomorrow night then you pick up the keys on Tuesday, and we make our final moves into position on Tuesday night. Mohammad, I have one more job for you. Can you have a look around for a van similar to Sean's?'

'Yes, do you want me to steal it if I find one?'

'No. Make a note of the plates then get copies made. Bring them here and change them onto Sean's van in the garage. We'll be using the van to move to the apartment, so we need to be as secure there as possible.'

'Sure, no problem, I'll do that right away.'

'Good, let's have a coffee then you can drop me off at one of the hotels near the airport.'

Fifteen minutes after Lyndsey and Costello had left the Hilton, April Grey had approached the reception desk.

CHAPTER THIRTY-FIVE

Grey spoke to the receptionist, then to the day manager, and last to the concierge. It always amazed her the reaction of people when she presented her MI5 Identity Card. People seemed to be relaxed and expectant when presented with a Police Identity Card.

Probably because of the glut of police TV programmes, she thought. But when shown a card from the security services, first there was a look of surprise, then a double take to be sure what they were seeing. Then a look of fear. To the everyday citizen this was a whole new world, completely outside their comfort zone, stepping into the unknown, this was serious. This meant they were only too pleased to help. A man fitting the description of the one in the photo she showed them had just booked out. It was the concierge who had been the most observant and gave Grey the information she needed to call Reece.

'April. What is it?'

'Can you talk?'

'Yes, I'm on my own.'

'I've just been speaking to the staff at the Hilton. It looks like our friend was staying here but left in a hurry about twenty minutes ago.'

'How can they be sure it was him?'

'I showed them the photo we have, and they weren't sure, but when I mentioned the baseball cap, they all agreed that the man fitting our guy's description never seemed to take his off and had just booked out. And here's the clincher, David, he may have been with a woman also staying here. They had different rooms on different floors, but they met in the Sky Cocktail Bar. It was the woman who booked and paid for both rooms using a credit card in the name of Karen Webb. If it is Costello, and I think it is, he was booked in under the name Paul Jordan? I've asked for the CCTV for the last few days. The day manager was a bit reluctant to let us have that but when I explained the arrest powers for terrorism under the Official Secrets Act, he phoned his boss and was more forthcoming.'

'Did you get any more about them when they left, a taxi, and if it was a taxi did the doorman hear where they were going? A forwarding address maybe?'

Grey laughed. 'We should be so lucky. The concierge is ex-army and the most observant of them all. He saw the man and woman leave together. Both were picked up by an Asian man in a black BMW which could be private hire as he opened the doors for them and put the bags in the boot before driving off in the direction of the station.'

'Can you get descriptions of all three, as well as the CCTV?'

'Sorted, I'll bring them back to the hangar for our briefing.'

'Good, call everyone and we can go over it later. I'll let Lockwood know after we've our debrief.'

'David, by the look of things they left in a hurry and not long after you spotted your tail. From what I've found out I think they're aware of you and most likely Mike, so you need to be twice as careful and so should she.'

'Agreed. I'll call with her and bring her to the hangar. I'm fucking angry that we were made, angry that he spotted us and angrier that I didn't spot him earlier, and now we are going to have to keep her much closer to the action. See you back at the hangar.'

CHAPTER THIRTY-SIX

'Hello.' At last, John Jo Murphy had called back.

'John Jo, it's Sean here I need you to do something for me, it's important.'

'Ah sure, Sean, no problem seeing it's yourself. What do you need?'

'Do you remember Mary McAuley?'

'The lovely Mary from Newry; the one that was married to Brendan?'

'Yes, that's her. Now, she's moved back to Belfast to be closer to her mother I believe, I think the mother still lives in the Beechmount area off the Falls Road, but she lives somewhere else in the city, I don't know where. I need you to call with the mother and find out where she is now. Can you do that for me?'

'Sure, Sean, I'll try to find out how soon do you need to know?'

'As soon as you can. Tell the mother you're an old friend up from Newry for the day and you want to catch-up with her daughter.'

'Leave it with me and I'll get back to you when I know anything.'

'Good man.'

Lyndsey had been listening to Costello's side of the conversation. Since they'd left the hotel and returned to Irlam, she'd been reassessing the plan. Imtaz and Waheed had taken the train to the city to look around the centre, now they joined her, Costello, and Mohammad around the table. After Costello had finished his call, Mohammad made another technical sweep of the room.

'Our plans have had to change. We always knew security around the conference was going to be tight but the fact that we've seen some people from Sean's past seems to indicate they know about the Irish connection to our operation,' Lyndsey said.

'I knew we were wrong to trust this infidel,' said Waheed.

'You and I are going to have a serious falling out, my friend,' replied Costello looking Waheed in the eye.

'That's enough,' Lyndsey cut in. 'Sean is not your enemy, Waheed. He is here, like everyone else, to strike a blow at the real enemy, the real infidel. On Tuesday night we move to the apartment and complete our attack on Wednesday morning. Mohammad, did you manage to get new plates for the van?'

'Yes, they're in the boot of my car. I can change them now.'

'Good, I've been thinking. Sean and I'll stay in the Radisson Hotel at the airport. Sean, you can park the van in one of the carparks near Terminal Three, then meet up with me at the Radisson. I'll book a twin room in the name of Mary Scott as they might be looking for Karen Webb already. Small hotels outside the city are unlikely to ask for identification so we should be all right as we will stay there until Tuesday. Waheed and Imtaz will stay here until Wednesday and move to the target area early that morning. Mohammad, you can drop me off at the hotel and meet up with me and Sean at the apartment block at 6 p.m. on Tuesday. Sean and I will stay in the apartment until the operation is over. Mohammad, you'll be in the Midland Hotel to give us the signal that the target is on the move, this will give Sean the few seconds he'll need. Sean, your van will be swallowed up in the airport carpark; it couldn't be in a safer spot. On Tuesday, we can move from the hotel to the NCP near the apartment and leave it there for the duration of the operation. Do you have some sort of carry case for the rifle that won't stand out?'

'Of course. The rifle has been broken down to fit into a small sports bag. I can assemble it quickly and it's already zeroed to my own specifications.'

'Good,' she replied. 'Now you can bring in the Semtex for Waheed and Imtaz to get to work on their side of the operation.'

CHAPTER THIRTY-SEVEN

Before picking up Mary, Reece had called Broad and brought him up to speed. Reece let Broad know of his concerns of interference by Lockwood. Because the operation was on British soil Reece felt the dangers posed by what he knew was normally a very proficient Police and Security service.

'I think I'll have to come up there if just to keep the likes of this Lockwood in check. He's been complaining to his Chief Constable, who's beginning to feel the pressure from him.'

'What's he doing?'

'He's asking for his ass to be covered in writing from the prime minister's office. How we want this to end is supposed to be Top Secret and I can see this idiot mouthing off to the press.'

'Idiot is the right word for him. He doesn't have a clue who we are or who he's dealing with here. He's a desk jockey jobsworth and to tell you the truth, I don't need his interference now that we're getting closer to Costello and his crew. We'll need police boots on the ground eventually, but until then, I want Lockwood to help without question when I ask them.'

'I'll be up there tonight. The Chief Constable and Mr Lockwood will be told where they stand. In the meantime, let him know in no uncertain terms that you're in charge and he will do as he's told. They can be replaced if needs be. See you later.'

'Let me know when you get here.'

Reece felt a little better knowing Broad had his back.

He waited in reception for Mary. When she came out of the lift her smile cheered up his day as always.

'What's up?' she asked.

Reece filled her in as they walked to the Range Rover.

'Hilton Hotel eh, a bit more upmarket from Newry.'

'Yes, but where is he now? We're going to check over the CCTV at our base location. That's why I want you there to have a look yourself. I also think it would be safer, being close to the team instead of out there on your own.'

'Where you lead, Joseph, I'll follow.'

There it was again, he thought, that smile that reached her eyes. Those dark brown eyes that seemed to see into his soul…his thoughts.

'Don't worry about booking out just yet, you might be here a little longer than I expected.'

'Again, I'm at your disposal. I'm not expected anywhere else, so let's go.'

As Reece drove to Barton, he watched her as she looked out at the passing shops, restaurants, streets, and cars.

'What are you thinking?' he asked.

'Thinking, now that's a question I don't hear every day. Not many people, especially the men, in my life are interested in what I'm thinking.'

'Well, I don't know about the other men in your life, but I'm interested, right now I'm interested.'

'I'm thinking, what am I doing here and what brought me to this place and time? Then I answer my own questions. I remember when I met you, I didn't know who you were at first, but I knew I wanted to get to know you. I wanted to get closer to you. Now I'm sitting beside you, driving through Manchester at night and I'm thinking despite everything, I'm exactly where I want to be. What about you? What are you thinking?'

'To be honest, I'm trying hard to keep my mind on the job at hand but you're making it very difficult for me.'

'I don't mean to.'

'I mean difficult in a nice way. It's the kind of difficult I could live with every day.'

'I'm sorry, I don't understand. I'm not sure what you mean?'

He pulled the Range Rover into the carpark of a pub just outside Barton.

'Why are you stopping? I thought we were going to your base?'

'I need a drink and so do you.'

The bar was surprisingly busy, maybe because it was serving food as well, but they were able to find a table all to themselves. A whisky and soda for him and a glass of pinot grigio for her.

'The only Irish they have is Jameson's, my favourite is Bushmills built these English bars never seem to stock it or rarely if ever. Did you know that Bushmills Whiskey comes from Bushmills in County Antrim in Northern Ireland?'

'Yes, I'm not a whisky drinker but I've heard of Bushmills.'

'Jameson's will do, but it's not Bushmills. Jameson's I would use for making hot whiskies. Bushmills I can drink straight on its own it's that smooth, did you know Bushmills is the oldest licensed distillery in the world 1608? The word licensed being the operative word. There were many other distilleries in places making the stuff before Bushmill's, but they weren't licensed or paying the tax man. I went to the Bushmills distillery once. Do you know what's written above the door?'

'No.'

'Here we turn water into gold.'

'The way you talk about it you might convert me.' She laughed.

'That's why I thought we should have this drink. Not just to give you a lesson on whiskey but, despite me needing one right now I just wanted some free down time with you on my own. You know nothing about me. We should get to know each other, who we really are.'

'Are you sure you really want to know the real me? You might not like what you hear?'

'That goes both ways. I know where you were born, where you were brought up, where you live now. I know your age, where you went to school, and that you were married to Brendan. The you I don't know is the one that made you who you are…the real you. What's your favourite book? Your favourite movie? What makes you cry? What are you afraid of? These are all the things that people in a normal relationship know about each other.'

'What's a normal relationship? I don't think I've ever had one. I was brought up by a strict Catholic mum and dad. My dad died when I was fourteen. I was at a convent school run by nuns who were even stricter than my parents. When I left school at sixteen, I was vulnerable and easily swayed. Brendan came along; the slightly older man of the world or so I thought. Someone who wanted to take care of me. Then, well, you know that part of the story and how that ended up, and here I am. What about you, what brings you to the here and now?'

He was sipping his whisky. It might just be Jameson's, but he wanted to take his time. He'd listened to her with interest in the way she was opening up beginning to relax. This was what he wanted. The whole thing with Costello would make anyone nervous and he was no exception.

'Well, believe it or not, I come from a large Catholic family myself. I was born in Larne which was then a predominately Protestant town. My father was a bit like Brendan; a bully when he had a drink in him. My mother who was a lot smaller kicked him out when she found out that not only was he having an affair with another woman, but he'd gotten her pregnant as well. I had a lot of Protestant friends and in those days, religion was never a problem. In the estate where I lived, the Catholic Chapel and the Protestant Church were the two buildings at the entrance gates to the local cemetery. On Sunday mornings both opposite congregations would finish their service at the same time and then everyone would stand between the two buildings chatting and laughing. Those were the good times when neighbours were neighbours before they started killing each other.'

'They're not all bad, Joseph. I have to believe that. You should too.'

'I know, you're right, I still have a few friends from those days but in my working life I've seen too much violence, too much hatred to know better. I fell out with the Catholic Church when the Priest at Mass started to spout off in his sermon one Sunday morning about fallen women. After my father had been kicked out, he moved to England with his new woman. My mother had originally been devastated. I was the eldest, only ten at the time and suddenly, I was the man of the house. After a while, my mother met and fell for another man, a Protestant. That day, in the Chapel, the Priest seemed to be looking straight at me, my brother, and sister. He was talking loudly about fallen women, jezebels as he called them. I knew he was speaking about my mother because everyone turned to look at us. I took the hands of my brother and sister and walked out. I told my mother what had happened when I went home and told her what happened. I also told her I would never go inside a Catholic Church again, and what's more, I would have nothing more to do with that religion.'

'My God, that was a big thing for a small child to deal with back then. You never went back?'

'Just once when I attended the funeral of a Catholic police officer who was shot dead by the IRA. I was reluctant to go inside the church. I waited outside thinking I would be able to sit at the back when the church had filled up, but my plan backfired. When I went in the only seats left were at the front beside the flag-draped coffin, and I was ushered to one of those seats. My anger for the Catholic Church was reinforced when the Priest said in his sermon, "If anyone knows anything about this terrible crime, they should tell the police."

'I nearly laughed out loud. I wanted to shout, you fucking hypocrite, if the gunman came into your confessional tonight and told you what they'd done, you would absolve them of their sin and give them six Hail Marys and three Our Fathers and let them go on their way to kill more policemen and you would tell no one.'

Mary could feel the anger in his words and feel the pain he was feeling. She decided to change the conversation.

'Where's your mother now? Is she still in Larne?'

'Yes, in a way. She's buried there.'

'Oh, I'm sorry, Joseph.'

'No reason to be sorry, everyone dies. If you smoked as much as she did then that time comes sooner than it should. She smoked all her life and the cancer sticks caught up with her in the end. It wasn't until she was gone that I really realised how hard life had been on her, yet she'd raised seven children practically on her own.'

'Seven? Christ that would be a struggle. Did you ever marry and have kids?'

'Yes, married twice and lived to regret it or should I say survived. I've two grown-up boys from the first marriage, one living in America and the other in the North of England, we don't talk.'

'What happened, or don't you want to talk about it?'

'Like all marriages the start was OK then come the children, both of us working to bring in the money to keep the roof over our heads. Then comes the drifting apart like passing ships in the night. We didn't know each other anymore. Then I found out she was having an affair with the husband of one of her friends. I challenged them both, but they denied it to my face. Then came the rows the arguments long into the night. I remembered how as a child I used to lay awake listening to my parents arguing, the loud voices the horrible words. It was then I decided I didn't want them to go through what I had as a child. One night after another long argument into the early hours I asked her what she'd do if the boys were grown up and left home. She didn't hesitate. I'd leave you was all she said. I told her I thought the same and there was no sense in keeping the marriage together for the sake of the children if there was no love anymore. We both agreed to see the solicitors the following day and that was it, really. The hardest thing was me leaving the family home leaving the two boys behind. I remember the first rented house I moved to after leaving the thing I noticed most was the silence without the boys running around. But she was the first-class bitch I'd been arguing with. She got the house. She squeezed me for every penny she could get always using the boys against me, telling them I didn't love them and trying to dictate when I could see them. It was a constant battel. After two years the divorce came through and guess what?'

'She took up with the other guy.'

'Not only that. He left his wife and kids, moved in with my ex, and married her.'

'How did that make you feel?'

'Strangely relieved. I'd been vindicated. It wasn't all my fault after all. She was the cheating bitch I said all along, but now she'd made her bed, she could lie in it. I concentrated on my work and any spare time I had was dedicated to the boys. I would have them three night a week, when work allowed, and during school holidays. But it was never enough and eventually, I guess they held things against me; blamed me for all their problems. As they got older, got married, had children of their own…we just didn't seem to talk anymore, we just got on with our own lives I suppose. They listened to the poison their mother liked to spout about me. It angered her that I could survive on my own, and when the boys finished school, and the money she was bleeding from me stopped, she hated me even more.'

'Families can hurt you more than enemies sometimes. I'm an only child so I was lucky, and Brendan and I never had children, thank God. Can you just imagine what he would have been like as a father? No, that side of my life worked out OK for me.'

Reece could see a sadness in her eyes as she spoke of something close to her heart. She would have made a good mother, he thought.

'But what about us, Joseph? Where do we stand?' She didn't ask about the second wife and divorce, and he was happy with that, another story for another time.

It was the question that had been keeping him awake at night but now it needed an answer, a decision for both.

'You know I said that while we're working on this Costello thing I needed to be as professional as possible and afterwards we could talk about our feelings for each other. Yes, Mary, that's right…I have feelings for you.'

She was quiet, letting him talk, she smiled. This gave him the courage to continue.

'I think I should be honest. I've had feelings for you since the first day I saw you in Newry then followed you to Belfast.'

'I'm glad you followed me.'

'This job can get in the way of relationships, you don't have to tell me, I know. But this time I won't let it. The Costellos of this world will have to wait. For this hour at least.'

He took her hand. He could feel the warmth of her soft skin as she squeezed his fingers. She watched him expectant but not knowing what. Then still holding her hand he said, 'Let's go.'

They left the bar still holding hands walking back to the Range Rover. She didn't feel awkward, everything with Joseph felt natural, meant to be, and if she was honest with herself, exciting. As they reached the Range Rover, she could see their reflection in its window. The street lights lit up the car park. Then without warning, he stopped and turning to face her she felt his arm around her waist while he held her face gently with his other hand. He pulled her closer towards him, then he kissed her. She felt the warmth of his lips on hers and she responded, kissing him back, and putting her arms around his shoulders. She'd never felt this way. She wanted him here and now. They kissed for what seemed like hours, then he just held her. Standing there with their bodies close enough to feel every curve and muscle without using their hands.

'I want you, Joseph, I want you.'

He felt a surge of strange energy go through him. This woman had broken through his barriers. There would always be secrets, things he couldn't tell her, things she didn't need to know.

'I want you too, Mary, so much,' he said through a dry mouth.

'But, for now we'll have to wait. Our feelings for each other will have to remain between us. I'm worried about the danger this mission can bring. That's why I don't want you exposed any more than you should be.'

'I'm a big girl, Joseph. I can look after myself.'

'I know you can, that's one of the things I love about you.'

'There's something else, Joseph. I love you.'

There they were. The three words that change everything. He knew they would come. The feelings he felt were more than just feelings, they were life itself.

'I love you too, Mary, and that's why I don't want you in danger.'

'Bollocks. You want me all to yourself.'

He started laughing as he felt all the tension and anxiety inside him evaporate as he held her tighter in his arms.

'This is how I want it to be, Mary, always close together and it will be. First let's get this job out of the way, nothing to interfere in our lives.'

'OK, agreed. But I'm waiting no longer than that. I want to be with you, to lie with you, to make love together.'

'This will all be over Wednesday one way or the other, then we can be together. It might mean you giving up Ireland.'

'For you, Joseph I'll give up the world.'

'That's always been my nightmares. Either someone is coming to kill me, and I can't get my gun to work or I'm too late getting there to stop someone dying. Sometimes I wonder is the world worth it.'

'It has to be, Joseph, or we all go down the pit with it.'

CHAPTER THIRTY-EIGHT

When they got back to the hangar Jim Broad had arrived in another Puma and he came bearing gifts. Some good, some not so good.

'Good to see you, Joseph. How are things?'

'Well, first we need to dispense with cover names, it will save any confusion as we go on.'

Turning to the woman standing beside him he said,

'Boss, this is Mary McAuley. It's thanks to her information we're all here. I think as names go; I'll stick to boss for you.'

Broad shook Mary's hand.

'Mary, I'm so glad to meet you at last, David has told me so much about you.'

'It's good to meet you and nice to know that Joseph is David.' She smiled. 'Although I think I prefer Joseph…it suits him better.'

'I'm sorry about that, Mary, another part of the job I'm afraid,' said Reece.

'Well, David, can you take Mary to the canteen and fix her up with a coffee then come back and see me as we need a chat?'

'No problem, see you in five.'

Reece left Mary in the canteen. She said nothing, other than, with a wicked smile on her face, 'I'll see you soon, Joseph.'

When Reece returned to the hangar, Broad and the rest of the SG9 team were watching the large TV screen on the wall. The hotel's black and white CCTV showed a man with a baseball cap leaving the Hilton with woman wearing a headscarf and sunglasses. A man wearing a dark hoodie with the hood up was waiting for them in a dark BMW and after putting their bags into the boot, he drove them away towards Deansgate Station. It could have been a private taxi or someone there to pick them up, the fact the driver appeared to be protecting his identity and was identified as a young Asian man, made the deliberate pick up a distinct possibility.

'We've looked at these pictures a number of times. The hotel staff confirmed that this was the man with the New York baseball cap who never seemed to take it off, and this,' April said as she pointed to the woman on the screen, 'they confirmed as the woman who paid both their bills. She used a credit card in the name Karen Webb. He was registered as Kevin Jones. The car is a black BMW registered to Hertz Car Hire here in Manchester, paid for by a man who fits the description of the driver but who used a credit card in the name of Kevin Jones. The address and driving licence he gave are fakes. He's hired the car until next Thursday, the day after the conference ends.'

'Do we have any more on the car after it left the Hilton?' asked Reece.

'They were picked up heading out of the city near Salford before we lost them. They didn't use the motorways but disappeared in the side roads.'

'This is good,' Broad said. 'We have them running scared and being scared they'll make more mistakes. They might even call the whole thing off, but I doubt it. These are dedicated terrorists who will do everything in their power to get the job done, so we can assume they're still on schedule.

'We need to make sure Lockwood understands where we are. I'll bring the Gold Commander up to date and they can continue to keep an eye out with their CCTV coverage and patrols. I'll be telling him if they are spotted, they're not to be approached but that intel will be immediately passed to us and to your team, David. The SAS can view the footage we have too and make any preparations they need, but the police and SAS will only move on my say so.'

Reece was pleased that Broad was now taking control as it would leave the SG9 team out on the ground where they would be more effective.

'As for Mike,' said Reece 'We've brought her fully on-board now there's a chance she was spotted so we're doing away with code names. It's Mary and David from now on. Boss, if you could arrange for a third vehicle for our use that would be helpful?'

'No problem, I'll arrange it when I have my little chat with Mr Lockwood. But now the bad news, people. I was contacted an hour ago by Tom Wilson from the PSNI. As you know, they've been working on their own operations against the dissident Republicans in Ireland, especially the ones in the north, and they've confirmed it's him and he's here. Costello knows we're here and most likely looking for him. That's why they were spooked and got out of the Hilton. With the BMW on the radar, we might just get lucky again so keep on your toes. Get out there and get the bastards. Realistically, David, now that Costello knows about Mary, we should keep her out of things; she's blown. But I'll leave that up to you.'

'We will keep her on board for the time being she also knows Costello and he will be easier for her to spot him than us. She can look at the CCTV, but I know she will only confirm its Costello.'

After Broad left, the team waited for Reece's instructions.

'I really can't say more than the boss. The next mistake they make will be their last. They have been spooked but I think they'll continue with their plan as it's too late in the day to change it now.

'Tomorrow's Saturday, let's go over everything we know tonight: CCTV, maps, the buildings around the conference area, then get a good night's sleep because God knows when we'll get another one.'

CHAPTER THIRTY-NINE

SATURDAY, 28 SEPTEMBER 2019

Just after midnight, Costello and the team sat around the table in the Irlam safe house. The plates on the van had been changed and they now watched Waheed expertly handle two small blocks of Semtex. He wore blue surgical gloves and from his rucksack he'd produced two sandwich-sized Tupperware boxes with small holes drilled in one end.

He handled and caressed the explosives as he would handle and caress the butt or stock of a gun he'd seen for the first time, thought Costello.

Waheed then removed two detonators from his bag. They were wired to a timer that looked like a buttonless mobile phone. Placing halve the Semtex in one of the boxes, he pushed the detonator through the hole and pressed it into the block of explosives. He placed the Semtex inside the Tupperware, accompanied by a bundle of five-inch nails secured together with Sellotape, closed the lid, and stuck the timer on the outside. Everyone held their breath as he repeated the process with the second Tupperware box.

When he'd finished, he produced two real mobile phones.

'The devices are now ready,' he said. 'These mobile phones – the trigger devices – will initiate the explosive. When they are switched on, they'll send a signal to here.' He pointed to the timing device linked to the detonator. 'Just switch it on, enter the code – which is 1,2,3,4 – and bang…off they go!'

'How close do you have to be for the signal to connect?' asked Lyndsey.

'The signal will bounce off the normal phone masts in the area, so anywhere up to one mile away.'

'I'm impressed, Waheed,' said Costello. 'I've seen and used explosives in Northern Ireland but usually with a line of sight on the target. This way you don't have to.'

'There will be large crowds at Piccadilly and around the conference itself. Mohammad said there will be many left-wing agitators demonstrating there all week. Imtaz and I will place the devices near both locations, retreat to the safe zone, and then detonate for maximum effect. We are both prepared to die for Allah, and to take as many infidels with us as possible. If we are cornered, we just need to press the send button on the phone twice quickly.'

'Mohammad, you'll go on Wednesday morning,' said Lyndsey, 'and then stay with Sean until the mission is complete, I'll be waiting for your call. Sean, you'll leave the rifle behind. I'll be in the van in the NCP car park, and I'll pick you both up when the job's done. In the initial confusion, we should be able to get back here and lie low until things cool down. Mohammad, make sure the kitchen is well stocked with food. After you've dropped me at the hotel, I want you to take the BMW outside the city and burn it.'

'Burn it?' said Mohammad.

'Yes, I'm sure the Hilton CCTV has you picking us up today and they'll be looking for the car by now. We aren't far from the airport, so you should be safe to drop me off then dispose of it. Waheed and Imtaz, you stay here until Wednesday morning and then take the train into Piccadilly. From the information Mohammed's given us about the conference and the PM's speech, we can expect him to walk out the rear door of the Midland between eleven and eleven thirty on Wednesday morning. Sean will be set up in the apartment ready and everyone needs to be in position for that time. It will be down to Sean to shoot the prime minister with the sniper rifle. Mohammad will send us all the text *ONE DOWN* confirming that Sean has completed his mission, that's when you tap in the code on the mobile phones then press the send button. The explosions and following confusion should give us the cover we need to escape the area. If you feel you can't get back, try to return to your own city and home.'

'I'll gladly offer my life for Allah, all praise to his name,' said Waheed.

'Me too,' said Imtaz.

Costello thought Imtaz looked a little more frightened at the thought of being a living sacrifice.

'If we kill the British prime minister and hundreds of people, we'll need all the angels on our side to get away, that's for sure,' said Costello.

Costello felt the buzz from his mobile phone in his pocket. Mohammad had already done his usual security scan, so he answered when he saw the number.

'John Jo, how are you?'

'Oh yes, hi, Sean, it's me, OK. Got a bit of information for you. Sorry it took so long. It took me a bit of time to track down Mary's mum. People are still very suspicious when someone starts asking questions. She lives in the Beechmount area on her own.'

'What have you got for me, John Jo?'

'Well, I told them that an old friend of Mary's had died and as I was up in the city for the day, I thought I'd call with her and tell her if she didn't already know. She told me Mary lives on the Lisburn Road, she didn't have the number, but Mary'd phoned her a few days ago to say she'd be away for a while and would call her when she got back. Does that make sense to you?'

'Yes, that would add up.'

'She believed my story, so she gave me Mary's number. I'll text it to you now.'

'That's great, John Jo, I owe you one. If you hear anymore, give me a bell.'

'Will do. Bye for now.'

The phone went dead and almost immediately, the text with Mary McAuley's number appeared on the screen.

Chapter Forty

When he parked the van at the airport, Costello thought that even he would have a problem finding it again in what looked like the biggest car park in the world. He made a special note of what lane and section the van was in in case he needed to find it in the dark in a hurry. He was thankful that all being well, he'd be coming back to find it in daylight.

He walked to the Radisson Hotel about a mile from where he'd parked up. A good distance for security purposes. He could check for surveillance and the van was far enough from the hotel it wasn't obvious where he was if the security forces found it. Had he flown out of the country, they would wonder, and if not, it'd be like finding a needle in a haystack.

Rain was falling, so he pulled his coat closed, slipping the Browning pistol into his right-hand pocket…the cold steel comforting in his grip. It reassured him knowing this was the final stages of the operation. He was happier now that the action was close. He felt more in control…this was his world now.

Lyndsey was sitting in the foyer of the hotel when he entered. They kissed each other on the cheek then he sat opposite her.

'No problems getting here then. You're parked up OK?'

'No problems. No one following, and you were right, safely lost in a car park for the night.'

I know someone who won't sleep tonight, he thought. Before he'd left Irlam, he couldn't resist calling the number John Jo had sent him. When the woman answered, he recognised her Newry accent.

'Hello, Mary. Surprised to hear from me?'

He could hear her breathing, the hesitation in her voice as she spoke.

'Who is this?'

'I think you know, Mary. I just called to let you know I saw you and your friend today. It took me a while to figure out where I'd seen him before, your Special Branch friend.'

'Who are you? I don't know what you're talking about?'

'Don't worry, you'll be seeing me soon, you and your friend.'

The call had only lasted seconds not long enough to get a trace but just long enough to give her and her friend a message.

'I could do with a bite…I will order a plate of sandwiches for the room What floor are we on?'

'The third, room 302.'

'I'll have a quick wash then a bit of kip.'

Ten miles away, in a field near Warrington, Mohammad had parked the BMW. He knew that a short distance away was the small train station of Glazebrook where he could catch a train in fifteen minutes that would take him to Irlam.

Plenty of time to do what he needed to and get to the station. He was sure no one had seen him turn into the field and the darkness would give him the cover he needed. Taking out the tea towel he'd brought from the Irlam safe house, he opened the petrol cap and stuffed the towel in as far as he could, then, using the lighter brought for the job, lit the piece of towel hanging outside. Making sure it was well alight, he turned and walked towards the road and, turning left, he walked the short distance to the station. Halfway there, he heard the loud explosion and saw the sky light up in the darkness as the car turned into a fireball.

CHAPTER FORTY-ONE

The prime minister had arrived in Manchester and was now in a meeting with senior ministers at his suite in the Midland Hotel when Jim Broad called to update him on progress.

He'd parked his car some distance away and had used the walk to take time the time to think, putting together in his mind what he would say to the PM. It was early evening and though the conference delegates had, in the main, left the main conference building for the day, there was still a large group of demonstrators in the area. The crowd were a mixture of all sorts. Some with placards showing their grievances and some more organised the rent a mob the kind that were always complaining about something and looking for trouble instead of getting of their backsides and doing something to change the problem. Then there was the usual Union and left-wing protesters and agitators with placards from Save our NHS to Tory Scum, Ban Foxhunting all accompanied by the usual chants of 'Tories Out', 'Tory Scum', 'Down with the capitalist system'. It was all meant to intimidate the delegates who had to pass them to get into the conference area.

Broad liked to think that he would fight for was the free speech these demonstrators represented, even if he didn't like how they used it. The thing that angered him most was that the puppet masters behind the demonstrators who organised the rent-a-mob would show up when the crowd was at its biggest, spout a few words for the benefit of the cameras, then having heated up the crowd once more, would disappear to the warmth of their limo and the expensive hotel being paid for with Union or taxpayers money.

Broad knew some of the history of the hotel that had been used by kings, queens, presidents, and now prime ministers. The prime ministers mostly staying when attending the Conservative Party Annual Conference which Manchester had shared every two years with Birmingham. The two main political parties in Britain had moved their conferences into the big cities away from the old costal resorts due to the fact the numbers attending had grown, now more hotel space was needed.

Broad had no problem getting through security and was now sitting outside the suite of rooms being used by the prime minister. He wasn't alone. There was a secretary behind a desk and standing at the door to the rooms was one of the PM's Personal Protection team standing quietly but alert.

'You may go in now, sir,' said the secretary.

When Broad entered the suite, Peter Brookfield came and shook his hand.

'Jim, welcome, thank you for coming. Please, take a seat.'

Broad sat in one of the large, winged leather chairs that made up a three-piece set surrounding a large glass coffee table which had two empty coffee cups and a buff folder with TOP SECRET across the top of the file and the words Operation Longshot in smaller letters below. Brookfield sat in the other armchair. Sitting on the large sofa were Sir Hugh Fraser and Sir Martin Bryant. After everyone said hello it was Bryant who spoke.

'Well, Mr Broad, where are we now, can you bring us up to date?'

His question indicated two things to Broad. He'd used the word 'we' which he could take to mean we're all in this together. But he'd started with a more formal, Mister, which Broad took as we're together in this but if the shit hits the fan, you're on your own.

Broad spent the next twenty minutes bringing them up to date.

'So, despite all the resources we have, we're not much closer to getting these people? You say we are, but how close?' Bryant asked.

There was that 'we' again, thought Broad, and he was sure Sir Hugh had picked up on it too when he smiled and winked at him.

'I do think we're close. We have them moving out of the Hilton in a hurry and obviously spooked. They exposed themselves and we can now confirm that the Real IRA and Islamic Jihad are working together. Most likely, led by Costello and Lyndsey. From the CCTV we have a full description of the driver of the BMW and its registration details. Thanks to the PSNI we've confirmation of Costello phoning Ireland, the conversation recorded, and the number of the burner phone he's using. CCHQ are monitoring it with the hope of pinning down his location.'

'Is there anything else you need?' asked Brookfield.

'Not now, Prime Minister. Can I ask, have you briefed your own protection detail or changed any of your plans?'

'Yes and no. We have increased my Personal Protection by two and my plans for the conference remain the same, on schedule.'

'The prime minister will be attending some Party events in the city tonight then back here to work on his speech and more meetings with ministers. We don't want the Press alerted by drastic changes to his security or itinerary,' said Bryant.

'Thank you, Martin,' said Hugh Fraser, 'I think we can let Jim get on with the job in hand. We must remember his team aren't policemen but a specialist unit with a specialist task as set out by the prime minister and the Intelligence Committee. Their job is to find the terrorists and deal with them.'

'Yes, thank you, Jim, for all that you and your team are doing, please keep me updated,' said the prime minister.

'Come and let me buy you a cup of coffee, Jim,' said Sir Hugh putting his arm around Jim's shoulder and guiding him to the door.

'Yes, good night, Mr Broad, and thank you,' said Bryant.

'Good night, sir,' said Broad before he left.

There it was again, the politician's language of formality. You're not one of us, you're on your own. At least Broad knew who his real friends were and who he could trust the kind of friend who would follow him through the door of danger. The politicians he'd come into contact with always looked for a scapegoat if things went wrong.

When they got to the hotel lobby, they found a seat in the corner of the crowded room still full of delegates talking in full flow.

Instead of the coffee he'd suggested, Sir Hugh ordered two large malt whiskies and a jug of water. Now, as he looked over his glass at Broad, he smiled again.

'I needed this, Jim. Any longer in that room with that jumped up one-trick pony, Bryant, and I would have shot him myself.'

Broad laughed. He knew Hugh Fraser hated the grey suit mob, as they called ministers and their lackeys, as much as he did. Bryant, because he had the prime minister's ear, could be a tough-talking mandarin one of the boys when he wanted to, but talk was cheap – action on the ground sorts the real men from the boys. Bryant was the kind of civil servant who had perfected the art of smiling to your face while stabbing you in the back. He would have been comfortable in the company of the gang that surrounded Julius Caesar on the steps of the Senate all those years ago. The locations might be different, but the tactics were the same.

'But, Jim, I want you know that no matter what we think of Bryant, he's smart and because he has the ear of the PM, we need to think like a politician. We work in the background of life not in the full glare of the British and world news cycle. The first people know about us is when something has happened, usually when people are dead.'

More people were filling the spaces in the bar. The conference and its fringe events were closing down for the day. The sound of voices filled the air and the two men found they could speak without being overheard.

'I know what you mean, Hugh. But the politicians might change but as far as we're concerned, their politics doesn't. Look at what they're now doing in Northern Ireland pandering to the Republicans and then getting the PSNI to hound old soldiers in their seventies trying to prosecute them for killings they were involved in during the Troubles when serving Queen and Country. The politicians did the same after Iraq; allowing ambulance chasing lawyers to lead spurious, made-up investigations on the behalf the terrorists we were fighting. That's what I fear now for SG9. Our people put their head on the block at the behest of these same politicians who are only too pleased to point the finger of blame when the shit hits the fan.'

Hugh took a long sip of his malt then leaned a little closer towards Jim.

'I know, and I agree with what you're saying. All our lives we've had to deal with these pen pushers. I've always stood by my people. I would never ask them to do something I wouldn't do myself. I don't want you and the team to have any worries. If push comes to shove, I have enough information on the skeletons in their cupboards to bring down the lot of them. In the meantime, let's get on with the job. I know your team have been briefed and trained to take these bastards out. But, if there is a chance to take Lyndsey alive, the information she has on the Islamic network would be more useful without a bullet in it.'

Broad understood what his boss was saying. It would give him the ace up his sleeve he needed to continue playing his game with the politicians.

'We will do our best. Now, can we get out of here and get some food, I'm starving, somewhere a little quieter?'

'There's a little club I just happen to be a member of not too far from here.'

CHAPTER FORTY-TWO

The call to the Warrington Police Station from a disturbed resident said there had been an explosion near Glazebrook, a small village on the edge of the Warrington Police Divisional Boundary with Greater Manchester Police. Detective Chief Inspector Kevin Connor, Cheshire Constabulary was old school, you always keep your senior boss up to date, and there was no one more senior than his Chief Constable so he was the first call.

'Kevin, I'll contact the Gold Commander and Chief Constable in Manchester to let them know what's happened. In the meantime, you can keep me up to date and I'll get their Gold Commander to speak with you,' said the Chief Constable.

'I look forward to hearing from him.'

'Call me at any time you need to, Kevin.'

'Will do, sir.'

The call came from the Gold Commander at 10 p.m. 'Usual commands keep me informed.' Lockwood came across to Connor as snappy and demanding.

'We need all the information we can extract from this scene, Chief Inspector, and we need it as soon as possible.'

When the phone went dead, Connor could only smile to himself as he thought, *you'll get it when I have it and not before.*

His mobile phone buzzed on the desk, he didn't recognise the number or the voice when he answered it.

'Hello?'

'Hello, Chief Inspector Connor?'

'Yes, speaking, who is this?'

'My name is David Reece and I'm leading a team working on the people who burnt the car on your patch. I would like to visit the scene and maybe meet you there for a chat.'

'Are you police, Mr Reece?'

'No, I work for the Secret Intelligence Service and as I say, we're after the people who burnt out that car. I'm not far away, I can be there in twenty minutes.'

'Well, we have floodlights and officers at the scene and you're welcome to visit it and I'll meet you there, but I don't think you'll get much from it.'

'I would still like to have a look for myself.'

'That should be OK, wait for me if you're there first, how will I recognise you?'

'I'll be in a black Range Rover. I'll stay in the vehicle until you knock on the window.'

Reece had been called to the comms room by April to be told they'd found the black BMW burnt out. The comms team had been monitoring the police networks, and it was just as well because they'd received nothing from Lockwood. Although just what Reece had expected, he was furious.

Reece found Mary still sitting in the canteen with a cold coffee.

'Sorry, but something's come up. Do you mind waiting here a little longer or if you want, I'll get someone to drop you back at the hotel?' After Mary had told him about the phone call from Costello and the confirmation of what they already knew. Baseball Cap man was Costello, and he knew Mary was working with the security forces, Reece was taking no chances with Mary's safety.

'No problem, I'm happy enough here. You take care.'

Reece could see the blue and white tape sealing off the approach to the car which was lit up with the bull lights making it look like a beached whale in the dark. He parked the car on the main road and waited for Connor.

He sat in silence watching the traffic go by and the police vehicles park up then leave after a while taking the evidence with them.

After ten minutes, a blue Renault Megane parked just short of the entrance and a large man in a grey overcoat got on and spoke to the officer at the field entrance. The man then turned to walk towards the Range Rover., Reece stepped out to meet the man halfway.

'DCI Connor?'

'Yes, Mr Reece, I don't wish to be formal but have you any identification?'

Reece produced his SIS Identity Wallet.

Connor was in his late fifties around six feet tall with receding grey hair and light blue eyes. He looked fit and spoke with a north-west accent but with a hint of Irish.

'Good to meet you. Now, how can I help?'

'To put it simply, sir, this car has been used by what we believe to be a terrorist cell operating in the north-west. We're on their tail and the car is just one more piece in the jigsaw to helping us catch them. We think they're in the final stages of a terrorist attack, so the quicker we can get the forensic information from this car the better.'

'Well, it would appear that when the car exploded after the petrol tank was lit the damage was mainly to the rear of the vehicle. These BMWs have a strong chassis, so I'm told. So, despite their best efforts to destroy any evidence, the front of the car is still intact, even the built-in satnav. Our technicians are working on it as we speak, and I hope to have the results within the hour. Hopefully we'll know where the car has been for the last few days.'

'You'll know the car was hired from a local Hertz dealer, we've already looked for the tracker they sometimes fit, but this one didn't have one – just so your guys don't waste their time looking for it. We need the info off that satnav.'

'I see that you've been working with Graham Lockwood the Manchester Gold Commander for the Conservative Conference, has this anything to do with that?'

'Yes, but I would appreciate you giving me a heads up on anything you get as time is of the essence.'

'Are you ex police by any chance?'

'Yes, RUC twenty years.'

'I thought so. My parents were from Northern Ireland. I have a lot of time for you guys. You held the line when some would jump ship.'

'I thought I could hear a bit of Irish accent.'

'Listen, between you and me, I know Lockwood and he's an ass of a paperclip pusher and I know he always wants to be the big boy claiming all the glory to himself. So, anything I get you'll be the first to know.'

'I know from experience how things can get bogged down in little kingdom battles at senior level. No pressure, but whatever you get I get before anyone else including your Chief Constable and I need it in a hurry. Nothing stops it or gets in the way. If you have any problems let me know.

You have my number. If we can find out where the car has been, then we have a chance of catching up with these guys.'

Connor smiled his understanding. 'You have my word. I'll be in touch later.'

Connor went back to the tape line and spoke to one of the SOCOs dressed in a white full body forensic suit. Reece returned to the Range Rover and started the engine. Using the radio, he spoke with Jim Broad.

'Just had a good chat with DCI Connor at the scene. I believe he knows where I'm coming from and that he's now working for me...we should get the information from the car soon. He doesn't like some of the top brass in Manchester that's for sure and he's going to work with us cutting out the red tape that slows things up. I would think that by the time I get back to the hangar, information will start to come through.'

Reece spoke as he drove. 'Have the SAS ready for a briefing when I get back.'

When he got back to the hangar, despite the time of night, everything was moving. Reece found the team and the SAS in the comms section of the hangar, checking their equipment.

'Great, you're all here,' said Reece who noted Jim Broad sitting quietly in the corner, the sign of a good commander. When all the training had been done, the recces complete, and the target known, a good commander would brief his troops with everything he knew then sit back and let them do their job.

'I met the DCI from Warrington who is in charge of the burnt-out car, and he'll be in touch soon giving us all he can. The good news is his forensic technicians just might be able to give us a location for these people from the inbuilt satnav which survived the fire almost intact. Our people could do it but considering they already had people there who could pull the information why delay further. It's going to be a long night people so make sure you have everything you need.'

Mary was watching from a chair at the entrance. Seeing Reece in full flow like this impressed her. This was the side of him that had been hidden, the professional side he'd talked about, and now, when she saw it in action and up close, she felt a little scared, and for the first time, she was aware of the real danger ahead.

'Where do you want us?' It was the SAS troop boss Kevin who asked the first question.

'Realistically, until we know a location to start from, we all stay here, conserve our energy until we have something to get our teeth into. But let's get everything ready for when we get the information. Everybody go through your equipment: your comms, your vehicles…everything needs to be right.'

Reece knew he didn't need to teach these people how to suck eggs but years of doing these things right had kept him alive and if people were going to die today, he wanted it to be the bad guys.

'Any questions?'

No one spoke.

'Good, I'll be back in a minute.'

Reece nodded for Mary and Broad to follow him. He walked them to the canteen and ordered three coffees. When he sat down with the hot drinks in front of them, he looked at Mary.

'Mary, you may have a very important part to play in this and there might be some danger. Are you still happy to continue and help us? I would rather keep you out of things, but we need to stop this fucker and to do that we need to spin all our cards.'

Mary took a few seconds before she answered.

'After the phone call, there's one thing I know, if we don't get him, he won't stop until he gets me so don't worry, Joseph, I mean, David. I still can't get used to David I still like Joseph and I might just call you that now and again.'

'I have no problem whatever you call me. Boss, can you provide a couple of cars for us to use? Range Rovers are comfortable but not practical when it comes to mobile surveillance as they stand out. By the look of things, we'll be involved in more vehicle surveillance than foot for now and we might have to move quickly in a built-up area.'

'No problem. We have access to the police vehicle pound in Manchester, I'll get you what you need, might take an hour or so.'

'By the time they arrive we should have something from DCI Connor for us to get our teeth into.'

'OK, let me make the call.'

When Broad left, Reece looked at Mary. She seemed to be calm, no signs of stress or pressure. This lady always impressed him but now, more than ever, he felt the deep feelings that were emerging every time he was alone with her.

'When we move, Mary, I want you to stick with me. I need you to be in a position to identify Costello if we see him. I know he may have changed his appearance and maybe wearing a disguise, you know the little things that make Costello, Costello. But I don't want you to take any risks…nothing that would put you in danger.'

'As I told you just now, Costello will kill me if he finds me. I have no choice. I need to find him first and you're my best hope of doing that. I'm in it to the end, Joseph. Yes, I prefer Joseph. I've known you longer as Joseph, so until this is over, and we have more time to ourselves, Joseph it is.'

'Well, there's not much more time, Costello and his gang have to come out of their hole soon and we need to be ready to cut their heads off when they do. Let's go back and see how the team are getting on. It's our job to wait until they make a mistake…then kill them.'

CHAPTER FORTY-THREE

Costello unpacked the few clothes he had from his bag and placed them in the wardrobe and drawers. The final item he removed was about ten inches long and in its leather sheath. He withdrew the Muela Pro Throwing Knife and felt the cold, solid steel as he balanced it in the palm of his right hand. He always thought of the knife as his get out of jail card to be used as a last resort if he needed to. When he first got it, he'd practiced for hours throwing it at a tree in South Armagh until he could pull it from the sheath secured in his boot, throw the knife spinning through the air, and hit the target dead center in a split second.

He'd sharpened the Blade producing razor-sharp sides. He'd taken the knife to a farm in Monagahan one night. He picked the farm for two reasons. The first was that the owner was old and slightly deaf, and the second it was a pig farm. He'd approached the pigsty quietly and stepping in, he picked out one of the larger pigs and approached it from behind. Pigs are like humans in many ways, they hear well and sense movement so the whole exercise made it all the more real for what he wanted to do. In one quick movement he stepped astride the pig pulling its head back and, just as it started scream, Sean cut its throat from ear to ear with the throwing knife. The blood spattered across the pen and the pig, now silent, collapsed its whole-body weight going limp. He knew the experience would be similar if preformed on a human being.

He felt the balance once more before placing the knife back in the sheath and secured it the boot on his right ankle.

He heard the door opening and Lyndsey came into the room.

'Have you picked which bed you're sleeping in?' she asked.

'The one furthest from the door…it gives me more time to react if we have unwelcome visitors.'

'Mohammad got in touch. He's burnt the car and was able to return safely to Irlam.'

'Good. Will he stay there until we move?'

'No. He has to pick up the keys of the apartment before he meets up with you. Before that, he'll attend the conference to see if there's been an increase on security and report back. Tonight, we relax, tomorrow we work.'

CHAPTER FORTY-FOUR

Mohammad had left Irlam Station and found the pizza shop was still open. He ordered two ten-inch pizzas, one with four cheeses and one with mixed meats but no bacon. When he got to the safe house it was quiet, but he found Imtaz and Waheed watching the TV in the living room, the sound down low, barely audible.

'Hi, guys, food's up.'

Both men smiled; Waheed showing the gap between his front teeth a smile but not a smile. He could see they'd been watching the news showing that day's report from the conference a government minister talking to the camera.

Getting plates from the kitchen, they all sat at the dining table.

'No bacon I hope, brother,' Waheed said.

'No bacon,' said Mohammad with a smile. Waheed wouldn't last long living in the west, he thought. There are times in war when you had to make sacrifices and Allah would understand.

'Where have you been?' asked Imtaz.

'Getting rid of the car. It's burnt, job done.'

They ate in silence, each in his own thoughts.

'What now is there any change to the plans?' Imtaz asked.

'No, we stay on track.'

'Can I ask a question, Waheed?' asked Imtaz. 'I've never seen what a bomb can do in a crowd, do you have any idea of a safe distance when I leave it?'

Waheed gave that wide gapped toothed smile this time it looked genuine thought Mohammad, like he was going to enjoy the answer.

'Of course, my brother, I can answer from personal experience. I was working with the Jihad and Taliban in Afghanistan, and we attacked a market of the enemy. I placed a rucksack bomb exactly like the ones we'll place in Manchester. I set it under a table in the centre of the market and went and stood about one hundred yards away, behind a wall, and pressed the phone button. When it exploded, many of our enemies died and many more were badly wounded.'

'Was it the Semtex and the nails that did the damage the most?' asked Imtaz.

'Not Semtex. This time I used captured Russian plastic explosives, but it's the same. The bomb had nails just like the ones I've used but you have to remember, when it goes off in a crowded place the blast tears bodies apart. The nails tear through the skin, breaking the bones underneath. Pieces of the broken bones fly like shrapnel, creating more damage to the bodies of people nearby. You can never believe unless you see it yourself, pieces of men, women, and children, still burning…the smell of charred flesh and hair. Sometimes, those closest to the blast disappear altogether, leaving nothing but a bloodstain where they stood.'

'It sounds like a scene from hell. How do you live with the memories, how do you sleep?' asked Imtaz.

Looking from one to the other, Waheed let out a long slow breath.

'You must always remember, my brothers, we're always at war. If these people support the Great Satan and refuse to acknowledge the one true God that is Allah, then they're the enemy and they must die, all of them, every one of them. Are you ready to carry the fight to the enemy for our God for Allah?'

There was silence for a few seconds as Mohammed and Imtaz thought about the question.

'That is why we're here,' said Mohammad. 'We know what needs to be done. We've already taken the risk that's needed, and we'll complete the task ahead with Allah's help.'

Mohammad then pulled his Glock from his coat pocket and laid it on the table. Imtaz and Waheed followed suit and placed their guns on the table too. The gesture was felt by all three. This was a battle they were determined to win, a fight to the death.

'Let us pray to Allah, let him give us strength, courage, and the wisdom we'll need,' said Imtaz.

All three knelt on the living room carpet and side by side, they fell forward, touching their heads and hands to the floor in a silent prayer to Allah.

Chapter Forty-Five

When the call came in from DCI Connor and it was Broad who took it. Reece and everyone else in the comms room watched for any reaction, but Broad gave nothing away. After he put down the phone, he turned to face the room and the expectant faces.

'It's good news. DCI Connor has just informed me that his boffins have been able to decipher the BMW satnav. The car has been all over Manchester but has been paying particular attention to a small area in Irlam near here. It parked up on at least three different occasions in the last few days. The DCI is sending us the location as we speak. I've asked him to keep his own people back and he informed me that as Irlam is the Greater Manchester Police jurisdiction, it won't be a problem. For now, this is a surveillance only operation to identify what and who we're up against.'

Broad then turned to Geoff Middleton the SAS commander.

'Geoff, I want you and your men mobile not too far in the background in case we need you quickly.'

The SAS officer nodded his understanding. 'Don't worry we'll be ready'.

'David, the extra cars you wanted have just arrived…two BMWs outside. They are fully fitted with armoured windows which I hope you won't need, and the up-to-date comms you will need.'

'The information from the Cheshire police is just coming through, sir,' said one of the two men monitoring the communications.

'Can you bring it up on the big screen and print off a few copies?'

'No problem, on the screen now.'

He pressed a few of the computer keys in front of him and a split picture appeared on the large screen at the end of the room.

Half of the picture was typescript detailing the movements of the burnt-out car the other half was a street map of Irlam with a red X showing where the car had been parked.

'Fuck they're only a few miles from us,' said Reece.

He then spoke to the SG9 team who were already pulling together what they would need, again checking their comms and weapons.

'I want us to work in two-man teams using the BMWs. April, you go with Steve, and I'll go with Joe, that way we have good coverage. Mary, you'll come with us, if we spot someone who fits Costello's description then your eyes on the matter will be a great help. I know you have Glocks, but I want each car to have some heavy fire power, should we need it, so each car carries a H&K MP5. We're all trained with them and I'm sure our SAS friends can lend us two with two, thirty-round mags for each.'

'Do you think that'll be enough?' asked Cousins with a smile.

'Well, as my old firearms trainer used to say, if you can't hit the target with everything you have in the magazine then you may as well throw the damn gun at them,' replied Reece.

'Let's go over the ground we need to cover,' said Reece as he walked closer to the screen on the wall to inspect the streets in Irlam.

'Comms. Can you blow up this picture of the map please and can you link it into the satnavs of our BMWs?'

'Yes, no problem to both,' came the reply.

'The car seemed to be parked here in Kings Road there's four other streets off it three avenues and one small close. By the look of things there's around one hundred houses so we take it slowly we don't want to spook them if they're there.'

'It will be tough to spot anything in the dark,' April said.

'I know,' answered Reece. 'We will do a foot and drive round of the area to get to know it. If they're in there, they'll most likely be in bed at this time of the morning. We also need to do a trawl of the CCTV of the Irlam train station which isn't far from this area so it's a good bet they've been using the train in and out of Manchester. Boss, can you chase that up for us?'

'Will do. Do you need anything else?'

'Not for now. I think we should get out there and see what we have. As Irlam's not far away if there is anything you need us to come back and see we can do so quickly, and while you're at it get them to check the CCTV between Glazebrook Station and Irlam for shortly after the time the car was discovered.'

Turning to the comms and the SG9 team Reece spoke slowly and quietly making sure they heard every word.

'We will need everyone to be on their toes tonight, guys. I'll be Alpha One. Joe, you're Alpha Two. April, Alpha Three. And, Steve, Alpha Four. Boss, you and the comms team here will be Alpha Control. We will all have the built-in radios in the cars plus our own body radios. I'll also borrow body armour from the troops. Make sure you all have your arm bands that were provided by the police just in case we need to move about in a hostile environment. Everybody happy?'

Everyone nodded their agreement.

'Right, I'm off to have a chat with our SAS friends to borrow a few items. Mary, stay here, I'll be back shortly.'

Reece found the SAS team already tooled up and ready to go.

'Geoff, I need two MP5s and four mags of thirty, plus a couple of flak jackets. Can you help me please?'

'No problem. Mickey, can you get these for David?' he asked of the nearest trooper, who left the room to return a few minutes later with the requested items.

'If you need to use them, I don't want it coming back on me so as long as you involve us in the fun, I'm saying nothing,' Middleton said with a grin.

'Don't worry, if we need to use them, you'll be the first one, I call.'

Reece then briefed the troops on what the SG9 team would be doing and their call signs.

'We'll keep things simple. I'll be Tango One and the rest of the team will use the Tango callsign followed by a number so that you know it's us. Can you get your boss to get the local police to put the area out-of-bounds so that we don't have any snoopy wooden top straying where they shouldn't be?'

'Good idea, Geoff, Northern Ireland Rules, eh?'

'Big boy's rules always worked for me.'

When he'd worked in undercover operations in Northern Ireland during the Troubles, they always put the area they were operating in out-of-bounds to local forces to prevent them spooking the targets or getting involved in a Blue on Blue where the security personnel could end up firing on each other by accident. Undercover people would refer to it as part of the Big Boys Rules when involved in operations that were likely to result in a shoot-out with the terrorists.

'David?'

It was Joe Cousins.

'The Cheshire Police are quicker than we thought. DCI Connor has just sent through the CCTV from Glazebrook Station, it's not great but there is only one person on the platform just after the car was set on fire. I think it's our hooded Asian.'

Reece and Geoff followed Cousins back to the comms section where the grainy black and white images were already on the big screen, they were in black and white and again the suspect had his hood up. There was no way they could identify him but this time he had a sports holdall with the Nike logo on the side.

'The bag gives us something else to look out for,' April said.

'Can we track where he went?' asked Reece.

'He got on a train for Manchester but got off at Irlam, then the cameras lost him when he turned right out of the station towards the streets where we know the car was parked up,' Broad replied.

'So, he goes back to the nest tonight. No one picks him up that we've picked up,' said Reece. 'We need to get out there and try to find out exactly where he went. OK, everyone, let's do this.'

This was the part Reece liked best; when they had something to go on, everyone knew the task ahead, and they could get out there and do something positive. Now the jigsaw was coming together Reece felt the same adrenalin he'd felt when extreme danger was around the corner in Northern Ireland during the troubles. The feeling you get when a car swerves towards you. You know the danger but the knowledge that in a short period of time you could be killed or seriously injured can spur you into the action that will make the difference over life and death.

Chapter Forty-six

'This is Alpha One, comms check?' said Reece.

His team responded.

'Alpha Two, clear.'

'Alpha Three, clear.'

'Alpha Four, clear.'

'Alpha Control, all clear signals.'

'Tango One, clear and on the edge of town, over.'

'OK, everyone, loud and clear,' Reece said. 'I'm going to take a drive around the Kings Road area. Alpha Two, park up on the main road through Irlam, Tango One, hold position.'

Two voices replied, 'Roger that.'

Mary was in the back of the BMW being driven by Reece. Sitting beside him, Joe Cousins had a clipboard with a notepad, watching every movement in the streets as they passed.

Mary soon worked out that Cousins was writing down the registration numbers of cars in the street and on driveways, passing them onto Alpha Control for a search of ownership. Every car registration they checked out came back to the house address they were parked outside.

The centre of Irlam appeared to be one long main street about a mile long with shops, bars, and take away food stores A typical English high street thought Reece, a bit run down with a mixture of old and new buildings.

As Reece had turned into the Kings Road, the narrow street had two more streets running to the left two dead ends with a further street running to the right another dead end. Kings Road itself was also a dead end all the streets surrounded by the fencing of an industrial estate.

The first street on the left was Henley Avenue which was the smallest of the three streets branching of Kings Road having about ten houses in all a dead end with a turning space at the bottom. Although it was dark, the street lighting was good, so Reece drove in slowly then, after driving through each of two other streets once and, making sure Cousins had all the registrations he needed, he drove to the top of Kings Road and turned left onto the main street stopping a few hundred yards from the Kings Road.

'Alpha One to Alpha Three, come in, over.'

'Alpha Three send, over.'

'We had a drive around Kings Road and the streets off it. As you would expect at this time of the morning it's all quiet, nothing moving, and only one or two with interior lights on. I'm thinking that although the satnav shows Kings Road, if they're in a house here then it could be any of about one hundred. The good thing is that if they're in there, they're going to have to come out of the top of the Kings Road. If we cover the road, we should get them coming out. We decide what to do next depending on what we see,' Reece said.

'Roger that. We've taken a drive down the full length of the main street and it's all quiet. We're on the Manchester side of the street away from Kings Road. On the other side of the Railway Bridge, can you see it from your side?'

Reece could see the bridge over the main street in the rear-view mirror.

'Yes, I see it.'

'Just as you drive under the bridge there's a side road up to the Irlam train station. We took a drive up to look and I must say the station looks in better nick than most of the buildings on the main road. It looks Victorian and has two lines going between Manchester and Liverpool. There's a tunnel walkway that goes under the lines for access to the two platforms then on down to the main road coming out at the traffic lights beside the overhead bridge. It would be ideal for anyone using the trains in and out of Manchester and staying near the Kings Road.'

Reece was having the same thoughts his memory went quickly back to his foot surveillance training with an MI5 officer who was one of the famous 'watchers' team who followed the Russian spies during the Cold War. This day one of the other instructors had been following Reece and his instructor when they'd gone down a walkway under the main road outside Madame Tussaud's in London. As they went down the subway steps and turned the corner to go down further the instructor in front of Reece just managed to avoid stepping on a Tramp sitting at the top of the steps with a large glass sitting on the step beside him. Stepping over the glass he told Reece to listen as they walked along the long tunnel. He knew that as there was a number of exits from the tunnel the instructor following would be following close behind concentrating on where they were and what exit they were taking. Suddenly there was a loud crash and smashing of glass with a burst of profanities. They had both looked around able to identify their following watcher as he picked himself up off the ground.

There was more than one way to get caught out when following someone and that was the point being made by his instructor.

'OK, we need eyes on the end of Kings Road to cover foot and vehicle surveillance. We will take another run around the Kings Road and make sure we have all the vehicle registrations, then we can all meet up in the station carpark for a quick chat.'

'Roger that,' said Grey.

Reece drove around the streets once more slowly this time to try to identify the driveways without vehicles on them. This was easy as only Henley Avenue had driveways and garages and only two houses had no vehicle the first number two on the left as you entered and one at the end of the street number ten, both could have a car in the garage.

Mary had been sitting quietly in the back but now she spoke.

'If you find them in one of these houses, what then, Joseph?'

'Then we decide what to do. That's what I want to chat to everyone about.'

He drove to the Irlam Station carpark where the second BMW was parked in a corner that avoided the span of the security cameras covering the station.

Everyone stood by the cars, the rain had subsided for a change.

'I'm happy where we are,' said Reece.

'We now know the basic lay of the land and I have to believe they're somewhere in the Kings Road area. The problem is, we don't know exactly where, or if they're together, or how many of them there are. We could call in a big squad of police and soldiers, seal off the area, and wait for them to show their hand, but there may be people we're not aware off, and again they might not even be there. We would be showing our hand what they don't know right now works in our favour. They don't know we're here. Now's the time to be patient and wait them out wait for them to make their move. It's three in the morning. I'm going to drop Mary off at the hotel, then Joe and I'll get back to the hangar for a little shuteye. April and Steve, you park up on the main road with a view of the entrance to Kings

Road anything coming out, especially on foot, make a note of it. If it looks like anyone we're interested in, follow them. Joe and I'll be back at 7 a.m. to let you get back for some rest. We know the target for these guys will most likely be Wednesday, so we still have time, let's use it. Any questions?'

'What if we think there's a danger to the public?' asked Harrison.

'We have a green light. We're here for one reason and one reason only: to find these bastards and take them out of the picture. If that means permanently, then so be it. This area has been put out-of-bounds to local police so if they need to come in here for any reason, they'll let us know for clearance purposes. That's the reason we don't carry handcuffs, that's not our job. The one thing we don't need is a blue-on-blue situation when they might run into us doing our job.'

When he dropped off Mary, he could see the tiredness in her eyes. He kissed her on the cheek and watched her walk slowly into the hotel, she'd turned to wave goodbye, but Reece was already gone. When he got back to the hangar the comms team were doing the same getting some rest leaving only one at the desk to cover the team out on the ground. All was quiet, so Reece and Harrison headed to the team section of the hangar. But as usual when he was in the middle of an operation, Reece found sleep hard to come by the different scenarios would constantly swirl around his head the questions he needed to ask the answers he needed but didn't know yet.

CHAPTER FORTY-SEVEN

TUESDAY, 1 OCTOBER 2019

The dawn light had started to come through the bedroom window where Mohammad was sleeping at the front of the house. Stretching, he got out of bed and looked out through the net curtains to the street below. It was 5.30 a.m. and the street, like the rest of the house, was quiet. There was a slight drizzle of rain with hardly any wind and the sky was a miserable grey hinting at more rain to come. After he'd showered and dressed, he went down to the kitchen and made himself scrambled egg and toast. Sitting at the table he checked his phone, no messages. He sent a text to Lyndsey.

Up and ready heading into town about eight.

A reply came back almost immediately:

See you later.

He switched on the TV, keeping the sound down, to get the early morning news from Sky. Alongside world-wide events, it dedicated lots of airtime to the conference. They were speculating on what would be in the prime minister's speech on Wednesday. As he watched, he could hear footsteps above him; someone was awake. A short while later, Waheed came into the room.

'Good morning, brother, did you sleep well?' he asked Waheed.

'Yes, soundly thank you. I'm going to make a coffee; do you want one?'

'Yes, that would be great. white no sugar.'

When he returned with the coffee, they watched the Sky reporters speaking to people attending the conference yesterday. It was too early to speak to any of today's delegates as the doors wouldn't be open until around 8 a.m.

'Are you nervous, brother?' asked Waheed.

'Not really. I've already sent a text to Sharon, and she is also awake. Today we move toward to the completion of our plan. On Wednesday we'll make the world shake with our Jihad. We just have to believe in Allah, and all will be well.'

'I agree, brother, my heart is set now that the end is near. When are you leaving?'

'I'll set off early to get there for eight.'

'I still don't trust that infidel. His agenda is not ours; his God is not ours.'

'He has his own agenda if he is successful and it suits Allah's purpose, then it will be in Allah's name that the word will go around the world. The false God he worships will be of nothing compared to Allah.'

They could hear Imtaz as he started to move about upstairs. Waheed looked at the ceiling. 'When he comes down, I think we should pray to Allah together,' he said.

April Grey had slept a little before the radio mike in her ear sounded the voice of David Reece waking her from her slumber.

'This is Alpha One, we'll be taking over the watch. Alpha Three, we'll be parking up close to you about 07.30, anything to report.'

'No,' said Grey. 'The world here is starting to awake. The road has been getting busy, it's coming up to rush hour. But nothing significant from Kings Road.'

'Roger that, we'll be with you shortly then you both get back and get some shut eye for a few hours.'

Twenty minutes later, Reece and Cousins pulled into the parking space behind Grey and Harrison. When Harrison pulled away, Reece moved his BMW into the space they'd vacated as it provided a better view of the entrance to Kings Road and two of the streets adjoining it.

Turning off the engine, they watched the traffic and the pedestrians moving about, starting their working day. The registration numbers taken down by Cousins earlier had shown all the cars belonged to residents who had lived in the streets around Kings Road for many years. But that didn't mean they were all clear.

One of them could be a long-time sleeper but the names had also been checked for criminal and terrorist links and apart from some with minor traffic violations nothing flashed up to show there was reason to investigate further. In the first few minutes they'd been there two cars had come out of Kings Road the occupants elderly grey haired and white skinned. After two hours it was beginning to look like a long day. It was as Reece was looking down Kings Road, he saw a man come out of Henley Avenue and turning right, he walked towards the top of Kings Road. Reece fired up the wiper blades to clear the slight rain sitting on the windshield. Yes, the man was definitely Asian, with a slight beard and glasses, he walked with his head down he was wearing a suit with a shirt and tie but what was more interesting was that he was also wearing a jacket over the suit with a hood pulled up over his head. Not only to protect him from the rain, Reece thought but also to protect his identification. Now Cousins could see the man. Both held their breath, straining their eyes to make sure, afraid to speak in case the figure disappeared.

'I think we have a hot one,' said Reece. 'He's not carrying any bags and he looks like he's going to a business meeting.'

Reece grabbed his Barbour jacket from the back seat and slipped his gun into the pocket.

'Alpha One, to control. I think we have our Asian hoodie. He came out of Henley Avenue, so we need to pay more attention to the residents there. There could be more of them in there, maybe even Costello and Lyndsey. I'll follow our friend on foot, I'm sorry, but get Alpha Three and Four back here as soon as possible, no sleep for anyone today.'

'Roger, Control, Alpha Two will stay and cover until backup gets here.'

'Roger, Alpha One.'

'Are you OK with all that, Joe?' Reece asked.

'No problem, David. Anything more comes out before help gets here, what do you want me to do?'

'Do what you can to check it out, anything moving try to stay with it; the street won't be going anywhere.'

'Roger that. Will do.'

Reece left the vehicle and started walking at the same pace as the target who was now about fifty yards ahead on the opposite side of the main road. Reece was watching for signs that the target was conducting anti-surveillance techniques, but he didn't appear to be. He was keeping a steady pace towards the junction at the railway bridge overpass. Reece pulled a tweed flat cap out of his pocket, it wasn't much, but the cap was also good protection when following someone as it would make it difficult for the target to see the concentration on the face of someone in a crowd.

As Reece expected, the man stopped at the main junction and waited for the traffic lights to turn green before he crossed the road to the side Reece was on before turning right once more towards the railway footway underpass to the station. Reece held back until he was sure the man had entered the underpass.

'Alpha One to Control, Tourist One now heading to the Irlam Railway station I will stay with him.'

'Roger, Alpha One.'

Reece took the turning into the underpass following the path under the railway line above and walked up the stairs on to the platform. The station was very busy with a large band of early workers on the platforms on both sides of the tracks. Looking around slowly, Reece took in the faces and spotted Tourist One buying a ticket at the machine then walking to the front of the crowd to wait for the next train.

Reece took his time and slowly moved to the same machine and purchased a ticket that would cover his travel for the rest of the day, then he moved behind the target. The man was about five-foot ten, with a lean build and smart appearance. His clothes looked like they'd been purchased from Marks and Spencer, and he wore smart black shoes. The shoes were important and made Reece smile. They were not the kind of shoes for walking long distances, more for working in an office environment. To Reece this meant unless Tourist One was stupid he wasn't going to be walking far today, and that was OK by Reece.

When the train arrived, the loudspeaker announced that it was the nine fifty to Manchester Piccadilly, calling at Manchester Deansgate. Tourist One boarded the middle of the three carriages by the forward doors, Reece boarded the same carriage at the rear doors. The carriage was packed, and it was standing room only, the passengers from Irlam filling the aisle almost to capacity. Reece could easily observe Tourist One for the journey. He faced forward throughout the trip, speaking to no one and Reece could see him move towards the exit doors when the train started to slow on its approach to Deansgate.

When the carriage stopped, and the passengers alighted from the train, Reece followed Tourist One over the walkway and down the steps then a sharp left street level. Reece followed him at the same pace from fifty yards behind.

'Alpha One to Control. Tourist One took the train from Irlam and we got off at Deansgate. We're on foot heading towards the city centre.'

'Roger, Alpha One. The rest of the team now in Irlam maintaining observation.'

Where are you going, pretty boy? Thought Reece. He walked with his right hand in his pocket feeling the grip of the Smith and Wesson helping to reassure him. There were fewer people on the street and Reece made a point of not gaining on his target and walking to his left rear as most people in Britain are right-handed, they'll look over their right shoulder when turning around to see if anyone is behind them, this would leave Reece in the targets blind side. If the target did turn to his left, Reece would definitely know he was looking for followers, Tourist One was making no effort to turn. Reece assessed that Tourist One was sure of where he was walking to, and that he wasn't carrying anything of concern, his steps continued in a set direction with the walk of a man who had no cares no fears.

'Tourist One now walking past the Bridgewater Hall following the tram tracks towards the Midland following the security barriers on the outside of the Conference Centre.'

'Roger, Alpha One.'

'Bloody hell he's just turned towards the main security entrance to the conference, wait out.'

Broad stared at the speakers in the comms section of the hangar trying to imagine what Reece was seeing and reporting, the rest of the room was silent.

'Alpha Control, you're not going to fucking believe this but Tourist One just produced a Conference Pass and went through the security checks into the Conference Hall itself. I closed the distance between us; if he'd made a wrong move, he's one of the bloody delegates. I'm heading to the security suite within the building to see if I can get him on CCTV, will phone you when I get there.'

'Roger, Alpha One, I await your call,' said Jim Broad.

CHAPTER FORTY-EIGHT

Costello had been up and had breakfast an hour before Lyndsey had appeared in the dining room.

'I must have been tired; I didn't hear you get up.'

'If you didn't hear me snore, then you must have been dead to the world,' he replied with a grin.

When she left for the hot buffet table, Costello called a waitress over and asked for a pot of coffee for two. The coffee arrived just as Lyndsey sat down with her bacon and eggs. Costello poured two cups of coffee.

'Any word from the boys?' he asked.

'I spoke with Mohammad before I came down, he was just leaving to catch the train into Manchester. He'll be in touch later when he's had a look around the conference area. I suggest we wait for Mohammad's call have lunch and maybe head in later.'

'Sounds like a plan. We can't do anything anyway until he gets the keys for the apartment on tonight.'

'Yes, a slight change of plan there. I have to be with Mohammad this evening at the estate agents with my passport to sign for the keys at five. The agents are on the main Deansgate street, so you can drop me off at the NCP and I'll let you know when we're inside the apartment.'

'Good idea, I don't want to be hanging about anywhere.'

'We can send Mohammad out for something to eat when we're in there otherwise we're just making it a longer stay than we need to.'

Now that they were close to the finish, and there was nothing more they could do, the hours would drag out, they knew this from experience.

'I can never think of food in the future when I'm eating, it's the same if I go to the supermarket on a full stomach,' said Costello.

'After tomorrow we can have a banquet wherever you want.'

'On a yacht on some beautiful ocean.'

'Sounds wonderful, it's something I've never done.'

'Let's make that a date then. Job done tomorrow then yacht in the Mediterranean for dinner. I'm off to get a paper and do some of that relaxing you talk about. See you later.'

Chapter Forty-nine

After he'd shown his identification to one of the security men, Reece was escorted to the security suite on the first floor of the Conference Centre. The Centre itself was full of delegates and the noise of a thousand voices in conversation was deafening. The security suite held around ten people who were either talking on phones or radios or watching monitors. Sitting at the back was Graham Lockwood, Gold Commander, who stood to greet Reece.

'Mr Reece, for what do we owe the pleasure?'

Reece sensed the question was in no way a pleasant greeting.

'Good to meet you again, sir,' he lied. 'We've been following a suspect this morning and it would appear he is one of your conference delegates.'

A look of panic came over Lockwood's face.

'You mean they're here, in here now?'

'It would appear he is on his own and completely clean, not carrying anything of danger to us but we can't take any chances.'

'Can you be sure? Where is he now? What are you going to do?'

There it was again, thought Reece, what are you going to do, the old swift two-step making sure he knew that if anything went wrong, it would be Reece to blame.

'That's why I want to use your screens to monitor him while he's here and try to get his details from when he scanned his conference card at the security tent.'

Lockwood knew Reece was in charge and he was only too happy to hand over control in this particular instance.

'Everyone,' shouted Lockwood attracting all the eyes in the room to look his way. 'This is Mr Reece I want you to give him whatever assistance he asks of you, this is important. Mr Reece, you have the room.'

Reece could see the questions on the officers' faces as they looked from Lockwood to him.

'At this stage, I need someone who can use the screens to cover the whole conference area from the main hall itself to the side shows and cafés, so which screen is best and who can do this for me?'

A young-looking constable put up his hand.

'I have good coverage, sir.'

'What's your name?' asked Reece as he pulled up a chair and sat down beside the constable.

'Jones, sir.'

'OK, Jones, first off, I'm not a Sir call me David. Second, show me what you can see.'

It only took Reece five minutes to spot Tourist One sitting on his own in the café area.

'That's him, Jones, keep your eye on him while I make a phone call.'

'Yes, sir, sorry, David.'

Lockwood had been watching over Reece's shoulder.

'Are you not going to grab him?'

'No, not yet. He's only a part of the plan. We need to see if he'll lead us to the rest. Where he is now is no risk to us, after all he's just gone through your security. He uses a false name of Kevin Jones. I checked with your people at the front security tent when I followed him through, and they confirm it's the name he's used to attend as a delegate. A quick check through my people shows the address he's given exists, but it's a dead letter drop; he doesn't live there. Mr Lockwood, as you can now see, these people are very professional and there has been a lot of thought put into their planning. We're close and this Kevin Jones, who I'm sure is no relation to our Constable Jones here, will help us bring the lot of them down.'

'I hope for all our sakes you're right, Mr Reece.'

'So do I, so do I. Now, if you don't mind, I need to speak to my people and let them know where our friend Kevin Jones is right now.'

Reece then phoned Jim Broad describing what had happened and where he now was.

'What do we do now, David?'

'We need to keep Tourist One under tight surveillance. We can't afford to lose sight of him. Send April here to work with me. Get her to pick up Mary we might need her insight to help us identify people we don't know if Costello is the only Irish connection here. Keep Cousins and Harrison in Irlam for now while you find out what house Tourist One came out of this morning. If we find that, then we can move in closer and work out if we use the troop to hit it or wait and follow whoever leaves it.'

'We might have some good news on the house. We discovered number two Henley Avenue is the only house in the street that's rented – the rest are long-term ownership.'

'That's great. Get the boys to walk past a few times to see if they can spot any occupants, but not to get close until after dark, by that time, with the conference more or less closing up around five, we should find Tourist One on the move again.'

Reece went back to the screens and Constable Jones.

'Anything to report, Jonesy?'

'No. He's just sitting there drinking and appears to be watching the world go by.'

'Is he watching anything in particular?'

'No, that's just it, just watching.'

'Keep watching but change cameras regularly; he might be watching us watching him. I haven't had a bite for some time, so I think I'll go down and see what they have to offer. If he moves, follow him and phone me.'

Reece wrote down his number and headed for the ground floor. It was easy to find the café and to mingle with the large crowd. He entered the open café behind Tourist One, who was still sitting at the table and reading a newspaper scanning the crowds. Reece ordered a coffee and a ham sandwich before sitting down six tables behind Tourist One. As he ate, he watched his target. Dressed like many here, a navy pin striped suit and shiny black shoes. His hair was short and neatly trimmed, a short-trimmed beard, and a round face with square thick framed black glasses.

He looked calm and relaxed, but Reece knew he was at work here, on a mission of his own. Watching the world go by was just a part of his reason for being here and Reece now knew he was assessing the security surrounding the conference.

Good, he thought, you're in my playing area now.

As he watched, Tourist One folded his paper and leaving it on the table, he got up and started walking towards the main Hall. Reece took another bite from his sandwich then left half of it on his plate. His phone buzzed. It was Jones to tell him his target was on the move.

'Yes, thanks, Jonesy. Stay with him I'm not far behind. Can you print up some close-up photos of him from what you've been seeing?'

'I already have, David, they're here waiting for you, and I've just sent one to your phone.'

'Good man.'

Reece followed Tourist One into the main hall staying about five rows behind him. On the main stage, the Conference Chairman was holding a three-way discussion on education with two company directors. This was followed with a speech by the Education Secretary.

Tourist One clapped at the appropriate places but he continued to move his head around making it obvious to Reece that he was also looking for CCTV and security but also checking for anyone watching him.

Near the end of the education speech, Tourist One left his seat and began to make his way back into the main area. Reece remained a safe distance away and watched as he circulated the stalls and displays, taking some of the freebies, one a bag to carry his goodies in before going back to the café and resuming his position with a pot of tea and a different newspaper.

Grey text him to say she'd arrived, so instead of resuming his position in the café, Reece went back to monitor Tourist One from the safety of the security room.

On entering the security suite Reece felt his spirits lift when he saw Mary sitting at the back of the room. Smiling he went and sat beside her.

'Well, how are you today?'

'I'm fine, Joseph, all the better for seeing you. Are you OK, you look tired?'

'I haven't had much sleep in the last twenty-four hours, but it's always the same when you get to the end game in these things, and we're definitely nearing the end. I hope you've had a good night's sleep because it might be a long day.'

'Slept like a baby, with some nice dreams involving you.'

April, who had been watching the screen from behind Jonesy, joined them.

'He's still enjoying his paper. Here are the stills, they're good,' she said handing over the pictures.

They were very good, thought Reece. Almost as good as a passport photo showing Tourist One's face looking directly at the security camera.

'Get these emailed to the hangar, the troop, and the rest of the team. We can hang on to these.'

'David,' called Jonesy from across the room.

Reece went over to look at the screen to see what Jonesy wanted.

'He's on the move again, heading towards the front door.'

'Keep on him. Can you access into the CCTV outside the conference in the general area around it?'

'Yes, no problem.'

'Good. Keep on him wherever he goes and record it if you can. If you see him make contact with anyone, record it or get a picture of them. If you need me call me.'

'Will do.'

Turning, Reece spoke loud making sure everyone heard him.

'As ACC Lockwood knows we are involved in a very important operation here which is protected under the articles of the Official Secrets Act, which means, as I'm sure you know, that what we've been doing here is of the utmost secrecy and is to be kept within these four walls.'

Reece could see Lockwood smile at the praise of his name, even though Reece had now specifically dropped him into the same well they were all swimming in.

'OK, let's go.'

Grey and Mary followed Reece down the stairs and towards the exit to find Tourist One. He wasn't hard to find; he was slow and deliberate…the pace of a man taking everything in as he walked. He'd turned left out of the main entrance and left the secure zone through the revolving gate onto the outside street.

Speaking into his body mike, Reece brought the hangar and the rest of the team up to date with what was happening.

'Tourist One on the move, now in the streets outside the conference zone, we'll stay with him.'

'Roger, Alpha One,' Broad replied.

'Let's break up,' said Reece as they walked. 'I'll cover him from the rear. April, you try to get ahead of him and cover from the front. Mary, you stay with me; a couple walking together is less conspicuous. April, where did you park the car?'

'On the other side of the Town Hall.'

'It doesn't look like he has a car, but we need to be ready just in case he gets one or is picked up. He's heading in the direction you've parked so we should be OK for the minute and Jonesy is keeping a watch on him too.'

April crossed the street and increased her step to get ahead of Tourist One. Reece and Mary stayed on the same side and about fifty yards behind.

'If he turns to look our way, Mary, I might have to grab you for a quick kiss.'

'I hope he does, then.'

Thanks be to God it wasn't raining, thought Reece.

There was nothing worse than having to follow someone on a cold wet day, it dulled sprit and moral. Tourist One continued to walk towards the Town Hall Square. Passing through the square, he turned left through the main crossroads stopping at the traffic lights to cross. April was still ahead of him on the other side. Reece and Mary stopped to pretend to do a bit of window shopping and when the lights changed, Tourist One crossed and for a moment, Reece lost sight of him, but April still had him.

'Tourist One now static, looking around slowly, don't turn into the street yet, Alpha One, he's looking for us. I can nip into a shop here and watch him through their window,' April said.

'Roger, Alpha Three. We'll wait for your signal.'

So now he was really at his game, thought Reece, what's he up to?

'He's entered a café halfway down the street,' said Grey.

'Roger, Alpha Three, we'll walk past and meet up with you.'

'Roger that.'

Reece and Mary walked past the café where they saw Tourist One standing with his back to the door at the counter. Further down the street, they stopped with Grey.

'He likes his tea and coffee this one,' said Grey.

'I'd like to get in there to see if he's making contact with someone from inside the café, but I've been close to him twice already.'

'I can do it,' said Grey.

'No, I want to keep you fresh for the surveillance later.'

'What if I go in?' offered Mary.

'I can't ask you to do that, it's too dangerous.'

'I won't get too close. I'll just get a quick coffee; God knows I need one. He's less likely to know me, and his sort don't have much respect for women, so already I don't like him.'

Reece looked into her eyes; every time he'd been with this woman her strength had impressed him even more.

'OK, but don't take any risks. Just a coffee, sit down, and observe without being too obvious. If he lingers, don't hang about. Leave when you've finished your drink. If he leaves, wait thirty seconds before you follow. If that happens and we're gone when you come out, make your way back to the Town Hall and go into the café there where I'll catch-up with you. We'll be out here so if you need help scream and we'll come running.'

Mary smiled the broad smile that always made him feel reassured by her. She kissed him on the cheek and walked away and into the café.

'You're going to have to marry that girl,' said Grey with a grin.

'You might be right. Let's split up to each side of the street and take an end each so we have him no matter which way he walks.'

Chapter Fifty

Broad had told Fraser that for the moment they had some sort of control but later the situation might force their hand and they might need to move. If they had to move, they could take Tourist One out of the picture alive or dead. His disappearance from the scene would make the rest panic and most likely call off the operation. But, in the end he couldn't take that chance, these people were fanatics and fanatics are unpredictable.

'Control, this is Alpha Two, over.' It was Joe Cousins who was still covering the Irlam address.

'Come in, Alpha Two.'

'We have another Asian male leaving the target street on foot. Heading up in our direction.'

Broad took over the mike.

'Roger, Alpha Two, stay with him.'

'Roger that. Alpha Four, with him on foot.'

'Control, this is Alpha Four. Target went into the local supermarket. Will go in and observe.'

'Roger that, let's put him down as Tourist Two,' said Broad.

Imtaz quickly browsed the shop for what he needed: milk, bread, butter, and a bar of chocolate for himself, he paid at the till and was back outside in just a few minutes.

'Following after buying a newspaper,' Harrison said.

'He bought some bread and butter, no chatter, now heading back the way we came. He's youngish with a shortcut beard. Wearing dark blue jeans and a padded black ski jacket, no hat. I can't take a chance following him down Kings Road, returning to the car.'

'Roger that. Did you get a photo of him?'

'No, he was too quick, in and out of the shop, he knew what he wanted, and he may have been there before.'

Cousins, still watching from the car, broke into the transmission.

'I managed to get a few snaps with my mobile and when I zoom in, they aren't bad, not quite David Bailey standard but will do at a pinch. I got a good shot of him when he was crossing the road and had to look right and left. I'll text them over now.'

'Good job, guys. Hold your position but it looks like he's settling in for the night and he may not be alone.'

The Kings Road and Henley Avenue will be getting a closer inspection tonight, thought Broad. Time to bring the troops back for a briefing.

'Tango One, can you return to base, over?'

'Roger, will do,' Geoff Middleton said.

CHAPTER FIFTY-ONE

Mary had entered the café thirty minutes before Tourist One walked out and turned left heading back towards the Town Hall Square. Mary did as she'd been told she finished her coffee then left the café. When she left, there was no sign of anyone, so she took her time walking back towards the Town Hall and phoned Reece.

'Mary, are you OK?'

'Yes, no problem. Thought you should know when I went in, he was on the phone. He mentioned something about keys and be there before five thirty.'

'Interesting…anything more?'

'Yes, he made two more calls. The first I'm sure he was taking in Arabic, so no help there, I'm afraid, but his last call was in English. All I could pick up was see you there at five. His accent was local I think.'

'You've done great. We'll make an agent of you yet.'

'I thought I already was.'

'You are, Mary, you definitely are. By the look of things, he is heading back into the conference so you just head for the Town Hall Café and I'll meet you there shortly.'

'OK, Joseph, see you soon.'

Tourist One returned to the Conference Centre the way he'd left and entered back through the security tent.

Reece and Grey followed, and he sent April to watch with Jonesy in the security suite. It was now 2.35 p.m. and from what Mary had heard, something would be happening around five.

Not long to wait, another few hours, and the picture should start to clear once more, he thought.

Imtaz had returned to the safe house with the food and made himself and Waheed a lunch of beans on toast with a mug of coffee.

'While you were out, Mohammad phoned. He said all is on schedule. The security is strong in and around the conference itself but less so the further he walked away from it.'

'If we go to Piccadilly, we'll be far enough away but there might be more security at the station.'

'I'm not worried about security. We can kill them too. We have the guns, the knives, and the bombs. Many infidels will die, and Allah will be happy with us.'

CHAPTER FIFTY-TWO

They had booked out of the room and left their bags in a locked storeroom behind reception. Lyndsey had gone out for a walk and some fresh air and now he could see her through the glass windows at the front of the hotel, speaking on the phone, the call only lasting a few minutes before she came back into the building and sat down opposite Costello.

'I just had a call from Mohammad. He says he has booked the handover of the keys at five. He has also been inside the conference this morning and there does not appear to be any increase in the security other than what you would normally expect. I'll collect the keys then leave on my own and go to the apartments, he'll follow ten minutes later. I'll phone you when we're both inside the apartment then we can buzz you in when you arrive.'

'Is there any change for the boys in Irlam?'

'No. As of now they're working on their own. They have their own part to play in this, so we leave them to get on with it.'

Mary had been waiting for Reece sitting in a table near the high windows she'd been reading a leaflet with information about the building when he sat opposite her.

'You know it's called The Sculpture Hall Café, and they do fantastic afternoon tea,' said Mary.

'Then let's do afternoon tea I could do with another bite the last couple of sandwiches were rushed and not very tasty to tell the truth.'

'What happened to our friend?' asked Mary.

'He's back inside the Conference Centre. Can you remember anything else he said during his phone conversations?'

'No, not really. He spoke quietly and quickly, and he was facing away from me the whole time looking out onto the street. I tried to be as natural as possible and even though I'm stunningly beautiful, he paid no attention to me.'

'I can't believe that, Mary, you're stunning,' he said with a smile.

She returned the smile and reaching, across the table, took his hand in hers.

'What next, what happens now?'

'I don't know, but he's more than just a tourist or a delegate and it would appear he is the link to the rest of the team we were looking for. We stay close to him, and the rest will lift their heads I'm sure of it, we already have at least one more in Irlam and the boys are keeping an eye on him. Either way we should know more tonight, and we can start to make our moves to wrap this up.'

'Do you think Costello is in Irlam?'

'I don't know. But the fact that Tourist One made at least three phone calls would indicate their team is split at the moment, which is something I would do in the same situation if it was me, this gives more options and less chance of the whole team being captured at the same time.'

Mary poured the tea and between bites of food continued the conversation.

'So, the plan is to capture them alive?'

'If we can. But that really up to them, to what they do. Our job is to stop them no matter what and if that means we kill them, then we kill them.'

'Or they kill us.'

'We always used to have a saying when I worked in Northern Ireland, our gang's bigger than your gang. We have to get these people, we have to stop them, and well, they just don't know it yet. For now, let's not think about it too much; let's enjoy this wonderful afternoon tea and the company.'

'I agree, Joseph, but I'll have to do some serious exercise to get rid of all these goodies and cream. You aren't looking as tired now, maybe it's the fresh cream perk up?' She smiled.

'I think the walk about helped but just being in your company helps.'

This time he reached across for her hand and as he did so his mobile buzzed in his pocket. Reece could see from the screen that it was Jim Broad who was calling.

'Yes, boss.'

'Ah, David. I believe Tourist One is still at the Conference Centre, but we now believe he'll be on the move to meet up with someone around five. Do you need any other backup in case you have two or more targets to follow?'

'Good idea, can we get our troop friends to keep an eye in Irlam and send Joe and Steve to me as backup, ask them to park up somewhere in the Deansgate area. The troop should use one of our Range Rovers.'

'I was thinking along those lines myself as long as you're happy with what you'll have there.'

'Yes, that'll be more than enough for now.'

'OK, leave it with me. I'll speak with the troop commander right away. We will also need to move in closer to the house in Irlam tonight to try to find out exactly what we have there. We can wait until well after dark just in case Tourist One goes back there. I'll get back to you later.'

Reece put the phone back in his Barbour jacket and poured some more tea.

'Things are starting to move up, we're getting some reinforcements which will help us keep a closer eye on our friend.'

'I'm glad, I was getting a bit tired there doing everything myself.'

Reece laughed out loud making the people at the nearby tables look round at the two people sitting holding hands across the table once more.

'Mary, you're the calmest untrained person I know in this kind of situation. How do you do it?'

'I've learnt to only worry about this moment, this time, and place. And being with you right here and now, I feel safe and secure, and I have to say, happy.'

'Then I'm happy too. But I still worry about you, and I like the fact that I can worry as long as you're here with me.'

'You're going to kill Costello aren't you, you're going to kill them all?'

He was slightly taken back by the question. She'd asked as a matter of fact, really knowing the answer herself without hearing his confirmation, but he tried.

'If we have to, yes…we'll kill them. It's really down to them. They are trying to kill innocent people. Our job is to stop them. If they come quietly, we'll arrest them, but if they don't, and it's the only option left to us then yes, we'll kill them. So, no matter what happens you stick close to me, Mary.'

'Oh, don't worry I will.'

April Grey had been watching the screens over Constable Jones's shoulder. Tourist One seemed to be repeating his movements of the morning. First sitting in the café almost at the same chair and table, drinking coffee, and pretending to read a newspaper. Then he'd walked into the main conference theatre took a seat and watched and clapped in all the right places then back to the same route before returning to the café again.

Not far from where Mohammad now sat, in a suite of rooms in the Midland Hotel, the prime minister was sitting with a few senior ministers and advisors, putting together his main conference speech that he would give to the Party faithful the next day.

CHAPTER FIFTY-THREE

Costello had been able to find the van in the giant car park easily, and that was only because he'd written down the details of the section it was parked in. After picking up Lyndsey and the luggage from the Radisson he took his time driving through the traffic and many road works that lead into the centre of Manchester. The journey had been uneventful, he drove past the Hilton Hotel to park in the nearby Great Northern NCP Multi Story Carpark.

'Mohammad should be starting to make his way to the estate agents. If I move now, I'll be there just before him,' said Lyndsey.

'You stay here. I'll text you and buzz you up when I'm inside the apartment. Will it take you long to get the gear out of the compartment?'

'No, it's easy to remove.'

He checked his mobile phone screen for coverage, which was good.

'Right, I'll wait for your text, see you soon.'

Lyndsey pulled her scarf around her head and face and left the van heading for the lift. The rain was playing its part. People would be expected to have some sort of head cover in the wet weather, she'd blend in nicely, she thought.

Costello opened the door at the back of the van and easily gained access to the hidden compartment containing the sports bag with the sniper rifle and ammunition inside. Sitting down again in the driver's seat he placed the bag on the passenger seat next to him. At the same time, he took the Browning pistol out from the belt at his back and keeping it in his left hand rested the weapon on top of the bag beside him, now he sat back and watched what he could see of the carpark.

The rain had stopped when Lyndsey crossed the Great Northern Square and turned onto Deansgate pulling the scarf tight across her face as the wind blew cold against her skin. She was glad she was wearing jeans with her short leather boots with a heavy woollen jumper covered by the dark blue ski jacket, all combining to keep her warm despite the wind. Her over the shoulder leather handbag weighing a little heavier with the pistol safely stowed inside. She could see the estate agents one hundred yards ahead on the other side of the street. She continued walking to the next major junction with Lloyds Street two hundred yards further down before crossing at the junction then turning to walk back down towards the estate agents now on the same side of the street, all the time searching Deansgate for the watchers, but none were there. She studied the faces of people walking towards her, but they were lost in their own little worlds some of them on their mobile phones or speaking into the hands-free cables hanging from their ears. When she reached the door of the estate agents', she studied the street behind her while looking at the reflections in the large glass window in front of her, pretending to study the laminated copies of properties on display inside the window. She could also see young Jake sitting at a desk just inside the front door reading the documents in front of him. When she entered Jake looked up with what appeared to be a genuine smile on his face when he saw her, a good commission that would come with the signing of this contract would bring a smile to anyone's face, she thought.

'Well, Jake, have you everything ready for me?'

'Yes, Mrs Webb it's all here. How are you today?'

'Very well thank you. But I'm working to a schedule today so can we get on with it?'

'Of course, I have all the documents here would you like to sit down?'

She sat at the desk as Jake sorted through the papers in front of him, producing them one at a time he asked her to sign in the appropriate places six times in all.

'I need to take a copy of your passport, have you got it with you?'

She produced the passport of Karen Webb giving it to Jake who continued to complete the paperwork. As he was doing this Mohammad entered the office and sat next to Lyndsey.

'Sorry I'm late. Have you been able to sort everything?' he asked Jake.

'Yes, no problem. Mrs Webb has been able to sign everything off and I now have the copy of her passport. I just need the deposit to go through and I'll get you the keys?'

'How much do you need?' asked Lyndsey.

'Including the security bond, three thousand pounds please.'

Lyndsey handed Jake her credit card.

'Thank you. I'll just go to our accounts office for the machine, back in a few seconds.'

When he left, Lyndsey leaned a little closer to Mohammad so that he could hear her without being overheard.

'When I leave, stay and talk to Jake for a few minutes then when you leave take a walk away from the direction of the apartments. Stay out for a couple of hours getting yourself a meal before heading back to the apartments and call me when you're coming towards them.'

'Are you worried about surveillance? I haven't spotted any. Did you?'

'No, but let's just be extra careful now that we're this close to the security perimeter.'

Jake returned with a hand-held card reader and punched in the payment figure then having inserted the credit card, passed it over for Lyndsey to provide her pin number.

'Thank you, that's everything gone through. I'll just get you the keys and you can be on your way. Do you want me to accompany you to check that everything is OK?'

'No, thank you for being so helpful we'll manage, I'm sure.'

'Right, back in a second.'

Again, he disappeared into the back office returning with a small set of keys and a document folder.

'Thank you for your business, Mrs Webb,'

He handed over the folder and the keys.

'In the folder you'll find all the information you need and details of how to get in touch should there be any problems.'

'Thank you for all your help, Jake, I'm sure everything will be all right.'

Lyndsey placed all the documents in her bag left the office turning to the right pulling her scarf up around her head once more.

Mohammad made the excuse of speaking with Jake for a few more minutes by asking to see any other brochures he had on similar apartments.

Reece and Grey had been watching the front door of the estate agents since following Tourist One when he'd left the Conference Centre and took a roundabout route to bring him to the estate agents where he'd entered a few minutes before. They had taken up positions at each end of the street. Mary once more stood and watched the eyes of the man she loved as he looked over her shoulder in the direction of the door recently entered by Tourist One.

'Do you know something, Joseph, you really do have beautiful blue eyes.'

'Do you mind I'm trying to concentrate here?' He smiled.

He'd noticed the woman who had left the offices pulling the red pattern scarf around her head, as she'd walked back in the direction of the Great Northern Square where Grey had been looking at the goods in a window display with some interest while still watching for the appearance of Tourist One, but that didn't surprise him, as the cold wind made it difficult to stand about Deansgate for any length of time if he had a scarf he would pull it round him too.

'What's happening, I'm beginning to freeze here?' Mary still had her back to the estate agents.

'Nothing much, wait a second. Alpha Three, let's swap and keep warm with some movement.'

'Roger that, good idea.'

Both agents carried out the swap with ease. Just as they'd done so Tourist One reappeared onto Deansgate. Reece saw him first and noticed he was walking towards Alpha Three who now had her back to him.

'Alpha Three, keep walking ahead Tourist One has left the building and is now walking to the junction again.'

'Roger, Alpha One. I'll turn left at the junction and find a closed location.'

Closed location meant a safe place from where she could observe without being seen. Reece and Mary moved after Tourist One on the same side of the street as he continued to walk towards the junction ahead.

Grey had turned left into Hardman Street junction and entered a shoe shop with a large window that looked out onto the street giving her a view of Tourist One as he crossed the junction continuing to walk straight ahead on Deansgate. She then left to catch-up as Reece and Mary crossed the same junction about seventy yards behind their target. All three continued to watch and follow Tourist One as he took his time walking through the central Deansgate area of Manchester without, it soon became apparent to Reece, any purpose whatsoever.

He eventually entered a Chinese restaurant in the China Town area of the city. Reece and Mary crossed to a Starbucks Coffee House opposite and waited for Grey to join them.

'OK, April do you fancy a Chinese?' Reece asked.

'Could do, I like Chinese.'

'We need someone in there just in case he is meeting someone. Mary was behind him earlier and I've been near him all day, so it has to be you. We will stay here for a coffee. If he moves on or you need us shout out.'

'Will do.'

She then crossed the street and entered the restaurant leaving Reece and Mary to order a coffee and continue to watch from the window.

'Alpha Control, check out the Deansgate Estate Agent office and see if we have anyone in there who's known,' said Reece.

Chapter Fifty-four

When she'd left the estate agents Lyndsey had turned into the wind coming down Deansgate pulling up her scarf to protect her face. Walking back on the route she'd come she noticed the lovebirds on the other side of the street in a couple's close embrace. It had been a long time she thought, since she'd held her husband so close, before he'd committed himself to Allah, becoming a martyr and leaving her behind to become the White Widow. Now she was back on the same soil with the intent to honour his memory and make the British feel even more pain for their support of a false prophet.

When she entered apartment C12, she noticed how quiet it was, having come up from street level and with all the double-glazed windows closed there was a strange silence. Looking through the rear balcony doors she could see the back door of the Midland Hotel in the distance now lit up by street lighting as the evening darkness began to descend.

The inside of the van was lit up as his phone began to buzz in the darkness of the carpark. He could see it was a text from Lyndsey.

I'm in will buzz you up when you get here.

On my way. Costello text back.

Lifting the bag beside him and placing the Browning into his belt at his back Costello locked the van and headed for the lift.

Costello walked straight to the Great Northern Apartment building and pressed the buttons marked C12 and then the call button. Immediately in reply he heard the open lock release the front door. The lift to the twelfth floor seemed to take an age but when the doors opened on the landing, he turned left to find the door to apartment C12 already open. Waiting inside he heard Lyndsey's voice.

'Come in quickly and close that door, there's an awful draft when it's open.'

'Nice to see you too. You want to try to sit in a cold van in a cold carpark.'

'You're here now. Do you want to set up? Jake has kindly left us a welcome basket with tea, coffee, biscuits, and milk.'

'I got bloody soaked just walking a few hundred yards, so a cup of hot tea is first on the agenda.'

Mohammad loved Chinese food and he'd used this restaurant before and knew the quality was excellent. Although it was still early, there were plenty of customers and he always thought that was a good indicator of quality. He was so engrossed with his menu he didn't notice the SG9 operator sitting at a table at the back of the room behind him. Grey asked for a menu and spoke quietly into her body mic.

'Tourist One alone, looks like he's only here for the food just eating, no calls, will report.'

'Roger, Alpha Three, we'll stay here and enjoy our coffee or two.'

A voice cut across the conversation.

'Alpha One, we're in position parked up on Deansgate if you need us.'

Harrison and Cousins had arrived.

'Great, Alpha Four. Keep position we have Tourist One in a restaurant in Chinatown, but we might need your help if he meets up with anyone.'

'Roger, Alpha One, we're dry, at least for the moment.'

CHAPTER FIFTY-FIVE

Jim Broad was now sitting in the comms section of the hangar listening in to the conversation of his team. Broad knew the final decision when to move, when to act, would be down to him and Fraser would back him all the way whatever he decided.

'Sir, a call from Sir Ian again.' It was one of the communication operators speaking, interrupting his thoughts. Right on que it was the MI6 Chief on the phone.

Calling back so soon, this should be interesting.

'Sir Ian, how can I help you?'

'Jim, I don't know if it's good news or not, but as you know we've been monitoring the airwaves for Costello's phone conversations, but it seems that our friends in GCHQ in Cheltenham can also monitor any text messages.'

Broad knew that the Government Communications Headquarters were good at monitoring things, but he was surprised they could also break into the text messaging facilities of the target's phones.

'Any news will be helpful if it clears the mud from the picture a bit more.'

'Well, it appears that our Mister Costello is somewhere close to the Conference Centre as we speak. A text message he received about an hour ago shows him to be near there. But we can't pinpoint exactly where.'

'Do we know the message?'

'Yes, I'm in. Will buzz you up when you get here, Costello replied, On my way. That was all, but we now have the phone the other person is using so we're monitoring that as well. We're starting to link all these people together, so we hopefully will get more which will help you and your team. I've organised the GCHQ for you to get these phone communications in real time through your comms there which will save time. No sense in me getting a breakdown here and then having to contact you. Have you the means to work that?'

'Yes, no problem, that'll be helpful. The team have been following that one guy around the conference and then the Deansgate area all day as you know. We don't think he's contacted anyone other than by phone earlier. He's currently sitting having a meal in a Chinese restaurant in China Town and we have people covering him. We have the troop on standby in Irlam at what we think is the safe house ready to move in close later tonight, so I believe we've at least two of their people covered.'

'What about Irlam, Jim? Are you thinking of hitting the house?'

'Not for now. We'll try to get close enough to find out who's in there first, but I think we're getting close to the end game. If there's people in there and they're the kind of people we believe they are, then we can't let them leave and get mixed up with the public.'

'Agreed, but if we move too soon and the rest of the terrorist outfit are already gone, we may only get the small fry and the big fish will disappear. It's something we have to think about. Either way, call me back before you make your move. If I get anything more, I'll let you know right away. I'll bring Bryant and the PM up to date. I also think that now we have Costello and at least one other close to the conference area we should get the Gold Commander and the prime minister's security team to beef up their cover. I know we expect Costello to make his move tomorrow, but I don't like him being this close without an actual location or eyes on him.'

'Agreed…but an increase in cover needs to be discreet not the Normandy Landing. I still think Costello is working to a schedule so let's give our teams a little more time.'

'Thanks, Jim, I'll keep in touch.'

The call ended, Broad studied the electronic maps on the wall once more one of China Town and one of Irlam both with a red dot showing exactly where he believed, at least two dangerous terrorists were currently located. Blue dots showed the locations of the SG9 team in Manchester and the SAS team in Irlam.

'Tourist One on the move,' April Grey broke through the silence in the room.

'Roger that, all teams be aware,' replied the comms operator.

The next voice over the network was that of Reece.

'Alpha One, I have him. By the look of things, he's heading back towards the conference area. Alpha Two can you cover the foot approach to the front of the Midland Hotel, Alpha Four stay mobile in case we need vehicle cover.'

'Roger, Alpha One' replied both agents.

The voice of Broad broke in on the conversation.

'Alpha teams from Control. We have been informed by our friends that there are at least two more, including Costello, in your area. GCHQ have picked up a couple of text messages which indicate they may be holed up somewhere close to the Conference Centre so be aware. If they get anything concrete will let you know.'

Reece acknowledged receipt of the new information and continued to follow Tourist One as he walked straight by the conference entrance and the front of the Midland Hotel.

Where are you off to now? thought Reece.

'Tourist One continuing on Peter Street past the Midland,' reported Grey, who was ahead of the target on the opposite side of the road.

'He's stopping and taking out his phone.' Reece could see him clearly from where he'd stopped with Mary outside the Midland front entrance.

'Now talking to someone, Alpha Four, can you come in from your end in case we need the help?' asked Reece.

'Roger, on my way,' Harrison replied.

Tourist One finished his call and started walking in the direction of Deansgate at the junction with Watson Street he turned left.

'I have Tourist One,' Harrison's voice spoke clearly over the air.

Now it was the turn of Jim Broad.

'Alpha Team, be aware your target has just spoken to a woman. He told her he was almost there. She replied she'd buzz him in. Looks like he is going to be meeting with his buddies, so stay on him.'

This was the time when the adrenalin would be pumping up in the watcher's systems. Now they were close anything could happen. Mary couldn't hear both sides of the conversation, but she'd been with him long enough to recognise the change in his voice when he spoke.

'On your toes, people, looks like our fox is going to ground.'

Reece kept up a steady pace fifty yards behind the target with April Grey behind Reece and catching up on the opposite side of the street. Harrison gave another update.

'Tourist One using intercom on the front of an apartment building. Now going in and waiting at lift, will try to get closer.'

As Reece and Mary followed, Grey reached the left turn that Tourist One had taken Harrison walked over to meet with them.

'He went into that block of apartments. It's called the Great Northern Tower, after the square in front of it, I guess. He was buzzed in. I can only say the lift definitely went up.'

'Great work, Steve, at least we know he's probably in there with Costello and a woman, so three here, and two in Irlam. Let's lock this down and see if we can zero in on what apartment they're in. Alpha One to control, did you get all that?'

'Roger that, Alpha One. I'm happy that we have this team narrowed down to two locations. Now we need to find out exactly which apartment they're in. I'll do some research here and keep an ear for more phone use and get back to you. Is there somewhere you can lie up in the meantime?'

'I'll keep two at a time in the car parked in Peter Street with a view of the front door. The rest of us will return to the security suite at the conference so we can speak more securely.'

'Roger, Alpha One, call me when you get there.'

'April, you've been out in the cold for some time so go and get in the car with Joe. Steve, you come with me and Mary back to the suite. Alpha Two, can you park up with Alpha Three in Peter Street with a good view of the front door?'

'Roger, Alpha One, on my way,' replied Cousins.

Less than a minute later the BMW parked in the ideal spot to observe the building's front door. Grey joined Cousins in the car leaving the other three to walk back to the conference suite.

Chapter Fifty-six

Mohammad had made himself a cup of tea and joined Lyndsey and Costello in the apartment sitting room. Both had been watching *Sky News* concerning the day's activity at the conference. The pictures showing the prime minister alighting from his car when attending a lunch with businesspeople in Manchester. The news reader then made a comment on what was expected in his speech to the conference tomorrow.

'He might have to speak through a hole in his head.' Costello laughed.

'Not might, will,' said Lyndsey.

'I'm just glad to be in from the cold for now,' said Mohammad. 'I'm thinking of tomorrow…how are we set up?'

'No change. Sean does his bit and Waheed and Imtaz do theirs. In the panic and inevitable lockdown, we leave by different routes. Sean is going to set up in the morning, you get into the Midland, and if you can give us a heads up when the prime minister is heading towards the back door, then Sean has some warning which will help. His conference speech is pencilled in for 11.45 so we can expect him to walk over around eleven so be ready from 10.45 onwards. I'll get the van and we'll drive out of the area which, if we're quick enough, should be easy to do in all the panic.'

As she was speaking, Costello went over to the dining room table where he'd left the sports bag sitting on top. Unzipping the bag, he reached in and removed three large parcels of bubble wrap and began to unwind the wrapping from the objects inside. Mohammad and Lyndsey silently watched him produce the rifle barrel then the shoulder stock then the breech and trigger mechanism. Next, he took a smooth dry cloth and wiped down each of the parts before assembling each part into the whole. Finally, he attached a tripod stand and sniper scope. When he'd finished, he placed the completed weapon back to stand on the table the barrel almost the same length as the rest of the rifle. Pointing to the rifle he turned to speak to the two silent watchers.

'This, ladies and gentlemen, is a TRG 22 Rifle with a match sight mounting set and foldable bipod for stability when using. It's one of the most accurate rifles around and one of the best sniper rifles in the world and in the hands of someone who knows how to use it, such as myself, a deadly killing machine. I've spent time zeroing the rifle in before I came here, so I'm ready to play my part.'

'I know you've had something to eat, Mohammad, but Sean and I could do with something. Could you phone somewhere for a delivery?' asked Lyndsey.

'I'll check Google. What do you fancy?' replied Mohammad.

'I'm in the mood for some Indian food. What about you, Sean?'

'Sounds good but not too spicy.'

'That's great. I know a good Indian down near the station I could go and get a carry out from there, be back in about twenty minutes. I'll get a bit of a mixture with some rice, that should be OK for both of you?'

'Suits me and some chips,' said Costello.

CHAPTER FIFTY-SEVEN

In his suite in the Midland the prime minister loosened his tie and kicked off his shoes as he pushed himself back further into the leather armchair. The almost finished speech lay on the coffee table between himself and the two other men in the room. Sir Martyn Bryant and Sir Ian Fraser sitting in similar chairs opposite both had a crystal glass of malt whisky in their hand. Peter Brookfield took a long sip from his own glass of the same refreshing spirit. The lighting in the room was low, adding to a relaxed atmosphere. Sir Ian had returned after his meal with Jim Broad and had updated both men in the room with the latest movements of Tourist One and the subsequent phone calls.

'So, Sir Ian, you believe you have these people tied down to two locations…one of them quite close to here. What now?' asked the prime minister.

'We're happy we have at least two under control at the house in Irlam. We don't know if there's anyone else there, so we're moving in closer later tonight to confirm one way or the other.'

'What then?' interrupted Bryant.

'We don't know what weaponry they have inside the house or how many to use it. Either way we need to keep them confided to that location without giving them the opportunity to blow the whistle on us to the rest of their friends, who we now think are somewhere in the apartment block not far from here.'

'And where are we with that end of things?' asked Brookfield.

'As I've said before there may be at least three in there, Tourist One surveillance observed going in. There is an unknown woman inside, possibly Sharon Lyndsey, who buzzed Tourist One into the building and we now believe from intercepted text messages, Sean Costello as well. We're monitoring all the phones both at Irlam and now the apartment.'

'I think what the prime minister needs is some sort of end plan. Do you have one, do you have an idea of how this will end, what about the people out there who know what your team have been doing?'

There it was again, the famous Sir Martyn Bryant ass covering, thought Fraser. *What are you going to do? Never mind what was agreed, I'm not letting you wriggle out this time,* thought Fraser.

'As you know, Prime Minister, from the very start, SG9 was set up for such a scenario and at the very start of all this they were given the heads up to track these people down and deal with them, to work ever in the shadows. Now is not the time to second guess us but to be determined in completing what we set out to do, not just for this operation but for the original idea of opposing this very kind of threat to our country and to our people. The SG9 team have completed the first part of their task by tracking these terrorists, for that's what they are, terrorists, down to a location where, with a little more work we can finish the task. I believe we have to send a message. We have to let the people out there know we'll protect them no matter what. The real people out there don't care how we deal with the likes of Costello and Lyndsey as long as we protect them. Fail and they'll crucify us. Fuck the media. A week down the road and it's another story they're chasing.'

He knew by mentioning the people out there that Brookfield would as a politician convert the word people to votes in his head and there was nothing the voters loved more than a strong leader.

'Of course, Sir Ian, I totally agree so let's get this out of the way as soon as possible. As things stand it's going to get more coverage than my speech tomorrow. It's just the timing and how we're going to deal with it.'

Bryant had said nothing, just nodding his head in silent agreement.

'Of course, Prime Minister, so if you don't mind, I'll get it out of the way as you put it.' Sir Ian finished his whisky and left the room.

'I want you to keep a close watch on things, Martyn. No mistakes and no comebacks.'

The politician was determined to cover his back.

Chapter Fifty-eight

April Grey had fallen asleep almost as soon as she sat inside the car. Cousins continued to watch the front door of the Great Northern Apartment building, he let her sleep. A few people entered and left the building but not his target. The rain had stopped, and the evening light had faded into darkness, the street lighting lit up the square and its buildings making identification of the people coming and going easier. Grey had been sleeping for an hour and a half when he saw him come out the main apartment door.

'I have Tourist One leaving the building and turning down Watson Street.'

April Grey woke immediately as the reply came over the radio from Reece.

'Roger. Alpha Two, can you follow on foot? Alpha Three, stay with the vehicle, we'll come to your location.'

'Roger, Alpha One, will do,' replied Cousins, he was out of the car and walking at speed in the direction Tourist One had taken.

Grey watched the door of the apartments to see if anyone else was watching or looking for surveillance, there was no one.

Cousins kept fifty yards behind closing the gap when his target turned a corner out of sight only to reacquire him once more. Target One didn't go far, he passed the front of the Hilton Hotel on Deansgate and walked towards the train station before turning left and into an Indian restaurant, The Raj. Cousins kept the team updated with every twist and turn. Cousins passed the restaurant and saw Tourist One standing at the counter with a menu in his hand. He found a safe place across the road where he could see the front door.

'Surely he's not eating again?' said Reece over the radio.

'No, he is still standing at the counter. He may be ordering a carryout,' replied Cousins.

'Feeding his friends in the apartment no doubt. Stay with him Alpha Two we'll meet with Alpha Three in the car.'

Twenty minutes later, Cousins reported Tourist One on his way back to the apartments. Reece, now sitting with Grey and Mary in the BMW watched as Tourist One pressed the door button and the apartment number he wanted to be buzzed into the building. Seconds later Joe Cousins joined the rest of the team in the car sitting in the back seat behind Reece.

'It looks like they might be settling down for the night, so we should try to run a sleep pattern for ourselves. I'm sorry but we're going to have to use the cars, it won't be comfortable, but we need to stay close to the targets. Mary, I'll drop you back at your hotel,' said Reece.

'I can sleep in a car.'

'No, you need to get some sleep we need you fresh in the morning to help us spot Costello if he's about, I'll pick you up at six. Joe and April can stay here, Steve, you come with me. No risks, if you see anything, let everyone know.'

'This might be a long shot, but apartment buildings of that size usually have a warden or security man. Do you think I should go and check at least if there is one, he might be able to tell us where in the building our friends might be?' asked April Grey.

'It's worth a try, April, but that building has 257 apartments, I googled it, so we don't want a panic or a situation getting out of control so tread carefully,' replied Reece.

Reece and Steve Harrison took Mary back to her hotel in the second BMW then returned to park up at the bottom of Watson Street looking back in the direction of the Great Northern Square and in line of sight with April Grey and Joe Cousins.

'All Alpha callsigns, this is Alpha One. I'm parked up on Watson Street one hundred yards from target door. Let's take turns, people. I'll start for the first two hours everyone else try to get some sleep. Any luck with the enquiry, Alpha Two?'

'No luck tonight there was a sign on the door that says someone will be available between eight and five tomorrow, so we'll have to wait until he or she turns up.'

'Right, let's speak to them when they do, we could also approach the estate agents where we saw Tourist One, they should be open around nine. Or better still.'

Reece spoke into his body mike.

'Alpha Control. Local police usually hold details of key holders in case of a fire or burglary of businesses. Can you chase it up and see if we can get some information from them on our friend Tourist One and if he got the apartment from them? They might just be able to tie it down to which one they're in. It's a risk as Tourist One might work for them but I don't think so I think it's more likely he is a client.'

'Roger, Alpha One, will get back to you.'

'What's happening with the Irlam address, Alpha Control?' asked Reece.

'The Tango Team are moving forward around 0200 to recce the building and place a mike on the window. Depending on the results, it's the intention to hit the targets when they leave the building and they have them under visual control.' This time it was Jim Broad who had replied.

'Roger that, Control, unless we get more information on which apartment they're using, we'll hold and observe here,' replied Reece.

'OK, Steve, you get some sleep if you can. This whole operation looks like it's going to kick off soon one way or the other, I'll give you two hours.'

'Thanks,' said Harrison as he pressed the recliner button for his seat and tried to get into a comfortable position. Within minutes he was asleep his breathing slow. Reece knew that Grey and Cousins would be able to do the same and would be asleep in the BMW across the square.

By now the local police would be told to leave the people in the cars alone. Putting the area of the conference and the hotel out-of-bounds to regular patrols wasn't on the cards.

There were too many dignitaries attending the conference.

Reece knew that when they moved on Costello and friends, they would have to be sure to wear the armbands provided by ACC Lockwood, even then they would be at risk of being mistaken for the enemy by over hyper police officers with little experience and the adrenalin rush of a gunfight going on around them.

The waiting while trying to stay alert was the hardest part of surveillance but Reece knew the waiting would be over soon, so staying alert was the most important part now.

CHAPTER FIFTY-NINE

At two in the morning the night was quiet and the darkness deep except when directly under the few street lights illuminating the shadows around the Kings Road and the few streets it serviced in Irlam. The troop team had sent the van back to the hangar at Barton to pick up a few pieces of equipment.

Four SAS soldiers in full assault clothing and equipment left the back of the van and made their way to the front of the target house.

Two of them took up positions at the end of the driveway at number two Henley Avenue, with their MP5 H&K rifles with suppressors fitted covering the other two soldiers who moved forward to the front downstairs window.

One rifle covered the front door while the other covered the window where the two soldiers in front now approached low down and quiet. All the curtains in the house had been drawn closed and the lights in the downstairs front room were still on.

The four-foot-high shrubbery and hedging gave them the cover they needed from the street. One soldier placed two sucker devices, sealing them to the glass while the other covered him with a SIG Sauer pistol. As close as they were to the window, they could hear muffled voices from inside.

A dog was barking in the distance.

Happy the listening device was securely stuck to the glass, both soldiers returned to the end of the short driveway and all four back to the van. The whole time they were outside and exposed was six minutes, another job well done.

Inside the van a signaller from the regiment sat facing the electronic equipment picking up the short frequency feedback from the sucker mike, now on the terrorist safe house window. He flicked a switch which would boost the signal back to the hangar where Jim Broad could listen in real time to any conversation in the downstairs area of the target house.

Surprisingly, at first the voices were still muffled then after the trooper swivelled a few dials on the equipment the voices came through clearly.

'Imtaz, hold the camera steady, that's it. I make this statement because I'm willing to die in the great battle against the enemy of Islam and Allah, blessings be upon him. I accept this task and will fulfil my destiny. The Great Satan America and her little Satan Britain, will be punished for their failure to acknowledge the one true faith and for the murder of the followers of that faith, this is why they must be punished. Allahu akbar, Allahu akbar, Allahu akbar.'

'Allahu akbar,' a new voice said.

The recording equipment in the troop van had picked up the whole conversation. Jim Broad realised he'd been holding his breath throughout the short clip of conversation. What he'd just heard only confirmed everything he already knew about the type of people he'd been dealing with they couldn't let them leave the house, a suicide bomber let loose on a public street didn't bear thinking about.

The voice that had given his statement of preparation for death spoke again.

'Now, brother, let us get some rest, our battle with the infidel begins in the morning.'

'Allah be praised, brother.'

'That's the downstairs lights out and a light coming on in the front upstairs,' reported a trooper who had eyes on the front of the building.

'Tango One, can you come back to control, we need to discuss an assault on the house tonight,' said Broad.

'Roger, Alpha Control, I'm on my way. I've ordered daylight aerial photos of the target house they should be there now can you have them available when we get back?'

'They are here, and we've uploaded them onto the big screen.'

'Roger that, I'm on my way.'

Jim Broad phoned Reece and brought him up to date with the details of the conversation. Reece answered the call on the second buzz of his phone which had been on silent but sitting on the dash the light had lit up the car interior. His Casio watch said it was 2.30.

'So, what happens now, boss?'

'What we've heard, means they've forced our hand. We can't let them get out of that house to mingle with the public and we can't have a standoff situation lasting who knows how long before the press gets on to it and help tip off their friends. In that scenario they could also phone the others tipping them off. I intend sending in a troop assault team on the house about 6 a.m. to take them out of the picture, from what we've heard and from what we know this is not going to end well for us unless we take the upper hand now.'

'I agree, boss, when you go in let me know. We will be ready for any movement here; these people need to be stopped whatever it takes. We also need the caretaker here right now. I need to talk to him and find out who we have here, there's at least three in there so we might need backup ourselves when we move on them. I'm sending you the number displayed on the building's door as the emergency contact number so you should be able to track him down.'

'Leave it with me, I'll let you know how I get on. I'll also be getting the police to give us a secure zone to work inside to deal with both locations and take care of civilians.'

When the call finished, Reece noticed that Steve Harrison had brought the seat up from the recline position and had been awake during the phone call.

'Sorry, did I wake you?'

'No, I've been trying to sleep but I never can in these situations, I get some extra energy from somewhere I don't know.'

'By the look of things, the troop are going to hit the house in Irlam before daylight. I hope we can talk to the caretaker here before then and work out where our friends are staying.'

'If we do find them what then?'

'We have some time to prepare an assault but if they get news that we've hit their house in Irlam we might have to move quickly, we can't let them escape. From now we start to prepare. I want everyone in their vests and armbands on and the H and K out of the boot we might just need the heavy firepower before this is over. I'll go over and tell the others. You stay here and keep watch.'

Reece walked across the square and getting into the back seat he found that April was asleep in the front passenger seat, waking when Reece opened the car door.

Reece quickly brought Grey and Cousins up to date, telling them to prepare their equipment just as he'd told Harrison.

'When the caretaker gets here, we need to have a quick chat with him. In the meantime, Steve and I'll pick up Mike as arranged. April, if the caretaker arrives before I get back, have that chat.'

'Are you OK with bringing her into a dangerous situation?' asked Grey.

'She's lived with dangerous situations all her life. Even with his face change I believe she could still identify Costello and if she gives us that advantage, the risk is worth taking. I've talked to her about the risk, now that Costello knows she might be working with us her days are numbered if we don't get him first. Our job now is to keep on the ball and get these people. The boss will be pushing the police to give us a secure zone for us to work inside and to stop civilians getting involved.'

'Will they know we're inside their zone?' asked Cousins.

'That's the plan, but I don't know when they'll take up position, so keep alert.'

Chapter Sixty

Middleton and his assault team studied the aerial photos identifying all the approaches to the Irlam house and the buildings surrounding the target area. The rear garden was surrounded by a five-foot wooden panel fence, difficult to get past but not impossible.

Middleton was thankful that the setup of the house was similar to the one at the SAS base and training ground that was used for assault drills and training. The fact there didn't appear to be any innocent civilians made the choice easy, a hard assault through the front door and window with two soldiers covering the back door in case of an attempted escape.

Every member of the team, including Middleton, who would go in through the front door were now dressed in their flameproof jumpsuits with full-face respirator masks to protect against smoke. Each trooper carried two stun grenades, a Glock pistol, and the standard Heckler & Koch MP5 machine gun – capable of firing 800 rounds of 9mm Parabellum rounds per minute. Each machine gun was fitted with a sound suppressor making it easier for the troopers to hear each other in a noisy environment which would already be overwhelmed with flashbang stun grenades and blast charges on the windows and doors.

Anything that can make the assault on a building where hostiles are expected inside was welcome and had come about from years of experience and practice learning what worked and what didn't.

Even then, SAS soldiers had it drilled into them to adapt as the circumstances arose. Put down overcoming firepower, cover each other, shoot to kill. The John Wayne wound in the shoulder, or the leg was movie stuff...not real life. A wounded man can still return fire, a wounded man can still kill you, so kill him first.

Geoff Middleton was confident he had the men to do the job. Each one knowing where he fitted in to the assault.

Middleton finished the briefing, and everyone broke away to make the last checks and to prepare in their own way. The practice drills were over. Some of the troopers had already experienced real fire situations, only two would be experiencing it for the first time.

'What do you need from me?' asked Broad who had been sitting quietly at the back of the room watching Middleton brief his men.

'Now that you've handed over to us it's the aftermath where we'll need your help. One of my troopers will be on comms here and you'll be able to hear the whole thing going down. Afterwards, we'll pull out quickly leaving the ground clear for the emergency services to go in and clean up. I'll be first through the front door,' said Middleton.

'I've already spoken to Mr Lockwood, and he'll have the locals on standby ready to move in with an ambulance and fire brigade. There will be a senior police officer on the ground who knows they'll have to seal the house and keep the residents tied down. There'll be a door knock, and statements will be taken.

'We'll put out the gas explosion story stating there'll be a press release when the area is declared safe and some idea of what has happened can be explained. This will give us time to find out where the rest of our friends are in Manchester. We will need similar backup there as well. I've informed the powers that be where we are and what we intend to do. We set our watches for 0600 and then with a bit of luck we'll be able to move on the Manchester address before 11 a.m. If they try to leave before then we have the SG9 team in position to intercept. Good luck, Geoff, I'll be here until this is over if you need me.'

'Good, sunrise is seven ten, so with any luck, it will be all over at the house and if needed I can let your team in Manchester have a few of my men to help there.'

Middleton turned and left to join his men and finish preparing his own equipment.

Chapter Sixty-One

With five minutes to go before 6 a.m., the police cordon moved in at the top of Kings Road.

The sun was starting to rise but it would be nearly two hours before the light would be strong enough to pick out the SAS team who were now moving in closer to number 2 Henley Avenue.

The attending police officers had been told very little. This was an anti-terrorist operation where they were only needed as backup and to stop anyone entering or leaving the road. The officers noticed there was also a fire engine and an ambulance parked up on the main road obviously under the same instructions as they hold back and wait for orders.

A minute before 6 a.m., a Transit van and two blacked out Range Rovers parked on the main road and eight fully combat dressed, heavily armed soldiers all wearing respirator masks left the vehicles and made their way, in twos, down Kings Road.

The police officers knew not to interfere or ask questions…this operation was way above their pay grade.

There was a fine rain falling and the grass, pavement, road, and windows of the surrounding houses glistened in the reflection of the street lights following the shadows left by the soldiers as thy moved forward in crouching positions. The police officers closer to Kings Road could see some of the soldiers were carrying what looked like small window frames.

These soldiers had their MP5s on slings over their shoulders while the others moved quietly with their weapons in the raised position pointing and sweeping to the front.

Middleton spoke into his face mike, constantly reporting to Alpha Control the progress of the mission.

'Alpha Control, Tango Team moving into position, will report when making entry.'

'Roger, Tango One, waiting out your numbers,' replied the SAS trooper in the control room.

Jim Broad had covered many operations like this, and it was the waiting that was the hardest. Waiting and hoping for the best. There was always the silence. The straining to hear every word coming over the radio waves. The communication rooms were always quiet at these times, leaving the professionals to get on with their jobs. It was always as if no one was breathing.

The SAS team on the ground had moved into their pre-planned positions: two troopers moved to the rear fence, two to the front downstairs window, and Middleton and three other men to the front door.

Middleton asked for a situation report from the trooper in the van who was monitoring the sounds in the house and was told that all was quiet. Middleton instructed the two soldiers at the rear of the house to move forward. This was part of the plan where they would quietly lift up one of the fence panels and slide into the garden before moving back door. The team had recognised the danger of being heard or seen from the target house, but it was a risk they had to take.

The silence from the house continued as the troopers moved through the fence panel, let it back down into its original position, and moved up to the rear door. There was still no sound or movement from inside the house as the soldiers at the front window removed the sucker mike and placed one of the framed charges up against the window while Middleton did the same at the front door.

The street was deathly quiet. Even the breathing of the SAS men was quiet and controlled behind the face masks. Middleton gave a thumbs up and the ten second fuses on the shaped frame charges were set and the troopers pulled back to the end of the garden path. The explosives were set in such a way that when the blast came the explosion was forced inwards. The flash, the bang, and the falling debris wouldn't only waken the residents in the street but many people in the surrounding the area but most definitely the people inside the house.

Before the last of the debris had hit the ground, Middleton's voice came over the airwaves, 'Go, Go, Go.' In seconds, the SAS troopers were inside the building, two taking the stairs, two inside the living room, and two into the kitchen after shooting off the back-door hinges. Two more men covered the building from outside. Inside the house, the troopers hit darkness and smoke was hindering their vision, but the respirator masks protected their eyes and breathing. Calling out 'Clear' as they moved through the house. The two troopers who had entered the through the kitchen door took over covering the living room while the two troopers who had entered through the front living room window turned to join Middleton and the second trooper who had headed up the stairs through the blasted front door.

As they reached the main landing, Middleton turned right with a trooper behind him. He moved to the main bedroom and stood with his back to the wall and opening the door, he threw in a flashbang. At almost the same time the two troopers who had entered the house through the front window followed up the stairs, turned left on the landing, and executed the same procedure at the door to a front facing bedroom. Both flashbangs went off at almost the same time, brightly illuminating the bedrooms followed with a loud bang. The final two soldiers were now covering the open bathroom and the third bedroom door which were both at the rear of the house.

As Middleton and his men were to discover, the front bedroom he attacked was empty. It had been Costello's room but was now vacant. The second bedroom contained a very shaken Imtaz who only had time to stand beside his bed and fire blindly with his pistol where he thought the door was, the blast and light from the flashbang had done its job. When the first trooper entered the room, he recognised the Asian man who'd been photographed going for the local shopping trip.

The rounds he fired hit the bedroom wall to the left of the soldier. With his Heckler & Koch already levelled, he fired back with a burst of five rounds hitting the man who, afterwards, reminded him of a rabbit caught in a car's headlights; eyes wide and scared. Three of the rounds hit Imtaz squarely in the chest and the other two hit his face and temple blowing his brains out the back of his head and spreading a halo of blood and gore over the wallpaper behind him.

Middleton's voice came over the airwaves, 'Contact, wait out.' That was the signal to the SAS radio operator and Broad that contact had been made with the enemy and there would be no more communications with them until the operation was complete.

Waheed had been in the rear bedroom of the house. His mind had been spinning about what the morning and daylight would bring. He and Imtaz had slept fully clothed to be prepared for all eventualities. The loud blasts had woken him from his light slumber, and he knew immediately what was happening. The enemy were here, and he was prepared to become the martyr he'd always known he would be one day.

That day was here.

He stood beside the bed facing the door as it opened. He could see for a split second the black gloved hand as the SAS Trooper threw in the flashbang. Waheed knew what to do he'd trained for this in the desert. As the flashbang sailed through the air, he dived behind the bed, closing his eyes and placing his hands over his ears. Even then the noise and flash that came burnt into his eyes and ears. He armed the small bomb he had beside the bed and tossed it towards the bedroom door as the first of the two troopers crept in.

The soldier saw the device flying through the air and instinctively dived to the left of the bedroom door when it exploded but the blast, in the confined space, killed him instantly. His body armour unable to provide protection at such close proximity to the explosion with the nails embedded into the Semtex doing most of the damage shredding his skin and penetrating deep into his body destroying the rear bedroom wall of the house. Waheed, still down beside the bed, had been protected although some of the nails tore through his back arms and legs.

He was still conscious and rose with his pistol in hand to continue his battle with the infidel. As he did so, he called on his God, 'Allahu akbar, Allahu akbar.'

SAS soldiers trained for such a situation: don't stop, keep fighting until it's over. The second soldier and Middleton, who had joined him, rushed through the door with rifles raised and they both fired at the rising Waheed hitting him twenty times and throwing him back against the wall before he fell forward onto the shredded bed. The wall behind him covered with blood and mixing with the cement and bone sticking to the bullet holes that peppered the wallpaper.

The SAS men checked their downed comrade confirming the worst.

There is a collapsible Clock Tower which is assembled on special occasions on the Parade Ground at the headquarters base nicknamed the Head-Shed by SAS operators but known the world over as the Hereford base of 22nd SAS Regiment or Stirling Lines after the regiments founder David Sterling. The Clock Tower also bears the names of every SAS soldier killed in action. Soldiers of the regiment who survive such operations call it beating the clock. Unfortunately, on this occasion another name would be added to the Clock Tower list.

Rolling the body of the terrorist over to take a photo of his face as they did with all such enemies, Middleton noticed the dead man was smiling through teeth that had a wide gap.

Middleton's voice came across the airwaves once more. Jim Broad listened with intent. 'Alpha Control, house secure, two enemy and one friendly KIA. Bring in a cordon.'

It was Broad who answered. 'Roger, Tango One, will do. Sorry to hear you've lost a friend. Return here as soon as you can for a debrief and reassignment.'

'Roger, Alpha Control, on our way.'

On the command from Broad, via the Gold Command in Manchester, the emergency services moved in to secure the house and the street.

The residents had been wakened by the explosion and the confusion that came from such a rude awakening. The troop Transit and Jeeps moved to the end of the street and Middleton and his men were quickly picked up having lifted two mobile phones and any documents they found they were driven out of the Kings Road and Irlam back to the hangar.

As the police, fire, and ambulance crews moved in to surround the target house and seal of the street, GCHQ, on the instructions from Broad, froze the phone, Internet, and mobile signals within a quarter of a mile of the street.

Gold command would, when asked to, release the agreed press release of a suspected gas explosion and the area would be sealed off until a full check of the area had been made.

Broad sat in on the de-brief of the assault team when they returned then phoned Sir Ian Fraser to brief him.

CHAPTER SIXTY-TWO

'What happens now, Jim?' asked Sir Ian.

'From the weapons and explosives used by the two at the house in Irlam, we can expect the rest of these people to be similarly armed, so we take no chances. We hit them hard, if they want to come peacefully, they'd better put their hands up quickly. We've been trying to contact the building society people and the building's caretaker without success. There's a company number with offices opening at 9 a.m. we will chase both. The caretaker comes on duty at 8 a.m. so we'll be there to talk to him when he arrives. Reece and his team have the building under close surveillance and the police are moving in a cordon as we speak.'

'Thank you, Jim, I'll update the PM and Martyn Bryant. My feelings are that this won't end well, but we all knew why the Department was set up, so let's get on with it.'

'The next few hours will tell a tale. I'll be letting Reece know after this call to get in there and sort it.'

The prime minister was an early riser even though he'd been awake until past three in the morning working on his conference speech. Now sitting in his suite with Bryant and Sir Ian he was quickly taking on-board the latest update from C, his head of Her Majesty's Secret Service. Although he'd been expecting the operation to come to a head, now that it was here, he still felt some unease in his stomach. He'd experienced this feeling many times before when he knew people would be looking at him for the leadership he'd desired all his political life. The decision had been made, the operation had started, and one of the reasons he'd been up so late working on his speech, was that he had to work on a different opening which would encompass the resulting deaths and what it would mean for the war on terrorism, the future of the country, and the type of politics he'd put in motion when agreeing to the formation of the Department SG9.

'All right, let's get on top of this, Sir Ian. When will your people move in?'

'We hope to have the details of which apartment the terrorists are in just after 8 a.m. We'll be moving in shortly after that. Now that the SAS are finished in Irlam, they're back at Barton being debriefed and reassigned to the apartments. In the meantime, SG9 have the building under surveillance and Gold Command are moving a police cordon in to secure the access to the area once our people move in.'

Throughout the briefing, Sir Martyn Bryant had said nothing. Now he spoke, giving both the PM and Sir Ian a chance to drink what was now a cold coffee.

'And you're happy we have the communications in Irlam screwed down so that the terrorists in the apartments have no idea their friends have already gone?'

'As much as we can. The media are only getting a small gas explosion briefing at the moment. Of course, we can't be one hundred per cent, but at the most they'll be confused. Mobile coverage has been closed down with no signals going in our out. If they do try to run, we'll be ready for them.'

The prime minister stood and shook the hand of both men.

'Thank you, gentlemen, I hope our next meeting sees the end of this. If you'll excuse me, I have meetings to get to. I'll also be briefing them regarding the operation in Irlam and the upcoming one here, under the strict embargo that they're sworn to secrecy until it's over.'

Bryant and Fraser shared the lift down to the foyer.

'You have my mobile number, Sir Ian. Keep me informed every step of the way. I'll be here in the hotel holding meetings with the police, and members of the Intelligence Committee and Cobra to update them on your progress.'

Sir Ian Fraser left by the rear entrance to the hotel. His driver spotted him and pulled up at the door. Sir Ian got into the rear seat behind his bodyguard sitting in the front passenger seat. Sir Ian always thought it less dangerous to him if he got into the car himself instead of someone having to hold the door open for him.

'Take me to the hangar at Irlam please.'

No more needed saying. He phoned Jim Broad and told him he was on his way.

Reece and Steve Harrison had arrived at the hotel a few minutes after 6 a.m. Mike was waiting in the reception area and smiled when she saw Reece come through the door.

'Ready?' asked Reece.

'As always,' she replied.

Reece was pleased that she'd dressed sensibly for the day, dark blue jeans, black trainers, and a blue hooded top with a white coloured blouse underneath. Reece thought no matter what she wore, she always looked beautiful.

'Steve is outside in the car. We will have to go near the apartments to keep up a surveillance presence for the minute. Are you OK with that?'

'Yes, no problem, let's go.'

By the time they got back to the Square, the troop assault on the house had started. Reece waited in the car with Mary and Harrison. From the little they could hear over the communications with the hangar, they knew that there had been deaths at the Irlam house. Reece knew not to radio the hangar or phone Jim Broad. There would be no answer while they were busy with the ongoing assault operation.

He waited in silence with the others until his phone buzzed with a call coming in from Broad. Reece listened without comment as Broad brought him up to date with the operation in Irlam.

'Where are you now?' Broad asked when he'd finished.

'We're waiting for the caretaker to arrive with eyes on the building as we speak.'

'Great. I'll try to get Middleton's people there after we've debriefed them.'

'Thanks, let me know when they're on their way. What about the police cordon?'

'I've spoken to our friend Mr Lockwood personally. He's been told from on high to give us any support we ask for. I know they have the equivalent of SO19 uniform police trained in building assaults, but I've told him we have enough people of our own to deal with this, so no mistakes, David.'

'No pressure there then. We have it covered for now and with any troop backup well covered. I just hope you can keep a tight blackout on the Irlam operation until at least 8 a.m. and we get the chance to speak to the caretaker and identify exactly where these people are in the building.'

'That's just over an hour away so I hope we can keep the lid on it until then. GCHQ are keeping all Internet and mobile phone communications closed down in the area until 8 a.m. at least. They will also be doing the same around the apartment once you find out where they are.'

'Any name for the caretaker yet?' Reece asked.

'Oh, yes, I forgot to say, it's Kevin Williams. He lives in Salford but has been out at a party all night not known where he's not answering his phones'.

'No problem. We'll keep an eye out for him, will let you know when he's here.'

CHAPTER SIXTY-THREE

Inside apartment C12, in the Great Northern Tower block, all three terrorists had been up for about an hour. Coffee had been made in the pot twice and the conversation had gone over the plans for the day. The clock on the wall said it was 7.45 a.m. There was no TV, but the radio was tuned into Radio Manchester and the usual traffic report stated the usual traffic jams around the approaches to Manchester City Centre on a working weekday morning. Mohammad was dressed in his suit and getting ready to leave for the conference after the eight o'clock news.

They had gone over the plan for the day a number of times. Mohammad would go to the conference then, at around 9 a.m. make his way to the Midland Hotel and from inside hopefully give a heads up to Costello that the target was on his way to the rear exit. Lyndsey laid out the plan of attack at the same time as the attack would be going down, she would be sitting in the van in the NCP car park ready to move to the front of the Great Northern Tower to pick up Costello. All would then get out of the area in the confusion when Imtaz and Waheed detonated their bombs.

Costello had looked through the scope of the rifle three times already since the light had improved. He could easily pick out people walking between the hotel and the main conference building. It was still too early for the delegates, so they had to be Party workers or security. There was little or no wind and as the light became stronger, he had no doubt in his mind that he could hit every target he'd looked at in the head, with a follow up to the main torso, in plenty of time before the target crossed the open ground to safety. He'd kept the sliding glass doors slightly open, so there was no need for movement which might be seen from the ground in daylight. This had made the room cold, so all three were wearing a coat over their clothes, even with the central heating on full blast the room was freezing at this time of the early morning, before any warming winter sun had risen in the sky. This was also why they were on to their third pot of coffee.

'I think I'll leave now and get a full English breakfast in one of the cafés, without bacon,' said Mohammad. 'I'll text when I'm through security and into the conference area.'

Lyndsey looked at her phone and noticed she had no signal. 'My phone signal has dropped out must be a problem.'

Both men checked their phones noting the same problem.

'All right,' said Lyndsey 'Let's not panic, it could be a local problem but let's not take any chances. Mohammad, you go ahead with the plan, go get your breakfast, get yourself a newspaper. If all is OK and you're happy you're not compromised, exit the hotel's rear door. If you think there is a problem, open the paper as if you're going to read it. If you do sense danger, we'll pull out and you do the same. It would be better to live for another chance than to get caught unnecessarily.'

'What about Imtaz and Waheed?' asked Costello.

'They will be martyrs to the cause and the distraction they'll make will help us retire to fight another day. Their deaths wouldn't be in vain, they'll strike a great blow in the name of Allah,' replied Lyndsey.

'Mohammad, walk out of the door at 9 a.m. exactly. I don't want to be bent down looking through the scope for hours.'

'I can do that.'

'We should be able to see you at a stretch from our view here anyway but that would help me.'

The radio brought their attention back to the announcer bringing the eight o'clock news. There was nothing significant and the mention that the Prime Minister Peter Brookfield would address the Conservative Party Conference at eleven thirty this morning meant to the three people in the room that the operation was still on.

Reece had been listening to the same broadcast in the car and the fact there had been no mention of the house in Irlam meant that Jim Broad had done his job and stopped any news of the suspected gas explosion getting out for the minute. The next broadcast at eight thirty would be different. As the radio station turned to the traffic and weather reports for the day, Reece noticed a man in a long dark coat with its hood up approach the door to the Great Northern Tower and press the buttons on the entry keypad. Reece could see the man through the glass door turn left and using a set of keys from his pocket open a door to the left of the lift and stairs.

'I think our caretaker has arrived. Mary, you come with me. When I question him, it might be good to have a woman with me to keep him calm two unknown men this time of the morning might spook him, and we want his quick support. Steve, you stay here and keep your eyes open.'

Reece pressed the radio mike. 'Alpha Team, I'm going to have a chat with our caretaker stay alert.'

April Grey and Joe Cousins replied, 'Roger that,' as did Alpha Control.

Leaving the car Reece and Mary quickly crossed the space to the door of the Tower Block and Reece pressed the button for the reception.

Chapter Sixty-four

When the man answered the door, Reece was surprised. In his mind, caretakers were always retired old men but then he remembered this young-looking man opening the door had been out all night at a party. Kevin Williams looked like a twenty something student wearing blue jeans with trainers and a Pink Floyd T-shirt. He was about six-foot with his black hair tied back in a ponytail. He was thin build with brown eyes on a thin face with a small goatee beard. Reece produced his security services ID, and he could see the immediate look of fear on the man's face although Reece thought that was probably to do with the strong smell of the pot he'd obviously been smoking at his all-night party.

'Mister Williams, my name is Joseph. Can we have a few moments of your time?' Reece didn't bother to introduce Mary as he knew Kevin Williams wouldn't ask, his eyes were still fixed on the identity card inches from his face.

'Yes, of course, come in.'

'Is there somewhere we can talk in private?' asked Reece as he returned his ID to his pocket and Mary followed him into the hallway.

'Oh yes, of course. This way.'

They followed him into the small office he'd come out of before answering the door. Reece noticed there was a real nervousness both in Williams's demeanour and voice, he would have to proceed gently if he was to get the help he wanted.

The office was small. More like a broom cupboard than an office with a desk with a laptop and a CCTV screen showing the front door and what Reece assumed to be the fire escape door at the rear of the building. There was two small swivel chairs and a small four drawer filing cabinet. Williams sat down on the chair at the desk. Reece and Mary continued to stand.

'What's this all about?' asked the nervous caretaker.

'You're not in any trouble, Mr Williams. Your party life is none of our concern,' said Reece.

He could see from the caretaker's face that he knew what Reece meant. His smoking habit was obvious but when he realised he wasn't in trouble, he relaxed.

'I'll help in whatever way I can.'

'We're interested in a new tenant who may have moved in yesterday. Do you have these records?'

'If they moved in yesterday, then the first I might know about it is if they're on my system here.' As he spoke, he pointed at the laptop.

'Can you fire it up please and check now?' said Reece.

He was glad he'd gone in softly softly with this man. He'd seen people in the past who, when being questioned by someone like Reece, automatically start to put barriers. Quoting their rights and asking for legal representation.

'Yes of course.' Williams turned to the laptop and after pressing a few buttons he brought up a screen showing the list of tenants in the building.

'The only new tenant moving in yesterday was a Mister and Mrs Grey in apartment C12.'

'What floor is that and what direction do the windows face?' asked Reece.

Mary was impressed how Reece had worked this man and got him onside without pressure.

'As the number says, it's C12 so on the twelfth floor. It faces to the back of the building with a balcony and patio type glass doors onto the balcony.'

'Did you see or speak to them?' asked Reece.

'No, they could have come in at any time to view it or move in. I didn't see them. I only see people when they have problems or if we cross in the hall. The estate agents that are registered with my system just update it remotely when people move in or out.'

'Does your front door CCTV record people coming in and out?'

'Yes, it's on a twenty-four-hour loop before it wipes itself and starts again at 9 a.m. every day.'

Reece looked at his watch 8.15 a.m. Something's going our way for a change, he thought.

'Can you bring the CCTV up from around 4 p.m. yesterday?'

'Yes, no problem.'

Again, the caretaker pressed a few buttons on the keyboard and a grainy picture of the front door entrance came up on the laptop screen. The clock in the corner of the screen showed the time running down from 4 p.m. As it was nearing the end of the working day and students returning from college, there was a lot of people coming and going.

Looking over the caretaker's shoulder, Reece asked, 'Can you fast forward it until I ask you to stop?'

'Yes, no problem.'

For the next few minutes Reece and Mary watched the screen, Reece asking the caretaker to freeze the frame on two occasions until at 5.23 p.m. he asked him to freeze the screen once more. The pictures were in black and white but even though the picture wasn't very clear, he could see it was a woman wearing a scarf, but Reece believed it was Sharon Lyndsey. Reece made the caretaker replay the frame five or six times and took a screenshot with his mobile as the caretaker informed him, he couldn't do it because of confidentiality for clients.

'Breach of confidentiality will be the least of your worries,' said Reece. 'If you obstruct me anymore, you'll be doing twenty years in Strangeways.' The look on the caretaker's face told Reece he got the message.

It was the best that Reece could do, and he didn't have time to argue. Playing the footage again, Reece pressed his hand hard into the caretaker's shoulder and shouted, 'Stop.' A tall man wearing a baseball cap with a clear NY logo had entered the building about twenty minutes after the woman carrying a large bag of some sort over his shoulder. Mary gasped, Reece could see from her expression and the fear in her eyes she knew who it was.

'Are you sure, Mary?' he asked.

She looked closer at the frozen picture. The man was looking straight ahead but had lifted his head slightly to see what floor the lift was on. It wasn't a full-face picture but enough for Mary to see the nose and mouth. This, along with the way the man had walked from the door to the lift, confirmed for her that she was looking at Sean Costello.

'Yes, I'm sure, I wish I wasn't.'

That was good enough for Reece. He stepped outside the office and spoke into his body mike.

'Alpha Control and Alpha Team, be aware that we've confirmed identification of Sean Costello in this building believed at this time to be in apartment C12. I'm going through the last twenty-four hours of CCTV, and we have him entering the building fifteen minutes after a woman who may be Lyndsey around 5.30 p.m. yesterday. I'll check the rest of CCTV which isn't great quality.'

Reece went back into the caretaker's office and took another photo of the man and sent both photos out to the team and Jim Broad. He spoke to the caretaker, 'Let's keep going through it until this morning.'

Stopping the CCTV on two more occasions, he watched their target, Tourist One, enter and leave the building returning with the carryout dinner they'd seen him buy the night before. Now he knew for certain it was food for Lyndsey and Costello and that all three were still in the building, most likely in apartment C12.

When the CCTV had caught up with the clock on the wall of the office, it was now 8.30 a.m. Residents were starting to come and go through the front door.

April Grey's voice came over the radio confirming that Tourist One had just left the building and had turned right in the direction of Peter Street and the front of the Midland Hotel.

'Alpha Four, keep with him, everyone else hold your ground,' instructed Reece.

Steve Harrison left the warmth of the BMW and followed Mohammad keeping fifty yards between them. April Grey stayed in the BMW parked near the entrance to the NCP car park and Joe Cousins sat in the car on the Peters Street side of the Square. Looking to his right he could see the front door of The Great Northern Tower Apartments and looking straight ahead he could see the disappearing figure of Tourist One followed by Steve Harrison.

Mohammad had stayed in the apartment to have another cup of coffee and listen to the radio. The fact there was still no signal on anyone's mobiles didn't bother him. He'd been living in the north-west of England for far too long to let what was a regular occurrence such as the loss of a mobile signal bother him. When he left and turned right at the front door of the building, he felt the fresh air on his face and realised the temperature had lifted slightly and the sun was breaking through the clouds with a little heat reaching the ground where he walked.

It's going to be a nice day, he thought.

Steve Harrison watched Tourist One cross the street and head towards St Peters Square where he entered the newsagent's and bought a copy of the *Daily Express*. He then walked to the security tents leading into the conference at the side of the Midland Hotel.

'He's heading back into the conference, what do you want me to do?' asked Harrison.

It was Broad who spoke first, 'Stay close to him.'

Reece spoke next, 'Stay close, Alpha Four, but if he makes any move that looks suspicious, take him out, for good if necessary.'

'Understood,' replied Harrison.

Steve Harrison closed the gap to around five yards and followed him through the security area. When Mohammed reached the body scanner, Tourist One showed empty hands and raised his arms to allow the metal detector to be swept over his body by the security guard. Harrison moved to the side of the scanner queue and showed his ID to the security officer before moving through to follow Tourist One.

Turning left, Mohammad entered through the rear door into the Midland Hotel. Harrison kept up a running commentary of their progress through security and as he followed Tourist One into the long corridor towards the front reception and lounge area of the hotel which was buzzing with the loud conversation of conference delegates.

Tourist One found a seat on his own and opened his newspaper. Harrison walked past him and sat at a table where two men were already seated and in conversation. They didn't pay any attention to Harrison but continued talking and making notes in their notebooks on the table in front of them. Harrison noticed that even though Tourist One had opened his paper he wasn't reading it. Instead, he was looking over the top of the paper his eyes moving around the room. Harrison had seen this ploy used by armatures the world over in his years as an MI5 watcher, to try to identify security forces or enemy surveillance.

Harrison leaned slightly forward as if he was involved in the conversation of the two men sitting with him.

After twice checking the room, Tourist One folded his paper and checked his watch. Harrison could see the large clock above the reception desk it was 8.55 a.m.

'All stations, Tourist One is looking for opposition and checking his watch, still sitting in Midland.'

'Roger, Alpha Four, it looks like he might be on a time schedule,' replied Reece. 'So be ready to move in if needs be, I'm still with the caretaker so now that we only have two in the building, we'll get ready to move here when we get backup but will remain ready to move if we have to.'

'Alpha Control to Alpha Four, I'll let the Gold Command know you're in the area and have them watch our friend on the CCTV system ready to back you up should you need it,' said Jim Broad.

'Roger, Alpha Control, I'll keep you updated,' replied Harrison.

'Alpha Control to all call signs. Local mobile signals are being unblocked at 9 a.m. After that, GCHQ will keep a close ear on anything from our friends.'

'Thanks, boss,' replied Reece. 'Things could start to be interesting now especially when they find they cannot contact the Irlam team.'

In apartment C12, Lyndsey heard her phone bleep indicating she was getting a signal again. She checked the screen but there were no messages, just a screen showing the network had been cleared and her phone was working again. Almost at the same time Costello noticed his phone light up for a few seconds as he had it on silent, he now knew he was back up as well.

Costello was leaning across the table looking through the scope on top of the rifle. He'd zeroed-in on the rear door of the Midland Hotel. At 9 a.m. on the dot Mohammad walked out of the hotel and stopped on the steps where he stood still for a few moments with a newspaper folded under his arm. He then walked across the square towards the Conference Centre. Costello followed him for a few seconds before swinging the scope back on the doorway.

'Mohammad feels OK, he kept the paper folded,' said Costello.

'Wait a second.' Costello held his left hand in the air as he continued to look through the scope. A man had just walked out of the door, and he was looking in Mohammad's direction. There was nothing strange in this but the fact he appeared to be talking to himself at the same time alerted Costello's senses.

'I think he could have a tail. A guy just behind him seems to be having a conversation with someone using a concealed mike. It might just be someone using a mobile phone now that they're up and running but I don't like it.'

'I don't like it either,' said Lyndsey. 'I've text Waheed and Imtaz with no reply, but they could be having the same signal problems we've had.'

'I'm beginning to not like this coincidence. Text Mohammad and let him know he may have company.'

'Alpha One, come in.' It was Jim Broad.

'Go ahead, Alpha Control.'

'Our friends in the apartment have been trying to contact the Irlam crew and now a text to Tourist One telling him he may have company. They must have eyes on Alpha Four.'

'Roger, boss. How quickly can you get the Tango Team here? We need to move on this soon.'

'They're leaving here now. I'll get the security cordon tightened as soon as they get to you.'

Chapter Sixty-five

Lyndsey spoke as she looked once more at her mobile screen. Mohammad had replied with a thumbs up emoji when she'd text him to be aware of possible surveillance.

'I'm not happy with this whole thing. No contact from Irlam and now possible watchers on Mohammad, I think we should abort and wait for another day.'

Costello was surprised. She was usually so positive and now she seemed afraid.

'There's always a possibility that they're on to us. But as you said Irlam phones might be having the same problems we were having and the guy behind Mohammad might just be talking into his own mobile hands-free mike or could be general security for the conference. We've come this far, and we're so close. We should hold our nerve just a little longer. At the very least I can do a lot of damage with this little baby.' He stroked the rifle with a look of love as he spoke.

'You're right. I might just be a little paranoid but let's take some precautions. I'll go down and have a look around. Then I'll wait in the van ready to take you away whatever happens. Now our phones are up and running again we can keep in touch. You OK with that?'

'Yeah, but before you go make me a pot of tea and I'll keep an eye on things. We're in the final leg and when Mohammad goes back into the hotel, he'll keep us updated.'

'Tea it is. Throw me the keys for the van.'

Steve Harrison was now in the operations suite in the Conference Centre watching over Constable Jones's shoulder as he zoomed the CCTV camera onto the face of Tourist One. He sat in the café drinking coffee and reading his paper. Harrison noticed that even though he was reading the paper for real, he still stopped to take a look around when sipping his coffee.

'He's looking for me but I'm not there. Let's keep him in view at all times, constable.'

'Will do,' said Jones.

The sound of the gunfire was loud and close. Reece reacted first. He turned and ran out of the caretaker's office while pulling out his Smith and Wesson. He could hear screaming from outside the building. They had missed Lyndsey on the CCTV as the machine was rebooting for its next twenty-four-hour cycle, she'd come out of the lift with two other residents and turned left as she walked towards the NCP car park.

As she'd passed April Grey sitting in the BMW, April had been watching her as she'd walked closer.

There was something familiar, something in the back of April's mind as the woman passed close by. April realised what it was as she neared, the red scarf. The same red scarf she'd seen the night before outside the estate agents. April let Lyndsey pass the car then started to open the door to follow, but it was too late, the woman had turned back towards her and now had a gun in her hand.

Lyndsey knew right away the woman was security forces. She'd seen enough surveillance officers in her life to know the way the woman had discreetly watched her as she'd walked by. As she passed the car, she knew this was it, she'd been spotted.

Turning back towards the car, she pulled her gun out of her shoulder bag, aimed, and fired twice. The woman in the car already had one foot on the pavement. The first shot hit her in the chest throwing her backwards, the second in the neck producing a spray of dark red blood that filled the inside windscreen and window glass of the car in a split second.

Lyndsey turned and ran towards the car park. She dropped the gun back in her bag and took out her mobile and tried to dial Costello. It took her two attempts before he answered.

'Get out, they're on to us.' Was all she said as she ran.

The screaming Reece had heard was from two young girls who looked like students. They were looking into the car, and at April Grey, not knowing what to do other than to scream. Reece, Mary, and Joe Cousins reached the BMW at almost the same time. Reece and Cousins pulled April out of the car and laid her down on the pavement.

'Alpha Control, get an ambulance here fast, agent down. And get the security cordon to move in,' shouted Reece into his mike.

Grey was unconscious but alive. Reece started calling her name and placed his hand down hard on the open wound in her neck, the blood pouring through his fingers onto the ground surrounding her. Her eyes were open, and she was trying to speak.

'April, April, can you hear me? Stay with us!' He started to pull her clothes apart with his free hand to see if she'd been hit anywhere else. He could see the brass bullet head wedged almost dead centre in the chest, but her vest had stopped it penetrating. From what he could see the only wound was to her neck where blood was pumping steadily through a large hole. Reece thought it had hit the artery there was so much blood. He shouted for Cousins to get the first aid kit out of the boot and when he brought the box, he tore the package of the solid bandage and pressed it hard against the wound feeling the warm blood against his fingers.

Mary was kneeling beside him.

'Mary, put pressure on the wound…press down on this bandage and keep talking to her. Help will be here shortly.' Reece could hear the sirens getting closer.

'What happened, Joe?' asked Reece.

'It happened so quick…a woman in a red scarf came out of the apartment block and was passing April's car. April must have recognised her and started to get out when the woman turned and fired.'

'Where's this bitch now?'

'She ran towards the NCP, but I lost her when I was running towards April. I thought her more important.'

Jim Broad broke into the conversation over the radio.

'Alpha Team, be aware that a female called the male in the apartment telling him we're on to them and to get out. The female is probably the one who shot Alpha Three. Backup and an ambulance should be with you shortly. Have you a sit-rep?'

'Roger, Alpha Control, Alpha Three's wound is serious. She's losing blood fast. We need that fucking ambulance here now. Mary will stay with her. We'll go after the woman and close down our friend in the apartment. Make the police aware we'll be wearing armbands for identification. What's the story on the Tango Team?'

'They're on their way to you but will be about thirty minutes.'

'That's too long. We can't wait. We need to move now. Alpha Four, can you have police move in quietly on Tourist One and take him into custody, then join us here at the apartment building? Mary, you stay here with April. Help's on the way. Just keep the pressure on the wound until they get here.'

Reece and Cousins started to move towards the apartment building.

'Be careful, Joseph,' Mary shouted after them.

When they got to the door and pressed the button for the caretaker, there was no response. It was then that Joe Cousins noticed the man's boot on the floor in the corridor to the right of the lift.

Costello had moved fast when Lyndsey had made the scrambled short call. Leaving the rifle where it was, he'd secured his Browning pistol in the waistband of his trousers then he decided to use the stairs instead of the lift he didn't intend to be cornered either in the lift or the apartment. He was almost out of breath when he got to the bottom of the stairs. He could see people running outside and could hear the approaching sirens. It was then he saw the *Emergency Exit* sign with the green arrow pointing to the left of the lift. He ran for the door and was pushing the bar cross handle down to open when Kevin Williams walked around the corner and asked him what he was doing. For the sake of silence Costello used his throwing knife. The caretaker's face registered both shock and surprise when he felt the pain – as if someone had punched him in the center of his chest – before looking down to see a strange piece of metal sticking out from his body and blood starting to pour down his clothes. In those last seconds before the darkness came, he realised it was his blood pouring on his best trainers. He doubled over then fell to the floor, the power in his legs and body gone. Death came quickly.

Costello pressed the escape bar and found himself at the rear of the building running towards a door in the fence about fifty yards away.

Reece moved fast when he saw the boots. He knew he only had seconds to react. He pulled his gun and fired two shots into the glass door, he didn't have time to use the buttons for access. The glass shattered, and he cleared the large shards of glass with the gun barrel before using his body to clear the rest and enter the lobby.

Pointing his gun in front, he took a careful look around the corner of the hallway where he saw Williams lying on his back with his eyes open, staring at the ceiling. Reece didn't need a second glance or to check the body for life; he'd seen that death stare too many times, he knew Williams was dead and he could see that his killer had used the emergency door which was lying open to make his escape.

'Follow me, Joe,' said Reece as he moved to the escape door.

Reece left the dead caretaker and ran through the open exit door, arms stretched forward in the standard V-shape, pointing his gun...looking over it ready to squeeze the trigger. As he passed through, he saw a man turning right through the open gate in the surrounding five-foot-high steel fence. As he watched, a hand appeared around the gate and the gun in it fired twice towards Reece and Harrison. Both men hit the ground hard, the bullets shattering the glass door behind them. Reece heard Cousins cry out, 'Fuck, fuck, fuck it!'

Cousins's face now had a stream of blood coming from a gash above his right eye from where a piece of glass had cut through his skin.

'Are you OK?' asked Reece.

'Yeah...that was too close for comfort,' he replied as he wiped the blood from his face with the sleeve of his jacket. 'Where is the bastard?'

'Can you see all right?'

Cousins wiped some more blood from his eye and his face.

'That's better, yes...I'm OK.'

'He fired blindly just to keep us back. We need to close with him before he gets away, com'on,' said Reece.

Reece was glad that Cousins had brought the MP5 from the car boot. They might need the heavier firepower yet. They now moved silently and as fast as they dared.

Mary had heard the two gunshots as she knelt beside April but with the echo of the sound in the city block, she didn't know where they came from or what direction.

She prayed that Joseph was all right.

The sirens were getting closer and Costello knew he needed to get away fast. He rounded the corner with his Browning held out. The woman kneeling over the body on the pavement looked familiar...even from behind.

Running forward, Costello grabbed her by the hair and pulled her to her feet. Jabbing the barrel of the gun into her neck he whispered, 'I told you we would meet again, Mary.'

The pain travelled right through her body from her toes to the nerve endings in her scalp. She tried to turn against it then felt the gun against her throat. Mary recognised his voice and tried to keep calm, but the more she tried to pull away from his grip the harder he pulled her hair and pressed the gun into her flesh.

Two young girls backed away: their eyes wide with fear. When they thought they were far back enough, they ran. Costello started to pull Mary towards the car's open door when a voice from behind made him turn.

'Drop your weapon, Costello, and let her go,' shouted Reece.

Costello turned slowly to face the man standing at the exit to the passageway. He could see the gun in his hand pointing directly at him. He could also see another man standing behind with what looked like a rifle pointing in his direction.

'So, Mary. This is your Special Branch friend,' said Costello. Mary struggled again to break free, but Costello pulled even tighter on her hair, the gun still hard against her neck.

'Now, now, there's a good girl, don't hurry me. I'll deal with you soon enough.'

'Let her go, Costello. Put down the gun and we can end this peacefully,' said Reece.

Costello started back towards the car using Mary as his shield.

'I don't think you understand, Mister Special Branch man. I remember you from across the interrogation table in Ireland. You know, like I do, how this is going to end. You're going to let me and Mary here get into this nice car and we're going to drive away, peacefully, as you say or it's not going to end very well. Your choice. Mary and I are going for a little ride and you're going to watch us go or she dies here.'

As he spoke, he moved closer to the car, taking a quick look behind him, he could see the keys in the ignition and April Grey's blood across the dash and the windscreen.

'I'm afraid I'm going to have to speak to your valet service about the mess but never mind, it'll do for now, so we'll be off.'

He used his foot to kick the body on the ground over and further away from the car.

'Stop, Costello. You're not going anywhere,' shouted Reece once more. 'For the last time, drop your weapon.'

Now, as Reece had been taught, he steadied his feet and his breathing and waited for the target to speak once more. Costello taking a breath to speak would be the signal he needed to ensure he didn't miss.

'No, you...' Costello never finished the sentence Reece fired once...the bullet hitting the middle of Costello's temple and blowing off the back of his head and spraying blood, bone, and brain matter out in a straight line behind him. The force of the round spinning him backwards, his grip on Mary lost, and the gun falling from his dead hand. His fall was broken partly by the boot of the BMW, and he finally rolled to a stop in the road on his back. His eyes open, staring in surprise at the sky. Reece moved above him and put two more rounds into Costello's chest. Make sure when they are down, they're down for good, so went the training.

It was then that Reece heard Mary screaming above the noise of the arriving emergency service vehicles. She was on her knees looking at her hands with tears streaming down her face. He could see there was blood on her cheek and in her hair. He knelt beside her stroking his hand through her hair, but he couldn't find a wound...the blood belonged to April and Costello. She was still screaming when he pulled her close to him.

'You're all right, it's over,' he said.

Her screaming stopped and she buried her head into his shoulder sobbing. The paramedics quickly hooked April up to a drip and started working on her in the ambulance.

'Can you go to the hospital with April?' Reece asked looking into Mary's tear-filled eyes. 'I need to stay here and chase up the woman and I want you to get looked at as well, can you do that for me?'

Her voice was hoarse with all the screaming, and she struggled to whisper, 'OK, but come and find me, I need you.'

'Call it in, Joe, get these two to the hospital, Steve and I will see if we can find Lyndsey. There was only one way it was going to end for this bastard, he knew it and he would have tried to take as many of us as he could before then.'

'No argument from me, David, if you hadn't shot him, I would have.'

Reece walked back to the car. Harrison had arrived at the same time as the ambulance and the armed police response teams. Reece was surprised to see ACC Lockwood.

'Mister Reece, I've taken control of the scene and circulated the description of the woman who shot your friend here. You can get your people off the ground now and leave this to me.'

'That's OK by me, sir. Did we grab the other man at the conference?'

It was Harrison who replied.

'We have him, David, he came quietly, and the Tango Team are taking him to the hangar as we speak. CCTV showed the woman who shot April go into the NCP down the street but then we lost her.'

'If she's as smart as we think she is, she's long gone but we can make a search through the car park and down to the train station. Lockwood, can you get your people to the station and continue to check the CCTV?'

'You still have priority when it comes to these people, Mister Reece, and to tell you the truth, you're welcome to them, but we'll help you look for her. In the meantime, we'll have SO19 clear the apartment,' said Lockwood.

Reece was pleased that at last he seemed to get the whole idea that the SG9 team were not the bad guys.

The three SG9 agents headed to the NCP car park, Reece in front, followed closely by Harrison and Cousins. The car park was like any other, large and cavernous, and there was no sign of the woman they were looking for. They continued to walk down to the Deansgate rail and tram station, still no sign.

'Alpha One, this is Alpha Control, come in, over.'

It was the voice of Jim Broad.

'Go ahead, Alpha Control,' replied Reece.

'David, we've been checking all the CCTV in your area through our live feed here. We have the woman in the scarf entering the NCP on foot but not leaving on foot. However, we do have a Ford van, similar to the one we were looking for, leaving the car park shortly after the shooting but we lost it heading towards the city centre. We've put out a stop with caution alert to all police in the area, but she may be well gone by now.'

'Understood, Alpha Control, we'll take a final look around the station area then come back to you for a debrief.'

'Roger that, Alpha One. See you soon.'

The further search produced nothing and the three SG9 agents returned to the hangar for the debrief to Jim Broad.

It soon became clear that with the two dead terrorists in Irlam and Costello in Deansgate, Lyndsey was now on the run and keeping her head down. It didn't take them long to interrogate Mohammad and get the full details of what the terror group had been planning. It appeared he was a willing talker and not as brave as he thought he was.

'Any word on April?' asked Reece.

'I'm sorry, David, she didn't make it. She died in the ambulance without saying anything. She lost too much blood. Mary stayed with her all the way, she's at the hospital now,' said Broad.

'Now that we have everything under control here, I'm off to the hospital to pick Mary up.'

Chapter Sixty-six

The prime minister and Sir Martyn Bryant had listened quietly when Sir Ian Fraser briefed them concerning the morning's activities.

'On the whole, your team have done a fantastic job, Sir Ian,' said the PM. 'I mean, tracking these people down to completely breaking up their plans, not to say anything about killing three and capturing one. Of course, we must remember the brave SAS soldier who lost his life and your dead agent.'

'It's hard to lose anyone, but she was one of our best and will be sorely missed. Her family will never know the true sacrifice she made. They never knew she was one of our agents, only that she was attached to the police in some capacity. And of course, we must not forget the regrettable loss of the caretaker, Mister Williams.'

'Of course, Sir Ian, and the fact that this woman who you believe to be Lyndsey escaped,' said Sir Martin Bryant.

'Yes, that's the only downside, that, and the sad death of our people and the innocent civilian. We have an all-ports bulletin out with her description, and I've instructed our agents and stations around the globe to find out where she is, but she knows all the tricks to keep her head down and has many friends in the Islamic world who will give her protection, but she'll stick her head out of her hiding place again and we'll be ready.'

Peter Brookfield held his hand up to take over the conversation.

'I'll be addressing the conference shortly. All I'll be saying is that our security services have prevented a terrorist attack in the streets of this city. I won't be specific on what the target was and that'll remain our secret.

'In the meantime, Sir Ian, I want to thank you and your agents for the great service they've done for our country. They were truly tested by fire and have come through with flying colours. Please pass on the thanks of a grateful nation. I'll see you at the next Intelligence Committee meeting with Sir Martin in London next week and maybe you'll have some more news on this Lyndsey woman.'

Two Weeks Later

Hurghada, Egypt

Reece and Harrison had arrived at the Egyptian Airport of Hurghada on a tourist flight from London Gatwick. The taxi to the 5-star Hilton Hotel resort in the city took fifteen minutes. The hotel itself overlooked the bay at the southern end of town.

Jim Broad had briefed Reece the day before in the SG9 office in London. As a result of the SG9 operation in Manchester and the follow up, they had sent full-face photos of Sharon Lyndsey to all European, Middle East, and Far East security agencies to look out for and report back to London.

Three days ago, MI6 had received a report from its embassy spook in Cairo that a woman they believed matched the photo and description of Sharon Lyndsey had travelled to the Hilton Hotel Resort in Hurghada after crossing the border from Sudan.

She seemed to like Hilton Hotels, thought Reece when he heard. The photo taken of her at the border checkpoint had been quickly matched using facial recognition confirming her to be Lyndsey.

Reece and Harrison had been met outside the airport terminal by the resident Cairo spook and given a large buff envelope in a handoff that took a split second.

When they had booked into the hotel, Reece opened the envelope in their room. Inside was a folder containing the up-to-date photos taken by the Egyptian surveillance team of Lyndsey sunning herself by the pool and swimming in the Red Sea of the resort. A short note confirmed she just seemed to be filling the role of a tourist relaxing and using the resort facilities with no sign of bodyguards.

The envelope contained two Berretta Semi-Automatic .22 pistols with fully loaded magazines. The pistol of choice for the assassin teams of the Israeli Mossad Kidon units. Each bullet would contain half the powder, this made the weapon just as deadly up close but with the noise given out of a silenced gun making it easier to conceal and use. The note had also said that in the short time they'd been watching Lyndsey each evening she'd taken a walk to a coffee shop and supermarket in the street behind the hotel. There was a small map with an X showing the café and a photo showing Lyndsey sitting at an outside table.

The spooks could also confirm through a contact that she was staying in the hotel for a week in one of the penthouse rooms and seemed to have plenty of cash. Reece took the note and map into the bathroom and burnt them in the sink, washing the charred pages down the drain. He used his encrypted mobile phone to let Broad know that it was Lyndsey, and they would confirm her movements tonight and move at eight o'clock Egypt time the next evening.

Reece and Harrison left the hotel at 7.30 p.m. and walked to the café taking seats at the back facing the street. From there they watched Lyndsey walk out the rear hotel door and cross the street to take up a table at the front, facing back the way she'd travelled.

She ordered from the waiter and lit a cigarette. Even though it was now dark, it was still warm. She wore large wraparound sunglasses, a silk scarf around her neck and pulled up to her mouth, and a white linen dress. She was carrying the same type of shoulder bag she'd carried in Manchester. No doubt containing a gun, thought Reece. There was no obvious sign of bodyguards, but they noticed two men of Middle Eastern appearance walk into the café and take up a table to the right of Lyndsey seconds after she'd sat down. To Reece they didn't fit. They were watching the street to the front of the café. Reece recognised the signs they were there because she was there. The Cairo spook had missed them because they didn't walk close to her. That could be a problem, but one they were prepared for.

If they got in the way, they were going down with her, thought Reece.

Reece and Harrison stayed in the café until Lyndsey left and the two men followed her a short distance behind. When Reece returned to the room, he contacted Broad once more and updated him on the two men. They weren't sure if they were bodyguards or Egyptian security, but either way the operation would go down at the café the following night.

As far as the two men were concerned, they would work to the rules used by Mossad: if they moved to become combatants then they would be treated as such and dealt with.

Reece and Broad had agreed the escape plan for afterwards. Nothing that would show who they were would be left behind. Lyndsey left the café around 8 p.m. each night so the operation would be aimed for that time.

The following night Reece and Harrison took up the same seats at the café and ordered coffee. As far as both could see there was no CCTV which was to be expected…Lyndsey wouldn't want to be caught on camera either. She arrived and sat at the same table as yesterday, closely followed by the two men. Their table was already taken by a young couple holding hands over a pot of tea, so they chose a different spot.

Reece watched Lyndsey closely. She looked every inch the tourist wearing the same wraparound sunglasses and light clothing similar to that from the night before. She sat facing the street watching the world go by as she took sips from her cup. The two men sat deep in conversation looking around them as they talked.

Reece and Harrison did the same and to anyone watching the scene, it was a normal café filled with everyday customers enjoying their coffee on a warm evening.

Lyndsey searched in her shoulder bag and producing her purse she left a note of money under the saucer on her table and started to rise. This was the moment Reece and Harrison had agreed to move. The two men were also preparing to leave, and one produced his wallet, starting to extract the money to pay their bill. Reece moved behind Lyndsey as she stood while Harrison stood in front of the two men blocking their view.

The two lovers told the police afterwards everything happened in seconds although it seemed to be in slow motion.

Reece got close enough to whisper in Lyndsey's ear, 'This is for April.' He pointed the Beretta at her right temple and as he pulled the trigger, he was close enough to see through her sunglasses and the look of surprise as the two bullets, fired in quick succession, blew a hole through her brain. The blood spray was short as it poured over the white linin cloth on the table in front of her. Reece held her as she fell, and he was able to set her back in the chair and rest her head on the table.

Harrison had the two men covered with his gun as they saw what had happened to Lyndsey. Both reached under their jackets but too late.

Thanks to being seated, their options were limited. They had become combatants. Harrison shot the one to his right twice in the chest while, as they'd planned, Reece did the same to the one on the left. Both men fell, knocking over the surrounding tables, both dead before they hit the ground.

The young lovers were in shock and looked on, mouths open as the two gunmen turned and walked casually down the street towards the corner of the hotel opposite and disappeared into the night.

They walked down to the deserted beach and within seconds a Royal Navy dingy with two Special Boat Service operators arrived. They sailed out one mile to where they boarded the Royal Navy Destroyer *HMS Ardross* which had, until two days ago, been on exercise in the Red Sea. The ship sailed to Cyprus, leaving the Egyptian authorities totally baffled that the two men had completely disappeared.

Not knowing who the men were and the discovery that their victims were Islamic terrorists, they believed the assassinations were the work of Mossad. The Egyptian authorities didn't want the world to know Lyndsey and her friends had been enjoying themselves in their country, so they decided not to look into the murders too closely, better to let sleeping dogs lie.

ONE MONTH LATER

MALTA

David Reece sat on the bench at the head of the costal walkway between Qawra and Bugibba watching the waves of St Paul's Bay splash over the rocks below. He always enjoyed the walk along this path first thing in the morning when everything was still fresh, and the sun was just above the headland in front of him. The walk took him about a quarter of a mile from his small piece of heaven on earth the Villa St Joseph. From where he sat, he could see the new motor carriageway as it passed around the headland heading towards the capital Valletta.

Mary sat down next to him. Even though it was the middle of November, the sun still radiated heat warm enough to allow them to wear light jackets over their T-shirts. When she sat down, she asked, 'What are you thinking, Joseph?'

He looked at her beautiful brown eyes as if for the first time. He loved how this woman could see into his soul and take away all the fears of life.

'You asked me that once before and I think I told you I loved you and we'd be together after the work was over. Well, the work is over for now but there'll be other times when I'll have to work, maybe be away from you and I don't know if I want to do that anymore.'

'Let's not worry about the future. Let's just have today, now, right here.'

'You're right. The work is done.'

'So, as I said, there's nothing for us to do now except drink our coffee and then head back to the villa where we can make warm passionate love all day.'

He loved her smile and the love they made together.

'Answer me a question. Why do you still call me Joseph even though the job is over? You're no longer my agent, you're the woman I love?'

'I know, and I love you too. I first knew you as Joseph, and you saved me from a life that was destroying me inside when you were called Joseph. So you'll always be Joseph to me. The one man who kept his promise.'

'All right, Joseph it is. But only for you. Now let's go get that coffee.'

She took his hand and looking into his eyes she smiled.

'Let's skip the coffee.'

LIGHT OF THE SUN

Dedication

I dedicate this book to my family and to all the brave men and women who stand on the wall.

Chapter 1

Barcelona

Take therefore no thought for the morrow: for the morrow shall take thought for the things of itself. Sufficient unto the day is the evil thereof.
Matthew 6:34 KJB

'Allah will bless you and keep you in the palm of his hand.'
The text on the phone screen was her signal to proceed. The Arab had told her the same words when he had helped her strap on the vest. With screws, nails, and TNT in the pouches around her, she noticed there was no smell only that from her sweat. She left the hotel and walking in the warm sun made her way to the La Rambla area of Barcelona. This was the main tourist area of the city, over one mile long with its pedestrian tree lined walkway through the centre. She had walked here twice, once with the Teacher himself. The streets were already filling with tourists and shoppers. The famous living statue street artists were picking the best spots to surprise those same tourists encouraging them to donate their money into the buckets, tins, and caps on the ground. No one looked at her, no one cared, they were all lost in their own little worlds, heads looking down at the phones in their hands or browsing the shop windows for bargains and holiday mementos. The pavement cafés were also filling up, with the loud chatter of conversation carrying across the street on the morning air. The suicide vest under her coat wasn't heavy or bulky, and her clothing was that of a Western woman with blue jeans and a coloured headscarf, leaving her face fully visible to all around. He had told her to go to the indoor market for maximum effect. Being early morning, the market was packed with local shoppers out before the severe midday heat. She could see figures of people in front of her, but not in any clarity, just the outline, her eyes did not want to settle on any one person, she didn't want to be weak, she was a soldier of Allah. He had told her to expect the fear, but that it would pass quickly as she passed through the gate into paradise. In her final moment she hoped someone would stop her, but then her voice took over, 'Allah Akbar, Allah Akbar,' she shouted. Her loud

voice surprised her for a second and she could see some of the people closest to her turning their heads towards the sound, some faces already with the shock of the realisation of what was about to happen, death was here. She pressed the button on the handheld device.

The explosive blast with the force of the TNT in the crowded space caused complete and utter devastation. Her body was blown asunder into minute fragments of bone adding to the shrapnel already created by the flying packs of metal spread through the crowded market with the speed of bullets. Forty died immediately: men, women, and children, with fifteen more who reached hospital dying later, 150 victims were injured many of them losing limbs. All that was left of the bomber was her head, almost intact with her brightly coloured scarf still in place around her face.

When the blast sounded and vibrated through the city the Arab was strapping himself into his passenger seat on the 10.30 a.m. flight from Barcelona to Rome. He had sent the text message before boarding, breaking the SIM card, he had thrown it with the burner phone into a waste bin. *God is Great*, he thought.

'Allah Akbar,' he whispered quietly to himself.

Iran

'Keep your face to the sun and you will never see the shadows.'
Helen Keller

The sun was at its hottest as Colonel Ali Shafi of Iran's elite Republican Guard drove the Jeep through the third security gate allowing access to the Parchin military site. Parchin was supposed to be a secret site southeast of the capital city Tehran. According to reports from the UN nuclear watchdog the International Atomic Energy Agency (IAEA) it was suspected of being a possible location supporting the Iranian nuclear enrichment programme working towards the production of a nuclear bomb capability.

Intelligence reports from the CIA and Mossad confirmed the fears of the IAEA inspectors. Iran continued to tell the world that it needed the nuclear material for a medical research reactor, yet despite numerous requests by the UN team to inspect the site, they'd been delayed; until, as they now believed, to allow time to hide the true purpose of the site.

Satellite pictures had shown the site had been sanitised to protect its secrets in an effort to remove and cleanse any evidence of illicit nuclear activity.

The clean-up activity had taken several months and included a large covering being placed over a steel chamber; this the IAEA believed was being used for explosive experiments in an apparent effort to prevent satellite monitoring of the location.

The IAEA report had detailed that significant ground scraping and landscaping had been undertaken over an extensive area in and around Parchin. Buildings had been demolished and power lines, fences, and paved roads removed. The IAEA assessment was that this activity was a deliberate operation by the Iranian government to protect the real work that had been going on at Parchin, and to deliberately hamper its investigation if the IAEA was to be granted access to the site. Their most recent report which was now available to the UN and other interested parties stated, 'The activities observed... further strengthen the agency's assessment that it is necessary to have access to the location at Parchin without further delay.'

This delay of access was not only of concern to the Secretary of the UN and the President of the United States. The Prime Minister of Israel had explicitly stated that Israel couldn't allow a government who had called for the state of Israel to be wiped off the face of the earth, to have a nuclear capability on its doorstep. The threat was implicit, 'we will act before you do.'

Over the last two years as commander of the secretive base Shafi had overseen the security of Iran's biggest gamble; to become an independent nuclear power. Today as he parked inside one of the covered bunkers he knew that the Western powers and supporters of the Zionist state of Israel would shudder with fear as the cause of Allah came down on them with the wrath of thunder.

Tel Aviv to Malta

Rachel Cohen looked down on the landscape of the island of Malta as the Air Malta A319 with 141 passengers on-board made its landing approach to Luqa, Malta's international airport. The flight from Rome had only taken one hour and twenty minutes. Rachel knew touchdown was only a few minutes away when she saw the cabin crew strap themselves into their seats facing the passengers in the aircraft's cabin. Looking at the ground below she picked out the landmarks on the almost treeless surface that she remembered from the many times she'd visited the island in the past. Then she'd come as a tourist. Looking now out the window she could follow the roads as they wound their way through the island and the small villages and towns to the larger tourist developments on the coast. She could pick out the hilltop town of Mdina. The fortress town had been the original capital of the island before the residents moved down to the coast for work. When most of the inhabitants left, the city became so quiet it soon became known as the Silent City. Yet she remembered it as a beautiful place to walk through its narrow-cobbled streets, then dine in one of the restaurants on the battlements that looked down on Malta spread out below. Now ahead to her left she could pick out the current capital Valletta, with its Grand Harbour one of the best deep-water harbours in the world, and the lifeline for the survival of the British Forces in the Mediterranean in the Second World War battle against Rommel's Afrika Corps and the Italian Axis forces in the battles across the North Africa and the Libyan desert. For the bravery shown by the Maltese people in that campaign the island was awarded the George Cross by King George VI. To this day it is displayed on the national Maltese flag as a symbol of pride. The people of Malta were fiercely proud of their history, not only during the Second World War but also when the Knights of Malta fought off a Muslim Army from the Ottoman Empire in the Great Siege in 1565.

Now as the ground rushed up to meet her Rachel thought of how she'd fallen in love with the island and its people. This time her visit would not give her the chance to relax. This time she would be looking through the eyes not of a tourist, but of a field agent in the employment of the Israeli Secret Service, Mossad.

Now, she would be going through customs using her cover name of Anna Stressor; the Italian housewife; accompanied by her husband Palo now seated next to her. Palo appeared to be resting his eyes but Ari Rosenberg, also a member of the elite Mossad Kidon teams was, as always, alert.

Passport Control was as usual simple enough to go through, with just a cursory look from the female officer behind the desk. *No problem so far*, thought Rachel. Was it only yesterday she was sitting in her apartment on the outskirts of Tel Aviv, when her mobile phone had buzzed a text alert? The words in capital letters *RETURN TO OFFICE* meant, *Urgent get there now!* Less than an hour later Rachel and Ari sat in the office of Mossad HQ in King Saul Boulevard in downtown Tel Aviv. Sitting behind the desk facing them was Kurt Shimon, head of the Mossad Counter Terrorist Kidon teams.

Rachel had met him a few times when training for the Kidon teams in the Negev desert. His reputation was legend in the Mossad. He had a desert tan with thick white hair; he looked fit and spoke with great confidence and authority. The Kidon or Bayonet in English, were the elite of the Mossad. Most members of Kidon came from a military background having served in the Israeli Defence Forces, IDF, and most of them had served in its Special Forces or elite regiments. On rare occasions a Mossad member could transfer into the Kidon when it was found they had that special gift or qualification. The training was tough, and few made it through to join the special clandestine killing arm of Mossad.

'We have a situation which needs your expertise immediately. Our intelligence sources in Iran have identified a clear threat to an unknown target somewhere in Western Europe. Scientists in Iran have perfected a small nuclear device using a small amount of plutonium which we believe is already being transported to Europe. This device could demolish most of London and leave a radioactive cloud to spread to the south of England and the coast of France, that's if London is the target. We do not know how it's being transported, but the triggering mechanism is travelling separately, and this is where you come in. An Iranian Colonel is travelling as we speak to Malta, with protection from the members of the Iranian Quads and possibly Hezbollah. In Malta he'll be handing the plutonium over to someone who will smuggle it into Europe where they'll meet up with members of a terrorist organisation, as yet unknown. We believe this Colonel is travelling from Iran on a container ship which is going to put him and his friends ashore at the Grand Harbour in Valletta in two days. This team will have the plutonium, and when it reaches their people in Europe, they will supply the explosives and trigger to set it off. The final target, and who their people are in Europe, are still unknown. That is where you come in. Get to Malta, pick up the trail, and try to identify the rest of these people. Combined with the explosive and the plutonium, this will be a dirty nuclear device. Any information we get here we'll let you know immediately.'

Every Mossad and IDF member knew the danger posed by the Iranian regime.

Iran had supported the terror group Hezbollah for many years, and its main operating base was in Lebanon, with Israel its main target. The Iranian Quads were really the Paramilitary wing of the Iranian Army, highly trained killers. Iran had told the world that the destruction of the state of Israel was their main priority. The Prime Minister of Israel had made it quite clear; Israel wouldn't allow a threat of nuclear attack against its people. Israel would carry out a pre-emptive strike before Iran had the capability to launch a missile attack on its country. The Western powers, especially the United States, feared such a scenario and that's why they'd put pressure on Iran to cease its nuclear strategy through inspections and sanctions. *This would be no picnic*, thought Rachel.

'Why Malta?' asked Rachel. 'It seems strange that if they want to get it into Europe, why tie themselves up on an island in the middle of the Mediterranean?'

Kurt Shimon smiled at Rachel when he answered.

'Believe it or not the Iranians still have contacts they trust in Malta even though we eliminated one of their friends there in 1995.'

Everyone knew the legend as part of the Mossad story. A Kidon team had travelled to Malta when intelligence was received that placed the leader of the Palestinian Islamic Jihad (PIJ) Fathi Shaqaqi, who had links with Iran, and who had been meeting with the Libyan leader Muammar Gaddafi in Tripoli, to organise training, weapons, and money to be supplied to his terrorist teams had stopped off in Malta. The Kidon team, that was quickly dispatched to Malta, soon tracked him down and shot him dead outside his hotel. It was a well planned and executed Mossad operation, once more showing the terrorist leaders, nowhere was safe from their reach.

'Anyway, it does not matter why they're back in Malta it's our job to find out why, so I'm sending you two. All the information you need will be sent by encrypted message to your smartphones. Go over to operations they'll supply you with false identity, weapons, and any information on this Iranian Colonel and his friends. I'll be keeping an eye on this, and in the meantime I'll be contacting our friends in the European Security Services to bring them up to date.'

The file on Colonel Ali Shafi was thin. A ten-year-old photo showed a round faced man with a heavy dark moustache and dark brown eyes. His family and military background were standard for a Colonel in the Islamic Revolutionary Guard Corps. Not only was he a Colonel in the guard but also a member of its Quads Force, the Unit with a specific remit to carry out unconventional warfare and intelligence activities, and responsible for extraterritorial operations. As Rachel expected, the Mossad files showed that the Quads worked closely with Hezbollah, Hamas, and the PIJ; all enemies of Israel. The interesting thing was his family. He had married into the family of the Grand Ayatollah of Iran Sayyid Ali Hosseini Khamenei. *This was no ordinary soldier*, thought Rachel. The files had been downloaded to the two Mossad agents' smartphones which could only be accessed through their thumb print to the screen. Anyone else trying to access the phone, would lose a finger or two when it blew up in their hand. A bit of *Mission Impossible* stuff but the science boffins of Mossad don't mess around. Next stop was the Grand Hotel Excelsior in the capital Valletta. Rachel had stayed there once before in another world a long time ago. The weapons would be supplied to them by one of Israel's Sayanim living in Malta. These are Jews and local residents living and working as normal citizens in every country outside Israel. They are recruited by Mossad to help its operators with everything from transport to money, safe houses, weapons and access to communications networks and other facilities, including official documents exclusive to that location. Sayanim dedicated their lives to the state of Israel and its existence and had indicated their desire to help in whatever way they could. First stop after booking into the hotel would be to contact the local Sayanim and collect their weapons.

A final piece of the message sent on their phones surprised both operators telling them that they would be contacted at the hotel by an agent from the British Secret Intelligence Service, David Reece.

Chapter 2

'I heard the voice of the Lord, saying, Who shall I send, and who will go for us? Then said I, Here I am; send me.'

It was raining in London, which made the River Thames that flowed through the nation's capital dark with churned-up mud, its colour more brown than usual. Sir Ian Fraser was looking out the window of his office on the top floor of Vauxhall Cross, the headquarters of MI6, the Secret Intelligence Service of the United Kingdom. Sir Ian head of SIS who was also known in the secret world of intelligence services and his employees simply as 'C', had his back to the room and the three other people sitting around the conference table.

Still looking down at the river he could see the spires of the Houses of Parliament to his right and the outline of Thames House the home of MI5.

'So, what you're saying is she was British?'

The voice from the room behind Sir Ian was that of Sir Martin Bryant the Chairman of the British Joint Intelligence Committee. Fraser turned to face the three people in the vast office.

'Yes, that's what I'm saying. Interpol have identified her as being British. She was originally plain Margaret Brown from East London.'

'But how did Interpol identify her as Margaret Brown. Surely there was nothing left to identify the woman?' again it was Bryant asking the question.

It was now the turn of the only woman in the room to speak.

'DNA and fingerprints.' Caroline Aspinall was the head of the Security Service or MI5 as it was better known. MI5 have responsibility for intelligence operations within the boundaries of the United Kingdom, while MI6 has the responsibility for intelligence gathering and operations on all borders beyond the UK and throughout the world. Both organisations have as their main remit, the protection of the citizens of the UK and its assets. Aspinall was a career Intelligence Officer having joined MI5 straight from university in Cambridge. She had earned her stripes and the respect of the men in the room working her way up the ladder, first as a field agent then as a top-class analyst. Her clear thinking and dedication had saved many lives, and as she progressed through the Security Service ranks, her qualities were noticed. After serving for ten years as head of operations, she had recently been promoted to the top job when her boss had retired.

'What do you mean, that the Spanish have the DNA of a British citizen?' asked Bryant.

Aspinall looked at Fraser and the other man in the room Jim Broad for approval to continue.

'Go ahead please, Caroline,' said Fraser.

She looked back to Bryant before continuing. Aspinall pressed a button on the table in front of her and the screen on the wall brought up the video of a young woman.

Margaret Brown looked every bit her young age. Her clothing was Western, her dark hair pulled back severely in a ponytail, her blue eyes looked straight ahead at the screen, and she seemed to be speaking without a script. There was a white sheet hanging on the wall behind her with words written in black in Arabic across it. She spoke clearly in English her London accent was still strong as she spoke.

'All praise to the father, Allah be his name. I am Margaret Brown, but my chosen name is Fatimah, and I am a soldier of the Islamic Jihad. My eyes were covered by the scales of the many false gods of the Western devils, but the work and love of the Prophet all praises to his name removed those scales and filled me with the desire to serve him however I can. Now I will bring his wrath as a soldier to those same infidels who blaspheme and ignore the will of the one true God that is Allah. I call on all our brothers and sisters to join our cause and attack these infidels wherever you find them.'

She then seemed to look at a space above the camera at someone hidden there for approval, then a male voice spoke in English with a slight Middle Eastern accent, 'Allah be praised, God is Great.' Just before the camera was switched off and the screen went blank.

'You see Sir Martin; this was no ordinary woman. Margaret Brown was originally as has been said from East London. The family still live there, and Special Branch are raiding the family home as we speak but I don't think they'll find anything. Margaret Brown left the UK over five years ago and as far as we know has never returned. When she lived here she got involved with a crowd of Palestinian activists and was arrested during a demonstration outside the Israeli Embassy here in London. She was only sixteen at the time but because of that arrest she was fingerprinted, and her photo and DNA taken. When she was questioned the report showed that she was into the whole Middle East scenario as she felt the Palestinians were being persecuted by the Jews and the rest of the Western World. She was thought by her interviewers to be a low risk and not of any use from a recruitment point of view. A few years later we find her name popping up again logged as a passenger on a flight to Egypt, but it would now appear that the trip was one way and she never returned to these shores. We, as you know Sir Martin, share a database with other European intelligence agencies and Interpol. After the Barcelona suicide bombing last week, the Spanish fed the bomber's DNA, fingerprints, and a photo of the woman's head, which considering she'd blown herself up, was pretty much intact, into the system and up popped that long-lost file of Margaret Brown. The video was released to the various Arab and Islamic Networks and put on social media sites which proves that the DNA and fingerprint evidence is correct confirming the bomber was indeed Margaret Brown or as she has now identified herself Fatimah.'

'Can we find out where she went, who she got involved with and why she did this,' asked Bryant.

Aspinall looked to Sir Ian Fraser once more before replying.

'As with all these situations, it will have to be a combined effort. The Anti-Terrorist Squad have already started with the searches and follow-up enquiries where she lived and grew up. They will be looking into her school life and any other involvement in Middle East activities. Five will chase up any information here at home, we'll also be checking the family's phones and computers for any contact with her. Then I believe it will be over to Six to see what she did outside the country.'

Now it was the turn of Fraser to present the part MI6 would have to play in researching the life of Margaret Brown.

'You have to understand Martin, although we have Embassies in most of the countries in the Middle East and Africa, we have very few actual agents on the ground. We have sent out the usual request, asking them to find out what they can as a matter of urgency. However, between ourselves and the NSA we do have good technical and eavesdropping coverage. The people at GCHQ and the NSA at Fort Meade have become experts in giving us a heads up on what they call chatter.'

'So, no heads up this time then?' asked Bryant.

'Not as such. They got nothing in the build-up, they're getting too smart for that, a few seconds conversation on a mobile phone can bring a Hellfire Missile fired from a drone down on their head. But GCHQ and the NSA did get some chatter afterwards when the jihadist groups started to cheer and celebrate Barcelona. They all started to mention the Arab. We have an idea who he is, from years of following any mention of him. The file shows he has been at this sort of stuff for some time. He may have even lived in this country for a time as a student.'

The MI6 chief sat behind his desk and pressed a couple of buttons on a remote control. The curtains on the large windows closed and the video monitor on the wall lit up to show a grainy headshot of what looked like a bearded man wearing sunglasses and the traditional Arab headdress a red and white checked shemagh. From the background it looked like the picture had been taken in what could only be described as any Middle Eastern town.

At the same time, a man of around thirty-five years came into the room and stood in front of the screen.

'Can I introduce for those of you who don't know him Matthew Simons our head of the Middle East desk.' said Fraser. 'He will talk us through all we know about the Arab. Matthew over to you.'

Simons was about six-foot-tall, slim, short dark hair with the tan and brown eyes of someone who might have been born in the Middle East, clean shaven wearing a short sleeved open neck shirt he had the body of someone who looked after himself.

'Thank you, Sir Ian.'

The voice was Oxford educated as Broad knew from his many past meetings with Simons. He also knew Simons was born in Gibraltar where his father met his wife while serving with the Royal Navy. He spoke Pashto and many of the other Arabic languages with the gift of sounding like a local when he did.

'This photo was taken at a Palestinian camp in Gaza by an agent working for Mossad. There was a party going on in the streets to celebrate 9/11, and the Mossad agent was there celebrating with the rest of them taking a few snaps with his camera phone. It turned out after questioning by the agents' handlers, the man in the photo seemed to be important. He had a few bodyguards and people referred to him as the Arab. Mossad then took up some interest in this man, and they've spent some time in finding out who he was. The reason Mossad told us all this and gave us some access to the file, was because it turns out our Arab friend here may have attended university in this country. Plus, we are inclined to think the job our SG9 people did in Manchester taking out the joint IRA and Islamic Jihad team might have endeared them to us for a little while. We like to think that when it comes to the Islamic threat, we are all in this together when sharing intelligence that affects everyone of us.'

These words stirred some recent memories in all present, especially those of Jim Broad who, as Director of Operations for the SG9 unit during Operation Long Shot, had seen his team take out three terrorists and arrest one with one escaping. The operation had prevented the assassination of the Prime Minister of the UK. SG9 was now, to put it crudely, the killing arm in the clandestine war against terrorist groups operating against the people of the UK wherever they might raise their heads, it was now the job of SG9 to find them and eliminate them. The decision to create the Department or SG9, was known to only a few, as a necessary evil to combat the rising war of terrorism that was attacking every civilised country in the world, especially in the West. It had been decided that prison only made Islamic Terrorists more dangerous for three reasons, being Martyrs to the cause, they indoctrinated their fellow inmates creating more terrorists, and they cost countries a fortune in security before eventually having been released after serving their term in prison, then they inevitably went straight back to their old ways, deadlier and wiser.

Broad remembered the words of Winston Churchill, when he said in the context of the Second World War 'The only way to defeat terror is with greater terror.' The Israelis, the Russians, the Americans had all come to realise this and formed their own Black Ops units to combat the disease that terrorism, especially Islamic Terrorism brought to the world. Broad thought you couldn't negotiate or talk to these people, they did not want to talk, they only wanted to kill you. It was now the job of intelligence agencies throughout the world to track them down and kill them first, 'Big Boys Rules' as it was known in the undercover war the Secret Agencies around the world now had to work in.

Matthew Simons turned once more to the screen on the wall and pressing a button on the remote once more brought up a file page marked *TOP SECRET*.

'Now let us have a look at what we have on the Arab, the man in the grainy photo. This file has been compiled by the analysts from many agencies working together, including our own intelligence agencies from Five, Six, and GCHQ. If Mossad are right, then this man did attend university in this country some time ago. If you can keep your questions until after I've finished we can discuss further at length. The file shows the basic background, and I have to say we should not get bogged down in all this, a lot of it is guesswork and speculation. Our friend is better known as Abdullah Mohammad Safrah. Born in Gaza in 1978 we first find him in this country attending the London School of Economics between 2002 and 2005 where he obtained a First in Economics. This part is fact, five have checked the records and he was here during that time and lived in a bedsit on Edgware Road. The usual student life, but no sign of student politics or groups. After leaving the LSE; he then, according to Mossad, turned up for more educational training at the Bir Zeit University on the West Bank, where he studied Physics, before moving to the Mansoura University in Egypt to study medicine, graduating as a Doctor in General Practice. Mossad believe this is where he may have been fully radicalised, becoming involved at first with the Islamic Brotherhood, and then moving on to the PIJ, an offshoot of the Palestinian Liberation Organisation. Founding members of the PIJ believed that the PLO had become too soft, and their founding charter is the destruction of Israel by Holy War or Jihad as we know it. Our friend Abdullah, it would appear, put his education to good use at first; practising medicine in Kuwait, Bahrain, and then back in his homeland of Gaza. It is believed he then joined up with his comrades in the PIJ to help Hezbollah in Lebanon in their war with Israel. While in Beirut we have him in the hospital there, putting his medical knowledge to good use, and according to reports from the Red Cross and the UN, he was good at his job and well liked. He is the eldest of seven children and the thing that might have changed his whole outlook on life from helping people to killing them, may have been an airstrike by Israel on a suspected PIJ commander in Gaza in May 2008. The bombs not only hit their target, but one at least overshot hitting a civilian area killing two of his family - a brother Hassan and a sister Yasmin. He then disappears off the radar in Lebanon, but it's believed he ended up in Iran, specifically Tehran where his links to extreme Islamic Jihad movements, such as Hezbollah and al-Qaeda, became stronger. Again, his masters recognised him as a leader, a man of quality. He was trained in all the terrorist ways on how to kill, using bombs, guns, knives, and his hands. But where he excelled, was as a planner. He would impress his trainers with his ideas and how to carry them out. As I said at the start, a lot of this is second-hand hearsay, but from our experiences of the Middle East and how these groups operate, it can be assumed to be fairly accurate. Over to you if you have any questions.'

As he spoke Simons had changed the pictures on the screen from the Red Cross and UN symbols to what looked like a terrorist training camp somewhere in the Middle East for effect.

Sir Martin Bryant spoke first.

'I can see your concern with the fact he went to university here, and that Margaret Brown also spent time in this country, but how does this link the two. I need to confirm there is a threat before I see the Prime Minister?'

'I understand Martin,' said Fraser, 'but as we said at the start it was through the chatter picked up by the technical spooks that has linked the Arab with Margaret Brown. We will put all our people on it and come back to you when we have more. In the meantime, I would suggest the PM say as little as he can about Margaret Brown. He should only state that for a time she lived in this country many years ago, and after she left there is nothing more known. That way we make the Arab and his friends think we are totally in the dark. In a slight fog maybe, but not totally in the dark. As you know, Martin, I'm taking the opportunity to meet with my fellow Directors of the CIA and Mossad in London before the end of December. At the same time, I've already asked them that we put the Arab top of the agenda when we meet.'

'So, while we wait for more information, we don't need to upgrade our state of alert for the moment?' asked Bryant.

When there is intelligence that indicates a threat to the UK mainland it is assessed by the Joint Terrorism Analysis Centre (JTAC) which makes its recommendations on the level of threat to the country, independent of government. Bryant knew that the threat level was currently at its second highest level out of a list of five, judged as severe meaning a terrorist attack to be highly likely.

'No,' answered Fraser, 'it should remain as severe for the moment, and I think we can leave it there for now.'

The highest state of alert in the United Kingdom was imminent and that would be only announced when clear information indicated an attack was going to take place. For now, severe indicating a threat of attack which realistically was always the case, would be enough. *No need to panic the population, the press, or most importantly the politicians just yet*, thought

Fraser. The meeting broke up with Bryant leaving to brief the Prime Minister on how to spin the Brown girl's story. But Fraser asked Jim Broad to stay behind.

Chapter 3

The Arab had stayed in Rome for three days, taking in the sights and relaxing in the sun while drinking black coffee outside the many pavement cafes. He always drank his coffee black when he travelled outside the Middle East. The Western coffee was not strong enough, and he missed the coffee of his homelands of Egypt, Palestine, and Iran. The coffee there would always be sipped with a side glass of water, and when he could get it some fruit, an orange or apple. His days spent in London had been good training on how to keep below the radar and fit in to the picture around him. People and waiters would pass him by, taking no notice of the clean-shaven well-dressed man of Middle East appearance with the Pilot Sunglasses, smart suit, and Italian leather shoes. After three days the Arab had booked out of his hotel. He took connecting flights first to Istanbul in Turkey then on to Damascus in Syria. There he had a meeting with his contacts in the Syrian intelligence to discuss a weapons supply across the border into Iraq, to be used by Islamic Jihad fighters. From there he took a plane to Iran. When he arrived at Imam Khomeini International Airport in Tehran the taxi from the airport took him north on the Tehran South Freeway to his villa in the district of Said Abad on the outskirts of the city. He opened some windows to let the air flow through. Although he had aircon, he had found that if he opened windows at the front and rear of the house the air flowing through created a natural wind tunnel making it more refreshing. He started up the motor to pull back the pool covering and went and changed, throwing his bag on to the bed, he could unpack later; he needed a swim first. After ten lengths of the pool, he went through his ritual of prayers to Allah kneeling on a mat on the grass beside the pool. When he was in the West his prayers were done in secret. He avoided any contact with the local Muslim communities or Mosques, which he knew were under constant surveillance by the intelligence agencies in those countries, why take chances when you did not need to. He dressed in fresh Arab clothing and ate a cold dinner alone. He made one phone call to let his masters know he was back and arranged to meet the next day.

The next morning brought a clear blue sky with a slight breeze that once more flowed through the house. He loved the mornings here best. It made him feel alive and alert, ready for whatever the day would bring. Today he dressed in light casual slacks and a white short-sleeved open neck shirt and pulled on his favourite Italian leather moccasins. Collecting his wallet, mobile phone, and keys to his white Mercedes, he left the villa and drove the car east towards the centre of Tehran. Traffic was busy even for the late morning, but he had given himself plenty of time to arrive early for meetings, taking that time to check the area and your surroundings for enemy surveillance. In the centre of Iran there should be no enemy surveillance, but he had been fighting his enemies far too long to take chances. The CIA and Mossad were more than capable and could operate anywhere in the world where they believed danger to come from. He parked in a shopping centre multi-storey car park in the Panzdah e Khordad city centre area and made his way on foot through the centre entering and leaving some of the shops but not buying anything until a newsagents, where he bought the Tehran Times. By the time he had circled the café twice, the two men he had come to meet were already sitting outside drinking their coffee. The café was on the edge of the city's famous Grand Bazaar, and hundreds of people were milling around the shops and stalls, making it easy to get lost in a crowd, or hard to spot someone in the crowd; so the café location had both its good points and bad. As he approached he could see at least four bodyguards, two sitting at one of the tables close to his contacts and two standing a short distance away. None of the four made any attempt to conceal who they were. They were here to protect their masters, not act as secret agents.

'Good morning gentlemen how are we today?'

It always amazed the two men that the Arab would always be in his in Western mode from his clothing to his everyday language and greeting.

'Good morning my friend and may Allah be with you.'

The Arab noticed two things, first, that General Malek Hasheem Khomeini greeted him in English, and second, apart from the Islamic blessing, was that he called him friend but no name. The two men stood, and they both kissed him on the cheeks three times in the Arab way. Both men were also dressed in the Western style, the General was taller at over six foot at least six inches taller than the man standing beside him who stood at five foot seven. According to the files in Mossad HQ in Tel Aviv he was Ibrahim Shallah, he was medium build but muscular, clean shaven with a slight scar under his lower lip which had been the closest he had come to an IDF bullet in the war against the Israeli Defence Forces in Gaza; he was the current leader of the PIJ. All three sat and ordered more of the strong coffee the café was famous for, with a side order of fresh water and some oranges for the sweetness. The reason they had met in a café and not in an office somewhere was at the request of the Arab. He did not trust meeting in government office buildings. Enemy intelligence agencies would always start with the offices of the States they were targeting, both for surveillance and the identification and recruitment of agents. For anyone watching, they would appear to be three businessmen discussing making money over a cup of coffee, rather than planning terrorist operations around the world. The General, even though he was dressed in civilian clothes, always had difficulty passing himself off as someone ordinary as he sat and stood in the fashion of a trained military man, ramrod straight. He also looked fierce with a heavy dark moustache and jet-black hair and with eyes to match he looked dangerous, not the kind of man you would pick a fight with. He was also on the files in King Saul Boulevard in Tel Aviv where Mossad records stated he was currently the Commander of the Clandestine Department of the Islamic Quads Force. He kept out of the media that so many of the Guards Generals were happy to be seen in and considered his job to be a secret one and always tried to live his life that way. With the coffee and oranges on the table they started to talk in general terms at first, both men inquiring how things went in Spain and how was the Arab's travels. The conversation business like, and matter of fact.

'You had a successful trip, making great press for our cause around the world,' said the PIJ leader.

'Yes, successful. The martyr will be in the arms of Allah now and the Western devils wondering what has happened,' replied Abdullah.

'Did you have any problems with your passports?' asked the General.

Iran had supplied the documents, training, and money for the Barcelona operation. The Western powers knew that the Iranian government supported many terrorist organisations with money, weapons, and training. Iran had become one of their main targets for surveillance and intelligence operations for that very reason.

'No problem at all. Having a Spanish passport, they just flagged me through. I felt comfortable just moving about their security which was very lax, even in a large city like Barcelona. They are not prepared for us.'

'I'm not so sure that will not be the situation in the future.' said the General, 'they'll be more prepared .'

'Abdullah, now that you are back, the General would like your help in something he has already set in motion.'

'How can I help, General?'

'My country, as you know, fully supports your actions in Gaza against Israel and throughout the world. We also support the Jihad as Israel is our enemy as it is yours. We can continue to carry out these smaller operations resulting in many deaths of the infidel. But, we feel, sometimes we must really hit them hard and make them listen. Since 9/11 the Western powers have become used to and accepting these small operations despite there being two wars in Iraq and Afghanistan. All we have really succeeded in doing is to bring down their wrath on those countries and increase the money they now pour into their security agencies which now direct their considerable attention and power towards ourselves. We need them to utterly understand that we will not be defeated, and we will bring the fight to their doorstep, not just the small villages of Iraq and Afghanistan, although we will still fight them there as well. We believe that 9/11 was such a great success that we must now follow the example of that success and move to a higher level of bringing the Jihad to their doorstep.'

The world knew the story of 9/11 when al-Qaeda terrorists had flown passenger jets into the Twin Towers in New York and the Pentagon Building killing over three thousand people.

'Your operation in Barcelona was just such a step but now we should move it up, move it forward.'

Abdullah began to feel a little of the intensity the General was trying to portray.

'Move it up?'

Now it was the turn of the PIJ leader to speak.

'My brother you must understand, Allah has a plan for you. There are other soldiers already on the move, your task will be to help them bring that plan to the Devil's door in London.

We cannot tell you everything now, but in the next few days I want you to visit our training camp where we train our European converts to the cause and chose for yourself soldiers of the Jihad who will aid you in this mission. When you've done that we will meet again. The Commander of the Camp has been told you will be coming and to give you everything you need.'

Abdullah knew the training camp the leader referred to. It was the same training camp where he had spotted a very committed woman from England named Margaret Brown. The Arab finished his coffee.

'Goodbye gentlemen until we meet again.'

'Inshallah,' said the General using the Arab word for 'if Allah wills it'.

Chapter 4

Jim Broad had filled his coffee cup and remained sitting at the conference table. Broad always respected the office of 'C' the head of MI6, so when Sir Ian Fraser sat opposite him, he would refer to him in one of three ways, Sir Ian, Sir, or Boss.

'Jim, we have a little problem which I think your SG9 team might be able to help us with.'

Broad sipped his coffee and waited for the chief to explain more. He knew if his Black Ops SG9 team were to be used it wouldn't be a little problem.

'I received a secure phone call this morning from Tel Aviv, to be precise Kurt Shimon himself.'

Broad knew who Kurt Shimon was and of his legendary Kidon teams and their operations around the world.

'As a heads-up he tells me they have an ongoing operation against an Iranian and Hezbollah outfit which may involve some sort of explosive device moving from Tehran towards Europe possibly even London. Now their people are following a Quds Colonel with his Hezbollah bodyguards to Malta. The problem is they do not think this Malta team have the full components yet, and the whole device won't be brought together until it reaches its final destination, which as I say could be London. They don't want to jump on these people in Malta too soon, when they might not have anything on them letting anyone else get away.'

Broad was not happy where this was going.

'So, tell me, why are they telling us this exactly?'

Sir Ian smiled. He could always rely on Jim Broad to hold him to account, the one thing Broad was not was anybody's *yes man* and Fraser respected that.

'I think three reasons Jubilee Centre Jim. The first is they have seen how we dealt with the Islamic group in Manchester, the Israelis respect that sort of action. The second is they're worried that this group might slip through their fingers and end up in London blowing up half the city when they had them under control for a short period, and third, I think they know we already have an experienced asset in Malta.'

Broad could understand the logic of the first two.

'David Reece, he lives in Malta?'

'Exactly Jim, he lives there, he knows the ground so to speak, and he is our asset, fully equipped to get a handle on things and report back what's happening. Not only that, but he can also take action if necessary.'

'What information have Mossad provided; do we have the full picture?'

'Mossad believe the Iranian Colonel arriving in Malta either has access to or is in the process of moving a small amount of plutonium which has been manufactured in Iran. He has a small crew of Hezbollah minders with him, and they're arriving on an Iranian merchant container ship which will dock in Valletta tomorrow night. Ships out of Iran are all well monitored since the Americans pushed up their sanctions because of the Iranian nuclear activity. Mossad were able to link into this coverage once they had some intelligence about the movements of this Colonel. They believe he is just moving the plutonium for a handover to another team who will continue with the operation to its conclusion. The Americans will use their satellite coverage wherever they can help. All we can do for now until we know much more, is get involved, so that we have the right information moving forward. Then we can better decide what we do next. That's why we need to get Reece close to the Mossad team, so that we have timely information, and we can decide what's in our best interests, not just those of the Israelis and Americans.'

'Why don't Mossad just bump off this Colonel, they did so in Malta once before?'

'They don't have enough information as to the full plans of the Iranian government and this Colonel. He is also being protected by at least four Hezbollah terrorists, making a shoot-out in downtown Malta out of the question. We need more information, Jim. The Prime Minister out of respect for our links with Malta, will, if necessary, let the Maltese government know if we need to move forward to a kill scenario. For the moment, our job is to gather information and identify more of this team and then as a last resort and only if necessary, move on them.'

'So, what do I tell Reece?'

'Just what we've been talking about, that there is an ongoing Mossad operation in Malta, and he might be of help to them. I know you're worried about us exposing one of our secret assets, but if a device is heading for London, we need our people in there, making decisions on our behalf. In addition, I'm sending Matthew Simons, he is on his way to Heathrow now to catch the next available plane to Malta, with his Middle East knowledge and language expertise he'll back-up Mister Reece in whatever way he can.'

'Is he ground operationally trained?'

'He's done all the firearms, surveillance, and anti-ambush training as far as a desk officer can be trained, no on the ground experience, but his brain and what he has in it will compensate for any deficiencies.'

'I hope so. Hezbollah are a dangerous outfit to come up against in the best of times. So, what you're saying boss is that this is now an official SG9 operation, and I have control?'

'I am indeed Jim, it's over to you and your boy. Simons has been told to contact Reece and brief him on what we know. Contact Reece and let him know he is on his way and give him the details of the Mossad people so he can link up with them that's where we will start.'

Broad drank the rest of his coffee and stood to leave.

'I'll get back to my office and get things rolling and keep you updated.'

'Thank you, Jim.'

The rain outside had stopped, and a weak sun had started to break through the clouds as Broad got into the back of his car.

'Where to, sir?' asked his driver.

At first Jim Broad was deep in thought and had not heard the question, then replied when the driver asked the same question again.

'The office please, Brian.'

The office of SG9 the most secret unit of MI6 also known as the Department was a non-descript building inside the perimeter of London City airport. As the car moved out of the car park Brian could see in his rear-view mirror that his boss was lost in deep thought and there would be little or no conversation during this journey.

Chapter 5

David Reece turned in the bed and looked at the face of Mary McAuley as she lay with eyes closed breathing slowly and quietly. The morning sun was shining through the linen curtains bringing a new day into the room and their lives. Mary slowly opened her dark brown eyes and she smiled at the face of the man lying beside her.

'Good morning sleepyhead,' said Reece.

'Good morning, have you been watching me long?'

'Long enough to realise how really beautiful you are when you're sleeping.'

Mary sat up, the thin sheet falling away to reveal her naked body. Reece turned on his back placing his arms behind his head. Reece was also naked, and Mary thought how strong he was sleeping or awake, but she didn't tell him that. She could see the five-inch ragged white scar on his right shoulder where the splinters from a bullet had entered his body. He had told her some of the story, how he had been involved in a shoot-out with an IRA gunman. He never complained about it, even though she knew he was in pain in those times when the metal moved in his shoulder, then he would let out a small groan or stretch his arm for some relief. If it were bad, he would take some pain relief tablets and the pain would soon settle down. She rolled over and sat astride him, his manhood now between her legs. Looking down at him she could see his clear blue eyes which always seemed to get darker when they made love. His hands held her hips and she could feel the firmness as he entered her, as their bodies now moved in sequence both looking into each other's eyes, no words being said.

The buzzing of his smartphone interrupted the moment. They both tried to ignore it, but it continued breaking into their thoughts. Mary stopped first and turning off him lay flat on her back.

'You're going to have to answer that.'

Reece was already reaching for the phone beside the bed, his mood in the moment broken. Whoever was calling at this time of the day better have a very good reason. When he answered the voice of his boss made him sit up and pull the sheet around him.

'David, I'm glad I caught you. I hope I didn't disturb you at anything?' said Broad.

Not for the first time Reece felt his boss had cameras watching his every move.

'No, just about to have breakfast. What's up?'

'Good, are you still in your home location?'

Reece noticed his boss was being secure with his words, not using the word 'Malta' meant he was being extra careful, even though the phone Reece was using had a secure encryption. Broad was obviously worried in case someone was listening to their conversation.

'Yes, I'm still at home.'

'We have a situation which might need your skills, at the very least an on-the-spot assessment, that's why I'm calling you. Our Israeli friends are in your city and running a little show that could have end repercussions for us at home. I want you to link up with them today.'

Again, Reece noted how his boss had told him that Mossad were working an operation in Valletta without specifically saying so. He knew Broad was old-fashioned when it came to talking over the phone even encrypted ones.

'I'm sending you Matthew Simons this afternoon and he'll be able to help you with the connection to our friends and bring you up to date. I'll send you a name and where they're staying. This person will be expecting you this evening and will be able to tell you what they know. You have my number call me if you need anything.'

The call ended without goodbyes.

Mary had sat up. Pulling the sheets around her, watching Reece throughout the call and noticed how his expression had changed from relaxed to one of deep thought as he put the phone back down on the bedside table.

'Work?'

'Yes, and it's come to visit.'

'What do you mean?'

'I have to pick one of our people up from the airport this evening. That was the boss, he's sending me the details.'

Right on cue his phone buzzed on the table. Reece read the message.

'It looks like our little holiday is over for now and we might have a guest staying over tonight. Let us go for a walk and some breakfast with a strong coffee and I'll explain what I know.'

Even though this woman had at one time been an agent in the IRA working for Reece and now they were lovers, there was only so much he could tell her. Need-to-know was always the way of secret organisations and now, she didn't need to know. He knew she would understand even though she'd asked him to leave that world behind. He always remembered one of his instructors when he was on a course with MI5 telling the class of agent handlers, 'The thing about keeping secrets, it's a lot easier if you don't know them in the first place. It's a need-to-know business.'

After they'd worked together in Manchester saving the life of the British Prime Minister in the process, she still felt she was an outsider in that part of his world, and she didn't like it, she felt there was that one part of him he would always have to keep hidden from her.

'OK, give me fifteen minutes to pull something on and brighten up my face.'

'There's nothing wrong with your face, or your body for that matter. Maybe we can pick up later where we were before that call rudely interrupted us.' He smiled.

They walked hand in hand along the promenade of the Qawra seafront to his favourite little café on the headland overlooking the Mediterranean Sea as it splashed over the rocks of St Paul's Bay. The early December sun was up and although there was a small breeze it was warm enough for the T-shirts and shorts they both wore.

With the coffee and croissants ordered, they sat looking out at the view. Reece had selected Malta and this special place to retire to after the danger of his days in the Special Branch of the RUC police force in Northern Ireland. That was before Jim Broad had caught up with him and invited him to come work for him at SG9. Reece had weighed up his options to retire at the young age of thirty-seven or work a little longer doing the job he loved and the one he knew he was good at. When he had told Broad that he intended to live in Malta, he had no problem with him living there as it was only about three hours flying time to London and the same for many of the main cities in the Middle East and Europe where Reece would be operating.

'Can you tell me what's happening,' she asked.

Reece knew the question would come and he was prepared for it.

'There's not much to tell now, London are sending a guy I know who will tell me more. I must pick him up at the airport this afternoon and then we are going to meet with some people in Valletta. Now you know as much as I do. At least the work for now is here in Malta. You can be sure I'm not happy having to work in my own back yard.'

'If I know your boss that won't last long. You will be on the move wherever it takes you.'

He could see she was already worried. Anything involving his work with the prospect of them being apart hurt her and he knew this. Her eyes avoided his gaze instead she looked at the waves crashing over the rocks at the entrance to the bay.

'Well, I'll keep the bed warm for when you get back.'

'That would be nice, but you better make up the spare. I think we'll have a guest to stay. As for keeping the bed warm, let's walk back slowly and see if it needs warming up now.'

'Calm down big boy, let me finish my breakfast first.' She laughed.

Chapter 6

The Islamic Jihad training camp was a good two-hour drive west of the Iranian Capital. After leaving the motorway, his drive continued along a dirty, dusty, bumpy track into the mountains through two small villages. The Arab enjoyed the drive in the open backed Discovery Jeep he used for such journeys. The wind in his face and hair was better than any car's air conditioning system, and he felt at one with the land around him which always reminded him of his Gaza homeland. As he went through the mountain villages, he could see the spotters in doorways, and some looking after the sheep in the fields. He knew all of them had been supplied with smartphones which they would be using to announce his journey as he got closer to the camp.

The camp had originally been a base for the Iranian Republican Guards Desert Warfare teams and covered two square miles, it had then been handed over to the various Islamic Jihad groups to help them with a location where, they could train their best recruits. Like any camp in the desert, the Portacabin huts and tents were mixed with a few concrete one-story buildings, everything the same sandy colour; the whole camp was surrounded by a fifteen-foot wire fence topped with razor wire. The Arab had trained there himself many years before where he was identified as someone special. He had his medical background, and he was clear why he had joined the cause, and why the West was the real enemy of Islam. His instructors noted how he not only picked up the skills of an exceptional assassin but also how he was able to talk to others, bringing them around to his theology and his plans for the future. He had taken two sharp bends in the road and when he came around the second, he could see the camp, just off the road to his left. He turned down the driveway to the entrance approaching the security barrier, where two men in desert fatigues and armed with Kalashnikov AK47 automatic rifles provided the security that had to be passed by anyone wanting access to the camp. He told the guard his name and that the commandant was expecting him. A quick check by radio and the guard told him he was to go to the first concrete building on the right where someone would meet him, and the barrier was lifted. As he drove through the entrance gate, some memories of his own training days came flooding back. At first, he remembered how the training was completely unexpected. The first few days were filled with how to keep clean in the camp, and how to make a bed properly military style. The recruits then filled out forms and were thoroughly questioned on their backgrounds and their reason for being there. It was nearly a week before they were given weapons to strip down and clean, before a basic firing test to start with, just to see how accurate they were. Evenings were always filled with prayers and religious instruction using the Quran. It was always emphasised they were the soldiers of the Jihad, the Holy War. They washed their own pots, pans, and plates, even though there was a kitchen separate from the recruits, they did their own cooking, cleaning up after they had eaten.

As he parked in front of the first building on the right standing outside, with a big smile on his face, was Kalil who had been the base commander when he had trained here and still in charge. He stood around five foot eight, with broad shoulders a large nose above a thick black moustache with his standard black beret placed over his short black hair almost covering his dark brown eyes. His smile of welcome told the Arab all he needed to know; he was glad to see him. He would always remember Kalil as a strict commander but who had now turned into a friend.

As he got out of the Jeep Kalil embraced him and kissed him on the cheeks.

'As-Salaam-Alaikum.'

'Wa-Alaikum As-salaam,' replied the Arab.

Kalil stood back and looked the Arab up and down.

'They have been feeding you too much my friend.' He laughed 'they told us you were coming. Let us go inside, I have some of your favourite coffee ready.'

'That would be wonderful I'm only beginning to remember how hot it can be under your blue skies. Why is it so quiet?'

At almost the same time he asked his question he could hear a loud prolonged burst of gunfire which to his trained ear was that of AK47 rifles on fully automatic.

'As you can see Abdullah our firing ranges are still busy,' replied Kalil.

The Arab remembered back to his own weapon training on the same firing range at the other end of the camp. Many hours of weapon familiarity and use until he could lift any gun, fire it quickly and accurately; then break the weapon down into its working parts to clean and oil them for future use. As he was always told by the instructors a clean weapon is a good weapon.

'So that's where everyone is. By the sound of things, you are busy Kalil. I hope you're not wasting too much ammunition?'

'Don't worry my friend, just enough to get the job done as we always told you. Since your day we have split the camp into different training categories, weapons, explosives, religious teaching, and now how to work with nuclear weapons.'

'Nuclear?'

'Yes, the Ayatollahs are pushing ahead with the whole nuclear plan, so they want our fighters to know how to use it. We have a few young jihadis learning daily from two of our scientists who come down from the city. Now come in and tell me how I can help you.'

Entering the large ground floor of the building he noticed nothing much had changed since his own training days here. The walls which had been painted white a long time ago were now a dusty grey colour. Many posters of the Ayatollah adorned the walls, and they showed their age. There were two wooden chairs behind a desk on which stood a laptop and a printer. The two large windows were closed, each were fitted with air conditioning units that were circulating cool air around the office. He knew there were three rooms at the rear, a toilet, a briefing room which could seat around twenty people and a large cell block, which on occasion had been used to detain traitors to the Jihad.

Near one of the windows was a large couch and two large leather chairs. On the coffee table in front of the couch was a large coffee pot with two small cups some milk and a bowl of sugar.

'Come Abdullah take a seat; the coffee is ready. When our lookouts reported you were on your way, I warmed the water.'

The Arab sat in one of the leather chairs facing towards the window. Kalil poured the strong black coffee and went to a small fridge beside the desk to bring back a bottle of cold water. The Arab took the offered coffee cup and poured a little water into the coffee taking away some of the bitterness from the Arabian beans.

'Just as I remember it, so strong you could stand up in it.' He laughed.

Kalil added a little water to his own cup then a little milk.

'I have become fond of the sweetness the milk gives it. Now to business how can we help you? Tehran did not tell us anything, only that you would be coming, and we are to provide you with whatever you need, no questions asked. All I can think is that it must be very important if it is to involve the Arab the man we call 'mu'alim' which means both craftsman and teacher, so which one are you today my friend the craftsman or the teacher or maybe both?'

Abdullah sipped his coffee which was still a little bitter and a little hot so he would let it rest for a while.

'Your coffee is good as always my friend. I have been given a little job to do which requires someone to help me, someone of a particular kind. I am hoping you will have just such a person here, someone currently training for the Jihad with rough edges who needs a little smoothing by myself to be the help I need. It can be a man or woman, but they must be able to take orders and do what I say. They must also be intelligent and street smart, be able to smell trouble without seeing it, and capable of dealing with it.'

'You are right to come to me and I think we just might have one or two people who fit your requirements. I like to think all our people are special, but as you know some are more special than others. I have our top five people on file here and you can use the laptop to read up on them. I'm needed down at the firing range for an hour, so I'll leave you alone to read, and when I get back we can discuss what you want to do.'

'Wonderful my friend, but can you leave me a fresh pot of your wonderful coffee to help me concentrate?'

When Kalil left, the Arab started reading the files on the laptop screen. He took his time, each file gave a little of what he was looking for, but in the end and after two pots of coffee, there were two separate piles of paper he had printed from the computer. He had been especially interested in where the people on file had come from; their age, their appearance, their special skills if they had any. He was looking for something the instructors hadn't picked up on, that something that made them special, and looking at a computer screen would only tell the basic story. He worked on the files one by one making notes as he went along. Two hours later he had two possible students; for that would be what they would now become, no matter what they had learned at the camp. If he selected either or both, he was the Teacher, and they would be his students, his apprentices, now he would need to see them and speak with them for himself.

When Kalil returned the Arab showed him the two files he had printed off.

'I need to speak to these two individually, are they still in the camp?'

'Ah, I see you pick the best fruit my friend. Yes, they are still here I will send for them now. Do you mind which one you see first?'

'No, just don't tell them who I am. When I speak with them, I'll do so alone. The less you know the better.'

Kalil nodded, then taking the radio from his belt he spoke a few words giving the instructions that the two students were to come to the office at once. Fifteen minutes later they could hear voices outside followed by a knock on the door.

Kalil stepped outside, then returned with a man dressed in desert clothing and desert boots. The Arab guessed he was in his mid-twenties and noticed how he walked across the room to where he sat watching him. The student was what would be described as of Middle Eastern appearance, with olive skin, dark brown eyes, and the beginnings of a beard, he was muscular at around five foot ten in height. So far exactly how he was described in the file on the desk in front of Abdullah.

'Please sit down,' said Abdullah as he pointed to the chair in front of the desk. Looking first through the file in front of him, the Arab then looked the man in the eyes.

'I've been reading your file and I know you speak English so please do. Do you know who I am?'

'No.'

Abdullah did not elaborate any further.

'It says in your file you originally come from London. Why are you here? I know the standard answers, but I want a truthful one. Why are you really here?'

The man across the table looked back into Abdullah's eyes and a slight smile appeared at the corner of his lips.

'Well...?' asked the Arab.

'I come from a strict Muslim family in Brixton and all my life white, mostly English and Irish men have asked me the same question. 'Why are you here?' This was even though I was born there, brought up as a child there, but just because I worshipped a different god and looked a different colour, they hated me, and I didn't even know them. I went to my local Mosque and, when I was older with some friends, I started to attend the

Finsbury Mosque, mainly because it had a reputation for the kind of worship to Allah that I thought I needed.'

'And did it?'

'For a time, but then I saw that the preaching of the holy book was pretty much the same as I had heard before. Then one day a Mullah came to speak. He came from Iran, he was in England illegally, and he talked of Jihad and the need for young men and women to be prepared to fight for the faith. The thing that struck me was that those present were not the usual men, but it appeared to me a select few, who had been observed and invited to this talk. He said something that made me think, he said it did not matter how we fought the Jihad in foreign wars and countries, or on the streets where we lived, but either now or one day soon we would have to fight for our God, our families, our people. I realised then that in my whole life I'd been going through the motions of being a good Muslim but without really committing myself to what that meant.'

'What do you believe now?'

'I decided that I had to be true to myself and Allah, and step forward instead of leaving it to someone else or to future generations. Now is the time of Jihad, of Holy War, and as the Mullah said that day, now is the time for action to get involved, no matter how small or big, you can get involved. Stop leaving it to others, and if you honestly believe now is the time, then step forward. So, I stepped forward with a few others that day and asked how. I'd never been involved with the police or as far as I'm aware I've never been under their surveillance, so I left my home and made my way to Iran, with an introduction from the Mullah to some people in Tehran and here I am.'

He had been leaning forward across the desk in the chair to help get his point to this man asking the questions. Now he sat back, to await the next question from this strange man who seemed to have an air of authority about him that he had never seen before.

'I see from your file you've excelled in firearm training and are quite the marksman.'

'Yes, I seem to enjoy that the best, especially the rifle. Maybe, I think, it's because it can do more damage and I can imagine the damage I can inflict on those people who not only cursed me for the colour of my skin but cursed the God I serve.'

The Arab could see a flash of anger in the student's eyes as he spoke these last words.

'It's easy to imagine killing another, but a far different thing to do so. Do you really believe you could do it? Men, women, children, Christian, non-believers wherever you find them.'

The student knew from the question and the way it was asked that this man had killed in the name of Jihad and that he knew how to kill.

'I do not hate non-believers. I'm sorry for them; they do not know Allah the Holy One as I do. That is not their fault. But they have been killing my people in the name of their God and will continue to do so unless they are stopped. They have the opportunity to convert but if they ignore that opportunity then according to the Holy Word they must die, and if I am to be the instrument of Allah, then I believe I could do it.'

'So, you want to die for Allah?'

'I'd rather fight for him, but if it's the wish of my God that I should die, if that is his purpose, then so be it I will die.'

The Arab had seen and heard enough.

'When you came in, I asked if you knew who I was. Now, do you have any questions for me?'

'No, I've answered your questions and although I've not seen you here in the camp before I believe you are here for a reason, a purpose, and if I'm to learn who you are or what that purpose is, you will tell me if I need to know.'

This was the answer the Arab was hoping for, and the file on the desk had indicated he had made the right choice when asking that the student should be brought to the office.

'Your name in your file is Mohammad Latif is that correct, your true name?'

'Yes, that is the one given to me by my father when I was born and the one on the passport I travelled with through Turkey and to Tehran. I did not want to risk being stopped with a false passport.'

'Where do your family think you are now?'

'When I went to the London School of Economics I lost touch with my family, living in student accommodation. When I finished my degree, it was then I decided to come here. As far as I know no one knows I'm here.'

'You might think that my friend, but the British Secret Service MI6, will notice your passport shows you've left the country flying to Turkey and you've not returned. Your passport will be highlighted for such a return where you would be detained for questioning. They may even be making enquiries about you as we speak, but they'll soon let it drop as you do not have a background that has been brought to their attention before, which is good. From this day on I will be your teacher and you will know me as such, that will be my name to you. Tomorrow you will leave here, and you will be brought to accommodation in Tehran where we will talk further. You will not speak of this meeting to anyone. Under my teaching and command, you will take part in a special mission for Allah. You will be given a new identity and passport and the skills you've been training for will be put to good use soon. Do you understand all this?'

Mohammad nodded, then stood then for some reason, he felt he should bow slightly before leaving the office.

The door to the office opened once more, this time it was Kalil.

'Are you ready for the girl?'

'Give me five minutes then send her in.'

'Was he what you are looking for?'

The Arab knew Kalil couldn't help himself asking, even though he would know it was wrong to do so.

'He will be leaving you tomorrow and he cannot talk about what we discussed so do not ask him my friend. After I've spoken to this woman we will have another cup of coffee and I'll tell you what you need to know - no more no less. This you understand…. yes?'

Kalil smiled. He knew he had just been rebuked in the nicest way for asking questions when he should have listened instead of speaking. He turned and went outside to find the next student.

When she entered the office, the Arab realised the file on the table in front of him did not do her justice. Her photo showed eyes that were tired and wary of the world. Maybe because the photo was black and white the true deep darkness of her brown eyes did not show through. He knew from the file she was only twenty-five, but the world had treated her badly according to the written words, but he wanted to hear everything about her from her own lips. She wore the traditional headscarf of eastern Islamic women covering her hair and most of her face and when Abdullah invited her to sit and to remove the scarf, he could see the surprise in her eyes as she obeyed the command without protest. Islamic women were not used to being without headdress when in the company of a strange man, however since being at the camp she had begun to expect the unexpected and to obey commands.

Abdullah smiled a smile of understanding, and this seemed to reassure her as she smiled back. She removed the headscarf to let her lush dark brown hair fall to almost cover her face but not enough to cover the three-inch scar on her left cheek, Abdullah noticed both.

'Please relax, Shama, you are not in trouble, and even if you were, from what I've read in your file you could deal with any danger if you had too. Yes, I've read your file and I know a little about you, your past, and why you are here. But I would rather hear from your own lips the answer to my questions.'

'Who are you, and why should I answer any questions?' she replied sitting straight backed in the chair. He noticed how her breasts pressed outwardly upwards against the brown linen shirt.

Again, the Arab smiled and spoke softly.

'For now, please think of me as your teacher and just simply call me Teacher. This is not some interrogation test or exam for your training. As I said, all I want to know for now is, what is not in the file and the real you, so please relax and help me out if you can.'

Now the woman nodded her agreement.

'Thank you. Can we start with a little bit about your background? I know you are from Baghdad and your family sent you here for your protection. The file does not clearly state why you need protection, maybe you can explain?'

Abdullah knew by her hesitation that talking of her past might cause her pain, he waited, letting her take her time to let her tell her story her way.

'I know you speak your native Arabic, French, and English, so if you could answer in English that would be helpful.' Abdullah wanted to see how good her English was. He was surprised just how good when she began to speak.

'My father was a teacher of languages at Baghdad University. He taught me different languages for as long as I can remember, some I remembered better than others and this helped me when I applied to be a nurse at the city hospital.'

'You are only twenty-five so you must have worked hard?'

'Another thing my parents taught me; you can be whatever you want to be if you work hard enough. I studied clinical medicine dealing with everyday illness and I loved my work.'

'And you had to give it all up because you killed a man?'

'I killed an animal.' She spat out the words with the flash of hate mixed with anger in her eyes.

'Please forgive me but I need to know why. All it says in your file is that you killed a man, so you had to escape Baghdad. What really happened?'

He waited as she took her time to answer, she moved from side to side in the chair and stared at the floor, before lifting her head to look him in the eyes. She began to speak slowly at first, getting faster the more her memory came back to her.

'As I said I was a nurse in the hospital, and I dealt with many kinds of injury. I had been seeing one of the junior doctors for a few months. With Asher, it was nothing serious, but I liked him, he was kind and my parents approved. Unknown to me he had been secretly treating injured Hezbollah coming back from Syria. I did not know he was under surveillance by the security police, not until one day they came to arrest him at the hospital. The police inspector leading the arrest was a well-known brute. We had treated many of his poor victims, from beatings to knife wounds, inflicted by him in the cells at the central police station.'

'What was his name?'

'Kamil Burgah,' before continuing she licked her lips and took a deep breath as if there was a bad taste in her mouth.

'When he came to arrest my Asher, he beat him badly while his thugs held him up so he could punch him freely without Asher being able to defend himself. I tried to intervene, but Burgah slapped me on the face knocking me off my feet and before I could get to my feet, they had already taken him. When I went home, I told my parents what happened. My father told me not to get involved, as he knew of this Burgah, and how dangerous he could be. I was not happy, so I decided the next day I would go to the station and ask about Asher.'

'You disobeyed your parents,' the Arab was interested to hear how far she would go to disobey a direct order.

'I know. I did not want to, but I thought it would do no harm to go to the station and ask about Asher; I had feelings for him, I cared for him.'

'What happened next?'

'Burgah took me to his office. The bastard was smiling when he told me that unfortunately Asher had been shot dead while trying to escape. My head was spinning, I couldn't believe it, I did not believe it. He just sat there smiling not caring, then he came around the desk and locked the door to the office. He told me his men knew not to disturb him when his door was locked. He looked at me as if I were a piece of juicy meat he wanted to eat. He asked me why I cared about this Asher, the traitor to Iraq. Was it because he was good in bed, and did my parents know I was a whore who slept around? Now I was too angry for words, I stood and tried to slap him across the face, but he grabbed my hand and forced me backwards across his desk. He was a big man overweight, and his breath smelt of stale tobacco. He pushed his full weight down on me and when I fell across the desk my hand found a long letter opener. I lifted it and tried to stab him, but he grabbed my hand and twisted it behind my back turning me around, and pushing me face down into the desk, he leant over me, and I could feel his whole body pressing down on me.'

The Arab could see the pain in her eyes as she tried to continue. Once again he spoke softly.

'I know this memory is difficult for you, but you need to get it out, to tell me everything to cleanse your soul and spirit. I do not judge you.'

Again, she took a deep breath before speaking, looking around the room then at the files on the desk before letting her eyes rest on the face of the Arab. She wanted to get everything out into the open and for once in a long time for some reason she believed in this man in front of her. There was something about him she felt she could trust.

'I could feel him thrust his body against mine. I'd never been with a man before, but I knew what he was doing. To put it in simple terms, he was inside me raping me, and calling me bitch and whore as he did it. I closed my eyes and gritted my teeth trying to think of Asher, my family anything other than what was happening. Soon it was over, I heard him breathe deeply and speak the words, 'Yes, yes, you bitch yes.' But it was not over. As he stood, he sliced the sharp paper opener across my cheek. From being raped to feeling the pain and blood pour from my face I stood in shock. He threw the paper opener on the desk and told me to get out and if he ever saw me again, he would give me twice as bad, pass me around his men and mark the other cheek, as you would brand a cow. Then he made his mistake. He turned his back to me to unlock the door. He obviously thought that his little whore had had enough and would want out of there, but he was surprised when I said is that all you have big boy, can we do it face to face next time? The one thing about being a nurse that he should have remembered was that we know exactly where the human heart is in the body, no matter if it's a good or evil one. I moved in close to him and I could see his eyes light up with surprise at what he thought I was going to do with him, but they were even more surprised when I shoved the paper knife deep into his heart the blade all the way into the handle. He tried to cry out, but I held my hand over his mouth as he fell to the floor dead in seconds.'

'Why did you kill him? Why not report him?'

'Who would believe my word against him? He made me feel scared, dirty, and he could blame me for inciting him to rape me? I could have been stoned to death, and he would have made sure that is how a Sharia Court would have found it against me. I thought about this afterwards; but not at the time, the anger in me just burst, yet I felt totally under control and justified. Since then, I have thought about it …. I know he got a quicker, cleaner death than the one I would give him now. Being a nurse, I knew how to test myself for infection or pregnancy and I was clear of both.'

She had answered a question he had been thinking about.

As she told her story Abdullah watched her face closely. He could see the strain the memory was bringing to her. A tear settled at the side of her eyes.

'Let us stop there for a moment,' said Abdullah.

'Let us have some of Kalil's fine coffee, then we can continue in a few moments.'

All she could do was try to smile and nod her agreement.

'Just black and strong for me,' she said.

'The way I like it,' he said as he filled the two small cups.

He thought he would change the subject of the conversation for a little while. The hot sun outside had started to go down on the hills in the distant horizon and the room had more shadow and had cooled slightly.

'How long have you been in the camp?' he asked even though he knew the answer from her file.

'Three weeks.'

'And from what I've read you're a good student. Is there anything you enjoy more than any other in your training?'

As she sipped the hot coffee slowly, she lifted her eyes to look at him to answer.

'I enjoy it all, and I understand how each part fits together to get the best out of me. But if I was to say one thing I enjoy more than any other, it would be the comradeship, how I've found people like myself who want something different for ourselves, and if that means we must fight for it, to kill for it, to die for it, then I will be ready and more prepared for the future with what I'm learning here.'

The answer he heard was spoken with clarity and passion. These were exactly the things he was looking for in his students. He had heard enough to stop the interview there and then, but he wanted to hear the full story to be completely sure and to let her totally unburden herself to him so that she would feel a comradeship with him, as with no other.

'Can we get back to your journey, the one that has brought you here? What happened after you killed this bastard as you called him? How did you escape; you were in a police station in the middle of Baghdad after all, how did you get to here?'

There was that deep breath again before she started speaking. The wounds and memories still strong. He sat further back in his chair and watched her face once more taking the strain of thought.

'He was dead on the floor without a sound, but with a lot of blood - much of it over me. My mind seemed to be clear and calm possibly from my years of training and being told to slow down and concentrate when I dealt with people in pain or when they had died. I remembered he had told me he always locked his door when he was with people like me, and his staff knew not to disturb him. Even though, I knew I wouldn't have much time. Using tissues from his desk I wiped the blood off my dress, blouse, and hands as best I could, but the stain was still there, so I used a simple trick, I put my clothes on inside out. People don't look to see if you've dressed backwards and with the time I had it seemed the best thing to do.

I took his key and left, locking his door from the outside to give me more time. I walked through the building and straight home, and no one stopped me or seemed to notice. My parents were shocked and at first they wanted to go to the authorities and complain about Burgah and what he had done and the situation he had put me in, but my father eventually realised the danger we were all in if I stayed in Baghdad.'

'I can understand that. Apart from him being a policeman did he have other connections?'

'Connections?' She laughed 'You could say that. He was known throughout Baghdad as the jumper, as he moved seamlessly from one faction to another from Saddam's Ba'ath Party through his security police, to the Americans as an interpreter and torturer, to a job as the city's chief political hunter, and all along the way he made himself a small fortune.

He was hated by the people of the city, and that included his own police officers who were genuine law enforcers.'

'It sounds like you did the country a favour. Please, tell me more of how you've come to be here?'

'That's simple. My father's brother is a member of Katib Hezbollah in Iraq, so within the hour my uncle drove me in his Jeep, and using roads he knew, he smuggled me to a small town across the border, the people there brought me here. I'd told my uncle and my parents I wanted to be a soldier of Jihad. Now I'm here answering questions from a strange man.'

She sat back in her chair her story told or so she thought.

'What happened to your parents when the authorities came looking for you which I'm sure they did?'

'Yes, they came and took my parents in for questioning but all they could tell them was that they did not know where I was, which was the truth. As I said there was no love for Burgah, so they were released, and they've not been bothered since.'

The Arab was satisfied. He closed the file, stood, and slowly walked around the desk sitting on it in front of her. Looking down he could see up close that despite the white scar on her tanned skin she was indeed beautiful with eyes that could persuade many a man to do what she asked and that was exactly what the Arab would need from her.

'Thank you for taking the time to tell me your story it has been of great help to me. I may have a mission for you to undertake are you ready to do that without question?'

'Yes.'

'Good. This will be your last night here. Tomorrow Kalil will bring you to another location. I will be there. You will be given a new identity and from now on you will know me as Teacher. You will speak to no one about this do you understand?'

'Yes.'

'Good, until tomorrow then. When you leave please ask Kalil to come in.'

He watched her as she walked to the door and the way she moved brought stirrings of his own basic animal passion. Many Arab men would look at her with disgust because of their deep-seated religious beliefs, but Abdullah only saw a brave woman who would be useful in his fight against the real enemies - Israel and the West.

The Arab instructed Kalil to have both students brought to his villa for three the next day. He instructed him not to ask them any questions and would only tell him they were needed for a mission of great importance. One day soon he'll hear of it and know that he played a part in training his people well for the Jihad and Allah. They parted once more as friends and soldiers in the war to come.

Chapter 7

The main international airport in Malta is busy throughout the year, but especially busy at the height of the tourist season from July to the end of September when the temperature on the island can start to fall and some heavy rainstorms from Africa can bring the island to a halt.

When Reece had arrived at the airport, the sun was still warm and the clouds small and white. The arrivals area was still busy but not that busy, making it easy for Reece to pick out Matthew Simons as he came through the customs screens and into the exit area. Reece had sat in on some of Simons talks on the Middle East, its politics, wars, and terrorist organisations. He had a lot of time for Simons and respected the easy way he spoke to get his subject across, taking time after his talks to stay and answer any further questions from his class. Reece had been one of those who stayed and living in Malta not far from the North African coast, he had asked Simons specifically about the risk of terrorist attacks on the island. He had smiled when he replied that they were unlikely but not impossible. Islamic terrorist groups were always targeting the many holiday destinations frequented by British tourists who they considered soft targets for extreme large-scale violence such as the attack on the tourist beach and hotel in Tunisia in the tourist resort of Port El Kantaoui. Thirty-eight tourists, thirty of whom were British, were killed by one gunman. The one thing Reece knew from his life of fighting terrorism wherever he had worked was never to let your guard down and trust no one.

'Matthew how are you?' asked Reece.

'Hi David, it's great to see you. A bit flustered to tell you the truth. I've had little time to breathe since this morning. I was glad the flight took three and a half hours; it's given me time to capture my thoughts and read the files I have for you.'

'Well, let's get going, my car's outside. We can talk on the way to my place, and you can tell me all about why you're here and how I'm going to be involved. You know the boss he likes to surprise me.'

As they drove from the airport Simons told Reece the reason he was here and what London wanted Reece to do.

'I have the files on my laptop which we can download when we get to your place, but basically we will know a lot more when we meet up with our Israeli friends later.'

The sun was almost gone and with it the heat of the day.

'Have you been to Malta before?'

'No this is my first time. I believe it's a beautiful island.'

'If we get the time, I would love to show you around.'

'Time might be a problem, David. I googled Malta on the way over, so I know a little of the history, but if we get free of work, I would love to take you up on your offer and look over the place; it looks fascinating.'

'It is. I love the mixture of all the different Mediterranean cultures from the east to the west, but as usual work gets in the way.'

'Is Mary at your place?'

It did not surprise Reece that Simons knew about Mary. The operation they'd worked on in Manchester and the connection between her and Reece was well known in the top circles of MI6 and the Department.

'Yes, she's back at the villa. She only knows that I'm picking someone up but not who or why.'

Reece knew the need-to-know aspect of his work was always paramount to getting the job done and staying alive.

'I'm not worried about that David. In fact, I'm looking forward to meeting her. I believe she is a stunning beauty.' He smiled.

'She's my stunning beauty you remember that.' laughed Reece.

The rest of the drive was in silence as Reece concentrated on the traffic which was busier than usual for that time of day, and Simons continued to look out at the architecture as they drove, passing under the walls of Mdina, the Silent City to their left and the Dome of Mosta Church in the distance, on their right. Malta traffic still moved on the same side of the roads as in England, but some of the local population drove as if they were in the crowded streets of Rome or London, cutting each other up, always looking for the short cut and sounding their horn loudly if they had to overtake a slower driver. It took Reece another forty-five minutes before he was able to park outside the Villa Joseph in Qawra.

'I can see why you don't want to live in London, it's beautiful here,' said Simons as they entered the gardens of the villa.

'You should see it on a really sunny day.'

'Maybe I will one day.'

Mary was in the front room reading a book when they entered.

'Mary, I would like you to meet Matthew, a friend from the office,' said Reece.

'Pleased to meet you, Matthew. Did you have a good trip?'

Simons, for the moment, couldn't speak. He was transfixed by the woman in front of him.

'Ohhh…pleased to meet you. Yes, thank you it was quiet, no bumps.' He smiled.

'I haven't made any dinner as I don't know what you want to do, Joseph?'

Simons looked at Reece with his eyebrows raised in question.

'It's OK, Matthew. She likes to call me by my code name. In fact, she insists on it. No, sorry we only have time for a quick drink and a chat then we must go out again. I'm afraid you'll be eating alone tonight but I hope we'll be back in time for a nightcap.'

'No problem. Matthew come with me, and I'll show you your room.'

'David, where do you want me to set-up my laptop so you can get a look at what I've brought?'

'Over there on the dining table then go with Mary and I'll fix us a few drinks. What's your poison?'

'Scotch and ice if you have it?'

'No Scotch here, only the best Irish, Bushmills OK?'

'Perfect.'

Reece went to the kitchen to get the drinks while Simons left the laptop on the table and followed Mary with his bag to his room.

Two Bushmills later, while Mary continued her reading in the bedroom, Reece gave a breakdown of the issue ahead.

'So, basically London wants us to work with Mossad to keep an eye on this Iranian and a couple of Hezbollah thugs. Find out what they're up to and if necessary, bump them off if it gets too sticky?'

'Well, let's hope it doesn't get too sticky, I don't fancy shoot-outs no matter what the odds.'

'Tell me Matthew, with your knowledge of how these buggers work, what's your gut telling you? My experience is from your everyday Irish cowboy. These Arabs scare the hell out of me.'

'And so they should. They're not just Arabs, as you call them. They come from many groups, religions, and on the odd occasion single people who just hate the West and their false gods. To them, and they honestly believe this, anyone who does not worship the one true God Allah, are infidels; devils who need to be converted or killed. To tell you the truth, the West hasn't helped with its many years of interference in the Middle and Far East, Iraq, Afghanistan, Syria, Libya. Yes, you and I know some of the interference was needed, but much of it was a mistake, now the birds are coming home to roost. Just as you saw in Manchester, when the Islamic side was willing to work with the Irish side to get the job done and again with 9/11 in the States and 7th July in London, they've decided to take us on wherever they can. The gloves are off, and the West has had to take off theirs in response, resulting in the Black Ops organisations such as the Department and you. These people will never stop I'm afraid until they kill us all and get their own version of an Islamic world whatever that will be.'

'Or unless we kill them first. I know what you're saying. I've seen these people up close, and they don't want to talk, to negotiate, they're willing to kill themselves to get the job done. Let's get moving, you wait outside by the car, I'll just say goodbye to Mary. We can grab something to eat on the way, there is a pizza takeaway at the end of the road we can eat in the car.'

Chapter 8

They ate as Reece drove into Valletta, the evening traffic light on the coast road that took them past St Julian's Bay and skirting the Harbour at Sliema, around the Yacht Basin and on into the city itself. Simons watched the beauty of Malta unfold with so many different sights to see, he again had appreciated why Reece preferred to live here instead of London.

'Have you ever worked with Mossad before David?'

'Just on the periphery once. I don't know if you remember when Colonel Ghaddafi shipped the Provos tons of weapons in the eighties and one of the ships, the Eksund, was stopped by the French with one thousand AK47 rifles, over fifty ground to air missiles and two tonnes of Semtex?'

'Yes, I remember the one that didn't get away.'

'Correct, it was believed afterwards that two similar ships had already got through. The Eksund was being monitored by Mossad, and RUC Special Branch had been informed to expect another shipment of weapons and an increase in attacks because of that information. The French who have always been sympathetic to the Arabs and wanted more cheap oil from Ghaddafi jumped on the ship first, releasing those involved within a short time. Of course, the British, Israelis, and the Americans, who all knew about the ship, were unhappy to say the least. My part as a Special Branch officer was to deal with the aftermath of these weapons getting through resulting in hundreds of dead. I've always respected the fact that Mossad face the same enemies and dangers that we have and that was one occasion when they wanted us to get these bastards as much as we did.'

'Well, these bastards as you call them have something that is far more dangerous than all the weapons in those ships, so let's hope this time your connection with Mossad will be more successful.'

Reece knew his way through the one-way system through the centre of Valletta City. Soon they were pulling into the car park near the ancient city walls and the five-star Grand Excelsior Hotel.

'Well Matthew, it looks like Mossad have a bigger expense account than SG9.'

Reece knew something of the hotel. It was a five-star experience throughout with stunning views from the Tiki Bar and Restaurant overlooking the Marsamxett Harbour and the historic Fort Manoel, with the entrance to the harbour and the Mediterranean Sea in the distance. When Mary had first come to Malta with Reece they'd spent an amazing afternoon relaxing in the sun on the terrace after a wonderful lunch while drinking their second bottle of white wine.

Reece asked the receptionist to try the room of Mr Stressor and to tell him Mr Reece was waiting in reception for him. He waited while the receptionist called the room and she confirmed that Mister Stressor was on his way down.

They took a seat at a table in the large reception area and waited. Five minutes later one of the lift doors opened and a man and woman walked towards where Reece and Simons were sitting. Reece noticed by the way they dressed and walked that they fitted right into the type of client the hotel preferred; people with class, both were the appearance of good health itself, fit and tanned. The woman wore jewellery to complement the white linen dress with a single string of white pearls around her neck.

Both men stood as the man reached out his hand.

'Mister Reece?'

Reece shook the offered hand.

'It's David and this is Matthew.'

'Both Jewish names from the Bible,' said the woman 'and if it's first names I'm Anna and this is Palo.'

'Both names, not from the Bible,' smiled Reece.

'Please let's sit here. It will be quieter than the other areas of the hotel,' said Palo.

As they sat facing each other Reece thought how beautiful the woman was, and how if she was, as he had been told by Simons, a member of the famous Mossad Kidon teams, how deadly she could be.

It was the woman who took the lead.

'We all know something of why we are here. You know our background and we yours. It's why we are here that matters, basically because that's what our masters want us to do. As time is of importance I'll get right to the point. We know that a ship carrying an Iranian Colonel will dock in Malta tomorrow evening. Our masters want us to watch him and find out what he is up to for now, nothing more nothing less. At least that is our understanding. Do you feel that is correct?'

'That's our understanding too,' said Reece.

'I'm sorry we didn't ask if you wanted something to drink?' asked Palo.

Reece had been waiting. He knew the prices and if Mossad was footing the bill, he would be happy to have a drink.

'Thank you a Bushmills Whiskey on ice,' said Reece who knew the hotel was one of the few places on the island that served his favourite tipple.

'Same again,' said Simons.

Palo called a waiter and ordered the two whiskies and a bottle of Chardonnay Wine with two glasses.

'Tel Aviv was impressed with how you dealt with that threat in Manchester,' said Anna.

'It was a team job, and we lost a few friends.'

'I think the innocent people who walk the streets of this world don't realise we are at war every day,' said Palo.

'I'm inclined to agree with you there Palo,' said Matthew, 'and for every one of these terrorists we kill, two more pop up. It's going to be a long war. As we are only four will that be enough to cover what you want to do?'

'For now, Matthew, I think we will have enough. If we are working together, I expect our masters will want daily updates. I'm sure if we need to increase what we need; like you, we can get extra resources here quickly.' Again, it was the woman who spoke, taking the lead in the conversation.

Reece had something to add to the discussion.

'The one thing we found in Northern Ireland; the more we killed the experienced guys, then those who stepped into the dead men's shoes were not of the same calibre, making it easier for us to close them down when they tried to carry out their operations. Cut the head off the snake and the body dies.'

'There's a difference David,' said Anna, 'the Irish terrorist knows there is a risk of being caught or killed but he always hopes to escape. The people we will be dealing with here and some of those you dealt with in Manchester do not care. To them it is an honour to die as a martyr for Allah. They don't worry about being caught which makes them more difficult to deal with.'

The waiter interrupted the conversation when he arrived with the drinks.

Reece raised his glass, 'Cheers.'

Both Israelis raised their glasses and spoke in unison. 'L'Chaim, to Life.'

'Do you have much information of this Colonel and what he is up to, and why he is coming here?' asked Reece.

Again, it was Anna who spoke.

'Not much more than you have already. I understand our boss has been in touch with your boss and a full file on Colonel Ali Shafi of the Quads Unit of the Iranian Republican Guard is available to us all. He is the head of the Security at one of their nuclear development sites. Another one that they deny having. From our information he is on his way here on an Iranian cargo ship; carrying, we believe, a small amount of plutonium for what purpose we are unsure. We do not know if he is going to use it himself or give it to or sell it to someone else. Malta has no strategic attraction or purpose for Iran so we believe he may pass the plutonium on to someone here, or the ship with him and his package will sail further to another port. In the meantime, it's our job to observe and report.'

Reece swirled the ice cubes around the glass. Looking at both Mossad agents he took another sip of the whiskey before he spoke.

'I presume you have all we need for tomorrow. Up-to-date photos of our target. The details of the ship, when it will arrive, and where it will dock in Valletta, it's a big harbour.'

This time Palo answered.

'Yes David, we have all those answers. The ship is expected around 6 p.m. Can I suggest we exchange phone numbers to keep in touch and we can send you all those details? Like you, no doubt, we all have encrypted phones so the details being passed won't interfere with our security or yours. We have contacted one of our people who lives on the island, and they've already supplied us with two cars and radio equipment we can use. They will also supply us with the details of a building close to where the ship will dock. A building we can observe safely from. We understand that as you live here in Malta you may know your way around fairly well, so that will be of great help if we need to follow this man.'

'I don't know every nook and cranny, but I have a basic knowledge of Malta. Do you have maps?'

'Yes, we have good maps,' replied Palo, 'the type used by tourists as we find they highlight important places of interest better.'

'Good, have you weapons?' Reece asked.

'From tomorrow we will have them,' answered Anna.

'Good. I understand that this Colonel will have some Hezbollah minders with him and if things go tits up we need to be able to get out of trouble,' said Reece.

'Tits up?' asked Anna with an inquisitive smile.

'It means if things start to go wrong or there's danger, we will also be armed,' said Reece.

'What are the local security forces and police like, are they inclined to get in the way?' asked Anna.

'The biggest danger is the police.' said Reece, 'It's not a big island so they don't miss much, and as we are out of the tourist season their problems are few leaving them free to catch-up on their own holidays and paperwork. I do not see them as a problem. There is a small naval unit based here in Valletta which concentrates more on smuggling from Africa and Sicily; again, this should not be a problem. There is a small military unit based inland. They do a lot of training in the other European countries with a small contingent on ceremonial duties. Again, with this being out of the tourist season, this is only on a couple of occasions. All have access to weapons, but in all my time here, I've never heard of a single shooting. Unless we are stupid enough to bring attention to ourselves, we should have no problems.'

'What if we have to use our weapons?' asked Palo.

'Let's hope that won't be necessary, but my training, and I am sure your training, is to shoot to kill when threatened. When I was undercover in Northern Ireland, two British soldiers in civilian dress accidentally drove their car into a place where a republican funeral was taking place; both were armed but tried to fire their guns in the air to keep the crowd back. Unfortunately, this did not work, they were overwhelmed, captured, beaten, and shot dead. I saw the whole thing afterwards as it was videoed from an army helicopter above the scene. It was not something I'll ever forget. After that any of us working that war made a promise to ourselves that if we were in a similar situation we would shoot to kill. We would rather face a twelve-man jury of our peers than be carried by six men to our grave.'

'I couldn't agree more David,' said Anna.

'Would you like another drink?' asked Palo.

Reece downed what was left in his glass.

'No thank you. I think we should all get an early night; we could have a few busy days ahead of us. Excellent, let us meet back here tomorrow at 3 p.m. and work from there. For tonight we will update London as I'm sure you will do the same for Tel Aviv.'

Standing they all shook hands.

'Until tomorrow then,' said Anna.

'Until tomorrow,' said Reece.

As they walked back to the car Reece could only think about the female Mossad agent and how her body moved in that white dress showing every curve when the slight breeze had caught it as she'd walked from the lift towards him. He loved Mary but he knew like all women she would want to know what the other women in your life looked like and how you felt about them. He would have to lie about Anna's beauty, but then he was good at lying.

Mary was still up when they got back. Simons went to his room to update London on the meeting with the Mossad agents, while Mary poured them all a glass of red wine.

At this time of year when the sun went down it could be cold, especially when you lived in a house on the shore of the Mediterranean Sea, when the winter storms could bring a strong wind directly off the top of the waves onto the shore.

'How did your meeting go?'

'It went OK, but I think it will mean more work for a few days for myself and Matthew so you might be on your own for a while.'

'What's it all about Joseph. Will you be in danger?'

'I can't tell you too much, the less you know about these things the better, but this I can tell you, it's basically a watching job. We will be working with other people to gather information for our bosses to keep them happy.'

'These other people you will be working with. Does it include a woman?'

There it was! The question he knew would come. Mary could read him like a book when it came to his job, and she knew if he was going to be working on a watching brief then there would always be the possibility that there would be a female operative working with him.

'Yes, one of the other team is a woman operator, why?'

'Oh, I don't know, just instinct I think. It's hard enough for me not knowing what you're doing all the time and I understand. The secrecy, the need to know, you've always explained but I know when you must work closely with others sometimes there will be a woman and I suppose I'm a wee bit jealous that it's not going to be me by your side. What's she like? Is she beautiful, no, don't tell me I'd rather not know? But is she beautiful Joseph?'

Reece smiled and taking her in his arms kissed her.

'You never have to worry about another woman beautiful or not, she is there like me to do a job, no more no less. I love you Mary, no one will ever be able to take your place.'

Now it was her turn to smile, and she poured a little more wine.

'Right answer, Mister Reece.'

Simons came out of his bedroom.

'I hope one of those glasses is for me?'

'Of course, help yourself,' said Mary.

'Great I needed that,' said Simons as he took a large swig from his glass, 'London updated, and we are to go ahead as agreed at the meeting but keep them informed.'

'By the sound of things, you're both going to be busy tomorrow, so I suggest we finish this bottle of wine and get an early night.'

'Matthew and I have a few things to discuss but it won't take long.'

'Then I bid you both goodnight, but don't stay up too late. Are we still walking up to the café in the morning?'

'Yes, and Matthew too if he wants to join us.'

'No thanks. I've had a long day and I'll need a lie-in if you don't mind guys.'

'Just me and you then Mary.'

Chapter 9

The Arab, as was his usual routine, began his day as the sun was rising, leaving the villa for a three-mile run then ten lengths of the pool before a simple breakfast of bread and fruit washed down with two cups of strong coffee. After a quick shower he drove to the Grand Bazaar in the city and once again met with the General of the Quads Overseas Operations outside the same café where they'd met before. This time they were alone and as far as he could see the General's bodyguards were keeping a low profile because they were nowhere in sight. The Arab told the General he had found the two students he needed for the next part of the operation. He also requested that he provide two new passports, giving him the details that were required, he would send him the photos later. The General described what the operation needed and how he should proceed. He knew the Arab would proceed as he would see it, and that the details he had given to him would only be used as the outline. The meeting lasted just over an hour. At the end of their conversation the Arab now knew the target and was pleased as he drove back to the villa that he had recruited the right people to complete the operation with success. As he left the café he did not notice the dust covered blue Toyota Hiace van further down the street. If he had, he would have noticed that the rear windows were black one-way reflective glass. The kind of glass that would protect the two Mossad agents inside, who could take their photos without being seen. Their target for the morning had been the Quads General. The man he had met with was unknown to them, and they had no idea that the batch of photos they transferred later that day would raise so much interest at Mossad HQ in downtown Tel Aviv.

Kalil brought the two students to the villa, not trusting the task of such an important assignment to anyone else, he appreciated that as the operation would be led by the Arab, the fewer people who knew of it the better. He did not stay long and after a coffee left for the city where he had business to see to, before returning to the training camp. The Arab showed the students to their rooms which were a great improvement on the tents and Porta cabins they had been staying in during their training. He told them to shower and change into fresh clothes to get rid of the desert sand, then meet with him on the open terrace where the cool breeze was blowing gently through the olive trees that surrounded the property.

One hour later the two students sat beside each other facing the Teacher who had a large file on the table between them.

'We will eat later. But first I'm sure you're both curious about a couple of things. First, why did I choose you and second, what are we going to do? So, do you have any questions?'

Both remained silent.

'I'll start with the first question which in a way answers the second. You both have the skills I'll need if we are to complete our mission. You both know how to use weapons and communications. You both know something of the use of nuclear weapons. More importantly, you are both committed to the cause even if your reasons for being here are different. But most of all to me you're still fresh, still with much to learn, skills that only I can teach you. I've been given a mission that consists of three parts. This is your first lesson, security, for your own part in the plan, you will work alone. You may have to kill someone to complete your part. Are you willing to do that if you have to, or if I ask you to?'

Both students nodded.

'Even if the person you have to kill is to your knowledge a good Muslim?'

Both students looked at each other before nodding once more.

'Good, because there may be a time or a reason when you will have to kill someone Muslim, Christian whoever. You must always continue to believe in the reasons you've joined this Holy War. The same reasons why I've chosen you. The Jihad is more important than our lives. If it is to succeed we must always believe that. As I told you yesterday, you're the students, and I'm the Teacher. For this operation you will be working in Europe under my command and with different identities. We are finished for now, so you may go to your rooms to pray and rest. Before you do, I need to take your photos for your new passports. We will talk more around dinner this evening when I'm sure you will have many questions which is only natural.'

The students never said a word and having posed for their photos taken on the Teacher's camera phone, retired to their rooms while he forwarded their pictures to the General.

The empty plates after dinner on the veranda showed the students enjoyed eating something better than the training camp food. The evening breeze was blowing gently through the trees surrounding the villa. The Arab, who liked to cook, had made the meal. The conversation included how the students felt about their training, world events, and the news of the day. The Arab spoke with a quiet voice, a voice that both students listened to with concentration, neither wanting to miss anything being said by the Teacher.

'I've chosen you both for an important operation. You each have in your own way a particular set of skills that Allah needs. You both speak English and from now on that is the only language we will use between us; here, now and wherever you are when you leave here on your tasks which I'll explain to you each in turn alone. The part you will each play will involve your own individual skills. At the start of the operation, you will be working on your own, but like the jigsaw, if you're successful, we will all come together at the last part to complete our mission. Therefore, I'll brief you alone. The less each of you know about the full jigsaw, the safer our security will be. When we each complete our parts and we come together at the end game, only then will you understand why this has to be this way.'

'Are we to sacrifice ourselves for the sake of Allah?' asked Shama.

The Arab could see no fear in her eyes nor hear fear in her voice when she asked the question. He could sense she did not fear death and he respected her even more for being brave enough to ask it.

'No, my child I know you both have dedicated your lives to the cause of Islamic Jihad. You both knew from the start that there would always be the possibility to give your life to that cause, to be a sacrifice to Allah if needed. The operation I will describe to you both will not require you to give that sacrifice, but to send hundreds of the enemies of Allah to hell and if the operation goes well to live, where you will be known among the soldiers of Allah, as one of his great heroes. If you do die during that operation then you will be among the greatest of the Martyrs and will pass easily into paradise to sit at the feet of Allah and hear him call your name. For now, you will rest tonight. With the early morning we will run, swim, and keep fit; then your education for the operation will begin, when I'll teach each of you what is expected. We do not have much time and there is much for you to learn and understand, so be awake with the sunrise and ready for the day and to fight as a soldier of Allah and Jihad. Inshallah, the future is in God's hands so until tomorrow, relax. This evening take a walk, enjoy the night sky, we will talk in the morning.'

Chapter 10

Jim Broad had spent the morning at his desk reading through the many intelligence reports from his SG9 agents around the world and the other files from MI6, MI5, and GCHQ, that linked into his own team's operations on the ground. Broad always tried to be in the office for 7am to get ahead of things before the day brought its own problems. He read for the fourth time the update from Matthew Simons, telling him what was happening in Malta and the meeting with the Mossad agents. The circulation notes at the top of the page showed the restricted readers who would have access to these reports, the Prime Minister, Sir Martin Bryant, the head of MI6, MI5, and Broad. The need to know strictly restricted to these few. Only they knew who and what SG9 were. Their job to find and eliminate those terrorists threatening the UK. It had taken Broad the full hour he allowed each day to satisfy himself that he had read enough, and to feel he was fully up to date with what was going on in the world he inhabited. The red-light button on his desk phone started flashing indicating that Sir Ian Fraser was on the secure line.

'Good morning Jim, how's things?'

'Not bad Sir Ian. What's up?'

'I suppose you're up to date with today's reports and the Malta operation?'

'Yes, just finished reading them it looks like our people have a grip on things down there.'

'Yes, but something has come in this morning which might interest you and have some influence on what your team in Malta are doing. Could you meet me at my office in an hour for a chat, I don't like spending too much time on these things.'

Broad knew of 'C' and his old-fashioned methods where he preferred to see people's faces over a table rather than a voice on the phone.

'Yes, that's not a problem see you in one hour.'

'Good man, see you then.'

Putting the phone down, Broad lifted the Malta file one more time to make sure he had all the answers for his meeting with Sir Ian, then buzzed his secretary to arrange for his driver to have the car ready in ten minutes.

London traffic was light and even though he was early for his meeting, Sir Ian had Broad brought into the office as soon as he arrived forty-five minutes after leaving his own.

'Have you read the overnight reports?' asked Fraser.

It was a question where Fraser already knew the answer. He knew Jim Broad was a creature of habit and was always in the office early just to make sure he could answer questions when they came. Fraser felt it was only good manners to ask his Black Ops Chief such a question.

'Yes, I think I'm up to date.'

This answer let Fraser know that Broad had read the reports but that he was aware that there was something he did not know, and that was why the summons to the office of 'C' instead of a chat over a secure line.

'I see our people have met up with the Mossad crew,' said Fraser smiling.

Seeing his boss smile when asking a question was a rare thing and it helped Broad relax. Whatever it was that Fraser was going to tell him it was not going to be trouble.

'Yes. Everything is looking good, and I expect them to get back to us later today after they do some work with the two Mossad agents.'

'It's early days and I want you to know that Sir Martin Bryant has been in touch with me, to say that if we need anything, he can contact the British High Commissioner in Malta to get it for us, no questions asked.'

'I'm not too happy with any involvement from civil servants, even Bryant or High Commissioners,' answered Broad.

'Don't worry, Jim. I told him the same thing while thanking him at the same time. Apparently, the High Commissioner is an old university chum of his, and, according to him, understands the need-to-know philosophy. But we should always keep contacts like these sweet. Do not burn our bridges as it were. But why I really asked you here concerns a call I had this morning which may have some bearing on what is happening in Malta. The call was from Kurt Shimon in Tel Aviv. It would appear they have an ongoing operation in Iran during which their agents photographed a meeting between a high-ranking Quads officer and another man, who from their files, they've subsequently identified as our friend the Arab.'

Fraser pushed a file across the desk to Broad before continuing.

'As you can see Jim the photos are excellent and better than anything we have on file here, so I suggest we get them out there to our people on the ground as soon as. I suspect knowing how Mossad operate, these pictures do not tell the full story, so we need to suspect everything we are being told. I like Kurt Shimon, but I don't love him. He's in the same business as us protecting his country and, like us, we have some secrets we don't tell everybody and that includes our friends.'

'You mean the CIA?'

'I mean everybody, but especially the CIA. Their big problem since 9/11, is any information they get they react on, and most of the time they react too quickly by sending in the heavy cavalry or just hitting everything with a drone. We are a bit more subtle. Let us find out what the bastards are up to first before we blow up half a city block just to get one guy.'

'Mossad haven't held back from doing just that in the past,' said Broad.

'I know that only too well, so let's keep some of our cards close to our chest as well. Like you, I read a report; but it only tells half the story. I want you to talk to Reece before he meets up with these Mossad people today. Send him the photos but tell him to keep them to himself and Simons. I want to see if their people have the same photos and if they share them with us. Tel Aviv will presume we will give them to our people in Malta, but I want to see if they've given them to their own people. There may be something going on here that Shimon doesn't want us to know, the full picture may be hidden, so let us play it slowly and let us see if they have any more cards up their sleeve.'

'I hope they aren't playing games. These people we are dealing with don't play for fun, they play for real.'

'I see in the report that the plan for today is to sit and watch, to try to work out what this Iranian is up to. Have you any thoughts on what might happen next?'

'It's a wait and see game, but if he comes ashore with anything that looks like a bomb or a weapon, between our guys and the Mossad team, we should be able to handle it.'

'You mean take him out?'

'If we need to, but he'll have those Hezbollah bodyguards, so let us hope it won't come to that. Reece is experienced enough and knows the land in Malta, so he'll make sure the Israelis know the score. We will work with them if the threat concerns both our countries, but we will not be taking orders from them. If we consider that threat needs to be eliminated, we will work alone if we need to.'

Sir Ian stood and walked to the large window overlooking the Thames. Broad could see he was deep in thought and waited to allow those thoughts to surface.

'Right Jim. You get back to your office and update Reece on the way forward. I have a meeting with the PM in Downing Street at ten and I will do likewise. The Arab is the terrorist poster boy and with this Quads Colonel arriving in Malta most likely working with him, they're up to something big. If we can nip it in the bud before it gets too far all the better, but for the moment we don't have enough of the picture to do that, so tell Reece what we need. After I have seen the PM I'll give Tel Aviv a call to see if I can push them for more information on what they think this meeting between The Arab and the Quads General in Tehran was all about.'

Broad sent the photos to Reece then called him.

'Good morning David. I thought you would like something juicy to start your day, a nice photo of our friend the Arab. Do you like it?'

'It's better than the one Matthew brought. So, do we still think there is some connection between him and our Iranian friend here?'

'We do, especially as he was meeting with an Iranian Quads General. 'C' thinks so as well. He is briefing the Prime Minister as we speak. We want you to be wary of our Mossad friends let them tell you the story of the meeting and the photos. Don't let them know you're aware of them yet. Have you everything you need?'

'Yes, for now.'

'If you run into any problems with the locals, the British High Commissioner to Malta is an old school buddy of Sir Martin Bryant. I don't know if he would be of any use but horses for courses when needed. His name is Sir Julian Richardson Smith. Good luck today, we can catch-up later.'

Bryant keeping his finger in the pie, thought Reece. Only if really needed was an understatement.

'Mary. Are you ready for our walk I need to do some serious thinking and the fresh air will help?'

'You know me, I'm always ready.' She smiled.

Chapter 11

After a run, a swim, and a light breakfast the Arab spoke to Shama first, now his student with the new name of Yasmin, at the table on the veranda. The male student Mohammad now Hassan having gone for a shower after his run.

'You are now Yasmin. Your previous life is gone. It was but a preparation for the life you're now going to live, the life of a soldier of the Jihad. You have already been told it will be a hard life, one of danger and test. Your new passport and documents will arrive today. Tomorrow you will fly from here to Rome, then from Rome to Malta, where you will meet with an Iranian Colonel who will pass to you a small package. You will then return to the airport and take a flight to London. There you will receive details of a safe house where you will stay until I come for you. Do you understand all this, what I say?'

'Yes, will I be supplied with a weapon?'

'Only when you get to London, you're training on how to use many different weapons will always be useful to you.

'I know it might not be what you expected to do on your first mission but the meeting in Malta and your transporting to London of the package you will be given, is vital to the success of our plan. That is why I asked you both yesterday if you could kill a Muslim. You must always remember you will be alone, and the Colonel will have Hezbollah bodyguards who are not your mission. The Arab spent the next hour describing in detail the part Yasmin had to play if the mission was to be a success. Your job is to collect the item and get to London safely. Have you any questions?'

'I'm to be alone until I get to London?'

'Yes, as I've said, this part of the operation is for you alone; an important part of the final jigsaw when we all meet again in London. You will be supplied with your documents, money, and a phone with only two numbers, mine and your fellow student Hassan. You can call me at any time but do not call Hassan until you are in London. The less we say over a phone the more secure we will be. Hassan will be waiting for you when you get to London. Let him know when you've landed.'

'Will I be able to recognise this Iranian, will I have the information I need?'

He could see she was worried and needed some reassurance.

'Do not worry Yasmin you will be given all the information you will need plus a photo before you leave. I have every confidence in you and the Iranian will be expecting you but will not know what you will be doing.'

'This package I have to pick up from him and transport to London, will it be easy to get through airport security?'

'Yes, it will look like a normal small walking stick and will be made of lead which does not give off any sign of what it really is; a small amount of weapons grade plutonium which on its own won't constitute a device. You will need to walk slowly with it as if you have a leg injury and you will be able to carry it on-board the aircraft and place it in the overhead locker during the flight. I don't anticipate any problems.'

'Thank you for placing your trust in me, I will not let you down.'

'Allah will be with you; you have nothing to fear so rest now and prepare yourself for tomorrow and the mission ahead. When you return to your room please ask Hassan to come here.'

The Arab poured himself another cup of coffee before sitting back at the table. He felt the cooling breeze as it travelled through the branches of the trees and could smell the orange blossoms that surrounded the villa. Hassan refused the coffee when he sat opposite the Arab.

'How are you today Hassan,' the Arab asked in English.

'I'm fine thank you. I've had my run, my swim and a good breakfast so I'm ready for the day.'

'Good, we need to get to work, now the operation has started. I've briefed Yasmin on her part which eventually will take her to London. You will fly to Paris in two days from now. Then I want you to take the Eurostar to London and contact our friend in London. You will then meet with Yasmin who, if things go to plan will already be in London. She will text you to let you know she has arrived. Tomorrow you will be given your papers and passport with any information you will need.

'Your part of the plan when you get to London will be to find rented accommodation with the help of a trusted friend who already lives there. His details will be in the papers I will give you. I'll give you a phone with only mine and Yasmin's number. I am number one and Yasmin two in the phone's address book, they will be the only numbers you will need, and the phone won't be used for anything else not even to call for an Uber or a pizza, do you understand?'

Hassan nodded.

'When you get to London text me one word, arrived. Once you text me, I will move from here to London. You will wait with Yasmin until I arrive. Have you any questions.'

'No, I'm sure the papers I have to read will explain more of my mission.'

'Inshallah, read them well, you will destroy them after you have done so. Memorise what you need, and I will see you in London.'

When Hassan had returned to his room the Arab found a quiet place in his garden and kneeling on the soft grass, he knew he had chosen his students well, he bowed and prayed to Allah for success.

Chapter 12

Mary recognised the signs; Joseph had been quiet after his phone call with London. He had still been silent as they walked to their café on the Qawra seafront for the usual coffee. It was a bit colder this morning, even though the sun was up, so they dressed for the day, each with hooded fleece and long cotton trousers. Reece wore his favorite black baseball cap with the flag of Malta badge.

'You're quiet, Joseph. Are you OK?'

He stopped walking and turned towards the sea and stopped to lean on the rail that ran alongside the path.

'You know, I love this place. Our morning walk, the sea, the air, and I never want that to change. It is our bolt hole from all the horrors of the world, some of that world we've lived in. But I always hoped that it would leave us alone here. Now the bastards have come here, and I must do something about it. I'm worried that if something goes down here, then our little peaceful, happy world will be finished forever.'

She wanted to hug him tight. To hold him and protect him from his world, but she knew she could only do so much, and she felt the hurt he was feeling.

'Don't worry Joseph they can try to get us, but we are stronger together than they will ever be. Remember what I told you many years ago when you worried about things, they can't make you pregnant.'

He laughed at her remembering something she'd taught him that he had passed on to others. There are always worse things in the world, if you only deal with the ones you must face, it's enough to be going on with. He put his arms around her and pulling her close he whispered in her ear, 'Thank you for being here with me, I love you.'

'I love you too Joseph and I'll love you even more if you buy me a warm cup of coffee I'm freezing.'

'You're right let's get on with the day.'

After the coffee and the walk, they returned to the villa to find Matthew Simons working on his laptop.

'Did you enjoy your walk?'

'Yes, thank you,' said Mary, 'have you had any breakfast?'

'I stole some of your lovely Maltese bread, it's delicious.'

'You're welcome to whatever you need. I'm off for a shower to let you two talk and plan your day,' she said with a smile.

'You have a keeper there David.'

'You don't need to tell me. That's one thing in my life I can be sure of. Now are you up to date with the latest from London?'

'Yes, I've downloaded everything for you to go through at your leisure, but I think you probably know everything anyway. What do you think will happen today?'

'We work to the schedule and plan already agreed with our two Mossad friends, but we take everything they say and do with a pinch of salt, we can't fully trust them. Like us they have a hidden agenda of protecting their own country. I don't fault them for that but let's keep our guard up when we meet them later.'

'The new photo of the Arab gives us a head start if he appears. Do you think he will?'

'I'm not sure. His kind keep their heads down until the last minute. But, if he does show himself he had better be prepared to die, because if the Kidon don't get him we will.'

'Don't you think we could capture him; he would be a great catch for our people to work on?'

'I don't think he would be willing to come along peacefully. I'm just saying that if we do see him we need to be prepared for someone to die, and after Manchester I don't want it to be one of ours.'

Simons knew about the shoot-out with Sean Costello and Sharon Lyndsey, The White Widow, in Manchester; when one of the SG9 agents, April Grey had been shot dead by Lyndsey who had then escaped. In the subsequent confrontation Reece had shot and killed Costello before he could kill any more people. He also had heard the story in the secret world, how Reece and another SG9 agent had tracked down Lyndsey and her two bodyguards to Egypt and shot all three dead.

'What about weapons? Do we have them?'

Reece went to the set of drawers in the dining room and took out a handgun.

'Are you familiar with firearms?'

'I've done all the usual courses and drills, but I'm a desk jockey. I fire words from a computer not a gun.'

Reece placed the gun on the table and started to break it down into its component parts; then taking a small piece of cloth and a jar of gun oil from the same drawer, started to clean each part of the weapon, the stock, the barrel, and the spring. This took a few minutes then he expertly assembled the gun and placed it on the table in front of Simons the fully loaded magazine beside it. He then unloaded the magazine one bullet at a time and left it on the table beside the fifteen bullets and did the same with the spare magazine.

'I've had this gun since my Special Branch days it has never let me down. A clean weapon will never let you down. Removing the bullets now and again will let the spring in the magazine rest so when you need it to do its job, it's unlikely to jam. As a government agent I have an International Firearms Licence which allows me to transport the gun over most borders if it's not assembled in its killing capacity. But as you can see, I've assembled this baby so many times I can do it easily and quickly even in the dark. I know the Department like more modern Glock pistols without the safety catch, but Smith and Wesson will do for me with one round in the breech and fourteen rounds nine mill parabellum in the mag. Fifteen in the spare for good measure. Today as it's basically a sit and watch and report back gig, I suggest you do without a weapon. We have the name of the High Commissioner on Malta, and we can get one if we need to. I think our Mossad friends would be able to get us one if we need one, trust me on that. Embassies and Consulates always have weapons available in case of an attack on their buildings, but we do not want civil servants getting their nose in the game, that's when things can really go wrong. Take it from me I know what I'm talking about, there's been times when I would seriously consider shooting one of them instead of a terrorist. From their little worlds they can do more damage than an idealist with a gun.'

'I'm happy with that. As I say, I'm just a desk jockey but I'm also OK to sit, watch, and report. If we must follow on foot or in vehicles then I can do that. I'm only too glad that they drive on the same side of the road as we do at home.'

'I don't think the Iranian crew will be looking for a shoot-out but if anything does go down, you take cover, and leave it to me and our Mossad buddies. A fight is the last thing I want here. I live here and hope to do so for a long time.'

Mary came back into the room, her hair still wet. Even though it was long she preferred to let it dry naturally, the heat in Malta usually taking care of the drying process quickly. Even though this time of year it was cooler it was still warm enough to get the job done.

'You two still chattering?'

'We have finished for now, so a fresh pot of coffee would be good if you're going to the kitchen,' said Reece.

'Watch it you, what did your last slave die off?' She smiled.

'Answering back,' laughed Reece.

'When will you be going into the city?' she asked.

'After lunch about two.'

'Any chance of a lift? You can drop me off near the bus station. I fancy a walk round the town and a look in the market.'

'Yes, no problem, but it depends on how good your coffee is slave.'

After dropping Mary off in the city, Reece parked up close to the hotel and with Simons, waited once more in the reception area for the two Mossad agents.

The reception area was busy with what appeared to be a bunch of new arrivals booking in. This was one of Reece's favourite pastimes to watch people and try to guess who they were, and where were they from. Then break down in his head what kind of business they worked in, it was his way of keeping his surveillance skills in tune.

When the lift door opened for what seemed the tenth time and the two Israelis walked out, he spotted them easily through the crowd of residents setting out for the afternoon in the city, or just going through for a late lunch in the hotel restaurant.

Standing to greet them Reece couldn't help but notice once again how beautiful Anna looked; now dressed in a blue polo shirt and tight-fitting jeans that seemed to enhance her full figure. She wore her dark hair in a long ponytail, and he was sure the leather bag that hung heavily from her shoulder carried more than just make-up. Following behind her, Palo wore his brown open necked shirt loosely around the waist of his linen trousers covering no doubt, as Reece did, the holster and pistol that agents always carried in the draw position. The Beretta .22 pistol was the favourite of Mossad, used many times in their operations and political assassinations around the world. Easily concealed, the .22 ammo gave off a reduced sound yet was deadly at close quarters. No James Bond shoulder holster for anyone who was trained properly in the game they played on the streets of the world.

'Good afternoon,' said Anna.

'Good afternoon. Are we ready for the day?' replied Reece.

'Always David. We have the details of where the ship carrying our friend will dock and we've arranged for an empty apartment overlooking the pier to observe from,' said Anna.

'You have been busy. Have you any other update for us?' asked Reece.

'Let us order a pot of coffee and sit and discuss our plan for today,' said Palo.

When the coffee had been poured Anna spread out a small tourist map of Valletta and the Grand Harbour. For anyone observing them they were just four tourists planning their day.

Pointing to the map Anna proceeded to show Reece and Simons where they needed to be for the ship's arrival.

'As you might know, David, I've visited the island on many occasions, but always as a tourist. This is my first time to look at everything through the eyes of an agent. I have good memories of the people and this city, so like yourself I'm familiar with the streets and the surrounding buildings and harbour.'

Reece only nodded and looked back to the map.

Anna pointed out the route from the hotel to the apartment overlooking the Harbour and the pier where the expected ship would be docking.

'That's about a mile from here,' said Reece.

'You do have a car, don't you?' said Anna.

'Yes, and I suggest we move it close to the harbour in case they use one. The traffic system around the city is mostly one way, so even if they do use a car, they won't be difficult to follow.'

'We can't afford to lose them, Mr Reece,' said Palo.

Reece looked at Simons and smiled before replying.

'No, Palo that would never do. Don't worry it's an island, they'll have difficulty getting off it without us knowing.'

Anna spoke again as she produced a file from her bag and handed round a photo.

'This is the latest photo we have of our Iranian.'

Reece and Simons both noticed that it was not the latest one of the Arab.

'This is our target Colonel Ali Shafi of the Iranian Republican Guards Quads Unit. As you are aware, our intelligence indicates he'll be carrying an item to hand over to a yet unknown person and our job is to identify that person then await further instructions from our masters.'

Reece could see that Anna oversaw the Mossad side of this operation; Palo sat observing both the SG9 agents as Anna spoke. The photo was in colour which Reece appreciated, black and white was OK, but it never really showed the person as they were; the suntanned skin, the eyes, the colour of the beard. Anna had not shown them the up-to-date photo of the Arab, they were holding back on full disclosure and that suited Reece. Why bring something into the game unless you're sure it's going to play a part, what part the Arab might play, if any, was still not known.

'Have you everything you need if we leave for your apartment now?' asked Reece.

'Yes. I have the address and the keys. I'm assured it is stocked with all our needs and I have two handsets for communications in my bag here. Shall we go?'

Reece finished his coffee and led the way to the car. The address wasn't hard to find. Reece had to park two streets away as there was no parking permitted on the main road. Across from the apartment was the Grand Harbour with the pier close against the road allowing only for loading and unloading.

The apartment was typical of the old harbour. The three floors had once been a dockside warehouse with a large, blue, wooden door with two windows showing to the front and with a small balcony on the two first floor rooms. Reece and Simons remained on the first floor while the two Mossad agents checked out the rest of the building. All the windows had wood shutters, that when opened could be fixed back against the outside walls with a metal hook. The shutters on the windows that Reece now looked through had already been hooked back and despite not having been cleaned in some time there was a clear view of the harbour pier across the main road. The pier for the moment was empty, while in the harbour beyond, shipping moved in and out from the Mediterranean Sea. The room consisted of a few large chairs, a table with four wooden chairs and in the back corner a small kitchen with a fridge and cooker, a kettle, a microwave, and all the paraphernalia a small family would need. Anna and Palo returned from their inspection. Both looked out the front window observing the same scene Reece and Simons had just observed.

'Well, what do you think David?' she asked.

'I've been in worse places.'

'There's two single beds on the next floor if we need to get some sleep.'

Anna took out her file once more and placed it on the table.

'I suggest we get comfortable and use our time to familiarise ourselves with all the information we have. The ship which is called the Qom is expected to dock around 5 p.m. and our satellites are confirming it's on schedule. It is basically a small container ship sailing between ports in the Mediterranean dropping off and picking up foreign cars. As we already know Shafi is coming to meet up with a contact to pass on what we believe is a small amount of plutonium, which has been manufactured in Iran against the wishes of the international community. Our job is to identify that contact and await further instructions. He will be protected by his Hezbollah bodyguard friends; at least four of them.'

'I'm still a little confused,' said Simons. 'Why Malta, why here?'

This time it was Palo who answered.

'Malta has always been close to Africa and the Middle East by its proximity to these countries. Hezbollah and Islamic Jihad have always done the dirty work for Iran, and we know in the past they have had some support here in Malta from a few who are not active but willing to provide somewhere for the terrorist masters and their operators to rest up between operations. The Islamic Jihad know this island as one where the security is weak and not likely to interfere with them. Another reason why Colonel Shafi will meet the contact here, believe it or not, is that he has a fear of flying and this ship voyage suits his purpose to carry out his side of the plan away from the prying eyes and ears of the CIA and our own services. Malta also has good travel links with the rest of Europe allowing his contact to move quickly from one place to another.'

Once more Anna reached into her bag and took out two Motorola wireless handsets.

'These are set to a secure frequency just for our use, so keep them on button number two at all times. They are fully charged, and we can recharge them here using that standard plug and cable beside the kettle.'

Reece had noticed the cable when he was checking out the room.

'How do you want to cover this,' asked Reece, 'we can't all sit looking out the window?'

Anna smiled and once more Reece noticed how beautiful this woman was. If Mary could see her now, thought Reece, she would be worried. But Reece decided to put on his professional head as he always did in this sort of situation.

'I'm sure we don't have to teach you anything when it comes to surveillance in any operation. We know about Manchester, how you and your team tracked the terrorists and dealt with them,' she replied.

'Then you must also know we lost some people there. People who meant a lot to me. We also know how the Kidon operate and your professionalism in dealing with your enemies. I always think of surveillance in percentages, 90 per cent filled with adrenaline and concentration, 5 per cent boredom and 5 per cent terror, keep thinking that way and we will be OK. So, I suggest we cover this from two fronts. Once the ship docks, we each take turns in the car with one of the radios. The person in the car ready to drive out here on the main road and pick one of us up if our target uses a car or taxi. Two of us can observe from here with the other radio and one of us can rest. If he leaves on foot then we have three of us here who can follow. If it drags out, we can all switch places at intervals, so we all get a chance to rest. What happens after that, is down to the target. Whatever he does will dictate what we do.'

'Exactly as we would do it David, but hopefully not so much terror,' said Anna.

'As we've all been briefed and shown this Colonel's file I think we need to consider the dangers here,' said Simons.

'The dangers, can you be more specific?' asked Anna.

Reece nodded for Matthew to continue, and he looked back to Anna and Palo to see if they reacted in anyway.

'The file and the intelligence we have shows us that this Colonel has a lot to do with the Iranian secret nuclear programme. The information that he may have travelled from Iran with a small amount of plutonium which he intends to hand over to a yet unknown person with connections to an Islamic terrorist cell can mean two things. One, this has been sanctioned by the Iranian leadership and two if I have any experience on how they work they intend it to be used by this terrorist cell in a deniable operation against the West.'

'I think we are all in agreement so far Matthew, so what happens now?' asked Anna.

'If he hands over the plutonium successfully that is his job completed, we let him go home. But in what form is the plutonium, how will he deliver it, and can we confirm he has it? There are so many questions that need answers.'

Again, it was Anna who spoke as she reached into her bag once more and produced a handheld device similar in appearance and size to that of an electric stunning device.

'You have answered your own questions. This little device has been invented by our boffins as you would call them. It can be carried discreetly, and it will register if plutonium is within a ten-meter radius. Yes, I can see you are thinking that means we will have to get close to this Iranian or his contact to confirm the presence of the plutonium. This is where our close surveillance comes in. It will have to be accurate and done in a way where we don't expose ourselves.'

Anna took out one more small package from her bag.

'These are ears mics, all fully charged and linked up to each other. When in your ear they will pick up the radios and we can speak discreetly.

'I suggest we use these when we are following or close to the target. Do you know how to use them?'

'Of course,' replied Reece.

'Can I suggest we keep the call signs simple,' said Anna.

'I'll be Alpha One, Palo Two, David Three, and Matthew Four. Are we all OK with that?'

They all nodded in return and proceeded to place the devices in their ears.

'You seem to have it covered,' said Reece, 'Can I suggest we relax for a bit before this ship docks, then Matthew or Palo can take the car and park up ready to pick us up if needed? I do not think this Iranian will want to hang about too long with a package of nuclear poison. He will want to hand it over and get out of here as quickly as possible. For all we know this could all be done by tomorrow; then we can all go home and get back to living our lives again.'

Anna smiled. 'We will be lucky if it's that easy. Let us hope so. The ship should be docking in the next few hours. I think we are ready, let us see where this Colonel leads us.'

Chapter 13

Before the Qom, with its cargo of cars and the Iranian Colonel and his Hezbollah minders, had entered through the entrance to the Grand Harbour at Malta, the Arab had watched as his two students were picked up by Kalil and transported to the Imam Khomeini International Airport in Tehran. Now the plan he had agreed with the Iranian General in the Bazaar was underway, he felt more relaxed; the wheels were moving. His own part in the plan would begin in two days and he was ready.

Hassan had the easier journey to begin with; a direct flight to Paris. The airport security in France was extremely tight, and for one moment he thought his documents wouldn't stand up, the only luggage he had was a shoulder backpack. He would spend no more than two days in Paris as a tourist before moving on to London. He only stayed one night in a city centre hotel. He found he didn't like Paris; it was too decadent, too noisy. The next day before catching the Euro Star from the Gare du Nord train station to London St Pancras, he followed the briefing from the Arab, wiping all fingerprints in his hotel room before making his way to catch the afternoon train. Travelling this way was to avoid the far stricter security at the British airports. It was the first time he had used the Eurostar, and even though the journey took two hours and fifteen minutes, at speeds of up to 186 mph, he was able to enjoy the whole trip feeling more relaxed than he had done for months.

The Arab had been right. The security at both stations was relaxed and Hassan, still using the excellent false documents he carried, passed through the checks without problem. Following his instructions, he caught a taxi outside St Pancras and told the driver to take him to the home of Arsenal Football Club and the Emirates stadium in North London. The driver was a Chelsea fan, so Hassan was glad to have a conversation about the past successes of the two clubs, as his knowledge of the current teams was little. He paid the driver and walked up the steep steps at the front of the stadium, then a complete circumference of the whole building bringing him to the statue of Thierry Henry the famous Arsenal footballer. He sat down next to the statue and took his time observing his surroundings.

Hassan then spent the next hour walking through the streets and roads using the anti-surveillance techniques he had been taught while in Iran. To the experienced eye he knew these would be spotted as basic, but nevertheless he would do his best to try to ensure he was alone in his travels. Although it was dry, and the sky was grey, he could feel the cold more than usual. He had been away too long in the warmth of the Middle East, and he had forgotten how different the climate was in England. He stopped to put on a sweater under his coat then found a coffee shop on the main Rock Street within walking distance of the Finsbury Park Mosque off St Thomas Road, his next destination for the day. As he settled down to a coffee and a sandwich he felt good that he had almost completed the first part of his plan and he was happy that he was not under surveillance. The Arab would be pleased with his student, but he had warned Hassan that when he approached the Mosque he would be under British anti-terrorist surveillance, as the Mosque had a history of involvement in the cause of the Islamic Jihad. He told Hassan to wear his shemagh scarf over his face on the roads approaching the Mosque until he was inside the building and again when he was leaving. He had timed his walk around the area and now a visit to a café to ensure that the time of day would see the sun start to go down and the light start to fall, making it more difficult for any observer to be certain about faces and descriptions.

When he left the café, he pulled the black and white shemagh from his backpack, putting it on, he made sure it covered most of his face with only his brown eyes showing and satisfied after one more full visual sweep of the road, he walked in the direction he wanted to go getting closer to the Mosque. In that area of the city, which had a large Muslim community, full face coverings were not unusual. Twenty minutes later he turned into St Thomas Road. He had gone over the maps with his teacher many times and now he was pleased that he had been a good student. His teacher would also be pleased, that not only had he listened, but he had put into practice what he had been taught. As he walked towards the building he watched for the spots where, if he were to carry out surveillance on the Mosque, he would place people to monitor the coming and going, recording vehicles and people. He knew it would be difficult for security agencies to operate in the vicinity of the Mosque as local people were mostly attendees and would expose any such surveillance if spotted. The building itself was not a distinctive construction; with a central Minaret and side windows which made the red bricked building look, from the outside, like a small block of apartments. The Mosque had a particularly significant history in the Islamic world. It had been a hotbed of insurrection and intrigue in promotion and support for the various Islamic causes and groups around the world. The British government, who had been monitoring the activities at the Mosque for many years, and its then Imam, a radical preacher Abu Hamza al-Masri, put pressure on the trustees to have the Mosque closed following an anti-terrorist raid. Although it was reopened in 2005, the British security services still considered it a place of interest in the war against the world terrorist threat. He knew from his own time in London that the building was more than adequate for what it needed to do, spreading the word of the one true faith. Hassan kept up his anti-surveillance and the only thing that aroused his suspicion was a Transit van at the top of St Thomas Road. The van at first glance appeared empty but was positioned in such a way that anyone in the back of the van could observe out of the rear windows, which were blacked out giving them a clear view of anyone walking down the road but not entering the building which was to the side of the van. Hassan walked past the van, paying it no specific attention, up the steps and entered through the main Mosque doors which opened to his touch. In the main entrance hall, he removed his shoes and stood to face a young man who approached him from a side room.

'Can I help you?'

'I'm here to speak with the Imam Mohammed AAyan. He is expecting me.'

'Who shall I say?'

'Tell him the one he has been expecting from the East.'

The young man appeared puzzled at the answer but replied 'Please wait here,' before going through the two large doors in the centre of the hallway.

Hassan dropped his backpack on the floor and keeping his face covered waited for only a few minutes before the large doors were opened once more. This time the man facing him was familiar to him from the media pictures he had seen.

Mohammed AAyan stood just over six-foot-tall with a long grey beard that still showed some of the black it had once been. His build was bulky, fat mixed with muscle, he was wearing a full-length shirt with a brown three-quarter length waistcoat. Half of his large face seemed to be covered by what Hassan could only think were cheap, black, thick lens NHS glasses.

'So, my brother you have come from the East. If so, you have a message for me,' he said through a smile that showed a full set of perfect teeth.

Hassan looked around for others but there was no one else.

'We are alone my brother; you can speak freely.'

'Our friend in Iran sends his best wishes and says the time has arrived for you to help him.'

AAyan reached out his arms and placing them around Hassan's shoulders with one arm and picking up the backpack with the other guided him to the side room the young man had originally came out of.

'I've been waiting for this day. Let us relax in here.' He showed the way to a small, empty office containing two large leather armchairs, a smart flat screen TV on a stand in the corner and a large prayer mat. There were no pictures on the cream-coloured walls only a large mirror.

As they both sat AAyan spoke again.

'Do not worry brother. Here we can talk freely. I have this room swept for electronic devices every morning.'

'Thank you for seeing me. I have a message here,' said Hassan as he removed a memory-stick from the zipped pocket in his jacket.

AAyan took the device and inserted it into the side socket on the TV, which he switched on. Taking the remote he found the information he needed and pressed play.

Almost immediately the face of the Arab appeared on the screen and his voice in English was loud and clear.

'My brother, thank you for helping us in the name of the one true god that is Allah. My brother Hassan who carries this message is just the first of what will be many soldiers in this war around the world against the enemies of our people. He has his mission for now, the details of which you do not need to know. This will not only protect him and those who come after him, but you also. As they say, what you do not know you cannot tell. For now, he'll explain to you what help you can give. Please give that help with my appreciation. I'll be in touch in person very soon. Allah Akbar, Allah Akbar.'

The screen went blank, the voice and picture gone.

'So, Hassan can I get you some tea, some coffee?'

'No thank you. I've been travelling all day and I need to rest. This is where I need your help.'

'Whatever you need in the name of Allah I will help.'

'For now, two things. Somewhere to stay that will accommodate up to four people safely.'

'And the second.'

'A secure burner phone number where I can reach you at any time.'

AAyan stood and moving to the mirror he pulled it from one side to reveal it was attached to the wall by a set of hinges. Opening a cavity behind it he removed a small Nokia mobile phone. And some keys and a piece of typed paper. Then closing the cavity and swinging the mirror back in place it became what it was minutes before, just a mirror.

Hassan was a little surprised and noticed that AAyan was smiling when he sat back in the chair once more.

'As you can see, we too have our secrets.'

'Indeed,' replied Hassan.

'These are the keys for just such a safe place; a flat on the Edgware Road. It's an apartment on two floors above a barber shop, the details and the secure number for this phone are on the document. I'll keep the phone on me from now on. I suggest you study them and destroy the paper when you're sure you know the address and the number. Now, be careful when you leave. I'm sure you noticed the Transit van across the road. It belongs to the British Security Services, and they'll have taken your photo when you came in.'

'I wore my face covering.'

'Good. Do the same when you leave. I do not think their finance is able to stretch to have a permanent surveillance team to cover this building, but we cannot be totally sure, so take whatever precautions you can when you leave. Use the Underground whenever you can as they struggle to follow our people through that system.'

Hassan stood to leave.

'Thank you for your help. I'm sure we will be in touch.'

'In the name of the one true God that is Allah, may you be safe and successful in your mission in his name.'

'Inshallah, God wills it.'

Hassan pulled the scarf up over his face, pulled his shoes back on and turning left out of the Mosque door, he walked with his head up appearing to pay no attention to anything around him. If anyone had taken his photograph, they would get nothing from it to identify him, and the casual way he walked wouldn't give anyone, who was not surveillance trained cause for concern. He walked to the main Finsbury Tube station and as far as he was concerned, today was a rest day for the anti-terrorist surveillance teams; he was satisfied he was alone.

Chapter 14

It was almost 5 p.m. exactly when the Iranian merchant vessel the Qom, started its docking procedure alongside the pier in Valletta's Grand Harbour. Reece watched through the high-powered binoculars that were perched on the tripod just back from the window. The ship was in a lot better condition than he had imagined. Showing very little rust, it looked like it had just slipped off the runners. *A newly built vessel, it must have had a full paint job recently*, he thought. He could see what looked like cars on the deck covered in waterproof tarpaulin to protect them from the salt water. On the same deck men were going through the business of getting the ship alongside the dock and secure. Ropes were thrown to men on the dock where they were pulled over the metal and concrete bollards securing the ship to the dockside. Within minutes the whole process of docking was complete. Palo and Anna who, were standing behind him could see the smoke that had been coming from the black funnel on the ship reduce until there was no more mixing with the still blue sky.

'It looks like there are cabins just under the bridge,' said Reece.

'I think we have some time yet. They will have to have the gangway pulled in and I'm sure the local customs people will have to check the manifest before our friend can leave the ship,' Anna replied.

Palo, who had watched the ship come into dock, now walked to the kitchen, and switched on the kettle.

'We have plenty of time for a coffee then.' He placed three cups on the table.

'Sounds good, make mine black,' said Reece.

'Do you think Matthew will be all right?' asked Anna.

Reece knew the one-way street he was parked up in. It was a slight hill, and he would be parked facing down towards the harbour and the sea. Reece picked up the radio.

'Alpha four, come in, over.'

He replied almost immediately.

'Here, over.'

'Good man you're awake. Just to update you our package carrier has arrived. We would guess nothing more for at least an hour, are you OK?'

'Yes, no problem, I'm in a quiet spot nothing much going on, happy to stay here.'

'Great will keep you updated, over and out.'

Reece looked once more at the blown-up picture of the Iranian Colonel.

'He should be easy to spot. There won't be a large crowd of passengers coming off at the same time, and if he has a couple of minders as we expect then we will be able to identify them too,' said Reece.

'Let us hope so. I always love it when they make things just that little simpler for me,' said Anna.

Palo brought the coffee and Reece took it and sat in one of the chairs allowing Palo to take over the binoculars.

Anna sat down in another chair.

'What about your woman David, is she all right after Manchester?'

Anna was letting him know they knew all about Manchester and the SG9 operation, but he wasn't going to be her best friend just yet.

'She's fine.'

'Sorry, I didn't mean to pry; just interested from a woman's perspective.'

'Then you will know how she feels. Having been involved in this stuff yourself it's not nice and she is the bravest woman I know.'

'She must be. That is why I asked if she was all right. By the sound of it she is indeed a strong woman. Maybe I can meet her sometime.'

'Once this is over I don't see why not. I'm sure she would like to meet you as well.'

Reece could only try to imagine the conversation there would be between these two beautiful women both now important parts of his life.

'What about you Anna? What is it like for a woman from Israel in this game? Your life must have been like mine and the women I've worked with, especially on the streets of Northern Ireland.'

'Similar? I would say from what I've seen of your war in Ireland terribly similar. Northern Ireland has a terrorist problem just like Israel, where fanatics want to kill you every day and the country is bordered by a country that gives safe ground to those same terrorists to operate.'

'There the similarity ends. Where we both have terrorist groups who want to kill us and wipe us off the face of the earth, the ones in my country don't want to commit suicide.'

'Ah, but there you're wrong. What about the ten hunger strikers. They committed suicide.'

Reece smiled at this attempt to drag him into a discussion that was seeking to learn more about him and his own wars.

'That's why we are here to try to stop more killings. Realistically that is why I do this. My own problem is that every time we kill one more of theirs, two more jump out of the trenches to take their place. When does the killing stop?'

Now it was Anna's turn to smile.

'That has been the question since man first stood on the earth. There is a story that a man was sitting on a bench beside Jesus, and he asked him, if you are truly God then why do you allow war, disasters, famine, and man killing man? Jesus replied, I was about to ask you the same question. You see David there'll always be these kinds of people and there'll always be those like us who are willing to put our head above the parapet and try to stop them.'

'For now, I will agree with you. But I know the time will come for myself, when I will want to leave the front line, leave it up to someone else. I just hope that when that time comes, I won't have enemies who are not willing to let me have a peaceful life.'

'As you say, let us hope that when that time comes, there'll still be people like us willing to stand between them and you.'

'I think I'll stretch my legs and see if Matthew is OK, he's parked two streets away and I'll still have the ship in view when I'm walking. Anything happens shout out.'

'You can be sure of it. But we should be all right for at least an hour allowing time for the custom check of the ship's contents and crew manifest.'

The first thing Reece noticed when he left the front door of the apartment was the temperature drop. The sun had started to go down and the air was fresh with a slight breeze coming in off the sea. He was glad he could stretch his legs and clear his head. Even though none of them smoked, the apartment was stuffy with the windows closed, no air was circulating inside.

Matthew Simons saw Reece turn the corner into the street. With the sun starting to go down, the streetlights were coming on and his view was just as good as when the sun was high in the sky. Reece climbed into the seat beside Simons.

'All quiet so far. Now with the ship docked we will have to wait and see what happens.'

'I know that. Do you think I'm stupid?' asked Simons.

'No don't be daft. I'm only here because I needed a breath of fresh air and I missed you.' Reece smiled.

Simons laughed.

'Well, that's all right then, I missed you too. Have our Israeli brother and sister got anything more for us?'

'No. Everything as it was. If the Iranian comes off the ship and gets into a car, you, pick us up and we follow. If he comes out on foot, we follow, and you catch-up. Let's hope he won't keep us waiting too long, I would like to sleep in my own bed tonight.'

'At least you will have the lovely Mary to cuddle up too. I've been thinking; he is here to meet someone and between our friends in the apartment and our own people we don't know who. If we are lucky and we do spot his contact, what then? Do we close them both down or try to follow both?'

'I don't think we have the resources to follow them both. We are doing this on a shoestring as it is. It seems when it comes to our Mossad and SG9 masters, it will always be down to money, and we are expendable and someone to blame if things go wrong. In this game if you remember to look after yourself and trust only yourself you will be all right. We know the Iranian is here to pass something on, so when he does that, we follow the receiver and wait for further instructions. Ours is not to reason why.'

'I know ours is but to do and die. It's the die bit I'm not too fond of.'

'And on that happy thought I'll get back to our Mossad friends. Is there anything you need?'

'No, I'm OK, thanks. If I do, I'll give you a shout. Nobody seems to be paying me any attention, so I'll just read my copy of The Malta Times once more and wait to see what happens, keep safe.'

Reece let himself back into the apartment and found Palo still sat at the window checking things through the binoculars. Anna was sitting at the kitchen table with another cup of coffee in front of her.

'Is Matthew OK?'

'Yes, no problem, probably a little bored like us, but OK. Nothing new then?'

'No but the coffee's fresh.'

Reece poured himself a cup keeping it black. He sat at the table facing Anna. He looked at his watch.

'I don't think it will be long now before we see some movement. The customs check will be short provided all the paperwork is in order, and I'm sure it will be, they won't want to bring any unnecessary notice to themselves.'

'I agree. We are ready. We can't do anything until they move, but we're ready.'

At almost the same time the Air Malta flight from Rome was landing at Malta's main airport. A young attractive woman passed through customs without any problem and taking a taxi from outside the arrivals building, she asked the driver to take her to the Casa Ellul hotel in Valletta, but first to stop off at a good souvenir shop on the way.

Chapter 15

Reece decided it was time to check in with Mary, God knows when he would get a chance again. She answered his call on the second ring.

'Hello sexy.'

'What if I had you on speaker,' laughed Reece.

'Then you would still be sexy, but I know there's other things I would rather have you on.'

'Enough of that I'm trying to do a job here.'

'So why are you calling me then and getting me to think I should put something nice on if you're coming home?'

'Not yet but hold that thought. I'll let you know when I'm on my way and you get into that something nice for me to help you out of. That is why I'm calling to update you. There's nothing happening here yet so, yes, I might be a little late.'

'Spoil-sport I'll just have to start without you then.'

'Don't you dare, I'll need all of you when I get back. Don't worry about food we can pick up something here.'

'OK but take care. I love you.'

'I love you too.'

When Reece cancelled the call, he looked across the room to see Anna smiling back at him. Realising he was blushing; he could only smile back.

'Don't worry David, we all need someone some time.'

At the same time Yasmin was arriving at the Casa Ellul Boutique hotel in the centre of the city of Valletta. The receptionist noted the details of the British passport that contained her picture and gave her name as Carletta Maguire from Catford just outside London. The Arab had booked all her travel arrangements and accommodation in this suite only hotel. Suite number five overlooked the narrow street outside. The rooms that faced this way all had the small iron balconies with a window door that opened inwards. When she opened the doors the iron protecting rails left the balcony just wide enough for the width of her feet to stand on. The open doors let a cool breeze into the room. There was the usual air conditioning unit on the wall, but it needed to build up the cooling fan after she'd switched it on. Lying on her back on the large four poster bed she realised she was tired. Yasmin took out the burner phone she'd been given and switched it on for the first time since leaving the Arab and Tehran. When the signal showed she could send her message she found the number that had been coded in and sent the words, *I am here room 5 Maguire*. Then lying back on the bed, she fell into a quick all enclosing sleep.

At the docks, Anna had taken over the binoculars and raising her hand she spoke to Reece and Palo without taking her eyes away from them.

'Guys. I think we are on.'

Both men went to the window standing behind her to look out. They hadn't switched on the lights as the sun had gone down, three people being illuminated looking out of a window was just not normal.

Reece could see three men coming down the ship's walkway but, without the benefit of the binoculars, he couldn't see their faces, but Anna could.

'It's definitely him, Shafi with two minders either side of him; both look the part, staying close, heads moving from side to side to see what they can. Shafi is using a walking stick which is strange, there is no mention of him needing one in the files. Here, have a look.'

Reece and Palo took turns to watching the men walk through the docks to the security hut at the entrance gate; then through and onto the main road, turning left and away from where they watched. Shafi looked just like his photo in the file. The two men walking each side of him but a step behind both had the look of young fit Arabs, each with a close shaved dark beard. If he were to describe them Reece would have said they were identical twins and only their jackets were different. One wore a denim coat while the other was wearing what appeared from the distance to be cheap imitation leather. Shafi from his bearing, sharp dark suit and open necked white shirt, emanated power.

'It looks like they're staying on foot and going in the opposite direction to Alpha Four,' said Reece, 'Let's move.'

'Palo, I'll stay with David on this side of the street to follow them into the city if they cross the road. You follow on their side and if they stop, we all pass by them to get ahead and turn back if needed I presume you're armed David?'

'Aren't we all!' he replied.

As they left the apartment Reece called Simons to let him know they were on the move.

'Stay where you are for now they might jump into a vehicle yet.'

'Understood,' replied Simons.

When they left the front door of the apartment the three targets were about 200 yards ahead of them still walking away from the docks.

Reece could see Shafi looking down at the screen of the mobile phone he was holding, then stop and speak to the two men following. All three then crossed the road to be on the same side as Reece and Anna. Even though they looked in the direction of Reece, they were paying attention to the oncoming traffic in the road while crossing. They then turned away from the watching pair and walked on with their backs to them. Reece noticed that each time Shafi looked at the screen he placed the walking stick he was carrying under his arm so he could work the screen with both hands.

'He's using the Sat Nav on his mobile. He is following it to a destination,' said Reece into his mic so the whole team heard at once.

'Roger that,' came the reply from Palo and Matthew. Anna just nodded her agreement having spotted the same thing herself.

'Why do you think they're walking?' asked Anna.

'For a number of reasons, I think,' replied Reece, 'They would know any taxi driver would be sure to remember picking up three Arabs from the docks and where he dropped them off. Then they have been cooped up on a ship for a while so they would like to stretch their legs and get some air. But I think the main reason is they will be taking their time and checking for surveillance following them. If they spot us, three things could happen, they could confront us, but they wouldn't be sure how many we are, so that is unlikely. If they do spot us, they might continue with their operation and try to lose us. Or three, they call the whole thing off, return to base and declare they have a spy in their ranks, all three of which will be bad for us so let's be careful.'

As Reece followed, he knew he would have to use all the trade skills he had been taught by MI5 on the streets of London many years ago and had used successfully to stay alive in Northern Ireland and most lately on the streets of Manchester; where in the end, he had to eliminate another terrorist. He was also thinking of Mary McAuley by his side on those streets, the woman he loved, when he thought of her he was glad she wasn't here now. He had put her in enough danger in her life, even though he knew she would give anything to be by his side instead of Anna the Mossad agent.

'They are turning into a side street,' said Anna breaking into his thoughts.

'I know the street, they'll be walking up a steep hill towards the city centre there's not much cover for us, no hotels just a few shops and the street will be quiet at this time,' said Reece.

'Alpha Four from Alpha Three come in, over.'

Simons replied to Reece immediately. 'Roger Alpha Three?'

'Our friends are walking towards the centre of the city, although they're taking the long way about it. Look up San Paul and Sant Orsla streets. Go there and find yourself a parking space. Don't know where they'll be going to ground yet, but that will get you closer to us, over.'

'Roger Alpha Three I'm on my way.'

'You do know your way round here David,' said Anna.

'Old habit. I'm sure like me when you did your surveillance training, they gave you a patch of a city to learn every nook and cranny, every street, every bus stop, taxi rank and subway station. They drilled it into you, so you didn't get lost up a dead-end alleyway. When I first moved here, I made a point of walking every inch of these streets and sat in a lot of cafes to watch the world go by. I still don't know every nook and cranny, but I think I know enough, at least I think I know more than the people we are following.'

'You're not giving away any secrets David, that's exactly as we are taught. Alpha Two let's keep this distance they seem to know where they are going.'

Palo waved from across the road and continued walking at the same pace as Reece and Anna.

The three men continued their walk, and Reece could see that they were relaxed by the way they kept walking straight ahead, not looking around, confident that they were in a city where no one knew them. The city was now a mixture of office workers going home and people going out for an early dinner in one of the many restaurants or perusing the tourist shops and buildings that were still open. Although the sun had gone down the evening was cool, but not cold; the street lights now bright against the dark blue sky. Once more the three men stopped while Shafi studied his mobile phone screen. Pointing, he said something to the men before they turned right into the next street.

'All call signs they've gone into San Pawl Street. Alpha Four be aware when you go into that area,' said Reece.

'Roger Alpha Three,' replied Simons.

The three men continued along San Pawl Street, then turned left into the next street.

'OK, everyone that's them into San Gann Street,' said Reece.

Palo and Simons replied 'Roger.'

Reece turned to Anna. 'I know this street. It leads up towards the centre and there are more shops and restaurants with a small Boutique hotel near the middle on the left as we go up.'

'Maybe that's where they're heading for?' said Anna.

'One of us must be psychic Anna, that's exactly where they're going.'

The three men had gone into the only hotel on the street. The last man of the trio, the one in the leather jacket, stopped for a moment to look up and down the street.

Reece was confident they were far enough back for comfort and not raising any suspicion. Appearing satisfied, the man had turned and entered the hotel.

'Alpha Four we have them at the Casa Ellul Hotel on San Gann Street. Can you park up nearby?' said Reece.

'No problem. I'm just round the corner in San Pawl Street,' replied Simons.

'What do you want to do now?' Reece asked Anna.

'Do you know this hotel?'

'Yes, it's a slightly upmarket one with a small reception area and a cocktail bar to the left when you go in. The rooms or suites as they're called are on three floors around an inside courtyard where they place some chairs and tables for dinner. There is a fountain in the centre of the courtyard with a statue of Heracles at the back end. I think there are only about twelve suites. It's called a boutique hotel because it's small but expensive.'

'You seem to know it fairly well. Have you stayed there?'

'No. I took Mary to dinner there once because the chef had a reputation for good food. The meal was nice but a bit too expensive for my liking. I hate it when chefs try to show off giving you microscopic portions which they call cuisine by using a special name of their own. I like the food to fill the plate. We didn't go back. As I said if we go in there and they're still in reception they'll clock us and that will make it difficult to follow them in the future; they might remember our faces.'

'We don't have a choice, David. We don't know who they might be meeting in there. I need to get close with the little device in my bag which might give us an indication if they have the plutonium with them.'

'I can't argue with that, and a man and a woman together will register less interest than one of us on our own.'

Anna spoke into her mic.

'Alpha Three and I will go into the hotel and find out what we can. Everyone else stay alert if we need you to come running.'

The affirmative replies from Palo and Simons came back.

'OK, David let's go and sample a cocktail, shall we?'

Colonel Ali Shafi was confident that, so far, his mission was safe, and he was now where he should be at this time. He did not need to approach the reception desk which at that moment was unmanned. He knew the room number and stopping to tell his two minders to wait, he turned to the stairs on the right of the reception with an arrow notice on the wall pointing up which said Suites 1 to 5 first floor. As he was talking to his minders, he noticed behind them, a man and woman coming in through the revolving doors: the couple continued past the men and into the cocktail bar. There was nothing special about them as they appeared to be smiling into each other's eyes and holding hands. He did not pay much attention to the man, but he did notice the woman, she was exceptionally beautiful, if only he had the time. A couple very much in love, he thought before he started to climb the stairs.

Reece and Anna were lucky, there was only one table which gave a view of the reception area, and it was free. Anna sat at the table, her back to the reception. Reece sat opposite Anna looking over her shoulder. Anna lifted her bag onto the table, looked inside and then at Reece.

'No alarm signal, nothing showing, he doesn't have the plutonium with him.'

'Provided your little device is working properly.'

'Let's hope so.'

A waiter came to the table.

'Can I get you something to drink?'

'Can I have a Bloody Mary,' said Reece.

'Make that two,' said Anna.

When the waiter left Anna looked at Reece once more.

'I think I heard him tell his men the room number. He said five. What are they doing now?'

'Sitting in reception,' said Reece looking over her shoulder.

'When the drinks come, I'll go to the little girl's room and update Palo and Matthew. Then we sit and enjoy our drinks for a while.'

The drinks arrived and Anna took her walk.

Reece watched the men without letting his eyes fall on them for too long. He could see they looked fit and were pretending like him, to be natural without drawing attention to themselves.

Reece pressed his elbow against his side and could feel the hard metal of the Smith and Wesson reassuring at his waist. He could also feel a slight stab of pain in his right shoulder the shrapnel from the wound received in that shoot-out with Sean Costello years before.

Ali Shafi knocked lightly on the door which after a few seconds was opened by Yasmin. She was always a light sleeper and the time she'd slept had rejuvenated her strength, she felt ready for the next part of her mission.

'Yasmin, I am the Colonel.'

It was the agreed approach, the one the Arab had told her, and she gave her reply.

'I am the daughter of Allah.'

'As-Salaam Alaikum, Yasmin.'

'Wa'alaikum salaam, Colonel,' replied Yasmin.

Introductions over, she opened the door and waved him into the suite.

'You have a nice place here. Will you be staying long?'

She knew his mission brief would only take him as far as where he stood now.

'Not long. You have the package for me?'

He noticed by her tone that she did not want to take any longer to complete the handover than she had to. *A pity*, he thought. She was quite pretty, and he would have liked to get to know her more intimately if they had the time. As a Colonel in the Republican Guard, he was used to getting his own way, giving orders that were obeyed instantly and having his way with women even though he was supposed to be faithful to his wife. He smiled as he remembered an old saying. 'There's no such thing as a married man a hundred miles from home.'

'The package as you call it you may already know, this is it.' He held out the walking stick in both hands like a Samurai handing over his sword.

She took it from him and immediately she could feel that it was heavier than she expected.

'You notice the weight I'm sure. That's because the outer shell is made of a special form of lead.'

She noticed that apart from the weight, the walking stick looked like it was made of silver with Arabic engraving on the outside.

He held out his hands once more and she placed the stick back in them.

'You are right, the outer casing is, as I say lead but, covered by sterling silver and the engraving you also noticed is very special too.'

'What does it say?'

'The Light of the Sun.'

'What does it mean?'

He walked over to the bed and beckoned her to follow him. Laying the walking stick on the bed he started to unscrew the silver knob at the top.

'As you can see you unscrew the top clockwise, this is opposite to the normal anti-clockwise as a simple security measure should anyone try to see if they can open it. Inside the hollow tube wrapped in another material to protect you is the weapons grade plutonium which if used in the way we want will answer your last question, it will light up the sky with The Light of the Sun. The lead of the outer shell and the material inside will protect against the x-ray machines and explosive detectors at airports and security checks from finding the plutonium. Is it your job to deliver the walking stick to its destination?'

'That is none of your concern. We each have our own part to play in this operation and to protect its security we only need to know our own part, no more.' she replied sharply using the words of the Teacher.

Again, the Iranian Colonel felt as if she'd slapped him across the face and he wasn't happy. *Maybe this woman needed a lesson*, he thought. Throwing the walking stick on the bed he pulled her two arms down by her side then pulled her in close to his body and tried to kiss her on the lips. To his surprise she didn't resist instead putting her arms around him, returning his kiss with her lips for a longer time than he expected. He relaxed his grip and when she pulled back from him he was surprised once more that when she stood in front of him, she was holding his gun in her hands. She'd removed the weapon easily from his shoulder holster when his attention was elsewhere. Now it was aimed at the centre of his chest.

'What are you doing?' he asked.

'A certain gentleman tried to force himself on me once before and I had to let him know his approach was not welcome.'

'That was not my intention. I thought you would like some company to help relieve the stress of your part in this operation.'

She smiled as she noticed the sweat on his forehead and the nervousness in his words. Suddenly he realised who he was dealing with, not the timid little woman he expected.

'I know about stress, and I agree. Maybe we should relax a bit to complete our part in the mission. At least let us lie on the bed and get comfortable.'

'I don't think I could relax with you pointing my gun at me.'

'It's a German Glock isn't it, with one in the chamber I presume.'

He just nodded never taking his eyes off the gun in her hand.

Waving him to lie down on the bed she moved to the opposite side.

'Now let's lie down and relax and to help I'll put the gun under the pillow until we are finished, then you can have it and be on your way no more to be said.'

'It will take a lot of foreplay to help me relax after this,' he said before lying down. She bent forward slowly slipping her gun hand under the pillow. This relaxed the Colonel seeing the gun placed out of sight and the fact that his two minders knew where he was helped reassure him.

Kneeling on the bed Yasmin placed her legs astride him and once more leant forward to kiss him. She could feel his manhood start to go stiff between them and his arms searching for her waist closing his eyes in response to her lips. At the same time, she stretched her right hand under the pillow and bringing out the gun she lifted a pillow with her left placed it over his face. The sound in the room was loud to her ears but she knew the pillow had deadened it to anyone outside. She left the scorched pillow in place, while the dark red blood spread slowly below it, then placed the gun on top of the body and pulled the duvet over it covering it up so it would look like someone sleeping there. Looking down at the form on the bed, she now remembered her final briefing from the Arab at his poolside in Tehran.

'When you receive the package, you will kill the Colonel. He is an enemy of the holy Jihad and a spy for our great enemy that is Israel.'

She had not questioned his instructions, if the Colonel was such a spy, then he should die. She was a soldier of the Jihad and that was her mission to kill the enemy no matter who and where she found them. She had been wondering how she was going to do it and once again in her lifetime due to the arrogance of a man, the weapon had been provided.

Quickly collecting her things in her backpack and checking she had no spots of blood on her clothes, she slid the walking stick down the inside of her jeans. When she walked, she was unable to bend her leg so she would pretend she had a slight limp. She would only have to do this until she was far away from the hotel. Placing a Do Not Disturb sign on the outside of the suite door handle, she took the stairs to the ground floor and reception. Leaving her key at the empty reception desk she walked past the two men sitting beside each other and without making eye contact walked out of the hotel to find a taxi from the stand at the end of the street.

'Malta airport please,' said Yasmin as she threw her backpack onto the rear seat then took her time to sit behind the driver and stretch the leg with the walking stick across the seat.

Anna sat back down at the table.

'Anything happen while I was away?' she asked.

'Not much, our two boys ordered coffee and a young woman left the hotel. What about the guys?'

'I updated them and told them to meet up somewhere near the hotel where they can observe the front door. Palo had already found a café with tables outside it with such a view and Matthew is going to meet up with him. Did the young woman leave the hotel because the coffee's bad?' Smiled Anna.

'She didn't seem to want to wait around to find out.'

'Shall we order another one while we wait? We don't know how long we will be here?'

'Good idea I like my Bloody Mary spicy and this one is exactly right. But we will have to take it slowly we need to keep our heads alert for this.'

'You're right let's make them Virgin Marys without the vodka. We will have to use our imagination instead.'

'Yuck. It will have to be good to imagine a Bloody Mary without vodka but let's go for it.'

Chapter 16

Having received the text from Hassan that he had arrived safely in London, the Arab closed his villa and left his car at the airport before catching a flight to Rome, then a connecting flight to London Heathrow. The new false British and European Union passport he was using identified him as Doctor Ali Hussein Mohammad. His cover story was that he was a pediatrician at Guys Hospital in London. The documents and the cover story put together by the Iranian Quds Covert Operations Directorate were of the highest quality. The one thing the Arab was sure of was that the British always respect their police and their doctors without question. As he had expected, the documents and his experience in using false papers allowed him to pass through airport security with ease. The fact that he only had a small cabin bag made the experience even easier. When he had landed at Heathrow, he took the Heathrow Express to Paddington Station in central London then, after a quick text message exchange with Hassan, took a taxi from the station to Edgware Road where, when he knocked on the door, it was opened by Hassan. *The mission is progressing to plan,* he thought, *each playing their part as he had asked.* At the same time Yasmin had arrived in her taxi at Malta airport. She made her way to the ladies' room and inside a cubicle she removed the walking stick from her jeans. Now she could bend her leg and using the stick as it was meant to be used walked to the departures desk to book in for her flight to London with Malta Airlines. If everything went well, she would be in London by midnight.

Back in the boutique hotel in Valletta, Reece tried to keep the conversation casual, smiling across at Anna each time one of the men in reception started to look around checking his surroundings.

'These Virgin Bloody Marys don't taste all that bad.' He tried to smile once more as he took a sip.

Anna could only laugh. 'They are terrible, and you're not a very good liar, Mister Reece.'

Reece laughed back.

'You're right, it's terrible. Our friends are looking a little nervous. Maybe it's the coffee?'

'Shafi is upstairs meeting someone we don't know maybe handing over the package. When he leaves, we will know the handover may have taken place. Hopefully, he walks out with the contact.'

'I hope it's soon. I don't think I could drink too many of these,' said Reece, holding up the glass that was now almost empty.

Palo and Matthew were into their second pot of coffee and getting to know each other while watching the front door of the hotel which gave them a good view of anyone coming or going. In the last hour, the only one leaving was a woman on her own, carrying a rucksack and walking with a limp. She was wearing some sort of scarf pulled in tight over her head. Looking round she spotted the taxi stand and left in one of them. Since then, there had been no one in or out. The evening stars were coming out. Although the temperature had dropped it was still warm enough to sit outside and the few tables that there were, were increasingly being taken up by the customers of the night. Those same customers of the night were also filling up the streets, making an atmosphere of the flowing life of Malta, with locals, tourists and business owners coming and going.

'I've never been to Malta before, but from what I've seen I would like to come back as a tourist sometime,' said Matthew.

'I've never been here myself. In a way it reminds me of Jerusalem, the buildings; the history involving the Mediterranean. Have you ever been to Jerusalem?'

'No, I'm sorry to say I haven't. That's another place for my list.'

'If you ever go there let me know and maybe we can meet up. I'll show you around the sites the tourists do not get to see, the ones protected by the security and the IDF, sacred sites to the Jewish people if you really like history.'

'I'll do the same if you're ever in London.'

'It's a deal. You never know, what happens here might see us both in London and Jerusalem sooner than we think.'

Inside the hotel, Reece had continued to watch the men over Anna's shoulder. He noticed they were getting more agitated, looking at their watches talking quickly to each other. The one in the leather coat had got up and walked back and forth while at the same time looking up at the lights on the lift numbers and then the stairs for movement. They had been there for almost two hours.

'I hate this waiting for something to happen,' said Anna.

'Especially when we can't drink real alcohol. We will give it another thirty minutes then we can swap places with the guys at the café. These two are beginning to look like cats on a hot tin roof,' said Reece.

'They must be like us. Starting to wonder what is taking so long. It's a waiting game for everyone but I think a change of scenery for us is a good idea.'

'I'll take a quick trip to the steps outside and let the boys know what we're thinking can you cover here?' asked Anna.

'Yes, no problem but avoid eye contact when you walk by them.'

'Of course, darling, I don't want to make you jealous.'

'I'm not worried about me, it's them I don't want getting ideas,' smiled Reece.

True to her word Anna walked straight past the two men without looking in their direction. Reece noticed the two men paid no attention to the woman but continued in close conversation with each other still looking at their watches and then at the stairs where they last saw their boss two hours ago. From years of interviewing terrorists across a desk Reece could see from the men's body language they were planning to do something soon.

Anna had returned and sat in front of Reece once more when the men made their move.

'I don't think we will have to wait much longer. Our friend in the leather coat just went up the stairs and his buddy is standing by the front door,' said Reece.

Anna spoke quietly into her mic to update Palo and Simons.

Ten minutes later Reece watched as leather coat came back down the stairs and whispered to his partner to which his partner asked a question. Leather coat shook his head in the negative. Both men then went up the stairs together. Although they did not seem to be in a hurry or panic Reece could see the concern on both their faces.

'Somethings wrong. They don't seem happy. I'll follow them you stay here. They have seen you twice and we've been sitting here for some time. If they spot me, they might think we are residents, but I think it's time to get a little closer. Tell Palo and Matthew to take up position outside and be ready for action if we need it.'

'OK David but take care. Our handover friend might not be here yet and that's causing them confusion.'

Reece passed the reception desk and noticing there was a young girl behind the desk he turned left, taking the stairs two at a time. Each floor of the hotel had closed glass fire doors giving a view of the long corridor leading to the suites. Reece could see the first floor was empty as he reached the second, he could hear loud knocking. Slowing down he took care to look through the glass doors in time to see both the Arab bodyguards shoulder charge the door which on the third charge they broke through. Reece turned and made his way back down to sit beside Anna, who had now turned her chair to face the reception area.

'I think we may have a problem,' said Reece.

'What's happening?'

'Our friends had to break down a door to a suite on the second floor. They are in there now so I think we will be seeing them soon with or without their boss.'

Twenty minutes later his prediction came true. Both bodyguards came back down the stairs this time a little faster than when they went up and left the hotel.

'Alpha Two and Alpha Four try to follow our two friends and see where they go. We are checking up on their boss,' said Reece into his mic.

'Roger that,' replied Palo, 'we have them, they seem to be heading back the way they came.'

'Anna, you stay here and cover my back if anyone else goes up the stairs '

'What are you going to do?'

'We have to know what's going on up there. The way those two left tells me there is something wrong. We need to act now.'

'Just so you know: I hear anything that sounds like trouble, I'm coming up gun blazing.'

'Just make sure you're aiming at the bad guys,' smiled Reece.

Reece passed the reception desk which was empty again and took the stairs two at a time once more. He had noticed there only seemed to be one CCTV camera and that was facing the reception desk. There didn't appear to be any on the stairs or in the corridors leading to the suites. Reaching the empty second floor, Reece walked slowly until he was standing outside the door to suite number five. He had intended to listen at the door, but he could see that despite the DO NOT DISTURB sign which still hung from the handle, the door frame was splintered, and the damaged lock set back from the closed position leaving the door slightly open. Reece pulled out the Smith and Wesson and gently pushing the door with the barrel, he slipped off the safety catch, ready to fire quickly if he needed to.

The lights were on and, with the gun in the fire v shaped position, with his arms straight he swept from left to right and focused on what he could now see was the body of Shafi lying face up on the bed. He didn't need to check if he was dead. Shafi's eyes were open looking at the ceiling and it was clear that a bullet had passed through the centre of his head, just above them. The bathroom, like the bedroom was clear.

Looking around he could see the bloody pillow with the scorched hole lying on the floor. He searched the pockets, and checked drawers and the room, making sure to leave no prints, he used his handkerchief to touch the surfaces. There was nothing to find or any more to be gained by staying and he returned to the bar where Anna watched him as he sat at the table her expression full of questions.

'We need to move. I'll explain as we go,' said Reece standing.

Outside the hotel Reece told Anna what he had found, and he passed on the information to Palo and Matthew as they walked back towards the harbour.

'What the fuck's going on here? I don't believe the bodyguards killed him. That's probably why they left so quickly. They need to get back to the ship and report home.'

'I agree,' said Anna, what do you think happened?'

'If the bodyguards didn't do, it then it could only have been the courier he was supposed to meet. I can tell you this, whoever did it was a professional, someone with training. And whoever they were, they were gone before the bodyguards broke into the room.'

'Then who?'

'I saw a woman leave the hotel. She was limping slightly and wore a scarf. She passed by the bodyguards without looking at them which, now that I think about it; is exactly what we would have done in her place.'

'Again, I ask if she was the contact why kill him?'

'I think that's a question for people on a bigger paygrade than us,' said Reece.

Reece spoke into his radio.

'Alpha Four, did you see the woman who came out of the hotel before the bodyguards left?'

'Yes,' replied Simons. 'She passed us on the other side of the street and got into a taxi.'

'Alfa Three?' It was Matthew Simons again.

'Go ahead, Alfa Four,' replied Reece.

'Our two friends are back on-board ship.'

'Roger that. Both of you go back to the apartment we will meet you there.'

'So, we go back to the apartment for a catch-up?' Said Anna.

'We need to contact our bosses, tell them what's happened and what we think needs to be done next.'

Chapter 17

Two hours later the four agents had gone over the operation so far and Anna and Reece had both updated their bosses. In the case of Anna to the Director of the Mossad Kidon Units Kurt Shimon in Tel Aviv and for Reece it was Jim Broad, Director of Operations SG9 in London. Both agents had spoken to their relevant bosses in separate rooms away from the hearing of the others.

'How did it go for you?' Reece asked Anna when she came back into the front room.

'Not bad, he seemed to take it very well. Then I don't think anyone can read Kurt Shimon when he's about to blow his top. How was it for you?'

'Jim Broad is going to get 'C' to phone the British High Commissioner to ask him to discreetly find out what the Malta Police find out. If I know anything, someone with a name like Julian Richardson Smith does not do discreet; they're more like a bull in a China shop but will always make sure to protect their asses making sure the shit falls on someone else.'

'I presume when your boss uses the Old Boys' network, they make sure this Julian won't know about us?'

'Correct. We disappear into the sunset or sunrise, as it will be coming up next. In the meantime, I think our bodyguard friends will stay on that ship awaiting instructions from Tehran. We also must assume that our lady friend who left the hotel and took the taxi is our courier and killer and headed straight for the airport. Why she killed him we have yet to discover. The last we saw her was over four hours ago so if flights were on time and I've checked on flights out of Malta dot com they are, then she could already be in London. Our technical people at GCHQ in Cheltenham are checking CCTV and manifests for passengers leaving Malta and landing in London for that timeframe. My boss wants me back in London as soon as possible. Matthew is to stay here and keep an eye on our friends on the ship and if necessary be available to link up with the High Commissioner and local security forces.'

'My boss told me I have to stay with you, so it looks like I'm going to London. Palo will stay here with Matthew as back-up.'

Matthew Simons, who had been watching the people coming and going through the harbour and on the ship through the binoculars, raised his hand in acknowledgement. Palo, who had been listening into the conversation, nodded in agreement. The lights in the room had been dulled to reduce Simon's silhouette at the window making the room seem secretive to the conversation it could hear, if, rooms heard secrets.

'I've been thinking about how the woman walked to the taxi,' said Palo, 'She seemed to be limping or had some form of stiffness in her leg. Do you suppose she had the walking stick down her trouser leg?'

'That's a good bet, especially if she's the courier and assassin. I saw no sign of the stick when I was in the hotel suite,' said Reece.

'But you did see Shafi with his face blown away,' said Matthew.

'Yes, and we still don't know why and that's the problem. There's something else going on here that we don't know about. Maybe we will know more when we get to London. There is plenty of stuff in the fridge, so I suggest you take turns at the window while the other gets some rest. Anna and I will take the car back to her hotel and my house to pick up our bags and on the way, I'll get London to book us on the first flight out. They probably won't notice they have a dead body in suite five until the morning cleaning. I left the DO NOT DISTURB sign on the door and closed it the best I could when I left. Matthew if that ship sails with our two friends on it, let our people know then act on their instructions.'

Reece and Anna left collecting her bag from her hotel room then Reece brought them to his villa at Saint Paul's Bay. Mary was still up and after introductions Reece left Mary and Anna to get to know each other when he went for a quick shower.

Within a short time, Mary realised she liked this woman and had nothing to fear when it came to Reece. Anna told her of her life in Israel and how she loved her country without adding anything about her work for Mossad. She spoke more like a travel agent making Mary respond by telling her of her own home country in Ireland. Mary made a pot of coffee, and they were just sitting down to a cup when Reece returned from his shower. He was carrying a small rucksack which Mary recognised as his quick travel bag for travel at short notice.

'Only time for a quick coffee I'm afraid. I've booked us out of Malta on the last flight tonight. It's going to Paris, but we can jump on the

Eurostar which will get us into London for six tomorrow morning. The first direct flight to London from Malta doesn't leave until ten thirty in the morning and I thought this will help us get ahead of the game. A game we are already behind on.'

Reece could see by the expression on her face Mary wasn't happy. Anna could also see Mary's face and excused herself for the bathroom.

'Mary, you know I don't want to involve you in this. I don't want to leave you here, but you know the business I'm in and I can only tell you it's not going too well now and that's why we need to get to London as soon as possible. I want you to stay here and wait for Matthew who will need to pick up his stuff. If he needs to fly back to London, why don't you jump on the same flight, and we can spend some time in Belfast when this is over. You're always saying you want to catch-up with your mother.'

This seemed to pacify Mary, she nodded and smiled.

'Good save, I would love that. You know I worry because I love you, so wherever you are and whatever you're doing it's important you stay safe for me.'

Anna who had caught the last bit of the conversation when she walked back into the room, said nothing but smiled at seeing the concern Reece had for the woman he loved.

'Mary, the flight leaves just after 1 am so we will need you to drop us off at the airport. I love you too and don't worry I intend to stay safe.'

'No problem, I'll get my coat.'

Chapter 18

The flight from Malta landed in London just after midnight and as she didn't have to wait on any hold luggage Yasmin found no obstruction going through the Terminal building. Following the lanes marked Arrivals EU she soon found herself passing through passport control where the officer behind the desk paid no special attention other than looking at her walking stick as she limped through. Outside the arrivals building she got into a black cab; the kind well known in London. She asked the driver to drop her off at the bottom of Edgware Road across from Hyde Park. When she'd sent the Teacher a text that she'd arrived, he had replied with the address she was going to. When she'd been with him at his villa in Iran, he had told her to get dropped off at the end of the road or street she was travelling to, and never to give the driver the exact address or to be dropped off outside. She was then to walk to the address looking for security forces who might be observing her or the address. In the taxi she soon relaxed in the seat, noticing two things, the large number of similar taxis leaving the airport and the drop in temperature which was a lot colder than the air in Malta. Forty minutes later she was knocking on the door of the apartment on Edgware Road, which was quickly opened by Hassan.

'Good evening,' said Hassan speaking in English as they'd been told by the Teacher.

'Good night I think at this time of the day,' replied Yasmin smiling.

Both embraced as if they'd not seen each other for years. Anyone watching at this time of night would think that they were friends or lovers. Hassan closed the door, took the rucksack off Yasmin's back and led her up a flight of stairs to the first floor above the barber shop and the street.

He pointed to a door on the right down a long corridor, which had stairs on the left leading up to what could only be another floor in the apartment. 'The Teacher is waiting for you through that door.' Yasmin walked to the door still in limping mode with the walking stick in her right hand. The room was well lit, bright with a set of wall lights and a ceiling light all switched on. The Teacher sat in a large soft chair facing the door with his back to the window that looked out onto Edgware Road, if the curtains were open.

'My child it is wonderful to see you once more,' said the Arab standing to greet her with a hug and kissing her on each side of her face. 'How was your journey? Tell me everything while Hassan makes us some tea.'

For the next hour during which Hassan joined them Yasmin told the Arab everything that had happened to her on her journey from Iran through Malta and then on to London. He made her go over her meeting and killing of Shafi three times, taking the walking stick from her as she spoke. Screwing the top of the stick clockwise he took off the knob and turning it upside down he let the contents, three long sticks covered in a thick plastic type of material slide out onto the couch. The Arab, satisfied, put on a pair of surgical gloves and slid the black sticks back into the walking stick screwing the knob back on. He took off the gloves and placed them in the bin in the kitchen.

'Do you think the bodyguards will remember you?' asked the Arab.

'No, I had my scarf pulled up and walked straight past them without eye contact.'

'Did you see or suspect anyone else on your journey?'

'No, I saw no one or suspected anything unusual.'

This satisfied the Arab as he stood once more. 'You will be tired. Both of you have done well and the first part of your mission has now been completed. You will both be staying here for the rest of the plan. I will be staying elsewhere, and you do not need to know where that is, it is not important. I'll return tomorrow morning and we will discuss the next part of our plan. In the meantime, rest, keep the walking stick here and you will know more tomorrow. In the morning make sure you pray to Allah that he will bless our mission.'

The flight to Paris and the train journey into London had gone well arriving on time at St Pancras just after 6 a.m. Reece had received a text from Jim Broad telling him that he should bring Anna to the MI6 HQ at Vauxhall Bridge for a 1 p.m. debrief and meeting. For now, he had booked them into apartments in Pimlico where they should get some rest. The Churchill Serviced Apartments in Pimlico were just as it said on the tin as far as Security Service Personnel staying and working in London were concerned. The stylish apartments were watched over by several ex-military personnel to ensure safety for the people using them. The smartly dressed concierge reminded Reece of a para regimental sergeant major he once knew in his days fighting the terrorist war in Northern Ireland. Built like a brick wall Reece was sure he could still jump out of a plane and hit the ground running if he had too.

'Good morning, Mr Reece, my name is Johnson. We have been told to expect you both. Here is your key, you're in apartment two on the first floor. The apartment has two bedrooms with a kitchen and bathroom ready for your use. If there's anything else you need just let me know.'

'Thank you, Johnson, to tell you the truth we are both knackered, and I know I need sleep, so if you could give us a wake-up call at twelve that would be great. I'm not confident I'll hear my own alarm.'

'No problem, Mr Reece, will do.'

Reece wasn't exaggerating. Anna went for a shower while he headed straight for one of the bedrooms where without taking his clothes off, he was asleep within seconds of his head hitting the pillow. Anna showered quickly and like Reece although the water jet had freshened her, she was asleep in the other bedroom ten minutes after Reece.

COBRA stands for Cabinet Office Briefing Room-A and is the British Government's briefing and meeting room when there is a crisis in the country. Different Government Ministers covering their own departments can chair the meetings usually with experts in the relevant issue that brings the committee together to deal with the crisis of the day. The meetings are usually called in times of great need. At 8 am. While Reece and Anna were catching up on their sleep in Pimlico, just such a meeting was taking place in the Cabinet Office Building at 70, Whitehall, just behind 10 Downing Street. The room was windowless, with one large central table surrounded by brown leather commuter type chairs. In front of each chair was a small computer screen and on the wall was a large screen visible to all sitting around the table. The room was the British equivalent to the more famous American Situation Room in the White House. Chairing the meeting and seated in the middle chair on one side of the table, was the Prime Minister, Peter Brookfield. Present were his senior advisers in the fields of Intelligence and Anti-Terrorism. From MI6, Sir Ian Fraser, known to those present as 'C'; from MI5 Caroline Aspinall; from the Metropolitan Police Commissioner, Sir Stuart Stevens, and his Deputy Commissioner in Charge of the Anti-Terrorist Squad, Helen Francis. There were three other people who because of their rank and expertise were attending to ensure the PM was getting the best advice possible before he made any decisions.

Suzanne Hughes MP, the Home Secretary; Sir Martin Bryant, Chair of the Intelligence Committee; and General Sir John Richardson, British Armed Forces Chief of Staff. For this meeting there was to be no civil servant present as notes did not need to be taken. This was a briefing and discussion meeting only. Any follow up or actions resulting from the meeting would be passed on to the various departments by the people present to carry out the final agreement made by those at the meeting. The PM opened the meeting by asking if everyone present had read the small file each had been given to bring them up to date with the issue before them. Everyone indicated they had, and he continued.

'Good. You will now be aware of where we are with this operation which I have sanctioned. Unless I'm mistaken 'C', we don't know where the plutonium, or the people that have it, are now?'

Everyone looked to where Sir Ian Fraser, sat opposite the PM, and waited for his reply.

'As everyone will see from the short report in front of them Prime Minister, we've been working with our friends in the Israeli Secret Service Mossad on this matter. From our end, we've identified the Barcelona Suicide Bomber as a onetime British Citizen and her connections to a Jihad terrorist known as the Arab, who attended university in this country before becoming the high-ranking terrorist master he now is. Intelligence received mostly from Mossad has indicated that the target for the use of this plutonium attack is somewhere in Europe most likely here in the UK.'

Although all those around the table were highly experienced in their own fields, some of them still took a deep breath as they thought of the serious threat that these words brought home to them.

'So, what you're saying Prime Minister, is that for now we don't know where these people are and there is an imminent threat of a terrorist attack in this country possibly here in London using a dirty bomb?' It was the Suzanne Hughes the Home Secretary asking the question.

'I think the question you're asking is correct in its assumption at this time Home Secretary,' replied Brookfield.

Feeling the tension in the room Sir Ian continued.

'In a joint operation with Mossad our own people have been working to track down the terrorist cell involved. The trail led to Malta where we believe there was a handover of the plutonium by an Iranian Quads Colonel to a member of the cell. This Colonel was, we believe then murdered by this terrorist, who we believe, from our people there, to be a woman. We don't know at this time why they killed him. From further checks it's thought she may have taken a flight into this country shortly afterwards.'

'But how did she get the plutonium through the airport's security checks?' it was Martin Bryant who asked the question. Sir Ian knew someone would ask.

'As anyone who works in the security business knows there are ways and means. Our scanners should show such items up, but with modern technology, ways can sometimes be found to circumvent our systems, as we have seen in the past with the shoe bomber and the bomber who nearly blew himself and a plane out of the sky when one went off in his underwear. Our people did see the Colonel arrive for his meeting in the Malta hotel with a silver walking stick, which they couldn't find after he was killed. We believe the woman, who may now be in London, was the assassin; and that she brought the walking stick with her into this country. We believe this walking stick contains the plutonium.'

'What are your people doing now Sir Ian?' asked the Prime Minister.

'We have been working closely with Mossad during this operation, and my head of operations Jim Broad will be briefing me further today and I will of course bring you up to date then. We are asking for the CCTV and passenger details of the flight from Malta to London which we think the woman used. Our agents on the ground were able to see what she was wearing and it's possible she did not have time to change clothes before her flight. We have agents in Malta watching the Iranian ship and the Hezbollah bodyguards on-board in case they go back into the city of Valletta. I would suggest that you contact our Commissioner in Malta to ask their security and police to help us track down this woman by releasing any information they get while investigating the Colonel's murder, and the woman's movements afterwards. This will include access to the hotel and airport CCTV and records. I also have GCHQ at Cheltenham checking their systems and our access to CCTV at the London airports, looking for a woman with a distinctive walking stick who might fit our target's description. This will also require the help of our police, anti-terrorist people and MI5, especially anything they're getting from their agents and technical sources. Information, however small, is vital. I have a specialist Matthew Simons. He's the head of our Middle East desk who is currently in Malta, and I've instructed him to return immediately and link in with all the agencies including those at this table to co-ordinate all the information we generate.'

'Of course, Sir Ian. As your people are already aware, I think you should take the lead in this country for now. Everyone here will give you whatever support you require. Going around the room does anyone else have anything they would like to add?'

'I think it's too early to comment now Prime Minister,' it was Sir Martin Bryant who answered on behalf of those there. 'The one thing I would like an answer to as soon as possible is, why was this Iranian Colonel killed? Is there something else going on that we are not aware of? How do we get these answers? We all know how Mossad operate. They've killed their enemies in Malta before. Are they at their work once more, and if anything goes wrong, would they leave us as the Patsy picking up the pieces? The Home Secretary will also have to consider if we should raise the current threat level now.'

'That is something to think about and I'm sure 'C' is on to it as well.' answered Peter Brookfield.

Sir Ian Fraser was waiting for something like this from Martin Bryant. Always the politician lining up someone to blame if things hit the fan. It was time to produce his ace up his sleeve.

'Correct Prime Minister. I can only answer Sir Martin with what I've already told everyone here, that this is an ongoing joint operation with Mossad. I think raising the threat level at this time might tip off our terrorists, and that might even bring an attack earlier than they planned if it's not already underway. Upgrading the level will bring questions from the press, the people, and fellow politicians, which could cause panic in the population. Without the intelligence Mossad have given us already, I do not think we would even be aware of much of what we do have. I can tell everyone here that I've been contacted by Kurt Shimon the Director of the Mossad Kidon agents. He tells me he is currently on his way to London as we speak, and he has asked to meet me at Vauxhall Cross this afternoon. I don't think he would be coming to London unless he has something of importance to tell us and he wants to be here when we progress this operation.'

Peter Brookfield looked around the room before he replied.

'I hope he has something for us. Because without a lucky break, as far as I can see, we might reach a situation where we will have to bring in severe restrictions on movements and increase searches. The people of this country will not be happy with that. Get out there and find these people as a matter of urgency. I do not want to see any leaks in the press that would cause panic and maybe tip the hand of the terrorists to change their plans whatever they are. If I think we will need another meeting Sir Martin will let you know. In the meantime, everyone, any information, give it to Sir Ian and his team so that they can catch these people. Sir Martin and Sir Ian please stay behind for a minute. Everyone else let us get our people hunting.'

After the three men were left alone Peter Brookfield spoke to the two men in a slow deliberate quiet voice.

'I think you will both agree with me, that this is probably one of the most dangerous situations we have been in. The reason I wanted to speak to you alone was because, once again, we find our most secret team SG9 deeply involved, from Malta to here. What I need to ask you. Should we keep them involved, bearing in mind that their original remit for their formation is not only to track down these threats but to eliminate them? From what you tell us, Sir Ian, they've carried out their mission as far as it was briefed to them in Malta. What I'm asking, I suppose is, do you think the national resources we have will be adequate to do the job without them now?'

'I understand what you're asking Prime Minister. SG9 has taken this as far as they could in Malta. The murder of the Iranian has muddied the water and they were tasked to find out who was meeting him and identify the item they were collecting. It was hoped we could have intercepted that person with the plutonium before they even got to these shores, but because of that murder and the assessment that the woman did the killing, we've moved on somewhat from the initial remit. Our SG9, and the Mossad agents at this moment are the only people who might have an idea of what this woman looks like and, who we are looking for. For now, I would like to keep our people involved if only to keep tabs on Mossad operating on our turf, even though they will deny it, I wouldn't be inclined to believe them. They are determined to get their hands on the Arab, and the niceties of good manners on their side will not be respected I'm sorry to say, probably because we would do the same in their place. I'll report back after my meeting with Kurt Shimon when I hope to have more information. The fact he is coming here personally means he not only is bringing something important to the table, but he wants to shoe himself into an operation on our soil involving his people.'

'All the more reason we should retain control Prime Minister,' said Bryant.

'OK. For now, we keep SG9 involved, but I want to be kept informed every step of the way, understood?'

'Yes, Prime Minister,' both men replied in unison feeling they sounded like a well-known pair of Civil Service Mandarins in a sitcom.

Chapter 19

Reece had slept deeply without dreams. He was awake before the wake-up call from Johnson but still replied with a 'Thank you,' when the phone had buzzed. Awake, he felt fully recovered from the exertions of the last forty-eight hours. Anna had heard the buzz of the phone and shouted from her room that she was awake. An hour later both agents were sitting in the outer office of the head of MI6 at Vauxhall Cross. To Reece, this office looked like so many more he had seen in government departments, modern furniture with the added flat screen computer screen on the steel desk. The secretary sitting behind it also looked like she'd come from a standard production line, white crisp blouse, dark pinstriped skirt, and black rimmed glasses. Reece thought her quite attractive for a woman who looked over fifty. She had asked them to take a seat as 'C' was busy now. She offered something to drink which both agents refused with a 'no thank you', then she returned to her typing.

'This is my first time here, what about you?' asked Anna.'

'A few times, and every time I came here the news was never good.'

'Well, the last time I spoke to my boss he wasn't happy so I'm ahead of you on that score.'

'At least you're one up on me. I've never been to Mossad Head Quarters. But when it comes to being told off, I've had some of those in the past, but I always think to myself, don't worry they can't make you pregnant.'

'Doesn't stop them trying,' smiled Anna.

The intercom on the secretary's desk buzzed. Pressing a button on the top of her desk, they heard the deadlock on the door open to the office of the head of MI6 release.

'You may go in now,' she said in her clipped educated voice.

The office was as Reece remembered it from the first time, when he was recruited by 'C' and Jim Broad into the Black Ops team that was SG9. Back then he realised he had been searching for a purpose in life, especially one where he could use the skill he had been trained in and used fighting the terrorist war in Northern Ireland all those years ago.

The same desk that had been used by every 'C'. Legend had it that it was the one used by Nelson on the Victory. The desk was clear of any files or documents, the only items being the tamper proof computer and a special desk communications console. Reece had been told the console allowed the director to speak securely with the Prime Minister as well as his equivalent in the CIA, Mossad and all the European Directors. In one corner stood the grandfather clock another item from a bygone age when the first head of MI6, Sir Mansfield Smith Cumming, who used the first initial surname to sign off all secret documents using green ink. The tradition stuck, every Director of MI6 afterwards used the prefix 'C', and the green ink tradition became protocol. Reece, when serving in the RUC Special Branch had always used the term Boss for his superiors. This was instilled into SB recruits so that an officer's rank was never spoken, protecting their identification as a police officer, especially in public, and in the undercover world they worked in. Reece rarely called Sir Ian Fraser 'C', using in the few times they met, the word Boss or Sir. The large bay window looking out over the Thames and London was fitted with windows that not only gave natural light but were bulletproof and made of a material that stopped audio or visual surveillance penetrating the room. Sitting at the large conference table, were three men. 'C' and Broad he knew, but the third man he did not know. Reece could see from the look of familiarity on Anna's face as she smiled but raised her eyebrows in question, that she did know the third man. Jim Broad stood to welcome them and gestured that they should join them at the table.

'Welcome David, welcome Anna,' said Broad. 'I think a quick introduction is needed for you both. Anna I'm James Broad one of the MI6 Covert Operations Directors.' Reece noted he made no mention of his department, SG9.

Pointing to the man at the end of the table that faced the bay window, Broad continued.

'This is Sir Ian Fraser, otherwise known in intelligence circles as 'C', the head of MI6 and of course you already know this man to my right, your own boss Kurt Shimon. For your information David he is the head of the Mossad Kidon teams.'

Both argents sat across from Broad and Shimon, wondering what was to come.

'I hope you were able to get some rest. I think you may be a little busy in the next few days,' said Sir Ian.

'Yes sir we did, thank you,' replied Reece.

'Good, then let us get on. Despite having the information that there was going to be a handover of terrorist materials in Malta we seem to have missed it. Instead, we lost the courier and discovered a murder. Not the greatest of operations, but from what we've learnt and discussed before you joined us it would appear none of these problems were down to how you carried out your part of the mission. I think Kurt can bring us up to date with some new information we were not aware of. It might help you understand a bit more about what happened in Malta.'

'Thank you, Sir Ian. It is good to meet you at last, Mr Reece. I've heard a lot about you. I hope you will forgive me but even Anna did not know what I'm about to tell you. The Iranian Colonel who was murdered was one of our agents. His own people would call him a spy or a traitor.'

Reece and Anna looked at each other, then around the table before looking once more at Kurt Shimon, who continued to speak.

'In a way, it was through Colonel Shafi that we first got on to what was developing in this terrorist plot. As head of security at one of the Iranian nuclear facilities he had been instructed by his masters in Iran to collect the plutonium and transport it and meet up with the courier in Malta. Anna, what you and David did in Malta was always going to be as good as the information you had at hand. The fact you were not aware of the information we had is not your fault. It was a matter of what you needed to know at the time, and I'd hoped that our dead agent Colonel Shafi would have given us the rest of the picture after his meeting with the courier. I would then have been able to brief you on the next part of your mission with a clearer picture of what was happening. We do not know at this time how our agent was blown or why they killed him without the torture that would be the norm for the Iranians and Hezbollah, but we will find out in the process of time. For now, we do not think your input to the mission has been exposed. We believe you are unknown to them at this time, although given by the fact they've killed Shafi, they must suspect we have some knowledge of their plans. I think the fact they appear to be continuing with their plans was deliberate. If we had had taken out the woman, the one we now suspect is the courier, then they would only have lost one member of what we believe is a bigger team. The other members of their team would regroup for a further operation; perhaps one we are not aware of. We believe this team is intact and will continue with its operation. It is now our job to find them and stop them. Now it looks like the target is here in the UK. I've told Sir Ian and our Prime Minister has told the British Prime Minister that Mossad are willing to work with the security forces in this country to help stop them.'

The room fell silent for a few seconds while Reece and Anna took in what they'd just heard. It was now time for Sir Ian Fraser to break that silence.

'As I told you when you joined us, we had already been briefed with the information you have just been given. I would think you might have some questions yourselves and the first question, I'm sure, will be what happens now? I'll hand over to Jim who is up to date. We've placed him in overall charge of the day to day running of this operation.'

Jim Broad had a pile of buff folders in front of him which he now passed around the table, keeping one for himself. Each folder had a large red X across the front with the words OPERATION SEARCH and TOP SECRET in capital letters across the top.

'I think the code name for this operation is very appropriate. This operation is now a country wide search.' said Broad standing to continue as if he was addressing a lecture hall.

Reece was laughing inside. Normally operation code names are selected by a computer so that they haven't been used before or the danger of being crossed over to another file. This name had either not been used before or had been deliberately selected by 'C' or Broad, who continued to speak, while at the same time reading from the folder in front of him. Everyone followed his voice while reading the words in their own folder.

'As of 10 a.m. this morning our two Hezbollah hoods have left Malta on the same vessel they sailed on into Valletta. We have instructed our two agents Matthew Simons and Palo to come to London on this afternoon's flight. When they get here, we've agreed they'll both run a combined operation desk at our rooms on the third floor, all information received will be fed through them. We have the resources of all the agencies at our disposal. All those agencies will be dropping everything else and concentrating their efforts solely on Operation Search. This will include the MI5 watchers, GCHQ at Cheltenham, the Met Anti-Terrorist Squad, and ourselves of course. David, I want you and Anna to work together on this. As you can see from the file, we still have little to go on, but we do believe this terrorist cell is here, somewhere in London. We do not think our girl in Malta hung around. We already have some feedback from Sir Julian Richardson Smith in Malta who has been speaking to his contacts in the Maltese government and police who are looking into the dead body of our Iranian Colonel. They inform him at this stage that they believe that he has been assassinated by the Israeli Secret Service, who I'm sorry to say Kurt, have form for this sort of thing previously in Malta.'

Reece could see a small smile at the side of Kurt Shimon's lips.

'Par for the course as you British would say,' replied the Mossad boss.

Broad nodded then continued with his report.

'Sir Julian was also able to tell us that a woman fitting our team's description booked into the same hotel room where the body was found and vanished without paying which we all know is a big no in the hotel trade.' It was Broad's turn to smile before continuing.

'The local police have been able to get the CCTV from the reception area of the hotel. They confirm through the local taxi drivers, that the woman went straight to the airport in one of their cars. Through his contacts and with a bit of persuasion from Sir Julian, who has told the local authorities the British government want to help in the search for the killer, he has been able to obtain the CCTV from the hotel and the airport security cameras.' Pointing to the opposite wall to where they were sitting Broad aimed the remote-control pen in his hand.

'If you would look at the screen the first video you will see is from the hotel.'

The video lasted about five minutes. Showing a young woman with Asian features with dark shoulder length hair. She appeared to know about the camera, keeping her head down the whole time, she was at the reception. They could see her talking to the receptionist but there was no audio. They watched as she handed over her passport which the receptionist appeared to scan with a scanner under the counter then handed it back with a key card before pointing to the stairs and lift. The video ended and Broad pressed another button on the pen.

The second time the video showed the woman carrying a small rucksack and walking with a limp. She was walking through the main doors and into the airport departures area of the building. After looking around, she walked to the ladies toilet where after a few minutes she reappeared, this time with a silver-coloured walking stick. Reece was not one hundred per cent sure, but he would have put a month's pay on it being the same one they had seen the Iranian Colonel walk into the hotel with, the one he couldn't find later. The woman on the video then booked in at the ticket desk before going through security, placing her rucksack and the walking stick through the security scanner before picking them up without problem on the other side. At the Departure Desk she had produced her passport, which had been scanned. The cameras, which had been in sweeping mode, picked her up moving through the airport and sitting a short time before moving through with other passengers to join her plane. Reece noticed she never lifted her head for a clear shot from the cameras. This woman knew what she was doing and wasn't going to make it easy for the security people who may be looking for her. The video screen went blank once more and Broad continued to speak.

'I'm sure you all noticed how she kept her head down and came out of the ladies with a walking stick, probably the one handed over by the Colonel, the one we believe contains the plutonium. How they've wrapped it we do not know yet, but however they've done it to get it past the airport security certainly works, because she was able to board a plane to London and we now believe she and her walking stick are somewhere in this country, most likely this city.'

Broad pressed the button once more and two full-frontal photos of the woman came onto the screen.

'These are the best photos we could get, but they are rather good. The one on the right is when she passed through the security search area at the airport. The one on the left is from her scanned passport. You will find copies of the photos in your file along with the details page of her passport.'

Reece looked down at the photo and tried to lock it into his brain.

'As you can see, even though Anna had the small Geiger counter and passed close to the Colonel when he had the walking stick in the hotel reception, it still didn't show any signal. We believe the Iranians have in some-way found a covering for the plutonium that protects it from scanners,' said Kurt Shimon.

'Yes. On that we can agree. So, you can see we have a huge problem,' said Fraser, 'The plutonium is now in this country and our scanners are useless. We need to find these people fast and eliminate the threat from them and the plutonium. Do we have anything on her arrival in this country Jim?'

Broad pressed the button on the remote device again showing a red dot on the screen which he used to follow the woman as she walked through Arrivals at London airport. The video was like the one showing her leaving Malta but this time staring into a camera at the passport desk.

The red dot then followed her outside the building for some distance before they could see she her climb into a black cab.

'As you can see, she arrived in London last night on the late flight from Malta and she still has the walking stick with her. We are currently trying to locate the taxi driver through the Met and MI5 but so far, we do not have any more information. We are also checking traffic cameras and APRN to try to track the taxi but nothing yet.'

Broad pressed the button once more and a screenshot of a passport came up.

'This is her passport document which is also in your folder. It shows her name as Carletta Maguire, twenty-five years old from Catford London. A quick check by the Met Anti-Terrorist Squad can confirm that a young lady of the same name lived there until two years ago when she appeared to travel to the Far East but did not return. There are two years left before the passport runs out. The photo looks like the real Carletta Maguire, but inquiries have confirmed it is not her. The passport has never been reported lost or stolen, so, I would worry about the real Carletta wherever she is. It would appear our lady who is similar in appearance is travelling on a false document, as we suspected. As of now she is our main target of interest. All resources are at our disposal. David if you could stay behind, I need to talk to you? For now, I believe Kurt has some information which he needs to update us with.'

Kurt Shimon stood as Broad sat back down at the table and walked over to stand in front of the wall screen.

'Thank you, Jim, and thank you Sir Ian for allowing us to help in this mission, which is critically just as important for us, as it is for you. As you've already heard Colonel Shafi, was indeed an agent of Mossad. Like you, we do not usually admit to who our agents are, dead or alive. Indeed, we have agents in the past, who have been captured and tortured before being executed publicly, hung from a crane in a square in an Arab town, just because we wouldn't admit they were one of ours. Shafi knew this when he became one of those agents. I have a quote in a frame on my office wall which keeps me going when I ask myself the question why am I doing this job? The quote from Golda Meir states, 'I understand the Arabs wanting to wipe us out, but do they really expect us to cooperate?' Golda is dead many years, but in my time I've come to understand that these Arabs don't just want to wipe us out, but anyone who supports us as well. This operation involves our two countries and our separate intelligence agencies. If we are to defeat these people, we need to work closely together on this. It might not suit some in our political or civil services, but we are at the coal face as you would say. The niceties of politics are not available to us, so we fight a common enemy every day together or alone. You are aware of our main interest in this. One of our agents has been killed and we will find out how or who exposed him. We believe everything about this involves the one we call the Arab. In your folders you will have the information we have on him and two photos; the one which was taken at celebrations just after 9/11, and the other just at the start of all this when he was photographed by our agents in Tehran in the company of the Quads General. The reason I'm here today instead of talking via a conference call is that I have something more to bring to the table. Forgive me, Sir Ian, but I wanted to wait until we were all here as this was passed to me from our London Embassy this morning. Jim, could I borrow your remote for a second.'

Taking the remote Shimon took a small pen-stick out of his coat pocket and finding the slot at the side of the wall screen inserted the device and pressed the button. The screen lit up to show a photo of people sitting at a distance around what looked like a swimming pool with a building behind them. Shimon pressed another button and the photo zoomed to a close-up stronger focus showing two men and a woman sitting at a table by the pool outside what now appeared to be a villa. Using the red highlight button Shimon rested the light on each person in the photo.

'The same agents who took the photo of the meeting between The Arab and the Quads General outside the cafe in Tehran, followed the Arab to the villa and at great risk were able to obtain this one photo. The first man is our friend the Arab; real name Abdullah Mohammad Safrah.' Highlighting the woman next to him he continued.

'This is the woman we've been speaking about; Shafi's killer and the courier of the plutonium into this country. The third man, we do not know. This photo was taken with a long-lens camera from some distance away. The villa just outside Tehran we believe belongs to the Arab and here we have him briefing his people. We again believe the briefing is for this mission in London.'

The photo showed the Arab and the woman from a frontal view, but the second man was side on, and they could tell that he was young, athletically built and dark skinned.

These photos are four days old and taken around the same time that Shafi was sailing down the Mediterranean towards Malta, so from the timeline we now have, we can safely assume that all three people in the photo at the villa are in this country.'

'Excuse me,' it was Reece who spoke, 'Considering how small the walking stick is and the Quads involvement why have the Iranians not just used the diplomatic bag and transferred it into this country without all this risk through Malta?'

Kurt Shimon looked at 'C' who nodded for him to answer Reece.

'A good question, Mr Reece, and one we asked ourselves when this whole mission came to our attention. I think we should look at a few important points. We think most importantly, the Iranian government have made a big thing of denying that they're working on any tactical nuclear weapons. They have denied access, as far as they can to the atomic energy inspectors, inspecting the locations, where we suspect they are creating the essential product to make such weapons. Because of this the West has come down hard on them with sanctions, leaving their own people suffering because of the Ayatollahs intransigent stance. If it was to come out that their officials were caught trying to use their diplomats to transport plutonium, then they fear those same suffering people would rise up and overthrow them. The Quads have always used the terrorist arm of Hezbollah and Islamic Jihad to do their dirty work. If such a terrorist was to be caught with such a weapon it's deniable. If they succeeded, then it suits Iran's purpose, namely, to damage the West, and in particular Israel, if they can. The people we have encountered so far are just such a terrorist arm and we know that the Arab has been involved not only with the Islamic Jihad but with the Iranians for some time. He is a willing partner and a dangerous opponent. This is the main reason why we are willing to work with anyone who is a target of this man to help catch him and his friends or eliminate them if necessary. Something I'm sure you have experience of yourself, Mister Reece, I hope that answers your question?'

It was Reece's turn to nod his agreement.

It was then the turn of Sir Ian Fraser to take back control of the meeting.

'Thank you, Kurt, everything is helpful if we are to stop these people in their tracks. As you can see, both our Prime Ministers have been briefed on this threat and both agree that we should work closely together on this. There are no state secrets at stake, just a threat from terrorists that both countries are aware of. That said, this operation because it's on British soil, will be led by MI6. The operations room to co-ordinate everything coming in and controlling reactions will be in this building. Matthew Simons will be the main conduit for the running of this operation from that control room. Everything will go through him. I expect him to be here in a few hours and ready to brief everyone on what we have at 5 pm today. Jim Broad will represent Kurt and myself at these briefings and report directly to us, so that we can then brief our Prime Ministers. Unless you have any questions, I suggest you go and make yourselves familiar with the set-up of the control room and collect what weapons and radio communications equipment you need from stores. We have laid on two BMW cars fitted with radios and tracking equipment in the underground garage. Does anyone have any questions?'

'If, as we expect, these three people are already in this country, what if they're ready to go now? What will we do?' asked Reece.

'A good question David,' replied Broad. 'We have put all our agencies on alert as far as we can, circulating the photos we have of our suspects. As everyone here will know, there are always many covert and surveillance operations ongoing in the capital at any one time. These can involve anything from counter terrorism to foreign spies and serious crime. We will divert some of the Watchers from the A4, MI5 and the Met Anti-Terrorist and Drug Squad teams from their own surveillance operations, to support the search for these people. The Met and the anti-terrorist team have extensive coverage of the city using a CCTV system with the ability for facial recognition, which will be monitored by a special team. On top of that, you have uniform police patrols who will be told to watch out for these people; not to approach, but to observe and inform us right away. Therefore, we need to have a strong control, with as much information as possible going through this building to prevent teams crashing into each other and causing more problems on the ground than the ones these terrorists will cause. We are not able to stop them if they were to go out this minute and carry out their attack, but with the information we are providing, these agencies can react quickly to such an attack, as they always can. The military have a Hazmat Nuclear and Biological Weapons teams at London barracks alongside our bomb disposal teams ready to move if needed. Our people at GCHQ and the Israeli equivalent are monitoring all calls between Iran and this country just in case our friends communicate with each other. Our next move is to get briefed up at 5 p.m. then get out there, find these people, and eliminate the threat. Anna, I know that Kurt wants to go to your Embassy to brief your ambassador, so if you could be back for five that would be great.'

Both Anna and Shimon stood to leave.

'As we are working together on this? I would like to have one of my people working in the control room with Matthew,' said Shimon.

'That will not be a problem your input will be greatly appreciated,' replied Fraser.

After the two Israelis left the room Broad and 'C' sat facing Reece across the conference table. Sir Ian leant across the table before he spoke directly to Reece.

'Now David, as I'm sure you know; this operation so far has not been going too well and we find ourselves in a dangerous situation where we have at least three high-powered terrorists in this country with plutonium for use in a dirty bomb. We all know the damage that would cause. I believe our Mossad friends have not been completely truthful with us. If they had been from the start, we could have nipped this whole thing in the bud. It is obvious they were depending on their dead agent to give them the heads up when to move. His death changed everything, it forced them to be more forthcoming with us. Pointing fingers now will get us nowhere, we are where we are. I'm saying this, because although we might appear to be working closely with Mossad, we should not trust them all the way. That's why anyone entering this building is scanned discreetly when they walk through the main doors. The scanners would pick up any bugging transmitters they would have on them if they wanted to leave one behind after their visit. Do not be in any doubt, we are in charge now. These people are in our country so we will run Operation Search our way, and if we can, we will deal with the terrorists in our own way, the way SG9 has been set-up for. Are you happy with that?'

'I agree as far as I'm concerned. I've told you in the past my reason for joining SG9 was for just this sort of situation. These people intend to kill us, our task is to kill them first. We have all seen the damage they are capable of. The only way they'll change is if we stop them and convince them this is not the way to progress their argument.' replied Reece.

Jim Broad stood up and stretched his legs, walking to the large window that looked out over the River Thames and London; raindrops were hitting the window. Turning back to face the men at the table he spoke once more.

'David, what this all boils down to now is, that we need to be as lucky as we were in Manchester. You were able to stop them then.'

Manchester was still fresh in his mind and always would be. The SG9 and SAS team had tracked down a terrorist cell which combined an Irish Republican sniper and Islamic fanatics.

'We had some luck, but we also had a good agent from the start which helped. This time, the agent has been killed and the bad guys are in the wind. And remember; in Manchester, although we stopped them killing the Prime Minister, we lost two of ours and a civilian.'

Now it was the turn of Sir Ian Fraser to join the conversation.

'Yes, but our experience tells us there is always the risk of losing some of our own. The case in Manchester being an example. But thanks to you and your team we stopped it being much worse and the whole cell including the woman leader who escaped to Egypt were eliminated.

In a way this operation is slightly similar. We are looking for these people, but this time we have a full-scale alert out there helping you, a lot more eyes and ears than you had in Manchester including, this time, Mossad. If you need anything more you will have it, but I want you to understand one thing; if you and your SG9 team do find these people and eliminate them; you're still a secret unit, which this country does not have or acknowledge. I know you understand this, but I'm reminding you. We have politicians who shit themselves that we have such people, who will always throw us to the wolves to protect their own skins if they have to.'

'You don't have to remind me Sir Ian. I remember how those politicians gave the terrorists everything they wanted in Northern Ireland, letting mass murderers out of prison after two years, and giving those on the run a free 'Get out of jail' card. The thing that makes me even more angry is that those same terrorists are now politicians with big salaries and big offices at Stormont, with chauffeur driven limos and bodyguards. Don't worry, when it comes to trust, then politicians are on a par with terrorists.'

Both Broad and 'C' smiled understanding.

'As Sir Ian just said David, anything you need. After this meeting, if you go to the control room you will find your colleagues from Manchester, Mr Cousins and Mr Harrison. You also have an SAS team at the London District Army Barracks waiting for your briefing as and when you need them. Their commander is also the same one you worked with in Manchester, Captain Middleton. And some more information I think you will be interested in; your lady is currently on route from Malta on the same flight as Matthew Simons and the Mossad agent you know as Palo. They should arrive in a couple of hours, and I've arranged for them to be picked up at the airport. I've booked a room for you at The Park Plaza Westminster Bridge Hotel so you can be with her later and get back here for the briefing at five. Tonight, the bill is on us. If you need it any longer, you're paying.'

Reece left the two men to their plans and when he walked through the outer office, he knew the secretary would be wondering why he was smiling.

Chapter 20

The windowless room was illuminated by light from a batch of screens. Two men sat in front of these screens, both using headsets to communicate to operators on the ground. The chat was familiar to the other occupants in the room, as they set up call signs, linking them to the control room and identifying each person they were communicating with and locating where each call sign was currently situated on the streets of London. Operation Search was underway.

Reece saw Joe Cousins and Steve Harrison as soon as he walked into the room. All three shook hands. 'Am I glad to see you guys,' said Reece.

'Malta seems to have been good to you,' said Harrison.

'If you think that Steve your eyesight's playing you up, you need a trip to the opticians.' laughed Reece.

'What's this all about?' asked Cousins.

Reece quickly brought them up to speed explaining the work with Mossad in Malta and the reason they were here today.

'Plutonium?' Henderson whistled softly to himself.

'Yes, and it's here somewhere in this country, most likely London.'

'Can I put in for my backdated leave now? For the first flight to somewhere sunny preferably,' asked Cousins.

'Afraid not Joe. Matthew Simons will have a more detailed brief, and hopefully an idea where these people might be when we get back here at five. In the meantime, get what you need from stores and catch-up on anything else that you can, and I'll see you both back here then.'

'I assume that includes weapons?' said Cousins.

Reece opened his Barbour jacket exposing his Smith and Wesson 59 resting in the holster.

'We can be sure the people we will be hunting will be armed so get what you need from the armoury. There are two BMWs ready for us down in the car park I'll take one, you two can have the other.'

Reece listened into the communications traffic coming and going through the airwaves, much of it familiar to him from his own days when working undercover in Northern Ireland when looking for a dangerous foe, always to be ready for the unexpected. *Nothing changes,* he thought, *the opposition might change but the threats were still the same.*

'Red Four to control in position three, over.'

One of the operators at the computer console touched the screen which displayed a digital map of London, a small red dot began to flash on and off showing exactly where Red Four was at that moment in time.

'Roger Red Four I have you,' replied the desk operator. Reece knew that in an operation this big, at least ten teams of eight would be spread out over the city, each covering a specific area. The teams would be colour coded to prevent confusion, White Team, Black Team, Red Team and so on. Each team would have a vehicle which could be a van, a black cab, or a motor bike; the rest of the team would be on foot. The teams would be a mixture of age with men and women from different ethnic backgrounds and skin colour.

His phone buzzed in his pocket. The screen showed a text message from Mary.

See you soon, can't wait xxx

Once again Reece was smiling as he headed for the lift. He picked up the BMW from the underground car park and drove out, joining the traffic over Vauxhall Bridge. Switching on the radio comms he could hear control continuing with its contacting teams in the city confirming their locations. Reece hated driving through London and would usually prefer to walk or use a taxi. The traffic was as always, busy and moved slowly. The good thing about the car he thought was that it had hidden blue flasher lights and a two-tone siren if he needed to move fast. He was sorely tempted to turn them on as he turned and drove slowly along the Thames embankment towards the Houses of Parliament but controlled the thought, for now.

The Park Plaza Westminster Bridge Hotel is located on the south bank of the Thames opposite the Houses of Parliament and Big Ben less than a five-minute walk from the London Eye. It was one of the hotels tourists preferred, with easy access to the historical buildings of church and government which, as Reece found when he entered his allocated room, he could see from the magnificent views across the Thames flowing three stories below. Reece threw his small bag onto the bed and checked out the minibar which was well stocked. The room had air conditioning with the usual large flat screen TV. The only whisky was Jamison which would have to do for now. He made a mental note to buy a bottle of Bushmills as soon as he could find an off-licence. It would be an hour before Mary arrived, so he asked reception to give her a key to the room 303 when she arrived; he sent her a text with the number and that he would see her later for dinner. He knew Mary would make a beeline for the hotel pool so she would be totally relaxed when he got back from his next port of call, the London District Army Barracks. The army based there carry out responsibilities for everything within the M25 motorway corridor that surrounds London. Having worked closely with the SAS on operations in Northern Ireland and most recently in Manchester, Reece had great respect for the men who made up the most secret unit of the British Army. As he drove through the traffic his mind went back to those days in Northern Ireland when once every six months, he would travel to Hereford to brief the next incoming Squadron from 22 SAS coming to the Province to take over the task from the current one leaving after their six-month tour. In what was once Stirling Lines, named after the founder of the SAS, David Stirling, he would stay for a couple of days in the officer mess and drink heavily with the men before and after his briefing.

At the main entrance to London and the South of England's Army Head Quarters he presented his MI5 Security Services Pass. This document was used by all SG9 operators as it gave the correct amount of impressive credentials when operating on the British mainland. The document told those who inspected it, respect the person who presented it, ask no questions, mind your own business, and carry out the instructions when asked. When Reece said he was there to speak with a Captain in the SAS, no further questions were needed. The armed military sentry directed him to park at an office building close to the entrance then go inside where he would be directed to a waiting room while they located the officer.

The waiting room consisted of a row of four chairs and a large coffee table. Reece checked his phone while he waited, there were no messages. Ten minutes later the door opened and Captain Geoff Middleton, 22nd Special Air Service Regiment entered. The recognition between the two men would have been obvious to anyone watching. Reece stood and, taking the offered hand to shake it, he couldn't help but think again how fit and healthy this man looked and how strong his grip.

'Geoff, great to see you. You look great, I'm glad it's you.'

'I don't know if I could say the same, remembering the last time we worked together.'

Reece laughed. 'If there's going to be trouble, I can't think of anyone better to get me out of it.'

'What is this all about David, we got the shout at the Headshed and told to get here asap?'

Reece knew that Captain Geoff Middleton and his team would be permanently on call at the SAS Headquarters in Hereford or as the men referred to it, the Headshed, ready to move at a moment's notice to anywhere in the world to deal with any imminent threat.

'What do you know, what have they told you?'

It was Middleton's turn to smile.

'Come on David. You know we are like mushrooms, kept in the dark and fed full of shit. They tell us as little as they can. At least with you I know I'll get the truth. So, what's happening?'

'You're going to want to be sitting when I tell you.'

Reece pulled a chair to one side of the coffee table and sat to face Middleton sitting opposite.

'Seriously Geoff, what have you been told so far to save me repeating something you may already know?'

'The Headshed told us to get here asap with equipment to assault a building or take out a terrorist cell on the streets of London. I do not even know who the opposition are, or their firepower. I'm hoping you can tell me that.'

For the next half hour Reece brought Middleton up to date, taking him all the way from working with Mossad agents in Malta, to the present, where it was believed that the terrorist cell was somewhere in London in possession of plutonium ready to use as a dirty bomb.

'So, let me get this straight. You lost them. You don't know where they are, and we could all die at any moment?'

'Correct.'

'Then I can see why you sent for us. Find them, stop them and kill them, easy.'

'We know a few things about them and what at least two of them look like provided they don't use good disguises. We have every agency you could think of looking for them, including Mossad. We have all current ongoing operations; with the surveillance, bugs, and informants, being directed to provide any information they can towards Operation Search. Everything will be co-ordinated and run by one of our top MI6 Middle East experts through a control room at Vauxhall Cross. We have a full briefing there at five this afternoon. You should be there. The feelers for information went out this morning, and I'm hoping we will have something then. So, you should come, it will be fun, and you will get the opportunity to put your questions. In the meantime, bring your own team up to date. How many are there?'

'Counting me, ten with the option for more from the Headshed if I need them.'

'Until five then.'

Reece shook Middleton's hand. Once more the strong grip still there.

Chapter 21

'Did you sleep well?' asked Hassan.

Yasmin pushed her hair back from her face and with her hands folded it to the back of her head then using the elastic hair band, wrapped it into a ponytail.

'Yes, thank you. The bed was soft and cool. Is there anything to eat, I'm famished?'

Hassan smiled. He had not cooked anything for two reasons; he didn't want to make too much noise as he wanted to let her sleep, and the second reason was there was nothing much to cook anyway.

'There's nothing much in the fridge. If you can wait, there's a chip shop across the street and I can get us something?'

Looking through the window across Edgware Road Yasmin could see several shops but didn't have a clue which one was a chip shop.

'Chip shop, what's that?'

Hassan realised they probably didn't have any such thing as a chip shop where she came from.

'It's like a takeaway café that sells fried food like potatoes that are cut into small pieces and fish covered in batter.'

'The Teacher told us not to go out unnecessarily.'

Now it was Hassan's turn to look out the window.

'I think the Teacher would want us at our best for our mission. To be our best we need to be well fed and the chip shop is just across the street, so I'll not be going far, and I won't take long. There is some bread in the kitchen. Butter me two slices and get out the plates. Do you like salt and vinegar?'

No, she thought. She'd not tasted fish and chips before. She wouldn't risk it.

Hassan had been true to his word and came back with the fish and chips wrapped in paper within fifteen minutes of leaving the apartment.

Yasmin had to admit her food was delicious, but as she was hungry the new experience would have been the same with most foods.

They had just finished eating when they heard the downstairs front door open and close, and the footsteps coming up the stairs.

The Arab had booked into The Beaumont Hotel in Mayfair, and he could walk to the apartment but, as it was raining, he took a taxi to Hyde Park corner and walked the short distance from there. To anyone watching he looked every inch the businessman; wearing a dark three-piece suit, he walked fast to get out of the rain as quickly as he could, again this wouldn't stand out as everyone was walking at the same pace to avoid the same wet stuff. He had always hated the British weather and longed for the warm sun of the lands of Allah.

'Good morning children, blessings be upon you,' he said when entering the room.

Both Yasmin and Hassan stood for the teacher as children would in class.

'Did you sleep well my children?'

'Yes, very well,' said Hassan.

The Arab sat on the chair at the window and faced both of his students.

'What is that smell, have you been cooking?'

Both knew the teacher was no fool and a lie would be worse than the truth.

'We have eaten from the takeaway across the street. There was nothing for us in the fridge or kitchen. It only took me a few minutes to collect it and return here.'

The Arab was silent for at least two minutes. Both students sat on the couch and looked at each other and waited before the teacher spoke once more. He spoke softly and slowly making sure that both heard him and would understand every word.

'I'm sure you both know why I chose you for this mission. This mission is not just for me or a cause. You are the representatives of Allah on earth. It is him you represent and him you disappoint when you let your earthly needs come before his will, blessings be upon him. You do not just disappoint me, but you disappoint Allah and that is unforgiveable. But you and I know that man's flesh is weak, and the only way to be forgiven is to commit yourself to the will of Allah completely. His will demands your full obedience, and I as your teacher tell you to give that obedience to me now, totally, and maybe then we can complete our mission on earth in the name of the most holy. I'll not tell you this again. There will be no next time, or your mistake will get you killed by the enemy, and that mistake not only puts the mission in danger but might get me killed as well. So, understand, if we were to survive such a mistake be sure I will kill you myself and you will die in sin before the eyes of Allah. Do you understand. Do I make myself clear?'

Both students nodded, afraid to look into those dark eyes they both feared.

'I've stayed the night in a hotel near here and I see everything. From now, you only leave this building on my order, to do what I tell you. I'll pick up some groceries later.'

Again, both nodded without saying a word.

Now the Arab produced two *London A–Z* street map books from his pocket and handed one to each of his students.

'No more will be said. Yasmin, can you bring us coffee and I will tell you what you will do next in our mission?'

Five minutes later Yasmin had brought back the coffee and poured for everyone. The Arab took the book he had given to Yasmin and opened it.

'Yasmin. Here you will see I've circled the area of Trafalgar Square. I want you to go there this afternoon and get to know the area very well. Take your time and find the place where the tourists gather the most in numbers. Use your mobile to take photos. You can walk from here, that way you will be able to look for enemy security forces. Hassan and I will leave right away. We have other parts to complete for the mission. Use the British money you have if you need to. Do not worry, we have more. Do you have any questions?'

'Will I have a weapon?'

'It is good that you ask and are willing to have one. Hassan and I will be collecting our equipment and we will all meet here at seven tonight when you will know more. For now, you must act and be like a tourist. The police do not randomly stop people in this country, the British shout and scream if such liberties are taken. Hassan, when you were given the keys for here, there were three on the keyring, I took one last night. Give one to Yasmin so she can return here if we are still out, then get your coat and come with me. We all have each other's numbers in the phones, so we can call each other or text as necessary. Don't worry about using them, just be careful what you say or text, the enemy may be looking for us at any time.'

Hassan followed the Teacher as they turned left out of the building and walked to the end of Edgware Road and turned left into Oxford Street. The rain had stopped so Hassan wore his shemagh as a scarf leaving his face exposed. Someone walking with his face covered in the Arabic style, while walking with someone in a business suit, might bring the kind of undue attention they did not need. Hassan could see the Teacher knew his way around. Using no map or looking for street signs, he appeared to know where he was going. He could also see the way he looked discreetly for signs of the enemy he had talked about. He looked for people behind him by studying the reflections in shop windows. He would take his time, looking left and right when crossing the road, not just for traffic but for anyone who seemed to be going the same way. Halfway down Oxford Street the Arab flagged down a black cab. When both men were seated in the back, he asked the driver to take them to Kensington High Street. They had not exchanged any conversation since leaving the apartment and remained silent until the taxi dropped them off.

'We are going to the Iranian Embassy. They're expecting us. You will remain silent; I'll do the talking. Do you have any questions?'

'No,' Hassan replied. They continued to walk and once more both men used the training they'd been given, and in the case of the Arab had grown up with, to look for the surveillance of the enemy. There are many cameras throughout the city of London; from the usual business cameras to traffic cameras and then the security cameras that most large cities and towns relied on to back-up their security and surveillance capabilities. Most of these cameras look down at angles that give a wide panorama of the whole area. Both men knew they should walk with their heads down looking straight in front and not to look up at any time, thereby making it difficult for anyone watching to get a full-frontal face shot.

'When we get near the Embassy you should pull your shemagh to cover your face as the cameras will be covering the building.'

The Arab then took a pair of thick rimmed glasses out of his pocket. Putting them on Hassan noticed how this simple move changed the Teacher's whole appearance.

The Embassy of The Islamic Republic of Iran is a building in a row of similar terraced buildings next to the Embassy of Ethiopia and overlooks Hyde Park in South Kensington.

The building was the location of a hostage siege, when the then British Prime Minister Margaret Thatcher gave the go for Operation Nimrod. The world watched on live TV as the SAS stormed the Embassy on the 5th of May 1980, using framed window charges and overpowering firepower and training, killing all the terrorists but one and releasing the hostages. On that day, the world found out that the British would not give in to terrorists trying to hold them to ransom, and the SAS who up until then had operated in secrecy became a household name around the world. The building had been severely damaged by fire as a result and rebuilt to continue as the current Embassy.

They pressed the doorbell and were admitted to the main foyer of the building. The staircase in front of them was still the same one where the SAS had practically thrown the hostages down from one trooper to another and out the rear door into the Embassy Garden; where they were made to lie face down on the ground, with their hands tied behind their back, until everyone was identified as a hostage. In this way they were able to identify one of the rescued as a terrorist who was lucky not to be shot as there would be too many witnesses.

The receptionist at the desk just inside the main door made a quick phone call to an internal number when the Arab asked for the Deputy First Secretary and told her to say, 'Your friend Abdullah is here.' Both men then sat and waited. Five minutes later a short, well-built man, wearing a dark business suit not dissimilar to the one worn by the Arab, came down the stairs carrying a large canvas holdall.

Both men stood to greet him as he came over to them with an outstretched hand. Shaking their hands, 'As-Salam-alaikum.' he said.

'Wa-Alaikum-Salaam,' replied the Arab.

The Arab knew the Deputy First Secretary was also the main officer from its VEVAK Intelligence Agency. He would have been told to be ready for a visit from an important person who would introduce himself with the words 'your friend Abdullah is here.' That friend was here, and his other instructions were to pass on a canvas bag and offer whatever assistance was required without question.

'I'm the Deputy Secretary please come through to the office.'

Walking ahead he showed them into a room behind the reception desk and closed the door behind them.

The room had high ceilings with a desk and four chairs. The desk had a laptop and a telephone; the walls were bare except for a large poster filled with writing in at least five different languages, two of which were Arabic and English.

'Please take a seat,' said the man as he sat behind the desk.

'I have my instructions. I'm to give you this bag which contains everything you requested and to offer my services if required without question.'

The Arab took the bag and handed it to Hassan.

'Take the bag and return to the apartment, I'll meet you there later as arranged.'

When Hassan had left the Arab turned to the man behind the desk.

'You have fulfilled your instructions. I may need more assistance in the next few days. Do you have a private number where I can call you at any time?'

The man reached into his waistcoat pocket and producing a business card handed it across the desk.

'Thank you. If I do need to call you, I will say this is your brother Abdullah. As you have been told, you will provide whatever I ask without question.'

Looking into the Arab's dark eyes, the Deputy First Secretary could feel a coldness surge through his body, as small beads of sweat trickled down the side of his head. He nodded rather than spoke as he thought the words would come out in a squeak.

The Arab tapped the number on the card into his phone and placed the card back on the desk before standing to leave.

'Allah be with you,' said the Arab.

'Inshallah,' replied the Deputy First Secretary.

Throughout the short visit Hassan had kept his face covered with the shemagh and continued to do so until he had walked a good distance from the building. The bag was slightly heavy, but Hassan could easily carry it in one hand. The rain had stayed away although a slight wind brought with it the cold feeling of more to come. Hassan kept to the main streets where he knew he could find a taxi more easily. The streets around Kensington were busy and he continued to look discreetly for anyone paying attention to this man with a canvas bag and a shemagh around his neck. Trying hard not to be obvious, he decided to find a café where he could have a coffee and sit at the window to observe the street, the people and traffic without attracting attention to himself. Kensington High Street is mostly high-end retail but there were still one or two restaurants and café's. The one he entered was exactly what he was looking for, a small café with a window seat, perfect for what he needed.

The Red Team from MI5 had arrived in Kensington High Street and the surrounding area at the same time. The team's brief, for the moment, to cover the streets leading to and from the Embassy of The Islamic Republic of Iran. Report anything considered of interest and especially be on the lookout for the woman and man in the photos provided. At the time they did not know the names, but the photo of the woman showed her face as she'd passed through an airport security system. The photo of the man was split into two separate images, one sitting outside a café, the other beside a swimming pool. Although MI6 now had all three targets' photos, the third man's face was not clear enough to use for the surveillance teams and would only cause confusion.

Hassan watched the street and the passing traffic as he sipped his coffee. He realised two things: the coffee was not that bad, and even if he did spot surveillance people, he couldn't be sure he knew exactly what he was looking at. People did not wear a deer stalker hat or wraparound sunglasses unless it was sunny or walked with the collar of a raincoat pulled up around their face. He realised it would be exceedingly difficult to spot professional surveillance people. Their job, like his was not to be conspicuous, to fit in to the surroundings and look as normal as possible. He felt himself relax. He would still be careful and try to spot the danger, but it might not be there; so better to relax and be natural, the more he did that, the less likely he would raise suspicion.

At the same time, the Red Team had passed where Hassan sat drinking his coffee and, took up positions around the Iranian Embassy. It was one of the female agents who spotted what looked like the man in the photograph sitting outside the café in Tehran leave the Embassy.

'Control from Red Three I have male resembling Target One leaving the Iranian Embassy.'

'Stay on him Red Three describe and give directions, over,' came the reply.

'Heading towards Kensington High Street wearing dark three-piece suit and wearing glasses. The glasses may be a disguise so not one hundred per cent sure it's him.'

'All Red Team, converge on Red Three it's all we have for the moment so let's get on it,' said Red One, the surveillance team leader.

The Arab spotted the woman at almost the same time. She had been walking away from him but had stopped to investigate a shop window where he could tell she was following him in its reflection.

The Arab increased his pace as he neared High Street Kensington Underground Station. Red Three saw him walk into the station. Informing the rest of the team, who had yet to catch-up from their original positions around the Embassy, they approached the Underground station from two directions. Apart from the people on foot, the first to get there and back-up Red Three was a car, with two operators and Red Five on a motorbike. Screeching to a halt they quickly followed into the station.

'Lost contact,' Red Three's voice sounded over the radio.

Allah had been with the Arab. He just made it onto the Circle Line train pulling away from the platform. The Circle Line could take him all the way to Edgware Road but that was the third stop from High Street Kensington and could take fifteen minutes giving plenty of time for the enemy forces to be there if he stayed on the train. He got off at the next stop, Notting Hill Gate; keeping his head down to avoid the cameras he knew would be looking for him. Exiting the station, he turned right and walked away from the station entrance. Over the next three hundred yards he crossed the road three times then took his time walking through the Notting Hill Market, all the while looking for the danger of enemy surveillance. After walking through the market, he climbed into the back of a black cab sitting at the end of the line of other black cabs and instructed the driver to take him to Oxford Street. He had the Glock pistol the Deputy First Secretary at the embassy had given him in his pocket. He would have used it if cornered, feeling reassured by the weight, it gave him more confidence. They may have been looking for him or just following anyone coming out of the Embassy, either way he felt he had lost them for now. He had no reason to go back to the Embassy, and London was a big place, with over eight million people; a great place to get lost in. After the taxi dropped him in the middle of Oxford Street, he walked the rest of the way to The Beaumont Hotel, again checking for surveillance crossing the road several times and going into two large shops, one of which had doors at the rear going out into another street. When he got to his hotel room, even though it had been cold outside with rain in the air, he felt the sweat sticking to his shirt. He stripped off his clothes, placed the gun under one of the pillows and had a shower. Feeling refreshed, he returned to the bedroom and, as an afterthought he sent a text to both his students.

Be careful our friends are looking for us

Hassan read the text. He was just finishing his coffee and all the time he had been sitting at the window he had seen nothing to raise his suspicions. He knew he had to keep control of his imagination otherwise he would see danger everywhere he looked. 'Keep calm, keep relaxed, be natural' he kept saying to himself. Leaving the café, he continued to walk in the opposite direction to the Embassy and when he saw a black cab with its vacant light on, he flagged it down and asked the driver to drop him of at Sussex Gardens, just off Edgware Road. Thirty minutes later he was back at the apartment. He placed the canvas bag on the kitchen table and poured himself a glass of water; and then sitting on the couch he turned on the TV, switching channels to *Sky News*.

Yasmin found her day less stressful. Acting like a tourist was easy, realistically that's what she was. She had never been in London before but had seen travel programmes on TV and had always wanted to go there. She had used the A–Z and had decided to walk the whole way to Trafalgar Square. The rain had stayed away; she felt the air cooler than what she was used to, but fresh despite the smell of traffic fumes. Everything looked so much bigger than she'd imagined: the shops, the historic buildings, the statues, the crowds.

Even though the day was cold, the tourists around the fountain and Admiral Lord Nelson's column were still plentiful. Yasmin took photos using her phone, the kind any tourist would take. She used the skills she possessed to observe the crowds, trying to guess who they were and where they came from, at the same time looking for the odd one out who could be surveillance. All she could see were Londoners and tourists, workers and families, no obvious surveillance; then again, good surveillance operators wouldn't be obvious. She took her time enjoying the excitement of the whole adventure. After a pot of tea in a café close to the square, she made her way back on foot to the apartment again.

Chapter 22

Reece found the traffic lighter when he drove across the city, once more he parked in the Park Plaza allocated car park. When he entered room 303, he found Mary smiling back at him from the bed. Her long black hair almost covering the pillow. She was wearing a dark skirt and a white blouse of silk that showed the outline of her breasts and Reece realised how much he had missed this woman, even though it had only been for twenty-four hours.

'You're a sight for sore eyes,' he said. 'What every man needs when he comes in from a hard day's work.'

'Well, if you feel you need to lie down be my guest.' She laughed.

The love they made brought back to Reece the memory of the first time, and the last time, always different, always better, always with love at the heart of it.

The room was beginning to get dark because of the rain clouds gathering around the city. Reece looked at his watch. He still had an hour before he needed to be at the briefing. He could walk to MI6 Headquarters in that time but even with the car he couldn't trust the traffic, or that he wouldn't get a soaking.

As they lay in the darkness of the room the clouds outside the window dark and foreboding, Mary curled up close to him, feeling the warmth of his body his skin against hers. She let her fingers stroke down from his neck to the scar on the right side of his shoulder.

'Any pain lately?'

Reece did not like to worry her, so he lied.

'No not much, just the odd stab.'

He didn't want to say that the pieces of shrapnel that remained in his body hurt like hell much more than usual. The pain killers that used to give him relief did not seem to hit the spot anymore. He knew he would need to see the surgeon again to confirm that the metal inside him had moved.

Lying close to her, he remembered that first time when he saw her in Newry, then followed her from a suspected IRA meeting house to a meeting with the head of the Provisional IRA Intelligence in the Europa

Hotel in Belfast. She had become a person of interest. He made it his purpose to get to know her, the unhappy marriage she was in, and when he had pitched his plan to recruit her as a source within the republican movement, he discovered that gunmen and killers like Sean Costello disgusted her. During the months of danger and covert meetings he had fallen in love with her but couldn't tell her until after the Peace Process and The Good Friday Agreement. That was when she'd once more searched him out, with the news that there was going to be the attempt to assassinate the British Prime Minister on the streets of Manchester.

'Have you any other injuries you don't want to talk about?'

'I fell out of a tree once when I was a boy, knocked myself out and broke my wrist.'

'What were you doing up a tree?'

'What does any boy do up a tree. Climb it then pretend you're a mountain climber or hiding from the searchers.'

'Which were you?'

'Hiding.'

'Not very well, you fell out of the tree.'

'Actually, I was jumping down the last bit, but underestimated the distance to the ground.'

'That will do it.'

'Every time.' Reece smiled.

'I'm sorry but I have to go again,' he said.

'Will you be back tonight?'

'I hope so, but I'm not sure.'

'Eating on my own again?'

As he pulled on his trousers, Reece lifted one of the hotel brochures from the coffee table.

'It says here the hotel has an award-winning Brasserie. I for one want to test the veracity of that statement. If I'm not back by eight, start without me.'

'That's no fun at all, try to make sure you join me.' She smiled.

'I'll do my best.'

'Is it dangerous Joseph?' she asked, using the undercover code name he had used when she'd been his agent.

He did not want to pass her off with a glib answer, but at the same time he didn't want to worry her unnecessarily.

'I'll be truthful as I am allowed because I know you will see through me if I don't. There is a serious threat of a terrorist attack here in London. We are pulling in every resource we have, not just me and my team, but everything. I'm going to a full briefing at five and I'll know more. Other than that, I want you to try to enjoy yourself tonight and I'll make every effort to join you for dinner.'

She had stood to pull her clothes back on. She shook her head to let her hair fall once more down her shoulders. He felt it would be so easy to stay here with her. To phone his boss and say he was resigning, take her to the airport, catch the next plane back to Malta, and live the rest of their lives making love and walking hand in hand along the beach.

But that was for the Mills and Boon romantic fiction books. This was real life. His job was, and always had been, to save lives and make that dream a reality for others, not just him and Mary.

'Joseph. I've been thinking I need to go see my mother. If you don't need me here, I should go.'

This caught Reece off guard. He had been too tied up in his own world and he forgot about Mary's. She knew that was his life, his work needed his total concentration. Everything else had to wait until the job was done.

'No, I can honestly say on this occasion you can relax. I think we have enough to cover everything. You know I would love you to be here, but to tell you the truth if you were not, I'd be happier, because of the risk to anyone not involved. You know that sometimes I can't tell you anything but are you sure you want to go to Belfast after what happened in Manchester?'

Mary had been deeply involved in helping to track down the rogue IRA man Costello and had been there when Reece had shot and killed him. To what extent her name had been blown to the Republican movement in Northern Ireland was not yet known.

'My mother now lives in my old house on the Lisburn Road; a relatively safe area for me. She is getting old, and I've not seen her in a while. You don't need me here. I'll be careful and phone you every night. I'll only stay for two days, three at most.'

'If you're sure you will be safe. I can let a friend in the PSNI know you will be there and to keep an eye on you.'

Mary knew Reece still had friends in the Police Service for Northern Ireland who he had worked with in the now disbanded RUC, people he could trust.

'I'll be all right on my own. You're not the only one who still has friends in Belfast.'

'I know but I would feel better if you had someone there who would get to you quicker than I could if you need help. His name is Tom Wilson, I'll give you his private number before you go, which is when?'

'I was thinking the sooner the better. Tomorrow morning if that's OK for you.'

'If you need to go, then go. I think this job will be over in the next few days so maybe I can join you in Belfast. It would be nice to see the city as a visitor instead of a job. I'm glad you're waiting until tomorrow to go. If I can't join you for dinner at least we might be able to lie in bed together tonight followed by breakfast, it seems an awful long time since we did that.'

Reece pulled on his Barbour jacket and put the Smith and Wesson 59 in the holster. Mary knew it was the signal that he had to go and quickly jumped off the bed and putting her arms around his neck kissed him long and hard. Reece felt the warmth of her body and could smell the perfume she always wore. Kissing her back he put his arms under hers and pulled her in to him as closely as he could.

Standing back Reece kissed her on the forehead and turned for the door.

'I'll try to get back for dinner, if not, definitely for later, either way I'll call you.'

'I'm counting on it.'

On the drive back to MI6 Reece thought deeply about the future and especially the one he wanted to have with Mary. He knew he needed to get away from work and spend some time alone with the woman he loved and to really discuss their future together.

The MI6 conference room at Vauxhall Cross was set up as a theatre, with two rows of chairs facing a lectern and a large screen on the wall. One of the control room operators was sitting at a computer linking images to the screen as they were needed. Sitting on the front row of chairs were Jim Broad, Caroline Aspinall, Helen Francis, and Sir Martin Bryant, representing the Prime Minister and Chair of the JIC. Reece knew that Bryant would be reporting through the Prime Minister to the Home Secretary nominally the overall political boss of MI5 and the British government's Foreign Secretary nominally the political boss of MI6.

Matthew Simons stood at the lectern and Reece sat in the second row between Anna, and Geoff Middleton. Reece could see others he knew including Joe Cousins and Steve Harrison before Matthew Simons interrupted any more hellos and introductions.

'Good afternoon everyone I'm Matthew Simons the MI6 Officer in Charge of our Middle East desk. I intend to brief everyone with what we have so far. Some of you may have more information to add, if you could wait until I finish to ask any questions or contribute to the briefing that would be helpful. Before I start, I would like to introduce Dr Ian McLeod. Dr McLeod is one of our senior biological and nuclear scientists at Porton Down, our scientific research department.'

A slightly balding man, wearing a three-piece suit with the chain of a pocket watch showing, who had been sitting on the front row beside Bryant stood and walked to the lectern. Facing the room, he put on half-moon spectacles and reading from his notes, looked over them when he addressed the room. The accent was Scottish, his back was slightly bent. He reminded Reece of his old headmaster at his secondary school.

'Good afternoon. Prior to coming here, I've been to Downing Street to brief the Prime Minister and Sir Martin Bryant on an update we received from the Israeli Government and Mossad. The original intelligence received indicated the terrorists had brought in plutonium for a dirty bomb. Such a device is not viable, as it would be almost impossible to assemble and transport without severe radiation damage and death to the perpetrators. Therefore, the material needs to be transportable with enough shielding to protect the carrier, but not so much that it would be too heavy to transport. The update we've had now indicates that these people have transported plutonium-238 which has been produced illegally in Iran. More easily transportable, and what is more can be used to make a dirty bomb. What is a dirty bomb you may ask? Put simply, on detonation, the explosives combine with the plutonium-238. The radioactive material is vaporised (or aerosolise) and is propelled into the air. This is completely different to a nuclear detonation. Plutonium-238 is not particularly dangerous as a radiation source on its own, but, when used with explosives it becomes what we call alpha particles in the air, which if ingested or breathed in as dust is very dangerous and carcinogenic. It has been estimated that 454 grams or one pound of plutonium inhaled as plutonium oxide dust, could give cancer to two million people. However, ingested plutonium is less dangerous as only a tiny fraction is absorbed in the gastrointestinal tract, 800 mg would be unlikely to cause a major health risk as far as radiation is concerned. So basically, what we believe these people have, is not nuclear, but more of a device based on terrorising the masses and damaging us economically. Nevertheless, hundreds could still die and the damage to not only this country, but to any country that values freedom and democracy would be devastating. Sorry about the political speech there, but I think you understand what is at stake. If you have any questions?'

The SAS Captain raised his hand.

'So, what you're saying is we believe these people have a small amount of this plutonium-238 and if it's used with an explosive device, apart from the initial blast, the main danger is what people breath in. Do we need to wear any special equipment if we are close to such a blast?'

Looking over his glasses at Geoff Middleton, McLeod spoke to everyone in the room.

'If you're not injured in the blast, get yourself and everyone to a safe distance which would be outside half mile perimeter from the blast. We have people on standby here in London with the right sort of clothing and equipment to go in and spray down the area. Unfortunately, such a spray down will take some time before we can give an all clear and depending on the size and where the blast takes place that could take months.'

With no more questions Doctor McLeod sat down, and Simons stood at the lectern once more.

Holding the red dot pointer in his hand he pointed to the screen and pressed a button at the side of the device. The screen was filled with a collage of photos showing the clear faces of the Arab, a woman, and an unknown man.

'You should already have these photos and a small page of intelligence showing their connection to each other and where the photos were taken.'

Everyone opened the folders that were sitting on the chairs before they sat down.

'I don't have to tell you that this operation, now known as Operation Search, is for the time being top secret. Between our own intelligence and Mossad, we are sure that these three people, possibly more, are now in this country, most likely London to carry out a terrorist attack involving a dirty bomb. We already have people out on the ground looking for them and I'll ask that MI5 and the Met update us on anything they have to add.'

Simons continued with his briefing for another twenty minutes, bringing everyone up to date with what he had so far, from the initial intelligence after the Barcelona suicide bomb, to the operation in Malta and finally to London.

Having finished for now Simons stood to one side and Caroline Aspinall stood at the lectern.

Speaking in her intellectual clipped accent she took the screen pointer from Simons.

'Thank you, Matthew. This operation may be moving fast but we are catching up. MI5 now has some more information which may be of help. We have a CI inside the Finsbury Mosque. His duties are to allow access to people coming through the main front door. Yesterday afternoon a young man wearing the Arab shemagh arrived at the Mosque. The interesting thing was that when this man arrived and left, he had the headdress fully pulled up to protect his face from identification. Like most people who attend the Mosque, they know that we try to take photos of everyone who goes in and out of the building. The confidential informant described the young man as being of Middle Eastern appearance but speaking with a London accent. He asked for Mohammed AAyan telling the CI he was expected. AAyan is the Imam at the Finsbury Mosque, and we have a thick file on him at Thames House. The CI reported that both men held a meeting for about fifteen minutes in a room which is used for special meetings and swept for bugs regularly, so we do not have the conversation. I can confirm that photos were taken of the man entering and leaving. We have them in colour as you can see but not of much use.'

Again, she pressed the button, and the screen was filled by the man leaving the Mosque. Reece thought that with the way the photo was taken with the Mosque behind, and the man's face covered by the shemagh he could be looking at a photo taken in any of the Middle East capitals. Aspinall continued.

'We have done follow-up checks on the woman who landed in London and took a taxi from the airport. Using the airport and traffic CCTV and APNR coverage, we were able to track down the driver and the cab and follow his journey. He picked up the woman and dropped her off at the bottom of Edgware Road. The anti-terrorist people spoke to the driver. He confirmed the journey. He does not know the woman and could only say she spoke English with an accent, only speaking to give him the location where she wanted dropped off, no specific address. He said she was young no older than thirty using a silver walking stick and dressed as a European. Unfortunately, the cameras didn't cover the drop-off or where she went afterwards. That's as far as we have her.'

'Why did the cameras lose her?' asked Martin Bryant.

Aspinall looked to where the question had come from.

'The drop-off and her movement from the car were in what we call a dark zone for our cameras. I do not know if she was aware of this but either way, we lost her. The good thing is we have a small area where we need to pay particular attention to.'

This seemed to satisfy Bryant. No more follow-up coming.

'If I could continue. We have some news on the other two men which I have only just received. One of our surveillance teams covering the Iranian Embassy were just taking up their positions when they spotted a man, fitting the description of the one we call the Arab, leaving the building. The team tried to follow him, but he was surveillance aware and made several attempts to lose the watchers. He knew where he was going, using the nearby Underground at High Street Kensington where he jumped on a Circle Line train before we could get to him. We put the word out for all the stations on the line to be covered before our teams could get in place, but we think he got off at the very first station on his route at Notting Hill Gate. We are looking at the station CCTV to confirm this, but we are fairly sure that is what he did.'

'You lost another of our targets?' again the voice of Bryant broke through the room this time a little higher pitched.

This time Aspinall looked straight back at Bryant. Her expression was that of a schoolteacher having to deal with a naughty schoolboy.

'Surveillance is never going to be perfect in a city the size of London. With millions of people getting in the way, and an Underground system which can move a suspect to numerous locations throughout the city. It is even tougher if the person you're following is surveillance aware as our friends will be. On this occasion our teams were just beginning to get into their positions after having received the basic information. The fact that they spotted this target, and at least have confirmed his awareness, and that we can confirm him in London, is a start, considering the circumstances I've mentioned. One of the stops on the Circle Line is Edgware Road, another pointer to that area so we should put extra resources into there. This meeting is to pull everything together that we have so far. The picture is starting to clear, we have two of our targets possibly working in the Edgware Road area of the city. The next time they're spotted we will have the resources on the ground and the camera coverage in support.'

With that Aspinall retook her seat and handed the pointer back to Simons who stood once more at the lectern.

'As you will know we will be running the operation from our control room here. All communications will be linked to our people running the boards. You should all know that this operation will be followed closely by number ten, but the final say on how it will progress will be with the MI6 Director, Jim Broad, who you all know. Mister Broad would you like to say anything?'

Jim Broad stood and turning to face the room and those seated behind him. He looked at Reece before speaking.

'Really it does not matter who runs this operation, because we all have the responsibility to work together if we are to succeed in our mission. Find these people, find them quickly because we do not have much time. In fact, we do not know how much time we really have. The operation will be running twenty-four hours a day so organise your plans to that schedule and be ready to move at a moment's notice. We will also be working closely with our friends in Mossad. Anna here, being their contact and another of their team Palo, who will be with our tech people in the control room. It is hoped that Mossad using their own people will be able to add to the information we already have. Now I believe the head of the Met anti-terrorist unit wants to say something.'

Helen Francis stood beside Broad and faced the room she looked into the eyes of Sir Martin Bryant. She wanted to make sure he understood the people in this room were united in their work, and that the message for number ten would recognise that unity.

'After the MI5 watchers followed the man from the Iranian Embassy, we had another look at our photo coverage of the Embassy around the same time.'

Taking the pointer, she pressed the button. Two photos were displayed on the giant screen. One showed two men walking into the Embassy and in the other, one of the men walking back out again.

'I want you to notice. When the men go in, we know one from his dress business suit, the surveillance, and photos to be the man we refer to as the Arab. The other whose face isn't clear; we don't know yet. After a while, the second photo shows this other man leaving the building on his own this time carrying what appears to be a canvas bag. Remember these photos were taken before our surveillance teams were on the ground.'

Pressing the zoom button on the pointer she brought the area of the man's face and head into sharper focus.

'I want you to take special notice of the black and white chequered shemagh around the man's neck. He walks with his head down to avoid a full facial photo which is partly successful as this is the best image we have of him.'

Pressing the buttons once more she brought up the photo of the man leaving Finsbury Mosque the day before, showing his face covered in a black and white chequered shemagh.

'I believe this is the same man in both photos and is our third member of the terrorist team. He favours the Arab headdress, and that might be his downfall if we spot him again, something for our teams to watch out for. This photo is being circulated to our teams as we speak, and copies are being sent to your phones right now.'

Almost on cue the mobile phone in Reece's pocket buzzed.

Francis sat back down and Broad spoke once more.

'This man was carrying a bag, and I'm sure it wasn't containing sweets from the sweet shop. You all have everything we have, and I believe enough you will need to get these people. I'll be available here until the end of this operation. To keep things simple, we've given the three people we know simple code names. The Arab, the man in the suit Target One, the younger man with the shemagh Target Two, and the woman Target Three. I'll keep everyone informed including 'C' and I'm sure Sir Martin Bryant will do the same with the Prime Minister. Unless there are any more questions let us get out there, people, and get a result.'

No one spoke and with everyone got up to leave, Broad beckoned Reece and Anna to stay.

'I've spoken with 'C' and Kurt Shimon and they both are thinking as one on this. Mossad and SG9 will work together on this to the very end. David you will work with Anna. Palo will stay here with me and Matthew Simons. No matter what comes in from the ground, we will try to give you a heads up to enable you to get there first and if possible, eliminate this threat. We don't want these people escaping or using the justice system to become heroes to their cause. Do you have a problem with this?'

'No,' said Anna.'

Having experience of killings on city streets Reece waited a few seconds before replying.

'We know these people are here to kill. They will not care how many, and from what we know already, the Arab has killed before either by himself or by using others to do his dirty work for him. They will not worry who gets in the way if we try to stop them, so from that point of view I have no problem. But the biggest problem for us is the hundreds of people who are on the streets, not including security forces who will be around at the same time. The ideal scenario would be for us to corner them in a building where either ourselves or the Special Forces get into a one-to-one situation and take them out. That carries danger as we saw in Manchester when one of the targets set off a suicide bomb during a house assault killing one of our SAS troopers. I think in the situation we are in, any action by SG9 in the open carries more risk. In such a situation, we can back-up the Security Services and take them out in whatever way we can, but that might also include capturing them alive.'

'I understand what you're saying, David. The terrorists need to be found first. Then we can decide what we are going to do. That is why I'll be here for every second, helping with that decision, are you happy with that?' said Broad.

'Yes.'

'Then let's get out there and good luck. Your team will have the call signs Alpha One and Two to help the control team know when you're around the other surveillance teams, so that, if necessary, we tell them to hold or pull back to allow you free rein. The SAS will be mobile in two transit vans with the call signs Tango One and Two to give you back-up. Your cars have bulletproof glass. In the boot you will find police marked baseball hats and protection vests with a couple of fully loaded H&K MP5 rifles. So, hopefully everything you need. Let me know if you require anything else. If we get any more information, I'll let you know immediately. Everything else you will hear over the air.'

'I've already had a run in the BMW, it's just what we need in London. Have you seen how many German built cars there are out there?'

'That's why our surveillance teams like them David, there's so many. They blend in and the bad guys can't tell which one is being driven by the good guys.'

Broad then sat down beside Sir Martin Bryant who had remained behind listening to the conversation. Reece, like Broad, did not trust politicians, and as much as Bryant would want everyone to believe he was one of the boys, they both knew his first loyalty was to the politicians he worked for. From his years of experience in Northern Ireland, Reece knew how the politicians had helped stoke the fires of war by protecting themselves, rather than allowing the security forces to take on the enemy. Instead of demanding a complete surrender, the politicians had let them off the hook, brought in the Peace Process and The Good Friday Agreement; allowing mass killers to walk out of prison after serving just two years and giving those not captured get of jail free cards. The politicians will always go the way of the next vote.

For now, it was time to get back to work and doing the thing he was best at, tracking down bad people and dealing with them.

'Do you fancy a coffee?' Reece asked Anna.

'Yes.'

'Let's head for the cafeteria, I'm sure we will find two people you need to know.'

Reece was right, sitting at one of the tables right where he expected them to be, were Harrison and Cousins. The building had three such places, one for the civil servants who carried out all the admin chores, one for the MI6 agents where they sat now, and a private dining room on the same floor as the office of the Director of MI6, where he ate and could entertain visiting politicians and fellow heads of the world's intelligence services.

'Anna, let me introduce you to Steve Harrison and Joe Cousins, hereafter to be known as Alpha Two. Gentlemen our friend from Mossad, Anna.'

The two men stood and shook hands with Anna.

'Welcome Anna, I hope you don't have to spend too much time with David, he can get you into trouble,' said Cousins.

'That's why I'm here, he already has.' said Anna laughing.

Reece left and returned with two black coffees with milk on the side. Anna was already deep in conversation with both Cousins and Harrison.

'Your friends are typical undercover David. They tell you a lot yet at the same time say nothing.'

'I taught them everything they know, but not everything I know. Can you imagine what the conversation would be like, if we really did know what each of us were up to in our past lives, we would all have to sit here with our mouths zipped shut. Someone once said, the thing about keeping secrets; it's a lot easier if you don't know them in the first place.'

All four raised their cups to toast the sentiment.

'OK people, we need to get out on the ground both on foot and mobile. The information points to them being somewhere in the Edgware Road area. It's a long road, so that's where we start. I know the basic outline of the road so we will start out on foot, parking up nearby. It's dark now and most of the shops will be closed, so it will just be the take-aways and restaurants open at this time of the day. The rush hour traffic that lasts for three hours in London will still be clogging up the streets, so if we walk the area for now, we will find it easier than having to negotiate the traffic. Do you have everything you need?' he asked the men.

'Yes, we picked up our weapons and ear radios and the car has all the extras required,' replied Cousins.

'Good we need to keep in close contact, and at the same time be aware of the other agencies operating out there.'

Reece had been right about the traffic. Despite there being a congestion charge for people driving in the city nothing had changed. The people somehow found the money for the charge and the traffic was still congested.

As they drove through the city, they tested the comms linking in with each other and letting the control room know they were out on the ground and available for updates.

It was almost 7 p.m. when they parked up on Connaught Street just off Edgware Road itself. The street was still busy and the two parking spaces where timed for payment parking was until 6 p.m., so they were now free to park until 7 a.m. the next day.

'Steve, you stay here with the cars while we go for a walk,' said Reece.

Reece knew it wouldn't go down too well if one of the cars was stolen with a high-powered rifle inside and full of equipment. Reece also knew that Harrison had a previous life as one of the MI5 watchers. He had spent quite a few hours walking the streets of London, following suspects and he would know this area better than the rest of them.

'No problem, I can listen to my favourite hour on Classic FM,' replied Harrison.

'As long as you keep one ear for us,' said Reece.

'Always.'

Reece informed control that Alpha One was moving on foot in the Edgware Road area. He knew the communications were encrypted to avoid listening radio enthusiasts or the opposition hearing the conversation, but he still had the instinct to say as little as possible.

The rain had stopped, the pavements wet and the air cold. *Why didn't I stay in Malta*, thought Reece?

Chapter 23

As the SG9 team parked up and started their reconnaissance walk around the area, the Arab, now dressed in a green parka and jeans, opened the door to the apartment on the Edgware Road and walked up the stairs to meet with his students as arranged. He had called in a supermarket to pick up a bag of groceries which he placed on a bench in the kitchen.

'Good evening my children,' he spoke.

They both stood to greet him.

'You both look worried, come let us sit down at the table and talk. Hassan, bring the bag.'

Yasmin poured them yet another mug of coffee and sat down with the two men.

'Let's see what we have.'

The Arab unzipped the bag and took out the contents, one item at a time. First there were two handguns; German made 9 mm Glock pistols. He checked that each had a full magazine. He then slashed the slide of each gun putting a 9mm round in the breach. The Embassy Deputy First Secretary had already supplied the Arab with the gun that now rested in the pocket of his parka jacket. All three guns ready to fire. Beside them he placed three fully loaded spare magazines.

'You will keep these with you at all times even when you sleep. You do not surrender if cornered. If you must die for the cause of Jihad then take many of the infidels with you.'

He reached into the bag again and produced three passports and three credit cards and handed one of each to his students.

'When our mission is complete, we will use these new identities to help our escape. The credit cards are in the same name as the passports, and you can use them to buy hotel rooms and flights. After our mission, take transport as soon as you can out of the city and go to Bristol, where you will find it safe to stay in a hotel for a few days. After this short stay you will get a flight from Bristol to any European airport. From there it will be easier to get back to Iran. Don't travel or stay together you will be safer on your own.'

Once again he reached into the bag and produced three plastic Tupperware boxes. The students could see they were just like the ones they had used at the training camp in Iran. The lids were closed, and they could see the plastic explosives inside with a detonator pushed into the explosives and two wires coming from the detonator through a hole in the lid. The wires were then linked to a mobile phone which was taped to the outside lid.

'You have both seen these at the camp?'

Both students nodded.

'Good, then Kalil taught you well. That is one of the reasons I've chosen you for this mission. You have learnt well my children. Now we are going to put all that training to real use in attacking the enemies of Allah. Do you have any questions?'

'We have trained in putting this type of bomb together,' said Hassan, 'the question is, how we detonate them.'

'A good question Hassan, it is my intention that we should not be near when they detonate. Today I spotted what I think was the enemy looking for us. I lost them easily when they started to follow. They know we are here, and they're out there in the city, so we need to be extra careful. The final part of our mission will take place in two days' time. Before I answer your question, Hassan. Yasmin how was your day as a tourist?'

Yasmin took out her mobile phone and opened the photos she had taken in Trafalgar Square and handed the phone to the Teacher.

'As you can see, the square was busy despite the time of the year and the cold weather. I saw nothing of the enemy that was not unusual, just some uniformed police on foot, no more than two at a time walking through the square. Any attack would be over before they knew what hit them.'

'That is good my child, and you're sure you were not followed?'

'As sure as I can be.'

'Good, good. On Friday it will be your mission to go to the square and leave one of these boxes.'

Lifting one of the boxes he pointed to the mobile phone.

'Now, my children, to answer your question, Hassan. You will notice each box has a different coloured dot on top. The one with the green dot will be left here. It has a one-hour delay. On each box there are two buttons. The blue one switches the phone on and the red one starts the timer, then you will have time to get away. When all our boxes have been armed you will get a train or to Bristol. The enemy won't expect you to go in that direction, they will think that you are still in the city, but the timer will give you enough time to get away.'

'And the second bomb?' asked Hassan.

'The mission is two pronged. The box with the blue dot is for Yasmin to place in Trafalgar Square. It has a two-hour delay giving Yasmin time to escape. It will attack the confidence of the population and their tourist industry killing many infidels. The third one with the red dot is the most important, which Hassan and I will deliver. It has a three-hour countdown giving us plenty of time to leave the target area. It will destroy the economic heart of the infidel for many years to come perhaps even for good. Have you ever heard of Canary Wharf?'

'Yes, it's mentioned in the A–Z book,' replied Hassan.

'What it might not mention is that it's the financial heart of Europe. All the big banks and financial companies are based there. This is our main target. Using one of these boxes with what we have in our walking stick will cripple these important institutions for years to come. It will be one of the greatest blows we can make against the Great Satan and the Jihad will praise our names.'

Both students looked at the Arab and smiled.

'Why must we wait for two days,' asked Yasmin. 'Surely we put ourselves at more risk of being discovered by waiting. We could go tomorrow.'

'Have patience my child. When we visited the Deputy First Secretary at the embassy today, he told me that on Friday there'll be the unveiling of a plaque at the opening of a new office building in Canary Wharf by the Princess Royal, the daughter of the British Queen. We will time our attack to coincide with the unveiling at 3 pm. As for the risk, the risk is no more than it would be if we went tomorrow. If you remain in this area and don't expose yourselves unnecessarily, we will be safe enough to fulfil our mission.

'There is no reason to leave, I'll return on Friday morning, be ready. You have your phones. Contact me if you have any problems. On Friday morning we will make a short video describing our mission to be put on the Internet after our mission is complete.'

He reached into the bag once more and produced three full face covering balaclavas.

'As this is not a martyr mission and we will be involved in many more in the name of Allah and the Jihad, we will have our faces covered for the video. Now I must return to my hotel. Do not forget your prayers tonight my children. Pray that Allah will bless you and our mission.'

The Arab stood and drank down the last of his coffee, before leaving the two students to their thoughts and prayers.

The Arab pulled the apartment door behind him and having a quick look around, turned to walk towards the bottom of Edgware Road and Marble Arch.

It was Reece who spotted him first, the man had just pulled up the hood of his parka as he walked along the street. Reece noticed the way the man kept looking from side to side and behind while trying to appear natural. It was the years of doing this for real that made Reece realise it was anything but natural. He spoke into his radio mic.

'Alpha One to control I have eyes on a possible for Target One.'

Immediately the reply came back from the desk operator at control.

'Roger Alpha One, confirm your location.'

'Edgware Road walking towards Marble Arch wearing a green parka with the hood pulled up and blue jeans.'

'Roger Alpha One. You are the only call signs in that area. I'm alerting the Red Team who are on their way to support you. Should be with you in ten.'

Reece continued with Anna thirty yards behind him, with Cousins walking on the other side but trying to stay close to be parallel with the target.

'Are you sure it's him?' asked Anna.

'Not a hundred per cent but there's something about him.'

'Did you see where he came from?'

'No, I noticed him as we came out of the side street. He seemed to be walking with his head down and looking discreetly around him.'

The target crossed the road again taking his time to look right and left, pretending to look at the traffic while at the same time watching for followers. It had started to rain again, and the dark evening light didn't help surveillance. After crossing the road, the Arab turned into the next street down.

'Target One into Upper Berkley Street.' It was the voice of Cousins, who was now closer than he would like to be because of the man crossing the road almost in front of him.

'Be careful,' said Reece.

'Roger that,' replied Cousins.

Cousins held back to give the target time to get a little further ahead. When he turned into the street, he could see the man turn into the first street on the right.

'Target now into first street on the right,' said Cousins.

'Confirmed, Seymour Place. He appears to be walking the square may be looking for you, over.' It was the voice from the Ops room following the movement on the board in front of them.

Surveillance teams knew the term, which referred to checking for surveillance by identifying the same people or vehicles taking the same route especially if it's an obscure route.

'I'm going to try to make up some ground to see where he's gone,' said Cousins.

Reece and Anna crossed the road, keeping to the opposite side as Cousins and increased their pace to make up the ground. The loud crack of three gunshots in quick succession split the night air. They had lost sight of Cousins as he had turned into the street on the right ahead of them. Both broke into a run at the same time pulling their weapons from their holsters. As they rounded the corner into the street Anna sprinted across to take up the further footpath while Reece swept the street looking down the barrel of his gun. The rain and darkness made it difficult to focus. He could see the body of a man, lying on the path forty yards in front of him. He could see no one else, the street was empty, even the traffic seemed to have deserted it.

The closer Reece got to the figure, the more he swept the area with the gun as his pointer. Anna crossed over and knelt by the man while Reece continued to give cover. Cousins was on his back, staring up at the sky, his eyes blinking and his breathing heavy, as the rain washed down his pale face.

'He's alive,' said Anna.

'Alpha one to control, I need an ambulance and back-up to my location now.' Reece spoke into his body mic.

Kneeling beside Anna there was no sign of blood. Cousins was fully conscious but in a lot of pain groaning and trying to move.

'Stay still Joe, more help is on the way. What happened, where are you hurting?' asked Reece.

'The bastard was waiting for me when I turned the corner,' Cousins said through gritted teeth and short sharp intakes of air. 'He was pointing his gun straight at me and when I went for mine, he fired. One just missed my head but the other two hit me in the chest.'

Cousins gave out another loud groan as he tried to pull open his coat.

Reece pushed his hand away and after putting his 59 in its holster pulled open Cousin's coat and saw two neat holes in the sweater. He pulled once more, this time exposing the bullet-proof vest where he could see the two heads of the flattened bullet rounds embedded in the material.

'Joe, you're one lucky son of a bitch.'

'Or one smart one,' said Anna.

'At this moment I'm not sure,' said Cousins still taking short sharp breaths.

'Take it from me Joe. A couple of broken ribs are better than a pine box,' said Reece.

'What about our man?' asked Cousins.

'Don't worry. He got away but he won't be far, we'll get him soon. For now, it's a warm hospital bed for you.'

Reece gave control a sit-rep on everything that happened while Harrison brought one of the cars to the street.

'Control. Can you have our CCTV people check all the cameras in my area to see if they can pick up our friend?' Reece also passed on the description of who he now believed to be Target One.

A few minutes later some of the Red Team and armed officers from the police SO19 unit arrived and sealed off the street. They were closely followed by the ambulance, which quickly lifted Joe Cousins, who gave a thumbs up as the doors closed.

'Alpha One from control,' it was the voice of Matthew Simons.

'Go ahead control,' replied Reece.

'CCTV has your man crossing over Oxford Street and halfway down North Audley Street. He entered a bar; we think it's called The George. SO19 and more back-ups are heading there now.'

'Roger that we're on our way,' replied Reece.

With Harrison driving, all three agents pulled into North Audley Street just as the police were sealing it off at the opposite end. Reece and Anna pulled on their police baseball hats and were getting out of the car before Harrison had completely come to a stop.

'There may be a lot of people in there so we try to do this as quietly as we can. Steve, go and tell our uniform friends that Anna and I will go in on our own and try not to look out of place. Tell them to hold back and don't shoot us by mistake.'

Harrison ran to where the police cordon was now set-up and speaking to them, pointed back at Reece and Anna who had now taken off their caps and putting them into their pockets walked through the doors of The George.

The bar was the style of a Victorian era pub with dark wood, with snugs to the left as they entered. The lights shaped as globes were connected to chains falling from the ceiling. On the right, the bar itself filled the full length of the room, with a mirror covering the wall behind. Being early, the bar was not yet full. A few of the snugs and tables were taken up mainly by couples, with at least ten people standing at the counter either drinking or awaiting service by the two women behind the bar. The light was bright enough for them to see everyone's face. It was one of those drinking establishment's where people were more interested in their own company and conversation than anyone coming through the door. Trying to look like customers was not a problem and they walked from the door all the way through to the rear with no sign of Target One. The only place left to search was the toilets. Anna checked the ladies while Reece waited. It only took twenty seconds before Anna returned to shake her head indicating no show she then waited while Reece searched the gents again after twenty seconds he returned.

'No show there either,' said Reece. There were two more doors one with the word 'Staff Only' and the other the rear emergency escape door which was closed with the bar still in place and locked. Reece stood at the end of the bar where the hatch letting the staff in and out of the bar service area was open. After a few seconds one of the women behind the bar noticed him and came over.

'Can I help you?' asked the girl who looked about twenty.

Reece discreetly showed her his Security Services ID which he always used on such occasions. He always found when people took a good look at the document their eyes would open wide with surprise and then with a touch of panic, they would always answer his questions quickly.

'It's nothing to worry about. We are looking for a man wearing a green parka who may have come in about fifteen minutes ago have you seen him?'

'It's been terribly busy. I think he was in, but he didn't get a drink.'

'Has anyone gone out the emergency exit?' asked Anna.

'No, the alarm would have gone off if it were opened.'

Reece took another look around the bar then came back to where the barmaid was standing.

'Where does the staff door go to, is there stairs?'

'No stairs they were concreted over years ago. The only thing back there is a small kitchen, the drinks store and a back door where the deliveries come in.'

Reece turned and pushed through the door followed by Anna and the voice of the barmaid shouting,

'Hey, you can't go in there.'

The room was small and filled with stock for the bar. A small cooker and a freezer made the path between narrow, leading to a closed door at the back. Both agents drew their guns once more and Reece pulled open the door covered by Anna. Outside there was a small closed in yard with another door which Reece opened to reveal a large car park. Reece swept the yard again using the gun as a pointer in front of him, but it was quiet apart from the gentle dripping of the rain from an overflowing drainpipe.

'He's gone. There's no cameras in here and about six exits out of the car park.'

They retraced their steps through the bar and Reece briefed the police on the cordon.

'You can go mobile again. Our bird has flown, thank you for the back-up. Steve, can you drop us back at the other car and we can take a drive around Edgware Road and Oxford Street? I think our friend was walking on foot for a reason, he could still be working out of somewhere local maybe even his two pals as well.'

On the way back to the car Reece updated the Ops room and requested that Jim Broad be informed.

'He knows Alpha One.' again, it was the voice of Matthews.

'Thank you. Can I request all teams to pay particular attention to the two-mile radius of where we first saw Target One? Can you also have our CCTV people check all the cameras coming out of the car park to the rear of The George within the last thirty minutes? If they get anything it would be helpful.'

'Roger that. The director asks that you return here to give a complete update before you stand down tonight.'

'Roger will do,' replied Reece.

It was then that Reece looked at the Casio G Shock watch. It was almost eight thirty. He dialled Mary on his phone. When she answered he could hear the noise of the restaurant in the background.

'Don't tell me something came up,' said Mary.

'I'm sorry I'm afraid it did. Can you forgive me?'

'Of course. I'm getting used to it, but I don't want it to be the norm between us. I hate it when you're not with me, and all I can think about is the danger you might be in.'

Reece didn't want her to worry. She was expressing the words that he was thinking about earlier in the day. The dangers were part of his life, but now he was sharing it with someone he loved it wasn't fair on her, or them both.

'No danger, just something that had to be checked out. How's the food?' Reece asked trying to change the subject.

'I don't know, yet I've just ordered, but from the smells I'm getting it's going to be good.'

'I'll get there as soon as I can. I'll pick up a bottle of Bush for the room and at least we can have a nightcap.'

'Hurry I miss you.'

'Miss you too, see you soon.'

'You should tell her you love her,' said Anna smiling.

'I do tell her, but when we are alone.'

'Knowing this type of work that won't be too often.'

'When we get back to the car remind me to find an off-licence and buy a bottle of Bushmills.'

The Arab had wasted no time in leaving the bar by the rear door. He had crossed the car park, keeping his parka hood up to avoid recognition from any cameras. He had spotted the man following him when he had crossed over Edgware Road. His suspicions were confirmed when the man turned into one street then heard his increased footsteps as he turned in behind him in the second street. He had pulled his gun and pointed it towards the street corner. It had been his plan to challenge the man, not knowing if he was just a criminal looking to mug him, or a serious threat. When the man saw his gun and went for his he fired. He saw him go down but did not wait around to confirm he was dead. He took many more diversions and checks after leaving the back door of the bar. He was confident he was alone, and he knew the shooting of the man would distract his enemies long enough to allow him to get back to the security of his hotel. He waited until he was in his room before he phoned Hassan.

'The enemy are close. I had to deal with one on the way back to my location. I'm sure they still don't know our locations, so I'll stay here and see you as arranged on Friday, understand?'

Hassan, who had listened the whole time, replied 'Yes' then heard the empty buzz of the call ended from the phone.

Reece and Anna spent the next hour driving around Edgware Road and the side roads and streets while Harrison did the same in the Oxford Street area. Calling it a night Reece dropped Anna off at the Israeli Embassy where she was now staying and headed back to the MI6 operations room to brief Jim Broad.

'Any word from the hospital?' asked Reece.

'Joe will be all right. Two broken ribs and severe bruising. He is a smart man. That vest saved his life.'

'I know. I think we all need to take a leaf out of his book. I put mine on when we got back to the car and before I went into that bar.'

Broad walked to the back of the room where there were a few chairs and invited Reece to join him. Reece could tell by his expression he wasn't happy.

'David, the record so far is not good. We keep getting close then we lose them again. We could have lost one of our own this time.'

'I feel your pain. It is not nice getting this close and nothing to show for it. What will we do now? There's a lot of agencies involved and I'm sure Sir Martin Bryant isn't too pleased. Probably sitting sipping whisky with the PM as we speak.'

'To say the least. The only good thing that came out of tonight's debacle was that our man wasn't seriously hurt. We can put it about that it was a mugging and keep the press and media away from it. Our people will go to ground, and if their operation is still on, which giving everything we know about the Arab, it will be, then we can expect their next move to be on the day they intend to move. We are keeping our people on the streets day and night and pulling in all the information we can from all our sources including CCTV and GCHQ. The next time they move we need to be ready. We cannot rely on them to make a mistake. When they do move, we come down on them hard no second chances anymore.'

'You're talking to the converted here. I'm heading back to the hotel to get a good night's rest.'

Broad stood and stretched.

'Good idea David. I'm staying here. If anything happens I'll let you know. Give Mary my best.'

'I will. I hope she's not too angry. I was supposed to meet her for dinner at eight, it's now ten fifteen.'

Reece went to the armoury, took the H&K from the boot of the BMW and returned it. He sent Mary a text to say he was on his way. She replied that she would meet him in the hotel's Primo bar.

Chapter 24

Mary was sitting at a table by the window looking out at the Thames. With its reflections of light, it made it look like the city was twice the size. When he looked at her, her smile made him feel that his day had just got an awful lot better. He kissed her on her cheek and sat down.

'What's in the bag?' she asked.

Reece placed the plastic shopping bag gently on the table.

'It's a bottle of that liquid gold I said I would pick up.'

'Your favourite Bushmills. The bar does serve alcohol, you know.'

'This is for the room.'

Reece beckoned one of the waiters and when he found they had Bushmills ordered a double and a Gin and Tonic for Mary.

'You look like you had a rough day, Joseph.'

Reece liked her calling him Joseph. It always reminded him how they met.

'You could say that, and it will be even busier in the next few days.'

The drinks came and Reece clinked his glass with Mary's before taking a mouthful of what he considered to be the best whisky in the world.

'I've already booked a flight for the morning to Belfast. I can cancel it if you need me here.'

'No, don't worry. Stick to your plans. This will only take a few more days and then I can join you there.'

Mary reached across the table and took his hand in hers.

'If you're sure, but please be careful Joseph.'

'I could say the same to you. You need to catch-up with your mother I know, but I'm not one hundred per cent sure about you going to Belfast. Don't be taking any risks.'

'I won't if you won't.' She smiled, as she clinked the side of his glass with hers once more.

Reece thought a change of subject was required.

'So, what was the food like?'

'Just as good as it say's on the tin.'

'What did you have?'

'I was a good girl. I had the salmon fillet with baby potatoes and a cold glass of Chablis. Every time I drink that wine it reminds me of our lunch in that beautiful restaurant in Grosvenor Street.'

Reece remembered the day just before he went to Manchester on the mission that would bring him closer to Mary moving from agent handler to lover.

'I remember. I'm a little hungry. Let us order a bottle of that nice wine and some sandwiches and get them sent to the room.'

'Now that's the kind of plan I like.' She smiled.

The wine was just as good as Reece remembered, the sandwiches excellent and making love to Mary, everything. Now he lay awake beside her, he watched her breasts rising and falling under the thin white sheet, her breathing soft in the night air as she slept the sleep of a child.

He had tried to sleep but the work of the day kept spinning in his mind. She was going to Belfast in the morning, a day that was already here. He was not happy about it. Too many bad memories of the dangers, the violence, the friends he had lost. Mary turned in her sleep and stretched her arms across his shoulders. He closed his eyes once more and at last sleep came.

The darkness of the winter morning was brightened by the streetlights through the window when he woke. A glance at his watch told him it was 06.30. Mary was up already up; he could hear the shower and her voice singing to herself. She didn't have a bad voice, and he had sung along with her in the times they'd a few too many drinks relaxing at the villa in Malta.

'You're awake.' She had come out of the bathroom a large white towel wrapped around her body.

'You're up early. I thought you would take the chance to sleep in.'

'Plenty of time for sleeping Joseph. My flight leaves at 11.30 and I want a decent breakfast before I set off. Anyway, you have a busy day ahead of you and a good breakfast will do you no harm.'

'You're right but before breakfast we have a little time.' He pulled back the bed sheet.

She smiled, then dropping the towel climbed in beside him.

Reece waved goodbye to Mary as her taxi pulled away from the hotel and headed to the airport just after 8 a.m. He had booked the room for another two nights, more for the convenience than anything else.

Twenty minutes later he was sitting with Jim Broad in the MI6 Operations Room. Broad looked like he had not slept well, and his clothes needed a good dry cleaner.

'We need to get something today David or the PM and Bryant will close down this whole city and cause a full-blown panic.'

Reece had been thinking along the same lines.

'You need to keep telling them that. You know how some of these politicians think. They will be shitting themselves. But if we catch these bastards, they'll be in front of the cameras claiming all the glory.'

Broad nodded in agreement.

'Have we received anything overnight?' asked Reece.

'We may have something. Have a look at the monitor.'

Reece crossed the room and watched the screen in front of one of the operators as Broad told him to bring up the CCTV from last night.

The black and white picture showed a man with a parka, red pointer arrows indicated the names of the location as he walked at a fast pace. The man had walked out of lower Duke Street before crossing Oxford Street and entering the upper part of Duke Street.

'Unfortunately, there aren't enough cameras in Duke Street to see where he went but he disappeared in that area.'

'He seemed to know where he was going so we could make a good assumption that he might be staying somewhere close to Duke Street. It's not far from The George and Edgware Road so we must concentrate most of our resources around there. Any spare resources should cover a roaming brief of the important high value targets in the rest of the city.'

Just then Anna and Harrison arrived, and Reece asked the operator to run the screen once more for their benefit.

'We still don't know where any of them are staying then?' asked Anna.

'No but I think we've them tied down to a smaller area and that's where we concentrate most of our resources,' said Reece.

'Alright David. I'll update everyone you get out there and see what they can do. We need a bit of luck,' said Broad.

'You know what we always say; 'They always make a mistake and when they do, we kill them.' I think last night was their first real mistake. Anna and Steve, we will stay together in one car. Steve, you drive. Then if Anna and I need to, we can follow on foot with you in the car as back-up. Happy with that?'

'Sounds like a plan,' replied Harrison.

Before they could move, Matthew Simons came into the room.

'Before you leave, GCHQ have just sent this.'

He went over to the console and typed a few words on the keyboard. The screen showed the ragged lines of an audio feed. They listened to the phone conversation between two men. The first voice was that of the Arab telling his friend of his close call with Joe Cousins and then the call finishing with a one word reply from the other man, 'Yes.'

'So, by the sound of things their plan is being set for Friday morning. We need to get the area where we believe they're hiding, screwed down as tight as we can.' said Reece.

'What makes GCHQ think these are our targets and do they have any idea where they are?' asked Broad.

'Believe it or not they've been keeping everything open for chatter and apparently Mossad were able to pass on a small voice clip from when our friend the Arab met with the Iranian General in the café in Tehran. That voice clip was very distorted, so it didn't tell them anything of significance, but GCHQ were able to keep it on their system and get a voice match when the call was picked up on their searches last night. They worked on it all night that's why it's taken until now for them to confirm it is the Arab. They were able to tie the calls down to a radius of two miles which would take in the same area where we believe they are,' said Simons.

'As I said. They would make mistakes, and this is one more. From the conversation, and the time of the call, the two men are holed up in different locations close to each other within that two miles. Today we get everyone to walk it, drive it, and get to know every nook and cranny so that when they do move, we don't lose them this time,' said Reece.

'Leave that with us David. We will get everyone into that area. You'll be tripping over each other, but we will keep you updated,' said Broad.

Reece was feeling a little better about the future as Harrison drove them across the city. Reece sat in front, with Anna in the back seat, first stop where they left off the night before.

Chapter 25

As the SG9 team drove across the city, the Arab was eating breakfast in his hotel room, the Prime Minister was holding a meeting in his private office in Number 10. There were four others around the table. The Chiefs of MI6 and MI5, Sir Martin Bryant and Kurt Shimon had all been summoned by the Prime Minister's office for a specific reason. He wanted to look them all in the eye and watch their responses to his questions rather than over the phone.

'I've been updated about last night's fiasco and the near death of one of our people, while these people make fools of us and get away again. What the hell is going on Sir Ian, your people have overall control?'

All eyes were on Sir Ian Fraser, and he noticed that Bryant had a slight smile at the corners of his mouth, he was enjoying this; if Fraser did not know better, this first question from the PM had been set-up by Bryant.

'The first thing we should remember is that these people we are dealing with are not amateurs. They are all highly trained. The Arab himself has experience of real time operations. Some of those operations have been against the best intelligence agencies in the world and I'm sure Kurt here would agree.' Shimon nodded and Fraser continued.

'We were lucky not to lose one of our operators last night, but the Arab was lucky too. We know they're prepared to kill but so are we if we have too. Taking in the whole of Europe and this country, starting from scratch, with hardly any information to begin with, we have them narrowed down to a two-mile radius in the city. We have now concentrated most of our resources in that area, if they raise their heads, we have a good chance of spotting them.'

'What has MI5 to say about this and has anybody got anything new to indicate what the target is?' asked Bryant.

Caroline Aspinall finished sipping her coffee before answering, ignoring Bryant she spoke directly to Brookfield.

'As you know Prime Minister, we are using all our people and working closely with all the other agencies to ensure a positive outcome.

The information you're getting is as up to date as the information I'm getting.'

Answered like a true politician, thought Fraser. Something he knew he wasn't good at. Caroline Aspinall had been taught how to deal with questions at a girls' private school and then at university in Oxford. Fraser had come up through the army ranks; the school of hard knocks, where the answers could sometimes be harsh but necessary to save lives. He still respected Aspinall. She was a strong personality in her own right, and would stand up for her people, just as he would.

'I believe everyone is doing their best. But I do not think it's enough. I've spoken to the Home Secretary, and she agrees that we should raise the threat level to Critical,' said Brookfield.

This time it was Fraser who spoke.

'Prime Minister, the current level is at Substantial, which, as you know means an attack is likely. The difference is that Critical is an attack that is highly likely soon. To everyone here and to the media that is a significant jump and would hopefully raise people's awareness. My own feeling is that the general population out there will not see much difference in the wording as they believe an attack is always likely. My only worry is that the press will start sticking their nose in and get in the way. It could even see our enemy changing their mind and bring forward their plan which now mentions tomorrow, Friday. It may also make them think we know more than we do, and they could drop everything disappear and come back on another day when we lack information.'

'I know what you're saying, Sir Ian, but I'm the elected leader of those people out there, and it's not only my job to protect them as it is yours, but it's also my responsibility to keep them honestly appraised of the danger they may face. We may only have twenty-four hours before this thing goes down and making the announcement now will not give the press enough time to interfere too much. The Home Secretary can handle the press for that period, and if anyone comes to any of you with questions, direct them to her.'

Fraser knew it was better not to argue as the decision had been made between the PM and Bryant before he had come into the room. It was the usual political decision. The one where they protect their arses and make sure that if things hit the fan, they can point the finger elsewhere. Then again, he thought, if he were in the same shoes as the Prime Minister, he would probably make the same decision. After all the experts had brought him nothing and the terrorists were still out there.

'I'm sorry Kurt, do you think it's the right thing to do?' Bryant asked.

The Mossad officer knew better than to get sucked into another country's political war.

'You must do what you think is right for your country. In my own country we would be kicking down doors and that would include the Finsbury Mosque. I would like to know what the Imam knows. But then you must do what you think is right for you.'

'I think you understand Mister Shimon. The British people cherish not only their own civil rights but the civil rights of others. Between ourselves I only wish I had the same power your Prime Minister has when it comes to dealing with these people.'

'Maybe that is why they think they can get away with what they intend to do, because they know you're vulnerable, and they believe because of that you're weak. In Israel we strike hard and that is the only way we can survive. We are surrounded by enemies who want to destroy us. I believe in the old saying, we call it the eleventh commandment, hit them before they hit you. I think from what I've seen, you have the resources to hit them, you just need the courage to do so.'

Fraser was impressed by the words of the Mossad officer which he totally agreed with. The difference was that the Director of MI5 and the Mossad were unaware of the true remit of SG9 that had been agreed at the highest level. To track down the terrorist threats to the UK and eliminate them wherever they were found.

'Don't worry Kurt we have the courage. If Margaret Thatcher could send the SAS into the Iranian Embassy, then an invasion fleet halfway around the world to the Falklands to kick out the Argentinians, then this country has the courage,' said Bryant.

'No offence intended we are with you in this, all the way,' replied Shimon.

The Director of MI5 had listened to this conversation and had to speak.

'You do realise Sir Martin that when we had the bomb attacks in July 2005, the Security Service came in for a lot of criticism and that's why we more than doubled the lawyers we had. The number of ambulance-chasing legal firms out there also increased because they could see big money through their distorted use of the human rights legislation. On one occasion we acted on poor intelligence that there was a biological weapon in a Muslim family house at Forest Gate. We raided it and found nothing. The intelligence was wrong, and the subsequent claims cost the British taxpayer £210,000 to refurbish the house and a further £60,000 to compensate the family. That one costly mistake almost cost the job of one of my predecessors, never mind the money. But since then, we tend to worry too much about getting it wrong, instead of doing our job despite the mistakes.'

She had made her point. Fear can freeze politicians into making mistakes. They think according to the amount of votes it could cost them, never mind the money or damage to the country. The Prime Minister stood before replying.

'Thank you for that Caroline. Can we get back to Operation Search? From my calculations we have about 24 hours, and we still need to find these people and the target. Keep me updated all the way. I'll give the Home Secretary the heads up to issue the increase to the threat level. All our forces will be put on full alert. Get me results and get them fast.' With that Brookfield and Bryant left the three intelligence officers to themselves.

'What now?' asked Aspinall.

'We find these people fast. The Prime Minister has given us more power without knowing it.'

'What do you mean 'C'? The press will be banging on our door as soon as that notice goes out.'

'Pass them on to the Home Secretary's office. In the meantime, we concentrate on the Finsbury Mosque and the two-mile area where we think our friends are holed up and knock down doors as Kurt suggests.'

'That will ruffle a few feathers,' said Shimon.

Fraser smiled.

'As I said, the PM has by his actions given us the go ahead to use all resources to find these people. If that means kicking down a few doors and ruffling a few feathers, then so be it. Better that, than hundreds dead because we did nothing. We start by putting pressure on their people. If things go wrong, we all might be dead anyway or at the very least looking for a new job. If it's war these people want, then it's war they will get.'

Reece and Anna had spent the last hour walking the busy streets between Oxford Street and Edgware Road. The winter day was cold, and both had made sure to wear warm clothes which also helped cover the fact they were wearing bulletproof vests. When Reece wore his Barbour jacket, he liked to keep his gun in the right-hand pocket rather than the holster giving easier access to it if needed. Anna was wearing a short parka coat and from the way she kept her hand in her right pocket Reece suspected she would be holding the grip of her .22 pistol.

Some of the streets being close together were not wide and they'd found on more than one occasion they'd crossed over the same road more than once. They had kept up a running conversation with Harrison in the car and Reece felt he was getting to know each street and alleyway the only way he knew best, by walking them.

'Do you fancy finding a café for something warm and wet?' asked Reece.

'Yes please, I need something to warm me up.'

'Let's walk back to Edgware Road and find one.' Reece radioed Harrison to let him know the plan. He would let him know where, and to meet them there.

They found a Starbucks, the kind of café he liked where they could get a seat by the window and observe the street outside. The café was quiet with only two other people sitting near the counter at the other end of the room. Harrison came in five minutes later and sat down with them after getting a coffee for himself.

'Do you know this area?' Reece asked Harrison.

'Yes, very well. I was part of a team a few years ago when we followed a suspected IRA sympathiser for days. He was over from Ireland working as a labourer on a building site. In those days there were hundreds of them over here working the sites throughout the city, some of them using it as cover for their other activities. Most, like him, were living in digs in Kilburn. The largest Irish area in those days. He never spotted us and went back to Ireland. But we identified his contacts and we arrested two of them later, they were planning to bomb Euston Station, not far from here. We had spotted him meeting them at a bar across from the station.'

Reece was looking out the window at the rain and the people, some of them with umbrellas for protection.

'I've stayed in Sussex Gardens a few times. I've always liked this area, its cosmopolitan shops, and restaurants. It always seemed to me to have a community atmosphere. I don't like driving in the city, it's too busy for me, and I think knowing the short cuts lets me get to where I want to be much quicker and at the same time I can admire much of what the city has to offer. If I need to travel further out like the MI6 building or the airports, I use a taxi or the Tube.'

'I'm like you, David. When I'm in a major city like Tel Aviv, I like to walk. You can see much more, and I feel more aware of what's going on around me.' said Anna.

'Talking about being more aware of what's going on around you. I see someone we should invite to join us.' Said Reece as he looked out the window.

'Tango One from Alpha One.' Reece spoke quietly and discreetly into the body mic on his collar.

On the other side of the street from where they looked out of the café window, they could see Captain Geoff Middleton SAS stop and reply into his own body mic.

'Tango One, go ahead.'

'Roger Tango One would you like to join us in the café across the road from you?' replied Reece smiling.

Middleton looked across the road and seeing Reece at the window did not reply but acknowledged by giving a thumbs up before crossing and entering the café.

Pulling a chair over to join them at the table, Middleton sat down beside Anna with his back to the window.

'Good timing, David I was just thinking about getting something to drink, but I suppose seeing we're working it will have to be coffee.' Middleton said with a smile.

'I'll get us some refills. What's your poison Geoff?' asked Harrison.

'A double espresso please.'

'David. I saw this man at our briefing, but I wasn't introduced,' said Anna.

'I'm sorry Anna. May I introduce Geoff Middleton, a Captain in the SAS. His team are working with us on this job. Geoff, this is Anna one of our Mossad friends.'

Both shook hands across the table and Reece couldn't help but notice both smiled a little bit longer than the requisite time expected for such an introduction.

'Nice to meet you Anna. I bet you're finding the weather here a little bit colder than where you come from.'

'If you mean Tel Aviv. Yes, but I work all over. Have you ever been to Israel?'

'Yes, on a few occasions on joint training exercises with the IDF and Sayeret Maktal. Or the Unit as you might call them.'

'Our Special Forces. I know them by both names, you must be good then.' She smiled once more.

'Oh, I'm very good.' He laughed.

Harrison came back with the coffees and placed them in front of the right people.

'Well David how is Joe? I heard he was lucky last night. Are you sure it was our man?' asked Middleton.

'A few broken ribs, but he'll be all right. We were not sure if it was the Arab when we first spotted him, but he started to take precautions right from the off. It was obvious he had done this before and knew what to look for. Joe was ahead of us when he followed him into another street. We heard the three shots. Joe said one missed his head but the other two hit him square in the chest. Lucky for him he had decided to wear his vest, or we would be talking about a dead agent today.'

'Thanks be to God he did. What's the plan now?'

'Have you been updated?'

'Yes, we've been told to get to know this area and remain on standby ready to go at a moment's notice.'

'Well, that's the plan. We are doing the same. We believe they're hold up within this two-mile radius and it's now a game of find them before they do anything, which we now believe will be tomorrow.'

Just then the mobile phone in Reece's pocket buzzed. It was a text from Mary.

'In Belfast. Call me when you can. XX'

'If you will excuse me, I need to make a call. Steve, give me the car keys where did you park?'

Harrison handed over the keys.

'Parked up in the next street down on the left.'

'Wait here. I won't be long.'

Reece found the car and pressed in Mary's name. He heard the phone ring twice before Mary answered.

'I didn't expect you to call me that quickly.' She spoke.

'You know me, you shout, and I come running. How's things?'

'Mum has had a fall and she's in the city hospital.'

'Is she OK?' He thought he could hear a sadness in her voice.

'She broke her hip. They are going to operate later today.'

'I'm sorry to hear that, everything will be all right. She's in the right place for now.'

'I know, I needed to let you know and to hear your voice. You know they don't allow people to use phones in hospitals. I didn't want you to worry if you couldn't get me if my phone was switched off.'

'Don't switch it off, keep it on silent. That way you will be able to read my messages or that I called.'

'How are you David, how are things going?'

It was one of the things he loved about her. She would always want him to be safe.

'Don't worry about me. You have enough on your plate. Everything is going well here. I should be finished here tomorrow and with you on Saturday.'

He could hear her voice change to one of relief.

'That makes me feel better. I'm heading for the hospital now. Please take care.'

'Don't worry. I'll see you on Saturday. Love you.'

'Love you too.' she answered before ending the call.

Reece sat back in the seat and thought about his day so far. He thought how Anna and Middleton had seemed to hit it off and compared it in his mind to the many meetings over coffee with Mary and the danger when she was his agent, code name Mike in Northern Ireland. He did not like her being there without him. There may be a so-called peace process, and the terrorists were supposed to have handed in their weapons. But the one thing that had kept him alive on many occasions, was never to trust anyone, and he certainly didn't trust the gunmen and bombers who tried to convince the world their terror was over. Reece could never believe them. They may have stopped killing for now but given the chance; because of the damage he had done to them through agents like Mike; he knew he would still be a prime target with old scores to settle. Much of this damage to the terrorist organisations was with the help of the SAS. He thought back to his close links with men such as Geoff Middleton. In his RUC Special Branch days, Reece had the job of travelling to the home base of the 22nd SAS Regiment in Hereford which had at first been named

Stirling Lines after the regiments founder Colonel David Stirling. The name had then been changed to Bradbury Lines but Reece always preferred Stirling Lines. Being an Ulster man himself he had also thought they could have named the Headquarters after one of the regiment's most famous officers Colonel Robert Blair Mayne another Ulster man. He would travel to the base for a few days every six months. His job was to update the incoming Squadron taking over from the current one in Northern Ireland. He would be picked up and dropped back at Birmingham airport. Over the next few days, he would stay in accommodation provided for him in the Officers Mess. He remembered the long corridor, with bedrooms on each side. The walls were filled with the plaques showing the badges of the different regiments and agencies throughout the world, who had visited the base and worked with the famous regiment. One of the plaques showed the harp and crown badge of the Royal Ulster Constabulary and had been presented to the regiment by himself. At the end of the corridor was the Officer's Mess, itself with a bar where, if no one was available to serve, officers and visitors could serve themselves and sign a chit which would be presented to them for their bar bill at the end of their stay. Reece had had a few beers in the mess with some of the SAS team and signed his chit, only to find at the end of his visit, he was presented with a receipt showing the regiment's crest of the winged dagger and the bill marked as paid with thanks. Above the bar there was two AK47 rifles presented to the mess by Major Mike Keeley. These were a souvenir from one of the most famous battles in the regiment's history. Keeley himself had fought against the communist backed guerrillas in the battle at Mirbat during the Dhofar Rebellion in Oman in July 1972.

Keeley had died from hypothermia during an exercise on the Brecon Beacons in Wales. Reece had a photo of himself standing at the bar with the rifles above him.

He would brief the incoming team in a type of theatre classroom on the current threat and intelligence in Northern Ireland using visual displays as well as answering questions. He would work with many of the men in the future months, and he would always remember the drinking session with them that evening after the briefing. The SAS men also took the time to show Reece around the main training areas of the base including the famous killing house, where the men would practise their close quarter combat firearm skills and hostage rescue. Reece had done most of his specialist firearms training and anti-ambush escape and evasion drills at a secret location in Northern Ireland. Over several days, he would fire every weapon under the sun; most of them captured from the terrorist organisations he was working against. Everything from Armalite and AK47 rifles to Thompson Sub machine guns. They would enter and clear buildings, engaging cardboard full size human silhouette targets. The last two days of the course included anti-ambush training that simulated the agent's car being attacked. He was taught how to fire and reload while still inside the car. Then the instructors brought in the bomb disposal officer (ATO) who would detonate a small charge in front of the vehicle to simulate disabling it. He had to get out of the car and moving up a narrow pathway that they nicknamed the Ho Chi Minh trail, engage more cardboard targets to the right and left taking cover to reload. It was as realistic as they could make it and after the course Reece felt a little like John Wayne in that he was confident he could draw his pistol and hit the target in the centre of the body every time. When he had joined SG9, his MI6 bosses sent him once more to Hereford to receive more specialist training. The SAS training was tough. They taught him the unarmed tactic of Krav Maga, a self-defence fighting style use by Special Forces the world over. They taught him that rather than back off in a fight it was better to engage quickly with your opponent to give you the element of surprise, especially if you don't have a weapon to hand. Reece ended up a qualified marksman with the handgun and could handle himself in a close combat fight, either with a weapon or his bare hands.

One of the main lessons he learnt was 'You are not John Wayne,' if you must take out your gun, you shoot to kill, two in the chest one in the head. If necessary, you keep shooting at the target until it's eliminated and no longer a threat. Lessons he would never forget.

Reece headed back to the café where he found Harrison standing outside.

'Are they all right in there?' he asked.

'Getting on famously. Two's company three's a crowd if you know what I mean. I was the gooseberry.' smiled Harrison.

'That good eh, lets break them up. We have work to do.' Reece handed Harrison the car keys. 'You head back to the car we will do another hour then head back to base to see how the other teams are doing.'

When Reece entered the café Anna and Middleton were laughing and leaning close across the table their hands almost touching.

'Right, you two, let's keep this professional; we have work to do. Geoff, I'm staying in the Plaza Westminster Hotel. I'm sure Anna would like to join us there for dinner tonight, say eight? Are you up for that, provided nothing happens in between of course?'

Sitting up straight in the chair with his eyes still on Anna.

'Sounds like a great plan. I look forward to it. See you both later then.' Middleton stood and turned left out the door to move in the direction Reece had first seen him.

'I've told Steve to shadow us in the car for an hour and then we can head back to HQ unless you have other plans?'

'No, none for now, or for dinner at eight.' She smiled.

Chapter 26

In a small hotel in Kensington the Deputy First Secretary of the Iranian Embassy was enjoying his second bottle of champagne in his bedroom. The woman he had just had sex with was showering in the bathroom. When it came to breaking Islamic law, he knew he would be hanged if his bosses in Tehran knew he was drinking alcohol and having afternoon sex with a woman who was not his wife. He had met her not long after becoming the new London Embassy Deputy six months ago. He had been out for a morning jogging session in Hyde Park when he spotted her. She had been jogging in front of him and he had noticed the firm shape of her body and her bouncing blonde ponytail hairstyle before he saw her take a bad tumble falling a few yards in front of him. As there was no one else around, he stopped to help her to her feet enquiring if she was all right. She had said her ankle was sore, and he could see a small amount of blood coming through a tear in her tight Lycra training tights.

She rested her hands on his shoulders as she got to her feet and he helped her through the park to the main road, where he flagged down a taxi to take her to the hospital. She smiled and thanked him for his help. Her accent was English, and she was softly spoken and educated. All he could think about the few days after was how stupid he had been not get her name or contact details or even introduce himself. It was to be three weeks later, when jogging the same route at the same time of day, that he saw her once more in front of him. Quickly catching up he had called out hello. She stopped, and turning, she seemed to recognise him so smiled and said hello back. He asked how she was, and she reassured him she'd made a full recovery. The ankle was twisted and the cut on her knee was only a scrape. She had felt foolish and when she thought about it afterwards, she was embarrassed that she'd not asked him for his name or told him hers. With everything now mended she had started back in her jogging routine only that day. He thought this must be fate. Fate had brought them together twice and he intended to make the most of it. He asked for her contact details and if he could take her out to lunch or a coffee. She had hesitated for just a few seconds then smiling agreed to lunch later that week. The lunch went well. He did not tell the Embassy security or the ambassador that he had met this beautiful woman. He had not told his wife either, she'd gotten fat from eating too much at the Embassy events. Sex with her was a chore and they hardly spoke anymore with more shouting arguments than talking. He had decided to keep this woman to himself, and he found the secret liaisons made the love making even more exciting. It had started with the lunch date where he had found himself laughing with the woman. He enjoyed having a glass or two of wine in the afternoon and over the weeks they'd met up when jogging, going for a coffee afterwards. The lunch dates had led to dinner dates and eventually, after about four weeks, to a hotel room and bed. There was no comparison between the young woman and his wife, her body was slim and fit. She was a single businesswoman, with the intelligent mind that went with it. She made love to him the way he wanted her to, he would tell her what he liked, and she obliged, seeming to know how to bring him to a special height of passion. He liked to think he pleased her, and he always felt relaxed in the time afterwards, when they lay in each other's arms and spoke openly about the world and their lives.

The woman in the bathroom was indeed beautiful. She looked in the mirror applying a little lipstick, just enough to keep a man interested, but not enough that he could get it on his clothes and give the game away. To her it was a game, ever since she'd been a girl of seventeen and realised that men liked how she looked and were willing to pay to be with her. She was twenty-six now and she'd made a small living from letting men enjoy the experience of spending a short time with her. That was until two months ago when she was having her end of the week glass of her favourite white wine in the Grosvenor Hotel in Mayfair. A man had sat at her table and asked if he could join her and buy another bottle of wine to share with her. She had been approached by men offering to buy her a drink many times but for some reason this time it was different. The man, tall and of athletic build clean shaven with dark brown eyes and hair, he was not the kind who needed to pick up women. *If anything*, she'd thought, *women would flock to him*. His open white shirt and dark grey suit were made of expensive material and design and his accent was foreign, although she couldn't place it.

He introduced himself as Ari and she readily invited him to stay while he ordered the wine. She was intrigued, and for the rest of that afternoon enjoyed the conversation finding he could make her laugh easily with his beautiful smile enhancing his appearance. It was when he had poured the last glass from the bottle that the conversation changed, he said he had a business proposition to put to her. He said his company were interested in the oil industry in Iran and hoped to complete contracts worth billions of pounds. Through business contacts he had been given her name and where to find her when she visited the hotel for her favourite glass of wine. He had given her a plain white business card with the words Eastern Oil and a mobile telephone number.

The proposal was simple and would bring her the kind of wealth that would make her immediate future financially secure. She was intrigued and invited him to tell her more, without asking anymore questions until he had finished speaking. The man ordered another bottle of wine and talked for the next hour. What it came down to he had said, was that his company needed inside information, and she was in an ideal position to get it for them. What they wanted her to do, was contact one of the Iranian Embassy staff in London, get to know him and let them know whatever he told her. He then told her if she could do this, they would be grateful and to show their thanks they would give her an apartment overlooking Hyde Park and pay her handsomely enough that she wouldn't need to have any other clients and she could concentrate on just the one.

When she told him she was interested but wondered how she could contact such an Iranian without raising his suspicions, he had the answer to that question as well. He would provide her with all the details and how to make such an approach without raising suspicion. It did not take her long to decide before the second bottle of wine was empty she agreed that she was interested but would need to hear more and see the apartment he promised before she signed on the dotted line. She had asked him would it be dangerous, was she going to be a spy? The question she thought was a sensible one and one she needed the answer to or there would be no deal. Once again, he calmed her fears. She would be doing what she'd been doing for many years, seducing men to like her and give her what she wanted. In this case the money would be coming from his company at a larger rate than her usual fee. She would only have one client, the Iranian, who wouldn't know she was working for his company. She would always have his phone contact details on speed dial if she should need him and they would meet after every date she had with the Iranian. Over the following weeks she'd moved into the Hyde Park apartment and met with Ari. He had provided her with the answer to the questions that she'd asked at that first meeting. She would go jogging in Hyde Park at a specific time on a specific day. He showed her photographs of the man they wanted her to get to know. They agreed she would instigate the meeting by falling. Before she would go on her run, she would tear her training trousers at the knee, and he would provide her with a small vial of blood to pour over the knee area. She was to pretend to be injured and allow the man to get her a taxi but not give him any information, just to thank him and leave in the taxi, which she should take back to her apartment where Ari would brief her further. It had all seemed a bit melodramatic, but she was intrigued, and if she admitted it, a bit excited at being involved in a new experience, where her talents were being used for reasons other than just for sex.

On the day she'd fallen in front of the Iranian everything went just as Ari had said and he was waiting for her when she'd returned to the apartment. She had done wonderfully well he said. Now that the first part of the plan had been completed, he gave her a bank card. He explained they'd opened a bank account for her in a new name which she was to use from now on so that the Iranian would never find out who she really was in case she wanted to call off the deal for any reason and go back to her previous way of working. From that day she was to be known as Martha Fleming. Ari had made her day complete when he told her there would be £5,000 per month in the account but not to go mad as lavish spending would bring unwanted attention to her. She was to say she'd received an endowment from her dead parents, and she'd worked in the travel industry thereby showing her interest in anything foreign. She was currently out of a job and was enjoying some time off. She knew this was a good cover as she loved to travel and had visited most countries in the Mediterranean, including Egypt and had travelled to New York. She had to wait for three weeks before Ari would tell her to go jogging again. The plan had worked just as he had told her it would and as she had dried herself down in the bathroom, she knew the man in the bedroom had believed everything she'd said and accepted the invented story of her past life as fact. He was like most middle-aged married men she knew. A little flattery and a glimpse of her cleavage and she could have most of them eating out of the palm of her hand. Over the weeks he had started talking a little more each time they met. He talked about his work, a little about his family and how living in London compared with his home in Iran. She had been an enthusiastic listener. It was his work that Ari was interested in, and he had told her to let the Iranian bring the conversation up and not to question him just to let him lead the way. It did not take many meetings before she found the Iranian beginning to talk freely about his work and his life. He was not happy with his work and was angry that he was only the Deputy Secretary at the Embassy. He believed he would be better at the senior job than his boss. Today she'd tried to get him to talk about the Iranian oil business with the intention of impressing Ari, but to her surprise the Iranian said he did not know much about it instead asking her why she wanted to know about oil. She was thrown for a few a seconds before replying that she was thinking of investing some money in the oil industry on the stock exchange. It was then that the Iranian told her he had a secret. When she innocently asked him what it was, he would only reply that he had recently met with an important man who had advised him that the financial district of London was about to experience some difficulty and it wouldn't be sensible to invest in a stock exchange that might not be there tomorrow. She pretended not to hear and replied I need a shower, but I'll be back soon so keep the bed warm. This seemed to please him. She knew that Ari would need to hear about the stock market and how the oil industry might be affected.

It was after ten when she left the hotel and pressed the number on speed dial for Ari. After a few rings he answered.

'Hello'

'Ari, I've just left our friend. I know it's late, but I think we should meet tonight.'

'I can be at the apartment in an hour.'

'Great see you there.'

Chapter 27

Alpha One had signed off for the night and Reece, after checking that there were no updates, returned to his hotel room where he cleaned up, changed his clothes, and headed down to the hotel bar. He sat on one of the stools at the bar and ordered a Bloody Mary. When he tasted it, he realised it wasn't as good as the last one he had drunk in Malta. Just then he saw his Malta drinking companion walk into the bar and walking closely behind was Geoff Middleton. *Did they come together or just happen to arrive at the same time?* Reece thought.

'I see you're having our drink,' said Anna.

She was wearing a tight-fitting white trouser suit and Reece thought she must have her gun in her purse as she couldn't hide anything in the suit.

'Hi David, what are you having?' asked Middleton.

'I'm OK. You two go ahead. I've booked us a table for eight.'

'Let's share a bottle of wine,' said Anna.

Middleton looked at the wine list then spoke to the barman.

'A bottle of Lindeman's Bin 65 Chardonnay please and two glasses.'

'Good choice,' said Anna smiling back at Middleton.

'Unfortunately, this will be about all we will be able to drink tonight and possibly until this bloody thing is over,' said Reece.

The dining room was busy, but their table was near the window overlooking the city and in one of the few quieter places in the room. It was obvious to Reece that his two dining companions had been speaking earlier. There were no personal questions. Are you married? Is there anyone else in your life? Where do you live? The kind of questions two people who are getting to know each other ask. Instead, they'd moved to the next phase. What do you like to do when you're not working? What are your likes and dislikes? Where do you like to go to get away from it all? Reece now knew what Harrison meant earlier in the day when he said he had felt like a gooseberry. When the time came to order dessert, Reece asked for the cheese and biscuits with a small glass of Taylors vintage port. Middleton said the same but Anna who asked for Cointreau with ice.

'Any news or updates?' asked Middleton.

'Nothing new on our side,' said Reece. 'The plan stays the same. There will be people out all night in the two-mile area we think, or should I say, hope they're in. We are back on the ground from 7am.'

'Nothing new from my side. All our people across the globe and here in London are working to find answers.'

'What if we don't find them? What happens if they get through?' asked Middleton.

'I don't want to think about that. You remember when we were in Ireland, Geoff? We worked night and day to stop attacks. The public didn't appreciate that we stopped nine out of every ten terrorist attacks. People only remember the ones that got through, the ones that took lives and devastated communities. We don't have the comfort of worry. We need to do our best and I'm sure if we do, we can stop these bastards.'

'Amen to that,' said Middleton.

'We have been stopping these bastards as you put it David for a lot longer than any of you. When they do get through the blowback is way above our paygrade,' said Anna.

'It's not only a time for good soldiers but good leaders as well,' Middleton replied.

'I don't like politicians at the best of times, but I have to say Brookfield is one of the strongest Prime Ministers we've had in a long while. I saw how he worked in Manchester up close. Even though he knew there was a terrorist hit squad out to assassinate him, he still went about his normal business and let us get on with our job, giving us the OK to take them out when we found them.' said Reece.

'It's always been my experience that politicians look for a way out to blame someone when things go wrong,' commented Middleton.

Reece raised his glass.

'Well, when I finish this port and cheese I'm off to bed. Early start in the morning provided nothing happens tonight.'

'Don't forget to call Mary before you go to bed.' Anna said.

'of course, she would never forgive me if I didn't say good night.'

Reece left the two diners alone and headed to his room. As promised, he called Mary to say goodnight. She told Reece her mother had come through the operation and was resting well.

'How was your day, Joseph?'

'Busy. I just had dinner with Anna and Geoff Middleton. Do you remember him from Manchester?'

'Yes, I think so, the SAS Captain?'

'Yes, that's the guy. I think him and Anna are getting on very well if you know what I mean?'

'If I know you, you're not happy about that, you're too much of a professional.'

'I know they are too, or I would have to remind them we have important work to do.'

'That sounds more like the Joseph I know. I'm tired my darling, so I think I'll hit the pillow. You do the same, by the sound of things you have a busy day tomorrow.'

'You're right, and that's exactly where I'm heading. All being well tomorrow, I should still be OK for Saturday in Belfast.'

'I'm looking forward to it and you can meet my mother. Good night. I love you.'

'Good night, Mary, sweet dreams I love you too. I'll try to call or text you tomorrow if I'm not too busy and you're not in the hospital quiet zone.'

He poured himself a small glass of Bushmills taking a few sips while looking out the window across the city. He thought about Mary and then his enemy across the river somewhere on the other side of the city. He was glad Mary was safe and far enough away to make his job that bit easier not having to worry about her.

Reece felt warm and decided to lie on top of the bed. Following old and trusted habits he placed his gun within reach on the bedside cabinet. He closed his eyes for what only seemed minutes when his phone, which he had plugged into a charger, started to buzz loud enough to wake him. Looking at his watch he could see it was only 2 am and he had been sleeping for two hours. Lifting the phone, he could see the name Broad on the screen. And he pressed the button to answer.

'What's up, Boss? I hope it's good news. I was having a beautiful dream.'

'Sorry to interrupt your dream but we aren't getting any sleep here. We have just been given some new information I think you need to know.'

Reece didn't know whether it was the warmth in the room or being awakened in the dark, but he could feel small beads of sweat rolling down his back and his forehead.

'Is it good information or bad?'

'Why don't you come here and see for yourself I'm in the Ops room.'

Reece took another look at his watch.

'I can be there in twenty minutes.'

'Try and make it fifteen.'

What the hell's going on, thought Reece, as he began dressing. No one likes to be rudely awakened and Reece knew from experience such awakenings were not only rude but not welcome usually bringing bad news. No matter how fast he moved it was seventeen minutes later when he walked into the operation room at MI6. He was surprised to see Kurt Shimon sitting at a table beside Jim Broad.

'What brings us here at this time of night?' asked Reece, sitting down opposite them.

The two men looked at each other then back at Reece before Broad spoke.

'I won't say I'm sorry to get you out of bed David, but if I have to be up at this time of the day then so do my people.'

'You know me Boss, you say jump and I say how high.' Reece smiled.

'Thanks for jumping. Kurt has some new information which you need to hear, I'll let him explain.'

Kurt Shimon pulled out a small notebook from his inside jacket pocket and started to read from it looking up at Reece as he spoke.

'As you might expect, like your Security Services, we have operatives all over the world especially in the major capital cities. This is not just for the benefit of Israel but also for our friends and allies in the war on terrorism.'

That's the politics out of the way, thought Reece, as he listened without commenting.

'One of our operatives has been working with a casual contact to obtain information from one of Iran's diplomats who works in their Embassy here in London. Late last night our contact was able to pass on something that the Iranian said. The contact thought the comment odd enough to pass on, and we think the same. The Iranian commented that your financial services might suffer a problem tomorrow. Our contact had been asking about investing in the stock market. On its own it could mean several things, even something as small as insider trading or a market slump concerning oil prices. But when we think that we are expecting the terrorists to attempt some sort of attack tomorrow it started me thinking and I contacted Sir Ian and Jim.'

Again, Reece kept quiet looking across at Broad as he felt there was more to come.

'Kurt contacted me just after midnight at just about the same time I received a call from the director at GCHQ. As you know they've been monitoring everything, and they found a text message that was sent from the Arab's mobile earlier. With the help of our friends in the NSA, we were able to clarify the message around the same time as Kurt contacted me, so I asked him here and then called you to join us.'

Broad pushed a piece of paper across the table on it he could see two lines of type.

'*Light of the Sun, Tomorrow Friday, Allah Akbar.*'

'Interesting. You are sure this was the Arab?' asked Reece.

'GCHQ are happy it was the same phone we identified earlier.'

Reece read the words once more.

'Were they able to say where he is?'

'Unfortunately, no, because the phone was switched off immediately afterwards, but they did confirm from what they were able to get that he's somewhere in the two-mile radius we are covering. At least it confirms our theory, and we will continue with our main efforts there.'

'Was your GCHQ or the NSA able to identify who he sent the message to?' asked Kurt before Reece did.

'Now that's where it gets interesting. The person at the other end of the text was none other than our Quads General Malek Hasheem Khomeini. Even though his phone is encrypted we can decipher the message.'

'Ah, more confirmation we are on the right track and looking for the right people. I'll contact Tel Aviv tonight and tell them to listen out for anything coming out of Iran. We have found in the past when these terrorist operations take place, we can expect a build-up of chatter to all their Arab friends to expect news from their Jihad friends.'

'Thank you, Kurt, between our people and the Americans, I'm sure we can point the finger in the right direction when this is over,' replied Broad.

'How are things out there right now?' asked Reece.

'As you can see it's quiet. We have updated everyone relevant with the information that our terrorist friends are still in that area and we believe the attack will be tomorrow. The police are going to hit the Mosque in the morning before Friday prayers. They want to be in and out before people start to gather so they'll go in at six. At the same time, they will hit the Imam's house and other suspect's houses.'

'I don't think they'll find much,' said Reece.

'Neither do I, but the powers that be want to send a message. If not to the Jihadis in our midst, then to the ones involved in this operation, in the hope it will scare them off, at least until we get more concrete information,' replied Broad.

'I know these people. They have come this far. They won't wait or run, they're here, and they'll complete the job or die trying,' said Shimon.

The phone on the main Ops desk began to ring and one of the two desk officers answered it before looking across at the three men and replying, 'Yes sir he's here. Mister Broad it's 'C' for you,' holding out the phone.

Broad crossed the room and took the phone and listened. As Reece and Shimon watched Broad's expression gave nothing away.

'Understood, Sir.' said Broad before putting the phone down and crossing the room to sit down at the table, joining the two men once more. They waited for him to speak. He was working out what to say and from his expression they knew the news wasn't good.

'As you will have gathered that call was from 'C'. When we spread the latest intelligence and all the other agencies were updated, he was contacted by both the Met Commissioner and Sir Martin Bryant who informed him that the Princess Royal is expected to open a new banking firm in the financial district of Canary Wharf today at 3 pm'

Broad waited for both men to take in what he had just told them.

'That's all we bloody need, a blue blood in the middle of everything. Can we stop her from being there?' asked Reece.

'Apparently the PM has already asked the Palace that same question. This is a new office in the city of the Bank of South Africa. The South African ambassador and a lot of high-ranking businesspeople will be there, and it's been arranged for some months. The Palace have refused to alter their plans, so yes, we have the added problem of the daughter of our Queen right in the middle of where our terrorist friends might be going.'

'Finding these people before they get there is more important than ever. I presume the Princess will have her own security?' asked Shimon.

'Correct, all the usual diplomatic protection. And Canary Wharf comes under the jurisdiction of the City of London police. It's my understanding they will all be briefed by the Met Commissioner and MI5 that there is an increased threat and that several security agencies will also be operating in the area. It's not unusual and something they've seen in the past, and they're happy they can work around it,' replied Broad.

'Have they been told it might be a dirty bomb?' asked Reece.

'No, that part they won't be told. With too many people knowing the full story, the worry is that someone will leak it to the press and all sorts of panic would ensue. The Home Secretary has increased the threat level so that's all they need to know for now.'

Reece looked across at the two men before speaking again.

'Realistically nothing has changed for us. The object of our task is still the same; find these people before they get to their target and stop them. With the added outside security for the Princess we need to ensure their people wear their identification such as the baseball caps and arm bands, we don't want people getting in each other's way. Our surveillance teams need to be aware of the Canary Wharf and especially the area that will be covered by the Princess's visit.'

'Agreed David. We will keep the night people out on the ground and have the day teams here for 7 a.m. for a full update and briefing.'

Reece looked at his watch.

'It's 03.30 so I'm off back to my hotel to try to catch a few hours' sleep. Can you organise a small A4 paper for the morning showing where the Princess will be with times and call signs for her protection? You could also give us a map of the area.'

'No problem I'll get Matthew Simons on to it. See you at 7 am'

'A good idea, Mister Reece, I think I'll do the same. See you here later Jim,' said Kurt Shimon.

Reece and Shimon travelled down in the lift to the underground car park.

'Thank you for looking after Anna for me,' said Shimon.

'Don't worry about Anna. I'm sure you know she can look after herself.'

'Oh, I know that, but still, it's her first time in London and she could be distracted.' Smiled Shimon as he got into his car.

Reece waved as Shimon started the engine and drove towards the exit. *I wonder*, thought Reece, *was he talking about the tourist attractions or a certain SAS Captain?* Kurt Shimon was the type of person who does not miss much, especially when it came to his Mossad agents.

Reece never slept well when he was in the middle of an operation and tonight was no exception. Between the dark dreams and the thoughts that were running through his head, he slept lightly for no more than two hours. At six he gave up and decided a shower would at least freshen him up ready for this day and whatever it would bring.

Across the city Yasmin was doing the same. She couldn't sleep, and a picture kept flashing through the screen in her head. It was a picture of herself playing as a child on the streets of Baghdad before all the wars and death. She got up and made herself a cup of black tea and scrolled through the photos on her phone, the ones she'd taken in Trafalgar Square and found the one she was looking for. A woman of about her age was smiling down at her daughter as she held her hand in front of one of the fountains, both laughing at the pigeons running around the feet of the people passing by. The young girl in the photo had triggered the dream of her childhood days on the streets of the Iraq capital. Carefree days when all she had to worry about was to be home in time for dinner when her father came home from work. She had always wanted to have children of her own and to meet and fall in love with the man of her dreams, but a cruel police inspector in the city of her birth had changed everything. It was no good to think of what could have been. She had taken a path to where she now sat, in a room in a foreign city, ready to complete her mission and punish the people who brought the war to her doorstep, and by their action changed her life forever.

She knelt on the floor and prayed to Allah for the strength to complete her mission to his honour and name. When she stood and opened her eyes Hassan was sitting in the chair watching her.

'I'm sorry, did I waken you?' she asked.

'No, I was awake, I couldn't sleep either. I hope you prayed for both of us.'

'Of course.' She lied. 'What keeps you awake?'

'I don't know. Thinking about the morning I suppose. All the training all the planning now it will be real. We will kill the enemy and they may kill us.'

'I was dreaming of my childhood in Baghdad. Before the war when you could play in the street without fear. The war changed everything and everyone. I suppose that is why I'm here. Everything changed for me I grew up from being the girl playing in the street and found that the circumstances changed to make me recognise the enemies in my life.'

Hassan stood and smiling he walked to the kitchen and switched on the kettle.

'Would you like another cup of tea?'

'No thanks.'

Bringing his tea back into the room he sat back down in the chair by the window. Yasmin was stretched out on the couch.

'What time is it?' she asked.

'Four,' he said looking at his watch.

'I'm looking forward to this being over and getting back to somewhere warm. I could never live in a country this cold.'

'I've lived here. You get used to it, and it's not like this all the time, the summers are usually great, but it's a different kind of heat to the one you're used to.'

Yasmin stretched, yawned, and closed her eyes. Hassan could hear her breathing change as she drifted off to sleep. He finished his tea and returned to the bedroom to kneel and say his own prayer to Allah and to try to sleep for the short while he had before the day's work would begin.

Chapter 28

Two hours later at 6.00 am. police had knocked on the door of Mohammed AAyan at his home in Finsbury, he inspected the search warrant, then accompanied them the short distance to the Mosque to find two police transit vehicles stuffed with police officers. Using his keys and switching off the alarm system he allowed them into the building under protest. Two officers stayed with him in the small office where he had met Hassan and made sure he did not use a phone. Two of the officers who continued to search the main building were in fact MI5 operators, they knew they wouldn't find much. They were aware of the informant working inside the Mosque and that he had brought everything he could find of worth to the attention of his handlers. They also knew that the building was swept regularly for listening devices, so it was part of their remit to leave behind two listening devices one covering the main hall and the other in the office where the Imam now sat. He would be brought into the hall to be questioned by the search team leader while they completed the task. What the Imam did not know, and because he lived alone, was that at the same time this search was taking place, another MI5 team were installing the same top of the range bugging devices in his home. He might carry out a sweep looking for them when he returned home but they would be left switched off for a few days until they felt sure the sweep had been done and then they could safely be activated. The Anti-Terrorist Squad contact in the Mosque was now able to let his handlers know when a sweep looking for bugging devices was to be carried out. When that happened, the devices would again be switched off reducing the chance of them being discovered; then turned back on to record again after the sweep had been completed.

It was when the Imam was brought into the main hall under more protest, that the two MI5 men discovered the hidden panel behind the office mirror. There were a few documents which they photographed before placing them back and closing the mirrored door. It took them another thirty minutes standing on one of the chairs to remove the main light in the ceiling and install the microphone and lithium battery pack above. They did not need to drill any tell-tale holes for the microphone, as the new equipment could easily pick up the voices below through the ceiling. When they screwed the light back into the ceiling, they used the small battery powered handheld suction device to collect any dust or debris left on the chair and the floor. They left the room looking exactly as they had found it. By 8 am the operation was complete. At the same time several suspect's houses had been raided throughout the city. Again, little was found and only one person arrested for breaking the nose of one of the search team.

As the searches were finishing Reece and the other team members had just finished their briefing. Matthew Simons had brought everyone in the room up to date with the latest information. They had the suspect's most recent photos, text, and phone messages. Everything indicated that the terrorists were still hold up in a two-mile radius, but in a city the size of London even this held thousands of locations and people. A small jungle to hide in and get lost, a needle in a haystack situation. The only good information from the day before was the possibility that the target was somewhere in the financial district of Canary Wharf. Simons had told those in the room that the Princess Royal was to open a new office at Canada House. He also told them that Canary Wharf, where the financial district was located, was an area of six million square feet with thousands of workers, tourists, and everyday Londoners: yet another needle in a haystack. Everyone in the team knew that GCHQ would be monitoring the phones and a special team would be looking at every inch of CCTV coverage. Anything of interest would be sent out to the teams from Simons and the men in the operations room. Reece had noticed that Anna had sat beside Geoff Middleton throughout the briefing and afterwards he sat down pulling a chair around to face them.

'I hope you both slept well last night, we are going to have a busy day,' said Reece noticing how Anna's cheeks turned slightly red as she blushed.

'We're well rested and ready to go,' replied Middleton answering for both.

'My boss has agreed for me to work with the teams today. Where do you want me?' asked Anna.

'You can stay with me and Steve Harrison today. He has gone to check out the MP5 and other bits and pieces. Have you any idea where you will be placed today, Geoff?'

'We have enough people to split them into two teams in two transits. One will be located near Hyde Park and the other near Canada Square in Canary Wharf. SO19 will have their own people on the ground. They will be working mostly with the Princess's protection detail during her visit to Canada House. They have the training and firepower to take down anyone who gets too close. Our job will be as a quick reaction force to back them up and deal with any fast-moving hostage situation. I'll be call sign Tango One at Canary Wharf and the other team at Hyde Park will be Tango Two. Both teams know what their jobs are so I hope you spot these people before we have to follow up, because if that happens, they will already be on the move with their bombs.'

'Any word on Joe?' asked Anna.

'I phoned the hospital before coming here this morning. He should be getting out today but with two broken ribs he won't be allowed out on the ground, but if I know him, he'll make a beeline straight for here to sit in on the operation.'

Jim Broad had been speaking to Simons and now came across to speak with Reece.

'David, can you come with me, 'C' wants a word before you go out on the ground.'

Both men took the lift to the director's floor where the secretary in the outer office told them to go straight in. Sir Ian Fraser was sitting behind his desk and invited the men to take a seat. Reece was surprised to see Kurt Shimon sitting in one of the three chairs.

'Gentlemen I hope you're up to date with the latest information. I've asked you here with Kurt so that you fully understand what we need to happen today when we find these people if you get the opportunity. David, you know the reason SG9 was brought into existence, not only to track and find the people who threaten this country but if you can, and the circumstances are right, eliminate that threat. It might surprise you David that I'm saying this in front of Kurt, as your team and your remit are most secret and only a select few know of your existence. Like MI6 the Mossad make it their business to know these things and I'm sure the existence of SG9 is known to them, just as we know about the Kidon teams in Mossad who are given similar tasks. Kurt told me this morning that the Israeli government have three people who sit on what they call the X Committee, the Prime Minister, the Minister of Defence, and the head of Mossad. They meet on a regular basis to discuss intelligence reports, specifically those concerning people or organisations that are a threat to the people of Israel. When they have enough information, the X committee then issue the order for the threat to be eliminated, just as we do when we use our SG9 team to eliminate specific threats against this country.'

Reece had known from his own Special Branch days of the existence of such a special force and committee in Israel.

Kurt Shimon waited for 'C' to finish before adding his own thoughts to the conversation.

'Thank you, Sir Ian. As you can see from what Sir Ian is saying the terrorists involved in this operation are also of great interest to Israel. We have been trying to find Abdullah Mohammad Safrah, known better to you as the Arab, for some time. This is the closest we've ever been. As you know from your own files and intelligence, it's for that very reason that the X committee have placed him on the list for elimination. This is also the reason I'm here today, the Mossad Director of the Kidon, sitting in the office of the directors of MI6 and SG9. Both our countries and our intelligence organisations have come together, to aid each other in the important task of protecting our people, by tracking down and if possible, eliminating the enemy of both our countries. I'm glad you've met Anna and Palo and that they'll be working with you today. You can be sure of their full support. I've briefed Anna and Palo that as we are working together on your soil, they should take their instructions from you. However, if they should find themselves on their own with the terrorists, then they should engage them and eliminate them.'

It was the turn of 'C' to add his voice to the conversation once more.

'So, as you can see David, your remit is just as clear today as it was on the first day you joined SG9. You know the target, go out, find it and eliminate it.'

Reece understood that the whole conversation was to reassure him that both governments and the directors of their various intelligence agencies were together on this. They knew the task was going to be dangerous, and the kind of people Reece was dealing with. It was also their way of giving him the go-ahead to use lethal force if necessary, even if not necessary.

Reece went back to the Ops room and found that Middleton had left to join his team and Palo was with Harrison and Anna. Like Reece everyone had dressed in suitable clothing that served the dual purpose of being inconspicuous and waterproof taking care of the British weather.

Anna had her hair tied in a ponytail again and as Reece had noticed before, she could dress in a bin bag and still look stunning.

'I left your vest in the car, and both vehicles have everything we need from baseball caps to the fully loaded MP5. The radios are tuned in to the Ops network and we have the most up-to-date satnav map displays with a back-up A–Z just in case,' said Harrison handing Reece a folder.

'Inside you will find the most recent photos we have of our targets which might come in useful if we find them.'

'Great, thanks Steve can you work with Palo and Anna will stay with me? I think we can leave the rifles back in the armoury. I don't think our enemy will have big weapons and between the SAS and SO19 there'll be plenty of those on the street. Our small arms will do for now. All we need now is a bit of luck and the rain not to be too heavy. There are other teams out there from MI5 and the police to the SAS and SO19. Everything goes through here so Matthew and the team will keep us up to date and stop us from running into each other. Everyone happy with that?' All three nodded. Reece turned to face the men covering the communications desk.

'Matthew?' Reece called over to Simons. 'That's Alpha One and Two out to Edgware Road. Will let you know when we are there.'

Simons answered back with a thumbs up.

'Don't worry, David. All those little dots you see on the screen are our people. When you're on the move the tracking device in your car will let us know where you are and that goes for the ear and radio mics as well,' said Simons.

'Nice to know Big Brother is alive and well,' replied Reece.

Chapter 29

The Arab had slept well, and had breakfast in his room, then leaving the hotel he walked towards Oxford Street, as ever checking for surveillance. He had dressed for the day to blend in with the employees of the financial district of London, a three-piece grey business suit, white shirt, dark tie, smart shoes, and a dark blue overcoat. To complete his disguise, he wore thick rimmed glasses and a tweed flat cap. He had watched the news in his room and there had been no mention of a shooting which was unusual and another indication that the Security Services might know about him and his plan. The rain was staying away for the moment, but the dark clouds gave an indication that it would come later in the day. He knew because of any heavy rain there would be less people walking the same streets as him. This would make it easier for him to spot surveillance. Turning down the side streets, crossing the roads checking reflections in windows; all to help him spot someone appearing in his line of vision more than once in the same streets.

The wind was strong, and people were walking with their heads down for protection from the biting cold air. A surveillance operative would more likely have to keep their heads up to follow a target. Even the weather was in his favour, he thought, Allah is with us today. After crossing a few streets and making the customary checks, he felt there was no reason to worry yet, so he flagged down a black cab and asked to be taken to Sussex Gardens. Just as before, when he was walking, he watched the traffic and noted the vehicles and motorbikes taking the same turns or keeping to the same speed. Everything had looked clear when he got out of the taxi and started walking towards Edgware Road. Near to the end of Sussex Gardens, and just before he turned right to walk down the Edgware Road, he noticed a dark BMW car in a parking bay with two men inside, even though they were talking, their eyes seemed to be focused on the street and the people walking along it. Immediately he was wary and concentrated his attention, watching the men and at the same time increasing his pace slightly so that he could turn right into Edgware Road and get lost in the larger number of pedestrians. Entering the road, he walked a few paces before crossing over to the other side and stopping to look back and then up and down the street. No one seemed to be paying him any attention and he walked further down the road before crossing directly and turning the key in the apartment door. He took the stairs two at a time and entered the living room where he found Hassan and Yasmin sitting at the kitchen table.

'Good morning, my children how was your night?'

Before they could answer, he took off his overcoat, threw it on the couch then went to the main window overlooking the road. He watched through the net curtains standing back so as not to be observed from below, but from where he could observe. He watched for the next five minutes without there being anymore conversation. To the untrained eye everything seemed normal, but the same man and woman had passed twice in five minutes then disappeared. Neither of them had paid any attention to the building he was standing in, but at this time of morning he expected most people on the street to be workers, heading directly to their place of work and not normally retrace their steps, unless perhaps they had forgotten something. Was he being paranoid? The couple could be early morning shoppers who were just browsing the shop windows but hadn't looked in any windows; he wasn't sure but still he trusted his instincts. He turned to his children who were watching him closely.

'You did not leave here since we met yesterday?' he asked.

'No, Teacher, as you requested we've been here all night,' replied Hassan.

'Good. We do not have much time. I feel our enemies are close, but they don't know exactly where we are yet. Have you both had breakfast?'

'Yes, we've eaten, and I've just made a pot of coffee,' answered Yasmin.

'Then I will have a cup of your coffee,' said the Arab as he joined them at the table.

Yasmin poured a cup for him and taking it black, he looked at his proteges and smiled.

'Don't worry my children. Today is the day when we will make the Devil nation fall to its knees and tremble. Our plan is unchanged. Yasmin you will bring your package to Trafalgar Square and leave it where it will cause the most pain to our enemies. Do not forget the timer is set so you must not press the start button before 1 pm, it is set to go off at 3 pm.

Hassan and I will be working to the same time so we must leave here at eleven. Hassan, please bring me the bag from yesterday.'

Hassan crossed the room and from behind the couch pulled out the bag and brought it to the table. Reaching inside the Arab brought out the three Tupperware containers with the explosives in them and set them on the table. Then he took out two plastic shopping bags, the walking stick, two small backpacks and finally what looked like a roll of brown packing tape.

'You remember which button to press?'

Both students nodded. The Arab then placed one device into one of the plastic shopping bags then into one of the backpacks and pushed it across to Yasmin.

'This is your weapon with which you will attack our enemy Yasmin. Treat it as your child, to deliver it in the name of Allah.'

The Arab unscrewed the knob of the walking stick and tipping it up, slid out the three six-inch-long items from its tubing. The items looked like sticks of black rock, the kind you would buy at a holiday resort each, wrapped in a thick plastic type substance. *In a way they also looked like sticks of black dynamite,* thought Hassan. The Arab placed them next to the container with the red dot. Taking the three black sticks he held them against the container and secured them with packing tape. Finally, Hassan noticed he secured the end of the tape into a slot at the side of the phone timer. Satisfied, he placed the box with the taped sticks into the remaining rucksack and pushed it in front of Hassan.

'The plutonium does not need to be attached to the explosives themselves. The blast itself will be enough to disperse the poison into the air and will not only kill many of our enemies but its financial strength as well. It has been that same financial wealth that has paid for its wars against our people and killed many of our children.'

The Arab moved the third container with the green dot to the centre of the table.

'This one will remain here when we leave. It will be set for ninety minutes after we've gone just by pressing the button. That way if they find this location, we will leave them a surprise, it will distract our enemy from our true target and give us the time we need to succeed.'

The Arab removed his mobile phone from his pocket.

'Are you ready to make your statement my children?'

Both Yasmin and Hassan stood, and the Arab placed two of the kitchen chairs in front of one of the white walls. Taking a black flag with white letters in Arabic, he then pinned it to the wall behind his two students. Yasmin and Hassan sat side by side facing the Arab. Hassan fixed his shemagh around his head showing only his eyes and Yasmin did the same placing her red scarf around her head, her brown eyes the only visible sign. The Arab set his phone to video and recorded their statements. Yasmin first, then Hassan; stating they were soldiers of Allah and the Jihad. Hassan with his English accent said that their actions were necessary as the West and Britain had killed the children of Allah and they had to pay for this sin. Yasmin then continued, her strong Middle Eastern accent coming through, by stating that the West had brought terror to her people, she quoted Churchill by saying, 'You have sent the wind, now you will reap the whirlwind.' Both finished together, 'Allah Akbar, God is Great, Allah Akbar.'

The Arab played the video back and satisfied linked it to a number in his phone and pressed the send button.

'Very good my children. Now, let us have some more of your wonderful coffee and we will talk some more about our mission.'

As Hassan placed the chairs around the table, Yasmin brewed fresh coffee while the Arab watched the street through the net curtains. People were going about their business. It was still raining, and many walked with umbrellas up. Satisfied he returned to join his two students at the table.

'What do you think our enemy is doing?' asked Hassan.

'A good question. If the other night is anything to go by and my close call when I came out of the Embassy, then they're working hard to find us, and we can expect them to be alert. When we leave here, we must be alert. If they find us, we cannot surrender, we must fight. We have our bombs and our guns, and we must kill as many of the enemy as we can but always try to escape. Today, we will be two teams. Yasmin, you leave by the front door at 11 am. You will travel alone to your target and then, as we discussed, try to get to Bristol. At the same time Hassan and I will leave by the rear door. The Arab then spread a small map of the city on the table.

'Yasmin, using your own route make your way to Trafalgar Square and complete your mission. Hassan, we will follow this route and take a taxi from here, then the train from here to our target. When we leave, I'll walk ahead of you and the only times we will be physically together is when we are in the taxi and when we reach this point, we need to travel alone in case one of us is compromised. When we reach this location, then and only then we will agree on the best place for our attack. By doing it this way if we are compromised there'll be a better chance for us to escape. You both must ensure you have the bank cards, money, and passports with you for we will not be coming back here. Only take what you need for today leave everything else, you can buy whatever you need afterwards. Leave the flag pinned to the wall as part of our message if the enemy finds this place before our surprise gift finds them.'

At that same time Reece and Anna were passing the apartment in the black BMW. He was able to turn the wipers to intermittent as the rain seemed to be slowing down against the windscreen.

'How do people live in this country?' asked Anna.

'What do you mean? I'm sure it rains in Israel.' replied Reece with a smile.

'Yes, but not with the coldness as well.'

'Warm rain. At least you could have a shower outdoors then and save on the electricity bill.'

Anna laughed at this idea.

'The neighbours might not like such a sight.'

'I don't know, maybe if it was me, but not you,' replied Reece.

Edgware Road was quieter than usual, thought Reece. Maybe the weather, the rain, would make it a little easier to spot someone, but it would be the same for them.

'You know I was just thinking in this weather with more people using umbrellas it will make it more difficult to spot our friends using CCTV, as most cameras are looking downwards. Our eyes on will be even more important,' said Reece.

Anna nodded in agreement.

'All the more reason we have cars and people on foot.' Anna replied.

'Therein lies a problem,' said Reece.

'What do you mean?'

'At any one time the likes of MI5 and the Met have at least three thousand active targets in the country. Many of those are already using up a great amount of their resources. I guess that's only one of the reasons that both our bosses are pleased for us to be working together, it reduces the odds of these people getting through, even though we haven't been too successful on that score.'

'Control to Alpha One come in over.' It was the voice of Jim Broad.

'Roger control, send over,' replied Reece using his body mic.

'Can you call me on your phone? Need a quick chat.'

'This car has a hands-free phone.'

'I know but apologies to our friend with you, but I need to speak to you on your own.'

'Roger, give me a few minutes to park up.'

Reece knew it could take up to five minutes to find a parking space in the area but in the event, as it happened it only took two as he parked outside a hotel in Sussex Gardens.

'Sorry about this Anna, but when the boss says on my own.'

'It's the world we live in. It must be important.' Anna smiled.

Reece left Anna in the car and found a low wall to sit on. He was glad the rain had stopped, and the wall was dry. The traffic, although noisy, was far enough away allowing him to hear Jim Broad's voice when he got through to him.

'Thanks for getting back to me,' said Broad.

'You asked me to call, so here I am. What's up?'

'The reason I don't want your friend to know, is that it's to do with the searches we carried out on the Mosque and suspect houses this morning. MI5 bugged the Mosque and the Imam home, so you know how they can be about need-to-know and especially when it's to do with their capabilities and the results coming from them. So basically, what their saying is that our friends from Tel Aviv don't need to know.'

'Understood. So, what you're saying is that you have something to tell me that's come from one of these devices?'

'Correct, it's not much, but it definitely confirms that we are on for today. Normally five would keep the device switched off for a few days to avoid it being found in a sweep, but on this occasion, it was decided by the gods on high that as all our intelligence indicates something is imminent they would keep it switched on. Our friend the Imam had a conversation in his office with an unknown male. The unknown lives in one of the houses we also searched so he's not a friendly. The Imam told him to stay at home today as the Jihad will be hitting the city. This is the interesting bit, he also told this unknown that the people who will be carrying out the Jihad are staying in an apartment he supplied to them on Edgware Road. So, you're in the right area. They must be close.'

That is what we've been thinking all along. So, if the target is Canary Wharf, then they'll be moving soon if they're not already on their way.'

'I hope we find them before they get to Canary Wharf. It is more open there with too many ways to escape.'

'Exactly David. But we have another problem now. The Home Secretary has been getting some sticky questions from the press. The kind of questions that would indicate someone is talking. That is another reason I didn't want to talk in front of your car passenger. I'm not saying it's coming from them. It might just be some over enthusiastic reporter throwing out some bait to see who bites. I think it's all down to the politicians raising the threat level.'

'More likely one of our own politicians. People in our line of work usually know how to keep a secret and why we keep it.'

'I'm inclined to agree with you there David. You can tell her we have information from a source. If she is as good as I think she is, she will be able to work it out for herself. Find these bastards David. Find them soon and deal with them.'

'I'm trying too. Do we have any air cover?'

'We are trying but the rain has made for low cloud which we hope will rise just enough to get a spotter helicopter up. I've authorised a CCTV and camera communications van to park up and cover Canary Wharf, especially where the Princess Royal will be this afternoon. That will give us access to all cameras in the area, with or without the permission of those who own them.'

'Thanks for the update, will you be there for the rest of this?'

'Yes, me and Matthew.'

'In that case I'll get back to the car and do some more passes up and down Edgware Road.'

Reece looked at the sky and he could see the greyness that indicated the rain clouds wouldn't be lifting any time soon. He returned to the car to find Anna finishing a call on her own phone.

'So, David, what's up, anything new?'

He wasn't going to tell her everything, but he knew she was professional enough to understand that what he did tell her was what she needed to know.

'They have definitely confirmed that our targets are in this area, so we can concentrate on this road. It's a lot less to cover than the two-mile radius we were working on initially. No air cover because of the weather, but extra cover to assist on the ground at Canary Wharf has been dispatched. The press are starting to ask awkward questions which might make our job a little more difficult. Do you have anything new?'

Anna held up her phone.

'That was Kurt Shimon asking how things were going. I couldn't tell him anything more than we had already been briefed. I did tell him that both Palo and I were embedded with the operational team, and we were out on the ground working the area. He told me he'll be in the office of 'C' until this is over. He also said that as we expect it to be over one way or the other by tonight, he has booked us on the late flight to Tel Aviv; so, let's get the right result when we leave.'

Reece started the car engine.

'Let's get the right result then.'

Chapter 30

In the apartment the Arab was looking out the window once more. The street below appeared to be normal, shoppers, tourists and workers all going about their business. The rain had stopped, and his watch showed the time to be 11 am exactly.

'Now my children it's time to complete our mission. Yasmin put on her red scarf, tying it tightly around her face. She pulled the rucksack over her shoulders placing her arms through the straps and pulled up the zip on her long brown overcoat. Hassan pulled his shemagh around his neck under his parka, using it as a scarf which he could pull up to cover his lower face if necessary. The rucksack he placed over his right shoulder.

'One more check, my children. Are you happy with your mission as soldiers of the Jihad and in the name of the holy one?'

Both students nodded.

'Good, you have your guns fully loaded and ready to use. You have your money and passports. I bless you my children, I have sent the video which will be circulated to the world at the end of this day.'

The Arab pulled on his own coat and placed his gun in the right-hand pocket. Then he kissed both students on their cheeks before he activated the small device they were leaving behind on the kitchen table.

Leading the way out of the room, he watched from the landing as Yasmin went down the stairs opened the front door and closing it behind her, stepped out onto Edgware Road.

The Arab and Hassan walked down the same stairs, turned at the bottom and left by the rear door that led to a small, enclosed yard.

'Keep close but not so close that someone would know we are together,' said the Arab. He opened the yard door and walked into the street that backed onto Edgware Road. He had memorised the names of the streets and locations he was to pass through to protect his identity. A London businessman would have no need to keep stopping to look at maps. He would know exactly where he was. He was happy with his new appearance; it was surprising how a simple pair of glasses and a flat tweed cap could change his appearance, adding to the confusion of anyone looking for him.

The Arab continued his walk; watching, ever watching pedestrians, cars, reflections.

He crossed Paddington Green and felt the rain starting to fall gently and he knew this was why there were not too many people on the green. In summer, the grass would be covered by people lapping up the sun and enjoying a bit of quiet peace in the middle of the city. Leaving the green, he turned and walked in the direction of the City of Westminster College that he could see in the distance, a quick look over his shoulder and he could see Hassan keeping his distance but stayed close enough to watch his every move.

Yasmin walked slowly to the end of Edgware Road, stopping occasionally to look in shop windows as any shopper or tourist would. At the bottom of the road, she took her time. Using the pedestrian crossings, she crossed over into Hyde Park to Marble Arch. She had read somewhere that parts of Oliver Cromwell's body had been buried near there. She stopped short of the Arch and taking out her phone took a photo of it and the park in front looking every part the tourist.

Reece and Anna watched Yasmin as she raised her camera. They had spotted her on their third drive pass down Edgware Road. Reece had let the rest of the team and control know that they might have eyes on one of the suspects, the woman. He did not want to do anything yet, until he was certain. Although she fitted the general description and looked like the woman he had seen for a fleeting moment in Malta and on the screenshot security photos, in the light of day and with her wearing a headscarf, he had to be sure. They had parked the car in one of the side streets off Edgware Road, then called for Harrison and Palo to stay mobile close by, in case any of the woman's friends appeared. Reece asked control to get the rest of the team to carry out a block surveillance for now. The team's mobile and on foot would now hang back and cover the routes the target would need to use when moving to another location.

'We can't jump on her yet. Until we confirm her identity, or if her friends are nearby, we hang back,' said Reece into his body mic.

'Understood, will wait for your instructions. But if she tries anything funny you know what to do. I'm moving the troop vans into the area in case you bump into the other two and need back-up,' replied Broad from the control room.

'Understood.' replied Reece.

Reece and Anna started walking on a path that was parallel with Yasmin, never taking their eyes of her, but watching in a way that would look like they were tourists themselves, taking in the bigger picture, rather than focusing on the woman who stood in front of the Arch.

'What do you think that rucksack on her back contains?' asked Anna.

'I think it contains exactly what you think it contains.'

Yasmin turned and walked back in the direction she'd come then crossed the junction into Oxford Street.

'We need to close-up on her. If she takes that bag off her back, we hit her. What's your location Alpha Two?' asked Reece.

'Just turning into Oxford Street from the Circus end heading towards you,' replied Henderson.

'Try and pull in and wait. We are heading towards you.'

'Roger, will do,' came the reply from Henderson.

'I don't like the fact she is moving into a more crowded area. It will be harder to close her down before she tries anything,' said Anna.

'If there is no sign of her friends by the time we reach Steve and Palo, then we will make a decision on whether to move in.'

Reece could see that the woman was taking her time. If she did have a target in mind, she was in no hurry to get there. The woman continued to look in shop windows and crossed Oxford Street twice, before reaching where Henderson and Palo were parked at the top end of Duke Street facing towards Oxford Street. Both men watched the woman cross over keeping to the main shopping street.

'Alpha One, that's her past us. What do you want us to do?' asked Henderson.

'She's going into the West One shopping centre. Stay in the car, we will go in after her,' replied Reece.

Reece had walked through the West One shopping centre in Oxford Street many times. He knew this would be the ideal place for the woman to carry out a suicide attack. Stepping up the pace Reece and Anna entered the centre twenty yards behind the woman. Her walking pace had slowed even further as she continued to investigate shop windows. Reece knew that there was a train link at the back of the centre. *Was she heading there*, he thought?

'Alpha One, I think the woman is the same one I saw in Malta,' said Palo.

'Roger that, I'm ninety-nine per cent sure it's her. She is still playing the part of the tourist shopper, but I'm beginning to think that whatever she's doing, today she's on her own. I don't want a Barcelona incident here, especially as I'm too bloody close to her now.'

'Take her out if there's any doubt.' It was the voice of Jim Broad in his ear. 'I have the Tango team deploying to you if you need them. We don't want a fuck up here and we don't know where the other two are.'

Reece could feel some of the pressure Broad must be under. He could imagine the calls coming down from Downing Street via 'C'. Reece remembered being under similar pressure when his bosses in his Special Branch days always wanted more. He used to remind them, *do you want it done right now, or do you want it done right?*

'I know the risks control. Tell Tango to hang back.'

Yasmin had looked in several shop windows before finally appearing to make up her mind. She went into the Starbucks coffee house and joined the small queue at the counter.

'What do we do now?' asked Anna.

Reece watched from across the corridor as the woman ordered coffee and sat down at a table near the window. Reece felt she was using the window as he would, looking for followers.

'I have an idea that might save time and a lot of lives,' replied Reece.

'What do you mean?' asked Anna.

'Stick with me and follow my lead,' said Reece walking across and into the Starbucks.

Anna couldn't believe her eyes but quickly fell in behind Reece.

Reece walked straight over to where the woman was sitting. She was taking off her backpack, placing it on the seat beside her. Reece sat down on one of the two chairs opposite her at the same time pulling his gun out of his pocket and pointing it at the woman under the table. Anna sat in the chair next to him. It took two seconds for the woman to register what had just happened. Her instinct kicked in and she started to reach for the rucksack, but Reece spoke first.

'My gun is pointing directly at you under the table. Don't make any stupid mistakes or it will be your last.'

Yasmin pulled her hand back to rest it on the table. The man's blue eyes were cold, and she realised she'd seen that type of seriousness before in the eyes of the Teacher.

'Who are you. What do you want?' asked Yasmin.

Reece was glad she did not panic or appear nervous. The one thing he did not want was a shoot-out in a packed coffee shop.

'I'm pleased to meet you and to see that you're not stupid. The last time I saw you was in a hotel in Malta,' replied Reece.

Reece saw the moment's surprise in her eyes.

'My question is still the same. Who are you and what do you want?'

'To answer the first part of your question, we work for the British government. As to the second we just want to talk for now. Do you mind if we join you in a coffee?'

Yasmin felt herself nodding even though she just wanted to run. The man never took his eyes away from her and she knew he was not joking when he said he had a gun under the table. She also knew from his eyes that he would kill her despite the many people sitting around them.

'Anna, would you get us three coffees please? I think we might be here for a while.'

When Anna had gone, Reece leant closer so that he could whisper the words directly.

'Do you have a gun and what's in the rucksack?'

Yasmin felt the weight of the gun in her left-hand pocket. For a second, she thought about going for it, but the next thought said *no he'll kill you.*

'I have a gun in my left pocket, and as you seem to know more than you should, there is a bomb in the rucksack.'

'Is it armed?'

'Not yet.'

'When Anna comes back you will hand her the rucksack with your left hand only. She will then sit down beside you and take the gun out of your pocket. Any stupid move and I assure you it will be your last.'

'What is your name?' asked Reece.

'I'll tell you mine if you tell me yours.'

'Joseph,' he replied using the undercover name.

'You can call me Yasmin. Are you Jewish with a name like Joseph?'

'No, I told you we are British.'

Anna returned with the coffee.

'Anna meet Yasmin. She is going to hand you her rucksack with her left hand. There is a bomb in it, she says it's not armed, she also has a gun in her left-hand pocket. When she gives you the rucksack, take it then sit down beside her and remove the gun discreetly from her pocket. Bring both outside and ask control to have the Tango team and ATO to pick them up and check the device asap.'

Yasmin handed over the rucksack and Anna sat beside her and neatly removed the gun, placing it in the rucksack. She left talking into her body mic as she walked back to the shopping centre exit.

'Now we can just enjoy our coffee and have a little chat as friends do. We are friends now aren't we Yasmin.'

Reece had decided to use his training and experience as a recruiter and handler of agents. His instinct was telling him this woman wasn't the dangerous terrorist they'd thought her to be; despite the fact she'd ruthlessly killed a man in a hotel bedroom in Malta. He saw something in her brown eyes that verged on the edge of tears. She took a deep breath and started to speak.

'I couldn't do it. I was awake most of the night and then this morning. I found myself going along with the plan but wanting to scream no, no, no.'

Reece kept quiet allowing her to continue now that she was opening up. He just hoped there would be time for questions and answers that would help find her two friends. Between sips of coffee and deep breaths she continued.

'To tell you the truth Joseph, I was hoping someone would stop me.'

'Why?'

'When I checked out Trafalgar Square and took photos. I was determined to return there today and leave the bomb to kill as many people as possible. But then when we reviewed my photos back at the apartment, I started to have second thoughts as you would say.'

'What apartment, where is it, are there others there now?' it all came out fast when Reece realised the Arab might still be there.

'The apartment on Edgware Road is an upstairs apartment number 137A. There is no one there now they've left to carry out their mission. But, oh my god, they left a bomb which is timed to go off ninety minutes after we left.' Her eyes opened wider as the memory came to her.

'What time did you leave?'

'Eleven.'

Reece looked at his watch the digital display showed 12.05 he grabbed her arm and pulling her to her feet made for the door and the street.

Anna was standing at the opened side door of a white transit. Two heavily armed SAS troopers stood beside her.

'Cuff this woman and get her into the van now,' said Reece to one of the troopers.

'There is a bomb in the apartment ready to go off in twenty minutes. We don't have time for bomb disposal all we can do is clear the streets and buildings.'

Reece jumped into the transit followed by Anna. Talking fast but clearly into his radio he informed control of the address and told them they were on their way with Tango One and one prisoner. Reece told the transit driver to get to the Edgware Road fast.

Anna held up the device they'd taken from Yasmin.

'What should we do with this?' she asked.

'It will only work if you press the blue button to start the phone, then press the red, it will explode two hours later,' said Yasmin.

Reece took the device and handed it to one of the troopers.

'There will be a bomb disposal team on the way to where we are going, give it to them. Tell them what you just heard about arming it but also tell them to trust nothing.'

The trooper nodded, took the device, and placed it inside the rucksack.

The transit driver had switched on the two-tone sirens and flashing lights while weaving the way through the city traffic. Turning into Edgware Road, Reece could see at least four police cars and two police motorcycles all with their blue flashing lights parked across the road barring the traffic from both directions. Police officers, some armed, were shouting at the startled pedestrians and herding people out of shops and buildings away from the area surrounding 137A. Reece was impressed at the speed they were closing the road.

'Have you the keys?' Reece asked Yasmin.

'No, I left them in the apartment. We were not returning.'

'Anna, you stay here with our friend. Two of you come with me,' said Reece pulling on the police baseball cap.

Reece had intended trying to break down the door. After that with fifteen minutes to go, he didn't have a clue. As they moved towards the building, a man in civilian clothing ran towards them from the opposite direction waving his hands in the air stopping Reece and the two SAS soldiers in their tracks.

'Stop, stop where are you going?' the stranger called loudly.

'Who are you?' asked Reece stopping outside the door with 137A written on it.

'I'm Felix,' replied the man.

Reece knew that Felix was the code name given to the bomb disposal officers or ATO Ammunition Technical Officer. When Reece had worked in Northern Ireland, he knew the code name Felix was because they were named after the cat with nine lives. He knew that once Felix was on the scene of a suspected device the rules were that he was in charge and must be obeyed. As a bomb disposal officer once told Reece when he was just a young police constable in Belfast and was sealing off the street because of a suspect package in a building, 'I get paid to do this you don't.' Another he met when dealing with an abandoned car bomb told him, 'I'm a bomb disposal officer. If you see me running, try to catch-up.'

Reece had great respect for these men and women who, no matter what the equipment they had, always had to take that last walk right up to the device to declare it safe. He knew the danger of any device being booby-trapped was one of the greatest dangers any ATO faced.

'I'm David Reece, Security Services. We've been told there is a device in the upstairs apartment in this building ready to go off in less than twelve minutes.'

'Is there anyone up there now?'

'We don't think so.'

'Well then, Mister Reece, if that's the case all we can do here is clear the street and buildings of people and sit back and wait for those twelve minutes to tick down. I suggest you and your team get back to your vehicle and park a bit further down the road.'

'In that case we have another device and the lady who was carrying it in the back of that transit. Perhaps you could use your time to look at it for me?'

'I will, now let us get away from this building.'

'You're the boss.' said Reece and turning on his heels with the two SAS men ran back to the transit. He was sure he could hear Felix shouting from behind him, 'You better believe it.'

Felix took the device out of the rucksack and having asked Yasmin once more how she was to set it, carried it further down the road, where he sat down on his own and spent five minutes inspecting it from every angle. From where he stood Reece could see that the ATO had a small penknife which he used to gently pry open the lid of the device, then he appeared to remove or cut something away before placing the lid back on and standing, walked back to the transit.

'I've seen this type of device before when I worked with the army in Afghanistan. One button, as the lady said, switches on the phone and the second usually sets a timer in motion counting down to detonation. But young lady,' He spoke to Yasmin while holding up the disabled device, 'in the case of your bomb, this one was set to go off as soon as you pressed the red button, and these little items are four-inch nails, combined with the Semtex there wouldn't be much of you left.'

'Oh no!' gasped Yasmin.

'Yes, young lady. Whoever gave you this bomb expected it to explode immediately, making you a suicide bomber. If you even know what that means.'

Reece saw that Yasmin was shocked at hearing these words, her eyes were wide and full of tears, and he thought, fear.

'Now, Mister Reece, if you're right we have two minutes left before the device in that apartment explodes, so if I could suggest you make sure everyone has taken cover before then and that the fire service is ready to go in to preserve as much evidence as they can. I'll get back to my own people before then.'

Felix then walked slowly back to his own green transit and Reece could see him waving his arms as he shouted for people to take cover.

Reece gave Broad a quick update over the radio and had just finished and was taking his place beside Anna and the rest of the transit passengers at the back of the vehicle when the bomb exploded. The blast was just as Reece remembered from his days in Northern Ireland the bright flash, followed by the loud low boom of the explosives detonating followed by the noise of flying debris and breaking concrete and glass tumbling to the earth from the sky. Then came the smoke followed by the smell and finally the flames starting to lick the outside of the broken windows. As the bomb was small and inside the building when it detonated, the flying debris had not travelled too far and fell well within the cordon perimeter reducing the danger to those taking cover. Reece slowly lifted his head to watch the flames start to take hold. He knew the fire service would wait at least five minutes to allow time for a secondary device to go off before they would approach the building, working from the outside to deal with the flames. By the look of things, no one was hurt and the agencies working in harmony with each other had reduced the chances of anyone getting injured. Reece was already thinking ahead. The Arab and his friend were still out there. If they had access to the Internet on their phones, it wouldn't be long before they heard about the blast. Reece hoped the news would please them and keep them thinking they were on track to finish their operation. Turning to Yasmin, he grabbed her by the arm.

'Now Yasmin. You know that your friend the Arab was happy to see you go up the same way as that building.'

The tears started to roll down her cheeks.

'No time for tears, many more people will be crying if we don't stop these people. They've shown they're no friends of yours. The Arab was happy to see you die, and he would have told everybody you're a martyr, now tell me where they are?'

Yasmin had been sobbing with her head down but at these words she lifted her head her eyes that were angry now, looking directly into the eyes of Reece.

'I don't know exactly where they are. They left by the back door when I left. All I know is they're going to Canary Wharf.'

'Do they have the bomb with them?'

'Yes, and the plutonium.'

For the first time Reece noticed that Steve Harrison and Palo had arrived and were talking to Anna.

'Steve says you need to talk to Matthew at control. With the explosion going off our radio mics were down for a few minutes,' said Anna.

Reece spoke into his body mic.

'Control, this is Alpha One, you have something for me?'

The voice of Matthew Simons came back.

'Roger Alpha One. We have had a couple of updates from GCHQ. Our friends have sent a video to Tehran which will go out when they complete their mission. We were able to confirm the end user as the Iranian Quads General so everything on for today. It then appears that the mobile phone this end has been switched off so we can't track it.'

Reece felt like saying, *no shit Sherlock*, but kept his thoughts to himself for now.

'Understood. The people here have things in hand, luckily no one hurt just some damage. The only problem is that the city will go into lockdown and the Tube will stop running. We need to get to Canary Wharf fast, so I need a chopper right now.'

It was Jim Broad's voice that came back this time.

'You're right about the lockdown Alpha One. The emergency Cobra meeting is already under way in Whitehall, and they're working to the book with boots on the ground and transport being brought to a standstill. The weather has cleared slightly meaning we only have one helicopter in the sky, just taken off from the city airport. I can get it to where you want it, but there'll be plenty of people on the ground at Canary Wharf so you could stay where you are and let them deal with it.'

'This fucker has got away before. Canary Wharf is a busy place, and we have the woman, we can use her to help us spot him.'

'OK, I can get you a Gazelle, where do you want it?'

Reece had flown in the RAF Gazelle helicopter many times, but he knew it only had five seats, the pilot and a spotter up front and three passengers.

'We can get to the top end of Hyde Park near to Marble Arch.'

'Leave it with me it will be there in fifteen minutes.'

'We will be there, and can you make sure there is an ATO at Canary Wharf, I have a feeling we are going to need one. The one here is following up on the bomb that has just gone off making sure there are no other devices. No matter what this woman tells us I don't trust the Arab and I don't trust her.'

'Roger will do,' replied Broad.

Reece turned to the others who were all hearing the conversation over their own radios. Yasmin was sitting in the back of the transit her hands tied with plastic cuffs.

'Steve and Palo go with the troop and use their sirens and lights to get across London as quickly as you can to Canary Wharf. I'll take Anna and Yasmin in the chopper and will be there before you. We will use Yasmin to help us identify the Arab and his friend, hopefully you will get there in time to take them out, if not, we will have to stop them on our own. Geoff Middleton already has an SAS team there. The more people we have the better.'

Reece leant in the door of the transit.

'Yasmin, you're coming with me.'

Chapter 31

The Arab and Hassan had continued their journey with Hassan walking a few yards behind the Arab. Outside the City of Westminster College, they had taken a taxi to Baker Street station, where once again, they separated before entering the station and the CCTV camera coverage. Keeping a distance between them, they had taken a Tube train on the Jubilee Line to Canary Wharf. The journey of almost one hour, brought them into the station at 12.30 just as the bomb had gone off at the apartment. They left the station and, with Hassan still behind, crossed over the road disappearing into the crowds of workers and tourists that filled the streets and walkways of Canary Wharf.

The Arab decided to use the next half hour to check out possible locations to leave the device, look for security surveillance, both people and cameras.

He crossed over Upper Bank Street and walked past the large building that was the home of Citibank UK then turned left and walked along the South Colonnade to the iconic skyscraper that was One Canada Square. He crossed over the square passing the Canary Wharf DLR Station and on into the shopping centre at Cabot Square. The square was named after John Cabot and his son Sebastian, Italian explorers who had settled in England in 1484. He had read on the Internet that Cabot Square is one of the largest in Canary Wharf. Passing the large fountain in the centre he knew that the inner perimeter had more fountains and was surrounded by trees, which would make it more difficult for observation via CCTV. What made it more interesting for the Arab was he knew there was a large car park under the square with glass ventilation holes to allow the car exhaust gasses to escape. He stopped by one of the fountains and sat down on the park bench. Turning he waved for Hassan to join him.

'We have made good time my child. Now it is time to complete our mission. I've not seen any of the enemy.'

Hassan looked around him. The rain had stayed away and now there seemed to be hundreds of people walking about. It would be almost impossible to spot surveillance in this crowd.

'Where have all these people come from?' he asked.

'You have to remember my child this is the very heart of the financial district of London. All these tall buildings hold thousands of offices and employees working there. It's lunchtime now and they walk about looking for their coffee lounges and restaurants. Our target is not just these buildings and banks but the very people who work in them, the same people and banks that have financed the killing of our women and children.'

'What about the Princess. When will she arrive?'

'According to our friend in the Embassy, she will be here at three, just around the same time we will send them a message from Allah they will never forget.'

Just then the roar of a low flying helicopter brought their eyes to the sky. The machine was flying low and appeared to be coming down to land somewhere nearby.

'Maybe the enemy is awake. We should find cover and set the timer. Follow me,' said the Arab.

Reece, Anna, and Yasmin had kept their heads down when they boarded the French Aerospatiale Gazelle helicopter when it had landed in Hyde Park, not far from Marble Arch. Reece could still hear many sirens above the noise made by the fast-whirling blades as they sped through the city, placing important areas into lockdown and the troop transit was now on its way to Canary Wharf. Strapping themselves in behind the two crewmen, Anna and Reece took the outside seats with Yasmin in the middle. Within seconds the machine took off and turned towards the Thames to follow the winding river towards the Isle of Dogs or as Reece knew it Canary Wharf. Looking at his watch he saw that it was almost 1 pm. Talking into the mic on the headphones they were all wearing, Reece decided to use the time to ask Yasmin more questions.

'Yasmin, can you hear me?' he asked above the noise of the aircraft. She nodded.

'What is the plan. What are they going to do now?'

Her voice when it came sounded weak and the radio static did not help.

'I only know they have a device like mine. They intend to set the timing switch at one to have the bomb go off at three, when they hope to be far away.'

'Where will they place the device?' asked Reece.

'I don't know.'

'You must know, you must have heard them talk about things and what they're going to do.' He could see her lip drop and the tears start to well up once more, but he couldn't be sympathetic. The helicopter banked to the right, and he could see that they were getting lower almost touching the rooftops of buildings.

'OK, tell me why Canary Wharf?'

'All the Teacher said was that they were going to deal a blow to the financial system in the West. He also said that a Princess would be there about the same time.'

Reece knew she was trying to be helpful. He had seen the same in many agents he had turned in the past who wanted to change their lives. Only in this case he believed it was too late for her, she'd gone too far down the rabbit hole.

'So, the device is the same as the one you had?'

Again, he could see from her expression she was thinking and wanted to tell him everything she knew.

'It's different. The Teacher placed sticks of plutonium in the bag with the device. He said it would disperse into the air with the explosion, that was the reason the timer was set to give them plenty of time to get to safety.'

'Where will they go?'

'All he said was that we were all to get transport to Bristol and book into any hotel there, where we could link up later.'

Reece could feel that the pilot was pulling slightly back on the controls, and they were slowing down getting ready to land. He looked out of the window and could see a large, grassed square between the skyscrapers and people in military and police uniforms pushing the public back to clear the landing area. Within a minute they were on the ground and opening the doors. Two men in military uniform ran up to Reece as he stepped down from his side of the aircraft, while Anna, took Yasmin out of the other side, her hands still tied with plastic cuffs. All three kept their heads down and moved out of range of the turning blades allowing the aircraft to lift vertically into the grey sky once more. As the noise died down Reece could see that one of the military men was Geoff Middleton.

'Good to see you David and you have one of our friends with you.'

'I'm sure you mean Yasmin here and not Anna.' Reece smiled.

'Correct, although I'm glad to see Anna,' he replied smiling at Anna as she approached holding Yasmin's arm.

'Where are we here? Any sightings of our friends?'

'No sighting yet, but we have this part pretty much tied down between ourselves and the police. The Princess is opening offices in One Canada Square at three and we've been told she refuses to change her plans.'

Reece brought up a google map on his phone. The location arrow showed they'd landed in Jubilee Place.

'This is a big area; we are a bit far from One Canada Square. When we were coming in, I could see there was many people about. That might be a problem when it comes to spotting our friends. Yasmin has told me they're probably already here. We do not know the exact target, but we do know if they're on schedule, they're setting a two-hour timer at 1pm on the device which is connected to the plutonium to give them time to get well away before it goes off. That is one of the reasons I brought Yasmin along, she knows them and if she spots them, then we have a chance.'

'There is a communications van in One Canada Square. I've been in it, and you wouldn't believe the radio and surveillance equipment it has. I would get over there if I were you, they might be able to help her spot our friends on the CCTV. I have our transit on the road it can get us there quickly.'

Reece looked at his watch as he jogged to the transit alongside Middleton and the trooper followed by Anna and Yasmin, the digital display showed 12.55.

'If they're here already, then we have five minutes before they set the timer running.'

Three minutes later Reece, Yasmin and Anna were in the back of the large HGV size communications van. Middleton wasn't exaggerating when he said it was well equipped.

Reece immediately recognised one of the two men sitting in front of the monitors.

'Jonesy, what are you doing here?' He had last seen Constable Jones doing the same job in the command room at the Conservative Conference in Manchester when the SG9 team had tracked down a terrorist squad and prevented the assassination of the Prime Minister. Then Jonesy as Reece had called him was doing the same job monitoring screens trying to identify suspects.

'Hello, Mister Reece. I decided the Gold Commander in Manchester was such a dickhead I just had to get away. London called and here I am.

'Great to have you on-board Jonesy. I presume you're up to date with who we are looking for?'

'Yes, sir. We have been looking and using facial recognition but so far nothing. There is a lot of people about so fingers crossed.'

'Everything crossed Jonesy and I'm not a Sir just call me David and as you're probably linked into our comms, Alpha One as well.'

Reece was looking over Jonesy's' shoulder at the screens and could see the problem. He suspected the crowds not only included shoppers, tourists, and workers but the extra people drawn to the prospect of seeing the Princess Royal.

'Tell me Jonesy does any of these screens do a playback showing say the last half hour of footage?'

'Yes, the one in the corner can do that and it can be divided into a four-square screen showing different angles and footage.'

'Can you get in front of it and run it through for us?'

'No problem,' said Jones, moving chairs and manoeuvring the mouse on the pad to show the four screens on the monitor. He typed on the keyboard and Reece could see all four screens flicker as the timers in the corner showed 12.30. Jones pressed another button and the screens started to run their pictures at normal speed.

Reece pulled two chairs and placed them behind Jones he pointed for Yasmin to sit in one while he sat in the other; Anna stood behind them. They were watching the screens over Jones' shoulder and Reece noticed each camera view on the screen was also imprinted with the name of the area it was covering, One Canada Square, Cabot Square, Churchill Place, and Columbus Courtyard. Reece looked at his watch again, 13.00. If the Arab was on schedule, he had just armed the bomb and started the countdown.

Chapter 32

The helicopter had passed over the square and by the sound of its engine the Arab knew it was preparing to land. The noise in the distance died down as both men walked through the doors into the Cabot Square shopping center. The Arab once more walked in front of Hassan. Leading the way, he could see a lift ahead and a sign which showed the types of shops on the upper floors, but he wasn't interested in the shops. Looking at the bottom of the sign he could see a downward pointing arrow and the words 'Underground Carpark'.

He pressed the lift button and waited with Hassan standing behind him. Both men entered the lift when it came, and the Arab pressed the button for the car park. They were the only two in the lift. The Arab turned to look into the eyes of his student.

'Now my son, I will not be getting out with you. The mission is now in your hands. Find a place under the air vents in the car park, set the timers and leave. I will meet you in Bristol or Tehran. Allah bless you and be with you this day.'

'Thank you, Teacher, Allah akbar.'

'Allah akbar.' replied the Arab as the lift doors opened.

As Hassan left the lift as two men got in to join the Arab on the upward journey to the first floor of the centre. Looking at his watch he noted that it was almost one o'clock. He put his hand in his pocket and wrapped it around the gun, he knew this was the time of most danger.

'You said your name is Joseph,' said Yasmin who had been listening to the conversation between Reece and Jones.

'I have many names and many faces Yasmin, a bit like your teacher. Now I want you to concentrate on these screens. Find your friends and maybe this day will end a little better for all of us.'

Yasmin leant closer to look at the screens, taking her eyes away from Reece, she had seen something similar in his eyes to the Teacher's, now she realised what it was, death.

'I'm going for a walk around the square,' said Anna.

As she was leaving the van Reece called on her to not go too far.

The phone in his pocket buzzed and Reece could see from the screen it was Broad calling.

'Yes boss,' he replied.

'Anything David? Everyone is getting a bit jittery now we've passed the one mark?'

'It's a bit jittery here too. We have hundreds of eyes looking and now our lady friend at the camera for the last thirty minutes footage. We are doing everything we can. I can assure you I would rather be somewhere else right now.'

'I know David. I'll keep out of your hair and let you get on with it. But let me know when you have something positive I can pass upstairs.'

'Will do.' Reece put the phone back in his pocket.

'David I might have something here.' It was Jones.

'What have you got?' Asked Reece, looking at the screen over the Constable's shoulder.

Using the cursor, Jones pointed at a man walking away from the shopping centre. He zoomed in and the man in an overcoat and wearing glasses looked familiar.

'Yasmin come here quickly!' called Reece.

Standing beside Reece she looked at the man being followed by the camera.

'Can you get closer?' she asked.

Using the mouse Jones zoomed in on the man's face just before he walked into the centre of the square and disappeared into the cover of the trees surrounding the park.

'I think it's him, but he is wearing glasses, it's hard to say.'

'The Teacher?' asked Reece.

'Yes,' she replied.

'Keep eyes on the exits from the park area Jonesy and inform control I'm going after him and to get people to the shopping centre and park. Yasmin, you're coming with me.' Reece grabbed her arm and opened the door.

Reece with Yasmin trying to keep up walked at a fast pace and pulled her along with him heading in the direction of Cabot Square.

It took nearly five minutes for him to reach the square. A five minutes which meant the Arab could be anywhere. In the distance he could see armed police and men in military dress starting to seal off the park exits. It was then that Reece felt Yasmin try to pull back on the grip Reece had on her arm. Turning to look at her he could see the look of shock and fear in her eyes as she looked over his shoulder in the direction they'd been walking. Reece knew instinctively there was danger and turning he saw the man in the overcoat and thick rimmed glasses ten yards in front of him. The man had stopped walking. Reece knew by his reaction that he had recognised Yasmin the same time she'd recognised him.

How is she still alive, and who is the man with her? he thought just before the realisation sunk in.

'It's him, it's the Teacher,' screamed Yasmin pointing.

The Arab was quick. He pulled the gun from his pocket and fired three times. Reece tried to pull Yasmin to the ground, but he heard her cry out and he felt the warm spray of her blood on his cheek as the bullet hit her. He pulled out his own gun as he hit the ground and rolled over once as rounds hit the concrete close to his head; he rose to his knee and taking aim, he fired double tap as he was trained. He could see one round impact the man's shoulder and spin him round. The man started to run. This time Reece took careful aim, controlled his breathing, and fired. The round hit the man squarely between the shoulder blades. He staggered for a few steps then fell, first to his knees then face down on the ground. It was only then that Reece realised there were people stood staring, some were screaming, some their phones already filming, him, then some running and Yasmin lying still. Anna came running up with her gun drawn.

'Are you OK?' she asked.

'Yes! See to Yasmin.' Reece shouted as he ran to where the man was lying face down, his blood, a small stream staining the pavement. As he got close to the man, he could see he was still breathing. Reece pointed his gun at the man's back, then he saw the man's fingers tighten on the grip around his gun. Reece fired twice more from the Smith and Wesson into the man's back, the 9 mm parabellum steel jacket rounds causing his body to rise in spasm, before he let out a loud groan, the last rattle of dying breath, letting the grip on the gun ease before it fell from his hand.

Reece remembered his special firearms training. Never take it for granted they're dead until they are dead.

Bending slightly, he placed his foot under the man's body and rolled him over. The glasses he had worn had fallen off his face, and although his eyes were closed Reece was able to reassure himself it was the Arab. More armed police started to appear, and Reece realised he still had his own gun in his hand and the police baseball cap was still in his pocket.

Kneeling beside the man's body he quickly exchanged both, his own gun to his pocket and the baseball hat to his head.

'Security Service,' Reece shouted towards the arriving officers who now surrounded the small area where the shooting had taken place, their automatic rifles pointing in his direction.

'Alpha One to control. Get a couple of ambulances to my location two people down neither of them friendlies.' Reece knew ambulances were not much use for dead bodies, but he wanted the scene tied down with as many emergency services as he could get, to move the crowd of curious watchers and their cameras.

'Roger, Alpha One, on the way. Update when you can.' It was the voice of Matthew Simons who would appreciate that Reece would be too busy to give a running commentary right now.

Turning to one of the police officers who seemed to be in charge, he told him that the ambulance was on its way and to seal off the immediate area and to start moving the crowd of onlookers away and if possible, seize their phones.

'And while you're at it, cuff this man, he's dead, but I still don't trust him.' He said pointing at the Arab who he could see was bleeding out fast, the pool of blood now flowing quickly into a drain beside the path. He ran back to where Anna was kneeling beside Yasmin.

'I'm sorry David, she's dead.'

Yasmin was lying on her back. Reece could see the ragged hole in her coat exactly where her heart would be, at least it had been quick but despite this he felt her death was such a waste.

'You're bleeding, David,' said Anna pointing at his cheek.

'No, it's Yasmin's,' he replied wiping his hand across his face.

He spoke into his radio mic. 'Control, can you get Alpha Two here to take control of the scene? Targets One and Three are dead.'

'Roger. They're on their way. Should be there soon.'

'Good, we will get back to the Cabot Square shopping centre. We still need to find Target Two and the device, we are running out of time. Get the comms van to keep looking at the playback on the CCTV to see where Target Two might have gone.'

'Roger understood. Units are sealing off the centre as we speak,' replied Simons.

Turning once more to the police officer Reece pointed to the Arab.

'Keep a close eye on him. Our people will be here shortly to take control.'

'Understood,' replied the officer.

'Anna come with me now,' shouted Reece over his shoulder as he ran towards Cabot Square and hopefully the third terrorist.

Chapter 33

Jim Broad had been standing behind Simons in the operation room listening to the ongoing communications from Reece. Simons was passing on the request from Reece to the communication van. Things were moving fast he thought: the end game not far off. He picked up the phone and spoke with Sir Ian Fraser who was now in the Cobra Room in Whitehall with the PM, Sir Martin Bryant, and the head of MI5 Caroline Aspinall. They had been listening in through the communications panels in what was effectively the government equivalent of the American situation room in the White House.

'I take it you've heard everything Sir Ian?' asked Broad.

'Yes Jim, thank you. We are also linked into the area CCTV and communications. At this moment I can see Reece and Anna running towards Cabot Square.'

Broad looked at their own screens and he could see the same feed.

'Can I suggest, in the light of what has happened, and given the time scale, there is at least one more terrorist out there. He's close and most likely has the device with him, given the current time he has probably started the countdown. I'm not happy that one of the Royal family and her security detail are going to arrive slap bang into what is a fast-flowing scenario. Can we not stop her?' asked Broad.

There was a pause and Broad could hear mumbled voices in the earpiece.

'Jim. The PM is currently on the phone to the Palace bringing them up to date with what is happening. Now, the Palace wants to go ahead with the visit but only on the understanding that the issue will be dealt with before they set out to drive to One Canada Square. Realistically if we've made no progress in the next thirty minutes bringing us to two o'clock, then the Prime Minister will have to order the evacuation of Canary Wharf. It is a massive area and thousands of people. I don't believe we could get everyone out by 3 pm. Your priority now Jim is to find the third terrorist and, more importantly the device, and eliminate the threat from both.'

'Understood,' said Broad as the line went dead.

'Matthew, we need to know where this guy is and fast. Anything, anything at all get it to Reece.'

Simons knew the pressure was on, and they were all under scrutiny. Not only were thousands of people and the country's economy on the line, but the very survival of SG9.

As Reece and Anna reached the trees and the park at Cabot Square, he could hear Jonesy's voice in his earpiece.

'Alpha One, come in, over.'

Reece slowed to a stop taking a few seconds to catch his breath.

'Go ahead Jonesy,' replied Reece.

'I've been looking at the feedback from earlier and I can see both men from the time they were together until they enter the Cabot Square shopping centre. The man with the glasses walking slightly in front of the younger man. I'm currently trying to get access to the CCTV inside the centre to see where they went. I've looked at the pictures from then. As far as I can see only the man with the glasses has left the centre so by the look of things the younger man is still in there.'

'Great work Jonesy. Can you capture a headshot of the younger man and send it to me?'

'As you speak, sending now,' came the reply.

'Thanks, Jonesy I'm going to cross the park and enter the centre. As well as trying to find this man's movements, can you also try to find where he is now?'

'Ahead of you. No sign of him currently but hope to have info of where he went shortly.'

'Thank you, Jonesy. Control, we are going into the centre. Please have uniform seal off entrances to prevent anyone going in and check people coming out and let them know we are on the ground inside the centre.'

'Roger Alpha One, on it,' replied Simons.

Reece and Anna continued to walk across the park and then into the centre. The time on his watch showed 13.40.

The shopping centre was crowded with lunchtime shoppers, many of them queuing up at fast food take-aways and filling up the restaurants. Reece took off his police baseball cap. No sense in giving the third terrorist any early identification of himself and Anna. Surprise, in any operation, was important. The faces of the many people around them seemed to swamp them. Reece felt it was like trying to find that needle in the haystack.

It was Anna who spotted Hassan first. He had just come out of a lift about fifty yards in front of them and was walking towards them. He was still wearing the black and white check shemagh; the same as the one in the most recent photo sent by Jonesy.

'David, I think that's him, just coming out of the lift straight ahead,' she said coming close enough to Reece to whisper in his ear.

Reece pulled Anna in front of him her back now to Target Two. Reece looked slightly over her shoulder and could see him walking towards them. Reece was pretending to talk to Anna as two friends might talk, up close and indifferent to the world around them. He whispered in Anna's ear.

'I've just realised that we need to take him alive. He is probably the only person who knows where the device is. When he gets close, stand in front of him as if you're going to ask a question.'

Hassan had felt relieved when he had completed his task. The buttons had been pressed, the countdown had begun, now to keep moving and find his way to the nearest train station to take him to Bristol. He was thinking what the evening's news would be like, the word of his mission being flashed around the world. An attractive woman was standing in front of him asking something about Boots chemist. The next voice he heard was a man speaking into his ear from behind. At the same time, he could feel something cold and hard pressed into his neck.

'Hassan don't make any sudden moves, or I'll blow your head off.' said Reece quietly.

Hassan thought for a split second to pull the gun from his pocket. His hand had been holding it tightly since he left the lift. The woman changed his mind moving closer she pushed a gun into his stomach reading his thoughts.

'Now don't be a naughty boy Hassan,' she said as she pulled his arm backwards and with a quick movement took the gun out of his pocket and placed it into her own.

Reece was impressed at how fast Anna had moved. No one had noticed how quickly and quietly this danger had been removed from their midst as they went about their daily lives.

'Now Hassan let's move quietly outside I have a few questions for you,' said Reece moving the barrel of his gun downwards to press it into the man's side. Gripping him with his other hand Reece moved Hassan towards the exit while Anna walked on his other side.

Being so close, Reece could smell the fear in Hassan as small beads of sweat trickled down the back of his neck. Maybe this was one terrorist who wasn't too sure about wanting to die for Allah.

Outside the exit armed police were stopping shoppers from entering the building. Reece could see the SAS transit with Middleton standing beside it and he guided Hassan towards it.

'Captain, can you get this man cuffed and place him in the back of the transit? I'll update control and start to get this place cleared.'

'No problem,' said Middleton pointing his MP5 at Hassan. 'Right this way sir.' One of his men quickly pulled Hassan's hands behind his back then searched him before placing him in the back of the vehicle. The only items on him were a mobile phone, a wallet with a bank card, pound notes, and a passport.

Reece quickly briefed Broad in the control room.

'He was coming out of the lift. When he went into the centre, he had a rucksack with him but now he hasn't so it's still in there somewhere with the device in it. Can you order the centre to be evacuated while we try to find it and get Felix here asap?'

Broad's voice came back. 'Will order the evacuation right away. That's a big place to search in time. As for Felix we only have one available and he is trying to get to you through heavy traffic after clearing up on Edgware Road, so it will be cutting it fine for him to reach you. At least we have some good news. The Princess Royal has decided to postpone her opening and stay at home for today. Do what you can but be careful David.'

'Oh great. I was always told to stay away from bombs. I'll have a word with our friend here and see what he can tell us.'

Anna was already in the transit and Reece sat beside her to face Hassan. The terrorist stared back at both his dark brown eyes filled with hatred and thought Reece, a little fear. Reece decided to take it slowly even though the clock was running down.

'Hassan. As you already know we do not have much time so do not fuck around with me. Your two friends are dead.'

Reece could see the change in the man's expression and the look of surprise in his eyes, but no reply.

'To tell you the truth, I'm surprised to see you alive. I bet you didn't know that your friend the Teacher had given Yasmin a suicide bomb to go off when she pressed the button on the phone timer.'

Again, the surprise in the man's eyes.

'We know you and the Teacher went into the shopping centre together and you had the rucksack with you. He left on his own, leaving you to finish placing the bomb and setting the timer. Now we can sit here until it goes off meaning we all die, or you can tell me where it is and stop this madness.'

Hassan continued to stare back but saying nothing. Reece decided to change tack.

'Alright Hassan, if you're not willing to talk we can clear this whole area, and no one will get hurt but as you know the plutonium will damage not just this country's, economy but the world's economies for many years to come. If you think it through that will bring great hardship to the many countries in the Middle East including yours. Families will suffer, many of them will starve, and all because you thought it a clever thing to do. I don't think you realise how much you've been used by your friends in the Jihad.'

'That's why it's called a Holy War, because in war people die and if the people who die are true to Allah, then they'll enter paradise to be with him,' said Hassan.

'That's funny. Because when we stopped you in the shopping centre you could have been in paradise already, but you decided not to. Do you think you're not good enough?' asked Anna.

Hassan looked at the woman but said nothing. Reece knew from experience they were getting nowhere fast.

'OK Hassan. We will go and search for the bomb without your help. I know it's supposed to go off in one hour. If we do not find it in thirty minutes, I'll pull everyone out of here, chain you to a pillar and let you count down the minutes to your meeting with your teacher in paradise.'

Again, no reply.

Reece and Anna left Hassan in the care of Middleton and his men and returned to the entrance to the shopping centre.

'We need get as many people in there as possible to find this thing,' said Reece.

'David this is Jonesy. Come in over.'

'What have you got Jonesy?' Reece replied.

'I have the two men on CCTV taking the lift down to the car park level. The man with the glasses stayed in the lift, came back up and left the centre. The one with the shemagh and rucksack got out. I then have shemagh man with no rucksack getting out of the lift twenty minutes later, just before you jumped him.'

'He didn't get out anywhere else other than the car park. You are sure, Jonesy?' asked Reece.

'Yes, I'm sure, down to the car park and return to the same floor.'

'Thanks, Jonesy that's helpful,' replied Reece.

Reece called to the police officer who seemed to oversee the evacuation.

'Chief Inspector can some of your officers search this floor and the upper levels, they should look for an abandoned rucksack. If they find it, they are not to touch it. Bomb Disposal are on their way, and they'll deal with it. Can you let me have two of your men to help us search the car park level?'

'No problem, understood.' Replied the Chief Inspector as he returned to his people, Reece was pleased to see he was the kind of officer who got things done without question.

'I guess the car park will be down to us, are you up for it?' asked Reece.

'That's why I'm still here,' replied Anna.

They took the lift to the underground car park accompanied by two uniformed police officers.

There were more cars than Reece expected, but they all seemed to be here on one level. Reece asked the officers to cover the area to his left and Anna to search to his right. He would take the central isles.

'Don't forget our man was down here for no more than twenty minutes he's fit enough to use the stairs, so that's why I've asked for the upper floors to be searched, not only for the rucksack, but for anyone still stupid enough to have ignored the evacuation call.' They had been searching for ten minutes. Reece knew that Hassan wouldn't have left the rucksack under a car or anywhere else it could easily be spotted. It was then he saw the large cabinet containing the emergency fire hose attached to the wall at the end of the aisle. He moved closer taking his time to check the outer door of the cabinet. He could see the wood where the door lock had been damaged. Someone had prised it open with something sharp. It could have been damaged by vandals, but Reece didn't believe in coincidence. He carefully pulled the door open and there squeezed below the curled firehose was the rucksack.

'All right, everybody stop. I think I've found what we are looking for,' shouted Reece.

Turning to the police officers he told them to return to the main entrance and tell the Chief Inspector to move his cordon further from the building. The officers quickly left using the stairs. 'Smart', thought Reece if this thing goes off the lift could be a death trap.

Anna had joined Reece and looking over his shoulder she blew the air slowly from her lungs through pursed lips.

'I don't know about you, but I don't like being too close to these things,' said Anna.

'I know what you mean. I thought my days of being this close were long over.'

'What are we going to do now?' asked Anna.

'We can't use our phones or radios they might trigger the thing. But it will only pick up transmissions over a short distance so we should be OK upstairs. The last time I spoke to control they said Felix was stuck in traffic. If we are to believe Yasmin, we should still have around one hour before this thing detonates but we can't trust these bastards especially the Arab. He was willing to make Yasmin a suicide bomber without her permission. He left Hassan to plant it and again he made sure he would be out of the way when Hassan pressed the button. I have no choice; I must check it out, at least that way I can give Felix the best information possible allowing him to deal with this thing quickly. You get out of here, no sense in both of us taking the risk.'

'No chance, David. I've been with this all the way from Malta to the back streets of London to here. A young woman died in my arms today, I'm not going to see you die as well. You might need someone here, right now I'm the only one.'

Reece knew by her voice this was an argument he wouldn't win.

'It's your funeral.'

'I hope not.' She smiled.

Reece slowly and gently pulled the rucksack out from under the fire hose. Turning he placed it on the ground and knelt on one knee beside it. He could feel rather than see Anna's eyes looking over his shoulder. Again, taking his time he pulled back the zip on the top of the rucksack. He switched on the torch on his mobile phone and pointed it into the rucksack. He hoped no one wanted to call him right now, either way he wouldn't answer it.

He could see a square plastic Tupperware box with a mobile type of phone on top. The clock on the phone screen was counting down in large letters 57 minutes 32, 31, 30 seconds and on. The box was covered with what looked like packing tape that was holding three dark tubes, Reece assumed was the plutonium.

'Well, here goes nothing,' said Reece as he steadied his balance and took hold of both ends of the box and lifted it clear of the bag, carefully setting it down on the floor beside him before standing and stepping back beside Anna, he looked around him.

'These bastards are clever,' said Reece pointing to the air vents in the ceiling.

'That humming noise you hear is the air vents to take the car fumes away from the car park and up into the air outside. If this bomb goes off the plutonium would get into the water system through the hose while the air vents would spread it twice as fast and twice as far, God knows how far. I need to separate that plutonium from the box and get it out of here. The bomb can then be dealt with by Felix if he gets here on time, if not, bomb damage can be repaired but not if it goes off with the plutonium. We have about fifty-five minutes, and I need something sharp to cut the tape around the box to release the plutonium.'

'I said you would need me,' said Anna pulling a small flick knife from her shoulder bag.

'You wouldn't happen to have the bomb disposal manual in there as well,' said Reece taking the knife.

He knelt beside the container taking a firm grip of the tape with his left hand, with his right he slipped the knife under the tape and pulled upwards. The knife was sharp and cut easily through the tape. Reece handed the knife back to Anna and gently began to roll the tape back from the foot-long tubes at the side of the box. When the tape was free of the box he lifted the tubes and placed them inside the rucksack. As he placed the last one in the weight and pressure of the tubes on the box was removed. At that moment Reece could see the numbers on the phone start to run down at a much faster speed as the minutes became seconds 30, 29, 28, 27. Reece picked up the rucksack and shouted to Anna.

'It's booby-trapped run, run!'

He did not have to tell her twice with Anna in front they ran to the door that led to the stairs.

Both made it through the door and Reece had slammed it behind him when he felt a powerful rush of air, heard the noise of the blast and he felt as if a giant hand was pushing him through the space. He landed at the bottom of the stairs, concrete and metal fragments shredding through the air around him. He lay on his back looking at the hole in the ceiling above him which held several large concrete slabs in a precarious position over his head. He started to stand, the rucksack still in his hand, but he felt a sharp pain at the back of his left thigh. He felt around and could feel what seemed to be a long thin piece of metal embedded in his leg. When he looked at his hand it was wet with blood. The air surrounding him was full of dust particles making it difficult to see.

'Anna! Anna!' he shouted but couldn't hear his own voice.

Moving around the space he almost tripped over her body lying face down at the bottom of the stairs. As the dust began to clear he could see she was covered in debris, and the hair at the back of her head had a small bloodstain, she wasn't moving. He turned her over and knelt beside her. Her face was untouched, but her eyes were open, staring at the ceiling, the light gone from them in death. Reece sat down beside her and lifted her head into his arms brushing the dust covered hair from her face and closed her eyes with his hand. Reece could see the trail of blood from his leg wound to where he now sat. It was then he realised there was quite a lot of it, and he felt cold, and it was getting dark but something yellow like a cloud was moving above him; then it went black.

·

Chapter 34

When Reece woke up in the London Hospital there were three people round his bed, Jim Broad, Matthew Simons, and Mary.

'Where am I, where's Anna, what happened?' he croaked. His mouth felt dry.

Mary rushed to his side and held his hand.

'You're all right my darling. You're safe in hospital, you're going to be all right.'

'I'm sorry, Anna didn't make it old boy,' said Broad.

The memory of her face came back to him, and he knew it was true.

'Mary, I know you want to be with David right now, but we need to talk to him alone for a few minutes then you can have him all to yourself,' said Broad.

Mary looked at Reece who nodded.

'Five minutes. He needs rest. I'll get a coffee but when I return your gone, understand?'

'Understood, Mary, thank you,' replied Broad.

She kissed Reece on the cheek and left the men alone to their secrets.

'I'm glad you're alive David,' said Broad.

'So am I. How long have I been here?'

'Two days. The doctors said that four inches of steel in your leg nicked the artery. If you had pulled it out you would have finished the job and bled to death,' said Broad.

'I could see yellow moving all around me before I blacked out what was that the plutonium?'

'No, it was the people in the Hazmat suits, they'd arrived just before the blast. Getting the plutonium away from the bomb was vital. You'll be glad to know the stuff it was wrapped in protected it from getting out into the atmosphere and the whole area including you was clean,' said Matthews.

'What about Anna? What happened to her?'

'One of those bad luck stories. A lump of masonry hit her on the back of her head. She died instantly I'm told. The ATO was badly stuck in traffic and according to him even if he had got there in time, he would probably have done exactly what you did. From his examination of what was left, the tape that surrounded the box had tiny metal strips running through it that were linked to the countdown of the timer. Any interference with the tape would set the timer in a faster count. He told me to tell you it's a good job you can run fast.'

There were still times when there seemed to be smoke in front of his eyes, but Reece knew it was the beginning of tears which he always held back.

'The Israeli Government have already flown Anna back to Israel where she will be buried on Mount Herzl in the graveyard for the heroes of the state,' said Broad.

'What happens now?'

'Your friend Hassan is being interrogated at one of our safe houses. When we are finished with him, he'll be handed over to Mossad who will take him to Israel. After that he'll no longer be our problem. The Prime Minister and the Queen want to give you a medal, but 'C' has told them you don't exist. Your instruction to the police to seize those mobile phones from onlookers was a good decision. The footage showed the Arab starting to move on the ground with his gun in his hand. The Met and the Attorney General have both agreed your decision to fire was the right one. The press has been told that he was shot by a member of the Security Services involved in a surveillance operation against a terrorist cell. David, I want to thank you myself. You had a tough job to do, you need to take time out to rest and recuperate. Get back to Malta with Mary and enjoy some of that sun.'

Broad's timing was perfect as he finished speaking Mary walked back into the room.

'Times up! He needs his rest,' she said.

'My words exactly, Mary. We will leave you two alone, David, you're in good hands,' said Broad. The two men left them alone.

Mary sat on the bed looking down into his eyes.

'You look tired my love. They say you should be ready to leave in a few days. Try not to worry. Mr Broad contacted me in Belfast and got me a flight back. He has told me to call him when you're ready to go and he'll take care of the flights to Malta. Mother's a lot better and getting all the help she needs.'

Reece pulled Mary close to him.

'I can't wait to get back to Malta. But first, we need to go to a graveyard in Israel to leave some flowers and pay our respects.'

OUTSIDE THE SHADOWS

Dedication

To my wife Helena with love, for always being there.

To the Head and Neck Cancer team at the Royal Liverpool Clatterbridge Hospital who helped me get through a tough time in the middle.

Don't envy evil people or desire their company
For their hearts plot violence, and their words always stir up trouble
Proverbs: 24

Chapter 1

London Hospital

He felt the noise of the gun rather than heard it, feeling the recoil in his hands as he pulled the trigger twice in quick succession. Double tap, as he'd been taught. Twice in the torso to put the target down, then once in the head to make sure. He held the gun double handed to ensure steady-aimed accuracy. The man in front of him had been pulling a gun from his coat pocket. He wasn't sure if the look in the man's eyes was surprise, fear, or pain as the first two bullets hit home, exactly where he'd aimed. The man on the floor didn't move. His eyes were open, staring, not seeing anymore.

Taking aim once more he shot the staring man squarely between the eyes, the hole smashing through skin and bone. The exit hole left a halo spray of blood on the ground that surrounded the man's head. 'They're not dead until they're dead. They're not dead until they're dead.' The words of his instructors reverberated inside his head, breaking through the image of the man now changed to the face of a woman lying on the ground. Dead. Bleeding. Then Mary's voice came through the flashing images.

'Joseph. Wake up. Joseph, it's me, wake up.'

He opened his eyes. Mary McAuley was the only person who still used his code name that he'd left behind years before, when she'd stopped being his agent and became the woman he loved. David Reece looked into her brown eyes and her smiling face as she leant close and kissed him on the temple. He could smell her familiar perfume and felt her long, dark hair against his head. He looked around the room of the private hospital ward. His vision slowly cleared, and he could make out the outline of a man standing near the door. His eyes, still blurry, slowly cleared, and he could see it was his boss Jim Broad, Director of Operations at SG9, the Black Ops unit of MI6, the British Secret Service. If he hadn't felt Mary's kiss or smelt her perfume or felt the touch of her hair, he would have thought he was still dreaming, still in the nightmare.

Mary was wiping his forehead with a cool, damp cloth, her smile reassuring.

'What's happening?' asked Reece.

'You have been having bad dreams, my darling. We nearly had to hold you down in the bed as you were swinging your arms about,' said Mary.

'You had a fever, old boy. Mary's been here every step of the way, and I've popped in a few times. Do you remember much?' asked Broad.

Reece managed to push himself up on the pillows supporting his back.

'What happened? Everything's sketchy,' he said.

Mary stood up from the bed.

'You were doing OK. The wound in your leg is healing well. But, for the last three days you've had a fever. You were asleep most of the time and sweated quite a bit. You cried out and moved about in the bed a lot, but this morning the fever broke. The doctors said your temperature has come down, nearer normal. I think you're back with us, Joseph. I was afraid I was going to lose you.'

'You sound like a nurse. You're not going to lose me that easily. Thanks for being here, boss.' Reece smiled.

'No problem, David,' Broad replied. 'You're my best agent, and your health is a top priority for me.'

'To answer your question, no, I don't remember much, just some of the usual dreams, the not so good ones.'

Mary poured Reece a glass of water and, holding the cup to his lips, helped him swallow a few sips.

Reece could still feel the dampness in the hospital gown he was wearing, which made the material uncomfortable against his skin.

'I'll need to get out of this,' he said, tugging at the collar of the gown.

Mary put her arms around his neck and untied the strings at the back.

'Yes, let's get that off you. I can get a fresh one from the nurse after you shower.'

Reece stopped her, pulling it all the way off. Stepping out of the bed slowly, he could feel that his legs were weak, but he could stand without help. The en suite shower room was only a few steps from the bed, and he found his strength was better than he thought.

'I think I'll be OK to shower on my own. Knock on the door when you have that fresh gown.'

'OK, but don't lock the door and shout if you need me. I'll give you ten minutes, then I'm coming in, ready or not.' Mary smiled.

'I'll wait, David, if you don't mind. I just need a quick chat on our own. If that's OK with you, Mary?' said Broad.

'I do mind. But if it means he'll get some peace, then you can have ten minutes, but no more,' she said firmly.

Twenty minutes later Reece was back in the bed, sitting up in a fresh gown, and Mary had left to get some coffee. Jim Broad pulled a visitor's chair close to the bed and in the secretive whispering style that he used when not in secure locations, he began bringing Reece up to date with what had happened while he'd been in hospital.

'You know we were lucky to stop that dirty bomb going off in Canary Wharf. Thanks to you and the team we were able to avoid a disaster. It's sad that we lost Anna, and the fact that you're here speaks about how close we came.'

'Tell me about it,' replied Reece, closing his eyes to help blot out the memory.

Broad continued. 'The prime minister would have liked to have come here himself to thank you, but as we don't exist, he felt the attention would bring too many questions. However, when you get out of here, he would like to see you at number ten.'

'No thanks. When I get out of here, I'm heading straight to the airport and a flight back home to my villa in Malta.'

Broad smiled. 'I totally understand, but I had to let you know, anyway. That brings me to the second point I want to bring up. David, you've been involved in two very dangerous operations in a short space of time. During those operations, you've killed three top terrorists. That's bound to have an impact on any man, especially as when you took them out it was up close and personal. I've spoken to the prime minister and Sir Ian, and we've decided you should take at least three months leave, to get yourself fully recovered from your wounds, both physical, and psychological. We even considered making available a Trauma Councillor if you think you need to speak to someone. Of course, such a person would have to be cleared at the highest level and there's not too many of those around.'

Reece lifted his hand to stop his boss. The fact that Broad was here and mentioning the top man, Sir Ian Fraser the Chief of MI6, the British Secret Intelligence Service and the boss of both Jim Broad and Reece. He understood the importance of what Broad was saying. You don't use Sir Ian's name unless you're trying to get your point across and Broad was letting Reece know he had the backing of C in everything he was saying.

'No head people. In my experience, they can make things worse, asking you to relive your experiences. No thanks.'

'Understood. As I said, the fact that you personally have put down three of the world's top bad guys, you know they'll be looking for you. So, for you, and Mary's sake, I want you to take those three months to recuperate. I promise we won't be in touch. We have enough people to get on with things, maybe not as good as you, but good enough for now.'

Reece raised himself up further on the bed.

'When I do leave here, it will be straight to the airport. As for coming back after three months, or anytime, I don't think so. There's only so much a man can do or take in this business, and I think this man has reached his limits. I thank you for your kindness to me and Mary, but I won't be coming back. So consider this my resignation as of now.'

Jim Broad was what people in the espionage business call 'old school'. He was thinking about the words he'd just heard. He also understood David Reece. He felt he had no other option than to agree.

'I hear you, David. I'll be sorry to lose you, but I totally understand. You have given more, much more, than any man should have to give. I'll always be here for you if you should need me. Mary is a wonderful girl. You should marry her and settle down to write your memoirs in the sun. But just remember you've signed three levels of the Official Secrets Act and you'll have to clear any book through the Whitehall D Notice Committee first. We don't want what's in your head out there.'

Reece laughed. 'Write a book? No, the only thing I'll be lifting is a large glass of Bushmills, then a good book to read by the sea. A fictional one that tells nice stories, not scary ones like the ones in real life.'

Mary came into the room carrying two takeaway mugs of coffee. Giving one to Reece, she turned to face Jim Broad.

'I'm sorry, Mister Broad, but as I thought you would be leaving, I only got the two.'

'That's fine, Mary. I need to be on my way.' Broad stepped forward to the bed and shook Reece's hand.

'Goodbye, David. Take care and remember what I said. I'm here if you ever need me. Same to you, Mary. Take care of this man. He's done more for this country than most people will ever know.' He kissed Mary on the cheek and left.

'What was all that about?' asked Mary.

'I resigned. I told him we'll be retiring to the sun and sea of Malta. What do you think? Are you up for that?'

She could feel the tears wet on her face. Setting down her coffee, she sat on the bed before putting her arms around his neck and kissing him.

'Up for it? Just watch me. I want to spend the rest of my life with you. Malta here we come.'

Reece was smiling. 'Yes, Mary, back to Malta, but via Israel first.'

Chapter 2

Israel

Funeral One

There were two funerals that week. The first took place amid the olive trees and sunshine on a hillside above Jerusalem. Rachel Cohen, an agent of Mossad, the Israeli Secret Service, had died while on a mission in England. She was brought home to the land of her birth, to be buried among the other heroes of her country in the cemetery at Mount Herzl.

The cemetery, dedicated to the leaders and people who sacrificed their lives for the state of Israel, was located on the southern slope of the mountain.

The Star of David flag-draped coffin had been transported from England on a special El Al flight to Tel Aviv. Present at the graveside of Rachel Cohen was the prime minister of Israel who, like Rachel had served in the Kidon unit of Mossad many years before she was born. Others saying their goodbyes were senior members of the IDF, the Israel Defence Forces, Mossad, and Rachel's own family, and friends. Her mother, still sobbing at her daughter's loss, stood beside Kurt Shimon, Rachel's boss. Her mother felt an immense sense of pride at seeing the dignitaries who were there with her today. Shimon, who had been in London with Rachel when she'd been killed, had accompanied her coffin on the flight back to her homeland, organising everything for the funeral through the government department that dealt with such matters. Rachel's father heard the Rabbi's voice but not the words. The thought of his daughter's smiling face, and the birds that were wheeling in the clear blue sky, distracted his gaze from her last resting place.

Kurt Shimon heard the Rabbi's words, the ones he'd heard at similar funerals in the past, *And the enemy shall know I am the Lord when I can lay down my vengeance on them.*

The Director of the Kidon Unit was distracted by his own thoughts, going back to the recent and last mission of the agent he knew by the code name 'Anna Stressor'. Working with MI6 and their Covert Black Ops team SG9, Anna had helped track down the Islamic Jihad terrorists intent on bombing the London financial district, using a plutonium based dirty bomb supplied by Iran. The SG9 team leader, David Reece, had worked alongside Anna from the streets of Malta to the streets of London, until they'd successfully removed the plutonium from the explosives that would have initiated the device, but not before a booby trap set off the explosives. Anna had been caught in the blast and killed instantly. Her final mission had been a success, and David Reece was also injured in the blast, but not before he'd shot and killed the terrorist leader known as 'the Arab'.

Chapter 3

Crossmaglen, Northern Ireland

Funeral Two

Later in the same day that Israel was burying one of its heroes, Irish Republicans were attending the funeral of a hero of their own. It was raining in the graveyard in Crossmaglen South Armagh, Northern Ireland. Not hard, but soft as the Irish called gentle rainfall. The graveyard was crowded. The coffin, draped in the green, white, and gold flag of the Irish Republic, contained the body of Sean Costello. Costello had been killed by a British Security agent on the streets of Manchester while attempting to assassinate the British prime minister.

The British had delayed returning his body by holding it until they'd finished all their investigations into the terrorist operation. For the mourners, the delay, taking many weeks, was not necessary, just one more reason to hate the Brits, not that any more reason was needed. The coffin had been brought from Dublin airport to the family home for an overnight stay. From there it was escorted to the graveyard by an eight-man guard of honour, dressed in black military style, wearing berets, and glasses to match, responding to commands in the Irish language. After a short service in the chapel, the coffin was carried by family and friends before being laid down on a stand beside the open grave. The local priest spoke more words of committal before a man stepped forward to deliver his words from a sheet of paper that he tried to control in his hand as it flapped in the wind and rain.

The speech was along the same lines that many there had heard before. The words describing the ongoing struggle against British occupation of the island of Ireland. The speaker repeated the famous words spoken by Patrick Pearse at the graveside of Jeremiah O'Donovan Rossa in August 1915, 'Ireland unfree shall never be at peace.'

Paul Costello, the brother of the deceased, smiled when he heard these words and thought, *nothing new there then.*

He knew the speaker well, and he knew his connections to his brother who was being laid to rest. Yet another martyr to an ancient cause. Brendan McDevitt, the Chief of Staff, and head of the Army Council of the Real IRA, the offshoot of the Provisional IRA, the organisation formed by republicans who did not accept the Good Friday Agreement, finished his speech.

'Sean Costello died at the hands of the British tyrant. He was a true son and soldier of Ireland. We will never forget him. We will make his killers pay. Our day will come.'

The mourners cheered as three men in full military camouflage clothing, wearing black balaclavas, stepped up beside the coffin and pointing automatic rifles towards the sky, fired off a volley of shots. Again, the crowd cheered as the men turned and were quickly swallowed up by the mourners. This was South Armagh, known during the war as Bandit Country because the security forces couldn't travel by road for fear of the well-placed landmines blowing up their vehicles, and the men inside them, apart. Any surveillance by the security forces would produce little other than a video or photo taken from long range. The security forces had suspected such a scene, but any idea of trying to interrupt or try to arrest at the funeral would only have led to unnecessary violence and bloodshed. Better to stay at a distance using undercover surveillance teams, to try to identify the main players and the movement of any weapons such as those involved in the firing of a salute over the coffin. Then, follow up with arrests and searches later. Anyway, the new Police Service of Northern Ireland, the PSNI, did not have the will, the resources, or the political backing, to enforce the law in South Armagh and the people attending the funeral knew this to be true.

Both sides knew the rules and the risks. Paul Costello was an MLA, an elected member of the Northern Ireland Assembly at Stormont in Belfast. During the war that was known as 'the Troubles' to the British, he'd fought them as a member of the South Armagh Brigade of the Provisional Irish Republican Army. In those days, along with his brother Sean, they'd helped to make the hills, fields, roads, towns, and villages of the South Armagh and border with the Irish Republic, a no-go area for the British Security forces, the army, and police. The only way they could operate was from behind their security base walls and by helicopter. But Costello had seen the end coming long before his younger brother.

The thirty-year war had become a war of attrition, and although the South Armagh Brigade had lost few men, mainly down to premature explosions, the rest of the PIRA units throughout the country had been decimated by the security-force's infiltration through their intelligence agencies. Many of the organisation's top people had been killed or imprisoned. The leaders of the Republican movement could see the way the wind was blowing. They knew to continue with the campaign would mean losing people needlessly and they'd decided that it was time to change tactics and go down a political road of calling for a ceasefire and negotiating a form of peace that would ensure the progress of their aim of a United Ireland.

Thinking back, he could still hear the anger in the voices of the South Armagh members opposing what they saw as treason to the cause and surrender to the British occupier of the island of Ireland. His brother Sean had been one of the loudest, his anger even stronger when Paul had told him he agreed with the leadership that they should stand down, and the stockpiles of hidden weapons be handed over for destruction before any peace talks could be formalised. He remembered at one meeting Sean had stood to his full height, his fists clenched, his face red with anger. Angry words led to bad feelings, to a falling out, and a parting of the ways. Paul helped bring the South Armagh Brigade round to agree with the leadership.

A specially held Provisional IRA General Army Convention backed the pro-ceasefire line. Sean Costello along with others, who opposed the peace process formed a new organisation styling itself Oglaigh na hEireann, which was to become the Real IRA. The fall out between the two Republican groups was severe. Real IRA members pilfered weapons from PIRA weapons dumps before they were handed over for destruction. The South Armagh contingent of PIRA had no intention of handing over all its weapons to what they saw as a British instigated so-called peace process. They would never fully trust the British. The weapons they retained were put into cold storage for the day when they expected the collapse of the whole process. The Real IRA had stolen weapons from PIRA and used them in attacks opposing the peace. A car bomb in Omagh in August 1998, killing twenty-nine innocent civilians being one of the worst attacks in the history of the Troubles. Despite this atrocity, the peace held. The Real IRA became the enemy not just to the security forces and the political world including the United States, but also the Provisional

Republican Movement and the Irish Government. Their members were told to leave the weapons hidden in the PIRA hides alone on threat of death and an all-out war with PIRA. The death of Sean Costello, a onetime member of both Republican terrorist groups, had on this occasion, brought both groups together in peace to the room at the rear of Sherry's public house. Those remembering the dead Republican filled the main lounge, many drinking pints of the black stuff, Guinness as it's known to the world. The voices of the men and women, many of whom had fought in the recent war with the Brits and a few who had been fighting even longer, became louder as the black stuff was poured freely and downed quickly in the style of a typical Irish wake.

Paul Costello sat in a corner of the room with some of his local family and friends. Looking round, he couldn't help smiling as he remembered the old quotation.

'God invented alcohol so the Irish couldn't rule the world.'

It was then that Paul Costello noticed a shadow across the table blocking out the light from the ceiling's fanlight. When he looked up, he recognised the tall, broad-built man looking down at him.

'Hi, John Jo.'

'Hello, Paul. I was truly sorry when I heard about Sean. Please accept my condolences for you and your family. You're all in my prayers.'

'Thank you. Thanks for coming.'

The other people at the table continued in their own conversations, appreciating that the conversation between Paul Costello and John Jo Murphy was one they didn't want to get involved in.

'I know you're with your family, but Brendan has something important he'd like to discuss with you. If you're all right with that…can you come with me to the back room?'

The MLA man knew that anything Brendan McDevitt wanted to discuss with him wouldn't be something he'd want to hear. As a member of the Provisional Movement, he did not trust the Real IRA faction or its leader. Crossmaglen was PIRA territory, so Costello knew McDevitt wouldn't step out of line while in the village. Whatever he wanted to say must be important or he wouldn't have taken the risk of asking for a meeting with such a prominent local Republican.

Without any further discussion, Costello followed John Jo to the back room of the pub, which was normally used for small private parties. As he passed through the bar, he was aware of eyes following his every move.

Everyone would have their own thoughts on what was happening, but all who knew a little of these things also knew to keep their thoughts to themselves and to keep their mouths shut.

John Jo Murphy came from a South Armagh farming family just outside Forkhill. The family had originally moved to the area from Dundalk across the border in the Irish Republic. His accent when speaking was more southern than northern, softer less guttural. He was around six-foot-tall, broad build, and his dark beard, hair, and eyes gave him a Middle Eastern appearance.

It had been some time since Paul Costello had been in the back room of the bar. It hadn't changed much. The small square tables each with four straight-backed chairs, he remembered would give you a sore back if you sat on them too long. The room was cold. Everyone said the owner, Peter Sherry, was tight with money, so that would explain the radiators being switched off.

Brendan McDevitt was sitting at a table and a young, dark-haired man stood and left the room without speaking, before Costello sat down. He recognised the young man who came from the same estate Costello had grown up in. He also knew that Kevin Kelly had once been a member of the same PIRA unit in Crossmaglen as the two Costello brothers. Now, it would appear he too had crossed over to the Real IRA. Costello knew that young Kevin would now be taking up position outside the door to prevent anyone from disturbing the meeting inside. John Jo sat down at the table, a pint glass in his hand.

'Thank you for agreeing to see me, Paul. I ordered you a Guinness,' said McDevitt as he placed the full pint glass across the table, setting it on the coaster in front of Costello.

'To Sean,' said McDevitt, raising his own glass at the same time.

'To Sean,' Paul replied. 'What do you want, Brendan?'

McDevitt smiled. 'Straight to the point. I thought you politicians were more subtle, playing your cards close to your chest.'

'Thank you for your words at the graveside, but today I must be with my family and friends and you, I'm sorry to say, are neither.'

'Straight to the point once more. Then let me return the favour as I don't want to waste anymore of your precious time today.'

Paul Costello took a long drink from his glass, then looked at McDevitt and John Jo.

'I'm listening.'

'I'm here not only as Chief of Staff of the Real IRA, but also on behalf of the Army Council.'

'I recognise neither. I recognise only one Republican movement, the Provisional one,' replied Costello.

'I don't want to go over old ground. That's not what I want to talk about,' said McDevitt, cutting across Costello's comments.

'As I said, I'm listening,' said Costello quietly.

'Sean died fighting for a cause we both might agree has still to be won,' said McDevitt.

Costello took another sip from his glass before replying.

'You will know that Sean and I went our different ways some years ago. I'm here today because he was my brother and my mother's son. Not because he died on an English street wasting his life in fighting when the people of this country want change. They want us to fight for that cause in a different way.'

'Again, you're going over the very reasons why we stand on different sides of the fence. That's why Sean decided to do what he did. To die for that cause, the one I believe, despite what you say, will still need to be taken up. But leaving those arguments aside, the reason I wanted to speak with you in person today, away from long ears, and prying eyes, is to tell you what happened in Manchester and why we buried your brother today,' said McDevitt.

'I know what happened in Manchester. Sean was there to kill the British prime minister. As usual, he was acting on his own. He even acted without your permission. A lone wolf willing to destroy the peace process and start another bloody war that would lead nowhere and only slaughter more of our fellow Irishmen,' answered Costello.

McDevitt downed another large portion of his glass before continuing.

'I think we can both agree on one thing. Despite what Sean did, he was doing it because he believed this country is still divided, despite what we both think about the so-called peace process. I think his plan, although he operated as a lone wolf as you call him, would have the backing of many republicans on this island, and if he'd been successful, he would have been regarded as a hero by many.'

Paul Costello looked at both men before speaking.

'No matter what would have happened, I still believe he was wrong, and most of the people on this island would agree. We can go back and forward with this argument till the cows come home and that won't change. You knew that before I came in here. Stop wasting my time. What's this all about?'

'Don't speak to the chief like that,' growled Murphy, starting to stand before McDevitt took hold of his arm.

'Sit down, John Jo. We must remember where we are and whose funeral we're at.'

John Jo sat back down, his eyes never leaving Costello, who was now smiling back at him.

'Yes, John Jo, as Brendan says, remember where you are.'

McDevitt took a drink from his own glass, then leant across the table to ensure Paul Costello heard every word.

'I don't want a fight with you or anyone here, Paul. I wanted to meet with you to tell you the things I don't think you know about Manchester, and what we intend to do about it.'

'I'm all ears,' replied Costello.

'Despite the whys of what happened in Manchester, and the fact Sean was operating without sanction from the Army Council, how he was killed, who killed him, and what went wrong has been clarified to us,' McDevitt continued.

Paul Costello remained silent, his eyes watching McDevitt for every expressive detail. He didn't trust these men, but Sean was his brother, and he was at least willing to hear what they had to say.

'As I' said, we've been getting more and more information about what Sean was doing and what went wrong. Yes, he'd linked up with some Islamic people, one of them originally from the North here.'

Costello cut into the conversation once more.

'I know Samantha Lyndsey. 'She's an old friend of Sean's. He trained with her in Lebanon. I guess they met up again, and that's how he lost his mind and went on that crazy mission. He got killed, and she escaped.'

'You're partially right. But your brother didn't lose his mind. It was a well-planned operation which would have been successful if not for two things.'

'And what would they be?' asked Costello.

'First, Sean was betrayed by an informer and second the informer's handler was an ex-RUC Special Branch man now working with the British security services.'

Costello sat up straight in the chair. What McDevitt was saying was news to him.

'I thought it was down to good luck by the British and their technical capabilities through bugs in buildings and phones.'

'You can be sure the British used all that sort of stuff, but not before they were given a heads up by their tout. To be on the safe side today, I've had this room swept for those very same bugs and it's clean.'

'How can I be sure you're telling me the truth? How do you know about this tout? Who told you?'

'It is true, Paul. But in case you didn't know, we believe Samantha Lyndsey was tracked down by the same people, then murdered in Egypt not long after, probably by the same Special Branch man. As for how we know these things, I'll let John Jo here tell you his part of the story.'

Costello could see John Jo Murphy was smiling.

I hope he's smiling because he knows something no one else does and not because Sean was dead, he thought.

'I want to say how sorry I am about Sean. I was with him on a few jobs, and I drove the van at Bessbrook when he took out the Brit with the fifty calibre. I heard the rumours that he was on a job in England, but like the rest of the army, I had no idea what. It was only afterwards that I found out it wasn't sanctioned, but as I'm sure you know, Sean wasn't one to worry about taking orders.'

'No, he was always one to do things his own way, go his own way and cause nothing but deep shit for everyone else,' said Costello.

Again, John Jo smiled and nodded before continuing.

'Well, the first I knew Sean was up to something was when he called me. I think he was already in Manchester where he'd seen a face from the past. A woman he knew from his days in PIRA. He told me he wanted to know where Mary McAuley was. You might remember her from the old days?'

Paul Costello tried to hide his surprise. Of course, he remembered Mary McAuley. He'd met her at high-ranking meetings of the Provisional Movement during the war and the subsequent peace talks. She'd disappeared off his radar during the talks, and he thought that she'd just stood down from involvement like many others when the peace process brought about the ceasefire, the Good Friday Agreement, and the dominance of the political wing of the organisation. She was privy to many of the movement's secrets, and if what he was now hearing was true, she was not only a spy for the British deep inside the movement, but she'd betrayed its secrets, which he had no doubt had ensured the arrest or death of many of his friends and now maybe even his own brother.

'Yes, I remember her. But why did Sean want to know where she was?'

'As I said, he thought he'd seen her in Manchester, but not only had he seen her he'd seen her with a face from his past, a man from the war days. I made enquiries in Belfast about where Mary had gone to live. She was nowhere to be found. Even her own mother didn't know where she was. I told Sean this and passed on her mobile number to him, which I'd received from her mother. I'm sure, knowing Sean, he would have called her, and with the Brits' technical ability at their GCHQ this helped track him down. We have made more enquiries since Sean was killed. She was back in London recently and according to our contacts at Belfast airport she flew here when her mother fell and broke her hip. She flew back to London the day after that Islamic Jihad team was taken out at Canary Wharf. Some people took photos of the gunman who shot dead the Jihad leader. Even though they seized the cameras, we managed to get one photo from our Islamic Jihad friends.'

John Jo reached into his jacket pocket and placed a photo on the table for Paul to pick up. The picture showed the side profile of a man kneeling beside a body on the ground. He could also see the man had a handgun in his right hand and he appeared to be checking that the man on the ground was dead. John Jo then placed another photo on the table.

'If you place both photos side by side, I'm sure you'll agree they're the same man.'

Doing exactly that, Costello could see the likeness, even though the second photo appeared to be older. Taken from a distance, it gave a full-frontal view of the man's face.

'OK. John Jo, they do look like the same man. Who is he and what's his connection to all this?'

Costello could see John Jo was enjoying this when he smiled and winked back at him.

'Another little part of the story which I'm sure you're not aware of is that the man in the photos is David Reece, an ex-RUC Special Branch man. He's the one that Sean phoned me about. I think Sean recognised him from the old days when Reece would have interrogated him in Gough Barracks in Armagh City. During the war, the PIRA unit in Dundalk circulated that second photo to ask units in the north to try to tie him down for assassination. One of the people who had one of those photos was Mary McAuley.'

Paul Costello could see where this was going, but he waited for John Jo to lay out the whole story before commenting.

'We don't think it was a coincidence that both Reece and McAuley were in Manchester together at the same time when Sean spotted them. We also believe that when the photo of Reece was circulated, she tipped him off, and that was one of the reasons he seemed to disappear from the South Armagh and Newry area. Then again, we find her flying in from London, and then returning there the day after the Islamic Jihad operation was intercepted and their leader killed by the man in the first photo, David Reece, who we now believe works for the British security services.'

'A lot of circumstantial evidence, John Jo. Why have you not lifted Mary and questioned her?'

This time it was McDevitt who replied.

'For the simple reason that she was so high up in the organisation she was beyond suspicion. To lift someone in her position for interrogation would need a lot more than circumstantial evidence, no matter how strong. I think if Sean had been successful in Manchester, and bearing in mind what he saw, he would have been on good ground to have her brought in for questioning by the Internal Security Team. I believe the evidence we have is strong enough to do just that.'

Paul Costello realised what was being asked of him. He knew about the Internal Security Team also known as the Knutting Squad for the way they would torture their victims before shooting them in the head, then dumping them somewhere along the border between the north and south.

'So, you're looking for my support as an MLA and ranking member of the Provisional Movement in letting you interrogate her to confirm your theory? Because she'd still be considered a ranking member.'

Taking another sip from his glass, McDevitt stood, and walked round the table and sat down next to Paul Costello.

'Paul, I think you misunderstand us. We know all about the risks and your high rankings, but as we said at the very start, the difference in the directions we took after the Good Friday Agreement mean we don't have to respect each other's rank anymore because of those differences.'

McDevitt was leaning closer to emphasize his point and Costello could smell the cigarettes and booze on his breath. Just a couple of more reasons for not liking this man. He knew of McDevitt's reputation for wanting to pull the trigger himself after they'd tortured someone into confessing their work for the security forces as an informer, a traitor. Paul Costello knew that a few of them were innocent of the charge, only confessing because they couldn't stand the torture, for that's what McDevitt liked to dish out. Costello knew his reputation and his nickname: Doctor Death. McDevitt was smiling as he continued and looking into his eyes, Costello thought the room had just got colder.

'We are not asking your permission. We know your stance and that of the Provisional IRA. Peace at all costs, even if that means letting someone who was a member of your movement and at the same time a spy for the British walk freely around rather than jeopardise that agreement you made with the Brits. We made no such agreement. But now this spy has caused the death of one of our people by her friendship with the British agent David Reece. We cannot let that stand, and we intend to make her answer for her crime and if at the same time we can make Reece pay, that would be a bonus. I'm telling you this because Sean was your brother and I want you to reassure your leaders that we are not looking for a fight with them.'

'You don't need my permission,' replied Costello. 'I know you only too well, and that you and your people will do what you must do, despite my feelings or thoughts on the matter. If what you say is true, and you succeed in speaking to Mary McAuley, before you do anything to her, or for that matter David Reece, we'll want to hear the genuine evidence from their own lips before you do anything to them. The Agreement, as you call it, is stronger than you think. Both sides will take action to protect it. If people see that you're acting without evidence, that will only make things worse for everyone. We know the Brits will act. They won't want you having them because of the information they have in their heads. The one thing I do know is that my leadership won't be happy if you carry out a killing on the soil north of the border. For myself, I can only say that I won't stand in your way if what you say is true. Whether my brother was wrong or not in trying to do what he did, he was still my brother, another Irishman killed by the British. But I won't support a death in the North that threatens the peace process. If that happens, it won't only be the Brits you'll have to worry about.'

McDevitt sat back in his chair.

'I think we understand what you're saying. Leave this to us. If I need to speak with you again, someone will be in touch. Now, go back to your family. You need to be with them today. But before you go.' He took a small business card from his jacket pocket and passed it over the table where Costello lifted it. The white card only had a mobile number nothing else. 'That's my private number, and only a few people have it. Call me if you need to.'

Costello put the card in his pocket. Then, without speaking, he finished what was left of the black stuff in his glass and returned to the main bar to sit with his own people. He'd left behind the kind of violence McDevitt loved. The kind he'd been working to stop, and now it was back knocking on his door.

Chapter 4

Tel Aviv, Israel

As soon as the doctors had cleared Reece to travel, he and Mary had taken a direct flight from London to Israel. From the travel information Reece read on the plane, Ben-Gurion airport is about twelve miles from Tel Aviv and was originally named Lod Airport but was renamed after David Ben-Gurion, the first prime minister of Israel. Jim Broad had arranged everything, making it easy for Reece and Mary to be escorted quickly through the normal high security at the airport. Outside the main entrance, they were met by the Mossad agent, Ari Rosenberg, better known to Reece under his cover name of Palo Stressor. Reece had worked with Palo and his Mossad partner, Anna, before she was killed. After her death, Jim Broad was able to tell Reece that her real name was Rachel Cohen, the name she'd been born with and the name she'd been buried with, back in her Israeli homeland. The men greeted each other as brothers with a strong hug.

'Shalom, David, welcome to Israel. You are looking much better than the last time I saw you. Did you have a good flight?'

'Good to see you again, Palo. The flight was great, thank you. Mary, this is Palo, a good friend,' said Reece, stepping back to introduce the woman behind him.

'Pleased to meet you, Palo.'

'And so very pleased to meet you, Mary. David has told me so much about you, but he didn't say how beautiful you were,' said Palo, smiling before kissing Mary on both cheeks.

'That's enough of your chatting up my woman.' Reece laughed.

Taking their bags, Palo placed them in the boot of the limo, then held the door open for them to get into the back of the car. Driving out of the airport, Palo kept up a tour guide type conversation.

'I promised your colleague Matthew a tour of Israel if ever he came here,' said Palo.

Matthew Simons was the MI6 Middle East expert who had worked on the last mission with them in Malta and London.

'He told me, and I believe he promised to show you a bit more of England if you're ever there, and don't forget to come and see us in Malta anytime,' replied Reece.

'I would love to. That's a date then. I know you might be tired from your flight, but Kurt Shimon has instructed me to escort you to your hotel to drop off Mary. Then he'd like to see you in his office. If that's OK with you, of course?'

Reece looked at Mary, who raised her eyebrows knowingly. She'd seen too much of his secret life to expect to be fully included. She'd heard him say the words 'Need to know' too many times to think she'd be fully a part of that life.

'I would rather freshen up anyway than sit in a stuffy office,' said Mary.

'We changed your reservation and upgraded you to a nicer hotel, all expenses on us.'

'We're always happy with an upgrade, thank you,' said Mary.

'Yes, it's the Brown Seaside Hotel, one of the famous Brown Hotels group. It is in a great location right on the beach.'

'Then you're forgiven for taking Joseph away to a meeting.'

The hotel was everything Palo had promised and more. After dropping a happier Mary there, Palo drove the short journey to the headquarters of Mossad, the Israeli Secret Service. Like the MI6 and MI5 offices in London and the CIA building in Langley, Virginia, everyone knew where they were, but because of security, and the underground car parking, the people who worked in these buildings could enter and leave anonymously. Taking the lift to the top floor, Palo and Reece were seated in the office of Kurt Shimon five minutes later. Shimon, the director in charge of the Mossad Kidon Units, or Bayonet as it was known, was at his desk. The office wasn't as plush as Sir Ian Fraser's at MI6, the furniture more modern and functional. Reece noticed similarities: the same style of computer and telephone console, but apart from a small camp bed at the far end of the office, everything else showed operational functionality.

Shimon came around the desk and shook Reece's hand vigorously.

'David, David, it's good to see you again my friend. You are well, I hope?'

'Yes, I'm good. Thank you for sending Palo to pick us up and looking after us with the hotel upgrade. It's very kind.'

Shimon invited both men to sit in the chairs in front of his desk before returning to his own position opposite them.

'Nonsense, David. After what you've done, not only for your own country but for the state of Israel, it was the least we could do. When I heard you were on your way, I told my friend Jim Broad we'd look after you. Anyway, there's another reason I wanted to see you here. Excuse me for just a moment.'

Shimon pressed one of the buttons on the phone console and a female voice answered.

'Martha, can you make that call we spoke about, please?'

'Right away, sir,' answered Martha.

Because they'd arrived on the early flight, it had been cool at the airport, but Reece noticed that now it was getting closer to midday. The sun was heating the room through the large windows that looked out over the rooftops of Tel Aviv. Reece had never liked too much heat, that being the reason he always left Malta for cooler climes during the summer months. He thought it was something to do with his growing up and living in the land of his birth that was Northern Ireland. The summers there were always comfortable, even at the hottest times.

He still loved that land and would return there for family occasions: weddings, birthdays, and deaths. The visits for deaths were becoming more frequent as they involved family and close friends from his Special Branch days.

'There is someone here who wants to meet you, David,' said Kurt Shimon.

As he finished speaking, the door of the office opened and a tall, lean man, dressed in slacks and an open-necked white short-sleeved shirt, walked into the office.

The two men sitting with Reece stood.

'David, let me introduce you to Danny Malkah, the Director General of Mossad,' said Shimon.

As Reece stood, he took the hand offered.

'I'm really pleased to meet you, Mr Reece.' The words were spoken with a soft middle European accent.

'Pleased to meet you also,' replied Reece.

The director general pulled a chair across the room to sit down, inviting everyone else to do the same.

'How was your flight? I hope your hotel is all right. Have you recovered from your wounds?' asked Malkah.

Reece was still coming to terms with the fact that he was sitting in a room with the highest member of the Israeli Secret Service.

'Flight good, hotel good, and health almost back to normal, whatever that is. Thank you.'

Malkah took a pack of cigarettes and a silver lighter from his pocket and lit one. He offered one to Reece, who, not being a smoker, refused with a 'no thank you'.

'Bad habit, I know, but we all have at least one. I know Kurt and Palo don't like them either. I know one day they'll probably kill me, but then no one gets out of this world alive – we all die of something.'

He blew a long line of smoke across the room and continued to speak.

'David. I've been fully briefed on everything that happened in Malta and London. I've spoken on the telephone with your boss Sir Ian Fraser, and with Jim Broad. Like Kurt here, they all speak very highly of you and what you've done not just for your own country, but for Israel and the rest of the world.'

'Just did my job,' Reece replied.

The director general took another long drag on the cigarette, blowing more smoke across the room. Reece noticed that he didn't seem to inhale that much and thought what he said about it just being a bad habit was just that.

'Danny, one thing you'll notice about David is his modesty. He is a unique individual who, even though works well with a team, 'is quite capable of doing things alone,' said Shimon.

Reece could feel his face getting warm. He wasn't sure if it was the sun heating up the room through the office window, or the fact he hated being praised in this way.

'You're right on one point, Kurt. I work as part of a team, always have, and the better the team the better the results. When I've worked alone, it was because I had no option.'

'I see what Kurt says about your modesty is true, but that's not the only reason I wanted to meet you. I know you're here to pay your own respects to our agent Rachel who you know as Anna. I've told Kurt that you're to be assisted in this, and Palo here will be with you. Tomorrow he'll escort you to her grave. I've spoken to Jim Broad this morning, and he tells me that you wish to stand down from operations. I must tell you I totally understand your reasons, but you should also appreciate that your dedication and skills will be missed, as I'm sure Jim Broad has told you. Despite this, I want you to enjoy your stay here. Be assured that if you need anything, either now, or in the future, you have only to contact Kurt and we'll help you no matter what you need.'

Reece was surprised that Jim Broad had told the head of Mossad about the future of his agent, but then again, Jim Broad would do, or say anything to have control of the situation that Reece had left him with. Reece understood that the offer of help at any time appeared to be genuine. He hoped he'd never need it. But it was a good card to have in his back pocket should he need to do so. Reece knew of the background to the close working relationship and history between the British security services and Mossad and his own recent experience.

Malkah stood to leave. The other three men also stood. Once again, he shook hands with Reece. 'Tomorrow, Palo will pick you up, so tonight relax, and enjoy your hotel. I've eaten there before, and the food is excellent. Do you remember Jacob Lavyan?'

Reece was surprised to hear the name again.

'Yes, we met once a few years ago in Belfast.'

'Well, my friend, he'd like to join you tomorrow on your visit to our country if that's OK with you?'

'Yes, of course,' answered Reece. The idea of meeting this man in his own country was something he'd never thought of or expected.

'Good, then have a good day tomorrow. If visiting someone's last resting place can be a good day.'

After the Mossad Chief left, Martha, who had been sitting in the outer office, brought in a tray of tea and fruit, leaving the men to serve themselves.

After pouring the three men black tea and offering a slice of apple to Reece, Kurt Shimon sat once more. Smiling, he leant back in his chair.

'You look a bit shocked, David,' said Shimon.

'It's not every day you meet the head of Mossad in person, and then for him to tell you someone like Jacob Lavyan would like to travel to a graveyard with you. You're right I suppose. I'm a bit shocked.'

'I'm sorry about that, but we wanted to surprise you, and at the same time show you in what esteem we hold you. Anyway, when you've finished your tea, Palo will drive you back to your hotel and plan with you the rest of your stay in Israel. Anything you need to let him know, and I'm always at your disposal if you need me.'

Reece took one more mouthful of the tea and standing, he shook Kurt Shimon's hand.

'Thank you for your kindness. For now, I'd like to have a swim and a shower and relax with Mary tonight. Until we meet again. Shalom.'

'Indeed, Shalom David, enjoy the rest of your stay.'

Chapter 5

Tel Aviv

The hotel was just as Palo had said, a definite upgrade. When Palo had dropped him off, Reece found Mary sitting in the spacious lobby with a pot of coffee in front of her. Despite the fact he'd been absent with a Mossad agent for a couple of hours, she was smiling.

'Oh, Joseph, you should see our suite. It's fantastic. We've picture windows looking out at the sea. I think your friends want us to feel good about being here.'

She was talking quickly like an excited child opening Christmas presents.

'It has beautiful marble floors, and the hotel has an indoor swimming pool.'

'Good. I'd like a swim,' Reece replied. 'But I would prefer the sea.'

'The sea it is, then. Let's go.'

The sea had been just what he needed; the waves refreshing not only his body, but his mind. Two hours later, he lay on the queen-size bed. Staring at the ceiling, he could hear the hair dryer in the bathroom as Mary dried her hair, and the low hum of the air con that kept the room cool despite the heat outside the window.

When he told Mary about his visit to Mossad Headquarters and his meeting, he could see her worried frown. He reassured her that they were going home to Malta after their visit and that he was retired. When he told her about the plans for the next day, she'd asked about Jacob Lavyan, he told her just an old friend from the past.

His thoughts went back to the meeting in Kurt Shimon's office, the genuine offers of help and the mention of Lavyan. He considered Jacob Lavyan a friend, in the same way fellow secret intelligence people consider someone in the same business, maybe not a friend as such, but respect for a fellow professional in the same line of business. He'd met Lavyan many years before when he'd visited Northern Ireland. Mossad had a close interest in the links between the IRA and Arab groups who, at the time were the enemies of Israel. Reece had been detailed to take him on a fact-finding tour of the border area of Newry and South Armagh. Lavyan was renowned in the world of espionage. Reece later found out that as a young man he'd been one of the Mossad team who had in 1960 kidnapped Adolf Eichmann. Eichmann had created a new identity and was living under an assumed name in Argentina when the Mossad team lifted him off a street close to his home and spirited him back to Israel where he was tried for his crimes, convicted, and hanged. He told Reece that his job was to help the British understand how Israel tracked down and dealt with their enemies throughout the world making sure the terrorists knew, that as far as Mossad and Israel was concerned, there was no hiding place. Lavyan had spoken of the similarities of the border, and how his own country found itself surrounded by countries, who, if not openly supporting the terrorists who attacked his country, at least gave them a safe living area from which they could attack Israel then return to safety. He also pointed out the army watchtowers on the hills along the border, which made it slightly more difficult for the terrorists to get through. He said they reminded him of the Golan Heights that looked down on Lebanon and from then on Reece had always used the same name for the hills of South Armagh. Reece had remembered the helicopter flights over the hills and looking down he'd think of the dangerous enemy who lived and operated below.

Afterwards, he'd taken Lavyan to one of his favourite bars in Belfast and introduced him to Bushmills Whiskey.

A few years later, he'd heard that Jacob had been part of a Mossad surveillance team that had been watching Mairead Farrell, Sean Savage and Danny McCann: three Provisional IRA terrorists who were planning to set off a bomb in Gibraltar. The Mossad involvement came about because they'd been watching a known Arab weapons smuggler near Marbella in Spain. At the same time, they were tipped off by British Intelligence that the three Irish terrorists were up to something in that area of Spain. The Mossad had followed the three but withdrew when they'd crossed the border into Gibraltar, where they knew the British also had an operation running. The SAS had then shot the three terrorists dead. The Gibraltar operation had resulted in loud condemnation in many political quarters and subsequently in more deaths directly impacted from the killings. At one of the funerals of the three dead PIRA at Milltown Cemetery in Belfast, a Loyalist gunman had attacked the mourners with a handgun and grenades, resulting in more death when three of the mourners had died. A few days later, as the cortege for one of the dead mourners was travelling to the same cemetery, two plain clothes British soldiers who had taken a wrong turn in their unmarked car, accidentally drove into the funeral path. The crowd surrounded the car and dragged the two men from their vehicle before handing them over to a PIRA kill unit. They were beaten, stripped, and shot dead. Reece could still see in his mind the video pictures taken from the Army Heli-Telly camera on the helicopter above the cortege showing the full impact of what happened frame by frame. The hardest part to watch had been when the video showed the two soldiers trying to make a break for it when the black cab had stopped on waste ground. Both men tried to fight their way to freedom before a gunman dressed in black shot both each in turn before running back down to the main Andersonstown Road and disappearing into the crowd. A lesson had been learnt by everyone who had watched the scenes of that day. If cornered, shoot your way out, even if your attackers are unarmed. As one of Reece's SB friends had put it, it's better to be tried by a jury of twelve than be carried by a team of six.

'Penny for them?'

Mary was standing beside the bed, the large white bath towel tightly wrapped showing the curves of her body, her long hair falling loosely around her neck.

'Bad, all bad, and they all involve you and what is under that towel.'

Chapter 6

Belfast

John Jo Murphy had taken the bus from Newry to Belfast. He arrived at the main bus station behind the Europa Hotel and walked through the city, using the time to watch his back and try to spot any surveillance following him, which was why he'd travelled by bus. He had plenty of time to check out the other passengers and make a note of any he suspected as security forces. He knew such teams would easily be able to follow the bus in cars, but when he walked through the city, he used pedestrian walkways where cars weren't allowed. So far, he'd seen nothing to worry him. Two men on the bus had raised his suspicion, but one had got off at Banbridge. The other had been met at the final stop at the Europa by what looked like a girlfriend or mistress by the way she kissed him.

Making his way through the main city centre, he walked through the Castle Court shopping centre, going in, and out of various shops, then stopping to sit, and take some time over a cup of coffee, to pay attention to the surrounding people. Looking at his watch, he saw he had an hour before his meeting at eleven thirty. He always liked to be at his destination at least twenty minutes early, allowing for one final check that he was on his own. He knew that despite all his checks for followers, a good surveillance team could cover him, but he wasn't going to make it easy for them if they were there. Apart from the two photographs he was carrying, it was a piece of paper in his pocket that might cause problems if he was stopped. But most of what he needed was in his head. So far, he'd seen nothing that bothered him. Finishing his coffee, he walked through the centre and out to the rear of the complex where there was a line of black cabs. These cabs mainly serviced the West Belfast Republican areas of the city, and the drivers were mostly sympathisers of that cause. If a Brit or security-force agent tried to use one of the cabs they would soon be spotted, and the word passed on to the IRA. The cab drivers would always engage in conversation with the passengers, and they would need to provide the right answers to the questions to confirm they had a genuine reason to travel anywhere in the West side of the city. Getting into the cab at the front of the line, John Jo asked the driver to take him to Beechmount Parade.

'Are you up from the country, then?' asked the driver, noting his passenger's accent right away.

'Yes, just for the day, just visiting friends,' he replied.

John Jo knew that even though the driver would take him to the Beechmount area in West Belfast, he would still pass on that there was a stranger in town. The local IRA would then send a couple of their young watchers to the Beechmount area to try to identify this stranger and note where he was going. The driver then tried a different tack with another question.

'My uncle Paddy McIlwaine lives on Beechmount Avenue. Do you know him?'

John Jo knew there probably was no uncle, and he wasn't going to play the game.

'No, I'm not familiar with the area. I just know where my friends live.'

The driver seemed to take the hint and drove away from the centre taking the main route up the lower Falls Road, passing the old site of Divis Flats on the left, then the main Sinn Fein offices on the right, just before the main junction with Springfield Road. John Jo could see the familiar mural of the hunger striker, Bobby Sands, on the wall of the offices. The phrase 'Sinn Fein' is Irish for 'Ourselves or We Ourselves' but known by many republicans as 'Ourselves Alone'. A phrase that many supported when it came to the many factions within the Republican movements. As the taxi continued up the road with the Royal Victoria hospital on the left and a Convent on the right, the streets, and houses around him were well-known to John Jo. When the Troubles had started in 1968, as a young man, he'd travelled to the city to support and fight for the local people who were being terrorised by Loyalists gangs from the nearby Shankill Road. The gangs were also supported by the police and the 'B' specials. He had fought these gangs at first with rocks and petrol bombs before the local IRA had brought in more guns, allowing them to fight back. When he'd travelled to the city in those days, it was from a true belief in the Republican cause for a United Ireland. and as a young man he'd believed the violence was only the start that would bring in the southern government in support of likeminded people in the north. That never happened. The rescue from the Republican Government in Ireland never came. When he'd been sworn into the PIRA in a house in Crossmaglen, the person swearing him in was Sean Costello. Like Sean and others, he not only mistrusted the Brits, but he hated them as well, and he now found himself as the Operations Officer on the GHQ Staff of the Real IRA. Sean had gone off the books with his plan to kill the British prime minister, but John Jo and the other GHQ and Army Council members would have welcomed him back if he'd been successful. Because he hadn't succeeded, Sean Costello had to be spoken of publicly as a rogue agent operating without permission of the Real IRA Command. And to prevent an internal war with the PIRA, they had to step back from supporting his actions. John Jo recognised the small terraced semi-detached houses as the taxi turned right off the Upper Falls Road into the Beechmount area along Beechmount Avenue, before turning into Beechmount Parade.

'What number?' asked the driver.

'Just drop me here please,' John Jo replied.

The cab pulled up at the kerb.

'That's four fifty please,' said the driver.

John Jo gave him a fiver. 'Keep the change.' He got out of the cab and waited to watch the vehicle drive up the Parade before turning right at the top and back towards the city. He started walking the same direction as the one taken by the cab. He walked slowly, paying attention to any movement in the street. There was no one, and no traffic. Everything was quiet. He walked on the left-hand side of the street, which was about two hundred yards long. When he arrived at the junction where the cab had turned towards the city, he saw a young lad sitting on a wall watching him. He had seen this lad before when visiting the city and he knew he was one of the scouts and lookouts for the local Real IRA unit. He nodded towards John Jo, who nodded back. He was telling John Jo everything was OK for his meeting. John Jo crossed to the other side of Beechmount Parade and started walking down it in the opposite direction to the one he'd come. The house he wanted was number 43, halfway down the street. The front downstairs curtains would be closed even though it was the middle of the day, another sign everything was ready, and he was expected. Looking at his watch as he walked up the short path to the front door, he smiled as the hands showed eleven thirty exactly. He liked things to be well-planned and that would be important if this operation was to succeed.

The door was opened by a small balding man, who with age, had gone overweight. Despite his appearance, John Jo knew that Brian McNally had a reputation for being a vicious hard man in West Belfast. Previously the Officer Commanding the PIRA Unit for the Beechmount and Lower Falls area, he'd left PIRA in protest at the Good Friday Agreement and had crossed over to the Real IRA with half the men under his command. It was well-known he'd personally looked the senior Republican leaders in the eye when he'd told them there was nothing good about any agreement with the Brits.

'Come in John Jo, and welcome,' said McNally.

The houses in the Beechmount area had changed little. They had mostly been built as semi-detached two up two down terraced houses in the 1930s before the Second World War. It wasn't until the sixties and seventies that grants were available for extensions being built at the rear to take in another bedroom and indoor bathroom. Prior to that, the toilet was in the backyard, and having a bath in a large steel basin in front of the living-room fire once a week was the highlight of the day. John Jo often thought the conditions people had to put up with then were justification enough to rebel against the Unionist and British Governments. A small three-piece suite almost filled the front room where McNally invited John Jo to sit in one of the armchairs opposite him. The fire was well alight with yellow and red flames, giving off a comfortable, warm heat. To John Jo, the furniture and the room looked like it hadn't been changed much since the house was built, with old, flowered wallpaper and family pictures in black frames.

'Glad you could see me at such short notice, Brian. I need your help with a project we are working on. Is it OK to talk here?' John Jo was only too aware that the Real IRA units had suffered badly because of the bugging and surveillance capabilities of the British Security and Police services.

'Yes, no problem. I had it swept for bugs this morning by one of our technical people. And as I'm sure you noticed, some of our boys are outside keeping an eye out for any of our friends. Your phone call said you'll need a couple of our guys who are reliable. I have two boys in the kitchen having a cup of tea. Now what can we do for you? How can I help?'

John Jo settled back in the chair before replying. He had been on the road since early morning, and it had been a long time since he'd had breakfast.

'A cup of tea and a biscuit, if you have one, would be good. Then we can get down to our chat.'

'Ah, no problem. How do you take it?'

'Black, one sugar.'

McNally went into the kitchen. John Jo could hear a muffled conversation before McNally returned with a mug and a small plate of plain biscuits, setting them on the coffee table.

'Help yourself. But watch out, that tea's hot.'

John Jo took his time, blowing into the mug before taking a small sip, then dipping one of the biscuits into the tea and eating it before it was too soft or dropped into the mug. He looked across at Brian McNally. He knew this man had been through much for the cause. He had been arrested while carrying out an attempted bomb attack on a shopping centre near Belfast city centre. A passing police patrol had spotted the false number plates on the car he was travelling in while transporting the bomb. He had been sent to the maximum-security maze prison where, in 1983, he'd been one of the 38 PIRA prisoners involved in the great escape.

Along with a few of the other escapees, he managed to get to the safety of the town of Dundalk in the Republic of Ireland. He stayed there as one of the OTRs or On The Run, and evaded capture by the British until the OTRs were given a 'get out of jail free' letter from the British government after the Good Friday Agreement was signed. While in Dundalk he continued to carry out operations with the border units, and on a few occasions delivered weapons and explosives to the Belfast and Tyrone Brigades, to carry on the war. John Jo knew that Brian McNally had made sure that much of those munitions was still under his control and now available to his comrades in the Real IRA to continue with the war effort against the Brits.

'The job I want you to do, Brian, is very simple, but there are two parts to it. The first is to knock down and either injure or kill an old lady.'

'Fuck me, John Jo. Are we killing old ladies now? I don't think that'll go down well with the boys or with me for that matter,' said McNally, taking a sharp breath before John Jo raised his hand.

'Hear me out first, Brian. When I tell you the reason why, and the second part of the operation, you might understand better why it must be this way. As for the boys. I'll leave that down to you, who you use, and how much you need to tell them. But the whole thing is top secret, only a small few need to be told or used.'

For the next hour John Jo told McNally everything he knew about Mary McAuley. How she was a tout working for the Brits, how Sean Costello had found out, and the evidence that she was working with her ex-SB man, who was now an agent for the British Security Service. He described how Sean Costello and the Arab Jihadist had been killed by the same man, and why they thought McAuley was now working with the Brits.

He could see from the expression of anger on McNally's face that this had all come as a total shock to him. He knew McNally had been at many high-grade PIRA meetings where McAuley had also been present discussing both military and political issues. He knew, like him, McNally would be thinking about the many volunteers killed on active service. Like the eight at Loughgall and the three in Gibraltar. They were some of the best people they had, and such deaths had helped bring the organisation to the talks table. You can only lose so many of your best people before you're crushed completely. This was the argument used by Gerry Adams and Martin McGuinness when they led the Provisional Movement into the talks with the Brits, and the breakup of the organisation, leading to the breakaway formation of the Real IRA.

'Fuck, John Jo, Mary McAuley? Are you telling me the truth? Are you telling me that bitch sat there in meetings then went to her SB bastard and told him everything?'

'I'm as shocked as you, Brian. But it's the truth, the bitch was, and still is a tout working for the Brits.'

'Bloody hell. So, what are we going to do?'

'This is where you and your boys come in, and why they need to knock down this elderly woman. The lady in question is Mary McAuley's mother. We know she recently fell and broke her hip and that's what brought McAuley back from London to visit her in hospital, before she returned to London to be with her SB man when the Arab was killed. Her mother has since been released from hospital, but she attends the City Hospital for Physio once a week. She currently lives in a small house on the Lisburn Road, which we think belongs to her daughter.'

McNally stood and threw a large log onto the fire, which had almost gone out. As he sat down, he stared at the ceiling in thought before speaking once more.

'So, what do you need?'

Taking a piece of A4 paper from his inside coat pocket, John Jo handed it to McNally.

'That is all the information you'll need about the tout's mother. I've had a couple of our own intelligence people watching her for the last few weeks. It details her movements. She uses a taxi when she goes and returns to her hospital appointments, but now she can walk a bit more. With the aid of a walking stick, she can walk the short distance to the shops on the Lisburn Road. On Tuesday mornings, she seems to meet up with two friends in the café in Sandy Row beside the shops. I would think the time to hit her would be then. Whether she ends up in the hospital or the undertakers, we believe that will bring her daughter out of the woodwork. Once your boys have done their part, I'll contact you to plan the second part, which will be to lift the tout and deal with her. You know the rule that has never changed, Brian, even with this agreement with the Brits. Once a Volunteer is Green Booked no matter what happens. To give information to the enemy is treason, and that means a sentence of death.'

McNally knew what the Green Book said about informing. The book was in effect the book of rules that volunteers agreed to.

'You can tell the boys in the kitchen the first part of the operation for now. I'll be in touch to brief them for the second part, but make sure they're aware of the secrecy needed.'

John Jo reached into his pocket once more, then handed a photo to McNally.

'That's a photo of the old woman. She should be easy to recognise and the fact she'll have a walking stick should help. Tell your boys not to fuck this up. You can tell them that this operation is on the instructions of the Army Council if you need to impress upon them how important it is.'

'Don't worry, John Jo. The lads are the best I have. They have done a few jobs, and they know how to keep their mouths shut.'

John Jo stood to leave, and McNally showed him to the door, shaking his hand before he walked away from the house. He turned left to walk slowly back towards the Falls Road where he would get one of the many black cabs. As he walked away from the house, he spotted the same youth still sitting on the wall, ever watching.

Chapter 7

Israel

The hotel lobby was bright, yet cool. Reece and Mary had gone for a swim in the early morning light, then walked hand in hand along the seafront promenade, watching the waves crash against the shore. It reminded Reece of his early morning walks in Malta. The water at that time of day was cool rather than cold, refreshing, clearing the mind of sleep and the extra alcohol they had in their system after staying up late in the hotel bar. The pain in his leg had been easing. *It must be the swimming, which was a form of physiotherapy*, thought Reece. Although, now and then, he could also feel a stab of the shrapnel in his right shoulder, an old wound that would never leave him.

Palo had sent him a text to say that they would be picked up at 11 a.m. This gave them enough time to return to the hotel and enjoy the superb continental breakfast, before taking a pot of tea to the lobby where they would wait. At five minutes to eleven Palo walked in, followed by an elderly white-haired man who, although slightly stooped, walked with determination. They stood to greet the two men. Reece had told Mary as much as he knew about Jacob Lavyan, a hero of the country he'd served all his life. Palo introduced Mary and Reece to the man standing by his side. The man, who wore large, black-framed glasses, put out his hand for Reece to shake. He carried a plastic shopping bag which he set on the floor beside the table.

'Shalom, David. It has been a long time, too long for friends,' Lavyan said, smiling.

'And Shalom to you, Miss Mary. I'm pleased to meet you also.'

Lavyan's grip was firm, showing there was still strength there if he needed it.

Jacob Lavyan had aged well, thought Reece. He had more hair than Reece and despite his age his brown eyes were clear and alert, his body looked strong, and he carried very little excess weight. Reece could see the muscles in his arms that filled the linen grey jacket he was wearing. He could imagine those arms around the neck of his enemies.

'Would you like some tea?' asked Mary, inviting the two men to sit down.

'That would be lovely, Miss Mary,' replied Lavyan his face beaming.

Mary waved for the waiter to bring two more cups and some more tea.

'You have come a long way, David. When I was told you were coming and the reason you would be here, I knew I should meet you once again,' said Lavyan.

'It's good to see you again, Jacob, although under the circumstances they're not the ones I would wish for.'

The tea came and Mary poured for everyone.

'Have you always lived in Israel?' she asked.

Reece noticed how Jacob smiled when Mary spoke to him.

'Yes. I was born in Israel on a Kibbutz. My parents were Russian immigrants who came to Palestine in 1928. My life has been Israel and everything I've done is for the land of my birth. My parents instilled in me a passion for what is right in life, and I've always tried to live up to that passion.'

He had given more in his answer than Mary had expected.

'Anyway, we should be going soon. It will take just over an hour to get to Jerusalem. But before we leave, I have something for you both,' said Lavyan before reaching into the shopping bag at his feet. He removed a boxed bottle of twelve-year-old Bushmills whisky, which he handed to Reece.

'I remember the headache I had the next day when you introduced me to this in Belfast, David. Still your favourite I'm told. I can tell you. It was difficult to find in Tel Aviv.'

'Your sources and memory are correct, Jacob. When we open it later, I'll toast your good health.' Reece smiled.

'Ah, you'll have to drink with Palo and Mary as I'm under doctor's orders.' Jacob winked.

Reaching into the bag once more, he pulled out two polished white pebbles and sat them on the table. Mary looked at them a slightly confused look on her face.

'Let me explain. These are very important stones. In Israel, it's a tradition that we don't leave flowers on a grave, so everything that's left is of equal value. It is our way of paying our respect that we leave a pebble, thereby letting the family know in what high esteem the person in the grave is thought of, and to let them know that we've been there.'

Mary lifted one of the pebbles and, holding it up to the light, she could see the sun shining off it and felt its smoothness.

'A wonderful way to pay respect. I feel honoured that you've brought these for us. I was wondering about stopping somewhere for flowers, but I think this is a much better idea.'

Reece lifted the other pebble and put it in his pocket. He took the now empty bag and placing the whisky back inside, walked over to reception, leaving it there until they returned.

Palo drove the air-conditioned car with Lavyan beside him and Mary and Reece in the back. During the drive, Mary seemed very excited, like a little child at seeing more of the country than just the sand and sea. Speaking like a true tourist she was asking the standard questions. 'What's the weather like all year round?' 'What's the history?' 'What's the local food like?' Lavyan and Palo answered every question both knowing that the questions were her way of distracting them from why they were here. Ever since the day Reece had first approached Mary to recruit her as his agent inside the IRA, he knew they'd both lived with danger and death in their lives. Reece knew that the death of the woman whose grave they were now going to visit had been felt a lot harder by Mary than she was letting on. That was one of the reasons he'd made the decision to retire now. They both had seen enough of death and had been too close to it for some time. The drive out of Tel Aviv and onto the motorway to Jerusalem had taken them through built-up suburbs to the valleys and hills surrounding the city then into the green countryside. This surprised Reece, as he'd expected the land to be like Malta, with little vegetation and brown dusty ground. Instead, olive, cypress, and eucalyptus trees filled the scenery with lush green grass. Now and then, Lavyan would point out a house or a hill. 'The prime minister has a summer house there. My family would picnic in those trees occasionally.' Reece could see Mary was hanging on to Jacob's every word. Like Reece, she was soaking in everything, and he knew they would talk about this experience many times in the future, over bottles of wine back home in Malta.

Now and then Palo would chip in with memories of his own, indicating where he had grown up and where his family lived. Where the best seafood restaurants were, and the best place to drink coffee. The time passed quickly, and now Palo took the scenic route through the hills. As they came round a bend, a few miles ahead, they could see on a plateau the outline of the city of Jerusalem. The dome of the Temple Mount shining in the sun like a giant upside-down orange. The city, half modern, half ancient, with its famous walls, and places of importance to Judaism, Christianity, and Islam did not disappoint from its description in the brochures. It took the breath away when seen for the first time.

'It's beautiful,' said Mary.

'It is,' replied Palo.

'It's a World Heritage site,' said Jacob. 'There's a mixture of Jews, Muslims, and Christians living there. And despite all its wars and troubles, is still sacred to all. We will take you there later. The old city has the most important sites to visit. Temple Mount, the Western Wall, the Church of the Holy Sepulchre, the Dome of the Rock, and the al-Aqsa Mosque to name the most important ones. The city has something for everyone old and new.'

As the city came closer into view, Reece could understand why it was held in such high esteem by so many religions and peoples. The whole view expanded across the horizon, seeming to rise above them into the blue sky.

'First, we pay our respects,' said Palo, as he took a side road to the left that ran parallel with the city.

The road now twisted around the mountain, winding higher, and higher. Reece could see many cars parked on one side of the road, narrowing the space to drive. The grey tarmac seemed to reflect the sun's light, and he noticed that Palo and Jacob had put on their sunglasses. Eventually they came to gates in the middle of a large wall with the words Mount Herzl National Cemetery written in large gold letters. Two soldiers with automatic rifles checked Palo's documents before they waved them through to park up near a large modern building.

'This is Mount Herzl, our national cemetery, named after Theodor Herzl, who we consider to be the father of Israel. It is also known as the Mountain of Memory. He is buried here on the top of the mountain. That building ahead is the Herzl Museum, which you can visit later if you wish, but first let us go to find Rachel. We will find her grave in the Military Cemetery,' said Jacob.

The heat outside the car was cooled by the breeze that seemed to surround the mountain. It was just after midday, and the sun was almost above them. They followed Palo who led them through another set of gates. In front of them was a large black marble stone raised on a mound with gold letters in Hebrew.

'That is where Herzl is buried. The letters just say Herzl, and they're engraved on all four sides of the stone,' said Jacob.

Palo led them down a path. Reece could see that the graveyard was on separate levels. As they walked down each level with similar headstones, on each level, the shapes changed.

As they reached the first level, Palo said, 'The leaders and prime ministers of Israel are buried here,' he said, pointing to the gravestones.

Looking across the ground, Reece could see how the spot had been chosen for its significance of looking down on the city of Jerusalem below them. They walked a short distance down to the next level. Again, Palo stopped, and pointing at the headstones, he spoke once more.

'Here are the graves of the heroes and military personnel who gave their lives to the state of Israel. Along this front row is where Rachel is buried among the heroes. Please follow me.'

The headstones were all the same and as they passed them, Reece and Mary could see the pebbles and small stones that had been left by those who knew them in life.

Then they reached the marble headstone carved with the name in black letters that stood out against the white: Rachel Cohen in Hebrew and English, with the Star of David above her name. They stood facing the grave and Reece had a sudden flash of the memory of seeing the woman he knew as Anna for the first time as she'd walked out of the hotel lift in Malta. He remembered the dress that showed the outline of her body as she moved, the smile, and the laughter she could bring to any situation. In one word, she'd been beautiful.

'If you would like to place your pebbles now? Place them here on the top,' said Lavyan.

Reece took the pebble from his pocket and, standing beside Mary, they both placed them on the top of the headstone. As they did, the cool breeze seemed to blow slightly harder. Reece felt it was Anna passing by saying 'hello,' saying 'thank you.'

'Would you like to say a few words of remembrance or anything? The prayer to the dead, which is a Jewish right, has been said, but if you like I could repeat it now on your behalf,' said Palo.

'Yes, that would be good. Thank you. Please do. Then I would like to say something and maybe you would too, Mary?'

'I have a short quote I know if that's all right?' answered Mary.

Palo nodded and, stepping closer to the headstone, he turned to face them, the city of Jerusalem in the background behind them.

'I shall speak in English, which I hope is acceptable to you as I'm sure it will be to Rachel and to our God,' said Palo.

'God, full of mercy, who dwells in the heights, provide a sure rest upon the wings of the Divine Presence, within the range of the holy, pure, and glorious, whose shining resemble the sky's, to the soul of Rachel, daughter of Israel, for a charity was given to the memory of her soul. Therefore, the Master of Mercy will protect her forever, from behind the hiding of his wings, and will tie her soul with the rope of life. The Everlasting is her heritage, and she shall rest peacefully upon her lying place, and let us say: Amen.'

They all replied Amen. Reece stepped forward, taking the same position that Palo had now vacated, and faced the way Palo had. Now, for the first time, he could see the city and looking at it, he thought, *this was a peaceful place to be if you were dead.*

'Thank you both for allowing Mary and me to be here today and thank you for those words, Palo. When I was in Special Branch in Northern Ireland during an operational break, I took a walk through a graveyard in the area I was working. I memorised the wording that I saw on a gravestone, and I think the words mean the same to everyone no matter where you are or what God you worship, and I hope you, and Rachel will understand them.'

'Think of me as you walk by, for where you stand so once did I, where I am now so you will be. Prepare yourself to follow me.'

Reece stood to the side to let Mary take up the same spot he'd spoken from. He could see the tears on her cheek, which she didn't try to hide or wipe away.

'Like David, I'm proud to be here, and proud to have known Rachel, or Anna as I knew her, even if it was only for a short time, but I thought of this quote while we were driving here, and I think it says exactly what we all want to say.'

'To live in hearts we leave behind is not to die.'

Mary touched the top of the headstone, then turning, took Reece's hand, and with her other hand wiped the tears from her cheek.

'Thank you for being here with us. It's made the whole experience more bearable. It's a beautiful place, so peaceful and quiet, even though the city isn't far away. I know Rachel is where she would have wanted to be. Back home among her people in the soil she worked so hard to protect,' said Reece as he shook both men's hands.

The breeze seemed to pass by them stronger again. Reece looked around, trying to take in the whole picture to lock it in his memory. The clear blue sky, the olive, and citrus trees, the green grass, the white headstones in rows standing strong against the world. Like the graveyard he'd walked through all those years ago, each one telling a story of a person's life in a few words, but in each, everyone was the same, everyone was dead, everyone was with their god or none. Their stories told their journey for now, finished.

Reece knew Mary well enough to know she'd want to go to the city and find a good cup of coffee and maybe something to eat. As they left the mountain, the road rose gently towards the city of Jerusalem, and it seemed to be bright white in the sunlight with the buildings rising above. It was obvious Palo had driven here many times using the streets off the main central road. The buildings were modern to begin with, then changed to those of older brick, most painted limestone white with closed shutters against the heat.

Entering the old city, Reece could see heavily armed soldiers patrolling in pairs, ensuring the safety of the citizens, *Jew, Muslim, Christian, or no particular faith,* thought Reece. It reminded him of his own days of service in Northern Ireland. keeping the two communities apart while trying to protect the innocent.

In a small square, Palo found the parking space he was looking for. Leaving the car, they walked the short distance to sit at a table outside one of the cafés that surrounded the square.

'This café is run by a friend and serves the best Arabic coffee in Israel,' said Palo.

The square was small and the buildings, at least three storeys high, had closed shuttered windows blocking the fierceness of the afternoon sun. It felt cool with a gentle breeze, and Reece could smell bread and coffee in the air. The coffee and pastries were as good as Palo had said.

'It's beautiful,' said Mary, looking around the square. 'It reminds me of some of the places in Valletta.'

'I don't know much about Malta other than what I saw when I was there, but I'll go there again when I'm not working,' said Palo.

'I've been there a few times. As you say, Miss Mary, it does remind me of this city. Especially the old part,' said Lavyan.

'You both should come and visit us, and stay for a while,' said Reece.

'It's a deal, but now let us show you around the old city, then we'll drop you back at your hotel,' replied Lavyan.

For the next few hours, that was exactly what they did. They visited all the holy sites and because of the identities of their companions they were allowed to go right to the heart of some, passing the guards who would normally stop the everyday visitors. Jacob and Palo were better than any tour guide, not only telling the history, but the secrets only they knew.

'The Temple Mount with its golden dome is one of the holiest sites,' explained Jacob. 'It has been fought over for centuries by many religions.'

The site that struck Mary the most, was when they came to the Church of the Holy Sepulchre with its two blue domes. Again, Jacob explained:

'The church was built over what your Christian faith believes is the site of the crucifixion of Jesus and then the tomb where he was buried.'

Again, because of whom they were with, they were able to go down into the area of the tomb which, having no natural light, was lit by many candles.

'It's so quiet and still,' said Mary, and tears rolled down her cheeks once more. Reece put his arm around her. Mary was one of the bravest and strongest women he knew, but she had a sentimental side to her he'd seen a few times before.

'Would you like to light a candle?' asked Jacob.

'Yes please,' said Mary.

Mary and Reece both lit candles, placing them in the holders against the wall, lighting up the small corner where they stood.

'I'm sorry about the tears. I felt so many memories here. They just seemed to come,' said Mary.

'The tomb affects many people, Miss Mary. I'm sure you won't be the first or last person to feel this way,' said Lavyan.

They left the church and the old city and drove down the coast. The city sat on a plateau in the Judaean Mountains between the Mediterranean and the Dead Sea. Reece tried to imagine what it was like to travel to from the days of Jesus, the Crusades, and right up to modern times when it was still being fought over.

This time, the journey seemed to take a little longer, because Palo had taken a route away from the motorways. At times they had to stop on the narrow roads to let other vehicles pass, and on two occasions having to let shepherds guide their sheep across the road in front of them.

Yet again, the land reminded Reece so much of Malta, and he started to feel a need to get back there, to what was now his home of peace and rest. The next few days, Reece, and Mary were left to explore on their own. Reece hired a car to drive wherever the mood took them and on two occasions had to turn back into Israel when they came to the border crossing with Jordan. They visited the main cities on the coast and in the evenings walked hand in hand through the streets and along the seafront of Tel Aviv. The night before they were due to leave, they dined at one of the many seafood restaurants near the hotel. The wound on Reece's leg had almost healed. The swimming and walking acted like the hands of a physiotherapist. He was taking fewer pain killers, even for the pain in his shoulder. Reece had noticed that Mary seemed more relaxed as well. She was laughing more. Her eyes had some of the old sparkle back. The sparkle he'd only seen when they walked and swam in Malta. He believed this was down to the combination of the trip and the fact that she now knew he wouldn't be going back to the old ways. They were halfway through their second bottle of Chablis, the dry cold wine that had, over the years, become a favourite of both when dining at a special place with special meaning. Reece felt the time was right and even though he didn't have a ring, he knew this was the woman he wanted to spend the rest of his life with.

'Mary?' he said, as he took her hand across the table.

'Yes?'

'I know this is maybe not the right time and place, and maybe I should wait until we are back in Malta, but somehow, I feel it should be now. You know I love you, and I know we've been through our fair share of things together, but I want to spend the rest of my life with you.'

'I want that too, darling.'

Reece smiled before he continued.

'What I'm saying is, I want you to marry me. I want to commit my life to you if you'll have me. Will you marry me?'

For a second, he could see those sparkling eyes start to well up with emotion. Mary stood and rushing round the table she just about gave him time to stand before she was in his arms, kissing him. When their lips separated, Reece held her at arm's length.

'I take that is a 'yes' then?'

'Yes, oh yes, yes,' she answered before kissing him once more.

'Where's my ring? And why didn't you get down on one knee?' She teased with a smile.

'What? With these knees? You would have to help me up, and as for the ring. I know a little jeweller in Valletta that we can visit when we get back.'

They didn't wait for dessert, instead walking along the promenade.

They could hear the sea as the waves crashed onto the shore. Above the sound, Reece could feel the buzz from the phone in his pocket.

Checking the text, it was from Jacob Lavyan. Before you leave tomorrow, can we've a quick coffee in the morning, just the two of us?

He replied yes that he'd see him in the hotel lobby at eleven. Once again, he felt his past interfering in his future, but he wasn't going to let it interfere tonight. This was his night, and he was going to spend it with the woman he loved.

'Who was that?' asked Mary.

'Just Jacob. He wants me to have coffee with him in the morning.'

'Why?'

Reece could see the concern in her face.

'Maybe to say goodbye and hopefully with another bottle of Bush? But don't worry, I'm not going back on my word. Those days are over for good. I just want to get back to our room and work off some of that food.'

Her smile was there again, but not as strong as the one when she'd said yes.

'But what about your knee?'

'As I said, you'll have to help me.'

Their flight wasn't until 8 p.m. so they had a full day to do a little more sightseeing and shopping. Reece had left Mary doing just that when he returned to the hotel lobby for eleven and his coffee with Jacob Lavyan.

He had ordered a pot for two. It had just been placed on the table when the old agent came through the doors, alone this time.

'Shalom, good morning, David. I hope you're well and ready for your journey home?'

'Shalom Jacob. Yes, thank you and you. Are you well?'

Both men shook hands. 'Yes David. For an old man, I'm very well on this beautiful day. I see you have coffee. Excellent, this will be my third of the day already. When I worked in operations, I became a coffee addict, having to keep awake for long hours.'

'I'm the same, Jacob, and for the same reason.'

Both men sat and Reece poured the two cups, leaving it black for each to decide on milk and sugar.

'So, Jacob, what are we here for?'

'Ah, the policeman is still there in you, the question right up front.' Lavyan poured a little milk into his cup and took a sip before continuing.

'First. Thank you for seeing me. I know it's your last day and I'm sure you and Mary are busy with your last-minute shopping and packing.'

'I'll always make time for an old friend,' said Reece.

'That is why I'm here, David, because we are friends. We both live in a world where they are few and our enemies many. It is about one such enemy that I wish to talk to you and my story goes back to the time we met all those years ago.'

Reece poured a little milk into his own cup. The coffee was strong and from what he'd heard so far, he thought he was going to need it.

'You remember when I came to Belfast? Well, I had many meetings with your senior officers and MI5 at your headquarters. We discussed many things, mainly about how your terrorists were suspected of linking up with the ones from my part of the world here in the Middle East. We knew the IRA was getting weapons and training from the various Arab terrorist groups and countries. Indeed, you must remember the shiploads of weapons from Gaddafi in Libya? Your security people even captured one.'

Reece nodded as he remembered the capture. The Eksund ship was loaded with everything a terrorist army would need. He also remembered Sean Costello the man he'd shot dead in Manchester. His file showed that he'd trained as a sniper in the Bekaa Valley in Lebanon with other terrorist groups, mainly Arab.

'Before I arrived in Belfast for those meetings. I received a full briefing of my own from our analysts here in Tel Aviv and then from our staff at our embassy in Dublin. These briefings were mostly in general terms regarding the situation at the time. However, there was one piece of information I couldn't talk about at that time, because it would have put one of our own agents in danger and made the close relationship we had with the British government difficult.'

Reece sat forward in his chair. 'Can I stop you there, Jacob? As you know, I'm no longer an agent of the British government as you put it, and I don't want to be pulled back into anything. Last night I asked Mary to marry me, and she accepted. We both want to live out the rest of our days in peace. Having been through such a life, I'm sure you understand.'

Lavyan poured himself more coffee and without adding any more milk took a sip. Smiling, his eyes were full of laughter.

'Congratulations, she seems a wonderful lady. Do not worry my friend. I totally understand what you mean, and I would never interfere with your plans. What I'm telling you hopefully might never bother you again, but I believe you should know, if only to protect yourself and Mary, in what I hope will be those peaceful years to come that you talk about. So, please hear what I have to say. It may be to your advantage.'

Hearing the word protect, Reece could feel his pulse quicken. The word usually meant trouble, and he wanted to avoid anything to do with protect or trouble.

'What do you mean?'

'As I said, I received briefings about the situation in Northern Ireland at that time. You may not know this but we, the Mossad, had agents who were members of the IRA especially in the border area of South Armagh where we had a particularly good one. The IRA man was part of a unit operating in South Armagh and he originally came from Crossmaglen but was living in Dundalk with others on the run from the North's security forces. For security reasons and to protect the source, I never knew his name.'

Lavyan stopped to take another sip of his coffee. Reece was not surprised that Mossad had agents within the IRA. If the terrorist organisation was working with the enemies of Israel, then it would be common sense to recruit agents within those organisations.

'Why should this affect me now?' asked Reece.

'Maybe it doesn't, but just in case, I think you should know what some of the reports mentioned, from that one agent. As I said the agent originally came from Crossmaglen and I need not tell you how we recruited him. You yourself, having done the same job at one time, would know only too well the how's and whys of the recruitment process along with the running of the agents once they're recruited.'

Reece merely nodded in response.

'The information this agent passed on alleged that a senior officer in the RUC Special Branch was working with the Provisional IRA. He was passing them information and protecting their people from capture by disrupting the British operations against them, especially in the border area.'

Reece continued to listen without interruption as he'd been taught many years before, to let the person across the table tell all before asking any questions. His stomach was turning. He could feel the anger inside him start to rise.

'We were only allowed to operate inside the Republic of Ireland. Our country had an agreement to operate jointly with the UK against the same enemies where there's a danger to both our peoples, but to operate only within the boundaries of each other's country with their permission. Our embassy in Dublin, like your embassies around the world, retains an intelligence-gathering remit. In that remit, especially during the terrorist war you were involved in, we targeted those people we were able to identify as being involved. Of course, our interest was, as you know, of any connection between the Irish terrorists and our Arab enemies.'

Reece was pleased to hear Lavyan call it a war and not the Troubles as the politicians labelled it. It was a war, not a simple case of trouble, with thousands being killed, and maimed.

Lavyan continued, 'So it was that our people in Dublin were able to target and in some cases recruit as agent members of the IRA living in the South of Ireland. This man was part of a vicious unit based in Dundalk. I won't say how we recruited him or why he agreed to work with us, but the information he provided we passed on to your security people. But, like all intelligence agencies, to protect our agent we kept back any information that would have exposed him to the other terrorists he was working with. Anyway, he gave us some information which helped with the interception of IRA operations, mostly those involving the movement of explosives across the border for use in the north and the British mainland. To our knowledge, he never took part in any murders or directed attacks on the security forces, but as you know, you can never trust an agent fully. Then later, he was able to provide briefings on the progress of the peace process negotiations and the thinking at the top of the terrorist organisation which we did pass on to London.'

'Trust an agent, tell me about it.' Reece smiled.

Jacob waved to the waiter walking through the lobby.

'Can I have a pot of tea with some fruit please?' he asked the waiter. 'What about you, David? Would you like some tea?'

'No thanks. I'll stick to the coffee.'

'Please bring some fresh coffee for my friend.'

When the waiter left, Jacob continued with his story.

'I cannot be specific on most of the intelligence this man brought to the table as I wasn't working in Dublin, but my briefing before I went to Belfast included the information that this Special Branch Officer was working with the IRA in the border area. The only thing our agent could tell us was that he held the rank of Detective Chief Inspector and was based for some time at Gough Barracks in Armagh City and his area of operation was the Southern Region of the province of Northern Ireland.'

'Can you tell me when this was? It might help me identify who he was,' asked Reece.

'My visit was in 1984, so it would have been around that time. The agent had been working for two years before then.'

It was a long time ago, and even though Reece tried to remember names and faces, the one thing he did know was that there was a frequent turnover of SB personnel to protect them from discovery by the terrorists they were working against. He knew that at any one time there were four or five DCIs working in Gough Barracks, the old army base in the centre of Armagh City. Reece had worked there himself for six years when he was attached to the Tasking and Coordination Group South, TCG(S), with responsibility of working with other agencies in the covert operations in the south of the country.

The tea and coffee arrived, and Reece watched Lavyan cut an apple into wedges and take a bite of one, then sip his black tea. The light of the sun coming through the large windows at the front of the hotel was now casting shadows where they sat.

'So, what you're telling me is that this man was working with the IRA against us, and your people never told our people?'

'Exactly. We thought it was too dangerous for our agent who might be discovered and tortured and murdered by the IRA. You must think of the kind of damage that could have done to our relationship with many countries not just in Ireland but Britain and the USA. The Americans at that time were supporters of the Republican movement in your country, mainly because of the Irish vote which a few presidents relied upon to get elected.'

'So why tell me this now?'

Jacob took another bite of the apple wedge and chewed for a few seconds before he replied.

'A few reasons, David. We know because of your background, and because of what you've done for your country and ours, you'll understand the secrecy in having to protect this information. The agent, although still alive, is no longer active, so he cannot give us any more information. The main reason I'm telling you this is that if you're ever in your own country again, you need to be aware of the danger that this Special Branch man, if he's still alive, could bring to you. Our people in this country believe you've done us a great service when you killed the Arab in London, and the respect we know you have for Israel. Therefore, we should let you have this information for your own protection in the future. So, what I'm telling you is, for now, for your ears only. Your people in London and Belfast have not been told, but if they're as good as we think they are, they must know about this man, and for their own reasons they choose not to do anything for now.'

'I'm finished with all that now. As you know, I've retired from SG9 and MI6 and I intend to go back to Malta tonight, to marry Mary, and relax with a book by the sea.'

Lavyan leant forward and smiled.

'I'm eighty-three David. I retired twenty years ago from the Mossad. Since then, I've run my own business still working with the various Israeli Intelligence organisations in a consultancy capacity. My work advises business groups around the world on their internal and personal security. Have you ever heard of the External Relations Department, the ERD?'

Reece shook his head.

'It was formed by Yitzhak Rabin in 1974 after several failed operations by our intelligence agencies with a remit to oversee future operations as a sort of watchdog and report back to him. The ERM has several departments, one of which is the Foreign Liaison, which works with Israeli military attaches and other IDF personnel working overseas. I'm the current head of that department within the ERM. I find I'm still contacted by Mossad and Amman when they need advice, or the use of my many contacts throughout the world when it's needed for the benefit or protection of Israel. What I'm saying David is this. Now that you're outside the shadows, as we say about someone like yourself with a past in the undercover intelligence world, you may find that your own country in the future may contact you when they have need of you. I think of you as a friend, but also someone I could contact if I needed your help or advice. You would be just one more of the large number of people in the world I could approach if I need help. The same goes for you, if you ever need my help or that of my organisation, we'd be here for you.'

Reece took his time before answering and filled his cup with more of the Arabic coffee. After taking a sip, he sat back, and tried to relax, taking in what Jacob had just told him?

'I appreciate your trust in me, and all you've told me. It goes without saying, that what you've said will remain confidential between us. As I've said, I really do want to retire from it all, but of course I would be foolish not to accept your offer of help if ever I should need it. So, in that context, you can come to me should you ever need my help. After all, what are true friends for?'

Lavyan's eyes lit up with a smile as he reached across the table to touch Reece's hand.

'Good, good. We are like the film Godfather, when they say I might need you to do something for me one day and that day might never come.' He laughed.

'Just don't ever let Mary know. I've made her a promise and I intend to try to keep it.'

As if on cue, Reece saw Mary come through the hotel doors into the lobby and looking around she smiled when she saw Reece. Both men stood to greet her.

Taking her hand, Jacob bowed, and kissed it.

'Shalom, Miss Mary, and congratulations. It's wonderful news.'

'Thank you. You are the first to know.' She smiled. 'So, what else have you two been talking about?'

'Would you like some tea or coffee?' asked Reece as Mary put down two shopping bags and sat beside them.

'No, thank you. And don't try to change the subject, Joseph.'

Both men laughed. 'We've been mostly catching up on old times,' said Reece as he looked across at Lavyan. Knowing that wouldn't be enough to satisfy her, he continued,

'Jacob has been telling me that, like me, he's retired from the spy business. He now works in his own right as a consultant to big business around the world.'

'Consulting on what?' asked Mary.

'Mostly on how organisations can beef up their security systems. From protecting their buildings and assets to the people who work for them,' answered Lavyan.

'And he's offered you a job, I suppose?' said Mary, looking Reece in the eye.

'No, not as such. I would just be his contact in Malta,' answered Reece.

'I totally understand your worry, Miss Mary, but I'll never ask David to go back to his old ways. I know only too well what it means to leave all that behind. Like myself, David would only help me in a consultant capacity. I'm getting too old to be running around and I've built up a network of people I can trust around the world. Each one is first and foremost a friend, and I insist they're not connected to any government agency. I run a respectable business, and some of the people who ask my advice would insist that I'm not connected to any such government. David and I'll always be friends, and we'll always be there for each other as friends, and that goes for you too, Miss Mary. I hope we'll be friends. For now, I would hope I get an invitation to your wedding, but at my age, please don't wait too long.'

Mary relaxed. Sitting back in the chair, she smiled at both men.

'Of course, you're invited, and don't worry, when we get back to Malta, the first thing on the agenda is setting a date. I've already got a few things for the day, or should I say, the evening.' She winked at Reece as she lifted one of the bags but didn't open it, leaving it to both men's imaginations.

'I think you've made him blush, Miss Mary. I look forward to your invitation, then. But now, I must go.' He stood to leave.

'Can you not stay for lunch with us?' asked Reece.

'Yes, stay please,' said Mary.

'I would love to, but I have an engagement of my own. You have a lot to do before your flight, and I would fear that when we get talking, it would be a long lunch.' Lavyan laughed. 'But I promise I'll see you again. Maybe in Malta and we'll have that lunch together as old friends do? You take care of this lovely lady, David. She's very special.' He kissed Mary on both cheeks, then shook hands with Reece.

'Shalom, my friend. Until we meet again.'

'Don't worry, Jacob. I'll take care of her and enjoy doing it. Shalom, until we meet again.'

The old man left without looking back or waving, and Reece thought he had a lot more on his mind than what he'd discussed with him.

After lunch, the rest of the day was spent relaxing and packing the two cases, which, with Mary's shopping, were now a little heavier. Palo picked them up at seven for the short ride to the airport. He made little conversation. At the airport, he escorted them through security and into a private first-class lounge where they were treated like celebrities by the staff before they were escorted to their seats on the flight to Rome, which took off on schedule at 20.00hrs. They booked into the airport hotel and after a late dinner returned to their room before catching the early morning flight to Malta. By lunchtime the next day they were at the Villa Joseph in Quara and having unpacked took the short walk along the seafront to the little café on the hill, where they sat, and looked at the waves crashing on the rocks below.

It was a cold day, so Mary squeezed up close to Reece, putting her hand in his jacket pocket for warmth.

'You'll have to meet my mum. I'll give her a call later,' said Mary.

'How is she since her fall?'

'She's recovered well. She walks with a stick and now she's living at my house on the Lisburn Road. It's a lot easier to get into the city or to see her physio at the City Hospital.'

'Why don't we get her a flight out here for a few days and she can meet me in nicer weather and circumstances?'

'That's a great idea. I'll ask her.'

'How do you think she'll take to me, an ex-RUC Special Branch man? If she's as good a Catholic as you say, she won't be happy that I'm a divorced heathen with kids.'

'Oh, Joseph. Don't worry, she won't bite you. She hated my ex as she knew he beat me, so anything is better than that. Anyway, it's me you're marrying, not her.' She laughed.

'That's good news. I'm not into fighting with old ladies.'

'Even though it's cold, Joseph, I'd rather be here than anywhere else in the world.'

'Me too,' replied Reece. 'But we can't stay long. There's somewhere else we need to be.'

Mary sat up and turning looked into his eyes, slightly worried at what he was going to say, not sure what to expect. 'Where, Joseph?'

'This afternoon we've to go to a little jeweller's shop I know in Valetta.' He smiled.

'My ring, I almost forgot.' She kissed him. 'Let's go.'

Chapter 8

Belfast

They had been watching her for an hour. In fact, they'd been watching her at the same time every day for a week. They had changed vehicles three times during that week to avoid being noticed. It was easy to follow the old woman, but boring for the two men watching her. Now, as Rosie Smith crossed the road at the end of Hugh Street and turned left onto the Lisburn Road, the two men in the white transit van watched once more. The old woman walked with the aid of a walking stick.

'What the fuck is all this about, Jimmy?' asked Frank.

'Don't ask me, I just do as I'm told. But it must be important, or Brian wouldn't have ordered us to do it. I thought we were two of his best. A couple of the kids could have done this. But ours is not to reason why.'

'Aye, I know, ours is but to do our die.' Frank laughed, which started off Jimmy, whose fat belly shook when he laughed.

Frank would be considered by some to be the better looking of the two. With his muscular body that showed time spent in the gym, and with the beginnings of a beard on his long face, he had his fair share of the opposite sex to play with. He started the engine as they watched a bus pass them, pulling into the stop where Rosie Smith always got on. They followed the bus, but both knew by now the routine, as it travelled down the Lisburn Road towards the city before turning into Sandy Row where the old woman always got off before entering the Food for the Day café, where she'd sit for an hour with two women friends, having a late breakfast before travelling back on the bus following the same route home. It always amazed Frank Walsh that these three old women could have so much to talk about and they each could eat a full Ulster Fry breakfast each day. Maybe it was their only meal of the day, but by the look of all three women and how they walked slowly, each with a large waistline, he could only believe that they also ate more when they got home. Having the walking stick, the old woman walked slower than the other two, who would walk in the opposite direction. Frank had always been careful with his weight and fitness. The way he looked at it, if he had to run, he could do, and he smiled to himself as he looked at Jimmy Bailey thinking if we must run Jimmy you're fucked. Rosie Smith had to cross the busy road to get to the bus stop on the other side and her return journey to Hugh Street. It was now 11 a.m. and her routine never varied. The traffic now was not as busy as the rush-hour two hours before. Once more Walsh started the engine, but this time, instead of following the old woman, he drove in the opposite direction to join the Grosvenor Road to its junction with the Falls Road. Turning left, he drove the final mile to Beechmount, where they parked around the corner before walking to the house and knocking the door of the home of the Belfast Officer Commanding the Real IRA, Brian McNally. Both men had been in the kitchen of the house when McNally had met with the man from South Armagh. They had heard a little of the conversation and after being briefed by McNally on the importance of doing a good job, they both felt they had. McNally answered the door and brought them through to the small kitchen at the back of the house.

'Everything OK, I hope?' he asked.

'Aye, boss, no problems,' replied Walsh.

McNally went to the cooker and, opening the oven, he put on oven gloves and took out a tray with a hot pizza on it and set it on a board on the kitchen table. Taking a circular pizza slicer, he cut the pizza up into triangles before placing two of the larger slices on a plate and setting it down in front of the two men.

'Help yourselves. I'm sure you're peckish.'

Both men sat at the table and took a slice.

McNally then filled two mugs of tea and set them in front of the men before joining them.

'Help yourselves to the milk and sugar. Now, fill me in on where we are?'

Both men were chewing the pizza, and it was Frank who spoke first, talking with his mouth half full, something his mother had told him not to do.

'Her routine is the same every day. Leaves home at the same time, then takes the bus to the café in Sandy Row. Meets up with two women friends, chats over a full Ulster then around eleven returns home by the same route she came.'

'Does she still use the walking stick?'

'Yes, she walks with a slight limp on her right side,' replied Walsh.

'What's this all about? Why all the interest in an old woman?' asked Jimmy.

'I know I've kept you in the dark, but that was for reasons of security. If you had been pulled in and questioned, the less you knew the better. You both have done a great job. Now, the time has come to move this operation to the next stage.'

Both men had finished eating, and in the quiet of the kitchen paid attention as their leader spoke. McNally told them the story of Mary McAuley and her betrayal of the Republican Movement with her Special Branch friend.

He elaborated how from her access to the senior people in the Provisional IRA during the war, then after the peace, she'd told her SB man the organisation's secrets.

'Fuck's sake, the bitch,' said Jimmy, interrupting.

'There's more, Jimmy. After the whole peace process thing and the Good Friday Agreement, she still gave information to the Brits. She might have gotten away with it if she'd not set up Sean Costello to be killed.'

Both men knew the story of Costello, who had been shot dead by the Brits in Manchester. They'd heard the rumour that he'd intended to kill the British prime minister, but he'd been shot down like a dog in the street.

His funeral had only taken place a few weeks ago, and he was buried as one of them, a member of the Real IRA.

'Are we sure she set Sean up?' asked Frank.

'Yes. he'd recognised her in Manchester, and she was with her SB friend. He was going to deal with her himself, but they got to him first. But all that's in the past. The time has come for us to deal with her. This has been given to us by the Army Council. You two will play an important part in the operation. It's Wednesday now, tomorrow you'll nick a car and store it overnight, then on Friday you'll knock the old woman down with the car and burn it afterwards. After you get rid of the car, I'll see you in the Wolf Tone Club and brief you on what happens next. Everything will depend on how well you do the job in the next few days.'

Frank thought of the words once more, *Ours is not to reason why, ours is but to do and die*. Still, he had to ask why. 'Who is this old woman and why do we have to do this to her?'

McNally knew one of the men might ask, and he didn't want to use his position in the organisation to threaten them into doing something they were not happy with, but he'd picked these two men for a reason.

'I thought one of you might ask. I picked you two because you're a team and because of the jobs you've done together before. You always do the job well, you know how to keep your mouth shut, and the fact that this is being sanctioned by the Army Council, I had to use my best people. We've looked at this woman who, I can now tell you, is the mother of Mary McAuley.'

Both men sat up at this information, keeping silent to let their leader talk further.

'We have an agent in the City Hospital where the old woman goes for her physio. The house she lives in on the Lisburn Road belongs to her daughter. We have looked at finding McAuley but with no luck. We think she might be in England. So, to get her back, the plan is to knock down her mother with a stolen car which will look like it's been driven by joy riders who have nicked it. Whether you kill her or seriously injure her in the process, when you do hit her, it will be enough to bring McAuley back here. When she does come back, we'll lift her to answer for her crimes. Are you both OK with that?'

Both men looked at each other before nodding in return.

'Will there be any kickback from the Provos?' asked Jimmy.

'No. They have already been told we intend to make McAuley pay for her treachery. Don't forget Sean Costello's brother Paul is an MLA at Stormont. They won't want anything done that might jeopardise their cosy relationship with the Brits. That's why it must look like a genuine accident. How we deal with the daughter is another matter. For now, you just need to work to my plan a bit at a time. The final part of dealing with her will be in the Republic, not in the north, so therefore not interfering with their fucking peace process.'

Again, both men nodded their understanding.

'Good. Now go home, get some rest. Nick the car and store it for Friday morning. Stay away from the bars and clubs until this is over. The part you're playing is most important. There will be further things for you to do down the road. Keep the van, we'll need it again.'

When both men had gone, McNally left the house, and walked to the main Falls Road. He used a phone box to call a number in the Republic of Ireland and briefed the man with a South Armagh accent to expect his package soon.

Chapter 9

Malta

Valletta, when you drive along the coast and the sun shines on the city from the sea, is like a pink cloud rising. Sparkling across the harbour from Sliema, the city shone in the midday sun. Reece enjoyed driving at this time of day with the air con on, when they were in the hot summer season, but now they were in what some would call winter. Although it was still warm, it wasn't needed. The fact that the traffic drove on the same side of the road as he drove in England and Northern Ireland made it even more enjoyable, not having to worry what way to go when roundabouts came. Mary was, as usual, quiet while he drove, just wanting to be lost in her own thoughts and watching the beautiful world go by. The radio was on the local station. Radio Malta played music they both enjoyed. Reece drove around the inner harbour and entered the one-way system of the city, before finding a parking space in one of the car parks outside the city walls.

'When we get the ring, can we find somewhere overlooking the harbour? I would like to celebrate with a glass of champagne,' suggested Mary.

'No problem. I think I know one or two places that would hit the spot.'

They walked hand in hand up one of the streets that led to the city centre and the long main street of the inner city. The street through the centre of the city went from the main entrance gate across to the city walls to the World War Two Military Museum. Where they were going was almost in the middle: a small jeweller's shop, just off the main central Victoria square. Mary took her time. The small, tanned man behind the counter smiled while he showed her trays of rings, none showing a price. Mary almost picked up one from the first tray but looked at three more before returning to the first tray and lifting the ring she'd seen before. She tried it on. It fitted perfectly, which to her was another sign it was the right one.

'Oh Joseph. I love this one. What do you think?'

Reece didn't care if she liked it. He was happy if she was happy.

'It looks great on your finger.'

The ring had a round sapphire with a diamond on either side.

'It might be expensive,' she said.

'If you feel it's the one for you, then you should have it. You like it, I like it, and I would rather you had something you'd seen and picked, than something I picked that was wrong for you. Let's get this one and go celebrate.'

The small man smiled as Mary handed him the ring.

'I'll take this one.'

'Does madam want to wear it now?' asked the small man.

'No. Can you put it in a nice box, please?' she replied.

'Are you sure you don't want it now?' asked Reece.

'No, Joseph. I want you to do it right.' She smiled.

Reece understood and paying for the ring they walked back down the street they'd come up to the walls of the harbour looking towards Sliema and the harbour mouth looking out to the sea. At the wall, Reece turned towards Mary.

'I guess this is right. You know I love you, and I want to make this commitment to you to spend the rest of my life with you.' Getting down on one knee and taking her left hand he slipped the ring onto her finger. He could see the tears start to stream down her cheeks.

'Oh yes, Joseph. I do. I love you.'

They kissed and hugged and stopped a passing tourist to ask her to take a photo of them on Reece's mobile.

'We have this photo, our moment in time. I'm so happy Joseph.'

'Now that we are committed to each other, and you have the ring to prove it. I want you to call me David. It is my real name, after all, Joseph is in the past and David is our future.'

'OK, agreed. Now, David, where are we going for that glass of champagne? Then I really must call my mother.'

'And I suppose we should bring her out here to help us celebrate.'

'Oh, David, I really do love you.'

Chapter 10

Belfast

The theft of the car was easy. As he always did, Frank Walsh just went for a walk around the Ballymurphy estate, to choose the car he'd take later. Then that night he'd return and using his two-foot-long thin metal ruler, he would put pressure on the side window, slide down the ruler, and press the release button to open the door. Before he reached that stage, however, he'd use the electronic device he bought on the Internet, which would deactivate the car alarm. He would then use a different switch on the same device, which, with a car such as the Vauxhall Vectra would overrule the electric key card, allowing him to start the engine and drive away.

During the terrorist war, the Provisional IRA had made it a kneecapping offence to steal cars in West Belfast without their permission. He had taken a bad beating, years before, for just doing a lookout for a friend who stole an old banger, so they could scream around the estates and do handbrake turns. His friend had not been so lucky. The Provos had shot him in both knees, leaving him to die in the alleyway after one of the bullets had ricocheted and nicked his femoral artery. Since the Good Friday Agreement, kneecappings were out, but steal the wrong car, one that belonged to a connected member of the Republican movement, and a beating from a couple of its hoods could do just as much damage as a handgun. Now Frank always made sure of the people he stole from, making sure they would do him no more harm than make a claim on their insurance. From his connections in the estate, he was able to establish that the red Vectra outside 94 Ballymurphy Road was just what he was looking for. He left it until 2 a.m. on Thursday morning before he was dropped off by Jimmy Bailey, who drove the transit van slowly past number 94, then turned at the top of the road before parking to take up the job of lookout. He flashed the lights twice to let Walsh know it was good to go.

Frank listened. It was quiet, no traffic or people. A couple of houses had their bedroom lights on, with curtains pulled, none overlooking his approach to the drive with the car he was going to steal. He had checked that number 94 had no outside lights or CCTV during his walk earlier in the day. Now working in the dark, he was in the car and driving it down the Ballymurphy Road with Jimmy in the transit covering his back within five minutes. They drove out of the estate and, taking the main roads, parked the car safely in a lock-up garage on the Andersonstown Estate. Both men were home safely in their own beds before 3 a.m.

The next day, Thursday afternoon, Walsh, and Bailey returned to the garage. They had picked up a set of number plates which would refer to another red Vauxhall Vectra – one that hadn't been stolen. They switched the plates on the car they'd taken from 94 Ballymurphy Road. Anyone checking out the registration would find that the car was clean. Both men cleaned the Vectra, making sure they'd left nothing that would identify them. Everything was set for Friday morning when an old lady might have a last day on earth. They locked up the garage and took the transit for a drive round the estate checking for any security forces surveillance teams; they saw nothing.

'Well, that's that sorted for tomorrow, Jimmy. Let's call it a day and get a bite of lunch.'

'Sounds good to me. I'm starving. You are paying?'

'You can fuck off. I paid last time.'

'Worth a try.' Jimmy laughed.

Chapter 11

Sandy Row, Belfast

Frank Walsh had driven round twice before he could find a space facing the right direction from the café. It was 10:50 and if everything went according to plan, the old woman would be coming out of the café soon. Walsh still didn't feel comfortable about having to knock down the old woman. Shooting at soldiers or police or blowing them up with booby traps was a totally different story, but trying to kill an old woman just didn't seem right. But an order was an order, and the order had come from the top man in Belfast. He just had to keep thinking to himself that it was justified. Bringing a traitor to justice was enough to satisfy his worry. He had been careful to look for any traffic wardens. Belfast City Hall loved the money that they brought in with their tickets. He knew the way they operated, checking the parking spaces over the lunchtime period when people were desperate to find somewhere to park while nipping in for sandwiches or lunch. And of course, it was one of those bloody wet Belfast days. The rain couldn't make up its mind whether to come down hard and fast or slow and steady. At least this might keep the traffic wardens away. He had seen none and now that he was parked up; he had a good view of the doorway of the café. The traffic was light, but he had to be sure of the distance he'd have to cover. He knew where she'd cross the road would be slippery. It would be difficult to keep control of the car when he hit her, he didn't want to end up crashing into another car and stuck in the road, with police, and emergency services coming down on him. It had to be quick and clean to get away safely. He had left Jimmy, who was parked up with the transit van, on the waste ground where he'd go afterwards. When he last spoke with Jimmy, he'd told him he'd hit the old woman at leg level so that she'd bounce off the bonnet and roll onto the road. *This way*, he thought, *there was a chance that she'd only end up seriously injured in hospital*. He still didn't feel good about knocking her down.

'Two. Can you hear me OK? This is one?' Frank spoke into the walkie-talkie.

'Loud and clear,' replied Jimmy.

'She'll be coming out any minute now. How's things your end?'

'All quiet. All good here.'

Both men knew that despite the walkie-talkies being end-to-end, there was still a possibility that they could be picked up, either by radio scanners, or by the security forces, so the less said the better.

'Good, see you soon,' said Frank.

Because of the rain, he had to keep using the wipers now and then, switching them on for their sweep to give him a clear view of the front door of the café. He also kept the air blowing on the windscreen as his own breath was steaming it up. Maybe because of the cold and the rain, she was running slightly late today. It was almost 11.05 when he saw her come out the door of the café. He put the car into first gear, keeping his foot on the clutch and moving up the revs slowly. He checked his mirrors, and he could see that there was nothing behind him. He watched her walk between two cars, looking left and right for traffic. He released the clutch and the handbrake to move the car out onto the road just as she started to cross. He accelerated, dropping down into second, and was almost in third gear when he hit her. She'd been looking in the opposite direction and was just turning her head enough to see him come, but not enough for her to get out of the way. Frank had steered the car to hit her dead centre on the bonnet. When he heard the thud as the car crashed into her body, he realised his calculations about her size had been wrong. It had happened so quickly. She 'had no time to react or even to scream or cry out. The impact, instead of hitting her legs, had hit her at waist level. The result of this was that she was swallowed up under the car and he could feel it rise and fall as it rolled over her body at speed. As he expected, because he had to accelerate to hit her, when he tried to brake slowly the car started to slide, but years of stealing, and driving cars at speed paid off. He was able to bring the car under control within 10 feet of where the old woman now lay crumpled behind him. In the rear-view mirror he could see her body lying still, smashed and broken, like the walking stick beside her. He could hear people starting to scream as they saw what had happened. It was time to get out of there. Putting the car into gear, he accelerated away towards the lower falls and the waste ground where Jimmy would be waiting. It had only taken a matter of seconds. Frank could see it all in his mind in slow motion: the surprise and fear in her eyes, the rain on the windscreen and her body smashed on the road. He concentrated on keeping his speed down, even though he knew the car would be damaged at the front, mechanically it was still moving to his commands. Within five minutes, he'd reached the waste ground where Jimmy was waiting. Taking the walkie-talkie and the 9mm Browning with him, Frank helped Jimmy pour petrol over the car, then set it alight. Leaving the blazing car behind they drove in the transit to a safe house in the Beechmount area where they changed into a fresh set of clothes. They handed over the boiler suits they'd worn to the lady who owned the house, so that she could put them through the washing machine. She also took the guns and the walkie-talkies which were to be taken away and hidden by a young, trusted teenager later. After they'd parked the transit van a short distance away, both men then walked through the Beechmount estate to the Wolf Tone Social Club where Brian McNally was waiting for them. McNally ordered three pints of Guinness and led the two men to a corner table to sit away from prying eyes and listening ears. The two men briefed him on what they considered to be a successful operation. When he'd heard everything, McNally told the two men to wait, while he went outside to a nearby phone box and once more dialled the number in the Republic.

When the man with the familiar southern accent answered McNally replied, 'Stage one successfully completed.'

'Good, I'll be up tomorrow,' replied John Jo Murphy, ending the call.

McNally returned to the social club and sat with the two men again.

'That stage is finished, boys. I think you deserve another couple of pints, but not too many as we're going to be busy over the next couple of days.' Both men smiled while emptying the glasses in front of them.

Chapter 12

MI6 Vauxhall Cross, London

It was very rare for Jim Broad to receive a call late on a Friday afternoon. Broad was in his office at London airport. The office was a front for SG9 the special Black Ops team that worked under his command. When he'd answered his phone, it was the familiar voice of Sir Ian Fraser's secretary.

'Can you please come to the office as soon as possible?' she'd said in her clear and perfect English accent. Nothing more, nothing less.

Forty-five minutes later, he was sitting in the office of the director general of MI6, looking out at the grey clouds over the Thames River and London. The rain that had been washing the streets of Belfast had yet to reach the streets of London. Broad knew that the clouds were indicating the rain was on its way. It always amazed Broad how the desk of the top intelligence officer in Britain always seemed so tidy in comparison to his own, which always seemed to be a maze of paperwork. The door to the office opened and Sir Ian Fraser and his secretary entered. The secretary was carrying a tray with a pot of coffee, sugar, milk, and three cups, which she set on the conference table. Then, to Broad's surprise, Caroline Aspinall the head of MI5 the British Security Service, entered the office. MI5 looked after the intelligence-gathering in the UK while MI6 operated overseas, so the fact that the head of MI5 was here worried Broad. The secretary left them to it, closing the door behind her.

'Sorry to spoil your Friday evening, Jim,' said Sir Ian, as he indicated for him to come and join him and Aspinall at the conference table. Caroline Aspinall started to pour the coffee, leaving the milk, and sugar for the men to serve themselves.

'I need this,' she said. 'It's been one of those days. I hate it when something comes in this late on a Friday.'

'No problem, boss. I was only going out for a show and dinner this evening, nothing important.' Broad smiled. 'So, what's it all about?'

'Something's come up that needs all our input and especially yours as it involves David Reece.'

Broad wasn't sure if he was happy hearing Reece's name in this room once more.

'What's he done this time? You do remember he retired. We can't use him anymore.'

'Caroline and I have been meeting with Sir Martin Bryant, chairman of the joint intelligence committee, and the prime minister this afternoon.'

These words didn't make Broad feel any happier. He waited to hear more.

'Earlier this afternoon, I received a call from Tom Wilson in Belfast. He tells me that the mother of Mary McAuley has been seriously injured in what would appear to be a deliberate attempt to kill her.'

Broad knew that Tom Wilson was the Assistant Chief Constable in the PSNI, the Police Service of Northern Ireland and that Wilson was the head of C3, which in David's Reece's day was the old RUC Special Branch. He also knew that Wilson and Reece were old friends.

'According to the reports Tom Wilson got from his people on the ground, McAuley's mother was knocked down by a car as she crossed a main road in Belfast. The car, which had been stolen, and had false plates, failed to stop, and was subsequently found burnt out on nearby waste ground. They are currently chasing up witness statements and carrying out an examination of the scene where she was knocked down and where the car was burnt out. Wilson tells me his people are not happy. They believe that this was made to look like an everyday accident caused by a joyriding car thief. We saw plenty of those in our day when we were in Belfast Jim. Witnesses at the scene reported that the driver deliberately aimed the car at McAuley's mother, so they're viewing this as attempted murder. Now, the reason he's kept us informed about this is because he obviously knows that Mary McAuley was once an agent working for Special Branch and David Reece. After I spoke with Tom Wilson, I asked him to keep us up to date. I also contacted Sir Martin Bryant, who informed the prime minister, as both are very aware of what David Reece has done for this country and your department. They are both aware of his links to Mary McAuley and through her to her mother. As this incident happened in Northern Ireland, a part of the United Kingdom, it was also thought that we should involve Caroline here and her MI5 teams in Belfast. The investigation, as I say, is still ongoing, and for the moment we don't have the full picture, but from what we know of Mary McAuley's background we can assume that this incident is aimed at her in some way and maybe even through her to David Reece.'

'Why, after all this time, and now that the peace process is in place would they do something like this?' asked Broad.

'That's the thing, Jim. From our people on the ground using our technical means and our human sources we don't think it's anything to do with the peace process or the Provisional Movement,' said Caroline Aspinall. 'Rather, we think it might be something to do with one of the breakaway faction groups such as the Real IRA or the Continuity IRA. Of course, we've sources in those groups as well and we are waiting for any feedback on why this happened. For now, we can only assume it was to get back at Mary McAuley's past. As Sir Ian says, we'll pass any information we get onto Tom Wilson and his team and, of course, to the prime minister's office and to here.'

'Have we anything at all which shows us who's done this?' asked Broad.

Fraser stood, and holding his cup, and saucer walked towards the large bay windows that looked out over London. With his back to the room, he answered Broad's question.

'Everything we've told you so far is all that we have. It's too early in the investigation to know exactly what happened and enquiries are ongoing.'

'What do we do in the meantime?' asked Broad.

Fraser returned to the conference table.

'The only thing we can do, Jim, is wait for more information. But in the meantime, we need to tell Reece and McAuley what happened. This is where you come in. You know Reece better than anyone, and you know his connections to Mary McAuley. I believe, as do the prime minister and Sir Martin Bryant, that you're in the best position to contact Reece and McAuley and speak to them directly. We'll be in a better position once we know what they want to do. If it was my mother, I'd want to be by her side as soon as possible. Can we leave it to you to contact Reece and McAuley and get back to me? In the meantime, Caroline and I have agreed to work together through the six and five teams. For now, the prime minister wants us to treat this as just another family matter, but at the same time, he wants us to keep an eye on things, bearing in mind the background of both these people, and especially David Reece. The British government does not want anything that would endanger the peace process, and this is where I want you to emphasise this to Reece, especially. Is that OK Jim? Do you understand what I'm asking?'

Broad always worried when he heard that the grey suits of politics wanted him to do something. He could feel the anger inside him rising, but he understood that at the end of the day, the politicians, and especially the prime minister, were his masters.

'Do we know how serious the injuries are to McAuley's mother?' asked Broad.

'According to Tom Wilson she's critically ill and on a life-support machine at Belfast City Hospital,' replied Fraser. 'So, you can tell Reece everything you know, or should I say everything we know, for now?'

'Are we going to give them any assistance? Any of our people or any of our equipment?' asked Broad.

'As I said Jim, the PM wants us to treat this as just another domestic incident, a joyriding hit-and-run. He doesn't want any attention brought to the peace process and accordingly the only assistance we'll give to David Reece and Mary McAuley is a sympathetic one. You can help them get to Belfast and arrange accommodation for them if necessary. But for now, we try to stay out of this. It's a personal family matter for McAuley and her mother.'

The more Jim Broad had heard, the more uneasy he felt. The politicians didn't want to get their hands dirty, but at the same time they wanted them to keep an eye on Reece and McAuley. What the bad guys did came second to anything else.

'I think I understand what you're saying,' said Broad, as he stood to leave.

'I'll head back to my office, so any more information you both have please pass on to me. I'll contact Tom Wilson to let him know that I'm going to call Reece and McAuley. But you know David Reece as well as I do. He won't stop until he finds out who's behind this and once he does, God help them.'

When Broad left, Caroline Aspinall poured herself another cup of coffee. 'You and I both know that Jim Broad is right. God knows what Reece will do if these people get in his face. Once we know they're heading to Northern Ireland, I'll give my teams the heads up to keep an eye on them.'

'Each one of us needs to keep the other in the loop, or this could get out of control very quickly. When Broad gets back to me, I'll update Bryant and the PM, and you can have a word with Wilson,' answered Fraser.

The rain Broad had known was coming was now battering the windows of the office. Looking out at the dark clouds, Sir Ian Fraser wondered how bad this day would be.

Chapter 13

Malta

The weather in Malta, compared to Belfast, and London, had been balmy. Today it had been sunny and warm.

At the Villa Joseph in Quawra, Reece, and Mary were in the middle of dinner. They had been enjoying a good day, having been to Valletta to pick up the ring. Then a nice glass of champagne in the midday sun overlooking the grand harbour of Valletta, before returning to the villa to make love and relax. Mary was already planning to call her mother later and tell her the good news of their engagement. Then they'd to book the flights and a visit to Belfast the following week. Mary cooked the dinner which didn't need much cooking as it consisted of fresh tomato and green salad with plenty of the island's delicious king prawns and the Maltese bread Reece loved so much. Reece had picked the wine, a crisp white local Green Label which they both liked. Mary couldn't hide her excitement. She kept talking about looking forward to introducing Reece to her mother and to showing her the ring. She was convinced her mother would be happy for her, knowing the problem she had in the past with her previous husband who was now languishing in jail for an armed robbery. Leaving the place he was robbing, he ran into the arms of a waiting police patrol that Reece had put in place, ready for him. Mary divorced Brendan McAuley when he was in prison. His favourite pastime had been to take out his temper on Mary, which on one occasion had led to Reece stepping in. He had stopped Brendan using his fists on Mary when the couple were on a night out in Newry town. On that occasion Brendan had found himself lined up against a man rather than a woman, a man whose fists were quicker than his, and who laid him on his back staring at the stars. Mary's mother had never liked Brendan McAuley. She'd seen the bruises far too often on her daughter's face and prayed for the day when she'd left him. But Mary, like her mother, had been raised a Catholic, which meant she tried to hold on to her marriage vows. When Mary had met Reece and had decided she'd enough of violent men, she started by working for Reece against the tyranny she saw around her. The feeling for her Special Branch man would change from working against all she'd known to trust, and eventually love.

As they were finishing their meal Mary had brought a notebook to the table and started writing down her plans, from calling her mother later to planning their trip to Northern Ireland, and what she needed to bring and pack. Reece took another sip of the local wine as he watched her, the pen in her hand working fast across the paper. He didn't know how many times he'd told this woman that he loved her. Sometimes he wondered if he'd loved her from the very start, from that first day, when he saw her while carrying out surveillance of IRA targets in Newry town. Watching her now, he knew how excited she was and how much his commitment to her meant.

'You're going to have to watch, or you'll set that paper on fire.' He laughed.

'There's so much to do, so much to remember. I must write it all down or I'll forget,' she replied.

'Don't worry, I'll go over everything with you afterwards, then we can get the flights booked for next week. I think we should stay in a hotel to make the whole thing more enjoyable. Make it more like a special occasion, which it is,' said Reece.

Before he could say any more, his phone on the coffee table started to buzz.

'I wonder, is that your mother? I always said she knew before anyone, so she'd know what's happening without you telling her.' He laughed.

But when he picked up the phone the smile on his face disappeared when he recognised the call was from his ex-SG9 boss Jim Broad. Mary watched the change in Reece's face and stopped writing her notes.

'Hello, boss, how are you?'

'I'm fine, David,' said Broad, getting straight to the point. 'I'm sorry, but I had to call you to let you know that Mary's mother is in hosp—.'

'She's in hospital?' interrupted Reece. 'Why? What's happened?' He held up his hand as Mary stood up.

'It would appear she was knocked down by a hit-and-run driver while crossing the road in Belfast.'

'How is she? Is she OK?'

Broad seemed to take an age to answer. 'She's in the City Hospital in Belfast. She's critically ill and on a life-support machine. All the information I have has come from Tom Wilson. It happened this morning, and he asked me to call you and Mary to let you know. David, I'm sorry. Tell Mary I'm here for you both if you need anything.'

Reece looked at Mary and beckoned her towards him and put his arm round her shoulder.

'Your mother's been hurt in an accident and she's in the hospital.'

The tears started to fall down Mary's cheek. Reece went back to the call.

'Thank you for letting us know, boss. We'll obviously have to travel to Belfast as soon as possible. Did they catch the person who did it?'

'Not yet, as far as I know. Tom Wilson will be able to tell you more when you get there. Do you need any help with the flights or accommodation?'

'No, thank you. We can take care of things from here. Thank you for letting us know.'

'No problem. Remember, David, I'm here for you if you need me.'

'Thank you,' replied Reece, ending the call.

'What happened? What happened to my mother?'

'She's had a bad accident. The boss said she's been knocked down by a hit-and-run driver in Belfast. He said she's critically ill and in the City Hospital.'

A strange sound came from Mary's mouth, like a cat crying. The tears were still coming, and Reece held her close.

'But why? Why?'

'We're going to find out, Mary. First thing we do is call the hospital to ask how she is. The next thing we do is book flights to Belfast in the morning. When we get there, I'm going to pay a visit to Tom Wilson. His teams will know what's going on. But your mother and her recovery are the most important thing for you now, so let's make those calls and get things moving.'

Mary took a deep breath. Pressing her hanky against her eyes, she dabbed the tears from her cheeks. She always looked at David in a crisis. Over the years, she knew the calmness in this man and the clarity of his thinking in a bad situation.

'I still have the hospital's number on my phone from when my mum was there for her hip operation. I'll give them a call now.'

'You do that, and I'll get on to the airport and book some tickets for the morning.'

Mary went into the bedroom to make her call, leaving Reece to call the airport. When Mary came back out, her face was showing pain and concern at the same time.

'My mum is on a life-support machine. They say she has a fractured skull and some internal bleeding, and they're going to operate later tonight. Oh my God, David, she might die! What am I going to do? What if she dies, David? What am I going to do?'

Reece held her. Brushing his hand through her hair, he kissed her on the forehead.

'I'm sure they're doing the best they can. I know if she's anything like her daughter, then she's a strong woman. I've had to book two flights for tomorrow. The earliest plane goes to Liverpool, then Liverpool to Belfast. We will be there before lunchtime. I also booked us into the Hilton Hotel in the city.'

'We don't need the hotel, David. I have my house on the Lisburn Road where Mum was staying. We can stay there. It'll save us the money.'

'No, it's on the wrong side of the city to the police headquarters at Knock, and it will save us time when I meet with Wilson. I can meet him on my own after we see your mother in the hospital in case you need to stay. Until we know more about what exactly happened, I think we should stay away from your house.'

'Why do you think someone did this deliberately?'

'I don't know. Until we do, we take precautions. I still don't trust the bastards over there. For now, let's pack a couple of small bags and try to get some sleep. I think it's going to be a busy couple of days and your mother needs us to be strong for her.'

'I don't know about you, but for now I need a strong drink. Where's your bottle of Bushmills?'

Reece produced the bottle from the drinks cabinet and poured a generous measure of the Irish whisky into two glasses.

'Maybe you're right. It can only help us sleep later.'

They took the Bushmills out onto the patio and sat looking at the stars. As he sipped the familiar flavour, his thoughts were of Belfast, a city he loved, and hated in equal measure. He had been born there, worked there, and loved there. But on many occasions, he'd almost died there. To Reece, Belfast was now a place to visit, to have a drink, and get out, to leave behind, only returning when he had a reason to do so. He knew Jim Broad, and his gut feeling was that he'd only given him the basic facts and not the full story. He was sure there was more to it than a simple hit-and-run. For Mary's sake, her mother's, and his own, he was going to find out what really happened.

The next morning, Reece, and Mary took the first available flight to Liverpool, then a flight that got them into Belfast just before lunchtime. Reece had paid for the flights with his own credit card, as he didn't want to take Jim Broad up on his offer of help unless he really needed to. From experience, Reece knew that people like Broad always preferred to be in control of the situation and for now, Reece needed to be in control. It seemed like Mary hadn't stopped crying, the silent tears always on her cheek. All night she'd lain close to him as he stroked her hair. On the journey to Belfast, he found he had to constantly reassure her that her mother would be well, even though he knew within himself there was a danger that she wouldn't recover from her injuries.

At the Aldergrove International Airport outside Belfast, Reece hired a black BMW saloon car from the Hertz car hire desk. He drove directly to the City Hospital between the Donegal and Lisburn roads in Belfast. Getting there just after lunch, he found the car parks busy. It took some time to find a parking space. After a short conversation with the receptionist, they were directed to the third floor of the hospital and the surgical ward for critically ill patients. At the nursing station, the senior nurse directed them to the private side ward and Mary's mother. Reece hated hospitals. The smell the constant noise always reminded him of his own visits and the pain from when he had bullet fragments removed from his shoulder after being shot by Sean Costello. Some were still embedded there to remind him now and then. Then the leg wound he was still recovering from the shrapnel from the bomb that had killed Rachel Cohen. Reece was expecting the kind of scene that he knew would scare Mary. The woman in the bed was looking old and frail, with dark purple bruising showing up on her forehead and cheek. She was hooked up to several machines, one of them helping her to breathe, another monitoring her statistics. There was a drip fed into her right arm. Mary had stopped crying but was taking short, deep breaths as she held her mother's hand. The nurse that was caring for her mother told them that even though her mother was in a coma, they should only speak positively around the bed, as sometimes it was believed the patient could hear exactly what was being said. She reported that her mother had come through a long operation to stop internal bleeding affecting her spleen, which had been removed. The nurse tried to be reassuring, telling Mary they were doing everything they could for her mother. All they could do now was monitor her in the hope that she'd make a full recovery, but it would take time. Mary spoke to her mother to let her know that she was there. For some reason she also told her about her engagement and of her new ring. Reece felt it was her way of letting her mother know that she now had a reason to get well. Reece hated hospitals, and he was sure most sane people felt the same. Anytime he'd ever been in one he'd been in pain, and he knew it was the business of hospitals to deal with the sick and the dying. He stayed by the bedside with Mary for an hour, but he sensed she wanted to stay longer.

'Why don't you stay with your mother a little longer? I can go and book us into the hotel and call on Tom Wilson at the police headquarters. He may have more information on what happened. Are you OK with that? Do you want me to get you anything before I go?'

For the first time in the last 24 hours, he saw a smile cross the lips of the woman he loved.

'Yes, you do that. I'm OK for the minute. If I need anything, I'm sure she's in good hands here. So, I could nip to the toilet or the canteen if I need to.'

Reece kissed her on the cheek. 'If you need anything, give me a call. I'll try not to be too long.'

By the time Reece booked into the Hilton hotel and drove across the city to the PSNI headquarters on the Knock Road in East Belfast, it was late afternoon. He had phoned ahead to make sure Wilson was there and to let him know he was coming. Feeling hungry, he stopped on the way to grab a burger in a McDonald's.

The badge at the entrance to the PSNI headquarters was different from the one he'd served under when it was the RUC Harp and Crown. The word had obviously been sent down from the top floor of the building that he was expected.

With a cursory glance at his driving licence by the guard on the entrance gate, Reece was directed to the visitors' car park and told to report to the reception desk on the ground floor of the building that covered most of the three-acre site that was now the police Headquarters for Northern Ireland. As Reece walked towards the main building, he could see the RUC George Cross Gardens of Remembrance. He had visited the site not long after it had been created. He remembered the water that poured like a small stream down the middle of the site which was surrounded by black marble slates engraved with the names of the police officers who had lost their lives serving the people of Northern Ireland. Many of the names he knew personally. Men and women who he'd worked with and lived with through terrible times.

The Portacabins that had contained the operation rooms of the special surveillance teams operating out of there during the war against the IRA and other terrorist groups had been replaced by a new state-of-the-art complex.

He walked up the short drive and through the front doors of the main headquarters building. It was as he remembered it. Three floors high. It was fit for purpose. To the left, as he entered the lobby, were the offices of the chief constable. To his right there was a glass cabinet containing a large book which was opened each day to a different page which contained the names of officers killed on that date.

At a reception desk on the ground floor, a young policewoman was on the phone. Putting down the phone, she looked up at Reece. 'Mister Reece, ACC Wilson is expecting you. He will be down in just a moment if you'd like to wait,' she said, pointing to the chair beside the Book of Remembrance Cabinet.

The headquarters building hadn't changed much from the days when Reece had worked there during the last ten years of his police service. The building itself looked like an old-fashioned secondary school from the outside. Reece had walked every corridor of this building during those years. Especially the third floor, which had been the operational floor for Special Branch. The floor contained not only the operational offices but also a vast registry of files and documents showing the terrorist and criminal threats to the country of Northern Ireland. Some documents stored were stored before the country came into existence in 1922, after the War of Independence. The country of Ireland had been split into the six counties of Northern Ireland, and the twenty-six counties of the Irish Free State, which was now known as the Irish Republic, or the Republic of Ireland. Reece saw Tom Wilson coming down the stairs. He was wearing a dark uniform with the insignia of the PSNI showing the rank of Assistant Chief Constable. Reece had to admit that the tall silver haired Ulster man looked fit and healthy. His slim body carried no excess weight, and Reece thought he was either a runner or a gym visitor, or both.

'You're looking well, Tom. The rank seems to sit well with you.'

'Thank you. From what I heard about your last operation in London, you're looking better than I thought you would.' Wilson had the same sharp blue eyes and spoke with the same mid-Ulster accent as Reece.

'I might look good on the outside, but you should see on the inside.' Reece laughed.

'Come, let's go to my office and have a chat.'

Reece followed up the familiar staircase to the third floor.

They still don't have a bloody lift in this building, he thought.

Walking down the long corridor that led through the double doors from the third landing, Reece could see that nothing much had changed. The office doors on the left and right were still there, still the same, but with different names indicating the new occupants. Halfway down the corridor was a door on the left with the sign ACC C3. Reece followed Wilson into the office, which was small with a desk, two filing cabinets, and three chairs. Wilson took the chair at the desk that faced the door. The large window behind Wilson reminded Reece of the operational office he'd worked in a few doors down. That office had two of these large windows looking out onto the same lawn below. He could remember how the windows increased the heat from the summer sun. So much so that they used to grow tomatoes on a pot on the windowsill. Sitting in one of the two chairs facing Wilson was a woman. Reece sat in the chair beside her.

'Would you like anything to drink, David?' asked Wilson.

'No, thank you.'

'David, let me introduce you. This is Detective Chief Inspector Heather Black. She heads up one of my teams in the city. I've asked her to investigate the circumstances of what happened to Mrs Smith. Heather, this is David Reece. An old friend and colleague. We worked together for many years. I don't think there's anything you can teach him about the business we work in.'

'Pleased to meet you, David. I've heard quite a lot about you.'

The woman had short blonde hair and dark-brown eyes. She was slim and dressed in a brown tweed jacket the buttons open showing a blue blouse underneath. What surprised Reece was that someone of her rank was now sitting in the office of her boss wearing tight-fitting blue jeans and white trainers. To Reece, this indicated this woman didn't care about what others thought. They had to take her as she was, whether they liked it, or not. The clothes could also indicate she was hands-on surveillance, ready to work with her teams. All this was a positive for Reece. *Then again*, Reece thought, *maybe I'm just a bit old-fashioned.*

'Pleased to meet you too, Chief Inspector.' Reece nodded to her.

'Before we start, I want you to know we're here for you. Anything that you need, just ask,' said Wilson.

'Thank you. We only want to know what happened. Mary is at the City Hospital with her mother, who is critically ill in a coma and on a life-support machine.'

'Understood. Heather, what have we got?' asked Wilson.

DCI Black turned her body to face Reece, her eyes looking straight at him.

'First, David. Can I call you David?'

'Yes, of course.'

'As the boss says, I know a bit of your background, so you'll understand something of the resources that we've been putting in place to try to get to the bottom of this. Our enquiries so far show that what happened to Mrs Smith was not a simple case of a joyriding hit-and-run. We have interviewed people at the scene, and looked at CCTV, but we haven't been able to identify the driver. The fact that the car was burnt out on waste ground not far from the incident may indicate that the driver had a back-up vehicle or someone waiting for them to assist a getaway. Any self-respecting joyriding car thief would simply drive the car as far away as possible, but somewhere near where they lived, or could hide, before abandoning the car, and leaving on foot. This has all the hallmarks of a planned and deliberate attempt to either seriously injure or kill Mrs Smith. Now, because we are looking at this as attempted murder it gives us the power to use all our resources to get to the bottom who is involved. At any other time we'd be baffled as to the reason why, but on this occasion, with the fact that she's the mother of Mary McAuley, previously your agent, code name Mike, we must consider that may be a reason for this incident. You will understand it's still early days in this investigation. Apart from the interviewing of witnesses and looking at the CCTV, we are in contact with our intelligence sources who are looking for any more information as to who may be involved. Photos from the CCTV don't give us much, only what appears to be a male driver wearing a baseball cap.'

She gave a grainy picture of the suspect to Reece. The DCI stopped giving an update. Then, looking at Wilson, she nodded.

From experience, Reece knew how the investigation would be running. He also knew because of who Mary was, it would be receiving a lot of attention from those in higher authority.

'Thank you, Tom. Thank you, Chief Inspector. Like you, I'm suspicious about what has happened. No offence to you both, but these days I don't like to come back to this country in any circumstances, never mind one that seems to be aimed at Mary and possibly myself.'

'I understand you, David, and I would like to talk to you about that. For now, do you have any questions for Heather? Otherwise, I think she should get on with things.'

'No. No questions. Obviously, if you get any more information, Chief Inspector, you'll let me know,' said Reece.

'In that case, I'll let the Chief Inspector get on with her work. If you get anything more, let me know right away, Heather, and I'll pass it on to David.'

'Of course, sir,' said the DCI, standing to leave. 'I hope Mrs Smith recovers. It was good to meet you, David.'

'Thank you, Chief Inspector,' said Reece. 'It's good to meet you too.'

After she'd left, Reece had a feeling that Tom Wilson had more to say, and what he had to say was not for the ears of his Chief Inspector.

'OK, Tom. What do you want to talk about?'

'Are you sure you don't want something to drink?'

'No. I'm OK, thanks.'

'David, I've some idea of how you and Mary may be feeling about this whole thing. But you must remember that my job as head of the PSNI intelligence-gathering operations is to find out if this is connected in any way to one of the terrorist groups in the country. Unfortunately, it's looking very much like that's the case. I can assure you we're leaving no stone unturned to find out who did this. I've been contacted by Jim Broad who has asked me not only to investigate and find out who has done this, but to watch over you as well.'

'Watch over me? You mean keep me on a leash? I don't care who gets these bastards. What I need to do is to keep Mary and her mother safe. Hopefully, you can do that, but if you can't I won't stand by and let them hurt the people I love. I saw too much of that during the war, when these bastards got away with doing things like this because the politicians were too afraid to take them on.'

Wilson leant across his desk to make sure Reece heard every word.

'I'm your friend. I know exactly what you're talking about, and I went through that war with you. As a courtesy, it's my job to let you know that I'll investigate this and catch these bastards, as you call them, and I'll do everything in my power to protect not only Mary and her mother but you as well. That's my job. Not only as the head of police intelligence, but as a police officer. I know the skills that you have, and I understand that if we need to protect you, then you have the skill to protect yourself as well. I hope things don't come to that, because in that instance I might have to be the policeman and not your friend. Jim Broad is obviously concerned that you and Mary are at risk. Ideally, he doesn't want you to be here, but he understands why. As for the politicians, they're only interested in keeping the peace, and I know that as far as the Provisional Movement is concerned, they want to keep that peace as well, and anything that would put that at risk needs to be nipped in the bud. I can tell you, it's for that reason and from the intelligence that I'm already getting from our sources, both human, and technical, that the Provos are not involved in this. As you're no longer working for Jim Broad, you'll understand that just telling you this bit of information is breaking the official secrets act. But hopefully you'll take this as a sign of our continued friendship and trust. I think it also shows you that this is a priority for me to get whoever did this quickly, and that you're all safe.'

'Have your people been able to find out the reason why this happened?' asked Reece.

'No, not yet. Like you, we can only speculate at this time that's something personal against you, but more likely, Mary. We must assume that whoever it is might know that Mary has worked for us in the past. They may even know she was your agent and who you are. By assuming this, we should expect the worst. That this was the reason they tried to kill Mrs Smith, either because she's Mary's mother and they wanted to hurt her, and through her you. Or they're planning something worse, maybe the capturing of Mary, maybe even you yourself. That's why am telling you to be careful, David. We don't have the full picture yet and we don't know who is involved in this, but we'll find out. Where will you be staying while you're here?'

'I've booked us both into the Hilton hotel and hired a car. Mary wanted to stay at her own house where her mother lives on the Lisburn Road, but I thought it would be safer staying in a hotel until we find out what this is all about. For the next few days, I don't see us doing much more than travelling back and forward to the hospital. You have my number, so anything at all, let me know.'

'Will do, David. In the meantime, I'll have extra police patrols cover the hospital grounds and the area of the hotel. Leave me the registration of the hire car so they'll know it's you. It was good to see you again. I'm sorry it was under these circumstances. As Heather said: I hope Mary's mother recovers and gets well soon. Maybe then we can all have dinner together.'

'That would be nice, but by the look of the injuries Mary's mother has, that might be some way down the road. We just got engaged, and we were about to tell her mother when all this happened, so hopefully she has something to live for now.'

'You old dog, congratulations! In the circumstances, I hope everything goes well. You should get back to the hospital. But be careful, David, these people aren't finished yet, I'm sure of it. Do you have a weapon?'

'No, now that I no longer work for Jim Broad, I can't carry it out of Malta.'

Wilson opened the top drawer of his desk. He took out a box and handed it across the table to Reece.

'I thought that would be the case, so this is for you, but be bloody careful, David. Only use it if you really need to. I could be crucified just for giving it to you.'

Reece opened the small box. He removed the contents, a Walther 9mm PPK pistol, a box of thirty rounds of the same calibre, two magazines, and a holster that would fit snugly onto his belt. Wilson watched as Reece lifted the gun and handled it, turning it from side-to-side Reece pulled back the slide to make sure the gun was empty.

'Are you sure about this, Tom? Are you not taking a risk?'

'I would rather there were some dead bad guys lying in the street than you or Mary.'

Reece lifted a magazine and opened the box of ammo, then removed seven rounds. His hands moved easily as his thumb pressed down on each round, pushing seven in total into the magazine. He pushed the magazine flush into the base of the handle. he slashed the slide once more to allow the top round to pass into the chamber. The Walther PPK was the first gun Reece had been trained in when he'd joined the RUC. It was a compact small gun, easily concealed, and packed a hell of a punch. Although Reece was a marksman with a pistol, he'd always remembered to be careful when firing the Walther as a novice. The slide was inclined to cut a small nick in the fleshy part of the hand holding the gun if you held it loosely. Reece knew that if he held it with a strong grip and pointed low at his target when he pulled the trigger, the front of the gun would rise slightly. This helped to hit the target square in the middle, just where he wanted.

'I appreciate you taking this risk, Tom, but what if I'm stopped while carrying it?'

Wilson reached into the drawer once more. This time, he withdrew a small, laminated card and passed it across the desk to Reece. Reece read: *Certificate to Carry* in one corner, and the crest of the PSNI in the other. Below this were the words, *Authorised to carry a firearm*. At the bottom of the card was a scrawled signature and in print beside it, *Chief Constable*.

'As you can see that card is signed by the chief constable. It's a new thing, mainly because 'we have so many visitors who've worked here before and now want to visit places of interest. This way, we don't have to give them twenty-four-hour protection. We've never had someone use one so far, and they've always been returned, so don't use it unless you really need to.'

Reece stood and slipped the holster onto his belt before inserting the Walther into it. He then loaded the second magazine with seven rounds, then put it with the box containing the rest of the ammunition into his jacket pocket. Reece felt a trust had been placed in him.

'Tell me something Tom, in all your days on the job have you ever heard talk of a high-ranking officer in Special Branch who may have been working with the Provos, most likely in the Newry and South Armagh area?'

Wilson sat back in his chair once more and took a few seconds before he answered.

'There were always rumours, but nothing concrete. Sometimes we found it was just bad feeling between two senior officers. Jealousy and lies can be spread easily. You know the game we were in, David. Lies and treachery were all part of it. The only people we could truly trust were ourselves. I heard some of those rumours, but as I say, nothing concrete, no definite names. Why do you ask? Have you heard something?'

'Because of your trust in me, Tom. I have something to tell you. What I'm going to say must be between you and me. No one else must know for now, understood?'

Wilson nodded.

'You are aware of some of the operations I've been involved in with MI6. These operations have brought me into close contact with Mossad officers both active and retired. One of these retired officers recently told me that during the Troubles he was in contact with the RUC as a liaison officer for Mossad. When he was in Ireland, he was briefed by his opposite number in the Israeli Embassy in Dublin. This Mossad officer was running an agent in the South Armagh, Dundalk Provos. This agent had given them information to say that a senior RUC Special Branch Officer, he thought, with the rank of DCI, was working with the Provos. This officer had tipped off the Provos when we had covert operations working in South Armagh and Newry. In this way, the Provos were able to avoid capture by either cancelling or abandoning their operations. The Israeli officer was able to say that as far as they knew, no police or army lives were lost because of the information that was supplied to the Provos. The reason my contact told me this was to make me aware of an extra risk when I visited this country. I don't know who the rogue guy is or whether he's still in the police or retains connections to the security services.

'I'm telling you this because of what you've done for me here today, to protect you as much as you want to protect me. If this guy is still in the mix, he could be a danger to both of us. We share the same past. We both worked at times in the same areas on covert operations and running agents, so this guy would have been around at the same time. Because of what has brought me here, I thought that you should be aware of it. Any information about who this man is will be important to us both. That's all I know for the present. But I'm just a little concerned about who is involved in this hit-and-run, and if, as is expected, his target is Mary, and me, all we'd need is a policeman from our past interfering in the present.'

'If I hear anything, I'll let you know right away. In the meantime, you get back to Mary and her mother. I think Mary will need you now more than ever.'

When Reece left the office Wilson made two phone calls. The first one to DCI Heather Black, who was now at the Belfast TCG office running operations in the city. He told her that Reece had just left the office and gave her the registration number of the black BMW hire car he was driving. He knew that Heather Black would be in radio communication with her surveillance teams, passing on the car details for them to follow Reece. The second call he made was to Caroline Aspinall at her MI5 office in Thames House in London. He gave the details of his talk with Reece, except the part about the rogue Special Branch Officer. For the second time that day, he let her know that he understood the political pressures of not letting anything happen that could cause problems for the peace process. After finishing the call, he sat back in his chair. Knowing David Reece as he did, this could get very messy, very fast. Now Wilson would take the short walk to the ground floor to brief the chief constable, who he knew, could be more political than the politicians, always worrying about his pension and a knighthood when he retired. Just like his conversation with Aspinall he wouldn't be telling him about the rogue officer, although he'd have to tell him that Reece now had a gun and what he could do with it if he was in danger.

Chapter 14

Belfast City Hospital

Before Reece had crossed the Albert Bridge that passed over the River Lagan into the heart of the city, he'd spotted at least two of the surveillance cars following. Reece had been trained in surveillance and anti-surveillance by the best in the E4A unit of Special Branch and the MI5 watchers' team. Being trained this way had saved his life on a few occasions. He had been watching for the surveillance teams since driving out of the PSNI headquarters and then turning left down the Newtownards Road. He had expected them. If he was Tom Wilson, he'd have done the same thing and set a team on him. Reece knew that anyone following would use the four-corner box type surveillance pattern: two cars ahead, two cars behind him, and a further two cars in reserve. He had spotted one of the front two cars and one of the ones behind. He wasn't worried if they were there, it was a form of protection, so he didn't try to deviate or lose them but instead drove straight through the City Centre and on to the Lisburn Road and the City Hospital entrance where he parked up. He found Mary sitting beside her mother's bed. There didn't seem to be any more tubes or any less for that matter. Mary's tears had stopped though her face was pale. Looking up she smiled when he walked into the room.

'How is she doing?' asked Reece.

'No change, although the doctors say she's holding her own. Oh, David, I'm glad to see you, it's so quiet in here.'

'I told you she was a strong woman.'

'The doctor's just been in, and he says we won't see much change for at least twenty-four hours. She seems so peaceful…if it wasn't for the tubes and machines.'

Reece put his hand on Mary's shoulder and, bending down, kissed her on the top of her head.

'I think there's not much we can do here now. we both need to rest. Let's head to the hotel, we can come back anytime you want, and we are not far away if there's any change.'

Mary stood up and held her mother's hand for a few seconds.

'I'm not going to be far away, and I'll see you again in the morning. Love you, Mum.'

Reece put his arms around her. He could see that she was exhausted, and she needed some rest.

'We can get something to eat at the hotel and then it's a shower and some sleep for you, my girl,' said Reece.

'I won't argue with you there. Suddenly I'm famished, and very tired.'

When they left the ward they stopped at the nurse's station and Reece gave them his contact telephone number to call any time. Mary told the nurse they would be back in the morning after nine. On the drive to the hotel Reece told Mary about his conversation with Wilson. He left out the part concerning the rogue police officer. Mary wasn't happy that he was carrying a gun again.

'Do you really think we're in danger, David? If what you're saying is true, someone tried to kill my mother and through her, maybe get to me, and you. Are the surveillance teams still following us?'

'If they're as good as I think they are, then yes. That might not be a bad thing for now, at least we've some form of extra protection. I don't think Tom Wilson or Jim Broad would like anything to happen on UK soil while the politicians are breathing down their necks to protect the peace process. Try to relax if you can and for now, let's concentrate on getting your mother well again.' Reece tried to lighten the mood. 'After all, her daughter's going to get married to the most handsome man in the world. And she can come and recuperate with us in the Malta sunshine.'

'I do hope so, David. I really do.'

The surveillance that was following were getting better, they'd begun to learn his driving routine: if he would indicate or not when making a turn or go through traffic lights on orange. He only spotted one surveillance car and wasn't a hundred per cent sure on that, but he hoped they were there, anyway.

The receptionist in the City Hospital who had taken details of the car when Reece had passed on his details, and the fact that he was visiting a seriously ill patient, made a note, and placed it into her handbag before leaving work that evening. She finished work at 5 PM and the traffic was heavy as she drove up the Falls Road and parked up in the Beechmount area. She then walked the short distance to her nephew's house on

Beechmount Parade. When she knocked, the door was answered by Brian McNally.

'Hello, Aunty. Come in, come in. I've just put the kettle on.'

The woman sat in one of the two wing backed floral patterned chairs by the fireside that matched the settee opposite and waited while her nephew brewed the pot.

'Are you still off the sugar?' he shouted from the kitchen.

'Yes, I'm sweet enough, and I have my figure to think about.'

He brought a pot of tea and one cup on a tray with a small milk jug.

'You want me to pour, or you do mother yourself?' he asked.

'No, just let it settle a bit and I'll pour it myself,' she replied.

'Well, Brian, I can see you keep a tidy house even though you're on your own,' she said, looking round the room.

'I try my best. The only time it's untidy is when the Brits call to give it a search.' He laughed.

She poured herself a cup of the tea, adding the milk afterwards. Lifting the cup to her lips she blew gently on the liquid before taking a sip.

'I need this, it's been a busy day,' she said, placing the cup back in the saucer.

'I'm sure it has been. Have you anything for me?' he asked.

She lifted her handbag and after searching around inside, produced the note she'd written before leaving work. Her nephew had called to her house in Andersonstown yesterday. He had asked her to keep an eye out for an elderly patient who had been knocked down in a car accident and specifically to get details of anyone visiting the patient. The fact that her nephew knew she might have an elderly patient who had been knocked down and be on one of the wards didn't surprise her. She knew not to ask too many questions and was always willing to help when her nephew asked.

'Just as you said, an elderly lady is in intensive care after being knocked down yesterday. She's only had two visitors today: a man and a woman. I believe the woman is her daughter and the man appears to be her partner.'

'Have you any names?' he asked.

'The patient's name is Rosie Smith and I think she comes from somewhere on the Lisburn Road. Her daughter is called Mary and her daughter's partner registered a BMW for our long-term patient parking under the name of David Reece. He had to show me his driving licence for proof of identity.'

McNally spent some time going over what she knew. She didn't know where exactly in the car park he parked his BMW. She described the man as being almost 6-foot-tall, dark hair and blue eyes. She remembered he was wearing a Barbour jacket with an open-necked shirt and, she thought, blue jeans. To her own eyes he was fit and healthy. The woman had long black hair; she was pretty, and was well dressed in a floral dress. McNally showed her the old IRA picture of Reece, and she confirmed it was the same man only older.

'Did they say when they would be back?' he asked.

'Not to me, but I was able to speak to one of the nurses on the ward who told me the daughter was very upset and had said she'd be back each day. The man left a telephone number with the ward and with reception.' She handed the note to McNally. 'I've written down everything that I know, including the number. It's there for you in the note. I don't know that I could do anymore without bringing attention to myself.'

'No, don't worry, Aunty. You've done more than enough. Leave the rest to me.'

She knew better than to ask any more questions, and realistically she didn't want to know anything else. It would be better for her if anything went wrong or anything happened.

'Right then, that's me off home for ma dinner. I'm famished.'

McNally kissed her on the cheek and escorted her to the door.

'Are you at work the rest of the week?' he asked.

'Yes, why?' she replied, worried about what he was going to ask next.

'Don't worry, Aunty. It's just in case I need to get in touch with you quickly, and I'll know where you are.'

'Just be careful, nephew. The world is a dangerous place out there.' She smiled.

'And you, Aunty.' He smiled before closing the door behind her.

After she'd left, McNally went to the same phone box on the Falls Road he'd used in the past. He made two calls. One to John Jo Murphy. He told him his guests had arrived and that he could expect visitors within the next couple of days. Murphy told him he'd prepare the accommodation. The second call was to Frank Walsh. He told Walsh to meet him in the Wolf Tone Club at eight o'clock that evening and to bring

Jimmy Bailey and Bailey's sister Mariad with him. As he walked home, a plan was now formulating in his mind. Brian McNally began to smile.

Chapter 15

Hilton Hotel Belfast

The Belfast Hilton hotel had been built after the Troubles. The hotel overlooked the Lagan River that runs through the city to the Irish Sea. Like all Hilton hotels the world over, the design was simple, yet classy, and functional at the same time. Reece liked the room on the third floor as it overlooked the river. Across from the large windows, they could see the two giant cranes of the old Harland and Wolff shipyard, indicating the site where the famous ship Titanic had been built. They had both showered and, with only towels covering them, they'd slept on top of the bed for an hour.

'Are you sure you switched the charger on when you plugged your phone in?' said Mary, opening her eyes.

'Yes, don't worry if they try to get us, I've also given the hospital our hotel number. If anything happens, they'll let us know.'

Reece was lying back with his hands behind his head, looking at the ceiling. Mary turned over and lay her head on his chest. He could smell the freshness in her soft dark hair. Her body was cool against his skin and although, like always when they were in this position, he felt like making love to her, he knew that was not what she needed at this time.

'I know, David, I'm just worried that Mum's there all alone with all those tubes. I'm glad you're here. I don't know what I'd do without you.'

Reece pulled her closer and tried to change the subject. He knew she was worried, and he also knew she must be strong. His mobile phone started to buzz. Reece left the bed and taking the phone off the charger lead he looked at the screen and could see the call was from Tom Wilson.

'Hello, Tom, what's up?'

'Hi, David. I'm just calling to see how you got on today. How's Mary and her mother?'

'Both doing OK in the circumstances, thanks for asking.'

'Where are you now?' asked Wilson.

'I think if your team are as good as I think they are you know exactly where we are, in the hotel.' He smiled to himself.

He could hear Wilson laughing. 'I told them you would spot them. How long did it take you?'

'Not long, but they're good. But it's good to have them there all the same. Thanks for that.'

'You're welcome. Just checking in to make sure you're all right. You have my number if you need to get in touch with me. I'm heading home now for the night. We can catch up tomorrow, but before I go, can you let me know when you'll be leaving the hotel so that my teams don't have to start too early?'

'Will do Tom and thanks again. Have a good night.'

'What was all that about?' asked Mary.

'Just Tom Wilson making sure were tucked up safely in bed for the night.'

'That's nice of him. I'm only realising now when we last ate. My belly thinks my throat's been cut,' she said, smiling.

'Let's get dressed and go down to dinner. I believe the views at night from the hotel's Riverfront Restaurant are spectacular. So whether they are or not, if you're there with me the food will taste spectacular as well.' Reece laughed.

The changes in Belfast since the end of the Troubles and the instalment of the peace process always amazed Reece anytime he returned to the city. New hotels, conference centres, theatres, shops, bars, and restaurants. Belfast had become a cosmopolitan city once more, but more modern than in the past. They'd rebuilt it from the rubble. As Reece looked out of the large restaurant windows that overlooked the river, he couldn't help but remember the days when, as a young policeman, he'd worked for one week a month in what was called the bomb transit. The job of the officers in the transit was to race to bomb calls to clear buildings and streets of civilians before a car bomb would explode, wrecking those buildings, and lives. Sometimes the week's duty in the transit would be quiet. at other times, they could be attending calls once or twice a day every day. It was during one of these calls that he came close to losing his life. The 999 caller had said a bomb had been placed in a grocery store at the top of the Donegall Road. As they drove up the Donegal Road, they could see a police Land Rover above the shop stopping traffic coming down the road. They pulled the transit across the road beside a garage to block traffic travelling up the road. Unknown to Reece and the other officers in the transit, the terrorists had placed a bomb in the garage as well. The owners had run out and seeing the police Land Rover thought they were sealing off the road for their bomb. As they'd got out of the transit and started to stop traffic, the bomb in the garage exploded. Luckily for Reece and the men in the transit, the blast went upwards rather than outwards. The memory of those few moments would always be the same: the blast lifting him off his feet and blowing him backwards, slamming him against the transit. As he travelled through the air, everything seemed to be in slow motion. Looking to his right, he could see a policeman on his knees with his hands over his head as pieces of glass fell like rain on his hands and cap. None of the officers were injured, but they were slightly shaken up. Reece later noticed a tear in his trousers: his knee had been cut by the flying glass and would need a few stitches later. He had been slightly deafened by the blast and just as the officers got their senses back, the second bomb went off in the grocery store that had been the reason for the original call. The terrorists had placed two bombs in two separate buildings before making their getaway. Another memory of that incident always made Reece smile. While stopping traffic from getting onto the road after the blast and the clean-up, one stupid driver tried to drive through Reece to get onto the road. Reece put up his hand, shouted three times for him to stop, but he kept coming. Eventually Reece put his hand on the gun on his belt and shouted that he would shoot him if he didn't fucking stop. That did the trick. The driver and his nervous legs somehow found the brakes.

'Penny for your thoughts?' asked Mary.

They had enjoyed the meal and the views from the restaurant window. Each table with its small vase of fresh flowers and lighted candle added just that bit of class that made the experience more intimate, more personal. There hadn't been much conversation as everything came back to Mary's mother in the hospital bed. Reece had continually tried to steer Mary away from thinking about her mother. The bottle of Chablis was still half full, which, being their favourite wine, was unusual. Mary wasn't in the mood for drinking and Reece needed to keep a clear head in case they had to drive back to the hospital at a moment's notice.

'Just thinking about how the city looks now, compared to the old dark days when we raced around trying to stop people from killing each other.'

'I remember how bad it was then before I married Brendan and moved to Newry. Newry wasn't much better. But I agree with you, the city looks lovely now. A place for people to come and enjoy themselves in peace and quiet.'

'I believe it's very popular with stag and hen parties. The flight from England on EasyJet are relatively cheap. At the weekends, bars, and restaurants are full. There is a whole new generation out there who hasn't got a clue of what it was like. They don't really know that there are still some bastards around who want to keep it all going. That's basically why I moved to Malta. I wanted to get away from this place as far as I could.'

'I know what you mean. If it wasn't for what happened to my mother, I wouldn't be here either. Malta and you are my home now and I only hope that after my mother gets well, we can all go back there to live in peace.'

They took what was left of the wine back to the room. Leaving the curtains open so they could see the light shining on the river, they both fell asleep.

Chapter 16

Belfast

They woke early. The sun was shining, sparkling off the surface of the river. Reece phoned down for a continental breakfast for both. They took their time getting ready, putting on fresh clothes, which, with the good night's sleep, left them feeling refreshed for the day. Mary was wearing a black two-piece trouser suit with a white blouse underneath. She felt that sitting for a day in a hospital, the way she was dressed, would make it more comfortable. Reece had no worries about comfort. He dressed casually in jeans and a shirt, the order of the day. Reece phoned Tom Wilson to tell him they would be leaving the hotel about nine thirty. Wilson thanked him and told him the surveillance team was already out on the ground.

'I hope Mum has had a good night's sleep as well,' said Mary.

'Well, no phone call is good news,' answered Reece.

Before he put on his Barbour jacket, Reece checked the Walther Pistol. It was a habit he'd carried out over the years. Make sure the magazine fits snugly and there was a round in the breech ready to go. Reece put the gun in the holster on the waistband of his trousers, then lifted the car keys off the table. Mary watched him. She didn't like the fact he was carrying a gun again, but somehow, she felt safer that he did.

'OK. Let's go and see how your mother's doing.'

Driving through the city on a crisp sunny day, when the rush-hour traffic had died down, was a nice experience. They could see all the new buildings they'd talked about the night before, the sun bouncing off the many windows looking out on the streets below. Reece had promised himself that he wouldn't look for the surveillance and just try to relax. But the professional in him was still watching, ever vigilant. He spotted two of the vehicles a black Volkswagen Golf and a red Toyota. The drive to the hospital only took 20 minutes. The lights and the traffic were in their favour. Even finding a parking space was easier than it had been. While Reece registered the car at the reception, Mary went ahead, eager to be with her mother. When Reece got to the ward, he found that Marys mother had been moved to a bed in a four-bed ward on the same floor. Mary had resumed the same position as the day before, sitting beside the bed, holding her mother's hand. Reece noticed that one or two of the tubes that had been attached to her mother's body had been removed. A young nurse came in to check the patient's pulse.

'Your mother had a good night, which is always helpful. Her signs are showing she's fighting back. The doctor will be around later to check, and he'll be able to tell you more, but try not to worry, he'll tell you more than I can.'

Reece pulled up the other chair and sat quietly beside Mary. Reece hated hospitals. They always reminded him of painful times. He always thought the quiet noise created by people moving about and talking in the corridors and on the ward made him sleepy, just like one of those self-help tapes or CDs designed to do just that.

'I still think she can hear us,' said Mary.

'I'm sure, keep talking to her. Tell her everything. Tell her about us and Malta, our engagement, and that the sun is shining today.'

Mary did just that. She talked quietly, telling her mother everything Reece had mentioned. Hospital chairs were never comfortable. They were not meant for people to sit for long periods of time.

'I think I'll go to the canteen and get a cup of coffee. You want one?' asked Reece.

'Oh yes, that would be nice, and a biscuit if you can find one,' she replied.

Reece left for the lift that would take him down the two floors to the canteen. When the lift doors opened, a nurse coming out almost bumped into him. The nurse smiled as she stood to one side, allowing him to enter the lift. He noticed she was wearing a different – coloured uniform to the ones on the ward: blue instead of light green. He thought maybe she was one of the nurses who specialised. As the lift door closed and he started to descend he remembered the nurse wasn't wearing a hat.

The nurse had continued to the ward where Mary was still sitting with her mother. The nurses' desk outside the ward was empty now that the nurses were carrying out their rounds in other wards and preparing the medicine trolley.

'Excuse me, are you Mrs Smith's daughter?' the nurse asked as she entered the room.

Turning, Mary could see the young, attractive nurse with blonde hair tied in a ponytail.

'Yes, I'm Mary.'

'I wonder, could you come with me? The consultant would like a quick word about your mother's progress. He's down in his office on the bottom floor, and I can show you the way.'

'Can we wait for my partner? He's just gone to get some coffee.'

'No, I'm sorry, the consultant needs to see you now as he only has a few minutes between his patient rounds.'

'OK, lead the way.'

The nurse walked in front of Mary towards the lift. Mary quickly sent a text message to Reece.

Going to see a consultant.

Inside the lift, the nurse pressed the button to the basement floor.

'Have they told you how your mother's doing?'

Mary noticed a small bead of sweat on the side of the nurse's face.

She's young and maybe in training, she thought, which is making her a little nervous.

It had been a while since she'd heard such a strong Belfast accent.

'They only say she's holding her own. I'm glad they took out a couple of those ugly tubes overnight,' replied Mary.

The lift came to a halt, and when the doors opened, the nurse turned left, and Mary followed. The corridor was quiet apart from two men dressed in a porter's uniforms pushing an empty bed trolley towards them. The nurse stopped walking, and standing to one side, she let Mary pass. Mary's thoughts had been about her mother's condition and the questions that she was going to ask the consultant. Looking ahead at the two men, she began to realise that something was wrong. She couldn't see any office doors in the corridor, only the exit door behind the two men. As she got closer to the men, the realisation that something was wrong became stronger. The men were wearing baseball caps. They let hold of the trolley and started to walk towards her. Mary turned to walk in the opposite direction, but her way was blocked by Mariad Bailey. Mary opened her mouth to scream for help when a sudden explosion of pain went through her body, sucking all the breath out of her, followed by a darkness as she fell.

The stun gun did its job. Frank Walsh had jammed it into Mary's neck, and as she'd started to fall Jimmy Bailey supported her body before she hit the floor. When Brian McNally had given Walsh the stun gun, he told him she'd be out of it for only a few minutes, so time now was of the essence. Walsh handed the stun gun to Mariad Bailey while he helped Walsh lift Mary onto the bed trolley. All three quickly pushed the trolley through the emergency doors and out to where Walsh had parked the transit. They opened the rear doors and the men lifted Mary's body into the back of the vehicle. Mariad Bailey and Jimmy got into the back with Mary. Walsh closed the doors behind them and, jumping into the driver seat, drove the transit through the main hospital car parks and, turning left, out through the Donegal Road exit. In the back of the transit Mariad tied Mary's hands in front of her using plastic cuffs. Walsh made sure he drove at a safe speed. not bringing attention was important now. Mary started to come round. the pain in her neck and shoulder started to subside. Taking a deep breath she opened her eyes, the headache forcing her to close them again.

'So, Mary McAuley, you're our patient now. Lie still and keep quiet. There's plenty of electric charge in this little device to help you sleep a little bit more if you don't,' snarled Jimmy Bailey.

Mary opened her eyes slowly this time. She remembered the man in the hospital porter suit. the same man was now kneeling above her. Turning her head, she could see the pretty nurse who had walked into the corridor with her. She didn't panic, there would be no use in doing that now, she decided to say nothing. She felt sick and fought to keep from gagging.

This wasn't the first operation that Mariad Bailey had been on. Now 28 years old, she'd been a member of the women's IRA, the Cumann na mBan. At nineteen she'd joined the Provisional IRA, then after the ceasefire, and peace process, with her brother, she'd crossed over to the Real IRA. When she'd met with Brian McNally the night before in the back room of the Wolf Tone Club she was not surprised to be asked to take part in the operation to lift the tout, a traitor to the cause. She'd done the same two times before and both the touts had ended up lying on a border road with a bullet in the head. McNally explained the operation and had brought with him a bag containing the nurse and porter's uniforms for them to wear. He gave Walsh the stun gun and explained its use and effect. McNally had also told the two men that one of their people would deliver two pistols to the garage before they left for the hospital. These guns were only to be used if things went bad. The main danger being the ex-Special

Branch man David Reece. McNally had said that it would be ideal if they could capture both Reece and McAuley, but the main target was Mary McAuley. She was a tout, and she'd to be dealt with.

Reece had a deep-seated instinct for danger from his days in Special Branch. The same instinct that had got him out of trouble and saved his life on a few occasions. As he stood in the queue at the coffee counter his mind was working overtime as he tried to understand why he was feeling a sense of that same danger now. He kept asking himself, what was it that was making him feel this way? His thoughts raced over what had happened that morning. His phone buzzed in his pocket, and he read the text message from Mary. Suddenly, he understood, and started to run back towards the lift.

Chapter 17

Belfast

The lift was in use, but Reece didn't have time to wait. Still running, he took the stairs three at a time, up the two floors to the ward. Mary was nowhere to be seen. Her mother was still lying peacefully on the bed, her eyes still closed. Reece tried to call Mary, but her phone seemed to be switched off, the call going to her answer phone. He left a voice message for her to call him back and sent a text message to the same effect.

He searched two of the nearby wards before he found a nurse in one of the small side rooms.

He questioned the nurse, but in his stomach he already knew what the answers would be.

'No. I've been doing the rounds, and I haven't seen her since I spoke to you both this morning when you came in. Why, is something wrong?'

'Maybe, I don't know. can you get somebody from security to come here now?'

'Yes, right away,' the nurse replied before locking the medicine cabinet and going to the nurses' station where she dialled an internal number on the phone.

'Can you send someone from security to ward C3 immediately, please?'

'I'll check the ladies' toilets just to make sure she isn't there,' said the nurse, putting the phone down. When she left, Reece dialled the number for Tom Wilson on his phone. His gut instinct told him that Mary wasn't in the toilets. She wouldn't even be in the building.

'Mary's gone,' Reece said when Wilson answered the phone.

'What do you mean gone?' replied Wilson.

'She's gone. I think they have her. I went for coffee and when I came back, she'd disappeared. The hospital nurses don't know where. They don't know what happened.'

'I'll get our surveillance people to block off the exits and search vehicles leaving. You understand because it's a hospital we must let people come and go. I'll get the local police to send a couple of uniform cars to take over from the surveillance people. If we are lucky, she's still there, but if I know these people, they'll already have gone. I'll get Heather Black, and we'll see you at the hospital in twenty minutes. Then we can decide where to go, and what to do. In the meantime, you continue looking around where you are, asking people if they saw anything. We need to look at the hospital CCTV and speak to hospital security as well.'

'I'm already on it. I have the security people coming to the ward and I'll get them to have the CCTV set up for when you get here.'

'I'll update the chief constable. He will implement a plan that we've in case one of our officers is kidnapped. It basically closes the roads into the estates in West Belfast and the roads going south. I'll see you in twenty, will have the blues, and twos on to get us there quicker.' The line went dead.

When an overweight security man arrived on the ward Reece told him what he thought had happened. He told them that the police would be checking vehicles leaving the exits from the hospital and that he needed to see their CCTV right away. The security man didn't ask any questions.

'I'll only need to talk to the hospital chief executive and let her know what is happening,' said the security man.

'I don't care who you talk to, but we need to move fast. Where's your control room? Where's the CCTV?' asked Reece.

'Follow me. I can call the chief executive from there, it's on the top floor.'

Reece got into the lift with the security man. He could smell the sweat from the man, who he suspected was the type who got nervous easily. Reece knew the man was already nervous as he was being thrust into something that had probably never happened to him before. He would have to keep pushing the security man's buttons to get him to move quickly. When the lift stopped on the top floor they went through double doors directly opposite. There were no windows in the room and one other man was sitting in front of a console of TV screens showing the views from the CCTV cameras around the hospital. The man with Reece told the man in front of the screens what had happened, and that they needed to look back over the footage right away. Reece didn't want to go too deeply into his own and Mary's background. These men didn't need to know of their connections to the police and security services.

'This woman may have been abducted from the hospital. She's not a patient. she was visiting her mother. I need to see the footage of the last 20 minutes showing all exits from the building and from the car parks. Do you understand?'

The man in front of the consoles nodded. Using a small joystick, he moved the screen video around and Reece could see the timer on each one recording twenty minutes.

They watched as the black and white images moved forward again at normal speed on all four screens. Each monitor was split into four separate screens, the total showing fourteen door exits and the two exits from the hospital. It was Reece who saw one of the screens show two men wearing porter uniforms accompanied by a nurse with a blonde ponytail and no hat pushing a trolley carrying what looked like a woman. They could see the men were wearing baseball caps. They lifted the woman into the back of a white transit. Leaving the trolley, the nurse and one of the men got into the back of the transit, while the other closed the doors then got into the driver's seat to drive out of the camera's view. Reece told the man at the controls to freeze what he'd just seen, then check the hospital exit cameras for the transit leaving, then try to get a registration number. Reece knew he'd just seen the abduction of Mary. The memory of seeing the nurse in a blue uniform came back into his head.

'Where does that camera cover?' asked Reece.

'The ground floor delivery door at the back of the building,' answered the man working the joystick.

'Is there a camera inside where they came out through the doors?' asked Reece.

'No, just the outside,' replied the security man.

'When I was going down in the lift for coffee, I passed a nurse coming out. Do your nurses wear blue uniforms?' asked Reece.

'Just the nurses that work on the maternity ward. most of the other nurses wear light green. The nurses at the Royal Victoria hospital wear blue.'

'Can you blow up the screen to show the two men with the trolley and the nurse when they lifted the woman into the transit, and can you slow it down please?' said Reece, now using a softer tone to his voice. He knew people would react better if they felt they were being asked rather than ordered.

'Sir, that looks like the transit leaving by the Donegal Road exit,' said the security guard, working the joystick, and pointing to one of the screens. They could see the transit turning left on the Donegal Road, driving away from the city.

The security guard was speaking to the chief executive of the hospital on the phone.

'She wants to speak to you,' said the guard, handing the phone to Reece.

At least the woman sounded like she knew what she was doing, asking him all the right questions. It didn't take Reece long to explain what had happened, what they'd seen on the CCTV, and that the police would be checking vehicles leaving the hospital. He told her that a senior police officer was on route from police headquarters, and he would be able to explain more. The woman seemed happy with this, and she asked Reece to put the security guard back on.

'Thank you for that Mr Reece,' said the guard, putting down the phone. 'The chief executive says we are to give you any help you need.'

'Thank you. I'm sorry, but I forgot to ask your name.'

'It's John, the man at the desk is Stephen.'

'Thank you, John, and you too, Stephen, I'm David.' Reece tried to keep his voice under control even though he felt like he wanted to scream, run somewhere, or just punch someone. He knew if he showed the panic, he felt to these two men then things could be missed, and it wouldn't help the situation. 'It's obvious from what we've seen on your CCTV that my partner has been abducted by these people and now this is a police matter. As I told your chief executive, there's a senior police officer on the way, he'll take over the search for my partner. The best we can do is to have all these screenshots saved and ready for him to see. They will be here in 20 minutes, so, as there's nothing else we can do. I'm going to take a walk down to that corridor and the back door to see if they left any clues behind. I'll be back before the police get here. How do I get to the corridor?'

'You take the lift to the basement, then turn left when you come out of the lift,' said Stephen.

Reece didn't take long examining the corridor and the doors out to where the transit had been parked. It was then that he saw what he knew was Mary's phone lying smashed on the road. It was obvious that the phone had been deliberately placed under the wheels of the transit that took Mary. He knew the men were likely wearing gloves, most likely surgical gloves, to help with their disguise as porters, and the fact that they wore baseball caps and kept their heads down showed they were aware of the CCTV. He was sure the woman who posed as a nurse had no gloves on and there was a chance she may have left fingerprints behind. Reece was careful not to touch where he thought there could be prints but he knew deep down there wouldn't be any. Experience told him these bastards would be making every effort to get Mary across the border, where they could work on her in relative safety. He could feel his heart rate pumping faster in his chest and the metallic taste of adrenaline in his mouth. He had felt the same sensation many times before when the covert operations brought sudden danger, and most of all he knew time was against him. He had to try to control the anger inside him, the anger that wanted to kick in every door in West Belfast until he found her. The professional side was kicking in. He knew it would be a waste of time to jump into his BMW and drive up the Donegal Road to chase every white transit he saw. He agreed with Tom Wilson that the best plan for now would be to seal off the estates and roads going out and into West Belfast. The kidnappers would be desperate to get Mary to a safe location in the South of Ireland, somewhere close to the border with the North where they could work on her. Reece had worked with the southern police, the Garda, and he knew from experience they never wanted to rattle the Republican terrorist's cages. Thoughts of his time in Special Branch, when based in Newry a few miles from the Irish border, he'd seen the aftermath of the IRA torture team when they left a body on a border road after they'd interrogated them. Again, his pulse started to race at the memory. Many of those victims had admitted to being informers working for the security forces, but he also knew under torture many of them had admitted what the terrorists wanted to hear rather than take any more pain. Their final pain was a bullet in the back of the head. Torture teams or the Nutting squad as they were known, would sometimes leave explosive booby traps near the bodies to try to kill the security forces responding. Because of the suspect traps this led to long delays, until the ATO could clear the area before the bodies could be recovered, which only led to more pain and suffering for the families of the deceased. He tried to push these thoughts to the back of his memory. Now was not the time to think the worst but to try to concentrate and get Mary back safely.

 Reece returned to the control room. He could see that Stephen knew how to get the best quality pictures out of the videos. He had transferred a running video with large still photographs to one screen. The face of the nurse was clear in the pictures. Because the men kept their heads down, the caps blocked any clear view of theirs. Reece knew any kind of mask would have brought unnecessary attention to them. He also knew they expected to be well away and in a safe location before the alarm could be raised. The PSNI were likely to have their faces on record, and the clear shots of the nurse might help to find them quickly. Again, Reece felt the pressure of time. The control room phone rang, and John answered.

'That was the chief executive. She's on her way up with your police officers,' he said, putting the phone back down.

Reece thought the chief executive looked younger than she sounded on the phone. She was dressed for business, wearing a dark blue trouser suit and dark rimmed glasses on a face that Reece would have described as oval, while her black hair was tied in a ponytail.

'Hello, Mister Reece, I'm Erin Johnson, the chief executive of the hospital,' said the woman, holding out her hand. 'Mister Wilson and my security people have told me what's happened. I think it's awful. I'm truly sorry and, of course we'll give you and the police whatever help we can.' Her accent was soft, almost lowland Scottish.

'Thank you. This is not yours or the hospital's fault. The people who did this have no respect for anyone. We have been looking at the CCTV and we've narrowed down the pictures you need to see. Stephen here has produced a rolling screenshot of what happened, plus the important still photographs of the people involved.'

Wilson and Black walked to the back of the room and asked Reece to join them so that they were out of earshot of the others.

'As I said on the phone, David, we've instigated a planned operation to seal off certain estates and locations in West Belfast. Because we've acted quickly, I'm sure they would have anticipated this, and will be hiding out somewhere in Belfast, instead of making a run for the border, which for the moment, is too far away, and full of dangers they don't want to run in to. We will search a few locations, but this will take time to set up and cause a lot of problems on the ground. I'm sure you remember from your own time on the job, the locals will react to any closing down of their area. It won't take long for the stones and petrol bombs to start flying. When that happens, the politicians will put pressure on the chief constable to pull out. Heather has her surveillance teams working to identify our suspects and to find where Mary is being held. I've also instructed our agent handlers to contact their people as soon as possible for any information they can get.'

'What do we do in the meantime? You know that every second counts and they'll be trying to get Mary across the border to work on her in some fucking shed where no one will hear her scream.' Reece could feel his stomach tense once more.

'You and Mary always knew the risk. For now, we are doing everything we can to get her back. I've asked Heather here to work with you and keep you updated every step of the way. For now, we'll send a copy of these photographs to our teams at HQ to see if they can identify these people quickly. I'll head back to headquarters to monitor everything and keep you both updated. Stay with Heather. She will be out on the ground keeping in touch with me and her own people using our secure comms.'

Heather Black sat down beside Stephen at the computer screens, plugged in a USB, and began to download the pictures he'd saved. When she'd completed the download, she plugged the USB into a tablet she was carrying, then pressing a few buttons on the tablet, she transferred the file.

'That's the file sent to headquarters. They will work on the photographs and video to try to identify them. Hopefully, it won't take long for us to identify them, but the men may take longer because of the baseball caps. Then we'll have something concrete to work on. From what I've seen, I'm pretty sure that the woman, the nurse, is Mariad Bailey, the sister of Jimmy Bailey. If it is her, then I must tell you she's one nasty bitch and anyone she's with will be just as nasty. We have run a couple of operations against both in the past. Her hair is black, I think that's a wig. If I'm right, then one of the men could be her brother,' said Black.

'Then we should hit their houses right away,' said Reece not feeling any better from what he'd just learnt.

'We will, but we both know they won't be home and there won't be any evidence to show what they're up to. By showing their faces they know we'll be after them and it's obvious that they'll be willing to go on the run and live somewhere south of the border out of our reach for now,' said Wilson. 'OK, Heather, take David here, and skirt round some of the estates where I have no doubt these rats are hiding. Your teams might get lucky and spot something. You can pull your people out of closing the hospital exits. I'll head back to headquarters to update the chief constable and keep an eye on what's going on. I've no doubt that as this is a public building, someone will have noticed the police activity, asked questions, and contacted the press. Before this gets out of control we need to move fast.'

Reece followed the DCI back to her car, a dark blue Audi. The car had been fitted with all the up-to-date surveillance equipment, from the hidden mic in the ceiling to the hidden camera showing the road ahead on a screen in the middle of the dashboard. Black had a running commentary going with her team. Reece could identify the callsigns. They hadn't changed much since his own days of operating surveillance in the city. He soon picked up most of the terms. The callsigns all reported they were covering the estates in West Belfast, Andersonstown, Ballymurphy, and Turf Lodge. Reece kept quiet as he listened to Black communicating with her operators and the control room back at headquarters. A radio message had broadcasted the registration number of the white transit van. There was no surprise to Reece or Black when they reported back that the plates were false and that they referred to a plumbing company in East Belfast.

Black asked HQ to look at any street CCTV to see where the van went after it left the hospital. Reece was surprised how quickly the reply came back. The van had gone up the Donegal Road and crossing over onto the Falls Road, it had last been seen passing Milltown Cemetery and heading towards the Andersonstown Estate. Black asked control to direct all resources towards that estate. Control confirmed the nurse fitted the description of Mariad Bailey but couldn't confirm the men.

Uniform search and arrest teams had been directed to go to the home addresses of the Bailey families and associates. Reece knew that if these people were as good as he thought they were, no one would be home. He asked Black to take him to Andersonstown, where the van had last been seen heading. It had started to rain heavily, and Reece remembered the old saying that rain was the policeman's best friend when it came to riot situations, the one thing rioters always seemed to hate more than the police was getting wet, it would keep them off the streets.

'Control to Red1,' Wilson's voice came over the radio. He must have put the blues and twos on to get back to headquarters that quickly thought Reece.

'Go ahead, control,' answered Black.

'Just to let you know, as expected, the press is onto what's going on. Our headquarters press office is getting enquiries from the Belfast Telegraph and BBC Radio Ulster. The teams need to be aware that there may be cameras out on the ground looking for trouble. I would think someone in the hospital has tipped them off.'

'Roger that. Understood,' answered Black. She looked across at Reece and raised her eyebrows. Both knew that once the press knew, politicians would know, and questions would start to fly, and answers demanded from the people back at headquarters. The pressure would be brought for them to pull back and avoid clashing with the communities in West Belfast. The politician's precious peace process was more important than Mary's life. This meant they didn't have much time. They drove around for another hour and despite the rain, the young hoods of West Belfast were coming out. Not only were they looking for police to throw the stones and petrol bombs at, but they were trying to stop cars which they would then hijack and set on fire. To try to stay undercover in such an area would be a mistake.

'I think we're wasting our time chasing our tails looking for these people. They will keep their heads down until things quieten down,' said Reece. 'My time would be better spent back at my hotel making a few phone calls. Can you drop me back at the hospital to pick up my car?'

'Yes, no problem. I'll let the boss know, and then I'll get back out to link up with my teams and see what we can do. I can pull them back to the edge around Andersonstown, so we can pick up on anything that looks suspicious moving about. I'm sure the boss will keep you updated. Try not to worry, David, everyone's out on the ground and we'll do everything we can to get Mary back safely. When I drop you off, I'll give you my number in case you need to get in touch.'

Reece nodded and forced a smile. He knew she was honest in what she'd said and that they were doing everything they could to find Mary, but he felt he needed to move things himself and that required a couple of private phone calls.

Chapter 18

Andersonstown, Belfast

They had reached the garage before the police road stops had been put in place. Jimmy Bailey had jumped out and opened the doors, allowing Walsh to reverse the transit into what realistically was a large hay shed which could have taken three transits. The shed was at the end of a lane that backed off the main Andersonstown Road and the estate which ran under the main Belfast to Dublin M1 motorway. Brian McNally had kept this building in his back pocket for just such an operation only known to himself and those involved. On the way to the shed, Mariad Bailey had put a gag around Mary's mouth. The gag almost made Mary retch. she could taste car oil on it, and she imagined it must belong to one of the two men. The woman in the nurse's uniform, who had now removed her wig showing her black hair underneath, seemed to be enjoying herself, grinning as she pulled Mary by the hair, she led her to a chair. The woman tied Mary's arms behind her, then each of her legs to the front of the chair, before removing the gag.

'Who the fuck are you? Why are you doing this to me? Let me go.'

The woman in the nurse's uniform came right up to Mary, then leaning over her, slapped her.

'You would be better to keep your tout mouth shut. We are not interested in your bleating,' the woman spat the words into Mary's face. Mary felt the sting of the slap and wanted to cry but biting her lip held back. she didn't want to show any weakness to this bitch.

'You had better do as she says and keep quiet. No one can hear you here anyway, so you'd be wasting your breath. If you're a good girl, we might give you some water and something to eat later. In the meantime, there's a bucket in the corner if you need to go to the toilet,' said Walsh.

Mary looked around her. The building they were in appeared to be an old shed or somewhere that farming machinery would be kept. She could hear the constant noise of traffic moving at speed and guessed they were near a motorway. It was dry and had three lit electric bulbs hanging from the ceiling. There were three made-up camp beds in the far corner of the shed with a card table and four chairs. Mary felt that it would be a waste of time trying to shout for help, as it looked like the shed had been well prepared for her arrival. The windows had been covered with sheets of PVC board.

'Can I have a drink of water? I can still taste that rag you stuffed in my mouth.'

Without saying anything Walsh took a small bottle of water out of a holdall sitting beside the table, unscrewed the top, then poured a small amount into Mary's mouth.

'Thank you.'

'You're welcome. Just to make sure you know what happens next, it's our job to keep you well until we deliver you to our friends south of the border. We are under orders to speak to you as little as possible and that you're well enough to make the journey, which might be a little uncomfortable for you. So, if I was you, I would save my breath and energy for what comes next. You're going to need it.'

Her arms and wrists ached where they were tied. The woman seemed to take pleasure in pulling them even tighter when she'd sat Mary in the chair. Mary tried to concentrate. She tried to keep her head clear even though it was buzzing with the whole experience. She had an idea of what they were planning for her, but she couldn't let herself think about that for now. She knew David and the others would be looking for her and wondering if these people were going to hurt her. For now, she'd do everything in her power to prevent that hurt coming sooner rather than later.

'You to keep an eye on her. I'm going to call the boss to let him know everything is on schedule,' said Walsh as he left by the smaller of the two shed doors. He walked to the bottom of the lane that joined the main road, then walked another 200 yards to the call box. When McNally had briefed the three of them in the Wolf Tone Club the night before, he'd given Walsh the telephone number of the club and said he'd be in the bar and to call there when they'd lifted the tout. The phone had rung out three times before it was answered. Walsh asked the man answering for Brian McNally. A minute later Walsh heard the familiar voice of his boss.

'Hello, what have you got for me?'

'First part done, but we only got the woman. We are back safe in the den. What do you want us to do now?'

'As we thought, the opposing team is bringing a lot of pressure to bear in our half of the pitch. We're going to have to play defence for a couple of days before we can move forward. You have everything you need in the den to play safe and lie low. Call me here again tomorrow at one. By then, we'll have a clear picture of what the opposition is up to. In the meantime, preparations are being made for the transfer to the next team below the line. Remember, they want her fresh, undamaged.'

'Understood. Until one tomorrow,' Walsh replied putting down the phone.

When he returned to the shed, Walsh sat at the table with the brother and sister. He told them of his conversation with McNally and that they would have to stay in the shed for the next few days.

'For fuck's sake, do you mean we've to clean that bitch's backside for the next two days?' asked Jimmy Bailey.

'You know better than I do, Jimmy. You don't disobey orders. If the boss had heard you now, he would blow your kneecaps off himself,' answered Walsh.

'Frank's right, Jimmy, and anyway, you don't have anything better to do. I know your love life,' said Bailey's sister.

'Right, we can keep her in the chair during the day and at night we can tie her to one of the beds. But one of us will be awake at all hours. We have the Browning pistol, which we'll use if we need to, but other than that we keep her fresh and well, as the boss said,' said Walsh.

Walsh left the table and walked over to where Mary was seated.

'Your friends are looking for you, but they won't find you here, so to be on the safe side we want to keep you happy and well for a couple of days. So, you be a nice girl and we won't hurt you. But any fucking about and who knows we may have to break a bone or two. Just nod if you understand.'

Mary nodded, but in a way, she felt relieved that she was going to be here for another couple of days.

Chapter 19

Hilton Hotel

The rain was coming down faster than ever when Reece parked the car back at the Hilton. He was still alert to any surveillance watching him. Not just the police surveillance, but anyone else, especially after what happened to Mary. He ordered a pot of coffee for his room and sat down at the dressing table to make two phone calls. The first call was to the office of the director of SG9, Jim Broad. When he was connected, the secretary put him through to Broad's office immediately.

'Hello, David,' answered Broad. 'I've been expecting your call. Caroline Aspinall and Tom Wilson have both been in touch to update me about what has happened. Have you any more news?'

'Probably no more than you already know. They have Mary and we must get her back. It's as simple as that. But the longer it takes the more likely she'll be dead.'

'I'm sure Wilson and his team are doing everything they can. I know that Aspinall has been in touch with GCHQ to make sure anything they pick up is passed to you right away.'

Reece had expected that. He knew that they would be using all the resources they had including listening into the terror groups' conversations through their bugging and telephone intercept operations.

'Boss, you know Mary, and I wanted to leave all this behind us, but these bastards just wouldn't leave it alone. Anything you can do to help me get Mary back safely is greatly appreciated.'

There was a few seconds' silence and Reece could imagine Broad either writing things down or speaking to someone else in the room.

'Understood, David. I have C here with me now, and we are both in agreement that even though you put in your resignation from the department, we'll give you whatever help we can to get Mary back. But I have to say, you must understand the delicacies of the shit that the Northern Ireland situation, the political situation, can throw up. Between Caroline Aspinall and the MI5 team and Tom Wilson with his people, we think you have enough there now to get the job done, provided we believe Mary is still in Northern Ireland. At this moment, it's basically an abduction, a kidnapping, so realistically a policing matter. So for now, work through Tom Wilson. To help you, I'm sending Joe Cousins, who can provide the SG9 footprint on the ground. He'll be with you in a few hours. I've booked him into the Hilton so that you can work together, and any feedback can be provided in real time.'

Reece knew that Sir Ian Fraser was in the office with Broad and as the head of MI6 he'd sanctioned the involvement of the SG9 input. To Reece this meant it was being taken seriously and at a high level.

'I appreciate your help, boss. I'll be in the hotel for the next hour or so waiting on calls from Wilson.'

'Good luck. If we get anything, I'll be in touch,' said Broad.

Putting down the phone, Reece looked out the window, the grey clouds and the heavy

Rain seemed to make the whole situation even darker. Somehow, the fact that Joe Cousins was coming to help him made things seem a little easier. Reece had worked with Cousins on a couple of operations recently. Both had ended in people being killed, one of them a female SG9 agent known to them both. He knew Cousins would be a calming and reliable influence on him and that the experience he would bring would be invaluable if they were to find Mary.

The next call he made was on his mobile phone. His thinking was that GCHQ and.

MI5 wouldn't have it bugged yet, or at least he hoped so. Anyway, he didn't care anymore. They either would help him, or they wouldn't. If he had to operate alone, he would. From his recent travels to Israel, Reece knew Tel Aviv was two hours ahead, which meant it was now early evening there. Jacob Lavyan had given him his personal number, so there was no worry about it being an office connection. The international dialling tone sounded at least six times before he heard the familiar voice.

'Hello, David. I didn't expect to hear from you so soon. How are you?'

'I'm well, Jacob. But I have a problem and I hope you'll be able to help me.'

'If I can, my friend. What do you need?'

It was the answer Reece had hoped for before he'd called the number. It would make the conversation easier.

'Thank you, Jacob. My problem is a big one.'

'Go ahead, I'm listening. Are there others listening too, do you think?'

'Probably, but I don't care. This is important.'

'I understand.'

'Mary has been kidnapped by terrorists. We are in Belfast. Her mother was injured in a car accident, which I think they carried out to get us here and while we were at the hospital this morning she was abducted.'

'That's terrible! What are you doing to get her back?'

'That's where I need your help. The police and security services here are doing everything they can, but because of the peace agreement and the political niceties they'll be hindered. When we met you told me of a source your people in Dublin had.'

'Yes, I remember.'

'If these people take Mary where I think they'll take her, that source might be able to identify where.'

'I don't know if the source is still available. I know from my own experiences time is important in these situations. I'll find out right away and get back to you within the hour. Where are you staying?'

'That's great, thank you Jacob, I'm staying in the Hilton hotel but maybe not for long. I'll wait for your call before I do anything else.'

'Shalom, David, shalom.'

'Shalom,' replied Reece, cancelling the call.

He called reception and ordered another pot of coffee. Before it arrived, his phone buzzed again. This time he could see the name Tom Wilson flash on the screen.

'Hello, Tom. Any news?'

'Yes, David, some good, some bad, I'm afraid. The bad news first. We have had to pull back the uniform people on the ground around the estates. As we expected, the young people were beginning to have a field day, attacking them with the usual bottles and bricks. Considering the weather, we didn't expect there to be so many and they appear organised, so that would indicate paramilitary involvement, someone controlling the response. On top of that the politicians at Stormont are bringing pressure on the chief constable and when that happens nowadays, he must consider everything, and try to cool the situation down.'

Reece had expected this but not so quickly. Someone or some organisation was behind this.

'And the good news?' asked Reece.

'For a start, we'll be pulling the uniform people back from the estates, but not out all together. They will set up traffic checks on the roads out of the city, mainly the ones going south. When things quieten down in the estates, Heather Black's team will be able to operate again with drive-through passes on the main suspect locations. We have had one source come in already to say that Brian McNally, the OC for Belfast Real IRA, has been spending a lot of time in the last 24 hours in the Wolfe Tone Club and taking calls. McNally is a nasty piece of work and I'm sure he has his dirty hands all over this. We will increase our surveillance on him and the club and listen in where we can. Two of his favourite men that he uses are Jimmy Bailey and Frank Walsh. So that would confirm who the men were, Jimmy being Mariad's brother, so we've everyone looking for them as well. What I'm saying, David, is that we are doing all we can, and we are starting to see some cracks to look through to help us find Mary.'

'Anything from Five?' Reece knew if MI5 were doing their job, they would already have several locations in the city bugged. They would have everyone on it listening for any scrap of information. If only to report back to their political head in Northern Ireland, the SOS, the Secretary of State.

'Nothing yet, but with them now knowing about our friend McNally and the Wolf Tone Club, they'll zero in on that and hopefully get something soon. Anyway, I'll keep in touch. Will you be staying at the hotel?'

'Yes, I've nothing else planned.'

'Right. Talk later.'

After the call, Reece thought about what Wilson had said. The politicians were getting jittery and putting pressure on Wilson and the PSNI. In his own way, Wilson had let Reece know he was on his side and trying to ignore them. He had also let him know that MI5 had the Wolfe Tone Club bugged, if not the building at least the phones. Reece had always hated the waiting for information when operational. He realised he'd been walking back and forth across the room willing for something more concrete to happen to let him know where Mary was so that he could be more involved. Reece was usually the one pulling the strings, but for now he had to be patient, and he didn't like being patient he was more a man of action. The mobile phone buzzed.

'Shalom, Jacob.'

'Shalom, David. Any news?' replied Jacob Lavyan.

'Nothing yet. We are still searching and hoping for some intelligence as to where they might be holding Mary. For the moment, we still think they have her in Belfast. The politicians and the press are sticking their noses in and that could only make things worse.'

'Do they know who might have her?'

'We have a few names. All not good people. They are knocking on their doors, but nobody's at home.'

'Well, I might have some good news. I've spoken to my contacts in Dublin, and they believe they can still contact the source in South Armagh. He's a lot older now and not as involved as he was, but he should still have his ear to the ground, as you say. So he might be able to point us to where they have Mary.'

'That's great, Jacob. Any help at all is most welcome.'

'In the meantime. I've asked one of my ERM people in Dublin to contact the source and you. His name is Ari, and he was a Katsa in the same business as you and is aware of what is needed. I've given him your number, so expect a call sometime this evening. If you need anything more, call me at any time, night, or day.'

Reece knew that Jacob was telling him that Ari was an ex-Mossad field intelligence officer who was now working for Jacob's company.

'I owe you one, Jacob. All being well, we can get together when this is over.'

'That would be good. I look forward to it, maybe another Bushmills. Shalom, David, Shalom.'

'Shalom, Jacob.'

Reece sent a text to Broad.

Need files on people over here who may have Mary. Can Joe bring with him?

A reply came back almost immediately.

Will send what we've and will contact Tom and Caroline to make sure they provide what they have as well.

Reece drank some more coffee even though his stomach felt like he could throw up at any time.

Chapter 20

West Belfast

'I need to go to the toilet,' said Mary. She couldn't see her watch, and she estimated they'd been here for at least three hours. Her shoulders, back, and wrists were starting to hurt. She needed to move. She needed to get the circulation back.

'No problem, little lady, there's a bucket in the corner you can use,' said Mariad Bailey with a smirk on her face.

'But I need at least to be able to get the circulation of blood back into my arms and legs. The hand ties are tight, and my arms are going numb. My hands and fingers are tingling. If your bosses really want me to be in good condition when you hand me over, then at least untie me and let me walk about for a few minutes. There's three of you with guns, so I would be mad to try anything stupid.'

Walsh stood up from the chair at the table and, standing behind Mary, he examined her hands and arms. He could see the skin around the ties had turned purple and bruised. Taking a clasp knife from his trouser pocket, he opened the blade, then cut through the ties.

'Just remember you're the one who said it would be stupid for you to do anything. I would hate to have to tell my bosses that you tried to escape, and we had to shoot you.'

Mary felt her arms fall loose by her sides. A sudden flow of blood through her wrists into her hands felt like an electric shock. She stood and shook her arms by her sides until she felt the tingling disappear. She turned to look Walsh in the eye.

'I'm not stupid, but I think you all are. No matter what happens to me there are people out there looking for us right now, and they'll find you. When that happens, we'll see who the stupid people really are.'

All three kidnappers smiled. Mariad Bailey walked around Mary slowly. When she stood in front of her, she laughed.

'If your friends are looking for us, and if they find us, you'll never know cos I'll put a bullet in your head before they get through those doors.

We don't know why our people want you, but we know you're a tout for the Brits. You might have had a wonderful background working for the Provos during the war. That all adds up to nothing if you're a tout.'

'And if I'm not a tout, what do you think will happen then? The war is over, and the peace process is more important than your little army,' replied Mary.

'Enough of the chat, Mariad. This bitch will get what's coming to her soon enough. We just need to concentrate on what we must do. Don't let her get in your head,' said Walsh.

Walsh grabbed Mary's arms from behind and shoved her back down into the chair.

'We'll tie your hands again if you try anything. Remember, one of us will always be watching you, so as you say, let's not be stupid,' said Walsh.

'Let's all have a cup of tea and settle down for the night,' said Jimmy.

Chapter 21

Stormont

Reece had dozed on top of the bed. The buzzing from his mobile phone woke him. Although it was still late afternoon, because of the time of year, it was already getting dark. He could see the name Tom Wilson on the screen.

'Hi, Tom. What's happening?'

'Hi, David. We still have everybody out on the ground looking for Mary and any information we can get. In an hour, we're going to have a meeting with the SOS at Stormont. I would like you to be there. The more ammunition we've in our back pocket the better. I know that your work for SG9 is still top secret and maybe even the SOS is not aware of the department. The meeting, as far as I can see it, is to bring up two things. The first is to brief him on everything we know so far about Mary's abduction. The second is to get him to use his political influence on the Republican side to show them that it's in their best interests to help find Mary and get her back.'

'Yes, I can be there. Where exactly in Stormont? It's a big place.'

'Not the big parliament building itself but round the side. Where the SOS has his own offices besides Stormont Castle. You will be cleared to get through security, and I'll meet you in reception, see you in one hour.'

The call finished, Reece decided a quick shower and fresh clothes were needed. When dealing with politicians he always felt that appearances and a clear head were important.

The drive to Stormont only took 30 minutes from the hotel. The view of the main building as you drive up the mile long entrance from the Newtownards Road was always stunning thought Reece. The building was the location of the first Northern Ireland Parliament which lasted until it was taken over by rule from Westminster at the beginning of the Troubles. From a distance, the building looks like it's been made of white marble, but it's the paint that was used to make it look that way. Reece knew that when he got to the roundabout, where the Edward Carson statue stands in the middle, that he should go to the road to his right and to the grounds of Stormont Castle. Reece had only been at the castle once before when he worked at Police HQ, and he had to drop off an intelligence report. He knew the castle was where the main civil servants of the government of Northern Ireland work. Beside the castle is the Stormont cottages one of which was the offices of the SOS for Northern Ireland. When he had finished his call with Tom Wilson, Reece realised he hadn't a clue who the SOS was. All he knew was that it would be an MP from the current British government in power at Westminster. He Googled on his phone, so he was able to find out that Gerald Freeman MP of the Conservative Party of Great Britain and Northern Ireland was the current SOS as they were known to the security services. He didn't have the time to research him further. He was waved through the main security gates by the armed PSNI officers, then through to the castle and the cottage. Wilson, as promised, had called ahead to ensure his clearance, bearing in mind that Reece would be carrying the Walther Pistol he'd given him. Reece parked the BMW in one of the visitor's parking bays. Entering the main reception area he saw another security guard standing just inside the door who nodded for him to go through. Giving his name to the receptionist he was asked to wait for a few minutes as she made a call to someone, letting them know he'd arrived. Within five minutes Reece could see Wilson walking down the long corridor towards him.

'David, I'm glad you're here. The SOS is in his office with a few people I think you know. Follow me.'

Reece followed, feeling like a schoolboy being escorted to the headmaster's office not knowing whether it was going to be good or bad. The corridor seemed very long for a cottage and at the end there was a pair of double doors leading into a small secretary's office where a woman sat typing behind the desk. Wilson didn't stop, but continued to walk through another set of doors, with Reece following. The room was well lit, as despite the large bay windows overlooking a lawn, the early evening darkness had descended, the grass still visible highlighted by spotlights pointing towards the sky from ground level. The office was palatial, with a three-piece leather suite and a large desk with two chairs in front of it. At the side, four people were sitting around a large circular conference table. All four people stood to greet Reece as he came into the room. Two of them, Jim Broad, and Caroline Aspinall, he already knew. *They got here fast*, thought Reece. He also recognised the SOS from his Google photograph, but in the flesh, he looked even younger. The Right Honourable Gerald Freeman MP came around the table and introduced himself, shaking Reece's hand.

'Mr Reece, I'm pleased to meet you, although I'm sorry the circumstances aren't better. Please, join us at the table. I'm sure you know Jim and Caroline here. This is Beverley, my personal secretary. As this is a special meeting, she'll take some notes. I find notes can be easier redacted than tape recordings.' He smiled.

Reece nodded in acknowledgement to the others at the table.

As he spoke while shaking his hand, Reece had the feeling the SOS was asking for his vote. Reece sat at the table beside Tom Wilson. The SOS resumed his seat and Reece noticed that there were yellow writing notepads and pens in front of everyone except Beverley, who held on to her notebook while continuing to write, no doubt adding Reece's name to the list already attending the meeting.

'Beverley has been cleared at the highest level,' continued the SOS. 'David, I can call you, David?'

'Yes, no problem,' replied Reece.

'You can call me Gerald or minister if you prefer.'

'I can assure you everything said in this room stays in this room. The notes will be kept on file but are mainly for my benefit, as I've found that with the many meetings I attend, they help me remember who I met with and what was discussed. I would therefore ask any notes you make yourselves to be left behind for Beverley to file or destroy as I see fit. After this meeting, I'll also be speaking with the prime minister. He has told me you helped deal with the situation in Manchester and that we can be assured of your full cooperation today. I've been fully briefed and updated about this terrible situation and what has happened so far. Tom Wilson has kept me informed via the chief constable of what action the police have taken. He tells me that it would be a waste of time to lift some of these people now. We are not totally sure of who they are or where they are. We don't have enough information to question them, and even if we did lift them, they would say nothing, wasting the time we need to find this lady. Then, to add to things, it could mean more riots on the streets, something we need to avoid at all costs. I was just about to be briefed by Jim and Caroline. Your arrival is auspicious and just in time. Before they start, I think I should tell you a little bit about myself because everything on Wikipedia isn't the whole story. Normally, posting to Northern Ireland as

SOS is seen as a dead-end job. Basically, a minister is sent here to keep the lid on things and to stop the two factions from getting back to killing each other.

'To tell you the truth, David, it's like keeping a bunch of unruly children from throwing their dummies out of the pram. You might not know it, but I come from a military background. I was a captain in 2 PARA, which didn't make the Republican side so happy, but the fact that I'd never served in Northern Ireland saved the day. I did two tours in Iraq, so I've some idea of what it takes to operate in a hostile environment and having been briefed by Tom and Jim on your background, and where you come from, and what you've done, I want you to know from the start that you have my full support.

'I know that London and the politicians here are not happy that your friend Mary has been taken in this way. The big worry, and you must appreciate this, is that the peace process needs to be kept on track, so from a political point of view I'll be taking the lead in that respect. Now we were just getting round to your involvement with Mary, so before we hear from Jim and Caroline can you bring me up to speed on how you got to know her, if you could tell me in your own words?'

Reece looked around the table. All the eyes were now on him. Both Wilson and Broad, who knew the background best, nodded for him to continue. Reece felt they were wasting time with back stories. But, from what he knew of politicians they always wanted a fuller story to protect their backsides in case the shit hit the fan.

'Well to save time, minister, I'll give you the short version. During my days in Special Branch, I recruited Mary McAuley as an agent, working close within the higher ranks of the Provisional IRA and their political arm, Sinn Fein. During those years she provided vital intelligence, saving many people's lives. In the run-up to the peace process and the talks they involved, she was able to give a running insight into what the Republican movement was thinking and saying to help move the peace talks along. There may have been other people doing the same thing at the same time, but I think the information she provided was so beneficial, we probably wouldn't be where we are today and have a peace process where both sides put down their weapons and are talking instead of killing.' Reece stopped talking and waited for a response from the minister.

'Thank you for that, David. My own view is that if it was not for agents such as Mary, and undercover officers working behind the scenes such as yourself, we may have taken a lot longer to get where we are today with the peace process. Can I ask you where you are today, I mean in your personal relationship with Miss McAuley?'

One thing Reece was beginning to realise about Freeman was that he took no prisoners. getting straight to the point and wasn't afraid to ask the difficult questions.

'Since the last operation I was involved in, which took place in London, you may be aware of, Mary and I'd hoped to retire to Malta and that's where we've been the last month. The night before her mother's accident, I asked Mary to marry me, and she said yes. So, answering your question, minister, our relationship is one based on solid ground where we both want a future together, hopefully living in Malta into our old age in peace and away from all this shit.'

'Thank you, David. I think we all understand where you're coming from. Now, Jim, as I understand it from the prime minister, both David and Mary played a significant role in saving his life during the recent operation in Manchester.'

'That's correct, minister. David has been working with the department for a few years after having retired as a detective inspector in Special Branch here in Northern Ireland. Just before the Conservative Party Conference last year, his old agent Mary McAuley made contact to say she'd information that there was going to be some sort of attack in Manchester. After further investigation and more intelligence from Mary, we were able to ascertain that the target was the prime minister attending the conference.

'We were also able to discover that the terrorist operation was a joint one between a member of the Real IRA, Sean Costello, and an Islamic terrorist cell led by Sharon Lyndsey. On this occasion, Mary McAuley put herself at great risk in helping spot Costello, who she knew personally from her days working within the Provisional IRA. We now believe that it was during the operation in Manchester that Mary may have been identified as working with us, this information then being passed back to the Real IRA, who we now believe instigated her mother's hit-and-run, putting her in hospital forcing Mary back to Belfast, into the open where she could be abducted. It is also possible that David is a target either for abduction or assassination.'

Freeman raised his hand and nodded towards Jim Broad.

'Just a quick one, Jim. This may be a bit of information that David is unaware of. The brother of Sean Costello is Paul Costello, and he's a senior Sinn Fein MLA or member of the local assembly here in Northern Ireland. So he would be one of the people that I'll be talking to as we try to get Mary returned. I've spoken to him in the past and I find him to be opposed to violence, but in the case of getting revenge for his brother's death, his views may have changed. Please continue, Jim.'

'I have much more to say, minister. As regards to the operation in Manchester, subsequent intelligence we received at the time confirms Sean Costello, who had been a member of the Real IRA after the peace process, had gone rogue, and was carrying out the operation without the sanction of the Army Council. It is our belief that Sean and Paul had both gone separate ways after the ceasefire and the signing of the Good Friday Agreement.'

'Caroline, can you bring us up to date with any new information from the MI5 and GCHQ point of view?' asked Freeman.

Reece noticed Caroline Aspinall had a small file in front of her, which she now opened.

'Thank you, minister. As soon as I was made aware of the abduction by ACC Wilson and our own offices based at Palace Barracks, I immediately requested that anything we had on the Real IRA, specifically the Belfast Brigade, should be forwarded to me, so that I could brief everyone here. From a few telephone intercepts, I can confirm that this abduction has been planned and carried out by the Real IRA, under the orders of Chief of Staff Brendan McDevitt and their Army Council. The police surveillance team has for some time been watching the movements of the Real IRA Belfast Brigade Commander Brian McNally. They noticed recently he was using a public phone box near his home on the Falls Road to make and receive calls. Because of the intercept on this phone in the follow up to the abduction, we noticed he made a call to a number in the Republic of Ireland. He had a cryptic conversation about having a package, which he would now deliver. We recognised the voice of the person in the Republic of Ireland as that of John Jo Murphy. We had his voice on record from when he'd talked previously with Sean Costello during the Manchester operation. On that occasion Costello had set him the task of tracking down Mary McAuley if she was in Belfast, because he believed he'd seen her in Manchester. John Jo Murphy is now a senior member of the Real IRA and we believe he's been put in charge of the operation to abduct Mary, then have her brought across the border for interrogation, and subsequently, no doubt execution.'

While listening to the director of MI5, Reece couldn't help thinking, *no shit, Sherlock*. Reece remembered back to his days in Special Branch and working with the MI5 bugging teams who operated out of the military base at Palace Barracks in Hollywood. He wasn't surprised to hear that they were still working out of the same building, as it was a relatively secure location outside Belfast city. Caroline Aspinall turned over a page of the notes. Pushing her glasses back on the bridge of her nose, she continued.

'Obviously goes without saying that everything I tell you in this room regarding our technical operations and transcripts resulting from them is top secret.' Everyone nodded.

'We have another operation running, which has been running for some time, covering the Wolfe Tone Club in West Belfast. The club is a popular drinking den for all the Republican factions in the city. We have both phones and the bar area itself covered, although you'll understand because of the noise side it's difficult to hear voice conversations sometime. I'm telling you this because although we do not have any voice conversations indicating anything to do with this abduction, we do have a phone call conversation between Brian McNally and an unknown male. The male confirmed that they had the package and were safe at the location. McNally told the unknown male that there was the expected security force's response, sealing off the areas, blocking roads. He told the unknown male they may have to stay where they were for a couple of days but that he'd be in touch to update him.

'We don't know where the unknown male is, but the phone number he was using refers to a call box in Andersonstown. Now that we've his phone number, GCHQ will keep a monitor on it, but from the conversation we expect the unknown male to call McNally again at 1pm tomorrow.

'I've told ACC Wilson the location of the call box and he'll have eyes on it if he can identify the caller and maybe follow him. We will continue to monitor all three phones. The call box used by McNally, and the one used by the unknown male, plus the Wolf Tone Club. I'm sure everyone agrees the conversations all indicate that Mary is being held somewhere in the North of Ireland, most likely still in Belfast. I'm sorry, I can't give you anything more at this time, minister. When we get more, it might give us the opening we need to track down these people, allowing us to react, and get Mary back.' Aspinall tidied up the papers in front of her and closed the folder.

Reece could see the evening being lit up by the spotlights on the outside lawn casting shadows across the grass. The SOS stood and looked at the faces looking back.

'Thank you everyone. David, I hope that what you've heard reassures you that we are doing everything we can to get Mary back safely. I want you to work with Tom and Jim, but please, no heroics on your own. This is a delicate matter and there's more involved here than just the recovery of Miss McAuley, as I'm sure you will understand. Everyone knows what they must do. For my part I'll have the senior members of Sinn Fein, including Paul Costello here for a meeting this evening, after which I'll speak with the prime minister. As for the press and media who are already onto this: my own Press Officer and the Press office at the PSNI will be the only ones to have any contact with them. For now, all we say is we've received a report of a possible abduction of a female, and enquiries are ongoing. Questions regarding the follow-up searches and police road stops in the West of the city can be covered by the usual answer that we are carrying out investigations into dissident activity. Let me not detain you any further. Caroline and Tom, can you stay behind? I need to go over a few things with you before I meet with the Republican politicians. Thank you, everyone. We all have a job to do, so let's get on with it.'

Reece could see Freeman as a commander of men in a military setting, but having nodded to the SOS his understanding, he had no intention of leaving this to a politician. As everyone stood to leave, Broad came round the table and shook Reece by the hand before whispering.

'I'm sorry about all this, David, but as you can see, we are putting everything into getting Mary back. Can I walk you back to your car?'

As they walked back down the long corridor and out into the car park, Broad said nothing more.

'Mine's the BMW,' said Reece, taking the keys out of his pocket and pressing the remote. The side lights flashed, and they could hear a loud click as the doors unlocked.

'So, boss, what is it you want to talk about?'

'That politician in there talks a good talk. We'll have to see if he walks the walk. I wanted to speak to you alone to reassure you of mine and Fraser's full support. We're taking a risk letting you know you can run your own investigation outside the parameters and restrictions of the local political scene. When you get back to the hotel, you'll find Joe Cousins and our friend from the SAS, Captain Geoff Middleton, waiting for you. They travelled over by Puma to the Hanger at RAF Aldergrove at the same time Caroline and I flew from London. Before they left, I briefed them at the SG9 office at the city airport. Everything you heard in there and more is in a file for your eyes only that they have with them. They also have equipment for you that you might need. I'll be available twenty-four seven but, as I might need to head back to London you should proceed as you see fit. I know you gave me your resignation notice but as it wasn't in writing I've told Sir Ian, you're still on the books.'

Broad took a small wallet out of his pocket and handed it to Reece.

'It's your old MI5 get out of jail ID. Only use it if you really need to and don't get caught with it on you or it might bring you more trouble than you need.'

'I don't know if I should thank you or not, but I do appreciate that you're putting your neck on the line. I'm not going to give any guarantee that this will end happily but, I can assure you if people hurt Mary or come after me. Then they'll know what hurt really means. Why are you putting your neck on the line, anyway?'

'Two reasons. The first is through the prime minister via Sir Martin Bryant and C. They all know your past and what you can do, and as they expect you'll do whatever it takes to get Mary back, anyway, they would rather we had some control of that. The second, as I'm sure you're sick of hearing, is the danger that this has brought or could bring to the peace process if it goes tits up and there was a shoot-out on the streets of Belfast between members of the British Security forces and dissident republicans. That is to be avoided at all costs and I suspect that will be one of the points the SOS is now pressing on Tom Wilson and Caroline as we speak. The Republican delegation he'll meet with later will be told the same thing.'

Broad reached into his pocket and removed a mobile phone which he handed to Reece.

'This phone is encrypted. It's the latest Samsung model and won't be picked up by anyone who wants to listen in. It already has three numbers on speed dial, Joe Cousins, Geoff Middleton, and me. If you need to add anyone to the list, feel free to do so, but make sure it's only people we can trust. This operation is off the books, David, as I'm sure you're beginning to understand. You get caught, you're on your own, and we'll totally deny you as having gone rogue. David, you know this country better than any of us. You know what makes these bastards tick, so I'm hoping you'll be able to get inside their heads. You will have noticed that at the meeting we just had, there were no files or photos provided of the people we think are involved. I think in all reality, the politicians are shitting themselves and just want this to go away. That means a body at the border. If it's been done in the Republic, they can do a Pontius Pilate and wash their hands of everything. I'll be in back in London and I'll keep you up to date from there. In the meantime, get back to the hotel and catch-up with Joe who has all the information you need to know about the bastards we think lifted Mary and the ones behind it. Geoff has a Smith and Wesson 59, which has the firepower you like. At least it's better than the Walther Tom Wilson gave you. He wants it back, by the way.'

Broad held out his left hand and Reece placed the Walther with the spare mag into it before shaking Broad's right hand.

'Thank Sir Ian for me. If this goes sideways, I know I'll only have myself to blame,' said Reece.

'If this goes sideways, we are all fucked for the future, but we all need a little bit of excitement now and then, and the one thing I've found since I got to know you, David, is that there's always a little excitement just around the corner.'

Chapter 22

Hilton hotel, Belfast

Joe Cousins and Geoff Middleton were sitting at a table in the hotel's main bar. It was Cousins who spotted Reece and waved him over.

'Normally, I'd say it's great to see you too, but under the circumstances...I'm glad you're here anyway,' said Reece, pulling up a chair.

'Good to see you too.' Cousins smiled. 'We just got a round in. Do you want one?'

'That would be good. It's been one bitch of a day. Thanks, Joe.'

'The usual?'

'Yeah, Bushmills, make it a double, thanks.'

Reece leant over to shake the hand of the SAS man.

'I'm glad your both here Geoff. I've just been to a meeting with the SOS for Northern Ireland and the security people involved and I'm glad to say we are starting to get some information on where this is all heading.'

Cousins returned and handed the whisky to Reece, who took a large gulp before setting the glass down.

'Thanks, Joe, I needed that,' said Reece.

'So, I see, but don't drink it too quickly. Have you seen the prices in here?' replied Cousins.

'London briefed us, and we've a file in my bag here for you to read later,' said Middleton, pointing to the grip bag beside his leg.

'Yes, Jim Broad told me, and I believe you have something a bit heavier as well.' Reece smiled.

'Also in the bag,' replied Middleton. 'We have booked into the hotel, but we're sharing a twin room. I hope he doesn't snore too loudly.'

'Let's finish these drinks and go to my room for a catch-up on everything. I think we are going to have a busy day tomorrow,' said Reece.

The three men talked for over an hour. They discussed what had happened so far and with the help of the file that the men had brought from London, Reece was able to quickly bring himself up to speed with the people they were up against. It had been a while since he'd interested himself so closely with the Republican Movement in Ireland and the main people involved. The file had one page of information on each of the named people he'd heard about and a couple he hadn't. Names, DOBs addresses, and places frequented with aerial photos and maps, and up-to-date full-face photos attached to each briefing sheet.

Now he knew what McNally, Walsh, and the brother, and sister Bailey looked like. Then at the back of the file, more information. this time the breakdown of the Real IRA high command including Brendan McDevitt, John Joe Murphy, and finally the MLA Paul Costello. Setting the file on the bed and spacing out the photos, Reece wiped his tired eyes.

'A nice bunch,' said Middleton.

'Yes, we've been over the file a few times on the way here. I don't think there is one of them who shouldn't be six foot under,' said Cousins.

'And this might be what's needed to do the job,' said Middleton as he reached into the grip bag and handed the Smith and Wesson with two mags to Reece.

Reece felt the familiar weight. He pushed one of the mags into the handle before pulling the slide back, allowing a nine mil parabellum round into the barrel before putting the gun into the right pocket of his Barbour jacket lying on the bed. It was always the way special forces carried a weapon, one in the barrel ready to go. He slipped the spare magazine into his trouser pocket.

'I have a few extra boxes of ammo in the bag as well if we need them,' said Middleton before lifting out an ear Mike. We have these for close comms, and the frequency won't be picked up by any nosey people.'

'So, David, we know from the files and today's updates who these people are. What happens next? What are we going to do?' asked Cousins.

'To tell you the truth, Joe, I don't have a clue. I would like to kick McNally's door in and squeeze the truth out of the bastard, but two things are stopping me. He would probably laugh in my face unless he knew I was serious about killing him, which, believe me, I would love to. The second reason is that whatever we do from now on in we've to be aware that these same bastards are under surveillance from a very good police team and maybe even MI5 watchers, so if they spot us we may become the targets taking the pressure off McNally and his friends.'

'In my past I did a little surveillance in and around the city. I don't know it as well as you, David, but from what I've seen coming from

Aldergrove it's changed quite a bit. But as we all know from Manchester, a city's a city, and you can get lost or lose a tail within a few streets, so I say let's get out there tomorrow and shake the tree to see what falls,' said Cousins.

'I agree Joe, we won't get Mary back sitting here waiting for news. News we might not get, if I know how these politicians operate. They believe in one thing only and that's knowledge is power. The SOS has already shown everyone that for this operation and the protection of the peace process he's in control of everything, and that will include what he wants us to know,' said Reece.

Reece lifted the file off the bed and looked through the pages. Cousins and Middleton both tried to read his thoughts as they watched his eyes scan the notes.

'You're both right. It's going to be a risk, but I'm not prepared to wait on any tidbits of information we might get. Jim Broad will do his best to keep us informed. Both him and C are putting their necks on the line by giving us the go ahead to find Mary. I think they understand there might be trouble if these bastards get Mary to a place where they can beat the information she has in her head out of her. If that were to happen, I don't think the SOS realises the damage it could do to his beloved peace process. Let's get a good night's sleep and meet back here in the morning about seven and we can go through a plan then.'

'I don't know about you Joe, but I'm famished, so I'm going out to find a decent chip shop and grab me a fish supper, said Middleton, walking to the door.

'Wait up Geoff, I'm coming with you,' replied Cousins. 'See you in the morning, David.'

After both men left Reece called down to reception and asked them to send up a double Bushmills.

Chapter 23

The Hayshed

'I really do need to go to the toilet and if it means that bucket you can turn your heads away,' Mary said loudly.

'Now don't you worry your little head. We have seen it all before.' Laughed Walsh.

'Let her piss in her pants,' said Mariad Bailey.

'OK, that's enough, Mariad, stop messing about. There's a small toilet at the back. Take her there but keep the door open and watch her,' said Walsh.

Mariad stood behind Mary and prodded her in the back with the Browning pistol to make her stand, then followed her to the back of the building, where there was what Mary could only think was another small bucket, but this time made of porcelain with no seat. It looked like it hadn't been cleaned in years.

'Sorry, but if you tell us what we need to know we can provide an upgrade,' said Mariad as she waved the gun upwards, a look of hatred on her face.

'For what I need that will have to do,' said Mary.

The woman held the gun and watched, never taking her eyes away until Mary was finished. Then, pointing the gun at Mary, waved it to direct her back to the chair.

'We are going to be here overnight, so let's all try to get some sleep. We will take turns to watch, three hours each. I'll take the first three hours, then you, Jimmy, and then you, Mariad,' said Walsh, who then turned to Mary. 'You. Get over to the bed in the corner and stay there. Sleep if you can, but if you can't, don't worry, you'll be sleeping soon enough. For good.'

Mary lay on the top of the blanket that was covering an old mattress. She could smell the sweat and urine from years of use and could feel the iron springs beneath the bed. *It must have come from an old doss house or hospital*, she thought. Walsh was standing beside the bed before he stooped down to tie a small metal chain around her ankle and pulled it tight before attaching the chain around the bed's metal leg with a small padlock.

'There now, all settled for the night. Do you want me to tell you the bedtime story of the wicked witch?' He laughed.

'No, thank you,' replied Mary before turning to face the wall. Her back to the room and her abductors, she struggled to hold back the tears.

Chapter 24

Belfast

All three men had breakfast together in the large hotel restaurant. Reece introduced Cousins and Middleton to the famous Ulster Fry, which, although both men had worked in Northern Ireland in the past, neither had tasted. *Probably*, thought Reece, *because both had been billeted on army bases, so had to put up with military food.*

'Now that's what I call a breakfast,' said Middleton.

'I agree,' said Cousins, as he burped loudly.

'It will keep us going. This is going to be a long day, and God knows when we'll be able to get another bite,' answered Reece.

'What's the plan for today, then?' asked Middleton.

The table Reece had picked for breakfast overlooked the city, and was away from other diners, so he could speak normally without the danger of others overhearing.

'I've been thinking about that. After breakfast, I'll call Wilson then Broad for any updates and check up on what they're doing so that we don't interfere with their plans.'

'Plans?' asked Cousins.

'Yes. I have no doubt, as I said last night, that they'll have surveillance teams out watching McNally, the Wolfe Tone Club, and the phone box used by his unknown male contact yesterday, so we don't want to expose ourselves for now. I think we need to get to know where McNally lives and the other two locations without bringing attention to ourselves. According to McNally's file, he always has lookouts watching over him, so if we need to get to him it will have to be done very carefully. The usual tourist maps are no good as they don't cover West Belfast, especially Andersonstown. First thing this morning I went to a newsagent across the road and bought two maps. On one side is the whole of Belfast, on the other is the rest of Northern Ireland down to the border showing Monaghan and Louth in the Republic,' said Reece, handing one of the folded maps to Cousins.

'I've already circled in red ink McNally's home and the Wolfe Tone Club. you can familiarise yourselves back in the car. What car do you have anyway?' Reece asked.

'It's a Toyota Avensis. Dark blue supplied by the military surveillance unit based at Aldergrove. It has local plates, and it has a local security radio, so we'll be able to monitor what's going on. It's not armoured but should be good enough for what we need,' answered Cousins.

'Good, I'll be in a hired black BMW. I'll take mine today and you can work in the Toyota. The encrypted phones will help us communicate alongside the ear mics, especially if we need to be on foot. So, I suggest we get out and spend a couple of hours getting to know West Belfast before McNally gets his one o'clock call. When that happens, if we are lucky, the surveillance teams will be able to follow the unknown male to where they're holding Mary. In the meantime, let's just stick to the tried and tested call signs. I'm Alpha One. Joe, you're Two, and Geoff, you're Three. If any of us has McNally on the move, we call him Tourist One and if we identify his unknown male contact, he's Tourist Two. Joe, are you sure these ear mics will work?'

'They'll be OK over short distances. I have two handheld walkie-talkie radios in the car, which cover a larger area. I don't know if they can be picked up by MI5, if they are, as we expect, listening in for any radio traffic.'

'That's good. We'll have one in each car and only use them in an emergency if we lose each other at an important time. Before they tie us down, whatever will happen will happen anyway,' replied Reece. 'For now, let's get out there, and get to know the land, then meet up in about two hours to catch-up.'

'Geoff can study the map as we are driving. I know a bit of the West Belfast area, at least the main roads which, I'm sure, haven't changed too much,' said Cousins.

The next few hours passed as Reece had expected, joining in with the traffic on the main roads and making sure they did not bring attention to themselves, especially when they drove through the heartland areas of the Falls Road and Beechmount where McNally lived. Then, keeping conversation to a minimum, they drove past the location where MI5 had indicated the phone box used by the unknown male during his call with McNally. Reece couldn't spot any surveillance on either, which was good.

He knew they would be concentrating their eyes on anyone approaching the phone box, so he made sure to pass it at a consistent speed in case they spotted his hire car. Either way, he only made one pass and didn't care if Wilson got in touch to ask what he was doing in the target area. He would tell him he wanted to know the area a little better just in case he could help in any way. Wilson had no idea that he'd be working with Cousins and Middleton with the blessing of SG9 and MI6. As the saying went, need-to-know, and Wilson didn't need to know. The biggest danger, as Reece could see it, was a blue-on-blue situation if they ran into the surveillance teams at the same time they were moving on McNally and his crew. They had agreed to work by the Israeli rule only to use their weapons if their lives were in danger or someone became an enemy combatant by their actions. Until then, their weapons would remain concealed.

The weather had been kind. Even though there were dark clouds threatening impending rain, it had stayed dry, but a cold breeze was keeping the temperature down. Reece was remembering the streets and routes before they came to him. The traffic, as in any city, meant he kept his speed down. When he drove off the main Falls Road and into the Beechmount area, the streets all appeared to contain the same red-bricked, small, terraced houses. Some with fenced-off front gardens, others with the doorstep right on the pathway passing the house. At the rear of the houses, there were long alleyways, or ginnels, as they would call them in England. It was through this alleyway system that IRA killers were able to attack army and police patrols during the Troubles before escaping out the back and entering another house on the other side of the alley. Then exiting on a completely different street to make their getaway complete. The satnav included with the hire car was ideal, in that it would show streets that were a dead end, where, if he'd entered them, he would have to turn to come back out. He knew from his days of surveillance this was dangerous in two ways: people living in the streets always noticed strange vehicles turning and not stopping. Also, they were ideal for boxing someone in for an attack.

Reece spoke into his mic. 'Let's take a break and meet for a coffee. There's a Starbucks on Boucher Road just the other side of the motorway. See you there in about twenty minutes.'

'Roger that,' came the reply from Middleton.

Reece remembered Boucher Road as a long straight road with a mixture of large retail stores, storage units, and some small shopping malls. The entrance to Windsor Park, the Northern Ireland national football stadium, was near the Donegal Road end of the road. Boucher Road was ideal for them to meet and catch-up, as it was just outside West Belfast but had easy access routes into the area they'd been working in.

Reece reached the car park of the Starbucks in ten minutes and used the time to phone both Broad and Wilson. The time was 11 a.m. In two hours, the unknown male was to make his call. Reece wanted to make sure there was no change to what was going to happen before he met with Cousins and Middleton. Broad assured him that there'd been nothing more to report and Wilson would only say his people were out on the ground but nothing unusual yet and that he'd let him know if anything changed. Wilson asked Reece where he was, and Reece lied when he told Wilson he was walking around the shops in the city centre. This seemed to please Wilson and Reece didn't care if it did or not.

The coffee house was busy, filled with the standard chairs and the smell of coffee Reece always felt that with the noise of the chattering customers and the large coffee machines, specialist coffee shops were a safe place to meet and talk. Most of the customers in the queue were getting their coffee to take out. Reece ordered his usual medium Americano with cold milk on the side and sat at a table by the large window just in time to see Cousins and Middleton park up. Five minutes later all three men looked out at the car park from the same table.

'Have you been all right finding your way around?' asked Reece.

'Yes, no problem. Joe knows the place better than he thought, and the maps are good,' replied Middleton.

'We did a drive-pass on the Wolfe Tone Club, the phone box, and McNally's home address. All quiet for now,' said Cousins.

'Yeah, me too,' said Reece. 'I think if things go as we understand them, then this whole thing could be over by two. We should park up just outside the areas where we think the surveillance teams will be operating. I'll cover the area where the phone box is and you two the Wolfe Tone Club. That way, we should be able to give further back-up if needed, but remember we are not supposed to be here, so we are in a wait and see situation for now.'

Joe Cousins nodded before speaking. 'We only did one drive past in Beechmount where McNally lives. We noticed a couple of things. There were two young lads obviously doing lookout. That's why we only did one drive through. We didn't want them to clock us. Then when we drove down the street Geoff spotted a security camera on the wall of the house which would cover the approach to the front door. If he's that security aware, then you can be sure he'll have one covering the back of the house.'

Reece let this information sink in before he spoke. 'I spotted the lads when I did my drive through as well. Because I was keeping my eyes on the road and the car at a constant speed, I didn't see the camera, so I want to change the plan. You two sit outside the area of surveillance at the Wolfe Tone Club. If, as I suspect, the lads doing lookout will be lifted when McNally is away, then I'll break into his house at the back.'

'What? Are you mad?' reacted Cousins.

'Probably. But I'm thinking, what if something goes wrong? What if the surveillance team loses the unknown male and they don't find Mary? If I'm in his house, I might find a clue to where she is and I could be there waiting for McNally when he gets home to question him myself. If Wilson's people find Mary and let me know, I can leave the house before McNally returns and we lose nothing by my having been there.'

'What if McNally returns with others or you get caught in there? Or there's a camera at the back?' asked Middleton.

'It's a risk I must take. No back-door camera, then I'm good to go. That's where you both come in. If I don't hear anything positive from Jim Broad or Wilson, I'm depending on you two confirming where McNally is and if he's with anyone.'

'What if he stays in the club? We can't hang around forever,' asked Cousins.

'If we've no word on Mary either by the surveillance or MI5 and GCHQ, then we'll have to go with my plan to wait for McNally to get home.'

Cousins looked at Middleton before replying to Reece.

'I still say you're mad. If everyone, including us, are the other side of West Belfast looking at McNally and the phone box you'll be on your own without back-up. If you're spotted or challenged, you're on your own. To be honest with you, David, it's a plan I'm not happy with.'

'That's why I must do it. No one, not even Wilson and Broad, will expect it. They'll be concentrating on McNally and if, for some reason his plans change, then we need to be ahead of the game. If we don't find Mary alive and well today, then I want to make sure Brian McNally gives me answers. We all know that if the local police lift him, he'll smile back at them over a desk saying nothing and his Republican-supporting solicitor will get him free after shouting about the violation of his human rights. McNally doesn't give a shit about human rights, and that's why Mary is in the danger she is now, if she's still alive.'

Reece felt he was raising his voice in frustration trying to get his argument across then remembering where he was, he continued speaking softly enough for the two men to hear him.

'Yes, gentlemen, I've had to think the worst that, if she's not dead already she will be soon and that will only be after they've tortured the life out of her. So, Joe, I'm going to be waiting for McNally if we don't find Mary this afternoon. Where you can help is to confirm when he's going home and if he's on his own. Then you can stay in the area where, if I need you, you can come quickly. I hope that we won't get that far, but it's something I must do.'

This time it was Geoff Middleton's turn to speak. 'We can see you're going to do this with or without our permission, or anyone else's, for that matter. So, of course, we'll be with you on this, but if you're going to have that face to face with McNally, make it quick, and quiet. We don't want a shoot-out on the streets of Belfast. We all know what that will mean. If we get out alive, we'll probably end up in jail and you might have started another war.'

'I know the risk, Geoff, and what I ask of you. But I ask it because we've been in those kinds of situations together not so long ago, and I can't think of any other people I would rather have backing me today.'

Both men nodded back at Reece.

'OK, thank you. We need to make sure our communications are working well. 'We'll have need of them before the day is out either way. We should leave the secure phones open when you have information on McNally. Switch them on and have the Bluetooth linked to the radio so I can listen into what's going on. Ideally, we'd have a team of twelve, but this will have to do.'

Once again, both men nodded. All three left. They split up, with Reece heading towards the Beechmount area of the Falls Road and Cousins and Middleton heading towards the area around the Wolfe Tone Club.

Chapter 25

SG9 Control Room, London City Airport

Sir Martin Bryant hated this place. He hated having to drive out of the capital to the offices of SG9 at the business section location of London City Airport. but today was one of those times when it had been necessary. The prime minister had insisted he be there to oversee what was happening in Belfast. Apart from the two communications operators manning the vast array of technical equipment in front of them, which included video feedback, the only other person in the room, sitting next to him, was Jim Broad. The large clock on the wall showed 12.40. They could hear the radio traffic from the Belfast surveillance teams. They had reported McNally leaving his home in Beechmount Parade and walking to the Falls Road where he flagged down a black cab which then took him to the Wolfe Tone Club in the Turf Lodge area of West Belfast. McNally seemed to be alone on his journey, without minders or lookouts. Broad had told Bryant it was probably because the operation McNally was involved in would be of the highest secrecy, and the less some of his people knew the better, in case they were lifted by the security forces. The prime minister, like all politicians, didn't like things being out of their control or blowing up in their faces. Having Bryant there would help insure, if things went sideways. The finger of blame wouldn't be pointed back at him. Jim Broad knew exactly why Bryant was there, and after he'd spoken to Sir Ian Fraser, the Director of MI6, they'd agreed with him that if things did go wrong in Belfast. He would have to throw David Reece to the wolves as an ex-agent gone rogue completely out of their control.

'Now we wait,' said Broad.

'I'm sure this is the part you hate,' replied Bryant.

'Yes, every time, and it never gets better with experience, either.'

'Do 'we have control of Reece?' asked Bryant.

'The Belfast MI5 team put a tracker on his car last night. One that only we here can see on the computer map of the city on the wall,' replied

Broad pointing at a large screen which had a red line electronically drawn through the map.

'The red line shows where he's been and is now. I know he told ACC Wilson this morning that he'd be walking about the city centre shopping while he waited on word from him. But as we both know Reece is not the kind of man to wait. And, as I suspected, that's not the case. As you can see if you follow the journey of the red line, he's spent most of his morning in West Belfast, passing by two of our locations of interest before most recently parking up on Boucher Road.'

Bryant crossed the room and standing with his arms folded across his chest he stood to get a closer look at the large screen in front of the operations desk. Broad walked over to stand beside him before speaking slowly so that Bryant would understand every word he said.

'As you can see. The surveillance car we provided for Cousins and Middleton has a built-in system that also provides live feedback on where the car is. That's the green line on the map. We know from that feedback that they've also been moving around the target areas in the West of the city. It parked up in Boucher Road at the same time as Reece, probably for a quick coffee and a chat about what happens next if I know Reece. Both vehicles are heading back into West Belfast and although we've this feedback, because of the distance between us here and Belfast, it has a delay of five minutes, so we'll always be slightly behind.'

'But what about the police surveillance teams? Will they not spot your people?' Asked Bryant.

There it was thought Broad the use of the words, your people, another pointer to the ass covering of the politician.

Broad took a deep breath before he answered.

'Reece and the other two are well trained and have been involved in this kind of operation many times. They know how to avoid being spotted and from the tracking we've seen, apart from them doing one drive past of the target locations, they've stayed just outside the circle of police surveillance covering each of the targets. You must remember this is West Belfast, and even the police surveillance teams will have to treat the area as working in enemy territory. Their concentration won't only be on their targets, but also in avoiding detection themselves, which could blow the whole operation. A car driving once by their target won't raise any suspicion and our people know that.'

The clock on the wall showed 12.50. Both men knew in ten minutes the route this operation was taking would be decided. For now, silence, apart from the odd bit of radio traffic coming over the airwaves. Although the operation room was large, for those minutes to Broad, it seemed the smallest room in the world.

Chapter 26

Andersonstown, West Belfast

Mary had found it hard to sleep. The bed was uncomfortable, feeling lumpy, and she could feel some of the springs and smell stale sweat. She was sure she'd been bitten on the back of her hand at least twice by something that was sharing the bed with her. She'd not been alone in the bed. She'd heard her captors swap over for their stint of guard duty during the night, whispering to each other as they did so, and then there was loud snoring. To her surprise, when she looked to see who it was, the woman lying on her back gave out another large grunt as she breathed ever-more loudly. Eventually dawn started to break and all three of her captors were up using what ablutions there were. Walsh made tea and from a holdall produced sandwich packs.

'I hope you're not a veggie, as I could only get ham or chicken,' he said, giving Mary a choice of the two packs he held out to her.

Mary didn't want to, but she was starving, not having eaten anything since breakfast in the hotel the day before. She silently took the chicken pack, and unwrapping it, took a large bite.

'Easy now, we don't want you to choke yourself. You might have a bit of travelling to do today,' said Walsh.

The rest of the morning passed slowly for Mary. They had placed her back in the chair in the middle of the shed, this time using one of the plastic ties to secure her right leg to the chair leg. She wasn't running anywhere soon. The woman tried to engage her in conversation, but always with a sneer and a sarcastic comment, so Mary ignored her. She wasn't going to waste her breath. Walsh and Jimmy Bailey sat at the table making conversation which Mary couldn't hear, but she knew by their body language and the way they kept their voices down they were discussing her and what was going to happen next.

Walsh looked at his watch and moved towards the door.

'Right, you two, keep a close eye on her. I'm away to call the boss. In the meantime, get packed up here in case we need to move quickly. Any nonsense from our guest, you have my permission to give her a good slap.'

Mary could see that Walsh was in charge and the other two knew it as well, so she had no intention of giving them an excuse to give her a slap.

Walsh walked down Owenvarragh Road with the large Roger Casement Park to his right and the Andersonstown Leisure Centre to his left. At the main Andersonstown Road, he watched for surveillance, noting the people walking about, what they were wearing, and where they were walking. He checked the cars and vans that passed him and any that were parked up with people inside them. He pulled the hood of his parka coat up, not only to hide his face from observers, but to protect him from the rain that was falling at a steady pace. Because of this, there were few people out and about, even though it was the lunchtime period. When they'd met with Brian McNally in the Wolfe Tone Club, he'd briefed Walsh on his own. Apart from putting him in overall control for this part of the operation he'd set out two scenarios which he called Plan A and Plan B.

Plan A was the abduction of the tout and if things were all right security-wise, they could have brought her straight from the shed down the main Dublin Road out of Belfast then hand her over to their people on the southern side of the border.

That plan had to be cancelled due to the quick and large security-force response sealing off West Belfast and the Dublin Road routes. They knew this was a possibility, so McNally had agreed a Plan B, which included them having to delay until they were sure they could move. This time, when Walsh came to the main road, he'd turned right and walked in the opposite direction to the day before. The traffic was busier, and he kept his head down to avoid the spray from the passing vehicles. He walked about two hundred yards to a Chinese takeaway where he went in and ordered four chips and rice with curry sauce. While the food was being prepared, he made a call from the public phone on the wall of the waiting area. It was 1 p.m. exactly. After the call he collected his order and leaving the carry out, once more he turned right and walked another two hundred yards to reach his destination, the West City Car Dealership. Walsh stopped and, pulling his hood tighter, he quickly looked behind him. He was alone on the road; the rain keeping other walkers from the streets.

Satisfied he wasn't under surveillance he walked through the forecourt of the dealership and, entering the main sales room spoke to the receptionist just inside the main doors.

'Is Frank Connor about?'

'Can I ask what it's about, please?' asked the receptionist.

'He's expecting me. I'm picking up a car,' replied Walsh.

'Mister Connor is in his office, just go through,' said the receptionist, pointing to a glass-partitioned office at the rear of the showroom.

Walsh walked to the office. Knocking on the door, he entered without waiting for a reply.

Standing looking at a white board showing sales figures on the wall was the owner of the dealership, Frank Connor. He was a short bald and overweight man wearing a tight-fitting grey suit. The man turned to see who this was entering without invitation and intruding on his concentration.

'Can I help you?' he asked Walsh.

'I hope so. Brian McNally sent me,' replied Walsh.

That was all that was needed. The words, by the look on the man's face, struck him like a thunderbolt but with a resignation of understanding.

'I was told you might be coming, but I hoped I wouldn't see you,' said Frank Connor.

'I've been told you have what I need,' said Walsh, not wanting to get into a long conversation with this man.

Connor looked as if he was going to be sick, his face white, and now showing beads of sweat under his chin.

'Well? I don't have much time,' said Walsh.

Connor fumbled as he opened the top drawer of a small filing cabinet and after a search, he produced a set of car keys and handed them to Walsh.

'It's parked at the back. A black Range Rover with the dark-tinted rear windows and a full tank of fuel as requested.' He realised he was talking fast, but he wanted this man out of his building as quickly as possible. The Real IRA Commander had sat down beside him a few nights before when he was in the Wolfe Tone Club for a quiet pint after work. McNally had spoken to him like the Don in the *Godfather* movie. 'I want you to do me a favour. You might never have to do it, but if you do, I'll owe you one.'

The favour was to provide a clean vehicle, which someone would call for. It was to be fully fuelled and have tinted rear windows. If there were no problems, he'd get the car back in its original condition. He would be told where to find it. If there were any problems, all he had to say was that it had been stolen. He knew who McNally was and his reputation. He wasn't going to argue. Walsh took the keys and left without saying more. Frank Connor sat down at his desk and felt he was going to be sick in to his bin.

Walsh always loved to drive top of the range cars and the Range Rover was exactly that, right down to that special smell you only get in brand-new cars. Despite what Connor had said, he checked to make sure the petrol tank was full. It needed to be, as they had a bit of a journey later. Walsh drove back to the shed and parked about twenty yards from the entrance.

'Right, here's some food, get it inta yeh right now, then get ready. I've spoken to the boss, and we'll be going for a bit of a drive and bringing our friend here with us,' said Walsh as he entered the shed.

'But they'll have details of the van. We'll get spotted,' said Mariad Bailey.

'Don't worry, we won't be using the van. I have a clean vehicle outside. Over lunch, I'll bring you up to date with what the boss's Plan B,' replied Walsh.

Chapter 27

West Belfast

When the secure phone buzzed, interrupting the comms connection with Cousins and Middleton, Reece knew it could only be Jim Broad.

'Yes, boss,' answered Reece, looking at the G-Shock watch which showed 13.05.

'David, a bit of bad news I'm afraid.'

'Tell me.'

'Our friend McNally received the call we expected at one on the dot. It was the same man's voice asking for him. The police surveillance teams had the phone box, but he didn't call from there. Five and GCHQ are trying to track down the location he made the call from, but I'm sure he'll be well away when they identify where.'

'For fuck's sake. What did they talk about?' asked Reece feeling angry, wanting to punch somebody, anybody.

'There we have another problem. The only conversation came from McNally who told our unknown male to go to Plan B immediately, to which the male replied understood. That was everything, no more I'm afraid.'

'What are the police and Five doing now?'

'Not much they can do. They still have the border roads and crossings sealed off with surveillance and road stops, and Five will continue to monitor all its resources. We don't know what Plan B means. It could mean anything from keeping Mary in a safe location in the city to trying to get her across the border,' said Broad.

He didn't want to mention the third option, that they may have already started to torture her and would shortly leave her dead body on a country road outside the city. He knew Reece would be thinking along the same lines.

'What about the politicians? What happened with the meeting the SOS had with the republicans and especially Paul Costello last night?'

Broad could hear the anger in the question and looking across the room at Martin Bryant he tried to pick his words carefully.

'Not much feedback. As far as I know, the minister laid down the law that Mary must be freed unharmed and if they knew anything about her abduction, they could tell the police anonymously if they wanted. Apparently, the Republican delegation wasn't too happy with the security forces' reaction, and they tried to say there was no evidence that republicans were involved at all. Costello was one of those leading with that argument. The minister left it with them that the British government would see it as a threat to the peace process if anything happened to Mary. I think that's as tough as he could be with them.'

Bryant nodded his approval at what Broad had said.

'Nothing more than I expected,' replied Reece. From the way Broad's voice was coming across, Reece felt he was being cautious. Instinct was telling Reece that someone was looking over Broad's shoulder, listening to the conversation. He sounded too formal, keeping straight to the point, which was unlike him.

'I've told ACC Wilson what I've told you, and I've let him know I would be telling you the result of McNally's phone conversation with our unknown male. You might get a call from him asking where you are. If he's the kind of policeman I think he is, he won't want you out there working on your own. Where are you now, anyway?'

'If he asks, you don't know. If he asks me, I won't tell him. It's now a need-to-know situation, and he doesn't need to know. I know the risks, but it's now time for you to let me get moving on these people.'

'That's why we sent you the back-up. We always knew this could go this way. I'll help in whatever way I can from here and anything I get, you'll get. But remember what I told you last night, David. If you're caught, you're on your own, and if you must shoot your way out of any situation, you will be classed as rogue.'

'Nothing new there, then. Understood, and thank you for the help.'

The line went dead and Broad could see the look of concern on Bryant's face.

'I'm not happy, Jim. I know Reece has the skills and we've used them to great effect to our benefit in the past, but this way we don't have complete control of him. I'm worried as I'm sure the PM is, to have him out there doing God knows what to get Mary McAuley back.'

'You're correct in saying we don't have complete control, but we've some. Cousins and Middleton are backing him up, and will be able to keep me updated as well. Personally, I wouldn't want anyone else out there tracking down the movements of these bastards other than David Reece.'

Bryant walked to the door of the operations room where he turned to face Broad.

'I'm sure you're right, Jim. But just in case, I'll speak with the prime minister in the hope this doesn't turn into a disaster.'

When Bryant left, Broad looked once more at the electronic wall map. He could see the red line that now showed Reece parking up in the Beechmount area of West Belfast and he thought, *Don't fuck this up, David, or we're all fucked.*

Chapter 28

Beechmount Parade

Reece parked up on the main Beechmount Avenue just off the Falls Road. He made sure not to park directly outside any of the driveways in the Avenue, but instead between two of the houses where he'd bring less attention to himself. Reece had been born in the Royal Victoria Hospital on the Falls Road not far from where he now sat in the car observing the street around him. All was quiet. there was no sign of lookouts or window curtains twitching, the rain keeping people indoors.

'Alpha One to Alpha two,' spoke Reece into the secure handheld radio.

'Alpha two send,' answered Cousins.

Reece informed Cousins of his conversation with Broad and the information that Tourist Two was in the wind.

'What's happening with Tourist One?' asked Reece.

'He is still in the club and the surveillance teams seem to be concentrating their focus on him for now.'

'As we decided this morning, I'll make a visit to his home location. When he moves, keep tabs on him and keep me updated by the secure phone. If he heads for his home location, I have the ear comms when you're close. That will give me time.'

'Roger Alpha One, be careful.'

'Will do.'

Reece left the car, gripping the handle of the gun in the pocket of his Barbour jacket. He felt a bit more secure in what he was going to do. He knew strangers in West Belfast could be spotted quickly and suspicions passed to the local IRA unit for investigation, so he didn't intend to hang about in the open. He crossed the road from where he'd parked his car and pulled the peak of the flat cap he was wearing tight down on his head. He turned into the long alleyway which stretched the full length of three hundred yards at the rear between the houses of Beechmount Parade on his left-hand side and Clowney Street on his right. Each house was protected by a ten-foot brick wall with a door leading into a back yard. Reece had raided many of these buildings in his RUC uniform days when he was stationed in Belfast as a young constable. The yards beyond the doors used to contain the outside toilets but were now most likely empty or a storage shed. Once inside the alleyway, he was protected from view. The high walls giving him protection from any prying eyes. If anyone else had been in the alleyway, it would have been difficult to avoid eye contact and the likelihood would be that he'd be challenged and asked who he was and what he was doing there. Again, the rain seemed to come to his aid. There was no one about, and the only noise were the footfalls made by Reece's canvas boots. He counted the doors in his head and when he reached what he thought was McNally's home he had it confirmed by the number 43 painted in white on the black door. The black refuse bin standing in front of the door with the same white painted number confirmed it. The door was made of wood and looked like it had been in place since the houses had been built nearly seventy years ago. Despite there being a Yale lock, Reece felt the door open with the slightest of pressure from his shoulder. He opened the door, slowly looking around for the telltale signs of cameras or alarm systems. He saw none, so pushed the door wider. No dog either. He stepped into the yard and closed the door behind him.

McNally's file showed that he lived alone and that his main security was his use of lookouts in the area when he was at home. The back door of the house with another yale lock and four panes of glass in the top half keeping it secure. The glass was single pane. None of the usual double glazed. Reece removed his cap and, placing it directly over the pane above the lock, used the butt of the Smith and Wesson to tap it gently. The glass broke easily and fell inside the door. Reece waited for a few seconds to see if there was any reaction to the noise, which was minimal, and with the rain hardly audible. He placed his hand through the broken window and reaching down inside, turned the lock, and opened the door. Once inside, he closed the door behind him and stood still, listening for any sound, for any movement. Again, he could see no sign of security cameras or alarms. He kept the gun in his hand, pointing it in front of him as he moved slowly. The kitchen was clean and tidy with dishes drying on the rack by the sink. Everything was quiet except for the buzzing of his phone in his pocket, which he ignored until after he checked the front living room, which was all clear.

'Hello.' He spoke quietly, noticing Broad's name on the screen.

'Hi, David, just an update. Our friend McNally has made a second short call using the phone in the Wolfe Tone Club. GCHQ tells us it was to the number in the Republic of Ireland that he's called before, speaking to the same man, who they identified as John Jo Murphy. All McNally had to say was that the package was on its way and will be at the handover at six tonight. Murphy only replied that in that case he would remain where he was to await the package and arrange things at his end. That's all we've for now, so they'll be transferring Mary as we speak.'

Reece felt as if someone had given him a kick in the stomach. Broad continued to speak, but Reece had difficulty hearing what he was saying. His head was spinning with thoughts of what to do next. Was being here the ideal place for now?

'Sorry, boss. What did you say?'

'Wilson's people are staying on McNally until he goes home, then they'll be moving about West Belfast and the motorway network, trying to pick up what they can, but I'm afraid it's a needle in a haystack for now. If I know anything about people like McNally, he's kept his distance from the operation, so he'll be heading home until he hears more. Do you want me to get Wilson to lift him and try to squeeze him?'

'No, not for now. Even if he did get something from him, it would take some time and we don't have time. And if he did talk, the bastard would probably lie to send us in the wrong direction. We couldn't believe a word that came out of his mouth.'

'You're the man on the ground, David. What do you suggest?'

'Leave this to us. Let the police do what they normally do, but if you can, keep them away from McNally for now.'

'Understood, whatever you do from now, be careful. I'll keep you informed if I get anything this end.'

The phone went dead, and Reece checked the two bedrooms and the bathroom. Everything in the house was neat and tidy, which was strange for a bachelor living on his own. Maybe McNally had a relative or cleaner who came in and looked after the place, although there was no mention of anyone in McNally's file. He went back to the living room and made himself comfortable in the large chair facing the front door. He rested the gun on his lap and took his time looking around him, noting the pictures on the wall and the top of the unlit fireplace. There was a framed copy of the Republican Proclamation, the one that had been read out by Patrick

Pearse on the steps of the GPO in Dublin, at the start of the uprising in 1916. That had eventually led to the War of Independence, Civil War, and the formation of the Irish Free State, now the Irish Republic. The window that looked out on the street was covered with a set of net curtains, making it difficult for anyone to investigate the house but easy for looking out. The room was warm but not hot enough to force Reece to remove his Barbour jacket. His stomach was still turning, but now under control, the professional in him taking over. The red light on the handheld radio, which was on silent, began to flash. He pressed the answer button.

'Alpha One come in, over.' It was Joe Cousins.

'Alpha One send, what have you got?'

'Tourist One just left the club. We can hear the comms of the surveillance teams following. He got into a black cab. He's on his own. Might be heading your way, over.'

'Roger Alpha Two. You're probably right but keep a listening to the comms and head closer to my location so we can use the ear mics.'

'Roger that, understood. On our way.'

Reece felt the gun in his hand and aimed it at the door.

'Now Mister McNally, let's see what you think when you have to face a man instead of a woman.'

Chapter 29

Belfast

Because Walsh had told them to have everything prepared, the brother and sister Bailey were ready to move.

'Do you need to use the toilet before we go? It might be some time before you'll get the chance again.' Walsh asked Mary.

'No I'm OK, but I'd rather stay here if you don't mind. You all go ahead and enjoy yourselves,' replied Mary, thinking that a little gallows humour might help her situation. She was still in the chair, her ankle strapped to the leg.

Mariad Bailey didn't want to miss the opportunity. She strode over to Mary and slapped her.

'That's enough,' shouted Walsh. 'She's only trying to goad you. Leave the beatings to our friends in the south. Remember she's not supposed to be harmed by us.'

'Well, the bitch is being smart mouthed,' snarled Mariad. 'And besides I don't like her anyway. A smack in the mouth is to little. She deserves a good kicking.'

Mary stared back at the woman. She desperately wanted to cry, and she could feel the blood trickle down the side of her lip and chin, but she wasn't going to let this bitch see the hurt. Instead, she just spat the blood on the floor and smiled back at her.

'Jimmy, cut her free from the chair before tying her hands in front of her.' Said Walsh. 'When we get to the car Mariad and I'll sit in the front, I'll drive. Jimmy, you sit in the back with her. If she plays up, gag her. Shoot her if she tries anything serious. Just so you understand bitch, we don't like your jokes or you. If you put any of us at risk, you're a dead woman earlier than you need to be.'

Walsh checked there was no one about before pressing the key fob to open the doors of the Range Rover, then signalled to his companions to move. Jimmy Bailey pulled Mary by the arm and pushed her roughly into the back seat before jumping in beside her. Mariad sat beside Walsh in front as he started the engine.

'This is the only way to travel. Sheer luxury, if only I owned it,' said Mariad.

'You never know. When we deliver our package we might get it as a bonus,' answered her brother.

'Let's deliver the package first. Keep a close eye on her,' said Walsh.

He drove down the Andersonstown Road onto the Falls Road, then through the West Link that connected the motorways through the city. Instead of turning right and taking the M1 towards the south and Dublin, he turned left, and headed for the M3, passing the George Best Belfast City Airport. They passed the towns of Hollywood and Bangor before driving down the coastal route away from the city. This way they travelled in the opposite direction to the one the security forces would expect. Mary watched as the familiar villages and towns passed. She knew the rear-tinted windows blocked anyone seeing into the back of the Range Rover. Jimmy held the Browning pistol on his lap, the barrel pointed in her direction. They were now travelling south on the Ards Peninsula. Mary knew it well and that the further south they travelled the less chance they would run into trouble. She'd travelled all over the area of the Peninsula in the past, from beach holidays with her parents to hotel stay overs with her husband. She'd travelled the full length of it, from Belfast down its east coast path to where it separated at Strangford Lough from the North Channel of the Irish Sea. If they continued to stay on this tourist route down the coast of Northern Ireland, instead of the direct route from Belfast using the motorways, she knew they would avoid the likelihood of running into a police roadblock. They had already passed two police cars that were travelling in the opposite direction, paying them no attention. The further they travelled from the city the more she noticed her three captors relax. Walsh had switched the radio on and tuned into BBC Radio Ulster. She noticed when the news bulletin came on there was little mention of her abduction, only that police enquiries were continuing.

'Even the local radio isn't interested any more,' said Walsh, looking at Mary in the rear-view mirror.

Mary didn't reply. Instead, she was trying to locate where they were and where they were going. The nearest area that boasted Republican sympathisers was South Down, but they were lightweights compared to the people in her old town of Newry, and then further into South Armagh, both of which they could be heading to. To get there by road they would have to cross Strangford Lough on the car ferry from the town of Portaferry to Strangford village itself, a ten-minute crossing where she hoped she'd be able to attract attention.

Chapter 30

West Belfast

'That's his cab approaching your location Alpha One.' It was the voice of Joe Cousins coming through strongly in the ear mic, making Reece jump. At least the equipment was working and now he knew that not only was McNally almost home, but Cousins, and Middleton were near enough to give him whatever support he needed. He pressed the button on the earpiece.

'Roger Alpha Two, I'm ready for him. Keep an eye out for any trouble.'

Reece sat up in the chair. He heard the cab pull up and one of its door's slam before it drove away. He heard the key in the front door, then it closed before McNally opened the inner door into the living room. The room was dark enough to make McNally stop and look twice to allow him to focus on the shape sitting in his living-room chair. He first identified the figure of a man and then the outline of a semi-automatic pistol pointing at his chest. He didn't know the man personally, but he knew his face from the pictures that John Jo Murphy had shown him. The one he'd said was the RUC Special Branch man, the one who had killed Sean Costello.

'Who the fuck are you, and what the fuck are you doing in my house?' he asked, pretending he didn't have a clue why Reece was there, his face an angry snarl.

'Oh, I think you know exactly who I am, Brian, and why I'm here. Now be a good boy and sit down,' answered Reece calmly, using the barrel of the gun to indicate for McNally to sit on the settee opposite him.

Knowing the man's reputation, McNally decided to play safe, and do what he was told, for now. He knew his lookouts would be back on the street soon.

'I'll ask you once again. What do you want?'

'You don't get it, do you, Brian? I ask the questions, you answer them, and you better answer quickly and truthfully, because we both know time is important.'

McNally didn't reply. The longer he dragged this out, the more likely his bitch girlfriend would be with John Jo in the south and his own minders outside knocking on his door. Given the extra time, he might have two rats in the trap.

Reece had sat across the interview table too many times with people like McNally. He could read his thoughts. The problem was McNally was thinking in the past. He was sure McNally had sat on the other side of those interview tables many times, knowing time was on his side. He would have known he'd have to be released without evidence against him, provided he kept his mouth shut.

'I know what you're thinking, Brian. The longer you keep me here the more likely the woman your people abducted will be dead, and maybe even me, captured, and dealt with by your scum friends. But as I don't have the time, I'm afraid I'm going to have to insist you answer my questions quickly. I have this gun for a reason. I'm willing to use it, as I'm sure you know. This won't be anything like the soft interrogations you had in the past.' Reece pointed the gun at McNally's right knee. 'You know the damage and pain a bullet can do to someone's kneecap. I know from your file you've pulled the trigger yourself.'

McNally's eyes narrowed, staring at the barrel of the weapon only feet away. He tried to calculate the distance between both men, but from a sitting position he knew it was too far and he knew the man pointing the gun would know that as well. Now he just stared back with hatred for the man in front of him.

Reece continued. 'As I said, Brian, I know we don't have much time, so I don't intend to keep you company much longer.'

In one swift movement Reece lifted a cushion from behind him and placing it in front of the barrel of the gun, fired a shot into the settee inches from McNally's thigh. The noise inside the room was loud, but the cushion had acted like a gun silencer which would sound outside just like someone hammering a nail into a wall. The black scorched hole in the middle of the cushion smoked but didn't catch fire. The smell of burnt material filled the room. Reece knew the kind of fear that McNally had spread throughout the community, especially with his neighbours. If any of them did suspect that it was a gunshot, they wouldn't come running. Reece also knew that the lookouts and minders were not in place yet, otherwise he'd have been given a heads up from Joe Cousins.

'Jesus, are you fucking mad?' shouted McNally.

'I told you, Brian, I don't have time for you to fuck me about. The next one goes straight in the kneecap.' Reece pointed the gun at McNally's left knee. 'Where is Mary?'

McNally looked at the gun, then at Reece standing above him with the cushion in his other hand. He could see a darkness in the man's eyes. He knew he meant what he said. He had seen men like this before where he couldn't decide if they were sane or mad. *This one was mad*, he thought. He also knew if his men were on the lookout positions and heard the shot they could come rushing in the door. This man was prepared to kill anyone getting in his way, including him. Again, he estimated the distance between them, which was now a lot closer, but he knew he couldn't move faster than a bullet.

'You can't do this. You're the law, you don't shoot innocent people,' said McNally.

'You see that's where you're wrong, Brian. I'll let you into a little secret. When it's war, the law comes last. So once again, and this time if you don't answer, you don't tell me the truth, you'll be one kneecap down. Where is Mary?' Reece said the last bit slowly and clearly.

McNally decided to play for time. 'Look. I don't know and that's the truth.'

Reece moved closer and placed the cushion over McNally's left knee, pushing the barrel of the gun into the cushion. McNally thought once more about making a grab for the gun, but he knew the man holding it could pull the trigger faster than he could react.

'Wait, wait,' shouted McNally, raising his arms above his head. 'OK, OK, I'll tell you what I know.'

Reece stood back, but kept the gun pointed at McNally's knee.

'Start talking. Answer the question, and don't waste my time anymore. Don't fuck me about.'

McNally dropped his arms and sat further back in the settee, trying to create more space between his body and the barrel of the gun. He pushed his right hand down the side of the settee arm.

'Are you looking for this?' asked Reece. Dropping the scorched cushion he took a knife out of his pocket, the serrated edge shining in the light of the room.

'I'm not that stupid, Brian. Bastards like you always try to have a back-up. Let's face it, I would too if I was in your shoes. Of course I searched the room when I came in. I also found the one that matches this down the side of the chair.'

It was then that McNally decided his only chance was to go for it. This man was going to kill him anyway. He used his dropped hands to give him the extra leverage to push himself up and with all his weight slam into the man standing in front of him.

Reece had expected McNally to try something, but the speed with which he moved surprised him. Reece knew from McNally's file that he'd been a champion boxer as a young man in West Belfast. He had used that skill to fight his way to the top of the Terrorist gang he was now in charge of, beating one victim to death along the way. Although he was older and looked to be slightly overweight, when he jumped against Reece it wasn't just body fat, but muscle. The force of McNally's lunge knocked Reece off balance, and he fell backwards knocking over a small table of ornaments, which crashed as they fell, the sound reverberating around the room. Reece fell back and felt the whole weight of McNally across him as he fell to the floor, McNally on top of him, his hands grabbing for the gun in Reece's hand. It was then that Reece heard McNally give a loud grunt, as if the wind had been knocked out of him with a punch. He rolled away from Reece onto his back, his hands now searching for the knife wound in his side. Reece realised that in McNally's own action of using his weight to force Reece backwards and grabbing for the gun, he'd forgotten about the knife in Reece's other hand.

Reece hadn't deliberately stabbed McNally. In a way, he'd done it to himself by jumping into the blade. Reece stood above the man lying on the floor, who was now taking quick, sharp intakes of breath. He could see the blood pumping in sequence with his heartbeat pouring through his fingers. His face was sweating, the skin pale.

'You're a stupid man, McNally,' said Reece putting the gun back in the pocket of the Barbour jacket and throwing the knife onto the settee before kneeling beside him.

'You fucking stabbed me,' said McNally through clenched teeth and short breaths.

Reece pulled McNally's hands away from the wound to get a better look at the damage.

'I'm not an expert Brian, but it looks bad. If you get help quickly you might live, but until you give me the answers I want, I'm willing to sit here and watch you bleed. At least that way I'll have the satisfaction of knowing you won't be lifting anymore women off the street for torture.' Reece searched for and found McNally's mobile in his trouser pocket before he sat down on the settee and waited. It didn't take long.

'The people that have her, have already taken her out of the city, she may even be across the border by now. That's all I know. You need to get me an ambulance.'

McNally could feel the wet blood flowing through his fingers. The pain of the wound and the difficulty in breathing made it hard to talk. He knew the man kneeling beside him didn't care, but he also knew if he didn't get help soon, this man would let him die.

Reece could see the small pool of blood under McNally's body getting larger with every short breath he took. He thought the knife had punctured McNally's lung.

'You're right Brian. You haven't much time, so tell me how are they getting her out of the city and across the border? What kind of car? How many of them? You need to talk fast otherwise you'll be dead, and I'll be gone. Tell me what you know, and I might just phone an ambulance. Your choice.'

McNally tried to get up, but the energy was draining fast, and he knew it, falling back down.

'There's three with her, two men, and a woman. I don't know what route they're taking. I only know it won't be by the main road. They already have a head start so you're too late.' McNally tried to smile his answers coming in short difficult breaths. The blood was now coming out of his mouth and down his chin. Reece knew McNally wouldn't tell him anything more, and whatever he did tell him would probably be a lie anyway.

Reece found the hole in the settee where the bullet had entered and using the knife he cut down to find it. He put the used bullet in his pocket and picking up the ejected casing he did the same. Stepping over McNally he went into the kitchen and wiped what prints he could off the knife handle and the door before returning to the living room and kneeling once more beside the man on the floor.

He quietly slid the knife under McNally's body.

'There now, Brian. I'm going to leave you now. I'll phone for an ambulance when I leave. They should be here within twenty minutes if they're not on an extended lunch break, so you should be all right, provided you don't exert yourself shouting or trying to stand.' Reece knew by the look of the blood loss already the man would be dead within ten.

'Please hurry. Call them now. I need help now,' McNally said gasping through clenched teeth.

'Don't worry Brian, I'll give you the same chance you give everyone else. When the emergency services come you can tell them you got injured fighting off a burglar. Then you'll be the hero bastard once more to all your friends.'

McNally could only grunt in reply, his eyes closing.

Reece left by the back door and walked back the way he came. He pressed the button on the earpiece.

'That's me out and on the way back to the car in the Avenue. Meet me there.'

'Roger,' replied Joe Cousins.

The human being inside of Reece felt sorry for McNally and he knew that if he'd phoned for an ambulance right away, he would probably be OK. But knowing what McNally would have done to him, and what had happened to Mary, he knew the world would be a better place without the likes of McNally in it. It would be hours before someone would find him, his minders, or a visitor, and by then he'd be long dead. Local police would describe the scene exactly as Reece had told McNally: a fight with a burglar had resulted in his death. Reece had an idea that knowing how those police investigators would feel about McNally they wouldn't be trying to find out what really happened.

When he got back to his car the other two SG9 men were parked behind him. Cousins, sitting in the passenger seat, pressed the button to open the car window. Reece quickly told both men what happened.

'Let's get back to the hotel. I'll contact Jim Broad and update him. All we can do for now is head for the border and hope he has something for us.'

Before you go anywhere, David, you need to change your jacket or wash that blood off,' said Middleton, pointing to the fresh stain on the pocket of the coat.

'Another reason to get back to the hotel. I'm sure Mary has left some face wipes in the bathroom. Let's meet back in the lounge once we all have a quick freshen up.'

Chapter 31
Hilton Hotel

On the drive back Reece spoke to Broad on the hands-free car phone. Broad didn't seem surprised to hear what had happened to McNally.

'I'm sure he got what he deserved, David. From what he told you, it would add up that his friends have a head start.'

'I know. There are dozens of roads crossing the border and we'd have to be lucky and need an army to find them and stop them before they get over,' replied Reece.

'I'll contact the PSNI and get as many of their people out, stopping as many vehicles as possible if they're not already doing that. We might be lucky, and God knows we need some luck. What are you going to do now?' asked Broad.

'I'm heading back to the hotel. I have no choice. I need to get after them. I need to close the distance before it's too late. I have McNally's phone, so if anyone tries to speak to him, I should know who it is at the same time you do. That might give us a slight advantage.'

'I agree, David, keep our two friends with you and in the loop. What might help is there has been a call monitored by GCHQ.'

'What?' asked Reece feeling impatient. *This whole thing was taking too long,* he thought, and he felt the politicians didn't care either way what happened.

'After the SOS spoke with the Republican MIAs we had a call going from Paul Costello to John Jo Murphy. He wants a meeting with him in Dundalk before they do anything to Mary. Of course, he didn't use those words exactly, referring to Mary as the package, but it was enough to indicate that's what the conversation was all about.'

'Did they say where in Dundalk?'

'No, but the meet is at ten tonight in the drinking hotel. Something that might help is the hotel these people used in the past. The Imperial Hotel is right in the centre of the town. I'll send you the details of Costello's Silver Ford Sierra. If you get there in time, Murphy might bring you to where they're holding Mary. We can't tip off the southern government or police. We can't trust them. From experience around the border and Dundalk, we know there were members of the police in cahoots with the IRA.'

'Thanks, boss. From my days in Newry, I know the Imperial. I know you're sticking your neck out for me.'

'You don't know how far, but you've been there for me when I needed you. Good luck. If I get anything more, I'll let you know.'

The line went dead just as Reece was pulling into the Hilton car park. Cousins and Middleton were already in the lounge with a large pot of coffee in front of them.

Reece quickly told them the details of the call with Broad.

'We have a little time. Not much, but a little. If what the boss tells me is true, Costello is putting some sort of hold on the kidnappers until after he meets with Murphy at 10 p.m. If that's the case and we are there, it might be our only chance to find Mary in time.'

'So, the boss is still backing us on this if we go across the border?' asked Cousins.

'Aye, but under the usual deniable rule if we get caught. Then we're on our own. I'll understand if either of you doesn't want to take the risk.'

Both men looked at each other before Cousins replied.

'We are with you all the way. We have Costello's details in the files we brought and his photo.'

'Thank you, guys,' answered Reece.

Before Reece could say anything more a shadow of someone standing above them blocked out the light across the table. The man looked lean and fit, about six-foot-tall, and he had that appearance of age that was difficult to tie down. Reece thought between thirty and forty. He was clean shaven with fair hair that looked untidy and long to his neck and shoulders. He was casually dressed in jeans, a polo sweater, and a brown leather jacket. He looked like he was heading to a rock concert.

'Excuse me, gentlemen, but is one of you Mister Reece? David Reece?' The accent was Mediterranean, and the tanned skin wasn't local.

Reece stood to face the stranger. 'I'm Reece.'

The man offered his hand. 'I'm Ari. Jacob Lavyan sent me.'

Reece shook the man's hand. The grip was firm.

'Ari, welcome, please join us. You may be just in time.'

Reece introduced Cousins and Middleton before he waved to a nearby waiter and asked for two more cups before pouring for himself and then Ari.

'Did Jacob bring you up to date with what's happening?'

'Only that your agent has been abducted by the Real IRA and you and your team might need some help to get her back.'

Reece couldn't help but smile at the understatement.

'You could say that. All we know is that they might already have the agent, as you call her, over the border in the Republic of Ireland. We understand that they'll do nothing to her until at least 10 p.m. tonight because they're awaiting a meeting between a Republican politician from here and one of her captors. The politician wants to question her himself. The agent's name is Mary, and we're engaged to be married. So you'll see why I'm determined to get her back. We were just about to leave when you introduced yourself.'

'I'm ready. I have my own car outside. What's the plan?'

'Can I ask if you have experience in this sort of thing? What's your background?' asked Middleton.

Ari's eyes seemed to narrow before he answered.

'If it's important to you, I'll tell you. I would want to know if I was in your position. I'm a retired Israeli Defence Forces, the IDF, officer. And, as Lavyan has told me to be honest with you, I was with Mossad for a while in the Kidon teams. I've been working with Jacob for the last three years.'

Middleton seemed impressed. 'Sorry, I had to ask.'

'That's quite all right. I would have asked the same of you, but Jacob has told me that anyone working with David is to be trusted.'

'I trained with the IDF and your Kidon unit in the past. I'm currently with 22 SAS. Have you worked on any kidnap situations like this?' replied Middleton.

'Yes, once, when a young IDF soldier was kidnapped by terrorists in Gaza. They held him for five days before we rescued him. We killed the terrorists.'

Middleton nodded his understanding of the briefness of the reply to his question. Such operations were not always successful. Reece cut into the conversation between the two men.

'We have our own GCHQ people monitoring the enemy's phones. We are going to head to Dundalk just across the border and hopefully spot this politician meeting with one of the abductors, John Jo Murphy.'

Ari smiled at the name. 'I know Murphy. He's been of interest to us for some time. I'm sure Jacob told you of my purpose in this country, that our organisation works through our embassy keeping an eye on people who may be a threat, and Murphy fits that category.'

'Then I don't need to tell you more, just that we need to move. The fact that you're aware of Murphy will be a great help. Do you know him personally? Do you know what he looks like?'

'Yes, I've observed him in the past. I know what he looks like. Can you excuse me? I must make a quick phone call before we go.'

Ari walked towards the hotel reception before using his mobile.

The three men watched him. At the same time Reece spoke quickly to Cousins and Middleton, briefly explaining who Ari was and his connection to Jacob Lavyan and the Israeli intelligence community.

'Whatever he brings to the table can only be of help and God knows we need all the help we can get. I'm sure if he comes from Jacob Lavyan, then we can trust him.'

Ari finished his call and sat at the table once more.

'I know Jacob has told you we have an old agent who knows the area and the people in South Armagh. He's been in cold storage for some time, but I've just called him and told him I want any information he has and to meet me at midnight. David, I know you have much experience in running agents. Would you like to come with me?'

Reece wasn't sure. Time was limited. 'Yes, I will, but first, we should concentrate on this meeting in Dundalk between Costello and John Jo Murphy. We must hope that one of them will take us to where they're holding Mary.'

'The meeting in Dundalk is at ten. It may only last one hour. You know surveillance as well as I do, David. It's risky at the best of times when you have a large team and plenty of back-up. But there are only four of us and a couple of cars operating in an area where we could lose our quarry very quickly. I'm not meeting up with the agent until midnight in the Ravensdale Forest, not far from Dundalk, so we can do both,' said Ari.

Reece probably knew the area better than anyone at the table. He had worked for many of his Special Branch years in South Armagh and on a few occasions across the border to Dundalk and Ravensdale Forest itself.

'OK, then I'll travel with you, Ari. We have two more cars outside. Geoff can take mine and Joe the other. That gives us three vehicles to watch John Jo and Costello. If we lose them, I'll go with you to meet the agent at midnight.'

This seemed to please Ari, and he nodded his agreement.

'OK. We need to let Joe and Geoff book out of the hotel. I'm going to keep my room on because I intend to find Mary and come back here, then we can get this show on the road. Ari, meet us down here in 10 minutes,' said Reece.

Fifteen minutes later all four men stood in the car park of the hotel. Reece pointed out the two cars that they'd been using.

'The one Joe will be driving is government issue and has some sophisticated kit in it so if we must leave it behind, we burn the shit out of it. We can't let it fall into enemy hands. They would use it for propaganda purposes, and it could scupper the whole peace process. It's for that same reason we can't leave any one of us behind. We bring everybody home dead or alive.'

No one was smiling. All understood.

'In that case you need to see my little baby,' said Ari, pointing towards a parked dark blue Nissan Izuzu.

The vehicle looked huge parked beside small cars. It was the type with the passenger compartment in the front half and a covered flatbed on the rear. Reece noticed it also had bull bars covering the front radiator.

'Let me show you the luggage compartment,' said Ari as he pulled the tarpaulin that covered the rear of the vehicle slightly to the side.

Looking under the tarpaulin, the three men could see what Ari meant by his baby. Inside, there was an arsenal of weapons. Reece could see at least four AK-47 assault rifles, an RPG7 rocket launcher, and boxes of ammunition, a few of them marked *Explosives.*

'As you can see, I've brought everything we'll need 'to carry out an assault and rescue mission behind enemy lines.' Ari smiled.

'Holy fuck,' exclaimed Cousins. 'If you get caught with that lot you'll be doing a life sentence.'

'Don't worry, my friend, both the vehicle and I have diplomatic immunity.' Laughed Ari.

'Joe, get Ari an earpiece and then we can all hear and talk to each other,' said Reece.

When Cousins returned, Ari pushed the device into his ear. The earpiece, because of its colour and size, was barely visible, and with Ari's long hair, completely invisible.

'For the rest of this operation, we'll work the comms through our phones and the earpiece. As we'll be close to each other, I don't intend to lose anyone to the people who have Mary. It's going to be dangerous. We will be on our own when we cross the border. If anyone goes down, we'll bring him home with us no matter what. For callsign purposes we'll use the NATO mnemonic alphabet with our first names. So, Ari is Alpha. I'm Delta. Geoff, you're Golf and, Joe, you're Juliet,' said Reece.

They all laughed, except Cousins, who just smiled, and nodded. Reece continued. 'Mary will be Mike, which was her code name, anyway. Geoff, take care of the hire car. If we need to, we can leave it behind and damage to it will come out of my pocket, so try to return it without a scratch. I'm sure MI6 wouldn't appreciate the bill if it got shot up in a foreign country. I'll travel with Ari. Unlike him, we don't have diplomatic immunity to cross the border with weapons, but once over, it won't matter. Joe, Geoff, give me your weapons to keep in the back of Ari's truck until we are over the border, then we can pull in somewhere and return them to you.'

Both men followed Reece to the rear of the Izuzu. There they handed over two British Army issues 9mm Browning pistols with two spare magazines they were carrying, a total of forty-five rounds. Reece placed them under the tarpaulin cover.

'Right,' said Reece. 'Let's get on the road. We can link up just over the border. I just remembered. There's a lay-by just outside Killeen village just on the south side. We can do the handover there and check our times for the centre of Dundalk and the Imperial Hotel for Costello's 10 o'clock meeting with John Jo. Ari and I'll cut through Newry town. You two stick to the main Dublin Road. The lay-by is just outside Killeen. If you're there before us just wait, we still have plenty of time.'

Chapter 32

Warrenpoint

At the very moment the SG9 team were leaving the Hilton hotel Mary was being bundled down a boat jetty and forced at gunpoint into a small boat. The journey had brought them to the town of Portaferry on the northern side of Strangford Lough. There they'd queued with other cars before boarding the small ferry which made a 10-minute journey across the Lough to the village of Strangford. Mary thought that she'd be able to raise the alarm and escape from her captors. But the pressure of the gun being pressed into her side ensured she kept quiet. There were only about twenty cars and a small van on the ferry. The crossing was smooth. Walsh drove them off the other side through the village of Strangford and onwards towards Downpatrick. After driving through Downpatrick and Hilltown they took a long straight road through the Mourne mountains down through Rostrevor and on to Warrenpoint. The winter fading light made the mountains look even darker. With the mountains behind them they pulled up at a small slip road in Warrenpoint leading down to the waters of Carlingford Lough. It was almost 6 pm and Walsh had timed his arrival perfectly. The Warrenpoint main harbour could dock large container ships but just outside the main harbour and nearer the main town square there were a couple of small jetties and slipways to accommodate smaller vessels. At the bottom of one jetty was a small boat. The owner was tying it off, making it secure against the side of the sea wall. The man had the look of someone who knew what he was doing. if anything, he reminded Walsh of the actor in the captain Birds Eye adverts. He was wearing dark overalls and a baseball cap, his face covered with a grey, almost white beard that made him look like the hardened sailor that he was. The man stood and without speaking nodded. He knew who they were as the two men and two women walked down the jetty towards him.

Gabriel Murphy had used this 19-foot fibreglass dory to catch lobsters in the Lough for the last 10 years. The boat had a 115 hp mercury engine and a small two-berth cabin under the bridge. Walsh nodded back. nothing was said as all four people boarded the boat. Once more Jimmy Bailey stayed close to Mary, making sure she was aware of the gun that was sticking into her back. Mary frantically looked around to see if anyone could see them but with the darkness descending and the cold rain falling there was no one. She even considered throwing herself over the side once they got onto the Lough. But that idea was soon thwarted when Jimmy and his sister pushed Mary down into the cabin, both sat facing her. Mariad had hated to leave the beautiful Range Rover behind. Walsh had left the keys in the ignition, keeping his promise that Frank Connor could get it back in good condition. Gabriel untied the ropes. jumping into the cabin beside Walsh he started up the mercury engine.

'Do you know what's next?' Walsh asked Gabriel.

'Yes, I'm to give you a lift across the Lough to Omeath where a van will be waiting to take you on. Any more than that I don't know, and I don't want to know.'

Gabriel Murphy had answered a knock at his front door the previous night to find his cousin John Jo Murphy asking to come in. Gabriel had never been involved with the Republican movement. His life was spent dropping off and picking up his lobster pots in a daily run along the shores of the southern side of Carlingford Lough. The lobsters he trapped in the pots would never make him a millionaire. The ones he did catch provided him with a simple life living in a cottage close to the shoreline and drinking in his local pub at night, joining in some of the singsongs that broke out when people were in the mood, known to local people as a bit of craic. John Jo had asked this favour ensuring him that he wasn't in any danger and that it would mean John Jo would owe him in return. He could have said no, as he had so many times before. John Jo knew that Gabriel only wanted the simple life, but Gabriel agreed only to this simple task knowing it would put John Jo in his debt. A debt he could call in if ever he should need it. The small boat easily cut through the light waves. The journey took just over ten minutes. No one spoke, the only noise being the outboard engine and the waves cutting through the bow. When he pulled into the jetty in the small harbour at Omeath in the Irish Republic, all was quiet. A dark blue Toyota Hiace van was reversing slowly along the top walkway above while Gabriel was tying up to the jetty wall. Once the boat was secure all four passengers left the boat and quickly walked up the jetty to where the Hiace was now waiting. Still no one spoke. Everyone seemed to know what their job was, although Gabriel did notice that one of the women seemed reluctant to move, being forced to keep moving by the man who had sat below with her on the journey across the Lough. When she leant back into him, it was then that Gabriel noticed the black handgun being used by the man to prod the woman, encouraging her to keep moving forward. All four got into the rear of the van, the doors being held open by the man who had reversed it before. Within thirty seconds everyone was in, the doors closed, and the van moving away, its headlights cutting into the darkness disappearing into the distance. Gabriel returned, untied his boat, started the engine, and steered it in a direction along the shoreline that would take him to his cottage, where he'd tie up for the night. After lighting the log fire inside he'd open a bottle of Jameson whisky, job done.

The journey for Mary continued, but now she knew she was in the Republic of Ireland across the border. Her stomach was turning. she could taste the fear in her mouth. Although it was dark in the windowless rear of the van the front driver's cab, windows gave enough light as the headlights of cars coming in the opposite direction lit up the inside of the rear. When they did, she could see Mariad, and Walsh whispering to each other and Jimmy holding the gun and smiling back at her. She tried not to show her fear, instead staring back at her captors when she caught them looking at her. There were no chairs in the back of the Hiace, so everyone sat on the floor. This was OK when they were on the main roads, but she felt the hard bumps when 'they'd driven onto what she thought were country lanes a couple of times. She estimated they'd been driving for almost an hour when the road changed once more to one of those hard pothole filled tracks, which seemed to go on forever, then suddenly stopping, braking sharply to a stop.

Jimmy jumped down from the back of the van first and waving the pistol he indicated that Mary should be next. Mariad decided to help her down by shoving her in the back. Mary landed on her knees in a muddy hole that saved her from any leg damage.

'For fuck's sake Mariad, would ye catch yourself on?' shouted Jimmy.

Mariad Bailey was laughing. 'She lost her balance.'

Mary struggled to get to her feet, but on the way she grabbed mud in her hand and threw it straight at the bitch as she was laughing. She caught a full mouthful of the mud before she could close her mouth.

'Not laughing now, bitch,' said Mary.

It took all Jimmy's strength to hold his sister back.

'You asked for that, Mariad. Now stop it. She'll get what's coming to her, so stop it, for fuck's sake.'

'When you get that bullet in the back of your head, I'm going to be the one pulling the trigger,' said Mariad, wiping the mud from her face.

Looking around her, Mary could see they were in the large yard of what looked like a farmhouse, with two large barns one at each end of the house. The whole yard was lit by the beams from two lights on the house roof and one of each on the barns over the doors. Two men came out of the farmhouse and walked towards them. Mary recognised both John Jo Murphy and Brendan McDevitt. Her blood ran cold. She knew of McDevitt and that he was now the head of the Real IRA, but it was his other nickname, Doctor Death, that reminded her of the stories she'd heard of how he liked to torture his many victims before killing them himself. It was McDevitt who spoke first.

'Ah, at last Mary, you're here. I hope you had a comfortable journey?'

To Mary the crooked grin was as unpleasant as his guttural voice. She tried to put a brave face on it.

'Why have you brought me here, Brendan? You have no right to do this.'

'Ah, now let's not get into all that now. We will have plenty of time to talk. We will be asking the questions, and you'll answer, one way, or another. Right, John Jo, show Mary to her new quarters while I get our Belfast guests something to eat. They have had a long day and I'm sure they're starving. Kevin, you watch over her.'

Kevin had been the driver of the Hiace that brought them here. As Murphy led Mary by the arm towards the barn to the left of the house entrance, Kevin went over to a Land Rover parked outside the barn. The only other car in the yard was a red Volkswagen.

The Land Rover looked like it belonged on a farm, the paint rusted, and the bodywork covered in bumps and scratches. Kevin opened the rear door and took out a black Armalite rifle before following John Jo and Mary into the barn. Everyone else followed McDevitt into the house.

Looking around her, Mary could see two chairs placed in the middle of the large space. The inside of the barn was well lit by two large arc lamps on stands. Along one wall there appeared to be empty cattle stalls with a feeding trough in front of them. On the opposite side there was what appeared to be a large steel tank filled with water which stood on top of two oil drums. Above the tank attached to one of the beams was a pulley of sorts made with ropes and chains and a large hook on the end. John Jo spun Mary around and sat her down in one of the chairs facing the barn doors. He quickly tied her hands behind her back with plastic cuffs and then an ankle to each leg of the chair with the same type of cuffs.

'There now, Mary, all comfortable. You won't need a gag as no one will hear your screams here.' He smiled. 'Now, Kevin here will keep you company and we'll be back later for that little chat. I must meet up with an old friend, but I'll be back later.'

Looking back, Mary decided not to answer. It would only inflate his ego. Kevin took the other chair and, placing it so that he could see Mary and anyone coming into the barn, he sat down. Placing the rifle across his lap, he said nothing.

Chapter 33

Dundalk

Reece and the rest of the team had no problems crossing the border. They had all been waved through at the PSNI traffic checks on the main Belfast to Dublin Road just outside Newry. The traffic being held up had slowed them down to a crawl in line. This gave the officers manning the checkpoint time to note the number of people in the vehicles, or if one of them was a woman, note the registration which would then be flashed through to the PSNI HQ Control in Belfast. At the same time they would still pull in the odd vehicle for a search and question stop. Reece knew if they were on the ball it wouldn't be long before Tom Wilson knew that one covert military car and his hire car had just crossed the border and into the Republic. Wilson would call Jim Broad, who Reece hoped would then tell him to forget what he knew. Then in the future, if he was asked, he could deny all knowledge. When they'd parked up in the lay-by just outside Killeen on the Republic side of the border, the lay-by was empty. They were protected from view and the car headlights passing on the main road by a row of fern hedges. Reece had used it years before to pick up and drop off agents. Ari handed all three SG9 men their personal weapons and at the same time invited them to take something more powerful in case they ran into serious trouble, which was to be expected. Joe Cousins took his time before selecting an AK47 and two full magazines.

'This is going to be fun,' he said, placing the weapon in the back seat of the BMW. Geoff Middleton looked the weapons over and made his selection. An Armalite rifle and two magazines. One he inserted in the rifle and pocketed the other as a spare then he placed the rifle in the well of the front passenger seat.

Ari turned to Reece. 'Do you see anything you would like, David?'

'Plenty, but not for now,' replied Reece, looking over the small arsenal.

'OK everyone, let's get into Dundalk, and find out the lie of the land. Costello or Murphy may be early so we need places where we can observe and not be spotted. I don't need to tell you how to suck eggs. You have all done this before and we are only going to get one chance at this. Joe and Geoff, you might have to stay with Murphy on your own while I go with Ari to meet his agent at midnight. Try to keep the comms short and to the point. Thanks again guys, be careful.'

They drove in convoy fashion until they reached the outskirts of Dundalk. Reece and Ari branched off to take a circular route into the town while Cousins and Middleton continued along the main route to the centre of the town. The hotel was on Park Street, one of the main thoroughfares through central Dundalk. When they drove past, Reece could see the hotel had been upgraded from the years when he used to visit the local Garda Police station to liaise with his opposite Special Branch officers in the Irish Police. That had all stopped when two senior RUC officers had been ambushed and killed by the PIRA on their way back from a meeting in the station just after they'd crossed the border into South Armagh. It was felt they'd been set up by someone in the Garda station who tipped off the Provos.

The hotel front now had a Continental-looking outside café with a dark blue slate finish to the front entrance. Although the rain had stopped and it was cold, there were still a few customers in the outside café, the hardy ones with thick coats and scarves. The surrounding area, with restaurants and bars, was busy, and finding a suitable parking space was difficult. Ari drove on, continuing for a short distance before turning to come back the way he had come. Then a car pulled out, leaving Ari a space to reverse into that had a good view of the front door of the hotel. Reece looked at the time on the dash. It was 21.25, so a good thirty minutes before their targets would be meeting. Because of the cold air, there weren't too many people hanging about. Reece lowered his window by an inch to prevent the windows misting up.

'Delta. Juliet in town centre. Where do you want me?' asked Joe Cousins on the radio.

'Roger Juliet. I'm watching some cars turn into the car park at the rear of the hotel. I just realised they probably have a rear entrance to the hotel as well. Can you go in and find somewhere to discreetly park and observe? If you find you're being compromised come back out, but at this time of night it should be busy enough with coming and going to give you the cover you need,' replied Reece.

'Roger. On my way,' answered Cousins.

Then the voice of Geoff Middleton.

'Delta that's Golf in town, where do you want me?'

'That's great Golf. We have the front and rear of the hotel covered for now. Can you park up on the road going north out of the town centre as that's the most likely direction our targets are going to come in and leave by, so you can give us a heads up?' answered Reece.

'Roger, Delta, will do,' replied Middleton.

'I think we've it well covered, David,' said Ari.

Reece watched as Cousins, driving the BMW, turned off Park Street, and into the rear car park of the Hotel.

'Delta, that's Juliet parked up with plenty of cover from other vehicles. Waiting for my Romeo,' announced Joe Cousins two minutes later.

'That's a good one, Juliet. Everyone, let's give JJ the code name Romeo and our visitor from Belfast, Hamlet,' answered Reece.

'Romeo and Hamlet it is, then,' replied Cousins.

It didn't take long for things to start moving. Ten minutes later it was Geoff Middleton who spoke first.

'Everyone. Hamlet is coming into the town from the north.'

'Roger Golf. Good job we were here early,' answered Reece. 'Stay in position Golf. Romeo might not be far behind.'

'Roger, will do.'

Five minutes later Reece and Ari could clearly see Paul Costello slow his Silver Sierra and turn into the rear car park of the hotel.

'Juliet, that's Hamlet into your car park,' said Reece.

'Roger, I have him,' answered Cousins. 'Hamlet is parked up and out and into the hotel. Not appearing to look for surveillance.'

'OK let's keep on our toes,' said Reece.

'I do believe Romeo has just passed me in a red Golf, going a bit fast to be sure, but in your direction,' said Middleton.

A few minutes later a Red Volkswagen Golf slowed and without indicating turned into the car park.

'That's definitely Romeo,' said Ari over the radio network.

'Are you sure?' asked Reece.

'Yes, I've observed him before a few times.'

'Good enough. Juliet that's Romeo into your area,' said Reece.

'Roger. I have him. Romeo out of car and into hotel,' replied Cousins.

'We don't know how long this is going to take but let's keep our current positions,' said Reece.

'Roger that,' came the reply from both Cousins and Middleton.

Reece knew that on occasions such as this conversations were brief in case the operatives carrying out the surveillance were distracted so everyone remained quiet, watching, waiting, ready.

'Delta, do you want me to go in and have a look?' asked Cousins.

'No, Juliet. In there, everyone notices strangers.'

'Roger, understood.'

In the darkness Ari didn't see Reece smile.

For Ari's benefit Reece explained.

'We don't take unnecessary risks in Bandit Country. And the Imperial Hotel has always been a favourite haunt of the Bandits from South Armagh.'

'Now I understand,' said Ari.

'Even if you went in, Ari, there would be questions asked about who you are, and with Mary's life on the line we've to be as careful as we can, so they don't know we're here.'

They returned to the silent watching. An hour later it was Murphy who came out first.

'Delta that's Romeo out and into his car. No sign of Hamlet.' It was Cousins' voice breaking the silence.

Reece answered quickly. 'Roger Juliet, you, and Golf stay with him but don't spook him. We will back you up as much as we can, but we've the meeting at midnight so may have to pull off in thirty minutes at 23.30.'

Both callsigns acknowledged with a 'Roger that.'

'Are we leaving Costello here?' asked Ari.

'By the look of things, he's staying for some reason. We must stick with Murphy. he most likely knows where Mary is, and he's Real IRA whereas Costello isn't. I know it's a risk, but we must go with the most likely target who will lead us there and I think that's Murphy.'

They watched as Murphy's red Golf turned left and headed north up Park Street. A few cars behind was Cousins giving a running commentary over the radio of Romeo's progress. Ari pulled into the light traffic and followed.

'He's not doing any anti-surveillance as far as I can see,' said Cousins.

'He's on his own turf and he'll be more relaxed. If we get onto country roads, we may have to hang back further,' replied Reece.

'That's Romeo on the main north road out of town,' said Cousins.

'Roger that. Golf, get ready to join us. With three of us, we can interchange,' said Reece.

'Roger that, Delta,' replied Middleton.

The three following vehicles spaced themselves out and when Cousins thought he had been behind Murphy too long, he pulled in to let Ari take over with Cousins joining the rear of the convoy.

'That's Romeo left, left, left onto the Kilcurry Road. Golf take point,' said Reece.

Ari pulled in and let Middleton take over point behind the red Volkswagen. Ari then took up the rear of the line of cars behind Cousins as he passed. Now they were on a country road the lack of street lights sharpened the white and red lights given off from the cars. Middleton braked slightly so that his headlights appeared further back. It was at that moment that Murphy accelerated at a bend and when Middleton drove around it, there was no sign of the red taillights of the car that should be in front of him.

'Romeo lost.' Middleton spoke quickly into the radio.

'Lost? What happened?' asked Reece.

'He accelerated just before the last bend and when I came around it, there was no sign of him.'

'Everyone pull in. We just came around the bend and there are two smaller country roads, one on each side. He must have taken one of them. Let's talk,' said Reece.

All three vehicles pulled up at the side of the road. There was very little traffic, so they had a few minutes before losing Murphy for good. Ari had reached into the glove compartment and brought out a map. Using a penlight, he quickly highlighted where they were. Placing it on the bonnet of the Izuzu they could see the two small roads, one that led across country towards Cullaville near Crossmaglen and the north in South Armagh, and the other towards Jonesborough and close to the border in Northern Ireland.

'He must have taken one of these roads and they're both going to South Armagh. There are a lot of farms along each road so we'd have a job checking them all, but we must try,' said Reece. 'Ari and I'll have to leave now to meet with his agent at midnight, so it's down to you both taking a road each.

'You will have to be very careful. The best way would be to park up when you see a farm and if you can approach on foot to try to spot Romeo's car. He may have already driven across the border.

'If that's the case, God knows where he is. That's why I must go with Ari and hope his agent knows exactly where they have Mary. I know it's splitting our resources, but it's the best we can do right now.

'For fuck's sake, don't expose yourself, and get caught. If you must shoot your way out from a bad situation, then do so. Everyone understand?'

'Yes, understood,' replied Middleton, answering for the two men.

Reece looked at his watch.

'It's now eleven thirty. We have half an hour before we meet the agent, so do what you can. We'll catch-up with you after the meeting.'

All three vehicles moved off with Cousins taking the small road towards Jonesborough and Middleton towards Cullaville, while Ari turned around, and headed back towards the main Belfast Road north, heading for the Ravensdale Forest.

Chapter 34

The Barn

Mary heard the car pull into the yard, followed by footsteps, but not to the barn. She could hear loud voices and she knew one of them to be John Jo Murphy's. Then the footsteps were coming closer, and John Jo and Brian McDevitt entered the barn. Kevin stood and moved behind Mary.

'Well, Mary, how are you feeling?' said Murphy, asking a question when he didn't care for an answer. 'Sorry to keep you waiting, but these things happen sometimes when we've to get everything in order before we can start. But it won't be long now before you and I can have that nice little chat we've been promising you.' He grinned.'

McDevitt came right up to where she was sitting, putting his face so close she could smell his bad breath, which reeked of cigarettes and whisky. She also noticed he hadn't cleaned his teeth for some time.

'We're waiting on a very special visitor who you'll know. He wants to see you before we put a bullet through that pretty head of yours. But that doesn't mean we can't start. So here's what's going to happen, Mary, and it's up to you whether the whole process is bad or very bad.'

Mary's stomach was turning, and she felt sick. She watched as he stood and walked around her, talking all the while in voice that she felt was full of menace.

'Our Belfast friends wanted to be here and watch, but I told them there's plenty of time. That Mariad one doesn't like you, does she? She especially wants to do bad things to you. But again, there'll be time for everyone. I wanted you and I to get to know each other a little better first.'

Mary noticed how he had lowered his voice almost to a whisper as he moved behind her. Then he pulled her hand back and, taking hold of the finger with her engagement ring, he continued to talk quietly.

'I see you're engaged. I hope your Special Branch boyfriend got what he needed from you. And I don't just mean information.'

Murphy was smiling. 'I saw the ring, Brendan. It looks expensive. I hope it was worth all the pillow talk.'

Still holding the ring finger, McDevitt squeezed it before pulling it in the opposite direction to dislocate it from its socket. Mary screamed at the sudden pain exploding in her brain, then the bile, and vomit surged into her mouth before she spat it out on the floor.

'You bastard,' she shouted.

McDevitt was standing in front of her once more.

'I've been called that before.' He smiled. 'I can assure you, it's going to get a lot worse. Now, this is how we're going to proceed. First, you'll receive little bouts of pain such as the one you just experienced. That's just to make you feel at home and for us to get some satisfaction before you tell us everything…and take it from me, my dear, you will tell us everything. You want to resist, you want to try to make us believe we've got it all wrong, but we've done this before. We know the process works.'

'Go fuck yourselves,' Mary shouted between the pulses of pain running up her hand and arm.

'Ah, that's my girl. Before we are finished you and I are going to have some fun. For now, this is how it's going to go. John Jo?'

Murphy reached into his jacket pocket and brought out a small cassette recorder, placing it on the ground a few feet from where she was sitting.

'It's not on record yet. That will be just for you a little later when you want to tell us everything, and you will, and there'll be a surprise guest here to hear you confess,' said McDevitt, smiling.

He's enjoying this, thought Mary. The pain was now a constant throbbing and the feeling of wanting to be sick was still in her stomach.

'No matter what I say you won't believe me. You enjoy this too much, so, as I said, go fuck yourselves,' said Mary through clenched teeth.

'Keep your mouth shut. That will only make my job even more enjoyable. Then when you beg for it to stop, we'll tape what you want to say,' replied McDevitt. 'Kevin, light the drums, please.'

Kevin handed the rifle to John Jo. Then going over to the drums below the large water tank he used his lighter to light the logs and kindling in each drum. The flames, high at first, soon settled, the heat slowly warming the water in the tank above.

'You see, Mary, when that water is hot enough, we'll lower you slowly feet first on that block and tackle into the tank. That's when you'll really confess and answer for your sins. I've used it many times before and I can assure you it works every time,' said McDevitt.

'And they say you're a great Republican leader. You're just a butcher of women and children and those who can't fight back,' said Mary, angry at herself for even speaking to this monster.

McDevitt just laughed. 'Well, in the meantime, while your bath warms up I'll leave you with Kevin. He will give you a little taster of what's coming. Kevin, keep those drums burning. John Jo and I'll go and get a cup of tea and bring you one back later. In the meantime, show her what you can do.'

John Jo leant the Armalite against the barn door and both men headed back to the farmhouse. Kevin lifted a couple of logs from a pile next to the water tank and placed them into the drums. Mary watched him as he made sure the fires weren't going out. Kevin walked deliberately towards her then suddenly punched her on the side of her head. The side of her face felt like it was going to explode with the pain, then she blacked out, the last feeling she had was when the chair toppled over.

Chapter 35

Ravensdale Forest

At ten minutes to midnight when Ari pulled into the car park it was quiet and dark.

Reece had expected the blackness, the trees drowning out any light from the night sky. He had met agents in forests many times in his Special Branch days and it always scared the hell out of him. Instinctively he took out the Smith and Wesson and held it on his lap.

'Are you worried?' asked Ari, noticing his actions.

'Not worried. I just never take these situations for granted, better to be prepared.'

'I've met this man here once before. He was on time and the meeting went well without problem,' said Ari.

Just then they could see the headlights of a car approaching. Reece flicked the safety catch off, ready for trouble if it came. Reece made sure not to look directly at the headlights, as he knew he'd be temporarily blinded when they were switched off.

'It's him,' said Ari as the car pulled into the space beside them.

The driver turned off the engine and quickly moved to the back of the Izuzu getting into the seat behind Ari. Reece wasn't sure. He had only caught a glimpse of the man in the reflection of the rear window when the interior light came on in the few seconds when he entered the car. Reece had seen his face before. He knew him from somewhere. Then it struck him like a bolt of lightning, the files he had read in his room in the Hilton hotel in Belfast with a photo of the man now sitting in the back seat, the MLA Paul Costello. Reece turned towards him, passing his gun to his left hand so that he could aim squarely at the man's chest across the back seat. Costello remained calm, staring back at Reece.

'Surprised, Mister Reece? That makes two of us and I can assure you I'm not armed, unlike my brother, when you shot him.' The accent was South Armagh, a bit north Irish, and a bit southern, but softer than most that Reece had heard.

'Why didn't you tell me?' Reece asked Ari, without taking his eyes, or his aim off Costello.

'You didn't need to know, as they say. You know our first rule is to protect our sources of information and I didn't tell you in case he didn't show up. His code name is Prefect but of course you will know him as Paul Costello, the Sinn Fein MLA, and brother of the late Sean Costello.'

'Prefect. This is David who I believe you know, anyway. Thank you for coming. David, I think you can lower your gun now. We have some serious business to discuss.'

Reece noticed his own breathing had been shallow, but when he lowered his gun he moved it back into his right hand. He wasn't going to trust the man in the back seat just yet. If Reece knew one thing in life, it was that to keep alive, the only person he truly trusted was himself.

'Nice to meet you at last, David. You're probably wondering why I'm here and what brought me here to be working with Ari's people? Let me give you the quick version.'

'That would be nice, but for now can you keep your hands where I can see them?'

'Understood. To answer the first part. Yes, I was a member of the South Armagh PIRA during the war.'

Reece was pleased to hear Costello call it a war not the political speak of 'The Troubles.'

Costello continued, 'I could see a lot earlier than some that it was a war we couldn't win. Your inroads into our organisation by your intelligence teams were starting to hit us hard. You were killing or imprisoning more of us, and we couldn't afford to lose good men at the rate we were. I'd started to think politically, but I never wanted to work with the British, especially the RUC and Army, or MI5 for that matter. To make matters worse, the new young recruits we were bringing in to replace those we were losing were amateurs and more innocent people were being killed. They didn't care, they were fanatics of the wrong kind. You couldn't talk to them, they wouldn't listen. I was on the run and taking a break in Dublin. The papers were all talking about back-door moves by the British government to try to bring about some sort of peace. It was then I had the idea of approaching the Israeli Embassy. I wasn't sure how it was going to go, but they were very open to my help and willing to pass on my information through diplomatic channels. The rest you probably know through Ari and his friends. I joined the Adams, McGuinness faction of

Sinn Fein and worked for the peace process to succeed and to convert the minds of the military mindset in the Republican organisation. Unfortunately, there were those like my brother who wouldn't, or couldn't change. I know you killed my brother, Mister Reece. If you hadn't, someone else would have. Try to understand. I loved my brother, but in the end, I didn't like him. We didn't agree on the way forward and no matter what, I couldn't change his way of thinking. I'd decided that the killing and bloodshed, especially the blood of the Irish people, was not the way to go. I don't know if the current process will ultimately be a success, but to my mind it's a better way than that chosen by my brother and people who think like he did. That's why I'm here now and when Ari contacted me, I decided to help him once more. Don't get me wrong, if the Real IRA kill you or your woman, then that won't help the peace process at all. It's a process that has come through worse and is still on track although those tracks would be wobbly for a while, like the time after the Omagh bombing in 98 that killed twenty-nine innocent civilians. The thing that has made the difference to me this time is that these people are using my brother's and my family's name as an excuse to try to derail the peace and start the killing all over again. These people came to me at my brother's funeral to tell me they intended to do something and weren't asking my permission. That's where we are now.

They have your woman and my agreement with them is that they do not kill her until I hear a confession from her own lips that she was a traitor during the war with the British. I knew Mary McAuley. I'd met her on many occasions at high-ranking meetings during the peace talks. She was highly regarded, and I had no reason to doubt who she was. My plan is to have them exile her. I'll try to convince them that the current peace is the only way forward. I'll tell them that by their actions they'd proved they still had the resources but that they could demand a place at the table. I know it sounds naïve of me, but until Ari contacted me, it was my only plan. So, that's my plan, Mister Reece, as far as it takes me.'

Costello took a long, deep breath, and sat back further in his seat, keeping his hands on his lap where Reece could see them.

'What evidence do they have that she worked for us? After all, you know her from your own meetings with her. Is this just a fishing expedition or, as you say, a way to try to break the peace and get back to war?' asked Reece.

Costello took a few seconds before responding. 'That's where you come in, Mister Reece. At my brother's funeral, they showed me photos of you and Mary McAuley, and they were able to say that my brother spotted her with you in London during his operation there. Further checks by them showed that she was also in London when that Islamic Jihad terrorist was shot. They also showed me the photo of you with the body of the Arab. They are happy that she's an informer, and they have the evidence. They had hoped to get you as well. That's why they deliberately knocked down her mother, hoping you would both come to Belfast and help make their job easier.'

'You keep saying they! Who are they?' interrupted Reece.

'I'm sorry. I thought that as we've come this far, you knew who they were. After all, the press has said it for days. They are the so-called Real IRA, and I can assure you they're right. This has nothing to do with the Provisional Republican Movement,' answered Costello.

'So, you mean the likes of Brendan McDevitt and John Jo Murphy?' answered Reece.

Reece could see a look of surprise come across Costello's face. 'So, you've kept your fingers in the pie?'

Reece smiled. 'We're not stupid. If the whole world knows, we know.'

'Yes, Murphy and McDevitt are involved. It was them who approached me at the funeral.'

'I'm sure we all agree we don't want the war back. Where is she? Can we get her out? Is she still alive, then?' Ari's voice broke through the two men's conversation.

Ari had asked the questions that brought them here. Reece waited for Costello to reply.

'She's being held at the McDevitt farm near the border with Jonesborough just inside the southern side. They won't kill her, at least not until I've heard her confession from her mouth. They are expecting me at 2 a.m. so if you're going to do something, you haven't got long.'

'Do you know this farm?' Ari asked Reece.

'Yes, we covered it during the war, but that was some time ago, and we'll be going in the dark at short notice with little time to plan. Anyway, we're putting our faith in Costello here. I'm not sure we can fully trust him.'

The sound of Costello laughing filled the car.

'You don't trust me? Now there's a dilemma because you're asking me to trust you, the man who killed my brother. The man who, no matter what happens, could expose me to the world as working with our sworn enemy. Do me a favour, get with the programme. The peace process is bigger than all of us here and everyone out there, including your own bosses. While we talk here, your woman's life hangs in the balance. If you're serious about her, we need to move soon. Besides, what kind of life would I have if your people and Mossad were hunting me down? A short one, I think.'

Reece knew what he said was true. No matter what he felt about Costello, he had no choice but to take the information he had given them and act on it now.

Ari opened the glove compartment and removed the map he had used in Belfast.

'Perfect. Can you show me on the map where the farm is? Have you been there before?' Ari used the small penlight torch to light up the map.

'It's just here, up a long laneway,' replied Costello, pointing to what looked like a small set of brown buildings that were almost exactly on the line that divided the border.

'Do you have any idea how many people are there?' asked Reece.

'There will be at least a half dozen, including both Murphy and McDevitt. They will want to be there when she confesses and anyway, torture is McDevitt's favourite pastime.'

'It's just coming up to one. How long will it take you to get there?' asked Ari.

'From here, the best way for me to go is back across the border and cross back to the farm from Jonesborough, about thirty minutes. If you do hit the place, make sure I'm not in the line of fire.'

'If we can get in and out without any shooting, I would be happy. But if shooting starts, you get down fast and stay down until it's over,' answered Reece.

'Oh, that really reassures me,' Costello replied sarcastically.

'Just make sure you're still wearing that sweater if you go there. We can't miss it,' said Reece, pointing the barrel of the gun at Costello's chest once more.

'Thank you for your help. We should all move and do whatever 'we have to do,' said Ari.

'Before I go, this little gem is just for you Mister Reece, a sign of good faith let us say,' said Costello.

'Good faith is important,' answered Reece. He still didn't trust Costello, and he didn't like the way he called him Mister.

'During the war and still working with the Real IRA for money is a rogue RUC Chief Inspector called Wilson. His son, Tom, is the top man in the Intelligence Department of the PSNI. So, watch what you tell Tom Wilson because his dad has big ears and deep pockets as far as the Real IRA is concerned.'

Reece felt as if someone had kicked him in the stomach. He knew DCI Paddy Wilson from his days in Newry Special Branch when Paddy Wilson was one of the senior officers in Armagh.

'How am I supposed to believe you?' asked Reece.

'Believe me or don't believe me, it doesn't matter to me. All I can tell you is that he did it for money and plenty of it. He told us when you were expecting us to carry out attacks and by doing so, we were able to identify some of the informers within our communities and deal with them. I tell you this because he has a gambling habit he needs to feed and now he's working with the likes of McDevitt for his pay day. By his actions, I consider him a thorn in the side of the peace process. The main people in Sinn Fein think to expose him wouldn't be believed but would reflect badly on them. I'm telling you this in the hope you can do something from your end.'

Reece and Ari remained silent.

'Well, there you have it. I'll have to go as they'll be expecting me,' said Costello, starting to open the door.

'Wait,' said Reece quietly. 'How many people are at the farm?'

Costello sat back in the seat. 'As I said, I would think at least six.'

'What would be the best way to approach the farm? How many buildings? What's the security like?' Again, Reece was looking for answers, for information.

Costello listened. he knew why Reece was asking these questions. Taking his time, he looked directly at Reece before answering.

'It's been a while since I was there. The family has CCTV, but if the coverage hasn't been changed, it's looking to the north, because that's where they always expected trouble to come from. They had one dog, a sheepdog, not a guard dog. It's friendly and licks everyone's hand. The farmhouse is a large two-storey building with a large yard in front of it.

There are two large barns and the one to the south is usually where McDevitt does his dirty work, so my guess is that's where you'll find your woman.'

'Thank you for your help,' said Ari.

'Don't get me wrong. When McDevitt and Murphy first showed me the evidence they had and the photos proving that Mister Reece and Mary McAuley were responsible for my brother's death I wanted them both dead in return. But then, I took the time to think about what could happen if they were killed. How it would affect the peace process and the danger of going back to the bloodshed again? My gut feeling said no, I cannot let that happen. As I already said, my brother was on his own destructive path and sooner or later he was going to end up doing a long prison sentence or dead. That was the choice he made, and the fact it was you, Mister Reece, who fulfilled his destiny. I can understand. Now I really must go.' Without waiting for an answer, Costello was out of the Izuzu and into his own car and away.

Both men silently watched the red taillights of the car disappear into the blackness of the forest.

'What do you think? Do you think it's a trap?' asked Ari, breaking the silence.

'To tell you the truth, I'm not sure. I'm still getting over the shock of who your agent was. But I don't think he'd take the risk of what would happen to him if it was a trap. It would be bad enough if my people were after him, never mind yours. I think he's genuine about keeping the peace. He's more of a politician now than a terrorist, so the peace process is his bread and butter now.'

'Bread and butter?'

'Just an expression we use to indicate what is more important to a person.'

'What now?'

'We meet up with Joe and Geoff and put together a quick plan to hit the farm around 2 a.m. before any decisions are made to kill Mary. Let's drive north and we can meet outside Jonesborough. I'll get onto my boss and get him to lift the police road checks on the Belfast to Dublin Road. Realistically they're looking at traffic coming from the north but if they're there when any shooting starts, we might have a problem if we want to escape back into the north. Let me have the map. I need to look at something while you drive.'

Reece quickly worked out the map reference number for the McDevitt farm. Then he opened the Google Earth application on his phone and typed in the number. The search brought up an aerial daylight photo of the farm complex and the surrounding fields and roads.

'Got it. Thank you, Google. That will do nicely,' he said out loud.

'What will?' asked Ari.

Reece explained what he had found.

'That will do nicely indeed,' agreed Ari.

Reece hit some buttons on his phone and heard the ringtone before the voice of Jim Broad answered.

'David? It's good to hear from you,' said Broad, but Reece recognised the sardonic tone in Broad's voice.

'We have been kind of busy here, boss, but needed to catch-up with you,' replied Reece.

'I've already had phone calls from Wilson and Bryant, both concerned that my SG9 operators are in the Republic of Ireland's jurisdiction. I could only tell them you'd gone dark, and I didn't know what was happening but that they should keep quiet for now. So I'm glad you called, hopefully to tell me good news and what the hell you're all up to.'

Reece quickly brought his boss up to speed from Belfast to the reason they crossed the border. He told Broad about Ari and the agent, but without mentioning the agent's name, instead just referring to him as Prefect, Costello's code name. He kept the Costello part to himself. Instead, he just told his boss that Prefect was able to provide them with the details of where Mary was being held.

'You believe she's still alive, then?'

'Yes, until 2 a.m. at least, when Prefect has agreed to meet with the abductors at the farm.'

'I take it you have a plan?'

'Formulating one and that's why I called you. We might need your help.'

'I can't give you any more resources if you're in the South of Ireland. I'll be in enough trouble for sending you Cousins and Middleton, which, I might add, my bosses don't know about.'

'I know and I'm truly thankful, but if we are successful, we'll be running for the border, crossing into the north near Jonesborough. If we get that far, a chopper would be greatly appreciated.'

Broad was silent for so long that Reece thought he had lost the connection.

'Hello, are you still there, boss?'

'Yes, I'm still here. I don't know who you think I am or what I can do, but something like getting you a helicopter is no small task. Do you really think you'll need it? Getting one will raise all sorts of questions.'

'I'm not sure. But having one on standby would be helpful, especially if we run into more trouble than we can handle. It will only be needed if we are being chased when we get across the border into the north. We'll be in the Bandit Country of South Armagh, and you know from your own experience how quickly those bastards can call up reserves.'

'Leave it with me. I'll see what I can do, but for God's sake, David, try to be as quiet as you can. This could raise an international stink to say the least. We will need a code name for any help team.'

'Let's go with Extraction Delta. It should do the trick,' Reece answered.

'Sounds about right. What about this ex-IRA source? Can you trust him?'

Reece was aware of Ari trying to follow the conversation as he drove.

'You know me. I don't fully trust anyone. We will be prepared for any problems. I'm sending you a Google Earth shot of the farm with map reference to where it's located along the border. If you get the chopper back-up, let them know and get them to send you a safe location nearby where they can land to pick us up if needed.'

'Leave it with me. I'll work from our operation room here. Another late night.'

'Tell me about it. Will be in touch.' Reece ended the call.

'Thank you for protecting the name of my source,' said Ari.

'He's your source. It's not for me to tell, but I think he gave me the extra titbit about naming the police traitor for a reason. To show good faith and to have the name in my back pocket should I need it in the future.'

As they travelled back across the border, Reece could see many landmarks that brought back memories of his days of service in the same area. There were new houses and now a motorway that started in Dublin and ended in Belfast. They took the country back roads and before long they were parked up on the outskirts of the village of Jonesborough South Armagh. Reece got on the radio.

'Delta to Golf and Juliet. Pull out from what you're doing and meet us just outside Jonesborough in the north. Take the main roads. We now know where Mike is.'

Both SG9 men replied, 'Roger, Delta.'

'You would know this area pretty well then?' asked Ari.

'Too well. It was in these fields, roads, and hills that some of the most vicious fighting took place. The IRA here was the deadliest unit in the land at the time. Most of their fighters had lived here all their lives and were related. That, more than anything, stopped them from becoming sources of information for us. Most of our intelligence came from army road stops and house searches or when we lifted them in early morning raids. We took them to holding centres for questioning for a maximum of seven days. They had been schooled in anti-interrogation and would just sit there saying nothing. They knew we couldn't hold them any longer and were back out home. Back again to their killing. They controlled the area so well that the security forces could only move around by helicopter. Most roads had landmines and booby traps. The other thing the South Armagh unit was good for was shipping large lorry bombs across to England where they caused devastation in places like Manchester and London. Yes, Ari. I know this area very well and I'd hoped I would never have to come back here.'

Chapter 36

Jonesborough

The SG9 team sat in the Izuzu twenty minutes later. At one thirty in the morning, there was no one else about in the village of Jonesborough in South Armagh. There was no light inside the car other than that from a half-moon shining in the sky when the clouds cleared. Cousins and Middleton arrived at almost the same time and, sitting in the rear seats they listened as Reece laid out his plan.

'According to Ari's source we now know where Mary is being held and we've an idea of what we are up against. I've sent everyone the Google Earth pictures of the farm complex and the map reference.

'The farm is only five miles south from here on the road through the small townland of Drumbilla, with a lane about a half mile long leading from the road to the farm. The best plans are simple ones, no need to complicate things. Anyway, we don't have the resources to do anything bigger.

'I propose we work in two teams. Ari will drop us off at the bottom of the lane, then park up. The rest of us will go forward to the complex. We know that there'll be at least six of the opposition there. The farm itself will probably be lit up with security lights. There will probably be some sort of CCTV, so our approach needs to be ultra covert. Mary is most likely being held in the southern barn in the complex. Ari has kindly provided me with a Baretta with a silencer, so I'll move to the southern barn with Geoff backing me up if things get noisy. I'll still have my own weapon for back-up.

'Joe, you'll make your way to the side of the northern barn to cover the yard and farm building for any opposition trying to prevent our progress. Ari's source might be there.

'We've told him if shooting starts to hit the dirt and stay there. He will be wearing a bright green sweater, so you'll recognise him. I just hope no one else is wearing one.

'Both Geoff and Joe will be using the heavy firepower. The enemy should be relaxed. They know the local police won't bother them and they'll feel safe in their own little castle not expecting visitors, especially at two in the morning, and that's when we need to be in there doing the job. Any questions so far?'

'Assuming all goes well, and we get Mary out of there. What's to say we won't encounter more of their friends? I'm sure they could get the word out quickly for reinforcements if they needed to,' asked Cousins.

'No matter what happens the plan includes an escape. After Ari has dropped us off at the bottom of the lane, we'll approach the farm on foot, down this ditch, which runs down the side of the lane.

'When we have Mary inside the barn, Geoff and I'll stay there with her while when I give the go over the radio Ari drives into the yard we all pile in and drive out.'

'Now that sounds simple, if the opposition play along we should be all right,' said Cousins.

'Hopefully, if we've caught them by surprise we'll be in and out before they know what's hit them. We will then drive back across the border where we'll go our separate ways.

'Ari back to Dublin and you and Geoff back to the Hilton in Belfast with Mary and I as passengers. I've asked Jim Broad to get us the use of a helicopter in case we run into trouble where we can't use the cars. But again, we can't depend on that,' answered Reece.

'Well as they always drilled into us in selection training, adapt and overcome,' said Middleton.

'Let's do that if we must. Now any more questions before we move?' asked Reece.

No one replied, with only Cousins nodding his head.

'OK,' said Reece looking at his watch. 'It's now 01.32hrs We get going and if as expected most of our opposition will be in the barn with Mary at 02.00hrs then we hit it at the same time.

'Take no chances, don't think for one minute about how killing one of these bastards will affect the peace process. They don't give a fuck about the peace process, and neither should we. As my trainers always told me Geoff, keep shooting them until they're dead.'

'My trainers told me the same,' replied Middleton.

'And mine,' said Ari.

'All right, let's go and good luck,' said Reece.

Ari put the IZZUZU in gear moving slowly at first towards the border. The half-moon cleared the clouds lighting up the road ahead.

Chapter 37

The Farm

Mary came round slowly. Her head ached, the pain mostly around her nose. Her head was down and as she opened her eyes a bit at a time, she could see her blood drying on her blouse. The bleeding had stopped but had dried in her nostrils, making it difficult to breathe through her nose. She didn't know if her nose was broken. it felt like it. It reminded her of the punches and slaps she used to get from her husband Brendan and how one night David Reece had saved her from further beatings in a street in Newry when he knocked Brendan out with one punch.

'Where are you now, David? I need you,' she thought. It was painful, but lifting her head she could see Kevin sitting in his chair watching her, smiling, with the Armalite across his knees.

'Don't worry bitch. If I wanted to I would have broken your nose and you wouldn't be awake for a while yet,' said Kevin, grinning.

Mary spat blood from her mouth in Kevin's direction. Her nose was sore and slightly swollen but when she tried to breathe through it she realised she could, just. It wasn't broken.

There was the sound of a car coming into the farmyard. Kevin got to his feet and walked to the barn door. Then she heard the voices. it sounded like everyone was in the farmyard talking over each other. Kevin stood back as the barn door opened. Brian McDevitt entered followed by John Jo Murphy, then a man she recognised both from her days in the movement and the media, Paul Costello. For a moment her body seemed to freeze as she realised here was Sean Costello's brother and she'd been there when her lover David Reece, code name Joseph, had shot Sean dead. Now she began to understand why they waited to get on with it. They were waiting for Paul Costello, brother of the dead Sean, and MLA in the new Stormont Government. The three men stopped at the door in deep conversation which, being too far away Mary couldn't hear, maybe because her ears were still ringing from Kevin's punch. McDevitt looked in Mary's direction as he spoke to Costello, then pointed to the water tank being heated by the burning logs. She didn't need to hear, she knew McDevitt was in his element pointing out Mary's future, and how he was going to progress it. Conversation over, the three men walked over and looked down at Mary.

'I thought you were going to wait until I was here?' said Costello when he saw Mary's bruised and bloodied face.

'We did wait, we just said we wouldn't kill her until you were here to hear her confession. We had a little fun letting her know what to expect and what was coming. I must admit she's stronger than you think, it might take her some time to really understand pain,' answered McDevitt.

'Yes and just for fun the bastard broke my finger as well,' said Mary through clenched teeth.

Costello walked behind the chair to look at her dislocated finger which protruded in the opposite direction to that normally done by a finger.

'I'm sure that's painful. But if you tell us the truth and quickly, then this will be over soon,' said Costello.

'The truth, the truth about what?' replied Mary.

McDevitt started laughing. 'Oh this is going to be fun if you keep that up, bitch.'

'The truth about your working with the Brits and setting my brother up for them to be murdered by your Special Branch boyfriend. You see we know. we've photos of him, and we know the both of you were together in London when Sean was killed and then lately when the Arab was killed. Denying everything means it will just hurt longer. And in the end you'll want to tell us everything.'

'I couldn't have said it better myself.' McDevitt laughed again.

'You're both enjoying this. I don't know what you're talking about. I know you, Paul. I sat in meetings with you when we both worked for peace in this country. I'm no traitor. The cause I worked for is over, there's a new cause, peace, and that's the cause I would work for now. Not the one these fanatics support.'

Costello stood closer, putting his face directly in front of hers.

'Then I'm sorry, Mary. The peace you talk about doesn't mean we can't deal with the things that happened in the past. Especially if those things involve someone who worked with our enemies to destroy the cause we then fought for, and that those people might still be working with the same people who killed my brother. If that means being here with you to deal with a spy, then that's what we must do.'

'No matter how you try to justify this, you know it's wrong,' said Mary.

'I'm sorry you feel that way. I wanted to hear the truth of your deals with the Brits before Brendan and his people get to work on you, to try to understand why you did what you did. But, I guess it will have to be Brendan's way, and as I said, before they execute you for your crime I'll still be here to listen to that confession. I'll go and have a nice cup of tea and when I return you should be a little more helpful. Brendan, can we've a few words outside please?'

'Of course, I'm sure Mary can wait. In the meantime, John Jo, and Kevin can make her a little more comfortable.' When he answered he pointed to the pulley hanging above the water tank. Both John Jo and Kevin knew the signal. they'd been here before when another traitor had to be dealt with. Mary could see from their reaction that this wasn't going to be good. Kevin set the rifle on the chair near the door then walked to stand beside her with John Jo. John Jo produced a long-bladed knife from his belt and quickly cut the restraints from her ankles and hands. Kevin held her arms behind her while he pulled her to her feet. As she stood, the blood in her body rushed into her arms and legs causing her to stumble in pain, but John Jo held her in front. She could smell his stale breath as he smiled through smoke-stained teeth.

'Ah, now, Mary, don't hurt yourself there's a good girl,' he said.

'Let me go, you bastards.' She tried to struggle free, but, from the hours of sitting she felt weak. The grip of the two men holding her felt like a vice squeezing her arms.

John Jo stood slightly back, then slapped her across the face with his open palm.

'Struggle all you like, you're going nowhere,' he said.

Two things struck Mary as they dragged her across the barn towards the heat of the steel drum and the logs burning. Her broken finger ached more than her cheek and nose, and she could hear the raised voices of McDevitt and Costello just outside the door. They were arguing over her, and she was sure she heard Costello say something about amnesty and exile. John Jo and Kevin must have heard it too because they stopped and stood still, holding Mary up between them, just feet from the burning logs, listening.

Then the argument stopped, and McDevitt stormed back into the barn, the door swinging backwards to smash loudly as it crashed against the barn wall.

'Right, you two, what are you waiting for, get her up there!' he shouted at the two men holding Mary.

'What was all that about?' asked John Jo.

'He only wanted to give her an amnesty and exile her from the country. Would you believe it? And her a fucking traitor that set up his own brother. Says it would be good for the peace process. Well fuck the peace process. This bitch is not getting away with what she's done.'

'Maybe you need to listen to him Brendan, there's a lot more at stake here than just torturing and killing me. Think what happens afterwards. You will have no friends anywhere if you damage the peace and that will include here in the south as well as Britain and America,' shouted Mary, still struggling to get free.

'You know what you all can do with the bloody peace process. Remember Ireland will never be at peace if she's not free,' replied Brendan. 'Now get her up there, no more talking.'

The two men dragged Mary closer to the water tank and Kevin swung the pulley away from it to lower it before he helped John Jo hold the struggling Mary to tie her hands with the rope hanging on the large hook at the end of the pulley.

Mary could feel the rope tighten and the strain on her arms as Kevin switched on the electric motor to operate the pulley. Her arms being lifted above her head, John Jo let her go and she started to feel her legs slowly rise above the ground. She stood on tiptoe to try to take the strain off her shoulders. Then her feet left the ground as Kevin pressed the raise button on the handheld control. She felt the pain in her shoulders like they were coming out of the sockets.

'Stop it!' she screamed. Looking down, she could see the bubbling water tank below her. Kevin took his hand off the button and the pulley stopped, with Mary swinging gently above the steaming tank.

'Don't fret, my dear, the water will soon warm you up and when your toes touch it, you will want to talk, but by then I might not care one way or the other. Now tell me the truth and we'll get you down and everything will be over quickly. Were you an informer for RUC Special Branch?' asked the grinning McDevitt.

'Stop this now. I've done nothing,' she answered through gritted teeth, the pain in her shoulders getting worse. She could feel the bile in her stomach rising once more. Her body was shaking uncontrollably. Sweat started to fall down her forehead. She had never felt such terror in her life, and she knew she was losing control of her senses.

'I can see you don't think we'll do it,' answered McDevitt.

Ari had dropped them off at the bottom of the lane. Driving quietly in low gear with his headlights switched off, relying on just the side lights, he drove on for another 500 yards before finding a gateway to a field, where he turned, and parked facing back along the road he had come. He parked up with the engine running. Reece and Middleton had reached the end of the hedge cover by sticking to the trench alongside the lane to the farm. Joe Cousins had done the same on the other side of the lane. Although the whole yard was brightly lit, there was no one about to see Cousins with the AK47 as he swung it right to left as he ran crouching across the yard to take up position at the side of the north barn where it was in dark shadow.

'Juliet in position. I can cover the yard,' said Cousins into the radio.

'Roger, Juliet. We're ready to move,' answered Reece.

Reece could see three vehicles in the yard. John Jo Murphy's red Volkswagen, Costello's car, and a battered Land Rover. There was no dog. Hopefully, he was lying by a fire in the house. The downstairs lights in the farmhouse were on, but from what he could see through the windows, no one was looking out into the yard. Reece felt calm. He had been trained to control his breathing at times like this. He was about to move towards the southern barn, where he hoped they were holding the still-alive Mary, when the barn door opened. He crouched lower where he was, as did Middleton just behind him. He watched as Costello and another man, who he'd identified as Brendan McDevitt, stood outside the barn, seeming to have an argument.

Costello seemed to be making the argument he'd said he would, telling McDevitt that it would be better if he let Mary live. McDevitt was having none of it. Then he stormed off back into the barn. The sound of the raised voices had also brought faces to the farmhouse windows. Reece could see a woman and a man, but not clearly enough to identify who they were. Costello, head down in thought, entered the farmhouse, and the faces disappeared from the windows.

It was then that he could hear Mary's loud voice swearing at her captors. For a moment Reece was glad she was still alive and in fine voice, but then he realised she was really pleading for her life. He knew they didn't have long and now they needed to act fast, no matter what the odds. Again, he worked to control his breathing. The anger inside him had to be controlled and aimed in the right direction. Even though he wanted to charge through the barn doors and shoot every enemy fucker in there, he knew any rushing would only lead to mistakes. The kind of mistakes that could put Mary in even more danger.

'Everyone from Delta. We have identified where Mary is being held. Golf and I are going in. Everyone ready now, go, go, go,' said Reece, taking another deep breath.

Reece ran straight for the barn door while Middleton just behind him swept the front of the farmhouse with the Armalite rifle for any enemy response from there. When they reached the door, both men waited each side of it for a few seconds. They could hear McDevitt give the order to get her up there, then the noise of the pulley, squeaking as she was being raised.

Reece held up three fingers for Middleton to see the countdown.

When the last finger dropped both men moved as one. Middleton pulled open the barn door and Reece entered first with the Baretta pointing straight ahead at the three men standing in front of the water tank. Middleton followed, the Armalite sweeping the barn for any other opposition before settling back on the three men. It was Kevin who moved first. He let go of the pulley control and ran towards the chair where he picked up the rifle but before he could swing it into position Reece had aimed and squeezed the trigger of the Baretta three times, the silenced weapon making hardly any sound: Putt, Putt, Putt. Kevin made no sound as he fell, two holes in his chest and one in his cheek, all torn, and pouring thick red blood. As he fell the rifle fell from his hands. John Jo started to move towards the rifle, but the voice of Middleton cut through the barn. 'No, no, John Jo, unless you want to join your friend here.' John Jo froze when he saw that the man speaking with an English accent was pointing the Armalite rifle straight at him. One thing John Jo knew from all his time of killing people was that you can't outrun a bullet, and this man knew how to send them.

'That's a good boy, now both of you move away from the tank and put your hands behind your head,' said Reece, directing their movements with a wave of the gun in his hand.

Both men did as they were told while Middleton covered them.

'Am I glad to see you. Get me down from here,' said Mary, still swinging gently, her toes only feet from the boiling water.

'I'll as soon as I work out which button is which on this thing,' said Reece grabbing hold of the controls.

'Don't mess around, David,' said Mary.

Reece pressed the button to swing Mary from over the water tank and then lowered her to the ground before untying the rope from around her wrist.

Mary collapsed into his arms. her strength almost gone. He carried her over to the chair she'd been tied to earlier and let her sit to get her breath back.

He could see the damage to her bloodied bruised face, and the dislocated finger. He could feel the anger inside him, and he swung round, the Baretta pointing straight at McDevitt's head.

'Give me one reason why I shouldn't blow your fucking head off,' said Reece quietly, the menace in his voice clear.

'Do you think you'll get out of here alive, Mister Special Branch man?' McDevitt leered.

'That's the plan McDevitt and you and John Jo here are going to help us. We are all going out to the yard where our transport will pick us up. Any stupid move by either of you will be your last. As you've seen, I've no hesitation when it comes to pulling this trigger. Delta ready for pickup,' said Reece into his ear mic.

The response from Ari was immediate. 'Roger on way.'

'That's two men and a woman out of the farmhouse. Both men have AKs and the woman a handgun, walking towards the barn,' came the voice of Joe Cousins over the radio.

'Roger, Juliet. We're ready to move. Can you cover from your side?' asked Reece.

'Yes, but will have to make sure you don't get in my firing line,' replied Cousins.

'Will do. We will break right when we come out the door towards the lane entrance,' answered Reece.

Reece lifted the AK47 and checked there was a full magazine before handing the Baretta to Mary.

'You know how to use this. Use your good hand. The safety's off, you just point, and pull the trigger. Geoff and I'll go out first with these two in front of us. You follow and stick close to me, keep low. OK you two front and centre,' said Reece pointing the rifle at Murphy and McDevitt.

'Fuck you. You will shoot us anyway. Why should we help you?' shouted John Jo.

Reece swung the rifle in one quick movement, the butt of the weapon connecting with John Jo's cheek. He fell to the ground, grunting with pain, holding his face.

'We don't have time to argue. Now get to your feet and move,' said Reece, once more pointing the rifle at both men. This time they both moved slowly, just then he heard Joe Cousins AK47 firing. Geoff Middleton was pleased to note that Joe had the rifle on single – aimed shot mode.

It was Mariad who had seen Reece and Middleton on the CCTV monitor in the farmhouse, as they were crossing the yard and entering the barn. They had quickly grabbed the weapons from the store under the main stairs in the farmhouse. Now as she ran outside with her brother Jimmy and Frank Walsh they came under fire from some other place in the yard. The shots didn't hit them but were close, smashing into the farmhouse wall behind them as all three dived for cover behind the Land Rover.

Jimmy Bailey could see where the fire was coming from and fired on fully automatic, splattering the wall, and windows of the north barn. Joe Cousins lay flat and aiming, fired two quick single shots, hearing the man cry out as one of the rounds hit home.

Jimmy fell behind the Land Rover clutching his right leg. Mariad could see that the rifle round had torn a large gash in her brother's leg just above the knee. The blood was gushing through Jimmy's fingers and his face was white and sickly looking. Right then she was so angry she just wanted to kill someone and if she could see the traitor bitch in her sights that would be a bonus. She pointed the Browning pistol over the bonnet of the Land Rover and fired blindly in the direction of where Cousins was lying. The rounds hit the wall high above him and he returned two more rounds, hitting the windscreen of the Land Rover to keep the enemies head down.

'Go, go, go now!' Joe spoke into his radio mic.

'We are out and moving,' replied Reece. He could see one of the men at the back of the Land Rover break cover slightly and point his rifle in their direction.

'Stop where you are,' shouted Frank Walsh. Where he stood gave him cover, from both Cousins and the people bringing McDevitt and John Jo out of the south barn.

It was then that Ari and the Izuzu screamed into the scene. With a roar of the engine and a screech of brakes he broke the tension as he entered the yard, driving straight between Walsh, and Reece. Walsh couldn't fire anyway in case he hit his people. Instead, he swung the weapon to take aim and fire at the Izuzu and Ari. Middleton fired off three rounds, forcing Walsh to take cover once more.

'Get in,' shouted Ari out of the lowered driver's window.

Reece grabbed Mary and, opening the rear passenger door, he practically threw her onto the back seat.

'Keep your head down,' shouted Reece before turning back to help Middleton cover the two IRA men.

'Get in,' he told Middleton.

'What about these two?' asked Middleton.

'Leave them to me. Juliet, jump in the back of the truck,' he shouted over the radio.

Joe Cousins was already on his way. When he had seen Walsh dive back into cover he didn't need to be told twice, he ran for the Izuzu. Mariad saw him running and fired the pistol at him, but missed before the chamber stayed back, empty. the unaimed shots she'd fired, had quickly emptied the gun.

Reece turned to face McDevitt and John Jo. Both still had their hands behind their heads.

'Get down on your knees,' shouted Reece, aiming the rifle at the men.

Both could see a coldness in his eyes.

'So this is how you kill? In cold blood on unarmed men?' said McDevitt.

'No. That's your way, McDevitt. But don't give me an excuse. Just stay where you are.'

Middleton jumped in beside Ari. 'Come on,' he shouted back at Reece, who turned, and jumped in the back beside Mary just as Cousins jumped into the back of the truck, landing on more guns, and ammunition.

Walsh did not stand and wait. He ran around the Land Rover and seeing the key in the ignition he jumped in and started the engine. Putting it in gear he drove in a wide circle before stopping it parked across the entrance to the yard, blocking any escape. He then took cover behind the bonnet, then aiming the AK47 fired at the Izuzu, which was moving in a circle in the yard. Ari had seen what happened. He revved the engine and taking his foot off the brake he accelerated straight for the Land Rover and Walsh.

'Hold on,' shouted Ari above the noise.

Two of the rounds fired by Walsh hit the windscreen, but it didn't shatter. It was then Middleton realised it was bulletproof. Smiling, he reached out of the passenger window. holding the Armalite he fired three rounds towards where Walsh had taken up position. He didn't need to bother. Walsh could see the large vehicle racing towards the Land Rover and he jumped to one side just as it smashed headlong into his temporary barricade. The bull bars on the front of the Izuzu did their job. With a crashing noise of metal against metal, the Land Rover was pushed out into the side of the lane, leaving just enough room for Ari to reverse a little, then drive past it when he had straightened up. As Walsh got to his feet to take aim once more at the back of the escaping vehicle, he saw the figure of a man kneeling in the back of it taking aim and firing. Walsh dived for cover once more as the bullets from Cousins' rifle burst through the branches and smashed into the small stone wall at the yard gateway. He kept his head down as he heard the noise from the engine of the escaping truck disappear into the distance. Walsh thought the strange thing was that the old Land Rover, although badly dented and sitting almost on its side into the laneway ditch, still had its engine running. He could see the red taillights disappear as the Izuzu turned out of the Laneway onto the main road heading north.

'Are you all right?' It was Mariad standing beside him.

'Yes. We need to get after them,' answered Walsh as he ran to the battered Land Rover and, jumping in, he put it in low gear four-wheel drive and slowly steered it out of the ditch and straightened it up on the lane.

Brendan McDevitt and John Jo came running out of the farmhouse, both now armed with AK47 rifles. Paul Costello, unarmed, came out behind them.

'I can't get involved in this, Brendan. This must be your business from now on. Anything you do now is down to you and the Real IRA,' said Costello.

'Only to be expected from you,' said McDevitt sarcastically. 'The least you can do is take Jimmy and his sister to the local Parish House in the village and leave Jimmy to get a doctor. I need to get on the phone for back-up in Jonesborough.'

'I want to come with you. I want to kill that bitch myself,' said Mariad.

'You will do as you're told. That's an order. Anyway, he's your brother. He's more important to you right now. If we can bring the tout back, we will. If not, we'll kill her and her friends where we find them,' answered McDevitt.

McDevitt jumped into the passenger seat of John Jo's Volkswagen while Walsh drove the Land Rover behind them towards the end of the laneway and north towards Jonesborough.

McDevitt used a number on his mobile speed dial. The call was answered almost immediately. 'Tony. Get the boys out now. I need you to set up a reception for a Izuzu truck heading your way. If they stop, hold them till I get there. If they don't, shoot the fuck out of them.' McDevitt didn't wait for a reply. 'I don't give a fuck what time it is. Just get the boys out, now,' he shouted into the phone before ending the call.

'Do you think we've time?' asked John Jo.

'I hope so. But no matter what happens we'll track them down. Those bastards have killed their last Irishman.'

'What about Kevin, and what if the guards investigate the gunfire at the farm?'

'Don't worry about the guards. I have a senior officer in my back pocket, and I already told him to make sure we weren't disturbed tonight. As for Kevin, he'll get a secret burial on the farm. Let's worry about that later. Get your foot down John Jo, this is a straight road.'

John Jo knew these roads well. he did as he was told. Walsh, travelling behind in the old Land Rover, and didn't know the roads had trouble keeping up. even though he pushed the pedal to the floor he still could only get sixty out of the old engine.

Chapter 38

Irish Border

Reece hit the speed dial number for Jim Broad who, despite the time, answered after the first ring.

'David, what's happening?'

'No time to explain, boss, but we need to bring on Extraction Delta right away. Were you able to get the chopper?'

'I had to pull in a lot of old favours. I have one of the special forces' choppers from 658 Squadron. By luck they were on a training exercise in Northern Ireland. The pilot's one of the elite, a special forces man, so he'll have no problem finding you and picking you up. He had flown from their base at Credenhill outside Hereford earlier today. So you're getting picked up by the best.'

Reece knew of the Squadron and the secrecy surrounding them.

'This better work, David, or both of us could end up in the Tower. I've had Sir Ian on the phone and he's getting it in the ear from Sir Martyn Bryant and the Home Secretary.'

'Or dead at my end,' Reece answered.

'Where do you want it?' Broad asked.

'There's a large car park at the back of the Four Steps pub at the southern end of the village. We will be there in ten minutes. How long will it take for the chopper to reach us?'

Broad looked at the large digital map display on the SG9 operation room wall.

'I can see where you're talking about. The chopper is on standby at Bessbrook Mill so I guess twenty minutes.'

'Get them airborne. Tell them to push it as fast as they can. The car park is big enough for them to land and it will be empty at this time of the morning. I'll keep this line open for direct comms with them. They will only be picking up me, Mary, Joe, and Geoff. Ari will be heading back south.'

'David, remember, try not to have a shooting incident especially north of the border.'

'I'll try,' Reece answered, ending the call.

'Are you all right?' Reece asked Mary.

'Yes, I think so. A bit sore here and there. Thank you for coming for me.'

'What else would I do? I'm only glad you're not badly hurt. It's not over yet. Now we must try to get out of here and back to safety.'

Mary nodded her understanding. Her stomach still hadn't settled down and she felt an overpowering need for sleep.

They had already crossed the border. The road ahead was clear as they came to a crossroad just outside Jonesborough. Ari drove straight into to the car park of the Four Steps, where he parked up. Everyone exited the vehicle, Joe Cousins having a bit of a problem climbing out of the back of the truck. It was then that he felt the trickle of blood running down the side of his right leg.

'Ouch,' said Cousins, sitting down on the ground.

'What is it, Joe?' asked Middleton.

'I think I was hit back there,' he answered, feeling his leg as best he could through his trousers. Everyone gathered round and Ari removed a pair of small scissors from the first-aid kit he had in the glove compartment. He cut into Joe's trousers where the blood seemed to start.

'You're lucky Joe, it's just a flesh wound, no bullet,' said Ari.

He quickly swabbed the wound with gauze and placed a large surgical dressing over the wound.

'You've done that before,' said Joe.

'It's surprising what you learn to do quickly in the Golan Heights.' Ari smiled and patted Cousins on the back.

'Can you stand?' Reece asked.

'Yes, I think so,' replied Cousins, getting to his feet.

'Good man. We will leave the BMW here. The Hire Company can pick it up later. Joe, you go with Ari. We might have to move quickly on foot and the leg might slow you down. Ari you can get out of here now. You've done your bit and if it goes bad here, I don't want an international incident between the British, Irish, and Israeli governments on my hands. Go back to the crossroad and turn left to the south. That road will take you directly to Dundalk and the road to Dublin. They know we went north. They won't expect you to head south. Thanks for everything.'

'OK Joe let's get moving. David, you're welcome. Jacob Lavyan asked me to give this to you and he's looking forward to seeing you and Mary in Malta,' said Ari, handing Reece a sheathed knife. Reece pulled the combat knife out of the sheath. In the street lighting he could just make out what looked like writing on the shiny blade.

'The engraving on the blade in Hebrew is part of the Mossad motto: "By way of Deception." 'Don't worry about Joe, I'll get him to our people in Dublin then home to London on a comfortable flight.'

'Thank Jacob for me. Now get going. I'm sure our friends are not far behind. Good luck Joe. See you in London,' said Reece, pushing the sheathed knife into his trouser pocket.

'You can thank Jacob yourself when you see him. Right, Joe, let's get you up front with me. Oh, I'd leave all the rifles here when you leave. If the authorities get hold of them for examination, they'll find they came from a PROVO weapons dump. That will throw some confusion into things in case you have to use them. As the motto says: "By way of Deception".'

Ari reached into the back of the truck and removed two full magazines, one for the Armalite, and one for the AK47.

'David, you can keep the Baretta. It came from the same hide as the rifles, so if you need to use it and leave it behind that would be no problem.' He then helped Joe into the jeep before leaving with one more wave and a thumbs-up.

Reece watched the lights of the Izuzu disappear into the night. Turning to Mary and Middleton he could see they wished they were going with Ari.

'OK, you two, I know what you're thinking. We could all have jumped into the jeep with Ari but if the word gets out to the southern security forces, they'll be on the alert and it's a long run to Dublin. They will be especially looking for Mary and that would only put Ari at greater risk of being captured and arrested at the least. Another diplomatic headache we don't need. Anyway, I don't trust the Irish security forces. Too many have sympathies with the likes of McDevitt and John Jo. The helicopter will be here shortly, and we'll be in a safe location before Ari gets anywhere near Dublin. His diplomatic immunity will protect him. Let's find some cover. We could have tried to make a run for it in the cars, but I have no doubt McDevitt will be phoning ahead to have his cronies intercept us. We can't take that risk. The nearest safe place for us would be Newry, about fifteen miles away.'

'What about the military car? Do we set it on fire?' Middleton asked.

'We will just have to leave it. They won't be looking for it and it's well parked up. The military can come back for it on a future date.'

Looking around the car park Reece could see it was surrounded by a large stone wall and in one corner there was a small garden including two trees and a few large shrubs. That was as good as anywhere to hide, and it gave some protection against being seen. Anyway, they didn't have time to find somewhere better.

'Let's get into the cover of the trees and garden over there,' said Reece, pointing. He noticed Mary was shivering.

'Mary, you're cold, here put my coat on,' said Reece, putting his Barbour jacket over her shoulders.

'But what about you?' asked Mary.

'You need it more than me and besides, that's what these sweaters are for, to keep me warm.'

'It's heavy,' said Mary feeling the weight on one side of the coat.

'That's my old faithful. If you need to use it don't wait. Remember, if you don't kill them they'll kill you.'

Mary felt the grip of the Smith and Wesson in the pocket and had to admit it gave her a little reassurance. She remembered when she was David's agent inside the Republican movement. He had shown her how to use the gun, saying it was the same for most semi-automatic pistols. How to pull the slide on top to put a round in the chamber. Then how to push the safety catch into fire mode, before holding the gun with a two-hand grip in such a way that she could ensure more accuracy. This time she'd have to depend on a one hand grip. Above all take time and aim for the torso, the biggest target, then pull the trigger twice to make sure.

They ran to the cover of the shrubs and settled down behind them just in time to hear the noise of a car approaching from the south.

'Tony. Where are you?' McDevitt shouted into the phone.

'There's four of us on the northern road out of the village. We've set up a roadblock, but nothing has reached us yet,' replied Tony.

'Stay there. We are in John Jo's Red Volkswagen and will be with you shortly,' answered McDevitt ending the call.

John Jo drove north through the centre of Jonesborough Village for just over a mile when he stopped the car beside Tony. He stood in the middle of the road with a torch in one hand and a semi-automatic pistol in the other. John Jo could see the other three men, all armed with rifles, at the sides of the road. All were dressed in camouflage clothing. Tony walked to the passenger side of the car, where McDevitt had scrolled down the window.

'What's happening?' he asked.

'There's at least four men and a woman, all armed, trying to get north. They are all British enemy forces, and we need to catch them dead or alive. The last we saw them they were in a large Izuzu jeep heading this way,' answered McDevitt.

'We have been here since not long after you called, and nothing has come through. How far were you behind them?'

'Not far, a matter of minutes at the most. They might still be somewhere back in the village. You come with us. Tell the rest of your men to walk back through the village checking every nook and cranny. We will start from the southern crossroads.'

Tony shouted the instructions to the men before getting into the back of the car. John Jo made a quick three-point turn and accelerated back through the village.

They watched from the cover of the bushes as the Volkswagen drove past the car park into the village. Followed about one minute later by the old Land Rover being driven by Walsh. Both vehicles returned a short time later with Walsh parking the Land Rover across the crossroads, blocking access to the village. Walsh got out and standing beside it he was able to stop anyone trying to enter or leave the village. John Jo parked beside the Land Rover and the three men started to walk back into the village, checking laneways and side roads as they moved.

'Extraction Delta, we're five minutes out. Are we OK to pick up?' Reece heard the voice in his earpiece.

'Roger, this is Delta leader. We are ready for pickup. When you land, keep the blades turning. There's opposition in the area, so be aware,' answered Reece.

'Roger that. How many passengers do 'we have?' came the reply.

'Three. Two men and a woman. Do you have any back-up on board?'

'Yes, four Troop people,' the voice replied.

'Great, we'll be ready. The car park is flat and central, a good spot for landing. You'll have to use the street lighting. See you shortly.'

They could hear McDevitt. His voice carrying in the quiet of the night air. Then Reece could see the heads of the three men moving along the wall on the outside of the car park. They would disappear as they checked alleyways and gardens. Then reappear, all three armed with automatic rifles. It was Tony who walked into the car park first. Then crouching low, he swung the AK47 from right to left. The tree area at the bottom corner of the car park was a possible hiding place, so he took his time, aiming the rifle as he moved towards the trees and bushes.

The three fugitives kept very still their breathing shallow. Tony kept moving slowly towards them. Reece and Middleton had both taken up kneeling positions behind a tree while Mary lay face down on the ground behind them. Reece set the rifle on the ground and lifted the Baretta pistol into the two-hand grip he had shown Mary all those years ago. The silencer was still fitted, so that meant he'd have to let the target get close to ensure accuracy and effect when he fired. Middleton had been covering the man approaching since he had entered the car park. If the man looked like firing into their hiding place, he would be dead by the time his second round left his weapon.

Just then, the sound of an approaching helicopter distracted the man's attention. He looked up in the direction he thought the noise was coming from.

'Extraction Delta, I see the landing area. We're about to land. Be ready.' The voice of the pilot was loud in Reece's ear.

'Roger. We have at least four enemies in the area and may need to engage while you land. We are in civilian clothes. The enemy might be in camouflage clothing. One of our party is a woman,' answered Reece.

'Roger. Understood.'

The man being distracted and looking up gave Reece the chance to break cover and he started running to get closer. The man seemed mesmerised by the sight of the helicopter flying in close over the roofs of the village and it was only at the last moment that he realised there was someone running at him. He started to point his rifle to fire at the approaching figure, but too late. The man knelt, and pointing a pistol at him, fired twice in quick succession. The first round hit Tony's solar plexus, the second in the throat, knocking him backwards onto the ground. He tried to shout but realised his voice was drowning in the blood coming out of the hole in his neck. Reece stood above the man who had dropped his rifle and was now using his hands to try to stop the blood spraying from his throat. Reece had hit the man's carotid artery with his second shot. He had aimed the two shots for the biggest target, the man's torso, just as he had been trained, but he now realised the downdraft of the landing helicopter had blown his aim off course. Despite this, the man lying at his feet had given up the struggle to stop the blood, instead, closing his eyes in death. Reece stood above him, slightly out of breath himself.

Now he could see sparks bouncing off the ground around him, the noise of the landing helicopter drowning out the fire coming from McDevitt and John Jo who were standing at the entrance to the car park. The killing of the man up close and personal had left Reece frozen for a few seconds. Then Middleton was beside him, the loud noise of his rifle bringing Reece out of his thoughts. Middleton being the better trained than the two gunmen firing at him and aiming his rounds he brought down one of the men. His firing forced the other to take cover behind the wall on the street side.

McDevitt just made it to the cover of the wall when he heard John Jo cry out in pain as he fell where he stood. Brendan could see the bullet had blown away half of John Jo's face. He lay quite still, and, McDevitt realised, quite dead. He kept his head down as he could hear the smack, smack, smack, of the bullets hitting the concrete and stone protecting him. Then the loud noise as the helicopter began to land in the middle of the car park. The three local men and Frank Walsh came running to crouch down beside him.

'David, get Mary,' shouted Middleton, bringing Reece out of his thoughts.

Reece nodded and ran back to the trees.

'Mary, come on, we need to go now,' he shouted above the noise of the landing chopper, its landing lights lighting up the ground.

'Let's take these bastards on,' yelled McDevitt.

Now that Walsh had joined them the five terrorists, some standing, some kneeling, moved to the car park entrance and started firing in the direction of Middleton and the landing helicopter. Geoff Middleton returned their fire, bringing down another terrorist. The down draft of the helicopter almost knocking him off his feet as the giant machine landed, its three wheels settling on the car park tarmac.

The special forces helicopter was a Dauphin 2, coloured with civilian colours, the dark blue instead of the normal military camouflage which would confuse the enemy on occasion. The colour also made it easier to move to different locations without bringing unnecessary attention from prying eyes. As it touched the ground the four SAS men on board jumped down onto the car park and fanned out in a small circle at the front and side of the machine. With the blades still turning, Reece and Mary ran to the side door where Reece helped Mary into the cabin behind the pilot. Reece could see the sparks as the bullets from the terrorists hit the fuselage of the helicopter. Reece knew that the important parts of the machine, such as the engine, were protected with heavy-duty armour making the bullets bounce off safely.

It was then Reece saw Geoff Middleton spin around and fall backwards. Realising he had been hit, Reece and one of the troopers ran to where he lay. The other three troopers started firing back at the terrorists, forcing them back into cover, the shooting from their end stopping for now. The SAS men were under strict orders to regard the operation as an extraction. If they came under fire, they could return the fire, but only to improve the chances of making the extraction a success. They were not to go on a killing spree but get in and out of danger with the least possible casualties.

Reece knelt beside his friend. He was still conscious but breathing rapidly. Reece could see a wound in Middleton's right shoulder.

'Geoff. Can you hear me?' He had to shout above the noise of the aircraft engine.

All Middleton could do in response was blink his eyes.

'Don't worry we're going to get you home,' shouted Reece.

'Leave his rifle,' Reece instructed the SAS trooper as they pulled Middleton to his feet. Middleton was moaning loudly as he fell in and out of consciousness. Each taking a shoulder, they hoisted him quickly forward and into the back of the helicopter with the help of two more troopers, while the fourth trooper aiming his rifle at the car park entrance gave cover. Reece and the remaining SAS soldiers jumped into the aircraft and, pulling the cabin doors shut, it lifted from the ground. Nose down it made a fast-forward movement towards the rear car park wall. At the last second, the pilot pulled back on the stick and the engine roared as it quickly climbed up and, turning to the left, cleared the village of Jonesborough.

Geoff Middleton lay on the floor of the machine as one of the troopers quickly cut away the clothing around the wound and applied a field dressing. He was pale and sweating.

Reece pulled on a set of headphones so he could talk to the pilot.

'Our man is badly hurt. Can you fly straight to the military wing of Musgrave Park Hospital in Belfast? Tell them you're coming with a gunshot wound to the shoulder and to have a surgical team on standby.'

'Roger, will do. It should take us about twenty-five minutes.'

'Make it as fast as you can. We'll do what we can for him in the meantime.'

Reece looked at the rest of the passengers, including Mary. He could see their concern for the man on the floor of the aircraft. The trooper who had stopped the bleeding for now gave Middleton an injection of morphine for the pain. In every SAS team, for such a mission, Reece knew one of the troopers would be a medic and trained in treating combat injuries. Reece knelt beside his wounded friend.

'Stay awake, Geoff. It won't be long before we are at the hospital. Keep with us.'

'Now, let's have a quick look at you,' said the medic, taking hold of Mary's hand to look at her damaged finger.

'Dislocated. Can you bear a little pain for a couple of seconds?' he asked.

Mary just nodded, gritting her teeth.

The medic massaged the finger and then in one quick movement held the finger tightly with one hand and with the other pulled the finger towards him. There was the noise of a small snap and Mary cried out, the pain bringing the tears down her cheek.

'All done. I'll put a little splint on it.' Taking the small splint sticks out of his medic bag, he strapped the finger. Mary felt a gentle throbbing around the finger, but the strong pain had gone. The medic then reached into the first-aid kit and produced a silver foil strip of tablets.

'These are just paracetamol. You can take two of these now. Then another two in a couple of hours. Should be like new in a couple of weeks. The bruising around your face and lips will heal even quicker.'

'Thank you,' said Mary.

The medic kept checking Middleton's pulse.

For now, Geoff was in the best hands they could provide, thought Reece.

Chapter 39

Four Steps

Brendan McDevitt raised his head slowly from behind the wall. He had seen three of his men go down during the firefight with the Brits. Tony and John Jo were dead, and another of Tony's men were badly wounded. With the noise of the gunfire and the landing helicopter, he had no doubt it had wakened the whole village. Someone would surely phone the emergency services who, with the report of gunfire being so close to the border, would contact their counterparts in the Republic. Walsh and one of the other men from the village lifted the wounded man into the back of John Jo's Volkswagen.

'We need to get out of here now,' shouted Walsh to no one in particular.

McDevitt threw his rifle in the back of the car with the wounded man and got into the driving seat as Walsh jumped in beside him. The remaining two village men ran back through the village to get to a safe house, leaving their comrades on the ground where they fell.

Walsh jumped out and drove the Land Rover behind McDevitt back to the family farm across the border. McDevitt made a quick phone call to the local doctor, who was a sympathiser, and had been treating Jimmy Bailey at his house. McDevitt told him he needed him to look at another volunteer with a leg wound. He explained he expected to be raided by the southern security forces and he needed to hide stuff before they came. The doctor agreed to come to the farm and pick up the wounded man. He would drop off Jimmy who was now patched up.

When they got back to the farm there was no sign of Paul Costello or his car. He had obviously cleared out after the shooting, thought McDevitt.

The doctor arrived twenty minutes later and after dropping off Jimmy took the volunteer back to his surgery.

McDevitt and Walsh had been spending the twenty minutes moving weapons and ammunition from the house to a hide that had been dug into the ground about forty yards from the rear of the farmhouse and covered with a heavy sheet of steel with turf on top of that. They poured water over the bloodstains on the ground where Jimmy Bailey had been hit. Then they put out the fire under the water tank in the barn and made it look like a barn again.

Although Jimmy was still in some pain, the doctor had given him some strong painkillers and the address of another doctor who supported the cause who lived in West Belfast. He told Jimmy he'd phone ahead to tell him to expect him at his home early next morning. The Belfast doctor would then take care of Jimmy's ongoing medical needs.

'You should all try to get back to Belfast tonight,' said McDevitt. 'Take John Jo's car. If the police here ask why there are bullet holes in the ancient Land Rover, I'll just tell them the Brits shot at me years ago when I was crossing the border to sell my cattle. But in the meantime, I don't intend to wait around here to answer their questions.'

'What about the men we lost tonight? What about their bodies? Do they get a decent funeral?' questioned Walsh.

'You leave that to me. After tonight we'll all have to keep our heads down for a while, you three included. If we get another chance to pay back that bitch Mary and her boyfriend, we'll take it. No interrogation next time. No holding back because of the Peaceniks. we blow them away on first sight. Now get your stuff together and don't carry anything that will incriminate you. It's John Jo's name on the registration so if you're asked, he loaned it to you, and hope that does the job. If you're pulled in give them the silent treatment. they can only get you for theft. I'll be in touch as soon as I can. Good luck.'

The three got into the Volkswagen, Jimmy able to stretch out in the back. With Walsh driving they turned right out of the laneway back towards Dundalk. Walsh knew the back road to Omeath where he could cross the border into the north, well away from the main Dublin to Belfast Road.

McDevitt made another call this time to arrange for two of his local men to come to the farm help to him clean-up the mess and take Kevin's body and McDevitt to a safe house just outside Crossmaglen.

He needed time to think.

The whole thing had been a complete ball's-up. He had lost important men. And what was worse, his reputation as commander who carried out successful operations against the enemy. Now was time to keep his head low.

Chapter 40

Belfast

When they landed on the helipad at the military wing of Musgrave Park Hospital in Belfast there was a medical crash team waiting with a stretcher. Reece and the troopers helped lift Middleton down from the aircraft. The SAS medic told one of the doctors about the wound and how much morphine he had given. A young-looking doctor in green scrubs told them Geoff would be taken to surgery where their top surgeon, who had been woken at home, was now waiting. The team rushed the stretcher into the hospital, leaving Reece, and Mary to thank the men. The SAS medic told Reece they were heading straight back to Hereford for a complete debrief, and as far as they were concerned, they were never here. Smiling, he shook Reece's hand, and within a minute the chopper was airborne and flying to the east over the city. When they entered the hospital Geoff Middleton had already been moved into surgery. They decided to wait, and Reece got them two coffees from a machine which, he had to admit, the coffee actually tasted like coffee.

'What happens now?' asked Mary.

'We let the rest of the world worry about that for now. Let's just see how Geoff gets on. He didn't look too good in the chopper.'

'I'm nice and warm now. have your coat and what's in the pocket back.' She smiled as she removed the Barbour jacket and handed it to Reece.

He had deliberately left the Baretta on the helicopter. No sense in being caught with a weapon on him that had dispatched a couple of terrorists. He still had the knife in his trouser pocket.

'I'll have to find out about my mother,' said Mary.

Reece took out his mobile phone and found the number of the City Hospital, pressed the ring button, and handed the phone to Mary. 'Ask them to put you through to your mother's ward. If they start to ask you any questions about your abduction, just say you're with the police and you can't say anything for the minute.'

Mary waited and when the hospital switchboard answered she gave them the information to be put through to her mother's ward. She stood and walked around the waiting area while talking. When she'd finished, she came back and sat down, handing the phone back to Reece.

'Well?' he asked.

'They said she had a rough few days but was now doing well and sleeping comfortably. I really need to see her, David.'

'If she's sleeping, we can wait here to see how Geoff is, then we'll go there tomorrow,' said Reece, taking hold of Mary's uninjured hand.

The chairs were surprisingly comfortable, and Mary fell asleep, her head resting on his shoulder. They were the only people in the room apart from medical staff walking through. The noise of the staff talking seemed, to Reece, to be in the distance and it had a calming relaxing effect on him. Reece must have dozed off himself before he was wakened by the young doctor shaking his shoulder. When Reece moved Mary woke as well.

'Hello, are you waiting for news of your friend?'

'Yes, how is he, doctor?' asked Reece.

'He's in a bad way, I'm afraid. He lost a lot of blood, and the surgery went as well as could be expected. He has bone damage which will need more surgery when he's strong enough. But for now, he's on what we'd call the stable list.'

'Can we see him?' asked Mary.

'He's in recovery. The operation was a long one. You can see him, but we've him under deep sedation, so he won't be aware you're there. I'll tell the nurse to let you know when you can go through.'

'Thank you,' said Reece. Looking at his watch, he realised they'd been there just over four hours. He could see the sun through the window starting to lighten the day.

'We must have been more tired than we thought to sleep in these chairs for four hours,' said Reece, sitting back down beside Mary.

'At least he sounded positive,' said Mary trying to smile.

'You still look tired. I'm not surprised with what you've been through. Do you want another coffee? The last one wasn't too bad?' asked Reece.

'Yes, but while you're doing that, I'm finding a toilet with a sink to throw some water over my face.'

Reece was at the vending machine waiting on the second cup of coffee to fill when the phone in his pocket started to vibrate. The screen showed the call was from Jim Broad.

'Good morning boss,' Reece answered.

'That's to be debated. My phone has been red hot since you shot up half of Ireland. I thought I told you to keep things low key.'

'Things went beyond my control, boss. They didn't want to play quiet.'

'Two dead on their side and two wounded on ours. How's Middleton?'

Three dead, thought Reece but telling Broad that now wouldn't help things.

'He's recovering. They say he's stable for now. Bad shoulder wound. I'm going to pop in and see him shortly.'

Reece moved as he was talking to avoid the noise of people walking through the waiting room area.

Broad's voice sounded strained. Reece could only think the boss had been awake for the whole operation and now had the added problem of speaking to his superiors and political masters. Broad continued to speak.

'At least that's good news. Joe Cousins is doing fine and flying back later this afternoon. It seems your Israeli friend is a good friend to have. Anyway, you might have got away with this one. The Northern Ireland SOS, on instructions from the Home Secretary and number ten, will issue a statement later stating that the PSNI believe this was a shoot-out between a dissident Republican paramilitary group and a drug gang. People won't believe it, but if we stick to that story it's the only one they have. This way we can get the media on board, then the Dublin politicians. The SOS is working the phones to the northern politicians as we speak. We think Paul Costello, who represents that area, will come out with a statement condemning those who bring violence to his community. He will say the people support the peace process and they don't want these people anymore.'

Now Reece was starting to feel exasperated.

'I hope it works, boss. Mary and I'll stay here for a while, then head to the hotel to freshen up before we go to the City Hospital to see her mother. We deliberately left weapons behind on the advice of Ari. The weapons came from a PROVO hide so that will put even more pressure on Mister Costello to keep things quiet.'

There seemed to be a few seconds pause before Broad answered.

'That's good news. I must go to Downing Street with Sir Ian later this morning. It was good thinking to bring Geoff to the military hospital. That way we can keep things quiet concerning our involvement. We weren't even there. What are you going to say about Mary being free?'

'I've been thinking about that. We can stick close to the truth and say that she was abducted by, she thinks, a Republican group with drugs links. Maybe she could even say that she got the impression that they kidnapped her because of her previous senior rank within the Republican movement and her support for the peace process to try to disrupt it. The hayshed she was kept in should be empty now, so she can say where they held her, and she escaped when one of her captures was asleep. It's thin, but I think the police will accept it as they'll be following their own enquiries. If the SOS can put pressure on them not to chase things up too much to protect the peace process, then we can hopefully get away with how things really went down.' Suggested Reece.

'That's good thinking and something I can give number ten. They will be looking for a get out of jail free card, so I'm sure they'll be glad to grab your ideas. In the meantime, give my best to Mary and Geoff. Do you need anything else?'

'We had to leave two cars behind. One was my hire car. I can give them a call to pick it up. The other is a military surveillance car, which the military will need to pick up being careful when they do so.'

'The Troopers already told us during their debrief in Hereford and we've arranged for both to be picked up,' replied Broad.

Reece saw an opportunity and thought he'd chance his luck.

'That takes a load off my mind, thanks. Would there be any chance, seeing that you're in a helpful mood, to get me some transport here? I don't want to use taxis. We don't know who we can trust.'

'Leave it with me. I'll get one of the Belfast MI5 team cars for you. Should take about an hour.'

'Thanks, boss. I owe you one.'

'I'll remind you of that,' replied Broad, ending the call.

Mary looked a lot fresher when she returned.

'Ah, you look better. How are you feeling?' Asked Reece.

'I feel better. It's amazing what a little cold water can do,' Mary replied.

Reece told Mary about the call from Jim Broad and the plan to keep things as low key as possible. Mary was happy she could answer the questions when they came.

'If they get too rough, I could always say I don't want to talk about it anymore. It's too stressful, and just keep my mouth shut. Don't forget when the war was on we were always taught to say nothing if we were arrested by the police. I think I could do that.'

'Excuse me.' It was a young nurse interrupting Mary's thoughts.

'You can go through and see the patient now if you would like to follow me?'

Reece took Mary, holding her good hand, having an idea of what to expect when they saw Middleton. The room was bright and quiet apart from the constant beep of one of the machines that the patient was hooked up to. His eyes were closed and his breathing steady although, thought Reece, this was probably because of the tube in his mouth. Another nurse in surgical gowns was just finishing making notes on a laptop on top of a small trolley. When she finished, she left the room, taking the laptop and trolley with her.

'Will he be able to hear us?' Mary asked the nurse who had come for them.

'He's under very deep sedation, so I'm not sure.' The nurse had a strong Belfast accent and spoke quietly. 'They do say that patients can hear sometimes and that you should always be positive when around them. I'll leave you for five minutes. I'm sorry, but that's all the time you have, as we'll be monitoring him regularly.'

They moved closer to the bed. Mary was frightened in case she moved a tube or one of the wires that seemed to cover his body. There was a large piece of surgical cloth covering the area of the wound and it was stained with a little spot of blood that had seeped through.

'Oh, David, he looks so hurt,' said Mary.

'He's in the best place for now. The doctor said he was stable, and that's good news,' said Reece.

The five minutes passed quickly and the young nurse, true to her word, returned with a trolley of fresh medication and the laptop that she entered details into.

'Sorry, folks, but that's it for now. He will be like this for at least twelve hours. You can come back tomorrow, or you can phone the ward and they'll update you,' said the nurse.

Reece nodded, then bent down close to Middleton's ear. 'You need to get well soon old friend. You have a wedding to go to,' he whispered.

The promised driver, a girl who didn't look old enough to have a driving licence, picked them up in a silver Renault Megane. She didn't say much, only that the car was theirs to use for the rest of their stay and could they drop her off in the city centre.

After a shower and some sleep, they grabbed an all-day breakfast in the hotel bistro before heading to the City Hospital. Reece phoned Tom Wilson PSNI and told him the good news that Mary was all right, and he could see her later back at the hotel.

Chapter 41

West Belfast

Mariad Bailey was angry. The woman she'd wanted to see suffer and be there when she died had escaped. The brother she loved had been wounded and now he was back in Belfast in the safe house on the Ballymurphy estate. She couldn't stop thinking about what had happened. They didn't hang you for murder these days, so she felt she had nothing to lose. If she succeeded, she'd be a hero. if she failed she'd be either dead or in prison. Both held no fear for her. She didn't tell anyone, not even her brother, about her thoughts, or plans. She knew they would only tell her to do nothing. To keep her head down in the safe house and if by chance she was lifted by the police, say nothing, they need to prove things, it's harder if you don't talk, say nothing. Her brother Jimmy was happy to spend his day with his wounded leg up on the settee. Trolling the TV channels and drinking endless cups of tea. Mariad needed to do something, she thought. A plan started to formulate in her head. A plan she had to do on her own, one she couldn't tell her brother about because he'd try to stop her.

'What was the sense in stopping a war that was hitting the Brit enemy hard then hiding? A soldier doesn't hide, they fight,' she thought.

'I must get some air,' she said.

She stood from the chair and threw the magazine on the table. She had been reading it for half an hour but couldn't remember one word of the articles.

'You can't take the risk. It's daylight out there. At least wait until dark. Now that Brian McNally is dead everyone is lying low until they find out what happened. I don't believe the story that he was killed during a burglary. What fucker in their right mind would burgle the home of the top IRA man in Belfast? He was too well-known. Stay in until after dark, sister, or until we get more news.'

Mariad smiled as she pulled on her parka coat. Pulling the hood up, she stroked her brother's hair.

'Don't worry, brother. I'll keep the hood up and I'm only walking round the block. I'm going stir crazy here and if I don't get out, I'll go mad.'

She bent and kissed him on the forehead. She didn't know if she'd be back, but she loved her brother and of all the people in the world, if things went wrong, she'd miss him the most.

It was one of those grey Belfast days with a slight drizzle of rain but no wind. As she walked with her head down, the plan continued to form in her head. First, she headed to another part of the estate where, in the nearby grassland, she knew there was a small hide where she'd moved a handgun in and out of when it was needed. The weapons hide was hidden from view, protected by a large circle of trees. The hide was placed in such a way for easy access and close to the road and estate for a quick drop off or getaway. Making sure no one was following or watching her, she walked down the pathway from the road, then quickly into the tree circle. There she moved a metal drain cover that was hidden under the turf beside one of the trees. She quickly lifted the cover and removed the .357 Magnum revolver that was covered in waterproof gauze. Checking the pistol was still fully loaded with six rounds she put the gun in the right-hand pocket of the parka. Quickly replacing the hide covering she left the tree cover and, making sure once more that no one was watching, she walked back through the estate. She headed for the main road where she jumped in a black cab and asked to be taken to Roger Casement Park.

During the journey, the talkative driver told her the good news, that the heavy security presence had been lifted and now there was no sign of the police checks. She had seen the driver before. He was one of the regular cab drivers that covered most of West Belfast. She could just smell the smoke from his recently extinguished pipe tobacco that she knew he used.

'Probably because of that bitch being found,' said Mariad.

The driver looked at the woman in the mirror and, raising his eyebrows he thought she looked like someone he knew.

'I heard a short report on Radio Ulster saying she'd escaped. It said something about her being held by dissident republicans connected to drugs,' said the driver.

'Usual Brit propaganda,' said Maraid.

When she was dropped off, she knew she was taking a risk. She walked back to the hay shed where they'd held the bitch when they first lifted her, but she still had to take the risk if her plan was to succeed. The security forces might already be aware of the hay shed. She'd have to make sure as much as possible that it wasn't under any kind of surveillance. She crossed the road back and forth three times and walked down the side streets before coming back onto the main road, passing the hay shed, and walking on about 500 yards before returning. As satisfied as she could be that everything was clear, she entered the barn. She found and quickly changed into the nurse's uniform and pulled on the blonde wig before pulling on the parka coat, then leaving the barn to return to the main road. She flagged down another black cab, this time asking to be dropped off at the City Hospital.

Chapter 42

Belfast City Hospital

When she arrived at the hospital, Mariad sat nursing a coffee in the Starbucks just inside the main entrance and corridor. She sat in a chair that allowed her to watch the people coming and going through the hospital entrance. She was on her second cup when she saw Mary McAuley enter followed by Reece. Both were deep in conversation, paying no attention to the people sitting in the café behind the large plate-glass windows that looked out onto the corridor. They walked towards the lifts leading to the hospital wards. Mariad left the table and entered the ladies' toilet. There she found an empty cubicle and after locking herself in she hung the parka jacket on the door hook and removed the Magnum revolver from the pocket, covering it with a scarf from the other pocket.

Leaving the jacket on the hook in the toilet she walked to the lift and, confirming which floor was female surgical, she pressed the button, hoping the woman's mother was still in that ward and that would be where she'd find the bitch and her lover. If only the mother was there, she was happy enough to shoot her as well for bringing the traitor bitch into the world.

Mary was pleased to see her mother sitting up in her bed, propped up by pillows. She was looking much better, and someone had tidied her silver hair. She smiled when she saw Mary and held out her arms to embrace her daughter.

'Oh, Mary, it's lovely to see you. Where have you been? What happened to your face and finger?' Her mother never missed a thing.

'An accident, Mum, but I'm all right. It's good to see you up and about.'

'They insist you get moving as soon as possible. Do you know they've even been getting me to take a few steps along the corridor? Who's this?' she asked, looking at Reece who was standing just behind her daughter.

'Mum, this is David. We are going to be married and we want you to get well and come to Malta for the wedding,' said Mary, holding out her finger to show her the ring still visible below the splints.

'Married…. Malta who…. what?'

'Hello. It's lovely to meet you and I'm glad you're doing well,' said Reece, shaking the woman's hand.

She smiled, then looking at her daughter she asked, 'Wedding in Malta? When did all this happen?'

'It's a long story Mum, but you must get well so that I can tell you everything.'

Mary sat down on the only chair beside the bed. Her mother's bed was the furthest into the ward. The ward was warm but a comfortable warm thought Mary. Reece took off the Barbour jacket and hung it on the chair behind Mary and went to look for another chair.

Mary told her mother how she loved Reece but left out his secret background.

Mariad thought the gun felt heavier than she remembered. Leaving the lift, she walked down the corridor and entered the ward. There was a nurse sitting behind the nurses' station. She did not notice Mariad, the notes on the computer screen having her full attention. Mariad could see the bitch sitting at her mother's bedside, her back to Mariad. Looking around, there was no sign of the man. Removing the scarf, she lifted the gun as she got closer. A woman in another bed could see this strange nurse with the gun in her hand and started to scream. Hearing the scream, Mary started to stand, and turn towards the noise when she heard the loud bang, bang of the gun as Mariad started firing. Mary recognised Mariad. The same nurse who had abducted her from the same hospital, who had promised to kill her. The screaming patient meant that Mary had moved just before Mariad fired. The two shots missed. She started to dive to her left when she saw a strange expression come over the nurse's face. Then, as she watched everything seemed to be in slow motion. The hand holding the gun fell to her side. Blood started to trickle out of her mouth. She fell first to her knees, then slowly forward onto her face, the gun clattering across the floor before she lay still; the knife sticking out in the centre of her back.

Reece had only been away a matter of minutes and, not finding a chair, he was returning when the nurse without the hat in front of him started to raise a gun, aiming it at Mary. For a split-second, he realised his

Smith and Wesson was still in the pocket of the Barbour jacket hanging on the back of the chair Mary was sitting on. He was at least ten feet behind the nurse and too far to stop her from pulling the trigger. The scream from the patient gave Mary that split-second warning and time for Reece to pull Jacob's knife from his trouser pocket. He threw it with all his might directly at the nurse's back, but not before she got off two rounds.

When the nurse hit the floor, she didn't move. Reece quickly lifted the revolver and pointing it at her head, moved to her side, and turned her over. Her eyes looked at the ceiling with a blank stare. Mariad Bailey was dead. The patient had stopped screaming but then heard another scream and Reece realised it was Mary, who was holding her mother in her arms.

Reece ran to her side and his heart sunk when he saw the limp body of Mary's mother, the blood spreading across the bed onto the floor.

Mary was crying loudly, her blouse stained with her mother's blood. Reece held her before sitting her back on the chair.

'Mary, sit there. Let me help your mother.'

Reece could see the blood was coming from the centre of her chest. Mary's mother was dead, and he felt angry that this innocent woman had become another victim of the mindless violence he hated. Thoughts ran through his head. What happened? Why did it happen? Did the dead woman with the knife in her back not know these days were supposed to be over? What now? What a bloody waste.

Medical staff came running, but he knew it was too late for two women in the ward.

'I'm sorry, Mary,' was all he could say, holding Mary as she sobbed into his chest. She knew, thought Reece, that her mother was dead before he did.

Chapter 43

London

The two weeks after Mary's mother was killed were a blur of police interviews and meetings with senior politicians. The funeral took place three days after the shooting, as was the custom in Northern Ireland. Mary sobbed throughout the service. Reece caught her at times sitting alone and sobbing quietly. The politicians as usual were looking for someone to blame but in the end, with some persuading from Sir Ian Fraser and a threat of his and Jim Broad's resignations, they went with the original statement of Mariad being a rogue terrorist working on her own. The statement in the press stated she had mental issues and had opposed the peace process and her target was someone in favour of it. There was no mention in the press of how she'd died or who the target was. It was felt the less said the more people could use their own imaginations and decide for themselves. Mariad Bailey had a simple family funeral at which her brother Jimmy was the chief mourner. A week was taken up with dealing with Mary's mother's estate. There was a will leaving everything to Mary, which made things easier. Reece was determined to get Mary back to Malta. She needed time and that was what he was prepared to give her. Before leaving for Malta, they'd flown to London where Reece met with Sir Ian and Jim Broad in the MI6 building at Vauxhall Bridge.

'How's Mary?' asked Sir Ian.

They were in his office overlooking the Thames River. The large windows letting in bright sunshine which filled the whole room. Sir Ian sat behind his desk with Broad and Reece in chairs facing him.

'It'll take her some time to get over things. I don't think she'll want to go back to Ireland, which perhaps isn't a bad thing,' answered Reece.

'You'll be pleased to know that Geoff Middleton will make a full recovery. What about you, David? Where are you now in all this?' asked Broad.

Reece took his time in answering, as he knew there was much depending on what he said.

'You remember boss, that before the abduction of Mary I told you I was resigning?'

Broad nodded.

'Well, as far as that goes I'm still resigning. I know you both have put your reputations and careers on the line for me, and without your back-up when I was, as someone said, working outside the shadows, Mary, and maybe me would be dead. But for now, I must think of both our futures and that's why we need to get to Malta, where I hope she'll recover, and we can get married. I don't know how long that will take but I do know from the day I met her and recruited her as an agent I've brought nothing but danger and death into her life. In a way I feel I'm as bad as her Republican masters, using her for my own cause. No, my days of hunting are over. I'm going to retire to my island with the woman I love and live happily ever after.'

Sir Ian nodded to Jim Broad.

'Sir Ian and I both understand how you feel right now, but we want to reassure you we are here for you should you ever need us. You have been one of our best operators and of course we'll be sorry to lose you. When you talk, people listen. You are a leader and that's rare in someone who has come through what you've come through. That's why we put our necks on the line when you needed us, and we were hoping you would agree to remain in some sort of position that we could call on you if we needed your help.'

Reece understood the tactics. Make him realise he owed them and put pressure on him to stay in harness.

'I know how much you put on the line for me. But for now, I'm burnt out. I see no future for me and Mary if I stay in. She's had enough as well. The only way forward for us now is to leave all this behind. But, to show my appreciation for what you've done during my time in Ireland, I picked up some information which should be of concern to you and your political masters. The agent I met with Ari, told us about an ex high-ranking Special Branch Officer from my old RUC days who worked for the Provos during the war and is still working with the Real IRA today. I knew him when I worked in Southern Region. He was one of my bosses. Detective Chief Inspector Paddy Wilson, the father of the current head of the intelligence Branch of the PSNI ACC Tom Wilson.'

Both MI6 men looked at each other and again Fraser nodded to Broad.

'What do you think about this information?' asked Sir Ian.

'If he was right here in front of me, I would kill him,' answered Reece.

'OK, David,' said Broad, 'I'm sorry we can't persuade you, but you must understand because of the secrets you have in your head we may need to contact you now and again. Leave the Paddy Wilson information with us. I'll chase it up and deal with it. In the meantime, I'll keep you on the books from the point of view that you'll need some money to ensure you and Mary have a good start. It would also cover you for carrying your firearm through customs. Now go get Mary and enjoy your future together.'

'And I would like to thank you for everything you've done. You're a brave man, David. I've known a few and you're at the top of the tree,' said Ian Fraser, standing to shake Reece's hand.

Reece then shook Jim Broad's hand.

When he had left the room, Reece felt relieved. He knew that Broad's mention of keeping him on the books was his way of holding on to Reece, but now at least it would only be on Reece's terms. For now, he'd tell Mary he was out and that they would be married. That was the only thing that would get her out of her pain. He had kept in touch with Geoff Middleton, and they visited him in the Belfast Hospital before they transferred him to his local hospital in Hereford. Reece had asked him to be his best man, and he had accepted with a big smile.

Chapter 44

Malta

'In the end we are all alone and no one's coming to save you.'

It was three months before Reece started to see the change in Mary. Despite the sun and fresh air of St Paul's Bay, she still walked with her head down and the smile was gone. Reece made sure he was with her when she wanted him to be, then left her on her own when she wanted that. But nurse time slowly began to work and gradually her head lifted. She started to become aware of the change in seasons and the world around her, but most of all she started to notice Reece by her side. She began to make sense of what happened and how to deal with it within. It was something she could leave to her memory and just get on with life, with living for now, and Reece was the most important part of that life. At first Reece felt she blamed him for her troubles but now he knew she was determined to go forward with him, here in Malta, their home.

They had planned the wedding by the sea with a small group of guests. Geoff Middleton had recovered from his wounds well enough to attend as his best man. Middleton had to leave his beloved SAS regiment, but Jim Broad had taken him on board as his latest recruit to his band of waifs and strays in SG9. Broad was there along with Joe Cousins and from Israel, Jacob Lavyan, and Palo Stressor. Lavyan and Palo had both brought their wives, but really the only woman Mary would have wanted there was her mother.

The ceremony was carried out by a local Roman Catholic priest out of respect for Mary who still associated herself with that religion. The scene for the ceremony was on the beach below their favourite spot beside St Paul's Bay for the end of their walk and morning coffee. When it was over and the licence signed, they had the small reception on the terrace in a nearby fish restaurant overlooking the sea, it was a favourite of Mary and Reece. For the first time in months Reece could see the old Mary he had fallen in love with. Smiling, talking with everyone, and at one time after the vows he could see a small tear slide down her cheek, but he knew it was a happy tear.

When Mary excused herself to go powder her nose as she put it. Both Lavyan and Broad came and sat on either side of him.

'David, I know this is your wedding day,' said Lavyan, 'but we really need your help.'

'We won't discuss it now. But can you meet with both of us in Tel Aviv after your honeymoon?' said Broad.

Reece didn't want this day destroyed by these men and the world they brought to his life. Instead, he just nodded. Whether he would go to Israel or not was a decision for another day.

About the Author

After twenty-six years working in Counter Terrorism, David Costa brings the background knowledge needed to bring the reality of that world to the written page. From recruiting and running agents, to planning operations to stop some of the most dangerous operations that were being planned, his knowledge of how the terrorist thinks and operates earned him special commendations.

Because of that background, David Costa is a pseudonym.

He is married to Helena and now lives peacefully in the Northwest of England.

Outside the Shadows is the third book in the trilogy that follows the Black Ops Team SG9, a unit within MI6. Because of his background the main character David Reece has been head hunted to lead the team in the war on terror. The unit has one remit track down the threats to the United Kingdom and eliminate them.

David says:

'I've been a writer for many years and until now, I've only been writing for my friends and family. Now I bring to the page the hidden work of the security community and the hidden undercover work most people never see going on around them. I hope you read and enjoy, but most of all understand.'

If you like Lee Child, Tom Clancy, and Frederick Forsyth you will enjoy reading the books by David Costa.

A NOTE FROM THE AUTHOR

I hope you enjoy this story and if you would like to hear more or send me your thoughts, please feel free to do so.

www.davidcostaauthor.com
Email: David.costa.writer@outlook.com
Twitter: @Davidcostawrite
Facebook: David Costa

Printed in Great Britain
by Amazon